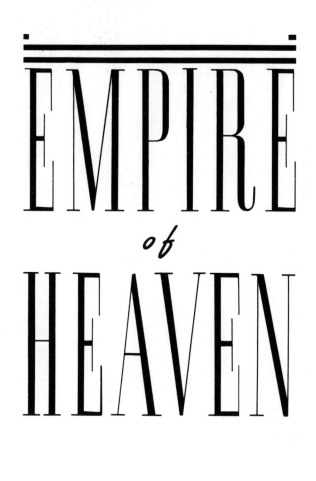

EMPIRE *of* HEAVEN

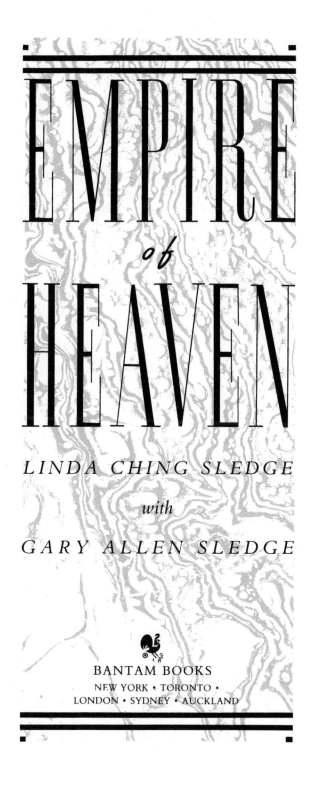

EMPIRE

of

HEAVEN

LINDA CHING SLEDGE

with

GARY ALLEN SLEDGE

BANTAM BOOKS
NEW YORK · TORONTO ·
LONDON · SYDNEY · AUCKLAND

EMPIRE OF HEAVEN
A Bantam Book / April 1990

Grateful acknowledgment is made to The University of Washington Press for permission to use adaptations from poems in The Taiping Rebellion *by Franz Michael, copyright © 1971.*

Library of Congress Cataloging-in-Publication Data
Sledge, Linda Ching
   Empire of heaven / Linda Ching Sledge with Gary Allen Sledge.
      p. cm.
   ISBN 0-553-05755-3
   1. China—History—Taiping Rebellion. 1850–1864—Fiction.
I. Sledge, Gary Allen. II. Title.
PS3569.L355E4 1990
813'.54—dc20   89-27863
                                        CIP

Published simultaneously in the United States and Canada

Bantam Books are published by Bantam Books, a division of Bantam Doubleday Dell Publishing Group, Inc. Its trademark, consisting of the words "Bantam Books" and the portrayal of a rooster, is Registered in U.S. Patent and Trademark Office and in other countries. Marca Registrada. Bantam Books, 666 Fifth Avenue, New York, New York 10103.

PRINTED IN THE UNITED STATES OF AMERICA

BVG   0 9 8 7 6 5 4 3 2 1

To my sons, Timothy and Geoffrey

Acknowledgments

I would like to thank the Rockefeller Foundation for the grant supporting the original project out of which this novel developed: a history of my family, the Yees and the Chings, who emigrated from Kwangtung Province in south China to Hawaii in the mid-nineteenth century. *Empire of Heaven* grew from a small seed, a Ching family legend about my great-grandfather, a foundling adopted into the clan during a populist rebellion.

Una Shih, the reference librarian at Westchester Community College, was a great help in scouring the New York library system for rare books on the Taiping Rebellion, which were invaluable to my research. Dr. Richard Hessney was kind enough to read the finished manuscript and give his expert opinion on Chinese language and literature.

I am also deeply grateful to the professional team that brought this book to fruition: my agent Ned Leavitt, gifted critic and generous friend; Linda Grey of Bantam Books, who took a chance on an incomplete and sprawling manuscript; editors Beverly Lewis, who guided the manuscript with sensitivity and vision through several complete drafts to its final form, and Nessa Rapoport, who helped immensely to clarify details of character, motivation, and plot; and copy editor Candace Levy, who read the manuscript with a fine eye for historical detail and chronology.

Preface

The Taiping Rebellion (1847–1864) was one of the bloodiest civil wars ever fought, claiming as many as thirty million lives and laying waste central China by bloodshed, famine, and disease. The Taiping rebels were originally a core of Hakka peasants in southern China who believed that their charismatic leader, Hung Hsiu Chuan, was the younger brother of Jesus Christ. Disciplined, ascetic, and fanatic about their faith, a curious and heretical blend of Old Testament theology and Chinese folk mythology, they won over the impoverished peasantry with the promise of a heavenly kingdom on earth. Their fearlessness in battle brought them victory after victory over the demoralized and corrupt government troops, and they very nearly took Peking, coming within sight of the rooftops of the imperial city before being turned back by Mongol mercenaries. At the height of their power, the Taiping controlled half of China from their base in Nanking in the fertile Yangtze River valley.

After their aborted effort to capture Peking, the Taiping continued to win battles, yet they never regained the momentum of their early successes before Nanking was won. The movement slowly unraveled due to fierce internecine wranglings and the avarice of the "kings," particularly Hung Hsiu Chuan, who locked himself away with his eighty-eight concubines in his palace after ordering the assassination of his top leaders, and went mad. When Nanking finally fell in 1864 to imperial forces under the redoubtable Confucian, Tseng Kuo Fan, those Taiping faithful who were not slain in battle set themselves afire and threw themselves from the walls of the city. An estimated one hundred thousand perished in this way.

The saga of the Taiping is as rich as fiction. Vivid characters abound, among them river pirates, white missionary soldiers of fortune, warrior women, mandarins who gave away their wealth to follow Hung, and peasants who rose from the mud of their villages to become, for a while, kings of the earth. In many ways, the struggle of the Taiping prefigures the struggles of the Chinese people in this century to throw off the yoke of one autocratic oppressor after another and rule themselves. Collectivism, the fascination with western thought (the same that underlay the mass protests in Tiananmen Square in 1989), radical land reform, the movement to free women from concubinage, prostitution, and foot binding—even Mao's Long March—all had their parallels in the Taiping era.

Although this novel evolves out of research into nineteenth-century Chinese history, it is informed more by imagination than by fact. Characters in drama, once created, have a will of their own, so experts in the period may find a revisionist view of Taiping history and the fusion of some dates and events. Characters such as Rulan, Pao An, Ailan, and General Li are entirely fictional. Among the major characters, only Hung, Wei, Shih Ta Kai, Jiao, and Yang are authentically historical, although I have turned them into creatures of my own imagining that may bear little resemblance to the portraits painted by scholars. Yang, the Eastern King, for example, is considered by most scholars to be an opportunist for speaking as the fraudulent "Voice of God." I have made Yang a hero, however, since he, not Hung, was the military and organizational genius behind the Taiping's astonishing early success. Mandley is a composite of several historical figures, among them Issachar Roberts and Augustus Lindley, westerners who lived with the Taiping in that period.

I suppose I should add a note about the English rendering of Chinese names and words. For the most part I have used Mandarin words rather than the Hakka or Cantonese that the characters actually spoke. In addition, characters refer to each other by personal name, as we do in the West, rather than by the elaborate title that depends on a speaker's relationship to the one addressed. I've also adopted the old-fashioned Wade-Giles system, eliminating hyphens and apostrophes for ease in reading, on the assumption that most western readers are still familiar with words translated in that fashion. My objective is not to have the reader labor but enjoy.

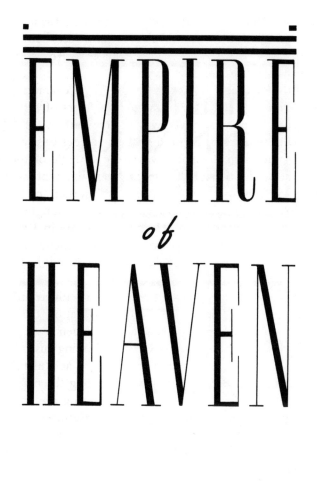

EMPIRE
of
HEAVEN

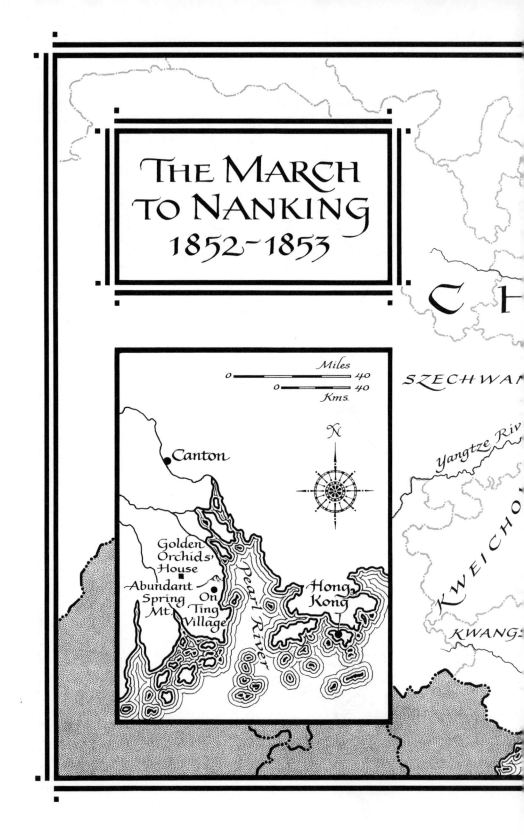

THE MARCH
TO NANKING
1852~1853

Miles
0   40
0   40
Kms.

N

Canton

Golden
Orchids'
House
Abundant
Spring
Mt.
On
Ting
Village

Pearl River

Hong
Kong

CH

SZECHWAN

Yangtze Riv

KWEICHO

KWANGS

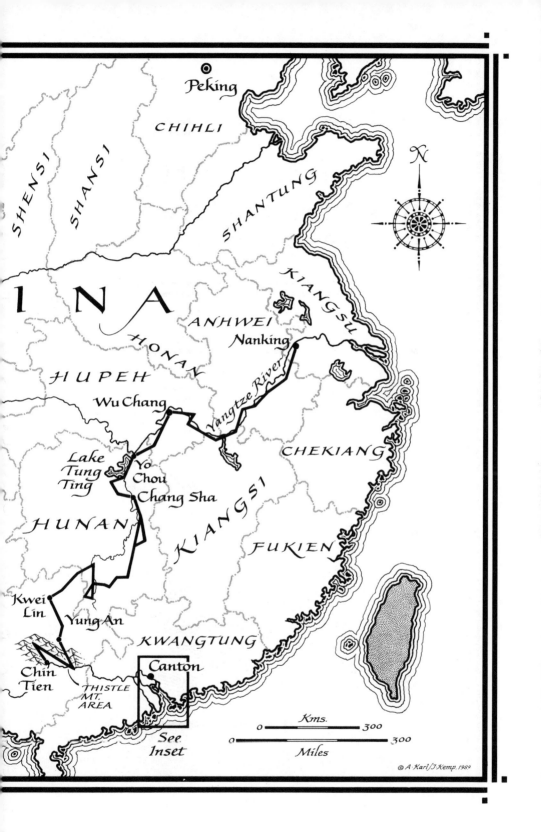

Peking

CHIHLI

SHENSI

SHANSI

SHANTUNG

KIANGSU

 INA

HONAN

ANHWEI

Nanking

HUPEH

Wu Chang

Yangtze River

Lake
Tung
Ting

Yo
Chou

Chang Sha

CHEKIANG

HUNAN

KIANGSI

FUKIEN

Kwei
Lin

Yung An

KWANGTUNG

Chin
Tien

THISTLE
MT.
AREA

Canton

See
Inset

Kms.
0   300
0   300
Miles

© A. Karl/J. Kemp. 1989

Part 1
SPIRIT WOMAN

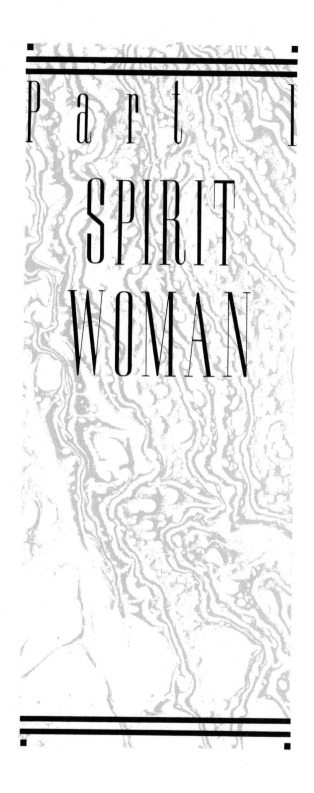

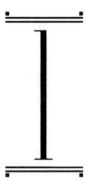

Hakka Village, Kwangsi Province, 1847

"Where is your mother, child?" croaked the old woman outside the door. A torch's flame coiled and hissed about the gray head, lighting her eyes with fire.

Was this the headman's wife, or a cunning *kuei,* a demon, who had eaten the spirit of that old, dry stick and now was hungry for new flesh? Rulan wondered.

The night world was full of demons: weasel spirits, water demons, fox-spirits, *ku*-creatures, drowned girl-ghosts. Rulan tried to clear her throat and spit, because spit warded off small demons, but her mouth was dry.

The crone thumped her fist against the door. Desperately, the girl wound the jute thong around the wall peg one more time, praying that it wouldn't break under the hag's pounding. A crimson stain of light flowed through the crack in the door and across the earthen floor as Rulan backed away into the rear chamber of the two-room hut. Dry, spidery branches of herbs hanging from the rafters caught in the girl's long hair.

"Little Stupid!" called the crone. "Move your big feet faster. The stranger in the clan hall is possessed. I saw him crawling on the floor like a snake. The headman wants your mother—now!" the old woman screeched. Her red mouth agape at the narrow door opening, she howled like a dead soul at the River of No Hope. "Ailan! Sister-in-law! Come at once!" she addressed the girl's mother. "If the stranger dies from the demon, then our clan is undone. His people will demand compensation, turn us in to the Punti officials at the county seat, spread lies about us among all the villages. Then what will our clan do for shame?"

"Mother! An evil one," Rulan whispered to Ailan.

Ailan stirred in the single bed the family shared. The naked baby curled against her began suckling again. "It's Auntie," Ailan told her daughter. "Tell her to wait a moment—quietly." Her body had grown as taut as a sea bird girding itself against a tempest, and the child, sensing the mother's alarm, began to whimper. Ailan touched a hand to the hard, brown body beside her, but Yang, her husband, was already awake. He held down her thighs with his leg and grunted his disapproval. Ailan heard the girl tiptoe to the door and deliver the message, then the old lady whine before choking into silence. The only beast more prevalent than evil this night, Ailan thought, was fear.

After a moment, Yang laughed gruffly and removed his leg. "More demon business," he said scornfully. Only then did Ailan rise to tuck the half-sleeping boy into the curve of her husband's arm. Yang was a proud, rough man with calloused hands stained black from coal dust and a face as worn as a mountain. He was a full-time bearer of rice and charcoal over the mountain passes, a part-time smuggler of salt and opium, or "black dirt," and a commander of men as rough and ruthless as himself. The only one he could not command was his wife, Ailan, the village spirit-woman and priestess of Kwan Yin, the Goddess of Mercy.

Breathing rhythmically, Ailan drew together the tips of her fingers in a rapid pinching movement, as if she were shaping an invisible lump of dough. She felt the space between her hands fill with heat. Slowly, she placed her hands on either side of a jar of medicine on the table next to the bed and blessed it.

"Demon business," the man in the bed repeated.

Ailan ignored him. "Where are your manners, Daughter?" she chided in a loud voice, while moving out of the dim corona of lamplight, as Rulan came back into the room where the family slept in a single bed. "Only a dumb lout girl would forget to ask Auntie into the house." In a different voice, she whispered, "Couldn't you tell she was not the *kuei*? She was afraid. Ghosts do not smell of sweat. The evil spirit crept into the village early this evening. All night I felt him—he is big, in the body of the stranger, with dark power to change the course of water under the earth!"

Ailan reached for the blue trousers that served her day and night, shook them for fleas, and pulled them up around her tall, thin frame.

Then she bound her breasts with a square of rough cotton, shrugged on the shapeless tunic that every village woman in South China wore, and secured the loose trousers with a length of hemp. Fully dressed, she was just another village wife, except for her height, unusual in a region of small women, her amber complexion, and heavy silver ear hoops, marks of the aboriginal Loi blood that ran in her veins.

"Shall I confess?" teased Yang from the bed. "Spirit-woman, it was I who sent the stranger to plague our turtle of a headman." His face softened unexpectedly when Ailan turned toward him. "What, am I as simple as that superstitious hag outside?"

"Snake spirits are cruel to unbelievers," Ailan replied more harshly than she'd intended. Squatting before a line of medicine gourds whose necks were tied with colored thread, she selected one, sniffed at the neck, and poured its dry contents into her hand. When she discovered the herbs were powdery with age, she threw them into a corner, set the gourd aside, and smelled the opening of another. To this second batch of herbs she added the potion she had blessed. Satisfied, she tied the gourd to the rope around her waist and approached the bed. "In my grandmother's time, snake-men hunted the world and ate men."

Yang laughed. "Snake-men want soft, oily flesh. The kind that clings to a rich man's bones. My meat is too tough. So let the evil *kuei* come! I will blow them away." When he puffed out his cheeks in murderous ferocity and crossed his eyes, Rulan squealed in delight. His "ghost" face, which he used whenever Ailan challenged him, never failed to reduce his daughter to helpless giggles.

Ailan scowled and undulated her hands across the space between them as if sweeping away her husband's words. "There is magic in words," she reminded him again after Rulan's hilarity had passed. "Don't tempt the spirits." She smiled down at the sleeping baby. "Boy-Boy," she crooned and reached out her hands to hold him, but Yang clutched the babe to his chest.

"Let him be," he growled and waved his wife away.

Ailan frowned. "Get up, Rulan. Go out and gather sticks. Wait—take this!" She pulled out a clove of star anise from a tiny medicine gourd and pressed it into Rulan's hand. "Keep it in your cheek and close your mouth. If the spirit tries to force its way into you, it will find the way barred. Then call the spirit by its secret name, *Ku,* and it will not harm you."

"You're taking Little Quail?" Yang asked, using the "milk name" by which Rulan was known in her family. "Let my daughter stay. It might be dangerous," Yang told his wife.

"I need her," she replied.

"So do I. Who will take care of me when you do not?"

"She has to learn the ways of spirit-women," Ailan said.

"Learn what? How to feed women's ailments and banish ghosts? No time for foolishness now. This land is gearing up for war, and girls as well as boys must prepare."

"What do you propose to teach her? To haul charcoal? To smuggle 'dirt'?" said Ailan.

"If need be. Or to carry a sword. If need be."

"No. That is not the way of the spirit."

Outside, the old woman called out impatiently to Ailan. Yang closed his eyes. When his wife and daughter were gone, he whispered to his year-old son, "Good. The spirit-women are away. Now we warriors of common earth are alone."

Muttering and quavering, the old woman led mother and daughter along narrow lanes to the clan hall. Rulan felt the night crackling with spirit energy. Looking up into the sky, she saw the moon scuttling through a dark bank of clouds like a frightened woman lost on a mountain road. Each bush, each tree had become something strange and other than itself. Then the curved roof of the Village Hall loomed over them, and in her excitement Rulan forgot about Yang lying with the infant in the narrow bed and her own suspicions that she had let her father down.

As the women stepped around the masonry spirit-screen that prevented ghosts from flying into the hall, the crowd in the courtyard surged against them.

"Spirit-woman, save us!" shrieked a wild-eyed woman, bent by the weight of the baby on her back, while another touched Ailan's medicine gourd with a reverent finger. Others plucked at Ailan's hair, shirt, and cheeks, wailing and swaying to the rhythm of their common terror. A huge mango tree stretched its limbs over the hall like a spider dropped from the skies.

The raw stench of fear assailed Rulan's nostrils as she followed her mother into the eating room. Dozens of wicks floated in oil lamps like glowing worms. Half a dozen elders of the village were pressed against the walls. Chairs and tables were kicked over; shards of broken porcelain were strewn on the ground. And a soft, bubbling sound, like the movement of the tide, quivered in the stillness.

In the middle of the room, the headman and two strangers—a man and a girl—stood with stricken faces around a heap of discarded clothing. Rulan dropped her sheaf of twigs near the half-eaten carcass of a bewhiskered carp lying in a dark puddle of spilled wine. The smell had grown unbearable: sweat and spoiled food mixed with vomit and feces. Suddenly, the headman squawked and the village elders scurried like frightened chickens around the edges of the hall; the rags had begun to writhe and twist as if an errant wind had spun them into life. The filth-encrusted rags became a living creature, a man. He rose to his knees and stretched his neck like a cobra.

The two strangers crept out of a corner toward Ailan. The man had the jerky intensity of a mongoose, with darting eyes that registered everything but saw nothing. He seemed more afraid of the crowd than of the apparition on the floor. The girl hanging on his arm was small, plain and sturdily built, with the same heavy features and dark skin as the snake-man.

"I am Wei, from Kuei Ping district. I own a pawnshop. I'm an educated man," he proclaimed, as if someone had challenged him. "I have powerful friends in Canton." Although his words were carefully chosen to make him seem refined, Ailan recognized the unmistakable country Hakka accent. She had heard of Wei's clan, a large and bellicose one in a rugged area called Thistle Mountain.

Pawnbroker Wei pointed to the man swaying in the dust and added boldly, "That is Hung Hsiu Chuan, a man chosen by the High God to right wrongs, but who knows what happens when gods contend for a spirit of a man? This is Jiao, his sister. We heard in the next village that your clan had trouble with the district authorities. We were going to offer our services, when suddenly, while explaining how our Manchu overlords have afflicted us too long, my friend fell down—"

"That—thing there—that is not my brother," the girl gasped through her tears.

Pawnbroker Wei gripped the weeping girl's shoulders and shook her sternly. "Enough," he chided. "We are not ignorant folk to fear a thing like this." Wei's attempt to keep up his dignity before the suspicious headman was beginning to flag. Under his breath, Wei spoke rapidly to Ailan. "Take your medicines and go away, Loi woman. We do not need you. Once before he was like this, when he failed the civil examinations for the third time. He was forty days in a sleep as deep as death. He awoke that time touched by God!" He regarded Ailan's impassive countenance with growing disgust. "Aiya, never mind. You are Loi, and cannot understand. All you need to know, woman, is that the sickness is temporary. When he awakes he will be charged with holiness, so tell your kinsmen to let us watch and pray for him in our own way and in the morning we will be gone."

"No!" protested Hung's sister. "Let the spirit-woman help if she can."

"No more, or you take away my face," he admonished the girl.

The headman spoke sharply to Wei. "You come as strangers to our village. You, who eat rice from our bowl, insult us. You read and write, so you think earth-magic and spirit-women are sham. You mock us even as you defile our ancestors' hall and insult our kinswoman."

The assembled elders muttered angrily. They too were offended by the rodent-faced man's peremptory manner and aghast at the evil he had brought into their midst.

Wei was not one to hold his tongue, no matter how menacing the situation. "This man and I are called by the High God to deliver you from unrighteousness."

"Throw the devils out!" someone yelled.

Hung's sister began to cry. "Auntie," she beseeched Ailan, "only love for my brother makes Wei speak so rudely. He does not know, as I do, that this spell is not like the other time. That is not the High God speaking through him, but a *kuei,* a monster, who has stolen my brother's soul. You know the old ways, Auntie, the Loi chants and potions—"

"Leave him alone, Loi woman," interrupted Wei. "Don't meddle in things beyond your understanding. He has been chosen by the High God to bring the rule of heaven to earth, and I am to be His scourge."

A long hiss interrupted Wei's angry speech. The snake-man swayed, spat, and farted. His red eyes gleamed.

Ailan peered at the twisting shape and said sharply to the pawnbroker. "But I know this *kuei.* He and I are old adversaries."

Ailan knelt and pointed to the stricken man's face. "I know your name. You are *Ku,* the viper. You suck the life from our sons and pull our daughters down to your watery house to bear your children."

He shot forward and struck Ailan's chest viciously with his head. Instinct made her roll away as he struck again, narrowly missing her belly. In rage and disappointment, he pursued her, while she darted left, now right, struggling to keep outside the arc of his whirling body. Finally he seemed to tire and curled upon the floor like a giant larva.

Squatting on her haunches, Ailan panted, "*Ku,* you are old and selfish. Why do you want this man?"

The thick lips barely moved. A thin, metallic sound echoed in his chest. "This is my chosen, my beloved. I cherish him for his evil ways."

Rulan's mouth was dry. She reached into her pocket, put the star anise behind her front teeth, and bit down hard.

"Old one, I know your true shape," said Ailan. "I have eaten the eyes of a crow. You cannot hide here. Kwan Yin, the Merciful Goddess, protects this clan and all who seek sanctuary in this hall. This man has done you no ill. Give him back," Ailan scolded, as if the demon were a naughty child.

The man began to wheeze and gasp; his gasps became long inhalations until in minutes his stomach had swollen to twice its size, and his face and limbs had ballooned. "The man is mine, Loi witch," he belched, while his pointed tongue flicked in and out of a face that bulged round and thick as a pumpkin. His red eyes blinked for a moment as Jiao screamed. Rulan thought she saw pain flicker in the depths of his gaze, but then the smile returned, cold and lizardlike.

"I say that you cannot have him," shouted Ailan. "You are unworthy."

"He is mine already," spat the demon.

When it seemed that the man might burst, the swelling suddenly stopped. For a long while, the bloated shape lay still. Then one small red eye popped open and rolled around in the gigantic head. Smiling, the creature began to emit a noxious gas that spread through the room. The mouth opened, spewing liquids hissing out of the orifices of his body. The smells of vomit and diarrhea sickened Ailan. Shrunken now, the man raised himself out of his filth and arched his back. Tiny tremors rippled up and down his spine.

The elders huddling against the walls began to wail and pray. In the courtyard outside, women shrieked and covered their children's faces with their hands.

"The sticks, Daughter," cried Ailan, sensing the panic spreading through the crowd, yet not daring to take her eyes from the man. "Set them there on the floor near me. But do not get in the way of the beast."

Taking the sheaf of twigs into her arms, Rulan scuttled to her mother, while holding the star anise behind her front teeth with her tongue. Why the sticks? Rulan wondered. Did her mother mean to build a fire to burn the viper out? She glanced once at the possessed man, afraid that his stained and sinewy hands were about to grab her as she passed, but his eyes were fixed on Ailan's white face. Nervously she tightened the old cord binding the twigs together. It broke. Ailan looked up in alarm.

"Quickly, take off your shirt and stuff it with the twigs."

In exorcisms Rulan had been taught to follow Ailan's instructions without question lest she jeopardize the victim's life . . . or her own. Blushing, Rulan pulled open the fastenings at the neck and shoulders and shrugged off the faded shift. Naked then to the waist before all the elders, she felt her skin prickle with embarrassment. Although only eleven, Rulan had the full breasts and dark nipples of a grown woman. The elders looked away in shame. But the demon-man so devoured her with his eyes that Rulan could feel the heat within the madness of his stare.

Uttering a sharp cry, Ailan shook out her hair and thrust out her arms. The gesture seemed to startle the demon, who turned from Rulan to hiss at the mother. Rulan was struck then with a new terror, not for herself but for Ailan, who was gasping for breath under the heavy veil of hair. It was as if the *kuei* were sucking the life from Ailan with every spell she tried to cast. Rulan had seen her mother confront tree demons and water spirits, drive off the flying heads who burrow in the riverbanks for worms; she had seen her mother make ghosts speak through the mouths of neighbors and cousins. Not once had Ailan shown weakness in all the encounters with ghouls and devils, until now.

"Fasten your shirt around them," Ailan commanded her weakly.

Rulan crouched low to hide her body from the men's eyes. She wrapped the cloth around the twigs, trying to tie the sleeves around the bundle. But the sleeves were short and hard to knot.

"Tighter," came her mother's firm voice. "The sticks must not come out. Use this." Ailan patted Rulan's waist.

Rulan's icy fingers fumbled at the cord that held up her thin trousers. In seconds, the sticks were tightly swaddled into a blue bundle the size of a baby, and Rulan stood naked before the demon, who squirmed upon the floor.

"Throw it here," Ailan commanded, tossing back her hair over her shoulder and holding up her hands. But as Rulan hurled the bundle, the man's body seemed to lengthen and his head catapulted forward. Ailan dodged the blow and caught the sticks as neatly as a boatwoman catches a child passed from boat to boat. The crowd cried out in surprise. But now the man, gliding on his knees, was slowly forcing Ailan against the wall. Panting and disheveled, she held the effigy before her and chanted

> *Ku,* who steals the soul of man,
> Turn back to the water, into icy sand,
> Sink in the slime of the Swollen Sea
> I am the Merciful. Hearken and obey me.

"Thou shalt surely die," the demon vowed. Now the body of the man seemed to fly across the floor. He hit Ailan with such force that the bundle was knocked from her hands and rolled against a table. His body pressed against hers, and he sunk his teeth into her shoulder at the base of her neck.

"Break the sticks!" Ailan shouted, flailing at the creature. The two grappled in a whirlwind of hair and spittle. Then her scream was all pain.

Dry twigs snapped as Rulan stamped on the sticks with the full force of her right foot. A sharp crack came from the demon's body. He arched his back in a spasm of pain. Blood ran from his mouth, but his jaws refused to give up their prize.

The villagers were frozen in horror. No one had the courage even to run. Jiao crouched like a small stone lion next to Pawnbroker Wei in the doorway.

"Again, quickly," Ailan groaned, "before he strikes once more."

This time Rulan landed with both feet on the sticks, which cracked like a spine broken by a mace. The demon contorted and screamed.

The sticks felt like burning brands on the bottoms of Rulan's feet. She felt them break as easily as brittle bones, and she tried not to listen to the awful sounds of the shuddering shape that was wrestling her mother to the ground.

"Harder!" said Ailan, struggling to pull herself upright. "It is the *ku*-creature you are trampling, not this innocent one."

Rulan had heard the loud, cracking noise in the man's back; still, like a dying beast, his teeth remained buried in her mother's neck. Rulan moved forward, but Ailan frantically signaled her away. The girl stopped, torn between duty to her mother and an overwhelming urge to save her, because Ailan was growing visibly weaker. The weight of the man had bent her body backward nearly in half. Ailan tried to shake him loose, tried to pull his jaws apart with her fingers, but he held on to her flesh like a vise. Her eyes were glazed with pain; blood ran over her shirt, his blood mixed with hers. Her hand went up, the fingers grasping nothingness, like a woman drowning.

Rulan sprang forward and grasped the man by the hair. His eyes rolled back in his head. With her left hand she forced her fingers into the side of his mouth to pry him off her mother's throat. Then spreading her legs wide and squaring her shoulders, she gripped his queue with her right hand and pulled hard.

Ailan dropped like a dead animal to the floor, as the man ground his teeth on Rulan's fingers. The pain was excruciating, but Rulan gripped the man's hair tighter until with agonizing slowness, his teeth began to loosen their hold.

Just as Rulan let go of the snake-man's braid, he lunged toward her, his teeth bared.

The gesture came as easily to Rulan as if she had practiced it for years. She lifted two gnawed and bloody fingers before her as she had seen her mother do when an intractable demon refused to leave a broken body. Heat surged from the center of her chest across her shoulder and down her left arm, jolting her upper body with its unexpected force. Some primal instinct made her jab his forehead with the tips of her fingers. The man clutched his skull as if he had been stabbed with the point of a spear. A terrible tremor shook his body from forehead to feet.

"Aaiiee!" he screamed, writhing in the dirt. His legs raked the ground like the tail of a wounded fish. Back and forth swung the legs in great serpentine strokes, leaving long tracks in the earthen floor before drawing back for a final, desperate lunge.

Freed, Ailan had found a wine pot that had fallen to the floor. Reaching into the medicine gourd that hung from her belt, she swirled the liquid once, twice, and wet her fingertips with wine. She flicked the drops in a circle around her. Wherever the droplets touched the snake-man, they seemed to sear his flesh.

Before the man could strike her daughter, Ailan lunged forward and gripped his head in the crook of her elbow. The demon tried to buck the spirit-woman loose, but Ailan tightened her hold. With iron-hard fingers, she pushed the spout of the gourd between his swollen lips. The man retched and drenched her shirt with vomit and tried to pull his head away, but he was caught fast under her arm. Mercilessly, Ailan filled the mouth with the brackish brew and kept pouring while the medicine flowed on them both, until, gasping and choking, he swallowed and was still.

"Rulan, sing the song of the silkworm sleeping."

The girl's tremulous, reedy voice broke through the sleeper's harsh breathing. Soon the song had charmed the man into sleep, but the singer could not forget the little star pricking the side of her cheek. The air inside the hall had turned to ice, making Rulan all the more aware of a pulsing warmth that flooded up from her throbbing heart across her chest and down her left arm. Half her body burned; the other half began to shiver. Crossing her hands on her chest as much to keep warm as to hide her nakedness, Rulan willed the tears of pain from her eyes and the trembling from her lips.

"Sleep. Sleep little darling. Into thy cocoon. Dream," Rulan sang, while the man in her mother's arms lay as still as death.

The song ended. For what seemed an eternity, no one moved. In the silence, Rulan could hear the dogs barking at the night ghosts in the village downriver. The moving river of heat had faded into a faint tingling; her fingers no longer throbbed, although her heart felt sore. Ailan rose from her haunches and shook out her stiffened limbs one by one. "*Ku*-dragon, awake and come this way," she called softly. In one graceful movement, the spirit-woman bent her body like a bow and trailed her fingertips along the floor, gliding backward toward the open doorway. The wall of terrified faces parted and vanished. There was the soft sound of scurrying feet.

"Go home, my darling," sang Ailan, flinging her hands toward the door. "Hide yourself far from here. Rest. Sleep." An eerie presence seemed to free itself from her and follow the direction in which she pointed; Rulan thought she saw something sear a path across the empty courtyard as the women fell back whimpering. It streaked across the village common, across the dark waters of the fishponds and spent itself among the tangled grasses of the swamp.

Ailan turned back from the doorway. But the man she expected to see broken and in need of medicine was standing upright. He looked up at her with eyes that were blindingly bright. Ailan thought it was like staring straight into the sun. She saw for the first time that his front hair was not shaved, but hung long and loose into his eyes. He tossed the lock of hair away from his broad forehead. Suddenly, his tongue began to move uncontrollably, triggering a strange ululation, a wild, barbaric string of liquid syllables. On and on he sang. Sometimes the notes cut through the air like a *jing wei* bird's jagged cries. Sometimes the sound plunged to a whisper.

Ailan was amazed. She had driven out the demon. Who was this new singer? And what was his wild song? There was nothing in her magic she could use against this music. Ailan, who knew where the mountain demons hid and where the *hsing-hsing* apes whistle in the high passes, had never heard such words before, and yet she understood their meaning. All her strength was pulled toward the sound of his voice, like the tide rushing back to the depths of the sea. A terrible yearning rose within her. Even the hairs on her head seemed to want to fly away toward the uncanny music. In his voice were sounds that men and women love and fear most: flames snapping, water lapping, earth shaking, heart breaking.

The man shook his hair like a lion, slapped his hands on his knees and roared

> My eyes see beyond the west and the north, the rivers and
>   the mountains.
> My voice shakes the east and south, the empires of the
>   sun and the moon.
> My arms enclose the narrow cloud-roads.

I turn over, without fear; I turn the stars in the sky.
I have swum with the dragon who dwells below.
Now I yield to the destiny that lives in my body!

"Are you *Ku*? What is your name?" whispered Ailan, shuddering. For the first time in her life, she could not recognize the essence behind the shifting emanation. "What do you want from me?"

"He comes, the Younger Son of God," Pawnbroker Wei shouted. Wei's pinched face was suffused with joy. He looked like a child about to receive a long-awaited prize.

The man turned his radiance on Ailan. "Sister, I am Hung Hsiu Chuan, Younger Brother to Jesus the Christ, Carpenter God of the sea barbarians. I have been asleep for these few hours, until just now when I heard a voice calling, 'You are still sleepy? You have not awakened?' "

Jiao threw herself into her brother's arms.

But Hung put his sister aside. "O ye of little faith, to trust in demons and witches of the old days more than in me," he chided. Weeping, Jiao pleaded for her brother's forgiveness, but Hung turned away from her and saluted Wei with a dignified bow. "I have no sisters among those who do not believe in me. This man is my brother for he knows who I am. Therefore will I give him a rod to hold over my family."

Pawnbroker Wei dropped to his knees, and Hung put both hands on his friend's head to bless him. "Faithful one," he said. "My Heavenly Father has said to me, 'I will make your descendants as numerous as the stars in heaven.' Go now, dear friend, and I will make the faithful flock to you. It is time you and I were about the Father's business."

Jiao wept bitterly.

"It was my voice you heard. My medicine that brought you back to life," said Ailan harshly. She dared not put into words the awful suspicion that blossomed at the back of her mind—she could vanquish *Ku,* the malignant reptile spirit of the south who dwelt in the watery pit, but not this man and his strange new evil whose essence she could neither name nor grasp.

Hung put a finger to his lips and shook his head. "What is your medicine? Witch's words? *Ku*-poison?" He and Wei exchanged smiles. "Loi sister, I know you from the place beyond." Then, seeing the curious village folk spill through the open door, Hung held up his hands before his chest. "Hear me, my Beloved," he shouted in a voice like a clanging cymbal. "Before I descended from heaven a moment ago, I fought the ancient demon and vanquished him. I dug out his eyes, I pulled off his tail, I turned him upside down and bid him hide in the Swollen Sea. But I did not slay him lest all the souls whom he had swallowed be lost forever. I have come to tell you of Taiping Tien Kuo, the Kingdom of Great Peace on the shores of the heavenly sea. The great ladder of power is upended—emperor, scholar, and slave—all are equal in heaven's eyes. No longer will the foreign Manchu ride Han people as horses. Listen to me.

> East, north, west, and south,
> Who—man or woman—will be my comrade?
> Cloud-dragons and wind-tigers.
> Who will march with me?

Again he turned to Wei. "Once more I have talked face-to-face with God and seen into the hollow gourd of the future," he said softly. "In the Empire of Heaven to come, you will be a king."

Wei hid his red, eager face in his hands.

Then Hung saw Rulan. Embarrassed by her nakedness, she crouched on the floor, her bleeding hand hiding her bare breast. His eyes warmed. Pushing his friend aside, Hung held out both arms.

"Come," he said, walking toward her. "I recognized you as my beloved when you laid your hands on me. You broke the serpent's back. The Holy Spirit flows through you. You are mine, the gift of the Spirit from God the Father."

"I do not understand, sir," Rulan said.

"You do not have to understand, only believe. Do what I command and I will make you first among women, first in heaven and earth." He lifted up the frightened girl, kissed her bleeding fingers, and presented her to the crowd like a bride.

Rulan found herself blushing at Hung's touch. She saw that Hung was handsome and forgot about the twisting, shuddering shape on the floor. His words resounded in her head like the echo of a gong: "First among women, first in heaven and earth."

Ailan snatched Rulan from Hung's grasp.

"You cannot keep her. She will return to me," he shouted.

"Never," cried Ailan. "Your evil cannot claim her," and she fled the hall with her bewildered daughter.

In the days that followed, Hung taught the villagers many things. At first they asked Wei, "Is this not the pig religion of the long-nosed barbarians, the very ones who steal Han babies and sacrifice them to the Carpenter God?"

Pawnbroker Wei answered them, "Do not put your trust in ignorant witches. Our Brother Hung is the incarnation of a new man. He brings a new dispensation. The High God, recognizing the special place of the Land of Flowers, has sent us His Younger Son to drive out the demon Manchu. In this task I am his prophet. The Canton merchant guilds are at my disposal. The Triad secret societies call me headman. Follow us and concubines, great estates, all manner of riches will be yours. You will enjoy the joys of heaven while here on earth."

The people were confused by these utterances, until Hung's words and songs convinced them. What he preached went against centuries of tradition, but reduced by famine and Manchu taxes, they threw off the customs of their ancestors to clothe themselves in hope. He made the headman kowtow to him nine times in the dust before the Village Hall, which he had taken as his residence. He declared Confucius the "King of Hell" and the Manchu officials "imps and demons." Then he ordered Wei to instruct the men in the purposes the High God ordained for them, while he addressed himself to the women.

"You are too fond of your husbands," he scolded. "You see how perverse and licentious you have become. Be ashamed!" He took his young sister Jiao to the Buddhist temple and made her topple the statues of Kwan Yin, the Goddess of Mercy, and Kwan Kung, the God of War. When Ailan, wracked with fever from the venomous bite, raged at him for the desecration done to the shrines, he pointed an accusing finger in her direction and said, "You must hasten to make yourself upright. Heaven declares you a demon if you continue to worship demons! Your daughter is forfeit." Jiao led the nuns, who had been Ailan's companions, to turn on her with sticks, forcing her to flee the temple of Kwan Yin.

Hung said all women were his sisters, and he praised the Hakka wives for not binding their daughters' feet in the fashion of the decadent Punti gentry. He sighed over the young girls, touching their cheeks and hair, and called them his "beautiful moons," until Jiao grew jealous and shooed them home. Wei brought men and women from neighboring Hakka districts to the village well to listen to Hung preach, and Hung's sister grasped the hand of each man and woman who promised to give "strings of cash," copper coins strung on twine through holes in their middle.

Sometimes Hung's words were filled with a sweet foreboding: "You will not err if you follow me. But people in the world will slander you, jeer at you, and despise you."

But the people liked best to hear Hung describe what he had seen on his last ascent to heaven. Then Hung's voice became a gong that made the young girls tremble with love and the young men yearn for a sword and the open road. He described the beautiful maidens dressed in saffron, the armies of angels who fought beside him in the forty-day battle with the serpent, and God the Father, in a tricornered hat and black dragon robe, whose golden whiskers brushed the ground. Using his long white hands, he showed them how God the Father had cut out his stomach, put in a new one and said, " 'You are my Youngest Son in whom I am well pleased. I send you into the world to exterminate the wicked and preserve the upright.' "

In the evening, Hung would sing the songs of the High Heaven for all to hear. His translucent eyes shining, he told them about Father Noah, the Ten Commandments, and always about the High God's judgment on his chosen.

"Beloved," he reminded his new disciples. "I am the true Younger Son of Heaven, next in line to my Elder Brother, whom the long-noses call Jesus the Christ. I have come down to tell you of the delights that await you if you follow me."

"He is mad. He is evil," Ailan warned them. "You were afraid of *Ku,* the snake demon that preceded him in that body, but this one is worse by a hundredfold." No one listened. When Ailan tried to restore the altar of Kwan Yin, Jiao roused the nuns against her. Together, they drove away Ailan and her daughter with stones and poured pig's blood over the food offerings Ailan had brought.

"Why do you despise that marvelous man?" asked Rulan in confusion as she stumbled after her mother.

Ailan grieved that her daughter, a girl who could read omens and see spirits, could not recognize Hung's evil.

By the end of a week, Yang, the charcoal-carrier, was sitting at Hung's feet. Night after night he would return to their cold house to argue with Ailan. Huddled on the bed next to the child, Rulan listened to her parents quarrel with increasing dread.

"Why do you resist him? You set him free!" Yang said.

"I have seen his light. It is dark, like coals in a deep pit. He brings war, dying, fire," Ailan replied.

"There are always such signs when a new dynasty begins. This man is the one to tear the rottenness down. After all the waiting—"

"A thousand pretenders arise every year, in every province, every village, and are crushed like beetles under the heels of the soldiers," Ailan reminded him.

"But you have felt his strength!"

"It comes from the wrong direction. He is north. Beware!"

Yang smiled. "A good omen! He will march north and shake the pretender off his throne. And those who join him will be first to reign in his kingdom!"

"Hung's evil will surely destroy you," warned Ailan.

"How do you know?" Yang retorted. "You say that about everything you don't understand. This man is different! When he speaks, people put aside their jealousies. They burn for love of him! Look how he made what was dead in me burn again!"

Ailan sat down heavily on the edge of their bed and stared hollow-eyed at the man who had given all he had to make her his wife. She hardly noticed the children huddled under the blanket beside her. "And after the fire rages across this Land of Flowers," she told him. "After the cities are ashes and stone—"

"Good! Good, I say!" shouted Yang. Only the tremor in his voice betrayed his anguish. "Burn out the Manchu! Pull down the great houses of the officials. Let beggars be kings and rule themselves!" Suddenly, with a cry, he dropped to his knees and pressed his face into his wife's lap. "Ailan," he whispered, "even beggars dream dreams."

He nuzzled the warm scented flesh through her thin trousers, felt her hot tears falling on his rough cheek, and found his own body quickening. When he gripped her thighs, she sighed. So often their quarrels ended this way—anger giving way to passion.

"No!" he said abruptly, twisting away from his wife's soft hands. "Your world is finished now that Hung has walked among us. Give them up, I say, the demons and paper idols and false charms and woman-gods. Hung needs your power!"

Ailan recoiled in dismay. "Kwan Yin will not let me!"

Angrily, Yang flung himself away from his wife. "Hung has issued a command," he announced. " 'Sell all you have and follow me.' The charcoal-carriers have agreed to go, and the fisherfolk, the rice farmers, the cutters of cane, and the salt gatherers. The sellers of pigs and ducks and dogs. The headman and elders. All the wives and unmarried sons and daughters and babes-in-arms . . ." His face was stark. "There is nothing I can give you here. But in a new place, where I can be fully a man, I will fill your lap with pearls and jade. Will you come?"

Despair seized Ailan, but her pride would not allow her suffering to show. "I can plant," she answered briskly. "Even without you, the children and I will not starve—"

Yang turned away, wounded. "Only the old ones will remain. Would you let the girl grow up among the dying?"

Ailan groped on the bed to where Rulan crouched with the child. She drew her daughter closer. "I haven't taught her all she needs to know. If there are old ones, she will be needed. A spirit-woman learns from childhood to serve."

Yang stumbled toward the bed. With thick, awkward fingers, he turned his daughter's frightened face to his. "Little Quail," he said gruffly. "Don't you want to be a warrior and ride a horse to battle?"

Rulan sat up and looked from father to mother in confusion. Jostled from sleep, the infant began to wail.

"She's a healer, not a killer," Ailan said, aghast, and pulled the girl away.

Ailan opened the front of her tunic and began to nurse the weeping child. The boy's cries ceased suddenly as he began to suckle. Silence cut like a sword between husband and wife.

"That is what you want?" Ailan said finally.

"Yes, yes," Yang told her. "I must be with him to do this work."

"And what about the children? What about the clan?" Ailan was too proud to beg for herself, but her hand pointed to her own breast.

Yang would not look into his wife's ravaged face. "This one thing I want for myself! And for you and for my children and their children. Is that wrong? The magistrates tell us to yield. Self, they say, is the root of evil. Self tears down family, clan, empire. But I am weary of bending."

"Husband," Ailan pleaded. "Who breaks first when the typhoon crashes? The upright branch, not the supple one. To bend is to survive!"

Yang laughed, but his face flamed. "What, am I a woman?" He grimaced as if she had struck him a blow. "Let me be a man. Let me be strong for you."

And Ailan knew that he had already decided.

The villagers too had made up their minds.

"I read his dreams before he awakened," Ailan cried to their departing backs. "You will perish by thousands and burn in a circle of fire. He will utterly destroy this Land of Flowers."

They paid her no heed, but instead sold their lands for copper cash, filled oxcarts with provisions, and set out on the road as their nomad Hakka ancestors had done in the last exodus from central China a thousand years before. They called themselves the Society of God Worshipers. By the end of the month, to the great rejoicing of the rival Punti "old-timer" clans who coveted the bleak hills that the Hakka "guest people" had wrested from them a millennium earlier, two-thirds of the Hakka families in the district had taken to the road to follow Hung, his friend Wei, and his sister Jiao. They left behind the tablets and tombs of their fathers, the sick, the timorous and the elderly, and Ailan, her daughter, and her infant son. One of the captains of the wanderers was Yang, Rulan's father, who led a column of charcoal-carriers on the long march north. He dreamed of pulling down the Manchu usurper from the Dragon Throne, putting Hung, God's Younger Son, in his place, and returning to make his wife a queen.

Ailan was fourteen when she was sold by the Loi to a rich Punti family named Li who lived on the monsoon coast of Heungsan county near the mouth of the Pearl River. The mistress of the house, the Tai Tai, kept Ailan as her personal maid until the day the girl turned eighteen and the contract was fulfilled. Ailan refused the Tai Tai's attempt to marry her off to a groom of the house and went instead to a *chai tang,* a Buddhist "vegetarian hall" where only women lived, in the next province. There she learned to raise worms and spin silk and chant sutras to their patron saint, the Goddess of Mercy, Kwan Yin. It was there at the women's house that Yang—the wild, exuberant Hakka charcoal peddler—spotted the girl in colorful Loi headdress and skirt who was loading bales of rough silk onto the backs of mules as easily as a man. He begged her to take him as her man, without ceremony, as Loi lovers do, but Ailan had learned civility from her former mistress and would not violate Han custom despite her origins. So Yang risked his Hakka clansman's disdain and paid one year's profits, all that he had, to the women's house to make a proper Han wedding: the feast was spare, a few cakes, wine, chickens, and oranges, and a rented gown for the bride. The "mother" of the women's house acted as Ailan's parents and the "sisters" of the commune stood in for her brothers and uncles.

It was a dangerous marriage. In the south, where many of warring races vied for the same rocky ground and fishing space, marriage with an outsider blurred the precious distinctions that kept a people unique. Aboriginal tribes such as the Miao, the Yao, the Loi, and the Tanka, who had been pushed by their Han conquerors onto remote islands, cliffs, and waters, had survived not by fighting the Han but by avoiding them. The Han themselves were divided in the south into two warring tribes, the Punti and the Hakka. These shared the same ancestors in central China but had convinced themselves that they were two separate peoples with distinct histories, languages, and customs.

In 1839 when Rulan was two, Yang was conscripted into the provincial army and sent to Canton to fight the British in the Opium War. The defeat of the Chinese army transformed Yang, as it did all of China. He turned sullen and withdrawn, shunning his wife to spend long days in the high country carrying charcoal and salt for wealthy merchants and nurturing his perpetual anger at the rich. He had done none of the great deeds he had dreamed of. In frustration, he committed petty acts of vandalism to annoy the Manchu officials and sold his services to the river pirates who were in league with the secret societies.

The Hakka rejected the surly Yang, although he was one of their own, but embraced his Loi wife. Ailan gratefully adopted Hakka customs, for the Hakka were the one Han tribe that endowed women with almost as much power as the matriarchal Loi. Energetic and proud, Hakka women considered themselves the equal of men and would not curb their tongues nor bind their feet like Punti women.

The Hakka revered Yang's wife not only because she was a kindred spirit but because she was a spirit-woman, one of the "ghost mistresses" or shamans of the Loi. Raised in the remote highlands of Hainan Island by descendants of an ancient race who still drank through tubes, worshiped snakes, and divined with eggs, Ailan had learned from her grandmother how to make the dreadful *ku*-poison, which could kill or bewitch men; how to heal knife wounds from the vine called "Thinking of You"; how to carve healing amulets out of amber; and make yellow paper charms against evil spirits. She could tell the future from tortoise shells, chicken eggs, and ox bones. She knew how to call up dead souls from the hidden places of the sky and earth. In the village, it was Ailan who mixed the medicines that cured female pollution. She purified a house of drowned girl-ghosts and made the lame walk by the vital energy called *chi* that passed out of her body through her hands. Spirits obeyed her. Women clung to her. Men dropped their eyes when she passed.

Yang alone did not fear her. Now, with her man gone, the life-giving essence of the spirit-woman began to wither.

■   ■   ■

Throughout the long, dry summer, Ailan worked to feed Rulan
and herself. They kept their garden and dug clams along the canal. The
village was nearly empty except for a few old or fearful ones who had
not followed Hung. Those who stayed barricaded themselves in their
hovels against bandits and marauding soldiers and blamed Ailan for the
dismemberment of their village. "The Loi witch betrayed us," they
murmured. "She healed the demon-man who stole our children."

When the wind blew through the streets, Ailan saw specters of
children playing and ghostly men going out to the fishponds. Once at
dawn she spied a crowd of demons setting up stalls for barter at the
margin of the water. She strode down to the water's edge, determined
to meet the goblins face-to-face, but when they saw her they scattered.
Even the ghosts recognized that Ailan was not one of them, not Han,
but an outsider from an ancient aboriginal race.

Ailan was sitting alone before her front door scouring a pot with sand.
The few villagers who were left, mostly the old and infirm, avoided
her. Hadn't she released Hung from his sleep? they reminded one
another. Hadn't she been the cause of their sons' and daughters' leaving? They turned their faces when she walked by and spat as if to foil
a bad spirit.

Rulan had gone with the boy to the village well. While she filled a
tall clay jar with water, he played in the sun with three small shells she
had given him. Neither of the children saw the aged folk until the mob
was almost on them.

"Drive the witch's whelps out!"

"Throw out the trash!"

"Remove the bad luck!"

Ailan came running when she heard the shrill cries of the children.
She saw the ragged circle of hags and doddering men chanting and
throwing stones at Rulan who was huddled against the wall, her body
shielding the boy. Rocks smashed against the side of the well and
bounced on the ground. The baby was screaming in terror.

"Mother!" Rulan cried. A stone hit her in the ribs and she winced in
pain. The baby shrieked.

"Stop!" Ailan yelled to the crowd. She pushed aside an old man
who tried to strike her with his cane.

"Get behind me, Rulan," Ailan ordered. She snatched up the terrified boy and turned angrily to face the crowd. "Be ashamed! Why are
you trying to kill my children?"

A crone called out, "My child is gone, dead to me! You killed this village!"

The stones flew harder and faster. One hit Ailan on the temple. Falling, she felt the baby slip from her arms. Vaguely, she felt Rulan pick up the child and urge her to stand. She leaned on Rulan as the girl pulled her through the crowd. She heard the old ones cry out as they struck her furiously with their fists. Why is the boy so still? Ailan wondered dazedly. Why isn't he crying? As if in a dream, she saw her house. Slowly, it seemed to walk toward her.

Rulan pushed her mother inside and barred the door.

Ailan saw in her stupor the bloody spot on the child's forehead. Painfully, she lay down on the bed beside him and pulled him to her breast, as the ancient ones howled outside. Only when they were hoarse from shrieking did they creep away. By then the child was locked in a ghost sleep, and Ailan too could not be roused.

Without warning, the boy's small body began convulsing.

"Mother!" Rulan cried in terror. But Ailan could not hear her daughter's distress.

The boy arched his back off the mattress as if someone were breaking him over an invisible knee. In desperation, Rulan held out her hands. She felt a wave of heat gather in the center of her body, at her heart, and pour out her left arm and into the baby's head. From there, the heat leaped up into her right hand, up her arm and back to her heart. She felt the warmth go round and round, a rivulet of swiftly flowing fire coursing along the invisible channels of her body.

Heat raced between sister and brother, and each time the river of fire made a complete circle, Rulan was left a little weaker. She was unconscious of time's passing; she knew only that a cock crowed. Then the spasms left his body and the child slept.

Ailan awoke with a jolt and reached for the boy. She saw Rulan with arms outstretched, saw the deep lines of fatigue on her daughter's face. She sprang up and grabbed her daughter's hands.

"Hold your hands together!" she commanded. "Kneel down!"

Rulan fell exhausted at her mother's feet.

"How long were you holding him with your *chi*?" Ailan said, aghast. She clutched the inert but still breathing baby to her breast.

"What?" the girl mumbled.

"With your spirit, with your vital essence. How long did you hold him?"

"All night. It made him stop shaking."

"All night! And you made the heat shift back and forth all that time, as I saw you doing now?"

"Yes, yes," Rulan murmured, frightened by her mother's intensity, yet too drained of strength to say more.

"Child!" cried Ailan, as she encircled Rulan with one arm. She was astonished that the healing fire had come of its own accord, like a hidden spring welling up without warning. Now the girl would have to be taught to control as well as summon it. She had to take her daughter out of this village. It was too dangerous for them now. She would take her children to the *chai tang,* the Buddhist community of women silk makers who had raised her as a child. There, in the commune, Rulan would learn to use her *chi* properly.

"I saw how you touched the snake-man's head, but I never saw such power in one so young. You could have killed yourself as you turned the heat with your heart. Oh, Rulan!" Ailan was sick with fear. What if she lost them all—Yang, the boy, and her daughter?

Rulan wept. "You would not wake up and Boy-Boy was shuddering so."

Ailan sat down on the bed, put the baby beside her, and pulled the girl into her trembling arms. She ached everywhere from the stoning.

"Please, can't we join Father?" Rulan sobbed.

"No, child. We must let him go." They rocked together, two women alone, while the small boy slept.

When their tears were spent, Ailan made the girl lie down on the bed. With her own hands, the mother poured a soothing heat into her daughter's body. In seconds, Rulan was asleep beside her brother. Ailan picked up the small boy and held him close, her heart breaking with each irregular beat of his own.

Now Ailan thought back to the night when the girl pierced the eyes of the *ku*-creature with the heat from her fingers. The heat was so strong then that it had forced the snake-spirit to the ground and made him slink away, blinded. The power had come unbidden, untaught, unlike Ailan's, which had been nurtured through years of secret exercises by her priestess grandmother, as with all chosen women in her line. Most practitioners of *chi gung,* the art of healing with hands, were men, but those rare women who possessed the power were said to be the strongest. And yet, there were some afflictions that *chi gung* could not heal.

The boy died at noon. None of Ailan's arts could save him, for he was only a shell; his spirit had flown away when the stone struck his head. Mother and daughter washed the tiny body, wrapped it in an old shirt, and bore it to the hills where the clan graves were dug. Ailan made a hole in the earth under a lemon tree and lay the small bundle in it. She put in a sack of rice and a packet of dried fish so that the child would not be hungry. She also buried with him the wooden tablets on which the names of her husband's ancestors were written.

"Let him sleep with his fathers," Ailan said, her face etched with grief as she tamped the earth down tenderly with her hands. "We women do not need these tokens. We know who we are."

Leaning together in sorrow, they stumbled down the rocky path into the empty village.

"Let me see your fingers," said Ailan, as they were pulling up wild onions in their small garden. Neither had spoken again of the tiny grave in the hills or of the man who had abandoned them. But Ailan knew that her daughter blamed her for Yang's leaving. The girl's grief over Yang's departure was causing a rift between them and jeopardized Ailan's hopes that Rulan would be a healer in her place one day.

Rulan sighed and held up the chewed finger of her left hand. After the battle with the snake-demon, Ailan had knit the broken skin together with silk thread. Only white rings remained of the infection, which had spread up to the girl's wrist.

"What you did to *Ku* was dangerous that night. But you had power. The same that kept your brother alive. I have it, too. Some of us have more. Although everyone can take *chi*, only those whom Kwan Yin blesses can give it. This is called *chi gung*, healing with hands. Father teaches son, or among my people, mother teaches daughter. A few, equally rare, are thieves of *chi*. These have the power but not the art, and in their hands, *chi gung* is like a dagger in the hands of a child. They are drawn to us healers as dark roots are to water. Beware of such men."

"Like Hung?" A spark flared in the girl's eyes.

Ailan nodded, rejoicing that she had finally stirred her daughter's interest.

Rulan thrust out her chin. "Father would never follow an evil man. And Master Hung does not look evil. After he was released by *Ku*, his face glowed. I never saw such a face. And such eyes. He called me 'Beloved.' Why would he hurt me?"

"Thieves wear different faces!" Ailan warned Rulan, appalled that Hung had beguiled her daughter as well as her husband. How could she convince Rulan that the snake-man was one of those beings who sought to devour the energy and warmth of women of strength? They sucked the *chi* from the healer and left her a mere husk.

"His eyes . . ." Rulan repeated stubbornly. "He saw straight into heaven."

"I have not seen heaven, yet the place he described in which he struggled with snakes and fought with imps frightened me. The sages teach that men are of heaven, all penetrating light, while we women are of earth, dark and absorbing. Yet there are men whose light burns everything before it. Hung is such a man. I never saw one who belonged more to death."

Rulan pressed her lips together tightly and looked down at her hands. She is only saying that, Rulan thought, because she is angry at my father, and because Master Hung is stronger than she.

"You think I am jealous of him," accused Ailan. "Hung's evil is real. His eyes coveted what he found in you. Tell me, were you tired when you touched the snake-man's head? And then when you held Boy-Boy with your hands?"

Rulan nodded reluctantly. "Why?" she asked finally in a small voice.

"Can you pour an ocean through the mouth of a jar? Can you press a hurricane through a keyhole? *Chi* is limitless, but the vessel is small. The healer grows tired. And when you are tired, thieves can hurt you. The disciplined healer learns to control and parcel out warmth in proper measure at the proper place. You feel it here." Ailan tapped Rulan's heart gently. "A young man grows into a scholar by memorizing books. A woman becomes strong by lifting heavy things. So it is with a healer. Practice. Make the heart strong, the mind keen, the hands gentle but absolute, so thieves like Hung cannot steal your life away."

Rulan shrugged one thin shoulder. "How can I practice? No sick ones will come to us now. The old people hate us here. And I hate them. They killed my brother. I wouldn't heal them even if I could."

Ailan swept her hands before her face. "You practice on the air. On unseen bodies. Like this." Ailan began to pummel the air as if she were performing the dancelike shadowboxing exercises called *tai chi chuan,* except that the movements of her hands were not inwardly circling but directed outward onto an invisible body whose outlines Rulan began dimly to perceive. "You try," Ailan said.

Against her will, Rulan felt excitement burn away her resentment. Her slender hands danced in the air, creating an invisible person standing before her.

Ailan reached out to caress her daughter's cheek. "Ah, child. See what happens when you open yourself? How good you are. You are made to heal." She was amazed at Rulan's quick grasp of the idea of an unseen body. It had taken Ailan months to understand what her Loi grandmother had tried to teach her, and yet her daughter saw it immediately. What was the child intended for? Ailan wondered with trepidation. Surely, one with such gifts—and such doubts and weaknesses—would be assailed by thieves like Hung and his minions. How could she make her daughter strong enough to stand alone? Ailan knew she had to find another teacher greater than herself, for her simple folk arts could not protect her daughter from those who coveted her gifts—or from Rulan's own reluctance to heal or lead.

Halfway through the wet season, Ailan realized that she and her daughter had no food to last through the month. One night, Ailan took ox bones and laid them in the coals of the fire. After the bones cooled, she brushed off the ashes and studied them a long while. Then she showed Rulan how the markings gave answers.

"I asked where we could find food and shelter, protection from bandits and ghosts of the unburied dead," she said.

"With Father and the others?" Rulan ventured hopefully.

Ailan shook her head.

"There is no other place that will have us," said Rulan grimly.

"You are wrong. See this line? It is cut off—destroyed by this great rift. But this line runs to the southeast. These other small lines feed it. It runs off the bone right into the future."

Rulan frowned. "What is there, Mother?"

"A place I lived in before I married, a sisterhood. The women there are strong. You could be like them. Remember what you did for your brother?"

The child's death was still painful to remember. Rulan felt her eyes prickle with tears. "Why was the power given to me, Mother? I don't even want it."

"Never say that, Rulan!" Ailan was hurt by the anger in her daughter's voice. The girl was growing increasingly aimless. All the more reason, Ailan believed, to spirit the girl away from the desolate village to a place where she could learn and grow. "I have nothing else to leave you except my arts, child. One day, you will be a healer greater than I. Maybe as great as the goddess Kwan Yin."

Rulan shook her head defiantly. "No, Mother, I am not worthy of being a healer."

In pained silence, Ailan studied her daughter. "You miss your father and blame me," she said finally.

Rulan bit her lip. She would not allow herself to be swayed by her mother's sympathy.

"Ah child," Ailan said. "Kwan Yin had a father too. She would understand your sorrow. Her father put her through cruel tests. Remember how he pulled her out of the nunnery where she was so happy? Remember how he killed her beloved abbess and set fire to their compound?"

Rulan felt her emotions rising. If she condemns my father and defends herself, Rulan told herself, I will not listen to her. I will not be a healer.

But Ailan said nothing about the man who had left them. "Kwan Yin never ceased loving her father, as was proper. And because she lived a pure and blameless life, she was able to heal her father of his error, and even to heal other people's suffering and despair. Why is Kwan Yin so beloved by us women? Because of all the gods, she alone loves the people better than the delights of heaven. Of all the gods, she alone hears a woman's prayers and knows a woman's heart."

A lesson on virtue and duty was not what Rulan wanted to hear. She grew stony faced and sullen. "I never understood why Kwan Yin turned her back on heaven when the sick on earth begged her to stay. Why retreat from heaven's gates when the gods invite you in? If I were Kwan Yin, I would have stormed heaven and forced the gods to change the world."

Ailan was shocked. "Child, child, we are only flesh. Kwan Yin was right to yield to those in need. Are you so hard-hearted?"

Rulan dashed away her tears. "No, Mother. But sometimes what I see makes me so angry. People starve. They fight and hate each other. The villagers despised Father because he carried dung and charcoal to make money."

"Then learn, so you can change things," said Ailan. And she held out her palms toward her daughter.

The rush of heat came like the kiss of an old friend. Rulan still did not know how it was done, only that her mother's *chi* lifted her hands and made her body swivel from side to side. When Ailan moved her fingers, Rulan's arms were tugged upward by invisible strings. She felt her spirit pulled by a sublime intelligence along a mysterious and ineffable path of light.

Thistle Mountain, Kwangsi Province, 1847

The moment before the morning sun slipped over the eastern ridge, Hung shouted into the fractured darkness, "Pray that the Light will come among you!" Hung tossed back his heavy mane of hair and strode with feline grace through the lines of adoring women to the highest point on the terraced hillside so that the multitude could see him. With his long hair, his thick, dark beard, and muscular body, he looked like a hero from an ancient legend come to life.

"Kneel down!" he commanded. Three thousand Hakka faithful went to their knees on the damp earth. Hung could make his voice as loud and long as a horn, or as gentle as a lover's sigh—and still be heard by every man and woman in the open air.

"Truly I tell you that the Light will come among you," Hung proclaimed to the hundreds of God Worshipers gathered there. "The Empire of Heaven will reign on earth. Truly I confess One greater than I. With my tongue I confess the Elder Brother Jesus." Hung lifted his strong arms to the sky, and at that instant, light flooded the barren hillside and the people trembled with awe and love for the man who led them.

As he knelt among the multitude, Charcoal-carrier Yang noticed that there were more new converts that morning than the day before. Those who came to see Hung out of curiosity stayed to listen to his ecstatic preaching and join in the songs and prayers—then they brought their uncles and brothers and cousins with them on the morrow. They were transfixed not only by his grace and beauty, but by what he made them see in themselves. Hung convinced them that they were not beggars but princes. Sometimes, like this morning, he made them see clearly a heaven they had only dimly imagined, a kingdom that belonged by right not to landlords and book-reading men and lily-footed women, but to those who sweated, toiled, served—and believed. Yet sometimes Yang thought his leader spoke unwisely. Sometimes Hung's vision of the treasures of heaven was drawn in gaudy colors and crowded with tawdry trappings. But more often, Hung's exhortations to the multitude to rise up against the Manchu "imps" and the "demon" Han gentry sounded like a personal vendetta against the scholar-officials who had failed to grant him a degree in the civil examinations. Then Charcoal-carrier Yang worried.

As he did every morning, Yang had prayed for his wife and children, and when the convocation had ended and the crowd melted away, he sought out Pawnbroker Wei to press forward his proposal that the God Worshipers abandon their camp in the Thistle Mountain region. Yang was reluctant to ask Wei for anything; he hated the pawnbroker for his vanity and his association with the outlaw Triad secret societies, an anti-Manchu rebel organization like the God Worshipers, although much more violent in its dealings with the people. But it was impossible to see Hung without Wei's intercession. Hung surrounded himself with trusted "advisers," such as Wei and Scholar Feng, who shielded Hung from the crush of the mob and interpreted his words to the people.

When Yang caught up to the pawnbroker, he found Wei wearing a new peaked hat, which Yang recognized as an imitation of an official's cap. "This is no place for warriors," Yang exclaimed to Wei. "We are like hens in a basket here. I've sent messages to the Younger Son, but he does not reply—" Yang had to run to keep up with Wei who was striding rapidly across the open field where the faithful had recently gathered. "Someone has to tell him to move the people out quickly. The local militia is garrisoned only a few miles from here," Yang warned breathlessly.

"What does a carrier of charcoal know about leading men?" Pawnbroker Wei shouted back irritably. "Besides," Wei asserted, "Thistle Mountain is our home. My ancestors' bones are buried near here. The narrow trails we Hakka know well. The viceroy of Kwangtung and his Manchu lackeys do not." Wei pointed proudly to the rugged hills of granite. "Here we live as invisibly as spirits among the pine trees and mist."

"And in a short while we will indeed be spirits," Yang retorted, "after the soldiers slay us all." He hated the tumbledown villages of the miners and charcoal-carriers of Thistle Mountain as much as his own home village. Although he had made himself a force among these men, he longed to turn them into real soldiers and prepare for the war that must inevitably come. And he was lonely. At night on his pallet, he yearned for Ailan and his children. What honor was he winning for them here? What would Ailan say if he returned to her a beggar after he had promised to make her a queen? Yang was beginning to fear that Hung was more content to drink in the people's adulation than to build the Kingdom of Great Peace.

"You need to learn humility, Brother," Wei admonished Yang. "You have talent, I admit. Talent for bossing work crews and loading donkeys. But it takes more than hauling rock to offer advice to the Younger Son. Look at those above you, all book-reading men. Scholar Feng is a learned man who translates the Younger Son's visions into edicts and odes." Here Wei paused. "My own talents, I admit, are small, yet I can make a poem. I have influential friends—"

"How does a pawnbroker acquire such 'friends'—from trading tin pots with beggars and housewives?" Yang interrupted rudely. "Or selling 'dirt' to unruly boys?" Yang was well aware that pawnbrokers were an unscrupulous sort, and pawnshops were places where Triads, spies, thieves, and murderers could make a quick transaction in opium, "black dirt," or stolen goods and information.

"I am a respectable businessman," Wei protested, stung by the insult to his dignity. "Great men call me by name, invite me into their houses, put money in my hand. Even Merchant Wang, the richest man in Canton, welcomes me—"

"At the back door," Yang retorted. "At night. And only if you are wearing a red turban and carrying dirt or stolen bracelets to trade." Mockingly, he lifted three fingers and placed them on his shoulder in the sign of the Triad greeting.

Wei flushed angrily. "You forget yourself. I follow Hung and the High God. I do not deal in opium. Still, I would rather do business with Wang than the viceroy any day. Wang has proven his respect for our cause. He sends us money and promises us guns and powder from the white devils and as many Tanka pirate boats as we need to ship barbarian weapons. And," Wei added smugly, "he swears that every Triad brother in the south is a true Han patriot who will join our fight to topple the Manchu!"

"I remember too well how Merchant Wang's Triads respect the

people," declared Yang angrily. "When I drove mule trains of charcoal through the mountains, they came to collect their 'squeeze.' Some of us were half-dead already, but still they took rice from our bowls and from our women and children. In the cities, I have seen how they 'stamp' female goods. Ten men rape a young girl, and when her family throws her out as too spoiled for marriage, the Triads sell her to a brothel. You call them patriots, I call them worse than thieves. If they join the God Worshipers, it's because Wang sees a good opportunity to fill his pockets."

Wei's scrawny body was rigid with indignation. "I will repeat your message to the Younger Son," Pawnbroker Wei said stiffly. "Every word."

A week after his argument with Wei, Yang and his men were rebuilding a bridge that had been washed out by a flood. The river was running high and wild, carrying broken trees and debris from upstream. The men were waist deep in swirling water, straining against the rushing current while stacking rocks for the new foundation. The storm had passed, and the day was bathed in pure, white light. The high mountain sky was clear, almost translucent, and the sun warmed the naked backs of the laboring men. Women were washing clothes and calling to their children, who played among the tall reeds along the bank. The entire camp was hard at work, digging ditches for waste, hauling drinking water, lugging baskets of rice and dried fish to the common cook fire, except for Wei, who was being carried on a litter by four men down the road that paralleled the river to the old farmhouse that served as Hung's sleeping rooms and the movement's headquarters.

When the men strung across the river put down their stones to gawk at the passing litter, Yang shouted angrily at them to keep working. How, he wondered, were they to build a new society if the leaders were intent on imitating the old one? Over the months of exile, Yang's love for the disenfranchised people of Thistle Mountain had grown more fervent, as his admiration for Wei and the other captains of the movement waned. Still, he refused to relinquish his devotion to Hung. Hung had courage and brilliance in far greater measure than any man he had known. Hung's sudden shifts of mood and outbursts of temper Yang ascribed to the stresses of leadership and the natural bent of genius, which did not follow the same rules as common men. Although he tried not to admit it, he missed Ailan, missed her soft thighs, and missed her implacable will, which had given him both comfort and strength. Lonely and troubled, he waded into the water with a huge stone and dropped it in the hands of the man next to him, who struggled through the water to pass it along to a man working farther out in the current.

Suddenly, Yang's head jerked up. Far upstream, women were screaming. The washerwomen had flung aside the wet clothes and were pointing toward the swiftly flowing river. There in the middle of the torrent was a small girl, her tiny arms flailing helplessly above the swirling brown water. Her hair streamed behind her on the flood like dark tendrils of seaweed.

"Grab her!" he yelled to the men working on the bridge foundation on the other side of the river. But they stood dumb and reluctant. One made a feeble attempt to catch the girl as she swept past. Yang read their thoughts: Why risk one's life to rescue a mere girl? The small form shot through the flue between the foundations and hurtled downriver. Yang scrambled to the bank screaming at the men.

Wei's retinue farther downstream was close enough now to help. "Catch her, stop her!" Yang called out to them.

The men carrying Wei hesitated, unsure whether to put the litter down, until, with a flick of his wrist, Wei motioned his men to continue.

"Mud-sucking turtle!" Yang shouted and began to race downstream, knocking aside a crowd of men who had put down their fishing nets to stare stupidly at the drowning girl. His stomach lurched when the girl's hair caught on a fallen tree lodged between two rocks. For a minute she bobbed above the waves, fighting to keep her head up, until the churning water pushed her under.

Yang flung himself frantically into the stream. The water was shallow, only chest high, but the current was so strong that he almost missed grabbing on to the tree when he reached it. Desperately, he held on to the broken trunk with one hand and groped with the other under the water for the small form. Nothing. He inched along the tree feeling below with his feet. Nothing. Nothing. Then something brushed against his knee. Yang let go of the limb and dropped headfirst into the icy stream. The water was too thick with silt for him to see clearly. But he found the place where her small body had been lodged in a notch by the force of the current. Yang caught hold of her streaming hair and pulled. She would not come up. He braced his feet against the rock and pulled again. She did not move. His lungs bursting, he reached down along the limp body and found where her foot was caught fast.

He struggled alone in utter darkness. Still she did not move. His

mind spun crazily, then focused like an inward eye on a single memory—
Ailan in the throes of childbirth. Their daughter would not be born.
All spirit-women were hard to bring into the world, Ailan told him
between waves of pain that left her exhausted, although she never cried
out. "This world is not our natural place. We belong to the place of
dreams," she gasped. Her words had sounded like a death knell.

Helplessly, he had watched his wife struggle to push the child out of
her womb. On the second night, the midwives gave her up for dead
and departed. Desperate to stop her agony, Yang reached into his
wife's body to touch the forbidden core of generation, turned his
daughter from her backward course, and pulled her from the world of
dreams into this one. The girl came out covered in darkness as Ailan
had predicted, her face and body shrouded in a caul. She had emerged
with tremendous protest, screaming not with the mindless, unfocused
mewing of an infant being born but with the rage of a grown woman.
Rulan had pinioned him with strange, reproachful eyes from which no
tears ran. And when he had wiped her clean and lay her on Ailan's
breast, she would not suck until he left the room. She was her mother's kind, he thought, a woman apart.

Just as he had done with his daughter, Yang turned and pulled the
small girl free with slow, steady movements. In seconds, he was
gasping for breath in the open air and holding the child aloft in his
muddy hands. She lived.

When he came back to his place with his men in the river, he
harangued them. "Turtles! Cowards! Master Hung tells you that if you
die in his service, you go straight to heaven. I'll tell you something
more. If we are really to turn the world upside down so that heaven
drops down to earth, everything must change. Girls will be worth as
much as boys, and women will have the rights of men." Such plain
speech won him little love among the men; if they had not feared him
so, they would have mocked him to his face.

Thereafter, too frequently for his own good, Yang complained to the
men about Wei. "The pawnbroker is a eunuch. He sits at Hung's feet
counting up his cash and fanning his brow and complimenting the
master in order to squeeze favors for his clan. He works all night, like
a eunuch sweating in the emperor's bed, to overturn what good I do
laboring all day long."

But Yang's tirades did little to diminish Wei's influence. While
Yang's men dug trenches for sewers, hauled water, and gathered
wood, Wei planted rice in Hung's ear and harvested it from Hung's

mouth in the form of edicts, proclamations, promotions, and awards. Pawnbroker Wei dismissed the charcoal-carrier as a jealous rabble-rouser, until Yang put together a work brigade of real force. Enlisting a few trustworthy men, Yang formed the camp police whose job it was to quell fights and enforce discipline among the warring families.

Hung was not oblivious to his lieutenants' jockeying for position, power, and attention, but settling disputes was not his mission; preaching was his only passion.

When he spoke in small villages about heaven and the High God and the prophets Noah, Moses, and Abraham, his eyes were bright with fires that burned within. "Worship God, your creator," he commanded the people. "On His favor all things depend. Why does He hold back his blessings from this Land of Flowers? Because imps and demons rule the land! Therefore, I say unto you, cast out the Manchu imps! If you die casting out demons, you will have honor and favor in heaven. Do not be afraid to die. I swear by my own Godhead that I will prepare a place for you in heaven. If you fail to do these things, you will suffer sores and wounds. You will burn in the fire of His eternal wrath!"

As Hung's fame spread, landlords, who were terrified of their tenants' rising up against them, sent troops to silence him. Once in a dusty, upland village, Hung grabbed a sword from the county bailiff and ran with it to the village school, where he smashed the ancestral tablets and the memorials of Confucius. At first, the impoverished peasants were as flabbergasted as the county officers; then they and the students, who had so often felt the sting of the teacher's and bailiff's thin bamboo, boosted Hung onto their shoulders and drove the yamen guards out of their village.

From that moment on, Hung carried a three-foot-long sword inscribed with the words *For slaying imps and demons*. It became a symbol of his power over Confucius, whom he called the "King of Hell" for having enslaved the people to the worship of dead ancestors rather than the one true God. Hung had only to wave it as he spoke and farmers left their plows, their wives and children, the land they loved better than themselves, even the bones of their ancestors to become a brother or sister in the Society of God Worshipers, which would build a heaven on earth.

Hakka tribesmen began arriving at Thistle Mountain in droves, more and more each day, to follow the High God and his Younger Son. The first core of Hakka was joined by a few adventurers from the rival Punti tribe, who were willing to set aside the centuries-old feuds for a common good. Soon there were men from every tribe and class of society—failed scholars, miners, porters, landlords, woodcutters, bankrupt merchants, displaced soldiers, barbers and other wandering tradesmen, Triads, rivermen, Miao outcasts. Unattached women came as well—runaway slave girls, whores too old and tired to ply their trade, and a bevy of discarded daughters: all of these were put into a women's unit under the leadership of Jiao, Hung's sister.

Hung further ordered every man to cut his queue and let his front hair grow to defy the Manchu, who had for centuries required all Han men to shave their crown and wear the queue to commemorate the horse, the animal they honored. Now every male God Worshiper wore his beard long and his hair down to his shoulders or tied into a loose topknot, as men had done in the golden age of the Tang and the Ming when Han men ruled themselves.

Among the men, five fought their way to power: Scholar Feng, Hung's trusted childhood comrade and the first of his disciples, who shaped Hung's proclamations into rules for the society; Farmer Hsiao, the headman of one village that converted; Landlord Shih Ta Kai, a handsome young leader of a large clan, eager to redeem his failure at the examinations by battling the imps; Pawnbroker Wei, clan head-man, whose influence among the newest Triad converts gave him a vast network of experienced spies; and Yang, commander of the charcoal-carriers, who had become the camp police.

Yang's leadership was the most tenuous of all, for it derived not from gifts or boyhood friendship with Hung but from his own raw strength over the work teams he headed. While the other leaders dreamed of heavenly kingdoms, only Yang had a vision that was as simple as sweat and as strong as the back of a mule. "You were dirt for the gentry and the Manchu to trod upon," Yang told his men. "But together our common earth shall rise up like a mountain and crush them. We shall own ourselves, and we shall possess our own land."

Yang gained compliance with a cudgel and assent with kicks to the backside. And he kept the fragile peace in the camp between Hakka and the increasing numbers of Punti, the two tribes who had brawled for generations. As their numbers spread out along the river and through the high valleys, Yang's camp police became a small army. He knew he could make them the core of a mighty military force when the time arose. Hung would summon the hopeless with promises on which they could feast, and he, Yang, would fashion them into war-riors the way a smithy makes a sword out of crude iron. The strategy he used to remake them he borrowed from the imps themselves. Whenever the government wanted work done on the levees or the roads, soldiers were brought in to police a corvée of conscripted villagers. Yang drilled his makeshift army in the same relentless fashion—but this time the work they were doing was for themselves.

Still, Yang was aware of a brutal irony: the God Worshipers were more vulnerable at ten thousand than when they had been only a hundred. Small, they were just another robber band, a plague on local clans, a distraction to provincial officials, not even an annoyance to the Dragon Throne. But as their numbers multiplied, they would inevitably attract the attention of the emperor's militia. Such was the fate of every grass-roots movement that flourished in secret only to be annihilated when its numbers thrust its members into the public eye.

Yang urged Hung's boyhood friend Scholar Feng to stop the preaching missions outside the area. "We have to grow like mushrooms in the night!" he told Feng.

"Hung is Younger Son. He must show himself before his people," Scholar Feng insisted stubbornly. Having witnessed the amazing power of Hung's oratory to end the tribal feuds and to keep the people's minds off their empty bellies, Yang reluctantly agreed.

So while Hung penned prayers and metrical versions of the Old Testament to fan the fervent spirit of the devout, Yang worked feverishly as Hung's practical man of affairs, to keep them all from starvation and from attack by local militia. If Hung was the spiritual source, Yang in a few short months had become the driving power of the body. Many nights he crossed the rugged mountains with his charcoal-carriers to rob the granaries in the next county. And he began to press the other four leaders into organizing their followers into military units, because he knew that an attack from the imps would come soon enough. His mind reeled at the danger—and the promise—of the mission they were undertaking.

As their numbers grew, Hung kept himself more and more apart from the day-to-day struggle, showing himself only to preach or to pray. From his farmhouse, odes, poems, and moral essays poured from his pen. The Ten Commandments were set into verse as the basic tenets of their community.

"Your preaching heralds a new epoch," Pawnbroker Wei asserted. "One day scholars will ask what acts and edicts set this mighty river flowing. Your words should be set down forever." And so Wei engineered Hung's favorite, Scholar Feng, into the honored position of historian and scribe—and out of the real arena of power.

One morning in late fall, Hung awoke from sleep with visions of blood and fire. By midafternoon he was spent, sunk in an inner twilight. He smiled dimly at Scholar Feng. "I am as idle as a fish in a deep pool." But Scholar Feng thought with alarm that Hung looked more like a lamp whose flame had gone out. Hung seemed deeply unsettled and impatient with Feng's request to review the plans that Pawnbroker Wei had brought for dividing up the camp police and putting them under the authority of the five leaders. Hung pushed aside the charts and figures, leaned his elbows on the desk, and stroked his thick, handsome beard.

"You must do something to check the greed of this charcoal-carrier," Wei argued. "How can a man who has married a Loi witch be trusted by followers of the one true God?"

The slanting rays of the sun, filtered through the papered window slits, fell on Hung's rapt face. Hung's beard was indeed tinged red, as the women alleged, Wei observed, and for a moment, he found himself staring like a lovesick girl at Hung's beauty.

Then Hung closed his eyes, and the light in the room seemed to fade. "We need Yang's crude power," he assured the two men. "He has absorbed the witch's yin. And the daughter . . . the daughter. . . ." He began to rock back and forth in his chair.

"What is the matter with him?" Feng whispered to Wei.

"He is fighting with devils and defeating them in realms we cannot see," replied Wei.

"Dear Brothers," came a low voice. "Listen. There is someone scheming against me. I feel his ire. I smell his sweat. With my inner eye I see him. It is the demon Manchu that squats upon my chair."

"Brother, you dream well," Feng replied admiringly.

"Yes, yes," Wei added, quick to see where a new advantage lay. "The authorities are aware of us now. They are sending troops against us. I was telling the other leaders: Let us fortify ourselves and build walls. I know where to buy arms from the long-nosed barbarians, from the West. But Yang does not trust me! How long would we have to wait for arms, he demands, how would we pay for them? Meanwhile, we are tethered here like a duck to a stick waiting to be slaughtered. We need arms and defenses."

"Ah, does *Ku* come for me again?" Hung replied vaguely. "Have I not wrestled with the evil one of the eastern sea and put him to flight? What is the emperor to me but another who must eventually bow! No. I will go out and meet him. I will strangle him upon the throne."

"And you will, Brother," Feng assured him.

"You may be invulnerable, but the rest of us are only common earth," Wei argued. "We need to build walls, buy barbarian weapons, choose men we can trust. We dare not leave the best fighting men under this charcoal-carrier's authority."

"But I say unto you, we do not need a walled city. A walled city is waiting for us, a city descended out of the skies. We do not need arms, we need feet," Hung declared. "As we move, the people will flock to us. They will sell their lands and bring us silver, which buys us swords and guns and food."

Scholar Feng saw in a flash what Hung's cryptic words meant. As a stationary camp, they were caught between the mountains and an attacking army, and were staked out, as Wei said, like a duck awaiting the knife. But on the move, the poor would flow to them like many small streams into a river. It was the same advice that Yang had been giving all along, but Feng chose not to acknowledge that. He inclined his head. "I will write your commands down and tell the leaders to move their people."

"Aaiiee, why should we move?" Pawnbroker Wei wailed. "Here is where our people are. All we need is defenses."

"We shall go, but without the little key we shall not open the gate," Hung intoned. "There is a gate to the Heavenly City—but only she can open it. The holy city cannot be made ours without her. She will break the back of the demon imp who squats on my throne."

And again, Scholar Feng could not read his friend's mind. "What is he talking about?" Feng whispered.

"I have no idea," Wei said as Hung drifted deeper into somnolence. But he knew full well.

"Again I say to you," Hung murmured sleepily. "She is the key. Bring her to me, and I will unlock the gate of the Golden City, and there we will create heaven on earth."

Scholar Feng ran his fingers through his long hair and tried to remember snatches of poetry or scripture that might contain clues to Hung's cryptic words.

But Pawnbroker Wei saw clearly the image of Yang's daughter, the wild child of the spirit-woman, as she broke the bundle of sticks and released Hung from the grasp of the snake-demon. If the girl was Hung's "key," she was also his own. With her he could control both Hung and the troublesome charcoal-carrier. Wei vowed to find her, buy her, even steal her if he could.

The House of Women, Kwangtung Province, 1848

Ailan packed her medicine gourds, her amulets, a few ox bones for divination, two quilts, two ceramic bowls, a few strings of cash, yellow unguents for the mountain imps who might waylay them, and enough rice for five days. Then she and Rulan set out on foot after the new year to a silk plantation across the border in Kwangtung, where women were allowed to live independent of clan or family.

At daybreak on the third day they arrived in a strange, secluded community of women who had set themselves apart in a women's house, or *chai tang,* in the hills. The headwoman, who called herself Ma Tsu Po, after the Taoist queen of heaven, was a girlhood friend of Ailan and greeted her as a sister. After Ailan turned over her few goods to the common treasury, Ma Tsu Po made them put their thumbmarks on a piece of paper to signify their joining the commune. Three teenage girls with straw brooms came to help Ailan and her daughter clean their allotted space in the sleeping hall and get settled. Each girl wore identical straw sandals and black pajamas and her hair in a single braid down her back. At first Rulan thought they were sisters. But when she had the courage to raise her eyes, she saw that one was as dark and suspicious as a Tanka boatgirl and towered over the others; the second was thin and quarrelsome, with a sharp nose and a ferretlike face; and the last was shy and beautiful, with small features, white skin, and a yellow orchid tucked behind one ear. The girls chattered and made coarse jokes, and when they laughed they did not cover their mouths with their hands.

Tsai Yen, the pretty girl with the orchid, stared at Rulan's chest and demanded, "How old are you?"

"Twelve," Rulan confessed, ashamed of her size.

"Ho! Old and ripe enough for a man to ride," accused Wing, the dark-skinned amazon. She ignored Tsai Yen's chiding and demanded of Rulan, "You girl, can you soak cocoons and pull thread?"

"I did once, but now we are both quite ignorant," Ailan said, encircling Rulan with her arm.

"We'll teach you everything," Tsai Yen promised, to the tall girl's annoyance.

"You make your own money here, and there's no father, uncle, brother, or any other man to cuff you on the ear and make you hop and lay like a hen," snapped the sharp-faced girl. She said her name was Harmony and stuck out her chin as if daring them to say how ill the name fit her.

The two hundred women in the commune called themselves disciples of Kwan Yin, the Merciful Goddess, but they did not act or look like her priestesses. They neither shaved their heads nor put on gray robes nor chanted Buddhist sutras. Instead they dressed like field hands to raise worms, prepare cocoons, and draw thread, for which they earned copper cash. Inside a stockade made of bamboo poles lashed with jute were vegetable gardens, five dormitories, open-sided sheds where the worm flats were kept, a weaving room, a small stable, a well, and a meeting hall. Although most of the money they made went to the upkeep of the shelter or to feed their impoverished families, the women were able to keep some for themselves. They thought nothing of wandering to the market town to trade or to the traveling opera in the villages. And although men watched them with hot eyes, none dared accost them, for it was said that they were in league with the Triads, the secret gangs of bandits who opposed the Manchu government. It was also said they knew magic charms to prolong sexual ecstasy or to strike men down.

As the days passed, Rulan grew more and more curious why her mother stayed, when it was clear that neither she nor Rulan belonged. The *chai tang* of Ailan's girlhood was unrecognizable. The sisters she remembered were old now. And the young girls were of a different breed: bold, immodest, irreverent. They called Ailan "Auntie," as they would any woman old enough to be their mother. But they did not ask her for healing because her methods were old-fashioned. Instead, when anyone fell sick, the leader, Ma Tsu Po, turned to the precise herbal recipes prescribed in books to stop pain and to cure. Unlike the people in the villages, the women here were unafraid of spirits. They practiced fighting with sticks in platoons and when they went into the market town they laughed at the young men ogling them, and did not see, as Rulan and Ailan did, the red-faced demon leaping in the crossroads at noon.

One night Rulan left her own pallet and crawled in beside her mother. "Why did we come here, Mother?" she whispered. "I lie here listening to the dead crying in the wind, but these strange women sleep undisturbed."

Ailan fell silent for a moment, remembering the nights that seemed a lifetime ago when her family had warmed each other in the same bed. All her world then was within her grasp: the passionate dreamer and revolutionary, who had made her his wife, the daughter so like her, gifted with the healing hands, and the sweet boy-child at her breast. Now all of them were lost on alien roads.

Ailan pulled her daughter into the curve of her hip. "Since the day you could grasp a tuft of grass in your hands I taught you about herbs. When you began to see the true shapes behind living things, I taught you the secret names of spirits, which roots heal and which can kill, and what songs and incantations make spirits cower. From the time you first bled, I taught you about the power women have over men. I will not teach you how to read the eggs or the bones yet, because you are not strong enough to know your fate. It makes the weak despondent, because everyone reads their own death. Now you know almost everything my Loi grandmother taught me. But songs and charms and plants are no longer sufficient in this age. You see how your sisters deride the old medicine. So I have brought you here to learn the healing that is written down in books, the same thing I would have learned if I had stayed here. It is too late for me, but not for you. These women are like an army of ants. They are marching to a place I cannot go."

Rulan lay her head on Ailan's breast. This was not the answer Rulan wanted. It made her feel lost and alone.

"Learn everything, Daughter," Ailan said sadly, "for the world is turning to water under our feet." Since the day she was wounded and her son murdered by the villagers, Ailan had been weak and slowly failing.

Rulan did learn new skills in the silkworm sheds, including how to keep the "little darlings" warm and well supplied with mulberry leaves that men brought from the nearby farms. By tradition, the silk industry had developed according to strict sexual divisions of labor. Men did the "outside," or heavy, physical work, such as dredging the fishponds. The ponds produced fish, which fattened on the drowned bodies of silkworms soaked and separated from their webs. The pond silt and fecal matter fertilized the mulberry trees that yielded leaves for the worms to eat.

The women did the "inside" work of tending the larvae raised on flat screens in the humid sheds. The division of labor went even further. Only unmarried girls like Rulan, whose spirits were not tainted by the pollution of childbirth, were allowed into the mat-sheds to separate the fibers of fully mature cocoons by dipping them into hot water before unraveling the white fiber. Matrons like Ailan spun the webs into thread, which was woven by hand or shipped to city factories. Men and women, ponds and leaves, fish and worms: the silk industry, like life at its most ideal, was a unity of balanced and harmonious parts. Silk was the most valuable of China's commodities, and nothing was wasted in its cultivation.

Ailan's task was to sit and spin with the old women on the steps. She could not see well, however. Sometimes she broke the thread. Sometimes her concentration lapsed and she dreamed about her husband, her son, and her old village. Her back pained her, and her head and fingers ached. Rulan was expected to shoulder the more laborious tasks of the young women. Wing took cruel pleasure in Rulan's clumsiness and teased the girl about fat "sausage fingers." Tsai Yen saw how the jibes pained Rulan, but every time she took Rulan's part, Wing teased the girl more.

One day, when Rulan was on her way into the groves, Tsai Yen and a sullen Wing waylaid her.

"Ma Tsu Po assigned us to train you," Tsai Yen said.

Wing's angry face betrayed her annoyance. "I am your instructor," she said threateningly. "Do what I do, and try not to make mistakes."

Wing steered Rulan into a dark shed where stacks of wooden shelves were covered with great sheaves of cloth. Tsai Yen raised a corner of the cloth and pulled out a shelf holding a thin layer of shredded mulberry leaves. She picked out a leaf and held it up to Rulan's face between thumb and forefinger. "See where it begins," she told Rulan.

Rulan tried but saw nothing. She didn't like this place and she didn't want to learn anything from the rude and bossy Wing. What was she supposed to see? She poked the leaf with a tentative finger, feeling Wing's displeasure. Stupid! she told herself. Look harder! Suddenly, she saw them. Tiny yellow dots on one side, like flyspecks.

"Eggs!" Rulan exclaimed.

Wing made a rude noise. But Tsai Yen smiled so prettily that Rulan's heart soared. Maybe they could teach her something useful after all. Rulan could see by the careful way Tsai Yen replaced the leaf on its wooden bed that the fortune of their community depended on the small dots. "We cool the eggs until the leaves are ripe enough for feeding. If the worms hatch before the leaves turn green in spring, they die. Not this year. This time, the leaves came early so we can afford to hatch many eggs. Look here!" And Tsai Yen drew Rulan to another shed where a group of young women were tending other leaf-laden shelves.

Wing shoved her up to the edge of the shelf and lifted a length of wet gauze. Rulan shuddered, for the leaves were alive! Hundreds of black larvae no bigger than a fingernail were eating through the trans-lucent shells of the eggs. As tenderly as any new mother handling an infant, an old woman began to scrape the newborn worms into flat baskets.

"This one won't soil her fingers with the little darlings!" sniffed Wing.

And in truth, Rulan was somewhat squeamish. How can she stand to touch them? she wondered.

The old woman seemed to read Rulan's thoughts. "They're like my own children," she said, smiling. And indeed she seemed genuinely to love the squirming spots.

Rulan swallowed her revulsion. She would show Wing that she wasn't stupid or clumsy or weak.

"You've seen enough. Let's go," Wing barked in Rulan's ear, and she pulled Rulan by her shirt out of the quiet shed across the chicken yard to a corner of the compound where there was much bustling and noise. Ducking under a long lean-to, Rulan saw a line of women carrying armfuls of leaves from piles heaped against the shed, which they dumped onto huge flat tables. Under the high-pitched laughter, Rulan heard a low, pleasant drumming rhythm that filled the shed like the pattering of raindrops. Wing tried to look grim but a smile played around the corners of her wide mouth. "You hear them, don't you? They're eating!"

Rulan peered eagerly over the tables and saw that the larvae there had grown to the size of her index finger. Some were white and others black. As each worm crawled hungrily along the leaves, nodding as it gorged, it sent out a tiny filament of silk from its lower lip to enable it to cling to the leaves as it ate.

Tsai Yen leaned close and touched one worm with her finger. The body was unmoving and stiff, its head raised up in the air as if it were listening to an inner music. "This one sleeps," she whispered, and Rulan understood that the stillness was only temporary. The worm would awaken to split its old skin and begin to eat voraciously once more. Tsai Yen looked closer and exclaimed, "Ah, here is one who has grown and left four skins." She carefully plucked up a long, fat worm and held it in the curve of her palm. The worm was as flaccid and inert as a thick noodle. "This one can eat no more," she told Rulan. "So now we take the little darling in here."

The next shed was filled on one side with wooden frames divided into small finger-size cells, each filled with what looked like a wad of white cotton. Tsai Yen carefully deposited the worm onto an empty shelf.

"Now she dances!" said Tsai Yen. Wing roared encouragement as the white worm uncurled and began to nod its head vigorously in a figure-eight pattern.

"Aiya! Look out, she spits!" Rulan exclaimed suddenly.

Wing rolled up her eyes. "Little Stupid! That's the silk!"

Rulan was too surprised to be hurt. She pressed her face close to the tiny cell where the worm was spewing forth a long white thread from its mouth. With rapid circular movements the head moved back and forth until the sticky filament had covered one wall of the cell with a thin veil.

Scanning the wooden cubicle, Rulan made out the nodding dark heads of the worms as they danced inside their tiny homemade shelters, spinning layers of silk from the inside.

"How long does she spin?" Rulan asked.

"Two days," said Tsai Yen. "She never rests. And look what she makes when her job is done!"

Wing yanked Rulan's braid hard and pulled her to another corner of the shed where egg-shaped cocoons the length of her little finger lay shrouded by layers of fine webbing in tiny cells.

"The worms are sleeping, I know," said Rulan. "My mother taught me the song. And when they wake, the gods give them white wings to fly to heaven."

"Gods! Heaven!" snorted Wing.

Tsai Yen silenced Wing with a frown. "Yes, yes, sometimes they fly away before we catch them," Tsai Yen explained. "The strong and handsome ones that have spun the most silk we save to lay more eggs. But most we kill in hot water." Rulan went with them into a lean-to billowing with steam; the mat-shed was as hot as the last level of the Buddhist hell. Inside, women were throwing handfuls of white cocoons into vats of boiling water and screaming to be heard over the crackling fire. Some of them were blowing on the flames under the water cauldron with small hollow reeds.

"Stay back," Wing ordered Rulan, elbowing her way toward one of the vats. "You!" she barked to one of the women. "Give those to me!" The girl wiped the sweat out of her eyes and slapped a pair of wooden chopsticks into Wing's hands. Then Wing spat into her palms and plunged her hands into the scalding water. Briskly her fingers flipped a cocoon over in the water, spun the white sphere around until a small thread had come loose; next Wing wound the end of the thread onto the chopstick and pulled hard, so that the thread, now stretched on the stick, could be secured to a wooden reel that stood outside the cauldron. "Turn the handle!" she yelled to Rulan. As Rulan cranked, Wing skillfully manipulated the cocoon with her fingers and chopsticks so that the thread was wound rapidly on the reel.

Long minutes passed. Rulan felt as if her arms would be wrenched out of their sockets, but she would not show Wing her fatigue. She yelled to Wing over the clatter, "I can pull harder! Shall I?"

Wing frowned and shook her head. "Be careful or you'll break the thread. It's only one thread. Sometimes it stretches almost a mile. Wait, it's almost gone. . . . There!" Wing pushed at something in the hot water, and through the steam Rulan saw that there was no more cocoon, only a small pink thing floating dead on the water. Wing grasped the worm with her chopsticks and dumped it into a basket heaped with small pink bodies. She looked at Rulan sharply. "Okay, now you try."

Before Tsai Yen could stop her, Rulan had grabbed the chopsticks, dipped them into the cauldron, and deftly lifted out a dead insect. But her fingers touched the boiling water, and she yelped in pain.

Wing doubled up with derisive laughter. She reached in with her calloused fingers and plucked out a worm.

"Enough!" scolded Tsai Yen, who turned to Rulan. "The water has to be hot to kill the worms and to melt the glue that binds the thread to the cocoon. Put only the tips of your chopsticks in the water. Work fast. Pretty soon your skin will toughen, and you won't feel the heat."

Rulan came home with red, wrinkled hands that Ailan swathed in the cool sap of a prickly aloe plant. Because her hands were too sore and stiff to hold chopsticks, she could not eat rice from her own bowl or take from the large serving dishes of meat and vegetables that the women shared. But Ailan gave her small balls of cold rice, which she was able to put into her mouth to staunch her hunger.

In a week when the worms were sleeping and there were no more cocoons to unravel for a time, Tsai Yen brought Rulan into the large buildings next to the dormitory where the looms and the pounding boxes were kept. Rulan loved the clatter of the looms and the camara- derie of the women who sang and gossiped while pounding the stiff cloth with wooden sticks into fabric as thin and translucent as butterfly wings. Envying those women, Rulan begged to be taken out of the mat-sheds to work a loom. But Tsai Yen said that the weaving and pounding were done only by a special group of sisters, all members of a family that had woven and pounded cloth for generations. These women were held in special esteem by the sisterhood for their ability, with a flick of the shuttle, to turn the thread into intricate patterns of many colors. They were given precedence at the dining table and freed from the ordinary drudgery of cooking and cleaning. They kept their pallets in a special corner and on feast days they sacrificed to their own deity.

In bed that night Rulan whispered in Ailan's ear the question that had plagued her all day. "Why are there two kinds of sisters in the *chai tang?*"

"In all life, there are those who labor like drones, and those who soar above the rest," said Ailan. "Which do you want to be?"

"A sister above all the rest," Rulan replied, tucking her sore hands between her mother's warm ones.

"Then you must learn to be stronger and smarter than the others. Know all that they know—and more."

The work was grueling, even for Ailan, who did not have to work in hot water but stayed in the hall with the old and the sick twisting the silk thread onto a spinning machine, two strands at a time. Mother and daughter had gone from being novices to true sisters; they worked every day of the week, with only a few days off yearly for lunar holidays or feast days devoted to Kwan Yin.

In the second month of the new year, strange men were seen in the mulberry groves behind the *chai tang*. Ma Tsu Po divided the women into "families" of five who took turns guarding the compound night and day. Ailan was named "mother" of a family that included herself, Rulan, Tsai Yen, Wing, and the ferret-faced girl named Harmony. By now Rulan and Wing had made an uneasy truce. Rulan had worked hard to earn the tall girl's respect, and although Wing no longer bullied her, the two still fought at times like peevish children.

The family's first work assignment was to clean one of the dormito- ries where fifty women lived. This was relatively easy labor and a diversion from the round of backbreaking "wet work" in the worm sheds. At first the girls tried to keep their voices low and their attention on brooms and mops, but within a half hour they were arguing and causing so much commotion that Ailan fled into the yard to escape the noise. Yet the girls were energetic workers; by midafternoon they had picked all the bedding clean of lice, scoured and packed away the cook pots, swept the rafters of dirt, and tamped the earthen floor with water.

Tsai Yen lit the brazier for tea and passed out cakes while Ailan went to take down the herbs she had been drying on a string in a corner of the hall. She had grown tired and gaunt; now only a shadow of her beauty remained. Her hair, which had become pure white, framed her thin face in pale radiance. Suddenly a fit of dizziness made Ailan nearly topple off the stool.

"Mother!" Rulan ran to steady her, but she pushed her daughter away and kept pulling down the dried grasses with trembling hands. Ailan blamed her growing debilitation on Hung's bite and refused to do more than sew amulets into her clothes to expunge the evil essences. But Rulan feared that no potion or charm would cure this illness. Ailan was wasting away over the loss of all that she loved—her husband, her son, and her home.

The girls were suddenly very busy, silent as Ailan fought for breath.

"Pfaugh!" coughed Wing, as Ailan threw down handfuls of yellow flowered stalks for them to tie up. "What is this rubbish? Matting for the outhouse?" She put her hands on her ample hips like a village scold.

Before Ailan could answer, Harmony grabbed the stalks away. "Wait, let me see. Aaiiee!" A cloud of pollen exploded in her face, and she was seized by a fit of sneezing.

"That's yarrow," said Rulan eagerly. "I helped mother pick it in front of the temple door last week, and now it's dry enough to pound for medicine."

"Now the monkey tells me," Harmony growled, handing back the stalks carefully to Ailan before wiping her dusty fingers on her trousers. "As if I didn't recognize the weed myself. And who lays out Kwan Yin's altar for the holy mother but me? I bet this sly monkey thinks she can cast the yarrow stalks too. Come, sit. Tsai Yen has a question about a lover."

Tsai Yen covered her face with her hands. Rulan had heard of casting the stalks, which, when interpreted by the ancient book the *I Ching,* could predict one's future. Her mother did the same thing by reading the yolks of chicken eggs or the cracks in bones baked in the fire, but Ailan could not read books or scrolls and therefore could not practice the divination laid out in the classic texts.

"Mother knows how to boil the powdered stems to make a strong tea. If men drink it, it increases their ardor, strengthening their yang."

Wing sneered, "No need to grow that here! What do you know about men's yang?"

Harmony's face took on a sly expression. "Didn't you hear this one tell how she bewitched Hung, the man-god? So overcome was he that the man-god's yang was as big as a staff and he offered to take her on his next trip to heaven. Isn't that so, monkey?"

"Me? I never—" Rulan began guiltily, cursing herself for bragging to Harmony about her mother's powers.

"Shame, Rulan, you should not mention that evil day," Ailan said sharply.

Stung by the rebuke, Rulan was about to make a retort when she saw the agony in Ailan's eyes.

The room was quiet again. Every sister in the *chai tang* was gossiping about Hung and his army of Hakka converts who were attacking the emperor's troops from their hiding place in the Thistle Mountain area. The maidens argued about what the man and the movement meant, for their legends predicted that a man would arise to lead them to freedom from the ancient law.

"Ma Tsu Po says it is too soon to tell if Hung is man or god," ventured Harmony, looking out of the corner of her eye at Ailan.

"He is not a god," Ailan snapped. "And worse than a man."

"Gods? Pfaugh. Men are pigs," Wing declared.

Rulan's eyes grew wide. "You hate men? Don't you want to marry one day, Elder Sister?"

Before Wing could make a rude answer, Harmony put her thin hands on Wing's cheeks and pinched the full lips into a fish mouth. "Can you imagine this bony carp cooking soup for her wailing brats, then kowtowing to her lord? 'My lord, will you favor me with your mighty warrior tonight?' And where will she find a warrior big enough to fill her up?"

With a cry, Wing knocked Harmony's hands aside and threw the girl to the ground. The two of them began to wrestle in the dirt. Ailan threw up her hands in exasperation and thrust the herbs into a bag, which she lugged out into the garden where she could sift through the contents in peace.

Over the grunts and squeals of the others, Tsai Yen said to Rulan, "Elder Sister had offers. She refused them all."

"But why?" asked Rulan, casting an apprehensive eye at Wing, who had straddled Harmony's back and was pulling her hair and ears. "My mother says that all grown-up girls must marry. Even here they must, otherwise, how will they have children?"

Harmony rolled away from Wing with a cry of triumph. Wing picked herself up from the floor, brushing hair from her eyes. Her broad face was caked with dirt. "You don't know anything, *hai ma?*" She glared at Rulan. "Why do I need smelly brats? Why do I need a man? I make more money pulling thread than my father and brothers do in the paddies. So why should I marry? I go wherever I want—to town, to the opera. If I marry I'd have to stay inside the house and jump when my man says jump. And then when my son is grown, I'd have to jump for my son."

Harmony's eyes were dancing in her narrow face. She planted her feet wide apart and pretended to sneak around imaginary trees and bushes. Then she called out softly, "Look here, look here, you lucky maiden! See what I have brought you?" Her hands shaped an erection. "Come test my sword."

Wing shook her fist and bellowed in mock anger, "I'd rather grind the bean curd than take the edge off that small blade."

"What did she say?" Rulan turned to Tsai Yen, but the girl was choking with laughter. Harmony leered at the red-faced Wing and began a comic serenade in a piercing falsetto.

Wing got up with an effort and turned her back on the giggling girls, taking mincing steps on her toes like a delicate Punti woman tottering about on bound feet. Slowly she twisted herself around, caressed her large bosom, and lowered her head shyly in a ludicrous imitation of a coquette. Then she stopped awkwardly with her sleeve before her face so that only her black eyes showed.

Rulan wiped tears of laughter from her eyes. "Elder Sister, you are too scandalous!"

A look of smugness came over Wing's wide face. "Oh, there's nothing wrong with marriage, Little Stupid. I am going to wed . . . only I will marry a woman."

The three maidens guffawed at Rulan's shocked face.

"Next full moon, Tsai Yen and I have the cutting-hair ceremony and offer vows to each one."

"What?" said Rulan. When she looked at Tsai Yen, the pretty girl grinned, her ears scarlet.

"You know," Tsai Yen stuttered in embarrassment. "The sisters pull out my front hair just like a real bride, and—"

Wing cut in, "And then the holy mother makes us take an oath before the others, and we are wed!"

Tsai Yen hid her small pink face in her hands.

"Your parents agree?" blurted out Rulan.

Wing sniffed. "Oh, them? My family disowned me long ago, said I was worse than trash. Tsai Yen's family did not know what to do with her. She's pretty, *hai ma*? So they set their sights on a rich husband and had her horoscope cast. But when the fortune-teller found that she had a bad fate, they were going to sell her for a whore. Tsai Yen threatened to kill herself. Out of shame, they made her come here. They were relieved when she told them she wanted to pledge herself to me. They already have grandchildren, and they don't mind now that she'll keep making money for *them* instead of for her husband's family. They're even going to make a party for us with pigs and cakes."

Harmony laughed ruefully. "Lucky Fish Mouth."

"Why don't you find a—a wife too?" asked Rulan, tentatively. These strange customs made her head spin.

"I can't. I'm already married," replied Harmony with a sardonic smile. "To a man. My father had a losing streak at fan-tan and when he had nothing else to bet, he bet me. I was only twelve when my husband's family adopted me. They called me 'Daughter,' but it was cheap labor they got. They were hoping their son would get me pregnant so I would have to marry him. That way they saved paying for a wedding, my father saved a dowry, and they got a maid and a daughter-in-law free. After one week, I ran back home. My father beat me and locked me in the outhouse and told my mother not to feed me. But they had to shit before I had to eat. When they let me out I ran away again . . . here. But they found me and brought me back. They made a wedding that time, a cheap one."

"Then why aren't you at your husband's house?" asked Rulan.

"You think I would let that son of a turtle put his thing inside me? You think I want to swell up with babies? I refuse to drown myself like a silly virgin so I did what the holy mother said. I wrapped a cloth around my bottom and took the herbs to stop my red snows. Even then that fool tried to force me, though he knew I was under Kwan Yin's protection, but I told him I knew incantations to make his yang juices dry up, and I showed him the amulets a priestess sewed inside my bindings. That scared him enough to send me back. Of course, I had to buy him a concubine who drops babies each year like a sow. And each year the babies die. My husband hates me. But every month he takes the money I send him. And the next month he asks for more." She spat on the floor.

Wing grunted. "What did I say? Any man who weds you weds Discord, not Harmony." She laughed uproariously until Harmony yanked her braid.

"It's true," Wing accused, rubbing her sore head. "And now that he is rid of her, his house is quiet and he doesn't have to work. Maybe he isn't so dumb. You think everyone is dumb if they cannot memorize books like you!"

Tsai Yen grinned. "Harmony taught herself to read. Now she teaches the sisters." She caught Rulan's hands in her own delicate ones. "We'll teach you so many things, Little Sister. How to catch river crabs, where to dig the sweetest mushrooms, how to kill a man if he tries to force you. Harmony will make you a scholar. Wing can teach you to fight with sticks."

Wing began to protest, but Ailan shuffled into their midst lugging a huge water jug between her legs by its handles. "Still fighting?"

Harmony barked, "And Auntie will teach us to use *chi* to chase away devils."

Ailan set down the jug, panting hard. "Be ashamed, you naughty girls. In the house where I was raised, our mistress the Tai Tai would have beaten us for such irreverence. Good girls do not mock devils unless they want to die."

Rulan's heart plunged. Ailan looked and talked like an old woman. She was frightened for her mother and a little ashamed of Ailan's old-fashioned ways.

That night, Tsai Yen set out huge plates of bean curd and cabbage on the long tables. After emptying their rice bowls and drinking bitter black tea, the four sisters sat close to the great hearth at the western end of the hall to listen to Ailan talk story. Many women from other families were gathered there too. The hall had a mood of mellow weariness after the long workday.

"There is magic in words," Ailan told them. "Words bind and unlock. They join the seen and the unseen. Once a bride found a knife in her bed. Being quick of wit, she picked it up and cut back and forth through the air, saying, 'Up I cut and across I cut, and I cut the tendons of poverty. May every year be more prosperous.' And sure enough, every year the family was more prosperous than ever."

Harmony shook her head. "I would say something like 'Is someone going to be murdered?' With my bad luck it would probably be me."

Ailan put her fingers against her lips. "Hush, Daughter. Don't tempt the gods with foolish words."

Harmony stuck out her chin. "A bad-luck girl like me has words and nothing else. Words are my weapons. My mother named me Harmony so that I would grow up modest and beautiful enough to attract a rich man. But no! Harmony chooses to yell and scream and screw up her face and say anything she likes to make the elders cover their ears and men run away. How can spirits hurt me if I'm not afraid to die?"

"You can die many times, Daughter," warned Ailan. The crowd grew quiet in anticipation of a story. Ailan smiled and nodded. "Two times in my life I have died. Once when I was a young girl and my mother sold me out of the Loi village into a rich Punti house. It was big, so big. It covered the whole side of a mountain—house, court-yard, garden, pagoda—I thought it was the palace of the Jade Emperor. Higher and higher this house climbed, to the very summit of the mountain. When I went to the top for the first time, my head was in the clouds. The Tai Tai of the house came into the garden dressed in white silk with a headdress of jade—or perhaps it was a ghost. I fell to the third level of death. I spoke with the spirits of the unborn."

Tsai Yen's eyes were huge. "Did you go to heaven or hell, Auntie?"

"I don't remember anything the first time. But coming back, there was a roaring, and then I vomited, and when I woke up there were people pouring water on me from the spring that flowed from a broken rock. I was all right after that. The Tai Tai was kind to me because I had called out the name she had just selected for her grandson. She sent me to bed and I was quite well the next day."

"And the second time?"

"The second time I was with Rulan on our way to the temple in our village, when suddenly I felt as if I were falling off the earth. There were tufts of grass on the side of the road; I grabbed them but they slipped out of my hand. I fell into a river that roared and foamed. It plunged me through a mountain gorge to a burning lake. There I saw a young man calling me from an island floating in the middle of the flames. The young man had red hair, a beautiful face, and eyes like two deep holes. When I reached the island, he tried to embrace me. But I knew by his eyes that he was a *kuei* so I pressed my hand, hard, on the top of his head, and in an instant he sank down into the earth. The next moment, I grasped a wriggling snake. I would have trampled him with the heel of my foot, except that I heard the nuns crying, 'Someone has died. Someone has died.' Then I heard my daughter calling, 'Mother, Mother, come back.' My spirit yearned to return to my daughter, so that when she called me by name, I came alive again and went into the temple. There were no ill effects."

Wing announced that she would like to live forever, like a Loi spirit-woman, and asked if ordinary women had as many lives as a healer.

"To live is difficult," said Ailan. "To die is easy. Remember Kwan Yin?"

Rulan shivered with anticipation. She saw other girls pricking up their ears to catch any new details this storyteller might weave into the old tale of the human princess who became the Goddess of Mercy, Kwan Yin.

"Well," began Ailan, "every girl knows that the princess's father would not let her become a nun, so he put her on an island without food or clothes. But the princess's body liked the cold, and she learned to drink dew and eat plants. Then the king was stricken with boils for his wickedness." Ailan paused and looked dramatically at the eager, tense faces. "And this was fortunate, for the girl was a healer. And every healer knows that only one thing can cure a person whose body is poisoned by an impure spirit—an elixir made from the eyes, hands, and feet of a living person. But it cannot be just any living person, only someone who has led a pure and blameless life. Otherwise, the cure will not work. So the princess, who was a healer, as I said, did not hesitate. She sent for a monk and told him, 'You see these hands? Cut them off. Cut off my legs too. Gouge out my eye with this stick.' The king drank the elixir that the monk made from his daughter's flesh, and the boils vanished. When the monk told him who had made this sacrifice, the father was ashamed. He journeyed for three months to the island where his daughter lived and fell down before her mutilated body, begging forgiveness . . ."

Rulan and Tsai Yen wept at Ailan's description of the father's reunion with his daughter, who was miraculously made whole again by her father's tears.

"I hate him," Harmony fumed, when the applause died away. Her voice was shrill and she stabbed the air with an angry finger. "He did not deserve a daughter of such quality. This is proof that fathers are the same as kings—heartless and cruel."

Ailan shook her head. "Suffering is the greatest teacher. The father loved his mutilated daughter better than when she was whole. And the girl became a saint."

Rulan thought of her father. What sacrifices could she make that would bring him back?

"The princess should have fought back," muttered Wing. "I like the story of the Warrior Woman, Fa Mulan. She did not bow down to any man. Better a warrior than a saint!"

To appease Wing and Harmony, who were calling for more exciting tales, Ailan brought out the bones that told the future. Although it was late, she stoked the fire and took out the ox bones she kept wrapped in brown paper next to her medicine gourds. After making small cuts with a sharp knife, she stuffed the bones with charcoal. Taking a long stick, she pushed the bones into the fire, and when the hall was swept

clean and the sleeping pallets laid down, the blackened bones were
raked out of the hot ashes and brushed off by eager fingers.

"Tell me first, Mother," said Rulan.

"Are you old enough?" Ailan teased her.

"Let me see! Teach me to read my fate."

"One day. Not now," Ailan replied, and held up the bones to the
light of the fire. Suddenly her face turned pale. She was not smiling,
but she did not weep either. She kept her face expressionless, as if to
stop it from cracking. "There is magic in words," she said. "My child
will have enough to eat. She will have a rich man and a poor one. She
will wear fine clothes and rags. She will hold life and death in her
hands. She will die by fire like a warrior in the outer world."

The women murmured their approval. Rulan shivered at the sound
of the words. Ailan seemed suddenly exhausted, so there was no more
reading of bones. Instead, at Harmony's urging, Wing chanted the
ballad of Mulan, the Warrior Woman who took her father's place in
the Khan's armies, while the women slapped their hands on the floor
in time to the beat. Rulan burned to go to war like Fa Mulan and to
heal the broken bodies of mighty warriors as Kwan Yin did. Her heart
was swollen with love for the maidens.

While the women slept, an ugly, grating noise came from the eastern
door. The door shattered and was ripped off its hinges. A dozen dark,
hooded figures trampled over the women uncurling from their quilts
on the floor and ran, with swords raised, directly to the crumpled
figures close to the huge stone hearth. They pulled up the screaming
women by the hair, thrusting torches into their frightened faces and
flinging them aside until they came to a small shape quivering against
the warm stones.

"This is the girl the spy described," hissed one of the men as he
dragged Rulan into the light and threw her at his leader's feet. "I
looked and looked, but the hag has vanished."

"Forget the witch. It's the girl they really want," laughed another.

"Mother!" Rulan cried, but the leader had snatched her up and
tossed her over one shoulder like a sack of rice.

"We have her!" shouted the leader, and the invaders turned to flee
with their prize.

Now, however, the women in the *chai tang* were fully awake. One
wall torch sizzled into flame, and a few women grabbed their fighting
sticks from racks along the walls and formed a phalanx between the
door and the intruders. The leader laughed and ordered his men

forward. They charged with a roar, swinging their swords. One woman fell, her throat slashed, then another and another. But one man dropped with the point of a stick in his eye and another screamed as his testicles were crushed with an arcing upper cut. The bandits circled left, for now all the women had weapons. Those without sticks threw pots, chairs, whatever they could get their hands on. The invaders retreated toward the great hearth. Outside, the bamboo clappers were sounding the alarm.

Shocked at the unexpected fury of the resistance, the bandit leader called his dwindling band into a circle and dragged Rulan in front of him like a shield. As she struggled, his hood fell back, revealing a bloated, tigerish face and long queue wound up on his head and tied with red cloth into a knot.

He shouted at the advancing women and held up his hand. "We only want the girl. We won't hurt you if you stand aside. There's a price for her and we mean to earn it."

There was a momentary lull of amazement before a piercing scream shattered the silence. A tall woman leaped forward, breaking the circle of armed men. The wild-eyed Wing whirled her stout stick around in a quick, two-handed movement, cracking the skull of one man and ramming the heavy base into the chest of the man who held Rulan. His breath exploded, but quick as lightning the man parried the next blow with his forearm, and a split second later his comrade caught the other end of Wing's whirling staff. A third punched her above the left ear, and then both Wing and Rulan were held like shields before the advancing line of women.

"This she-devil dies. I don't care if a bucket of silver is paid for her, I'll cut the girl's throat if you move another step," said the leader, turning his head quickly to spit out blood and broken teeth. He drew his knife across Rulan's neck and a rivulet of red seeped in the wake of the blade.

"Thou," said a voice as deep as the sea.

"Mother—" screamed Rulan.

"The witch!" shrieked one of the men.

"Take the old one too," growled the leader. But none of the raiders ran forward.

Ailan raised her arms and her sleeping robe fell like a dark shroud around her. In one hand she held yarrow stalks, in the other a small medicine gourd. The fire in the hearth sputtered behind her. Ailan's face was swathed in shadow.

"Your magic doesn't frighten us," the leader sneered, but his eyes darted nervously from side to side, while blood bubbled in the corners of his mouth. One by one, the men dropped behind him.

"Thou. Look upon thy death," she said.

Turning, Ailan cast her medicine gourd into the glowing ashes of the hearth, and the embers burst into multicolored tongues of flame. In the same instant, she leapt up with a sharp cry, whirled in the midst of the inferno, and sprang back into the room, her robe afire. With a high wail that seemed to last forever, she whirled like a top, spun, and whirled until sparks and pieces of burning cloth flew away from her and her hair was a flaming aureole. She spun toward the bandit band and its leader, who flung Rulan aside and began to run. Then like a sun-engulfed bird she jumped on his back and wrapped her flaming wings around him. They collapsed together in a ball of fire.

The intruders rushed to the door, but the women were upon them. In less than a minute, all the men were dead. Rulan got up and ran to her mother; she expected Ailan to spring up like a deer, but when her hand touched Ailan's shoulder, the burned flesh came away in Rulan's hand.

Ailan was dying and no charms or potions could bring her back to life.

"Mother! Come back," called the girl. She tried to will the heat to flow from her hands, but in her grief and terror, she could not find the center of energy in her heart.

"To defeat him, give him what he most desires . . . ," whispered Ailan.

"Who, Mother?"

Ailan raised her blackened hands before her face and pulled them with great effort through the air. Slowly, she turned her palms outward to her daughter. Her eyes closed. Through her tears, Rulan felt the heat leap across the space between Ailan's fingers and her own. The next moment, Ailan was dead.

All night, the three maidens rocked the stricken girl in the circle of their arms while sounds as ancient as the earth welled up again and again from Rulan's throat, as the daughter sang the spirit-woman's soul home.

Forbidden City, Peking, Spring 1849

The young eunuch An-te-hai betrayed no trace of his inner turmoil as he stirred the ink stick on the ink stone of white jade. He dipped the brush into the thick liquid, carefully shook off the loose drops of ink, and handed it to the chief eunuch with a graceful bow. The chief eunuch, his huge rump spilling over the fragile stool, was about to take the wet brush when a cough from the Tao Kuang emperor brought him quickly to the great bed hung with imperial yellow. An-te-hai was left holding the dripping brush over a cupped hand so that the ink might not soil the rare carpet. The chief eunuch had found yet another way to make known who was great and who was beneath notice.

The chief eunuch murmured over the shrunken shape in the bed while other beardless ones glided over the polished floors with hot towels and cups of medicine, or, like An-te-hai, stood like invisible statues awaiting the emperor's command to move or to speak. As the Tao Kuang emperor's body servant for twenty years, the chief eunuch was the only one among the thousands of half-men in the Forbidden City who could touch the Dragon's body unbidden and whisper into his ear. In this recent illness, the chief eunuch's command over the flow of messages to and from the emperor was absolute. If a eunuch had a message from a prince, he would have to pay a bribe or forfeit some useful piece of gossip to the chief eunuch.

Yet no bribe of An-te-hai was high enough to gain him access to the ailing emperor. The reasons were clear: as the eighteen-year-old heir's favorite, An-te-hai was by definition the chief eunuch's greatest rival. Nor did the Tao Kuang emperor wish to see proof of his own mortality in the shape of an emissary from the son who would rule after him. An-te-hai was also an ally of the minister of rites, with whom the chief eunuch was currently feuding. The day of ritual plowing was approaching and the minister was exercising his authority to prepare the sick emperor for the rite of propitiation to the spirits of land and grain. Knowing how much the chief eunuch despised him, An-te-hai greeted the summons to act as scribe for the emperor with surprise and trepidation. His life in the palace, with its conflicting jealousies and shifting alliances, was growing more difficult to manage than juggling plates on bamboo wands.

An-te-hai had heard in the harem that the chief eunuch was pushing his Han favorite, the doddering and obese viceroy of Kwangtung and Kwangsi, for chairman of the censorate. An-te-hai was guessing that an ally in the most powerful ministry at court would ensure the chief eunuch's continued ascendancy in the palace should the emperor die and power be placed in the hands of a ruling Council of Princes.

For the heir was clearly unfit to rule alone. No one knew that better than An-te-hai, who, as the youth's first lover, had fed the youth's penchant for lasciviousness. When the heir's eye had turned elsewhere, An-te-hai used opium to ensnare the youth, this time for good. An-te-hai had his own plan, one that would have given the chief eunuch every cause to kill him. When the old emperor died, An-te-hai intended to take the chief eunuch's place in the shadow of the Dragon Throne. Against that day, the younger man was backing his own Han favorite—a minor general named Li from an old and recently discredited family in Kwangtung whom he hoped to place on the viceroy's chair in the unruly south. The southern provinces of Kwangtung and Kwangsi were the gateway for opium and barbarian wealth, as well as the breeding ground for every kind of deceit and rebellion. General Li's secret correspondence with An-te-hai had shown Li to be a useful and intelligent man, hungry to win back face for his family. That Li's father, a Hanlin master, had ruined the clan was enormously fortuitous, for Li would be grateful for promotion and only too glad to curb the power of such families as the Wangs of Canton who had fattened themselves at his father's expense and who undoubtedly supplied the Triad bandit society with money and arms. Moreover, Li possessed the best qualities of the southerner: distrust of everyone, especially other Han. The game therefore had to be played subtly. How to discredit the viceroy of Kwangtung and Kwangsi, put his own favorite among the governors of the rebellious provinces and the Council of Princes and Ministers, and so ensure his place in the new order.

The chief eunuch rose from the floor with little grace. The long sash that covered his shame was askew and his moon face was streaked with perspiration.

The Fat One looks half-dead himself, observed An-te-hai with satisfaction as he proffered the now dry brush to his master. He waved the brush aside and motioned to An-te-hai to sit down at the desk to transcribe a letter.

Now the game begins, thought An-te-hai. Which one of us will win?

The young eunuch settled his lithe body on the mahogany stool that the king of Siam had given in tribute five hundred years earlier to an emperor who had been served by yet another half-man. An-te-hai liked the thought that although he had no progeny, he stood in a line longer and older than that of the emaciated man in the bed, whose Manchu ancestors had occupied the throne barely two centuries. Originally a band of castrated criminals made to serve the earliest emperors as punishment, the eunuchs had grown from shame and discredit to immense power as dynasty followed dynasty. An-te-hai, who supervised the care and feeding of the eunuchs, had counted five thousand the week before. This was a woefully small number compared to the seventy thousand eunuchs who had filled the palace at the end of the Ming era, when a eunuch nearly usurped the Dragon Throne; yet An-te-hai was confident that those days would soon come around again. Hadn't he proved that the lowliest kitchen boy in the Forbidden City might win the heart of a prince and thereby make his desire felt throughout the empire?

An-te-hai pressed the sharp bristles of the writing brush into the viscous ink. He had spent the day with the other half-men in utter silence, lifting, wiping, feeding the emperor, while the princes argued, cajoled, and harangued in the Audience Hall. But at night, An-te-hai and his brethren ruled. Because they were the only men besides the emperor allowed in the Forbidden City after dark, they had to draft and copy all the day's business and so exerted a powerful control over the flow of information. A memorial might be mislaid as it made its way from courier to courier through the labyrinth of passages in the palace. A convenient delay in the delivery of a letter had as much meaning as the message itself. A key word here or there might change a letter's significance. An-te-hai wondered if he dared shape the letter dictated by the emperor without his rival's knowing.

The man in the bed groaned. To think that the whim of such a weakling could raise a man up or cast him down. What would the emperor do for the viceroy of the joint provinces of Kwangtung and Kwangsi, a man as gross as the chief eunuch and equally inept at dealing with the God Worshipers in the Thistle Mountain region? The whole empire, An-te-hai believed, had grown too fat and old and soft to deal with its troublesome children. If only he could speak his mind to the Dragon, order him to appoint a strong and manly man such as Li to fill the crucial chair in the south. An-te-hai felt the rush of words pressing at the inside of his mouth. One word—Li—and the rebellion would be crushed before it began.

The chief eunuch was speaking softly into the emperor's ear. "But shouldn't we find a man of the south, one who knows about secret societies, to root out these unruly God Worshipers before they become too troublesome? And if not a southerner, surely there is some man here in the capital, some disgraced official or poet, that we could send to redeem his reputation."

The emperor protested feebly.

The chief eunuch continued to murmur insistently. An-te-hai felt the eunuch's small, piggy eyes focus on him.

The emperor sighed. "You there, scribe. My servant says that you are a wise and astute diplomat. How would you handle this trouble with the God Worshipers in the south?"

Here it was—the Fat One's trap. By speaking, An-te-hai would be forced to expose his hand. Then he would be under scrutiny, every word examined and censured if it were other than what the chief eunuch desired. Except that An-te-hai was prepared. The chief eunuch, in interpreting the emperor's wishes for so many years, had come to believe himself one with the Tao Kuang emperor and mistook compliance for assent. Condemned to the shadows for so long, An-te-hai had perfected the art of waiting. His plan involving General Li would take long to bring to fruition, but it would be surer and more devastating than the trap the chief eunuch had in mind for him. General Li himself had suggested it in his last correspondence when he spoke of the *tao,* the Low Way, the Way of Water. An-te-hai would take his cue from the wily southerner. Together, he and the general would work through the natural order of things and bring down their enemies as surely as water wears away a mountain.

Thus when the Dragon spoke as the chief eunuch prompted him, An-te-hai replied as easily as if he spoke every day in the presence of the emperor, the Ten Thousand Years. And he made an answer that the chief eunuch would love.

"Celestial, address the viceroy of Kwangtung and Kwangsi and strengthen his hand. Let the viceroy use the power of the Dragon Throne to quell the trouble brewing in Thistle Mountain among the Hakka of Kwangsi who call themselves God Worshipers. Give your faithful servant the viceroy the power to raise both men and taxes to suppress the vermin that afflict your kingdom."

Triumph spread slowly across the chief eunuch's fat face. Fool, thought An-te-hai. He believes that he has cowed me into submitting to his will and is already counting the presents when the viceroy of the southern provinces, his fat lackey, is raised to the censorate.

But An-te-hai had done exactly as Li advised. General Li's last letter had convinced him that force could not tame the wild Hakka tribesmen in the hills of Kwangsi. Leave them alone, counseled Li, and they will fight among themselves and fall apart. Every blow meant to smash them would only unite them and breed more resistance. Thus if the Dragon would grant the viceroy more power to tax and to impress peasants for war, the viceroy would strut and puff himself up, order an incompetent militia to scare the civilians. Then either the militia would fail and humiliate the viceroy, or the militia, starving as usual, would run from battle and steal the people's crops and pillage their homes, and so anger the prickly natives of the region that they would take up their pikes and hoes and join up with the God Worshipers and become part of the revolt themselves. That was the way it was from the time the first men of Han had gone into the unruly, barbarous south and been polluted by Yao and Loi and other snake blood. Either way, there was a good chance that the viceroy would lose face and fall from grace, bringing down the chief eunuch with him. And the doddering old emperor would be made to plow a fallow field. In time, An-te-hai would raise up this clever and so useful General Li to the viceroy's empty chair, and receive the gratitude and loyalty of the new emperor.

The old man in the bed was seized by a fit of coughing. After the chief eunuch held the emperor's head above the spittoon, the feeble voice of the emperor began again.

"Write my viceroy in Kwangtung that he shall have all powers to tax the people and impress an army for me to go against the God Worshipers. And if he acquits himself with alacrity, we will invite him to a new post in the capital."

When the letter was done, An-te-hai handed it to a small eunuch, who carried it three paces to the chief eunuch, who read it softly in the emperor's ear. The emperor waved his hand, and the chief eunuch took the imperial seal, which lay beside the bed, and put the stamp of the Dragon on the letter.

By then, An-te-hai was touching his forehead to the thickly woven yellow and red carpet for the seventh time. He was glad that with his face in the rug, he need not see the gloating of the chief eunuch's and could thereby hide the smile of victory on his own.

That night in his tiny room An-te-hai feverishly whispered his envy, his desire, his rage against his enforced silence . . . but softly, for there were ears pressed against the walls listening for shame and treachery. He had not transformed himself into an unspeaking, unspeakable half-man for nothing. He would throw a blow at his enemies that would kill.

Power was all. Food, drink, sex were nothing compared to that. Not simply because he was a eunuch. There was a legend among the people that eunuchs were insatiable engines of sexual potency. Without a sack to go empty, they were the consummate instrument of pleasure. Remove the impulse and the threat of procreation, thought An-te-hai, and one became pure appetite and desire.

Most eunuchs past adolescence grew seedy and fat. An-te-hai had worked to maintain the hard muscles and slim physique of his youth, but for power's sake, not love. In his first years in the palace, he had dallied with maids and with other eunuchs, but one maid had wanted him too much, too often, and by then, he had caught the eye of the heir, who was as jealous as a girl. The maid had threatened to expose his indiscretion, so she had had to be poisoned, at some trouble and expense, because the murderer had then to be poisoned and another paid off. What a miserable chain! All for a pleasure so transitory that it was easier to do without.

Thus feverishly whispering alone in his dark room, An-te-hai spoke at first to himself. But as the night shadows deepened, it seemed he was addressing a woman, one whose gigantic ambitions matched his, someone from the Manchu princely clans, someone to bring to the heir's bed who would bind that weakling forever to him. Who would this perfect woman be? If she did not already exist among the palace women, An-te-hai vowed to scour the old Manchu families in the capital to find her. Or he would create her himself.

Five furrows. Six furrows. The Tao Kuang emperor was gravely ill and still he drove the sacred plow deep into the hallowed ground. A light veil of rain blanketed the Temple of Agriculture where the eunuchs, princes, and officials had gathered for the annual ritual of "meet the spring." A propitious omen for the rice crop, the rain was nevertheless frigid and relentless; it seeped through the emperor's sable hat and ran down his neck under the thick layers of padded silk. It turned the red and gold sashes of the imperial princes into sodden rags and made their prized peacock feathers hang limp over their black caps.

The plow that the emperor pushed was ancient and most holy—a simple sharp point set into a curve of highly polished wood decorated with symbols of the land and the grain. It cut deep into the wet earth, leaving a fissure as raw and red as a wound.

Three more times the emperor pushed the plow into the wet clay as the chief eunuch drove the yellow ox forward. Thin rivulets of rain and sweat rolled down the old man's face. Once he slipped and nearly fell. The courtiers stirred in sympathy, but no one came to help. The Dragon had to do this alone to appease the rain-bringing dragon and the sun-producing phoenix and the spirits of land and grain, who had been stingy with their blessings over the last year.

An-te-hai pitied the emperor for having to leave his sickbed to wallow in mud and rain like a dumb ox—and only because this was always done every spring by every emperor before him.

With a feeble heave, the emperor drove the plow through the last furrow. The princes muttered their approval. In a final gesture to the gods, the old emperor bent to toss the sacrificial rice upon the wet earth and fell headfirst into the mud.

When the chief eunuch reached him, the emperor was already raving. "Old friend, the omens are clear. Heaven has withdrawn its hand from us."

"No, no. We will live forever," whispered the chief eunuch, rain dripping off his bulbous nose.

"Don't lie to me, old friend." And the face that so few ever saw or dared to look on turned up to the merciless sky.

How strange, thought An-te-hai, squinting through a veil of water at the man lying in agony in the dirt, that out of the thousands of sycophants, concubines, eunuchs, and princes, all professing their love, the One had no one. The Dragon of whom the empire stood in dread did not know his friend from his enemy.

The Dragon lingered for a year. And died alone.

6

Kwangtung Province, 1849

The society that became Rulan's new mother had a special name—the Golden Orchids. The community was unlike any other in China, for here, women governed themselves. Silk made the *chai tang* viable. Silk made the Orchids rich. No other Han women enjoyed such independence as these once-superfluous farm girls in the south.

Cut off from the villages by a range of hills, the Orchids were entirely self-sufficient. They paid rent for their land to the most powerful man in the region, General Li of Abundant Spring Mountain; yet they made their own cloth, medicine, shoes, and shelter, grew much of their own food, and sold what they could not eat. They pooled their cash for taxes, land rents, and funeral expenses. They took in extraneous women of all ages and classes: prostitutes, abandoned wives, pregnant widows, runaway slaves. The oldest was a former concubine of sixty; the youngest was three, rescued from the river after she had been pushed off a boat by her Tanka boatman father. Some weeks Rulan saw no men except the bell-doctors who hawked medicine or the farmers who brought in ox-drawn wagons filled with mulberry leaves for the little darlings.

The maidens gloried in their outcast status. They adopted rituals to enhance their yin, their female power. They used secret charms and incantations to frighten away aimless men, for there was always danger lurking in the mulberry groves. The Orchids practiced special calisthenics with long sticks to strengthen their bodies should any woman be required to fight for her life. They even developed a cryptic finger talk by which one sister could communicate with another. Like the Triads and God Worshipers, the Orchids were another faction of a people growing toward revolution.

There were other women's societies scattered throughout the region, but because the officials were embarrassed and jealous of those women who did not fit the pattern, these houses were neither acknowledged nor officially sanctioned. Still, corrupt magistrates and bailiffs came regularly to their door to extract extra squeeze.

Shortly after the new year, word was sent from the yamen, the county seat, that Lam, the newly appointed magistrate for the district, would pay a visit to the abbess. He was from Fukien Province. It was customary for officials to serve outside of their native province to curtail corruption, although it did not take most officials long to learn how to squeeze the locals. Ma Tsu Po took the usual precautions and had the women bundle up most of the finished silk and hide it in the mulberry groves. Then she ordered everyone to wear their worst rags and to bury half the pots, utensils, and temple treasures under the boards of the warehouse. Rulan watched from a storeroom window on the day that Magistrate Lam's retinue of bailiffs and bearers marched through the gate up to the stairs of the council house. Ma Tsu Po was already knocking her head to the floor as Lam's palanquin reached the bottom of the steps. Two women, the society's sergeants at arms, went down to escort the magistrate to the room where the governing council of the society met, for there the haggling over taxes and bribes would take place.

Rulan was surprised at the slightness of the man who alighted from the palanquin. Magistrate Lam was still a smooth-cheeked youth, but his heavy robe and the gold-buttoned hat of his office lent him the gravity of a much older man. Lam ordered Ma Tsu Po to rise and beckoned her to his side. When he spoke, he chose not to disguise his unmistakable country accent. "Call your sisters into the courtyard," he said. "I would like to address them."

Ma Tsu Po suppressed a gut-clenching wave of fear. Quickly she signaled the women guards with finger talk to bring forth only half the women. The youngest and strongest were to arm themselves in their hiding places.

When the courtyard was filled with nervous women glancing sideways at the magistrate's armed guards, Lam stood on the top step of the council house and began to speak in Hakka dialect, using homely, colloquial phrases that every woman could understand.

"Women of the *chai tang,* I've come to assure you of my friendship to your commune. In the past you have been badly used by my predecessors in office. It is not my intention to overtax you or demand a squeeze for protection. Nor will I allow robbers and brigands to cheat the people under my care. Pay what is dutiful and just, keep peace with your neighbors, and you have my goodwill. I know you are worried. And rightly so. You women have suffered since the long-nosed barbarians withdrew from Canton to the treaty ports they extorted from us. You lost fathers, husbands, and brothers in the war. Those men who still lived lost their jobs. Many of you came here destitute and without clan to build this community. Out of your sweat, the commune grew, and now you turn a profit from silk where others failed. I pray that your example will be followed by other villages and clans. Let us build together to restore prosperity to the poor folk of this province. Respect this."

The women were used to being exhorted in tired, time-worn phrases, not in words that touched on raw wounds and recent bitternesses and dealt directly with their status as women apart. There was a moment of true bewilderment and then applause and cheers. That night they entertained Lam with songs and dances and in the morning sent him on his way to the next village. He went with nothing but their goodwill, for in keeping with his word, he had refused the gifts they tried to press on him.

"My head is dizzy," Ma Tsu Po confided to the four elders who made up the ruling council. "I feel naked without paying for protection. Can such a worthy man be trusted? Aiya, he is too young and vulnerable. Officials with such love for the people and such probity never last long. They kick out the leeches from their posts, cane a few bailiffs for brutality, and confiscate the land of a couple of minor gentry for tax fraud. Eventually, they stir up so much ire among the corrupt that the landowners appeal to the viceroy and the magistrate is transferred or demoted. Worse, if the poor wretch has joined a secret reform society, he will be discovered and beheaded. Well, let us grow in this magistrate's sunshine, but labor all night against the day his term is done."

At Rulan's formal initiation into the society at the age of thirteen, the abbess pricked Rulan's wrist and finger with a knife and squeezed the blood into a wine cup. After the cuts were bound with a golden cord and Rulan had tasted the blood, the Council of Elders led Rulan in an oath while Ma Tsu Po held up a tiny effigy of Kwan Yin carved in peach jade. Two hundred voices welcomed Rulan, saying, "When persons have the same heart, its sharpness cuts gold. Words from the same heart have the fragrance of an orchid."

With heartache, she remembered what her mother had told her—she had to grow and learn and change in order to survive in the new world. How can I do this alone? she wondered. But she knew Ailan's spirit would give her strength, just as her mother's wisdom had provided her with a new family of sisters to protect her.

Ailan's sacrifice in the flames merited a sacrifice of equal measure. Rulan decided to lay all life's passions aside and remain a maiden forever. All men, she now believed, were like the renegade father she both loved and mistrusted: they chased willy-nilly after vain dreams, trampling on a woman's heart, taking her years and her beauty, begetting sons, and selling away her daughters.

One night, Rulan dreamed that her mother came to her in the shape of a phoenix that spread immense golden wings over her pallet. A winged serpent entered the house of women and sniffed about in every corner, from the rafters to the baseboards, but so long as her mother stood over her, the serpent could not find Rulan—until the light from a thousand fires lit up the night sky. The phoenix turned in apprehension toward the flames and disappeared. Then the red-eyed snake spied Rulan. His tongue flicked, his jaws opened wide, and poison ran out of his white wet mouth. Uncoiling, he leapt on her bed.

Rulan awoke screaming, and would not be comforted until Tsai Yen left the pallet she shared with Wing to lie beside her.

"Sleep, sleep, Little Sister," whispered Tsai Yen. "What do dreams mean?"

"Everything," sobbed Rulan.

"Nothing but misdirected desire," the beautiful maiden replied, stroking Rulan's back, while Wing tossed angrily on her cot.

Ma Tsu Po insisted the Orchids had to know all that was known by men. Every maiden in the commune learned to read—not the Confucian classics, which she claimed denigrated women, but edifying material or "good books" culled from heroic legends. After evening rice, Rulan sat in the great hall with the others while Harmony recited the sagas of dead heroines such as the goddess Kwan Yin, who had no husband to serve, no mother-in-law to please, and no children to constrict her. Afterward, under Harmony's sharp eye, it was the girls' turn to recite. Always the same lessons: men cannot be trusted. Refusing to marry is morally superior to marrying. Men and women are equal under heaven. It is a woman's right to seize leadership when men fail.

When the famine struck the villages, the maidens' stores of rice and cash were a temptation for aimless hunger marchers and seemed an easy target for thieves. In the year after Ailan's death, the commune was vandalized six times by bandits and a seventh time by frustrated Punti in retaliation for a raid by Hakka men whose home village they could not discover. Each time the maidens drove the attackers away; each time a sister died. Ma Tsu Po appealed to Magistrate Lam for an investigation; he acquiesced but the damage was done.

Anguished over the bloodshed, Ma Tsu Po decided that the Orchids needed protection, not an official inquiry. Although she suspected that the Triads were involved in the raid that resulted in Ailan's death, because the raiders were too organized to be simple bandits, she had to buy protection somewhere, and the Triads offered the best source of protection in the region. So she made a pact with the Red Turban Society, a local branch of the far-flung Triad secret society that claimed millions throughout the south. For a fee paid with finished silk, the "brothers" policed the villages around the commune and sent instructors to teach the women the arts of war. Except for their mustaches and dirty head rags, the men were the male images of the Orchids in their plain black pajamas and straw hats. The Turbans were like ghosts, rarely speaking to the Orchids, appearing without warning in their midst, only to disappear just as suddenly into the night.

The Red Turbans taught the maidens how to fight in squads with long bamboo pikes, short swords, and small bows. The leader of the Turbans was a giant of a man, a Fukienese whose Triad name was "Iron Fist." He was versed in all the arts of war from *tai chi chuan,* the dancelike exercises that underlay the martial arts, to stick fighting, to cannon, or so he claimed. He cleared a place in the stable yard, heaped soft grasses on it, and taught the most daring of the women the art of hand-to-hand combat. Iron Fist cursed them roundly when they failed and yanked their braids when they did well, treating them like rowdy boys aping soldiers.

"You, the tall ugly one, come here," he yelled in a gruff voice one day. He spoke Cantonese peppered with Fukienese words.

Wing stepped out of the circle, bowed, and squared off in front of Iron Fist. In a second he had swept her down with a raking move of his left foot. Then he drilled the rest of them on foot movement.

"You, second tall ugly one, forward." Tsai Yen giggled while Rulan bowed and confronted him. She steeled herself against his insults, which always unnerved her, because she hated to be shamed in public. Guessing correctly that he would feint a kick but attack with his hands, Rulan successfully avoided a lightning-fast blow that would have sent her toppling and managed to stay on her feet for almost a minute.

"Lucky," was Iron Fist's only comment, but a stern smile played on his lips, and he did not ridicule her when she finally fell.

After that day Rulan carefully watched all his movements. She noticed that although he was expert in all his techniques, he liked to win by trickery. Perhaps he merely enjoyed making the women look foolish, which was not hard to do, because he had years of practice and great strength. He especially liked to sweep them off their feet so that they fell on their backsides with a thump.

Rulan learned this lesson painfully herself when Iron Fist taught the sisters stick fighting. His favorite move was to aim a high blow to the left of the head, which would force his opponent to back up, and then quickly cross his arms and chop at her knees. When the woman tumbled backward, Iron Fist always gave a snort of appreciation.

While Wing seemed grimly determined to beat him, Rulan quietly studied his character. She admired his strength and discipline, but realized he was an actor who did not really give his heart to his work. He did not teach as her father had with a sort of wild joy. When her father had taught her to tumble, he gave his whole heart to the movements and to the teaching.

Although the *chai tang* could not afford to keep horses, Iron Fist showed a few of the best women athletes the rudiments of riding, first on a saddle slung over a barrel, then on the backs of two angry young ox calves. Only Wing and Rulan could stay on. Wing had the strength, but Rulan had an intuitive skill with animals, who calmed at her touch. Loi witchery, Wing scoffed.

On the last day of instruction, Iron Fist organized an exhibition. The Turbans had been with the women three times a week for four months, and by now there was an easy informality among them all. After an early evening meal, while there was still light, Iron Fist called everyone into the stable yard. The squads of women he had trained went through their exercises for the review of Ma Tsu Po and the elders.

After the women had performed, Iron Fist stepped into the center of the yard. "I asked the abbess if we could end our ceremonies with something special," he declared. He motioned to one of his men, who went into the stables and brought out two handsome horses, one black and one brown. Their saddles were of shiny dark leather, and the hardware decorating the reins was of gleaming brass.

"These two horses were—ah—'freed' late last night from a troop of Manchu bannermen in the next county." All the sisters laughed. "We're sending them to Canton tomorrow, but today they are ours for a race between warriors. Three times around the silk sheds for ten coppers," Iron Fist announced and pointed to where two poles were stuck in the ground at opposite ends of the yard. "My Turban brother has challenged me. If you've got a copper to bet, put it on me," he shouted.

The men leapt into their saddles. Their horses reared, then plunged ahead, as the dust of the courtyard rose like a cloud around their churning flanks. At the first turn, the two horses bumped together, and the sisters gasped as Iron Fist nearly fell from the saddle. But he regained his seat and pounded on after the other Triad who had taken the lead. They were out of sight behind a building, then racing back. Rulan had never seen anything as beautiful as the galloping horses. At the second turn of the third circuit, Iron Fist caught up with his rival. From there the two horses ran side by side until Iron Fist nosed out his cursing competitor at the finish line to the wild shouts of two hundred sisters. Iron Fist dismounted, bowed to Ma Tsu Po, took a string of copper coins from off his belt, and brandished it above his head.

"I held this from the beginning because I knew it would be mine at the end. But I will put it up as a purse for any two sisters who will race once around the track."

The women began to call out the names of their favorites. After a few minutes of prodding, the two whose names were mentioned most were pushed forward: Wing and Rulan.

Rulan stood nervously by the panting horses, feeling small and frightened. Iron Fist put the reins in her hands, told her again how to mount, but she barely heard what he was saying. All she could see were the angry red eyes the beast turned on her.

"Don't worry, Sister, they're tired. They won't run so fast," said the brother who had lost the race.

"I will win," Wing said over her shoulder to Rulan. "You do not have the strength to handle such an animal, whether he's tired or not."

"Are you ready, Sisters?" Iron Fist shouted. "Honored Mother, give the signal!"

Ma Tsu Po raised her hand. The silence was so deep that only the snorting of the horses could be heard. Her hand dropped.

Instantly, Wing catapulted herself into the saddle, but at the last moment, Iron Fist's great black whirled unexpectedly and threw Wing off balance while her leg was still in midair. Wing fell clumsily across the neck of the horse, clutching the saddle horn, while the horse whinnied and bucked, and the crowd cried out.

Rulan was still standing beside the brown horse looking into her wild eyes. She ran her hand under the silky hairs of her mane, and with a firm, slow movement boosted herself up on the stirrup and into the saddle. It felt as if she were rising to the top of a mountain. She leaned low along his powerful neck and spoke into her twitching ear. "Slowly, slowly."

She shook the reins and he started off at a ladylike trot. When she passed Wing, the black horse stopped bucking and fell in contentedly behind the brown filly.

Rounding the first shed, Wing lost her temper and began kicking her horse in the ribs. But her mount had decided that his role was not to please his angry rider but to pace the brown. With Wing seething in the saddle, the black horse cantered easily, its nose under the brown's tail.

"Move, you stupid pig!" Wing shouted, to the laughter of the assembled sisters. She shook the reins furiously and slapped the horse's neck with her hand.

Rulan lay down along the brown's neck. "Run!" she said in the lilting language of the Loi and gave him his head. The brown, her ears back, broke into a gallop. In seconds, the black horse was left far behind. When Rulan and her mount pounded across the finish line, the sisters were jumping up and down, roaring their approval.

Tsai Yen danced up. "You were wonderful, Little Witch. Your magic beguiled this horse and outsmarted that one," she said, laughing at the fuming Wing. She held out her arms to Rulan, who carefully swung down.

Iron Fist shouted for quiet and flourished the purse. "I used to call this one Number Two Ugly. Now I give her a new name. Number One Horsewoman!" A broad grin split his face. And for once Rulan did not chafe at his jibes.

When Iron Fist held up Wing's hand, the sisters loyally cheered their other favorite. But the attention made Wing more red-faced with humiliation. Coming after the laughter, even Tsai Yen's tender caresses could not console her. In the flickering torchlight that evening, the stable yard became a stage for an eerie, breathtaking spectacle of martial arts, as the Turbans, stripped bare to the waist, jumped and twisted in complex sequences of *tai chi,* from "push-hands" boxing to intricate swordplay. But Wing saw neither the gleaming, sweating men, nor the long-haired maidens waving their champions on; her eyes were filled only with the sight of the despised girl who had stolen the approbation of the Orchids.

Iron Fist's farewell the next morning was passionate but curt. "Not all battles are won with raw strength," he told the women. His dark eyes gleamed beneath the broad shelf of his brows. "Patience and cunning count as weapons too. Never give your true loyalties away. Do the unexpected, and you will defeat any aimless band of men that afflicts your house."

■   ■   ■

Ma Tsu Po observed Wing's growing hatred of Rulan with alarm, for
she had witnessed before how a rivalry between two strong-willed
women could divide the *chai tang*. All the signs of danger were present:
Rulan and Wing were clearly the only women capable of succeeding
her. Both had built up strong followings among the women, which
could easily split the community into opposing factions. What to do
with these two brilliant women who might one day replace her? Each
had talent, but neither was seasoned enough for leadership, and neither
could work with the other. The impetuous Wing, who appeared so
stern and closed-minded, was hiding a highly emotional and sentimental
nature under a hard shell of cynicism and disdain. If Wing were to
lead, she would have to allow herself to feel for others and to learn that
not everyone responds to gruff orders. Rulan was the opposite—
curious, open, and trusting. She had to acquire canniness, to think
sometimes like a trader, a thief, or a bandit. Ailan had trained her
daughter to follow ritual and discipline to the letter. The obedience
Rulan had learned complemented her natural gifts of sympathy and
healing, but blocked discernment and initiative.

While Rulan had more natural gifts than Wing, she was tentative in
all of them. Ma Tsu Po took heart from the observation that Rulan did
not live the earth religion whose magic she was trained to perform.
Perhaps there was some innate skepticism inherited from her rebel
father that prevented Rulan from falling into unquestioning piety.
Rulan's mind, Ma Tsu Po saw, was like quicksilver: brilliant yet
unpredictable and too easily steered off course. Rulan needed some
great cause to fill the gap left by the loss of her mother and abandonment by her father. Otherwise Ma Tsu Po feared that the girl might
fall under the sway of any personality stronger than herself. In Rulan,
yin, the female principle, warred with yang, the male; the solidarity of
ancient earth struggled with the restlessness of water. The combination
was volatile. In her there was potential for renewal and growth . . . or
violence and destruction. It was up to Ma Tsu Po to see that the
positive emerged to the benefit of the whole *chai tang*.

After the intense period of martial training, Ma Tsu Po apprenticed
Wing to the temple nuns in the belief that the example of the gentle
goddess would win the cynical girl to a softer life. If Wing gave her
heart to Kwan Yin, she would not be subject to bouts of envy or
self-hatred.

What to do with Rulan was a more difficult problem until an old
man was found wandering in a delirium outside their gates. He was an
impoverished, opium-ridden husk who claimed to have served the
Manchu court as physician to the Tao Kuang emperor. The Orchids

thought him preposterous. Yet washed, fed, and allowed to flourish in a Spartan atmosphere, Physician Sung proved a valuable addition to the community and a companion to Ma Tsu Po. Ancient as he was, he posed no threat or temptation to the sisters. On impulse, Ma Tsu Po apprenticed Rulan to him. He had arts that surpassed the lore of female folk medicine. If he could break the hold of Ailan's ancient magic on her daughter's mind, Rulan might finally gain the confidence to act decisively on her own.

Physician Sung's face was as yellow as parchment. His tiny ears were a forest of bristly hairs and his beard was so skimpy Rulan suspected that someone had pulled it out hair by hair. Three front teeth, all that remained to him, clicked like stones. He was a ridiculous figure. Yet as he grew in sobriety and self-respect, he began to display enough vanity, knowledge, and sharp-tongued wit to convince Ma Tsu Po that he might be the eminent court physician that he claimed.

Because male physicians were not allowed to touch the bodies of female patients, he diagnosed by asking questions and making the sisters point to the location of their pain on a ceramic doll covered with lines and dots that identified pressure points, meridians, and vital organs. But in time, familiarity and age exempted him from the sisters' natural modesty. The sisters called him "Kung Kung," Grandfather, and brought him sweets to slake the opium hunger.

Observing how the old man's cheeks had taken on a new glow whenever he spoke about his former life, the Orchids peppered him with questions about the Manchu, whom they regarded as strange and remote. There were few Manchu in the south, mostly high officials or generals whom the common folk rarely saw. The Manchu were like a race from the moon: they had adopted the culture and language of the Han race whom they had conquered, but they still existed on a separate plane.

"Kung Kung, forgive this impertinence," began Rulan, "but does one treat the emperor differently than one treats a mortal?"

The old man sniffed contemptuously. He was making an herbal poultice for Tsai Yen, who had strained her back in the mulberry groves.

"Of course, Daughter," he said, his voice heavy with irony. "One treats a mere mortal as if the patient's life depends on it. One treats the emperor as if your life depends on it. How do you think I got this opium habit—fear, anxiety, trepidation. My body was hot, cold, and in flux constantly. Did the August One fail to move his bowels today? Aaiiee! My dear friend Chu is sent into exile! Does the Dragon squeeze out a drop or two of bloody urine? Then Pharmacist Tan's medicine must be bad! Cut off his head! One treats the Son of Heaven at one's own peril. One does not practice medicine in the Forbidden City, one practices politics."

"And did you see the great concubines?" Tsai Yen asked breathlessly. "Are they very beautiful?"

"The concubines are as big-boned and big-footed as you and your sisters. They stick great wooden slabs on their heads and wrap their hair around them, and wear 'boat shoes' with the tips curled up so their flat feet look as tiny as that of a Han girl of good family. I know, I know, you sisters are women of a new age, but I'm an old-fashioned man. Give me a willow-waisted Han woman who sways on lily feet when she walks to enflame a man's ardor. Amazons like you make my yang wilt. Give me a small-foot woman any day," he sighed, while casting a sidelong lascivious glance at the pretty, petite Tsai Yen.

"And the castrated ones," Wing said darkly. "What is their preference?"

"Yes, what about them?" asked Rulan.

Physician Sung paled at the mention of the eunuchs whose evil reputation had spread even to remote villages. "They're everywhere. Thousands of them. The young ones look the same as any boy, but by the time they are thirteen, most are fat, with smooth, oily skin, double chins, and thick fingers. No one hears them, though. They're not allowed to talk unless the Dragon bids them. They move like spiders through the hall, listening, never speaking, weaving their poisonous webs. That's their weapon—the secrets they whisper to the emperor. They're the ones who rule, because no one knows the emperor better than they. Because they have no children, no families, they are a clan unto themselves. They hate everybody—woman or man—even the old emperor because he is whole. It comes from cutting off their sack.

"The Tao Kuang emperor is dying because he listened to his fat chief eunuch, not to me. I prescribed good, clean rice. Hard work. His eunuch gave him opium, wine, stuffed him like a duck with obscene delicacies that ruined his digestion, combed the empire for beautiful girls to set his old bones on fire. And they have already put poison into the heir. The heir is under the influence of a young eunuch named An-te-hai, a devil escaped from hell. He believes that the sackless ones are the true rulers of the Land of Flowers. Woe to us if he gains power! He had already taught the heir all the foul games that eunuchs play with each other. And I have heard that when the heir grows weary of the pretty young eunuchs, An-te-hai secretly escorts him outside the Forbidden City to the common fleshpots of Peking, where no perversion is too abominable for enough gold. The heir will be dead of the pox before he can sire another half-dead creature like himself."

"Then it is only a matter of time before the emperor falls," Rulan observed. Physician Sung seemed to confirm all that her father said. Perhaps her father's mission to topple the throne was not impossible.

"Cut your tongue!" said Physician Sung sharply. Then he laughed softly to himself. "Aaiiee, I forget where I am."

From this cantankerous, gossipy, ill-mannered old man, Rulan learned firsthand about the opium rot at the imperial court and in the army. She heard about the buying of honors and scholarly appointments by the gentry, who owned most of the land in the empire. She learned too about the classic pharmacopoeia set down in the *Canon of Herbs,* the first-century classic text of herbal medicine. The old doctor took her out into the fields, hills, and marshes to locate the 365 plant, animal, and mineral substances catalogued in the canon. And he made her memorize the names and characteristics of the diseases and conditions that each substance could cure. She learned which herbs to gather and dry, which should be eaten raw, which boiled in water, which steeped in wine, which ground and mixed with honey into a paste and formed into pills or suppositories, and which steamed into a rich tea. One plant could have many different properties. Fresh leaves of the trumpet flower, which grew wild on the riverbanks, would make a soothing poultice for boils or ringworm. When its roots, flowers, and leaves were dried and pulverized, a tiny dusting of it taken in hot water would soothe a hacking cough; one small pinch would alleviate pain. But a spoonful would kill.

There was only one thing on which the old man and his new pupil could not agree. He could not convince her that illness was not the result of unseen spirits meddling in the lives of living creatures.

"Demons," Physician Sung scoffed. "If you are going to learn from me, you must rid yourself of your mother's ignorant fantasies. Examine the symptoms, observe the emotions of the patient. Believe only in what you see, touch, and smell. If there is a boil, prick it with a needle. If there are worms or fever or loose bowels, give spirits of sulfur. Your goal is to restore the balance of nature. If you insist on seeing ghosts and spirits, you cannot truly heal."

Rulan thought that he chose, like the sisters in the *chai tang,* simply not to see. "But Teacher," she insisted, "I have watched my mother chase a flying head out of a villager's hut."

"Peasant incredulity spiked by fear, witch chants, and sheer stupidity!" he replied brusquely.

What would he say about healing with hands? Rulan wondered. He would make her a laughingstock before Ma Tsu Po! But she recognized that the old man's irritating way of putting every well-worn idea to the test made it possible for him to come up with new ideas, solutions for healing which Ailan, who was bound to the spirit world, could not. One of the techniques he taught was healing with needles, which had gone out of fashion in medical circles in recent centuries, but which a few classically trained doctors in remote corners of the countryside continued to use. For the old man, there was secret satisfaction too: implanting the nude bodies of young women with needles made him strut like a rooster. Even though the Orchids teased him by calling him "husband" and "wielder of the jade stalk needles," they appreciated his techniques, which worked wonders with the old and arthritic as well as the young and work bruised. It was a rare education Rulan was getting: the best medicine known to learned men imposed on the spirit rites of the shaman.

The old doctor believed that everything could be done better if one only tried. When he discovered that the needles Ma Tsu Po gave him were made out of the same iron used to make harnesses and thus rusted and caused infection, he found an ingenious answer. Remembering his years as a young doctor practicing in a poor town where porcelain needles were used, he figured out a way of making needles out of broken rice bowls. He taught Rulan how to knock the porcelain shards with the back of a heavy knife to produce identical narrow chips that could be worked into various shapes—chiseled like an arrow for skin diseases, egg tipped for massage, stiletto shaped for draining, round and thin for relieving pain, and thick and long for wrapping with burning herbs in the technique called moxibustion.

"See, Daughter," he told her, when they had amassed a quantity of clean porcelain needles. "If you are poor, you must be sure your mind is rich. Years ago, we could not afford gold needles, and iron taints the flesh, so we learned to use the useless—broken dishes. Remember that a greater principle than ritual, how a thing is done, is how to think!"

The old doctor was amazed at how quickly she learned; Rulan could soon determine the precise point of pain simply by watching a patient's expression and feeling along the bone. After insisting that she memorize the complicated charts of needling points, it was he who suggested that she could have a certain latitude in attempting a more risky technique. "Puncture wherever there is tenderness," he told her, "except for these places." And using his body as a map, he showed her the forbidden points over the eyeball, the scrotum, the carotid artery, the windpipe, and lung where needling could induce excessive bleeding. Then he put her fingers on his bald head and made her feel the soft places in the skull where the brain was exposed, like a baby's fontanel, the nose, and behind the ear, where a needle pushed too far caused death.

Physician Sung thought he monitored his pupil's every waking moment. But unknown to him, Rulan had a secret ritual: she would rise before sunrise, when the sky was pulled out of darkness, to talk to her mother's departed spirit. It became a habit to follow that with the *chi gung* exercises her mother had taught her. No one would recognize the gestures, she reasoned, or else they would think that she was performing some aberrant form of *tai chi chuan*.

One morning, after finishing a complicated sequence of movements, she found the old doctor watching her intently.

"What are you doing?" he asked.

"*Tai chi,*" she lied, rubbing the sweat from her eyes and steeling herself for his ridicule. "I know only a little of the dance."

He shook his head. "What are you doing with your hands? Who taught it to you?"

Rulan paused. Should she tell him? Her mother had sworn her to secrecy lest the evil ones, the thieves, try to steal *chi* from her.

"What are you afraid of? I'm not one of those, not a thief. Who taught you?"

"My mother."

He rocked back in surprise. "Mother? I thought *chi gung* was a man's art. In my family, fathers pass it to their sons, though there are legends that men stole it from the one great Mother."

"Will you keep my secret?"

"I have to." He laughed. "You know too many of my own. Here, let these old bones feel your warmth." He held up his palms to her.

Rulan laughed too, happy that he had given her face and that somebody now shared her secret. She held out her hands, the left one slightly extended, and pushed against the air as if moving an invisible load.

Instantly his right hand moved back.

"Aaiiee!" he said, looking down at his hand as if it burned. "I never felt that much heat before. And you used your left hand, not your right. That's backward. Come, let me look at you."

Rulan dutifully went up to him.

After glancing over his shoulder as if he were checking for a predator that had come too close, he pressed his fingers into the palm of her hands. "Where did you get your strength?"

"Mother said I stole it from a *ku*-creature, when I pushed a spirit out of a man."

"Oh. More spirits and devils!"

"You may laugh, but *Ku* is a fearful demon!"

"That may be how a spirit-woman explains evil. Reasonable people know that there is neither good nor bad in the universe. There are only alternating winds. Yin and yang, hot and cold, light and dark. A wise man recognizes the flow and does not try to move against it. I must teach you more control. You are too undisciplined. We'll exercise together every morning. You will push against my hands, and I will teach you to direct the flow. You are like a flood. You must come out like a stream."

"There is so much I don't know. Mother didn't know either."

"But you watched her heal?"

"Not often. She had me practice on an unseen body."

"Remarkable," he murmured. "You mean you invent the one you hope to heal. Yes, of course, that's what the ritual suggests. You teach me force. I will teach you control. The old arts and the new. *Chi gung,* needling, herbs. Sometimes one works, and sometimes another. A good physician knows and uses them all."

"And spirits?"

"A physician cannot use what does not exist."

"This one will make a superior healer," he confided to Ma Tsu Po.

Now there was another reason for the urgency in Rulan's training. It was clear to the abbess that rebels, such as the God Worshipers, all the various sects of the Triads, such as the Red Turbans, and the Small Sword Society were growing stronger in the south. There was talk among the leaders of the secret societies of a grand alliance proposed by the religious zealots in Thistle Mountain. Ma Tsu Po found the idea extraordinarily naive, for the societies had only their hatred for the Manchu in common. Other such alliances had been attempted in the past, only to degenerate into wholesale slaughter. The bargain she had made with Iron Fist was a cautious, one-time transaction; the Orchids needed to learn to fight, the Triads needed cash. She had no doubts what thoughts the Triad men might have entertained had they stayed longer in the company of young women. What role should the Orchids play in the rebel alliance? Ma Tsu Po wondered. Was there anything to gain by joining forces with other secret societies? She needed a strong young woman to assist her, a woman more intelligent than Wing, more cool headed than Harmony. What better ally than this strange witch's child, if she could only teach the girl how to think clearly and act with deliberation.

Ma Tsu Po confirmed her plan one day as she watched Rulan haul a net of fish from the dwindling stock in the compound's ponds, a man's work in another more typical village. She marveled at the young woman's strength. Rulan had worked all day, and it was now near sunset.

"Pull hard, Rulan, because only every other fish is ours," Ma Tsu Po called out. "The first goes to our landlord, General Li."

The young woman held up work-reddened hands. "I have not shirked my duty."

Those hands should be feeling for hurt, not hurting—stopping blood, not bleeding, Ma Tsu Po thought. But she gently scolded, "Why are you complaining? Do you think you are better than your sisters?"

"No, Mother," Rulan replied good-humoredly. She turned to grasp the net with her bruised fingers. "I will gladly fish for General Li, if that will help my sisters," she said over her shoulder.

Ma Tsu Po was touched by the girl's sincerity. To keep the girl by her side, she invited Rulan to be her secretary. There were no objections from the elders. And only Wing fumed and complained about favoritism when Rulan was excused from all other chores except her studies with Physician Sung.

But Ma Tsu Po soon had more pressing concerns than the rivalry simmering between Wing and Rulan. The turmoil in the nation was beginning to invade the *chai tang*. Beggars streamed to the gate for rice and money. Girl babies were abandoned at their gate. Drunken youths threw stones into the window slits or roamed the mulberry groves, calling obscenities to the maidens as they dredged the fishponds. For weeks, two local toughs had been harassing Tsai Yen, trying to pull her into the bushes.

The lessons after dinner changed. Gone were the ballads of patient, suffering widows or self-sacrificing daughters. A grim-faced Harmony led recitations of battlefield poems of fighting women. No one begged her to chant the tale of the Merciful Goddess Kwan Yin anymore. Instead, the maidens clamored for Wing's thumping rendition of the ballad of Fa Mulan, the legendary Yuan dynasty woman warrior who led a battalion of swordsmen to victory in the guise of a man.

One night at the end of summer, Tsai Yen did not return from the groves. After a frantic search, her half-naked body was discovered in a mulch pile, her neck broken. The girl had been raped. The two youths had waited until Wing was absent to seize Tsai Yen. Insane with grief, Wing tried to drown herself, and when that failed, she found the white powder used to kill rats in the storehouse and ate it.

Rulan forced the half-unconscious Wing to swallow raw eggs mixed with powdered alum to throw up the poison. Wing vomited a little but when her mind began to wander and her pupils shrank, Rulan became alarmed. The old doctor said that Wing was dying, but Rulan would not accept that diagnosis. If Wing would not fight back, Rulan would do so for her. Some perverse instinct in Rulan would not allow the rivalry between them to end in this manner. She tried to rouse Wing by the heat of her hands. Wing thrashed and moaned, fighting against the life-giving current, determined to die. As Wing slipped into unconsciousness, Rulan took her longest needles and jabbed them into Wing's wrist, between the thumb and index finger, and below the knee, the points which govern the stomach. Every few minutes, Rulan rotated the needles in an effort to bring Wing back to life by causing pain.

After many hours, Wing began to cough up a black, bloody bile, then to kick and punch, then to weep. Wiping the tears and sweat from her face, Rulan silently blessed her mother and Physician Sung. The girl would live.

Ma Tsu Po and the council appealed directly to Magistrate Lam and brought suit against the families of the two boys, pleading the case in person in court at the yamen. Lam acted swiftly. After an investigation, he found the youths guilty and petitioned the throne for their deaths. But the local clans bribed the bailiffs, and the boys were allowed to escape. The outrage shook the *chai tang*. Rulan began to wonder whether they were only vulnerable women after all. Ma Tsu Po contacted the Triads again; she decided to cast her lot with them.

Then as the cold season began, Harmony's husband stood at the gate to demand his wife's return. His concubine had died, and he had signed on as cook boy for a scholar in Canton. The job was for husband and wife. Again, the Orchids took the case before Lam. But this time the law worked against them. Bound by Confucian ethics, Lam ruled that the law was clear: A husband had rights over his wife that could not be bartered away by all the wages Harmony had sent over the years to keep him in rice and wine. Ma Tsu Po denounced Lam and his justice and vowed to fight the law, but after the magistrate sent armed guards to their gates, Harmony insisted on leaving to end the threat to the women's community. So the most brilliant of the Orchids was sent to be a drudge in the kitchen of a wealthy man.

With Harmony gone, there was only Wing and Rulan left of the original "family" of five. Rulan's life became centered on the desperately ill Wing, for Rulan was frightened at the thought of being left truly alone. It took several months for Wing to recover, and during that time Rulan left Wing's bed only to help the old doctor nurse those sisters who had been brought low by a coughing sickness. It was an evil season. Wing fought her, rejected her care, spurned her medicines, reviled her presence.

When Wing was strong enough to walk, Rulan took her into the groves. They were the same height now, although Rulan was temporarily the stronger of the two. Wing leaned like an old woman on Rulan's arm, but Rulan could feel the older girl's resistance. She decided to take a chance and confront Wing's ill feeling directly.

"I know you hate me. I've been afraid of you since I came here," Rulan told Wing.

Wing glowered. "That's wise. I'm an angry person. You never know what I'm going to do."

"Everyone looks up to you. Why are you so angry?"

"Because I don't need anybody's pity! I've been on my own since I was thirteen after my parents married me to a lout. I like it that way."

"You—married? But you never said—"

"Yes, I was married!" Wing retorted in exasperation. "My father said I was worse than a guest because I brought in nothing and ate more than a son. He was glad to pay a man in the next village to take me off his hands. My husband drank my bride-price away, beat me, forced me twice a day. His mother was no better. Then my clumsy husband fell into a grain bin drunk and was smothered. His mother turned me out. My father had other daughters and wouldn't take me back. For two years I sold myself to survive. When I heard about this place, I walked nine days to come here."

"I didn't know—" Rulan stammered.

"Your hand hurts! Take it away!" Wing said violently and thrust Rulan aside. She would not allow herself to be taken for a walk the next day or the next, but her resentment of Rulan seemed in some strange way to make her stronger.

Soon Wing could manage simple tasks. She was assigned to clean the dormitory, and Rulan made to assist her as she had done once before when she and her mother had first come to the *chai tang*. Rulan continued to dog Wing's heels, peppering her with questions and medical advice. Wing's surliness was a welcome change from her earlier hopelessness. Rulan was determined to nag, cajole, and browbeat Wing into facing her loss directly.

"Tell me," Rulan asked, "what does it mean when a woman loves another woman, as you loved Tsai Yen?"

Wing's eyes opened wide in anger. Suddenly, her face crumpled. When she replied, her voice was small and shaky. "If two women decide to live together, they swear an oath never to eat meat, never to be penetrated by a man, never to bleed in birth, for then they escape the 'bloody pond' after death and go together to the Happy Land. Then the abbess plucks the hair from the brow, as women do for any bride, and they become one."

"But isn't a woman's duty to bear sons?"

Wing shook her head. "Harmony used to say that heaven and earth are tainted when a woman gives birth. When you are a man's wife, you cannot avoid the bloodstained water after death, and you offend the sun and the moon. Giving birth is a sin."

Rulan hesitated. "And do you ever desire a man's stalk?"

"No," Wing said slowly. "I like a softer touch. And when I need to be filled, there is the silk sleeve filled with bean curd to use in play."

And a woman who has never had a man? Rulan wondered. How would she know if she desired one or not? She was too shy to ask, but she knew at least that she was no longer afraid of Wing and that Wing no longer despised her.

Aware of the changing tensions between both women, Ma Tsu Po decided to make Wing part of her staff as a sergeant at arms. Her intention was that the two most talented sisters should learn to work with one another. But Wing's jealousy could not be put aside so easily.

By the beginning of autumn, Wing was strong enough to propose a race. "No horses. Feet. To the end of the groves and back," she challenged Rulan.

Rulan was delighted that her patient wanted to be her opponent once again. She agreed, and on their first free afternoon they set off from the mulberry gate to the end of the groves one mile away. Rulan fell behind, but conserved her energy by keeping up a measured stride. She saw Wing disappear behind the thick leaves of the mulberry trees. The smell of the leaves and the moist earth was heady and exhilarating, as was the sensation of moving her limbs in time to the rhythm of her pounding heart. After two-thirds of a mile, she caught up with Wing and, taking two strides to Wing's one, she swiftly closed the distance between them. Rulan was so close she could hear Wing's labored breathing. Then the wide mouth of the drainage ditch yawned before them. They leaped, almost together. Wing's long legs stretched and cleared the gap. Rulan flew high, until her left foot struck loose soil on the opposite bank. Down she fell with a cry.

Wing whirled around. The look of triumph vanished when she saw Rulan lying on her face at the bottom of the trench, half in the water. She scrambled down to her.

"No, no, no," moaned Wing, again and again, as she caught Rulan under the shoulders and pulled her up out of the mud.

Rulan exploded with mischievous laughter. "I am too clumsy and stupid," she cried. "You beat me fairly, Elder Sister."

Wing caught Rulan in her arms, stroking her wet hair and sniffing her cheek as a mother does a beloved child. Suddenly Wing began to cry. "I thought, again . . . I thought I lost . . ." Unable to say more, she held Rulan tightly and would not let go.

"I do not know if I am a woman meant for a woman," Rulan said after a while. "I have never known a man—"

"How can you tell one rice grain from the next?" Wing replied. "Pleasure is pleasure. But when someone loves you—that is beyond compare."

As Wing held Rulan, the loneliness of a lifetime surged forth. Naked beseeching shone in her eyes. "Dear one," she wept as she kissed Rulan's face and hair.

Rulan leaned against Wing and felt the terrible beating of a woman's heart. She felt the heat of Wing's body, smelled her sweat. Wing's arms wrapped tightly around her. Slowly, she felt Wing's terror subside into the overpowering ache of need.

Rulan waited shyly.

After a while, when the racing of Wing's heart had shifted from the pulse of fear to the pulse of ardor, Wing opened her tunic and drew Rulan's face against her breast, encouraging the girl with a touch as gentle as the fluttering of a butterfly.

They tarried in the mulberry groves until twilight. And while Wing taught Rulan pleasure, she herself felt more love and sadness than she had ever known.

A month later, when Wing asked Rulan to exchange vows, she accepted. Permission was granted by Ma Tsu Po, who was delighted at the happy outcome of the rivalry and set aside a day following the mid-autumn Moon Festival, a few weeks hence, for the ceremony.

7

At dawn, a week before the exchange of vows, Rulan was jolted awake by an elderly sister holding a small oil lamp aloft in the humid darkness of the sleeping room.

"Quick, the holy mother wants you," whispered the woman.

Rulan was dimly aware that Wing's pallet next to hers was empty as she crept through the lines of sleeping women. They rapidly crossed the compound grounds and walked up the steps of Ma Tsu Po's cottage. Approaching the main room, Rulan heard angry voices. Her heart dropped; one of the voices was Wing's.

"Go on," the old woman urged, and pushed Rulan forward.

The door closed behind her. There before the abbess and the four women who composed the ruling council of the society was an ashen-faced Wing.

"Go now, Wing, while we talk to Rulan. The decision rests with her," the abbess said in a tired voice. Wing was trembling. As she passed Rulan, she moved her fingers in their secret talk; the signal was "farewell."

"Step up, child," Ma Tsu Po said.

Rulan stumbled forward on the icy floor, wishing she had thought to comb her hair or slip on her straw slippers. She felt as naked and vulnerable as a supplicant before a judge.

"Elder Sisters, how have I displeased you?" she said in a small, frightened voice.

"You do not displease us, child," replied Ma Tsu Po. "It is our turn to plead with you. You see, you can do a great service for the Golden Orchids."

Relief flooded through Rulan. They were promoting, not punishing her.

"It will not be without sacrifice."

"Ask me anything!" Rulan effused.

The five women stirred uncomfortably on their barrel stools.

"Youth is always eager. Hear us out before you pledge," said the old woman who was the society's treasurer.

"This house is one of five in our society," Ma Tsu Po began. "You know that life for us is not easy in the Land of Flowers. Women like us, who are bound neither to father nor husband, are considered strange. We suffer for that strangeness. Our mother house has twice been set afire. We try to defend ourselves, but each attack leaves us weaker. Now we have been offered help. Our brothers in the Red Turban Society have made a pact with Master Hung, leader of the God Worshipers."

Rulan's breath caught in her throat. Hung again! She could see once more his compelling eyes and hear his lilting voice describing visions of heaven, or summoning Yang, her father, to his side.

"We can be part of their pact. Each of our five houses is guaranteed security by the Turbans. Moreover, through a Canton merchant guild, the Turbans can arrange to have our silk sold at a price fixed twenty-five percent above our costs. 'Dragon Eye,' the master of that guild, is headman of all Triads in Kwangtung. He promises to secure a government license for our society to sell silk on our own without going through the agents of our landlord, General Li."

"What must I do?" Rulan began to fear the worst: perhaps Ma Tsu Po intended to sell her to Hung for a bride-price. She remembered how Hung had desired her and how Ailan had pulled her away from him. She still felt the man's compelling power over her, while fearing what Ailan alone had seen—the invisible snake coiled around him, the dark fire that burned inside.

"We want you to heal an old woman who is about to die."

"What?" replied Rulan, incredulous. "Is that all?"

"You heard right," Ma Tsu Po replied. "We have had word that a servant of General Li is searching this county for Ailan. Li's mother was the Tai Tai your mother served as a girl, and now that the Tai Tai is dying, she will have no other tend her but her old slave girl. That servant has been directed here by our Triad brothers. He should be arriving tomorrow. We want you to take your mother's place. Mix the Tai Tai's medicines and offer the appropriate prayers, since she too worships Kwan Yin. Keep her alive. Be our eyes and ears in the general's house. The Triads and Master Hung need information about Li's movements. The rumor is that Li will be appointed to lead an offensive against the God Worshipers. We will send a messenger to you on days that are sacred to Kwan Yin. Report everything you hear to her.''

Rulan took a deep breath, relieved that this was only another job of healing. "I can do it.''

"It could be dangerous,'' cautioned Ma Tsu Po. "If General Li finds out that you are our spy, he will cut off your head.''

"That's why Wing was afraid for me,'' Rulan cried. "Let me run and tell her the good news. How long after the wedding must I be away from here? Wing and I need to plan—''

"You cannot be married now, Daughter.''

Rulan's face fell. "Why?''

"You have to leave for Abundant Spring Mountain tomorrow!''

"But you agreed. You chose the date yourself!''

Ma Tsu Po shook her head.

Disappointment turned to desperation. "Then marry us now! Tonight!''

The Keeper of the Rites, who was also the oldest woman in the house, spoke with great compassion. "No, Daughter. You know that the rule of Orchid marriage is fidelity. When you marry, you marry one. And you pledge never to know a man.''

"No man has touched me!''

"But as a spy, your body must be our instrument,'' said Ma Tsu Po firmly. "You can learn as much from a lover as from an enemy. That is your sacrifice. You must give up Wing for a time and learn all you can about the general. Find out what his wives argue about. How much money he owes and to whom. What his plans are in the silk and salt trade. What he tells his mother. What rumors circulate through the house about his preparations for war. Put your will at our disposal. Remember what you swore at your initiation. Can you sacrifice body and soul for your sisters?''

Rulan's head was spinning. How could she give Wing up? Yet how could she refuse the women who had raised her as their own child for nearly two years? An angry thought nagged at her. If they truly loved her, they wouldn't ask her to do what every Golden Orchid abhorred—to leave the sanctuary of the house, turn her back on the teachings of Kwan Yin to become a whore and a spy.

"Wing would never allow this," Rulan declared.

"Wing objected to the danger and the calumny you might suffer. But Wing is a warrior. She knows what it means to sacrifice. In this case, her sacrifice is greater than yours, for you go with face and honor, and she must wait in fear."

Rulan remembered the sign Wing had made with her fingers. Wing had decided for her too. Something in Rulan rebelled. "I will not do it."

Ma Tsu Po was grim. "I know another who might convince you." She motioned to the Keeper of the Rites, who opened a door and beckoned. Four black-clad strangers slipped into the circle of light cast by the flickering oil lamp.

"Your manners, Daughter! Greet your teacher," Ma Tsu Po chided.

Through a veil of tears, Rulan looked up into the dark-browed visage of Iron Fist, the Triad warrior who had shattered Wing's pride.

"I have spoken to the girl," announced Ma Tsu Po. "She refuses."

Rulan made a perfunctory bow, trying to hide her confusion.

When the other strangers took off their conical straw hats, Rulan noticed with alarm that they had unshaven heads and no queue: there was a skinny flat-nosed man with hair tied into a greasy headknot, a youth with hair like a lion's mane and the fine features of a poet, and a short, bowlegged man in torn trousers whose head rag obscured his face.

"These gentlemen are God Worshipers. That one is Master Wei." Ma Tsu Po indicated the scrawny, sharp-faced man whom Rulan remembered from her first encounter with Hung in her home village. The abbess next nodded at the handsome youth. "This is Shih Ta Kai, a captain among them. That one says he is your father."

The bowlegged stranger in clothes as tattered as a beggar's unwound his dirty head rag. There was a fringe of hair covering his forehead that had once been shaved clean, but Rulan knew instantly the mocking eyes, the wide mouth so like her own.

"Father!" she exclaimed with joy as sharp as pain—and then the memory of his abandonment and the deaths of her brother and mother rushed in on her. She steeled herself against the treacherous onslaught of her wildly fluctuating emotions. "Forgive my mistake, Sisters," Rulan announced, regaining her self-control. "I no longer have a father. I am a Golden Orchid."

The man threw back his big head. "Little Quail," he cried, in a voice so familiar that Rulan felt her heart drawn into a net. "Would you clap your old father on the cheeks and pull his ears? Would you ride on his back? Even sisters of the Golden Orchid have fathers, and I am yours!"

"You left us to starve!" she said, rousing her anger to block the pull of blood.

"I took away a hungry mouth so you would not starve."

"Because you were not there to protect us, the villagers killed the boy."

The smile on Yang's face faded instantly. "I heard. I wept." Tears rose in his eyes and sorrow tightened his throat. "I have other sons now. Sons of a thousand dispossessed, whom I will soon make into an army."

"Mother died. I hold you responsible," Rulan accused him. In any magistrate's court she would be convicted of impiety and sentenced to death for her unfilial words. But she was her father's daughter—too impulsive to care about consequences.

Yang shook his head sadly. "I had to free myself from the village or be smothered. Ailan of the Loi was too powerful. How could I know that some measure of her energy and power depended on me? I never thought she would sicken without me, and I looked forward to the day when I could bring her to sit beside me on a throne."

"Don't pretend you don't know how she died, or that you are sorry. She was killed protecting me from bandits. Because your ambition had made you great, they wanted me for ransom. Your pride purchased her death."

"Impossible!" he cried. But Rulan saw that his confidence was shaken.

"Twelve men broke down the door of our dormitory," she said. "They came for me. My sisters fought them, but when they were beaten back, Mother leapt into the fire and fell upon the leader with her own burning body. After that, we slew them, every one."

"Well, Master Wei, headman of spies, your information seems faulty. Master Hung said nothing of this to me," Yang said to his scrawny companion.

"She is lying," Wei declared.

"This girl doesn't lie! My daughter doesn't lie. She is as sure as salt, *hai ma*, Holy Mother?"

Ma Tsu Po nodded uncomfortably. "Our Triad brother Iron Fist knows of our old complaint against—bandits." Ma Tsu Po did not say what she had long suspected: that the men who had tried to kidnap Rulan were like Iron Fist, also Triads. "That is why our assent to your proposition does not come easily," she said to Wei. "This girl lost a mother. We lost seven sisters that night. We take most seriously our daughter's risk as a spy in the house of a dangerous man."

"Do you think I do not?" Yang cried. "She is my only living flesh."

"Sister," hissed the monkey-faced Wei. "Guard your tongue!"

"You speak like a man with something to hide," Ma Tsu Po replied, losing her temper. "Perhaps those were not bandits but God Worshipers themselves, *hai ma?*"

Yang's eyes had lost their bright mockery. Rulan saw that he despised Wei. Obviously there were factions even within the universal brotherhood of believers.

"If I suspected for a moment that you or Hung—" Yang accused Wei, who seemed to shrink inside his baggy black pajamas. Yang turned back to Rulan. "Little Quail," he pleaded. "I swear I did not know. Wei told me that you and she had disappeared. Only a few days before we set out here, Wei told me about Ailan's death—and the boy's. I grieved when I heard the news, but I believed she went back to the Orchids because she had chosen her time to die, as Loi healers do."

"Fine words," said Rulan bitterly. "You never honored her."

"She was the only woman for me. There will never be any other. But the people—ah, I will put my heart in a snare for them. Ailan would not help me in this, you see—But you—if the old Tai Tai wants a healer, then no one but Ailan's daughter can satisfy her. No one can give our movement life but you. The old woman's son, General Li, is our enemy. Yet Li has a changeable nature. If the emperor offers him honors, titles, money, he will be the emperor's man. But at a propitious moment, if the emperor treads on him, his ambition could make him our ally. We need to know his secret desires. We need you to tell us if he can be turned to our side—or if he plans to move against us."

"Mother gave her life for me. You ask me to risk mine. She leaped into the fire, and with the flames of her own dying routed the thieves. You ask me to walk into the enemy's house alone and unprotected. Whom should I honor—you or her?"

"Honor your mother through me. She healed the sick. I mean to heal a dying nation. I need you, Rulan," Yang begged. "I know I can turn these aimless families into a mighty army! I can make warrior squads of them even as I did when I ran charcoal-carriers through the high mountains. Enough squads of angry men, and we can topple the throne!"

Wei tugged angrily at the wisp of hair on his chin and said, "You think you are first among us because you have taught the ruffians in camp to bear arms. Remember that all power is His. Hung is Younger

Son! You are mortal dust—charcoal dust." Wei laughed at his small joke while keeping out of the reach of Yang's strong arm.

Iron Fist gripped Yang's elbow with his enormous hand. "Ho, brothers! What's this? Two God Worshipers quarreling?" he scolded. "This is what comes of god talk. Save your wrath for the gentry pig Li. It's his house we want to sack, his pockets we mean to pick."

Yang shook himself free. "It's always money with you!" he said contemptuously.

"I don't complicate things with lofty principles," Iron Fist retorted. "I know my enemies: a headman with full pockets. A fat magistrate. I have a brother who is a magistrate—but he is a leech like Li. Kill the Ching, restore the Ming! It's a battle cry, not a holy creed! Why else does anyone fight but to fatten off the pigs who fatten off us?"

"For peace, for justice! To right the wrongs against the people!" declared Shih Ta Kai reproachfully. Rulan was stirred as much by the youth's dignity as by his beauty. He seemed to hold himself above his quarrelsome comrades.

"Brothers," interrupted Ma Tsu Po in exasperation, "we are not here for a war council or a family reunion. Rulan, make peace with your father and be done. Your mother is dead. The pattern goes on. Forget that evil night, I command you."

"I have no father," Rulan said defiantly. "I am a Golden Orchid. Nevertheless, if you command me to go to my death to help the sisters, I will go."

Ma Tsu Po ran her hands through her thick gray hair and sighed. "Rulan, Rulan. You must go consenting or nothing will come of your sacrifice. How can you serve the Merciful Goddess if you are so angry?"

"The brat is her father's, after all," Wei snapped, moving quickly to put Iron Fist between him and Yang. "He too serves no power higher than himself."

"Daughter," pleaded Ma Tsu Po. "We have a purpose and little time. Your sisters need you. No one else can save us but you. Make peace with him and go willingly."

Rulan stood in stony silence.

Yang gave an embarrassed laugh. "Then if you deny me as a father, let us be brother and sister. Father Moses says that to obey the High God is the first commandment, above the duty to a parent. Two warriors then, you and I, fighting for the people. Your mother would approve."

He touched the tips of his fingers together, and Rulan understood that despite his grief and shame, he was blessing her.

Ma Tsu Po leaned over Rulan, her voice ragged, and picked up a sheaf of papers from her table. "With the God Worshipers, we will have a place in a new order. Hung has promised us freedom to own land in our own names. Our own names! Freedom to take the examinations and serve in Taiping Tien Kuo, the Kingdom of Great Peace. Think, Rulan, of the lives you save! Think why your mother brought you here, why she perished so that you might live. So that you—and all women—might be free!"

"Within the four seas, all are brothers, all are sisters, and the Heavenly Father cherishes all," said Shih Ta Kai, spreading his arms wide and fixing his large dark eyes on Rulan.

"But you must smash your idols first. Hung has decreed that all the old gods and goddesses are sham," said the Wei. "Kwan Yin is vapor. Nothing. The High God is all."

Iron Fist groaned in exasperation.

Ma Tsu Po replied angrily. "I have decided. We will not give up the goddess."

"There is no room for demons from the old days," retorted Wei. "What other gods but the High God do you need? We are not ignorant heathens like our parents and grandparents. Master Hung carries a three-foot sword for slaying demons such as Kwan Yin. Come now, choose! You cannot serve the High God and this lump of clay you call a goddess. With these hands I have smashed scores of altars to this demon! I do the same with yours."

Ma Tsu Po put her hands to her ears. "Kwan Yin is not a demon! Kwan Yin is heaven's anointed!"

"Then let her strike me with thunder and lightning," shot back the scrawny Wei, his goatee trembling as he spoke. "I say she is a *kuei* like Confucius, the demon King of Hell, and all the spirits and demons of the underworld whom we call emperor and magistrate and high court officials. If I lie, let Kwan Yin strike me dead, I say."

"Stop!" shouted Ma Tsu Po. "Mock the Goddess of Mercy and you mock us too. Your words only make us more firm." To Yang she said, "You speak of justice. Remember the women who live as priest-esses among us. If she had lived, your wife would have been one. If you smash our altars, you crush their hearts."

"Aaiiee!" Iron Fist exclaimed. "My head hurts from all this shouting. Gods, goddesses, demons, devils. Call them what you will, the important thing is that we put a tick in the ear of the dog's head who squats in Peking." His frown was so deep that his eyes vanished under the hairy brow. "You told me your High God is patient. Show a little patience yourself, Brother Wei. He waited for you, you said. He will wait for the daughters of Kwan Yin."

"You work it out then," Wei muttered to Yang, blowing his nose with his fingers. "Let it be on your head if the Younger Son's will is thwarted."

Iron Fist followed Wei, pressing for a compromise. "Discipline must be maintained and the sisters must fight alongside our soldiers," he said into the God Worshiper's ear. "Hung will have to understand that some loyalties from the old days are not easily abandoned."

Yang stepped close to his daughter. "I meant to say nothing. I'll say this."

Rulan looked away.

He touched her chin, gently turning her face to him. "What I tell you could kill me," he whispered. He glanced at Ma Tsu Po. She was listening to Shih Ta Kai tell how he last evaded a government ambush. Seeing that no one was paying attention to them, Yang continued in a whisper. "At first I believed that Hung was a god. Now I do not. But Hung's tongue draws hungry people to him. I need Hung a little longer. I need you too, Rulan. Help me. Go into the house of Li, and together we can change the people's fate."

Rulan did not reply.

"You carry your mother's magic. Without it I cannot start a fire. We can give her spirit peace and your sisters freedom."

Rulan wanted to believe him. Her head cried out against it, but her heart wanted to believe. Reluctantly, she nodded.

Yang slapped his thigh in delight.

Ma Tsu Po looked up. Walking quickly away from Shih Ta Kai, the older woman demanded, "What is your answer then, Sister?"

"I will be your spy—"

Ma Tsu Po sighed deeply, unsettled by the victory. This coercion was not Kwan Yin's way, no matter how she tried to persuade Rulan that the cause justified her sacrifice. "Now you must show courage, Daughter."

Yang touched his daughter's wet cheek. "Do you remember when we played hunt-the-tiger? We used secret words and no one, not even I, could find you if you did not wish to be found." He rubbed his daughter's shoulder and chuckled.

The memory of the days when they had once been a family sleeping under one quilt flooded back to Rulan. Her father had made up animal names for every village elder. She had led a gang of ragamuffins in mischief, but it was her father who thought up their tricks: mixing dung into the headman's tobacco; filling the rice baskets owed to the yamen with stones. How Rulan wished for the innocence of those days.

"Yes," she said, her heart still hardened against him.

"That language will be our sign. That and these special code words I will teach you."

In order that she might instruct the messengers who would pass between them, Yang taught Ma Tsu Po the same code based on the games he had played with his daughter in a happier time.

After she was dismissed, Rulan crept into Wing's pallet, and they held each other all night.

"You must promise not to give anyone your heart, no matter who you love with your body," whispered Wing.

"I promise," Rulan said. "And you must promise not to harm yourself, not even think of dying until I return to you."

The next day, as Ma Tsu Po had foretold, a messenger from the Lis came searching for Ailan of the Loi, and was despondent when he learned she was dead. But his mood rapidly changed to jubilation when he found that her daughter, an orphan who lived in the community and who had learned all Ailan's arts, could be his for a small price. So he bought her and took Rulan as a *mui tsai,* a slave girl, to the great house on a hill above the Pearl River.

Part 2

WOMAN WITHIN WALLS

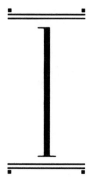

Abundant Spring Mountain, Kwangtung Province, 1850

Amazing! They can squat like that forever, Roderick Mandley observed to himself. The crowd of peasants, who were waiting as he was for the house steward to appear, crouched on skinny haunches against a bird-splattered wall just inside the gate of Abundant Spring Mountain, the Li family compound. He knew that most westerners would consider the chattering farmers little more than baboons—stubborn, brutish, and liars by nature, with small, hooded eyes and shrill voices. Mandley could never muster a proper western disdain for the Han, even to mask the fear he now felt. He saw instead in each beggar's face the marks of a heroic people conserving every grain of rice, every drop of water for the famine or drought that might befall it again. China assaulted his senses and left him dumbfounded by its sounds and smells, its stark beauty, its exalted view of human possibility, and its mundane cruelty in the imperfect now. Alone in an alien land, he had no sense of homelessness, only a heightened sense of astonishment.

Though it was early morning, Mandley found the subtropical midsummer heat unbearable, yet none of the farmers seemed to sweat as he did through the ridiculously inadequate disguise of his conical straw hat and blue peasant's suit. He stuck out all over—too broad in the shoulders, too long in the leg, too long in the nose. Too conspicuously a western "barbarian," he thought ruefully, and—because all but a few

port cities in China were off-limits to his kind—too carelessly dangerous. Still, white Bible distributors had roamed the southern provinces
for years in similar disguise, counting on their utter strangeness to
confound the officials they encountered.

A clown, he told himself. None of the petty tradesmen, except for
an old herb vendor who glanced at him out of the corner of his cloudy
eyes, looked in his direction. Nevertheless, Mandley sensed that they
were as keenly aware of his presence as chickens were of a hawk
perched on a tree. Although Mandley had been in China three years,
he had still not mastered the Han ability to close off sensation and,
amid the choking conglomeration of humankind, sink into a private
space as impassively as a mollusk at low tide. What he had attained
was a keen sense of wonder that made him a misfit among his stern
and unimaginative colleagues.

Six months earlier in Canton, at the beginning of the new year,
Mandley had met with General Li and the current viceroy of Canton's
representatives as part of a trade delegation of westerners attempting to
win back business for Canton from other recently opened treaty ports.
He liked the general, mainly because Li seemed to despise, as Mandley
did, the viceroy's man, a grossly fat merchant-comprador named
Wang, to whom all the other tradesmen pandered. The meeting was
ostensibly about exchange rates—the amount of silver foreigners were
to pay for Chinese commodities such as tea and silk. In fact, the
discussion was about opium, and hence it was conducted in language
subtle enough to constitute a code that Mandley could barely fathom,
despite his facility with the southern dialects.

More was at stake for the Han than for the barbarians from the West.
At the turn of the century, Britain had nearly bankrupted itself buying
tea and silk from China, while China bought nothing in return. With
opium, the relationship was reversed: China became the debtor nation
while British companies grew fabulously rich selling tea in Europe and
black dirt to the Chinese.

General Li was adamantly opposed to any "silk and tea trade" with
opium-peddling "barbarian" nations. Mandley remembered how Li
had castigated the other Han delegates for their greed and cowardice.
While the British traders seethed, Merchant Wang had dropped his
eyes in embarrassment at his colleague's diatribe—not at his own
reprehensible conduct. What inverted madness, Mandley avowed. Li
seemed to him the first man of principle he had found in China, the
kind of old-fashioned Confucian whom westerners extolled but rarely

met in the flesh. Mandley had sensed in Li an honesty that appeared almost—well, American. A pity that the only western commodity Li had shown any interest in was arms, particularly the Prussian rifles that had just come into fashion in England and America, which the Han armies—still dependent on swords, bows, and pikes—had never seen. Although he would be judged a traitor to his race, Mandley had made the decision to make the general a brother, for surely Christian principle was served in eliminating opium, which was sin pure and simple. How could the Gospel be espoused when the very nations who preached it brought along this devil's drug?

Mandley had sent Li the requisite letters, but after six months of waiting, he had now come himself to the general's door—only to be put off by the house steward.

Mandley kicked out his legs, unkinked his spine, shook out his six-foot length, and stretched like a man getting ready for a race, knowing that the line of coolies would be collectively aghast at his ugliness. He didn't care. Barbarians, even in disguise, were expected to be eccentric; he would not disappoint them. His bladder was uncomfortably full, but his sense of decorum wouldn't allow him to piss against the wall as a dozen or so of these "civilized" Han had done within the half hour, not six paces from where he had been sitting.

Instead he strode over to a guard lounging outside the steward's office and demanded in gutter Cantonese, "Where is your master, that turtle turd of a steward?" He had learned long ago that command was essential in dealing with servants, who otherwise considered you as worthless as themselves. And yet he was taking a chance in announcing his presence so boldly. Since he was traveling without papers in territory off-limits to all westerners, he could be executed, particularly if his mission to sell Bibles to the Han was known to the authorities. But the three days' wait had finally unnerved him.

Because it was beneath a civilized person to acknowledge that a barbarian could speak passable Cantonese, the servant grimaced, cocked his head to one side with a befuddled look, and emitted a sound like a riverboat engine releasing steam. "Aaeeeaah?"

"Forget it," Mandley said in English. He stuck his head in the door and caught a glimpse of the steward, dressed in morning robes and drinking tea at a small table between sacks of rice and bushels of produce. It infuriated him that every minor lackey aped the effete mannerisms of his gentry employers. The steward was being served by two women so small Mandley felt he could have put one in each pocket of his Tennessee greatcoat and walked off without feeling their weight.

How a man could be attracted to those doll-like creatures hobbling on mutilated stumps was beyond him.

"Not yet. My master is too busy. You go!" the servant scolded and pushed Mandley away.

The Chinese see no correlation between time and the importance of a task, Mandley thought in exasperation. That's why they'll soon be carved up by Britain, France, Germany, Russia, and every greedy Old World duchy with dreams of empire. That dismemberment Mandley intended to prevent, even if it meant he'd be dubbed a traitor to his race. His vision of China was of a Christian nation girding the stalwart ethics of Confucius with the armor of eternal salvation. His vision of himself was equally grandiose: to be Joab to a Chinese David . . . perhaps to General Li. Unlike his brethren who wanted to win goods and trading rights, Mandley wanted to win souls.

He attributed that evangelical urge to his Baptist mother, who determined that her only son would know God as deeply and personally as she. And so he was raised straight and hard in a backwoods oaken pew, although his father spent each Sunday morning drinking jug whiskey and throwing two-headed axes for money while the preacher read Romans 12. Only after Mandley had been in China for some time did he realize that the liquor of rebellion flowing in his father's veins ran in his as well, and that his passion for saving reprobate souls owed as much to a paternal lust for adventure as to his mother's piety.

But Mandley's dream of shepherding the growth of a new nation was quickly fading in the blistering sun of the crowded courtyard. Mandley fumed, sweated, and scratched for another hour before rousing himself to climb a small stairway beside the steward's office that curved up to a higher level of the compound.

He stood on a low wall to get a better view. The house itself was vaster than any plantation home in Kentucky or Tennessee, immense even by typically monumental proportions for mansions in south China. Spilling over five broad, curving terraces of a granite cliff overlooking the Pearl River, it was the largest and oldest country house in the region. The Portuguese Dominican priest he had met in Macao had offered the unbelievable story that the Lis could trace their history back a hundred generations, over two thousand years. "A line longer than the Hapsburgs," the priest avowed. Their founding ancestor was said to be a northern nobleman who had led a battalion of Han out of central China into the southern wilderness, crushed the rebellious and savage tribes, and made them swear allegiance to his lord, Shih Huang Ti, the first emperor of the Chin dynasty.

The reality, which the Lis over the centuries had contrived to forget, was different. Their ancestor was no nobleman, but a bandit chieftain who had cannily turned against his neighbors in Shih Huang Ti's bloody pacification of the defiant clans along the Yellow Sea. As a reward, Old Li was given the right to oversee a flood-stricken strip of the monsoon coast up from the mouth of the Pearl River.

In those early days, when the Chin rulers were winning and losing an empire, Kwangtung was a wild, luxuriant place. The hills were covered with groves of cinnamon, camphor, and the aromatic carda-mom. Persian princes dropped anchor at the mouth of the river to caulk the hulls of their vessels with the resins of the Kan-lan tree. The drums and flutes of tattooed peoples echoed along the banks of muddy rivers. Brilliant sunbirds darted through dark, wet forests, and turtles swam in the phosphorescent sea.

One day, while cutting through the tangled liana vines in the hills, Old Li was ambushed by mountain bandits near a spring. For two days, he held off the marauders until they finally gave up and slipped away. Taking his escape from death as a lucky omen, Old Li found the hidden source of the spring on the barren summit and built a fortified way station there. He quickly came to believe that the place was strong in earth-magic. The rocks, the curve of the river, and the silver spring itself formed a rare congruence from which flowed the "three trea-sures" of essence, energy, and spirit.

In time, Old Li took a river girl as a concubine to serve his wife and to warm him at night. The girl gave him five sons.

Long after Old Li's death and the quick collapse of the empire of Chin, the Concubine successfully directed her sons' careers in Changan, the capital of the Han emperors. By the time of her death at age ninety-three, the Concubine had channeled the spring's abundant wa-ters into spillways, fountains, and fishponds, and cut the second and third terraces around the prow of the mountain.

Two generations later, the house was complete: five great terraces dropping to the river like a painted scroll let down from heaven. Gardens filled the spaces between the halls and living quarters with the region's vivid vegetation: dwarf palm, gnarled trees heavy with five-fingered star fruit, ferns as broad and tall as a small horse. A twelve-foot brick-and-plaster outer wall crowned with sharp pottery shards enclosed the fifth tier or "Lower House" built for minor relatives and slaves. A road ran along the river's edge past the red-tiled roofs down to the dock, where two marble lions clutched the river between their paws. From that point, rice paddies and mulberry groves owned by the Lis fanned east and west across a plain dotted with fishponds and villages, and cut by brown canals. Outside the stucco walls, Hakka

farmers, Tanka bargemen, and brothers of the secret Triad societies
would gaze up at the Lis' sanctuary more in anger than awe. They saw
the house as a symbol of the avarice of imperialist officials who had
sucked the juice from the Land of Flowers. Beggar, boatman, bandit,
all longed to pull the great house down.

Now, Mandley studied the layout of the house in case he had to
make a hasty retreat. His chances of escape were slim, he concluded.
Guards stood at the gate. Inside the courtyard, peasants with baskets of
poultry and vegetables crowded around a huge cistern fed by the natural
spring, for this was the day that farmers and merchants came from
nearby villages to trade with the three-hundred-member household.
The smells of fish frying in oil, pungent peppers, and dung smoke
from the cook fires wafted up from the Kitchen Court. Men bare to
the waist were hauling water jugs up to the residences on the terraces
on the hill above. Other men were carrying down night soil, while
maids tiptoed through the throng carrying piles of silks and cotton and
hiding their faces from the glances of men.

What a curious cross to bear, he mused, as he watched the ancient
herb vendor rock back and forth on his haunches like a sleepy monkey
and ring a small brass bell in one hand; to be called to save a people
that attracted and repulsed him, a people of immense dignity and
unbridled pride, who revered their parents as gods, cherished their
sons, and despised their daughters.

A shadow fell across the stairway. Mandley looked up to see a
young woman descending from the terrace above. She was unusually
tall for a Han, and rather than hiding her face behind her sleeve at the
sight of a strange man, she stared down boldly at him. He found
himself staring back. One rarely saw Han women up close, for they
were hidden away like chattel. This one was startlingly different from
the women he had seen. She had strong features, a well-defined nose,
and deep-set, round eyes. Her hair was not oiled and pulled back into a
tight bun, but hung down to her hips in a single thick braid threaded
with red ribbons. He had once seen drawings of Amazon women in
Attica sporting the same braid as they rode their horses into battle. An
Amazon in China? It was an absurd, even shocking thought, except
that this girl was nothing like her tiny, rabbity sisters. Peeking out
from under her trousers, her sandaled feet were normal size, not the
three-inch stumps that all the other women hobbled about on. She
carried herself erect, so that even in the loose blue peasant pajamas,
Mandley could see breasts that were shapely and full.

"Don't be afraid," he said in Cantonese.

Her lips turned up at the corners in a half-smile that emphasized her wide mouth and black eyes. "I'm not," she retorted, and shifted a small round basket from one arm to the other.

He found her directness odd and intriguing. When she tried to pass, he stopped her. "I have an important message for General Li, but this steward has kept me waiting for three days now. Can you help me?"

"I am the spirit-woman here. The steward will not listen to me."

She started past.

"Don't go," he cried. "What's your name?"

"One must not ask names," she chided. "It's not polite—surely you know that. If you speak our language so well you must know our customs." Then seeing his evident distress, she seemed to soften.

"Young Mistress," begged Mandley, using the honorific reserved for young women of noble birth, "I must see your master. My news is important to him—to all China." On the chance that the girl might be a sympathetic soul, he added with an uncertain flourish, "Especially to your father's house."

She glanced up at him in sudden panic, then looked quickly down into the courtyard. They were attracting the attention of the crowd below. "This miserable person has no importance to this house," she said quickly. "I serve the Tai Tai, the master's mother." She hesitated, as if weighing a ticklish matter. Finally, she added in a voice devoid of emotion, "My father is far away. How could what you have to say to my master affect him?"

"You look kind. Can I trust you?" he pleaded.

Rulan had never seen such need before in a man's eyes. His openness frightened her.

"I have something the general needs," he whispered. He patted something hidden under his tunic. "A book called the Bible!" As he warmed to his subject, his voice rose alarmingly. "This book will redeem your people from the fiery pit. It will bring them out of the hands of their tyrant oppressors!"

Her silence only seemed to encourage him to greater indiscretion. "The general is a great man," he declared expansively. "He loves the people. With this book he can do for them what no other Han man has. This book proclaims the coming of the High God's only Son. This book makes the weak strong and the enslaved free!"

Listening to his impassioned speech, Rulan decided that the barbarian was either demented or a fool. He spouted wild, treasonous words with no concern for the swift punishment that would undoubtedly fall on a foreign priest who had wandered outside the port cities set aside by the emperor for barbarian preaching. He had come, moreover, to the very place where his life counted least.

"Can you help me?" Mandley pleaded. He grabbed Rulan's arm and found himself warming unexpectedly at the touch of her smooth skin.

Rulan pulled away, confused. The foreigner was like a lost boy who did not yet understand his plight. She pitied him, for he had the same desperate intensity that she recognized in her father before the coming of Hung to their village. She decided that she must stop the barbarian from throwing his life away on a man who cared nothing for the people.

"You've chosen the wrong man," she whispered. "General Li hates foreigners. On his last campaign, he slew three barbarian priests and made a fire out of their books."

Mandley was flushed and unbelieving. "It's not possible. Please, I beg you, let me talk only once to him—"

"The master cannot see you," she said firmly, marveling at the barbarian's thickheadedness. "He's in Peking."

"He's got to be here! The steward has been promising to send me to him for three days. I have this note."

"Nevertheless, he's away," she said coldly. "That's only the steward's seal. He's keeping you around to get the squeeze, so he can buy more dirt."

"Bribe money?" Of course! Mandley thought bitterly. What a fool he had been not to realize that the steward was stringing him along to make some extra cash to pay for his vices. He had risked his life and wasted his time for nothing. Mandley bounded down the stairs past three coolies huddled in a circle, sucking on rods of sugarcane.

"Liar! Philistine!" he yelled as he barged into the steward's antechamber. The two tiny ladies screamed, dropped their trays of crockery, and ran off. "Where is your master?" Mandley cried. "I have a message of life and death for him!"

The steward rose from his stool, his egg-shaped head bobbing on the thin column of his neck, and nervously turned toward the red-faced giant threatening him. His small eyes darted to the door. "Patience, patience. The master will see you. It can be arranged."

"When?" Mandley saw with disgust that the steward's face was the lurid yellow of the opium addict.

The steward shrugged his shoulders, embarrassed for the ill-mannered barbarian.

Rulan's face appeared in the doorway. "You were right!" he shouted to her. "This turtle dung is cheating me!"

The steward murderously eyed the girl he despised, but she returned his glare without flinching. "I said if you still want to see the master I can arrange it," he said. The flat, smooth surface of the steward's face cracked open in a wobbly grin. He picked an invisible piece of lint from the front of his coat and rubbed it between two fat fingers.

"I'd sooner squeeze your neck before I give you one damn copper to stuff into your pipe," Mandley snapped in English. He repeated it slowly and with venom in Cantonese.

This final insult was not to be borne. Recovering a measure of his dignity, the steward yelled for the guards. But his voice had shrunk to a mere squeak.

"You had better go," Rulan said. "The steward will order the guards to beat you to gain back his face."

Regretting his outburst, Mandley followed the girl outside. He saw that several men had joined the circle of squatting coolies, and that the rods they were sucking on were not cane but cheap bamboo pipes. His head began to hurt from the tendrils of cloying smoke. Peasants sold ducks and cabbages to feed their opium habit. The steward squeezed the peasants to feed his. And where was the master? If Li was in Peking with the other ambitious mandarins elbowing for favor from the new emperor, if Li could not keep his own house clean and free of error, he was not the man that Mandley wanted as a brother.

"I should not speak," Rulan whispered to him. What she was about to do was fraught with danger; yet for some reason she trusted this ungainly barbarian who came in the incongruous disguise of a civilized person to offer a preposterous plan to exactly the wrong man. "What I am going to tell you can cost many lives if you betray me. At Thistle Mountain in Kwangsi Province is a man named Yang. He, not General Li, is the kind of man you seek. The people he leads need arms. If you find him, tell him that Rulan—no, not Rulan. Tell him Little Quail sent you. Tell him where and how we met. Tell him that in the name of the High God, you want to free the people."

Mandley searched the girl's face. Could she be the one who would open the door to him—the door to China? The steward was screaming like a woman now and cursing the girl.

"That turtle dung is more angry at you than me," Mandley told her. "Be careful. Rulan." He said her name slowly, committing it to memory. She blushed. Then he sprinted toward the gate, nearly knocking the old herb vendor off his haunches.

The steward turned his fury on the girl who was the enemy of the general's wife, whom he served. "You have cost me silver, Hakka dogmeat. What lies did you tell him? That I take bribes? That I deal in opium!"

"Nothing. I saw him for the first time when I came down just now."

"You lie. You spoke to him about me. First Lady and I know you are Tai Tai's spy."

"The barbarian has unsettled your wits," Rulan replied evenly.

"Aaiiee! Impertinent! Neither First Lady nor I will hold back our hands forever!"

"Someday your hands will be caught in a sack of silver and Tai Tai will cut them off," retorted Rulan before turning her back on the steward.

If the steward had not feared the witch's powers and the sick old woman who protected her, he would have demanded that the guards turn the girl out immediately. Instead, livid with offense, the man resolved to take the matter to Meng, General Li's wife, who, like him, was waiting impatiently for her mother-in-law, the Tai Tai, to die.

Ignoring the babbling farmers at the door, Rulan strode into the court-yard, while a myriad questions whirled about in her head. What had possessed her to act so rashly? Why should she trust a total stranger—and a barbarian at that? Perhaps he was a mercenary, like the barbarians who sold opium, or an imperial spy sent to root out traitors. She was as impetuous as her father in such things. If she had only had time to talk to the stranger, she might have gleaned more information about his intentions. But the barbarian had exploded like a firecracker! Surely his anger was proof of his compassion for the people—or proof of a greedy and unstable disposition. And yet the barbarian was not en-tirely grotesque, for he was young and flat-bellied, although the hair under his straw hat was as pale and limp as flax. How ludicrous to think that any Han would be taken in by his disguise. His eyes had been kind, at least before his impatience made him lose control, and extraordinary in color. They were as light as the sky, as brilliant as Hung's. What did that portend? Had she acted rashly and compromised her father, the sisterhood, and her beloved Wing?

Rulan had been in the general's house for nine months. Every other week an Orchid disguised as a farm wife would come to hear what Rulan had learned about the general's movements. General Li was rarely home because of military business, for it was a rule in govern-ment that all officials served outside their home province to ensure their probity. Only twice in that time had Rulan seen the general, and then only from a distance, as the great man rode through the gates on the shoulders of his bearers while lackeys shouted his titles. But the women's courts were rife with gossip about him.

Rulan had reported the general's fights with his wife and son, the fights among the maids and concubines who enjoyed his current favor, the despair among the rejected, and the habits and opinions of every emissary who came to drink tea. Luckily, too, the Tai Tai talked about her son constantly, especially about his career at court. Li seemed to have a champion in some high office who was pushing him for greater rank. But was this petty woman talk useful and worth the risk? Bereft of Wing's and Ma Tsu Po's counsel, Rulan felt confused, isolated, and abandoned again by her father.

Yet she comforted herself with the knowledge that if the Orchids ignored her, the Lis did not. Rulan had nursed the old woman through a near-fatal bout of kidney disease and healed Liang Mo, the general's only son, of a minor lung ailment due to overindulgence in opium. Both the Tai Tai and Liang Mo had come to depend on her, so much so that the Tai Tai had assented to her grandson's pleas and allowed him to take Rulan as his personal slave girl—and into his bed. Liang Mo was a soft man, hesitant and unsure with women; she had cured him of that softness too. And she had discovered that although the love of a woman is sweet, a man's stalk is keen, so keen as to touch the very core of pleasure.

wiftly skirting the throng of merchants, Rulan returned to her search for the bell-doctor, the traveling vendor of medicinal herbs, from which the angry barbarian had distracted her. But the old man was nowhere to be seen. She listened for the sound of his bell, but heard only the cackle of ducks and the sharp cries of tradespeople. Pigeons pecking at dropped rice cooed and scuttled out of her way as she ran past.

"Aiya! Slow down, girl. Watching you dart like a goat upon a mountain makes my blood hot." The fat slave woman Moon was perched on a low stone wall nearly hidden by an overhanging fringe of ferns at the eastern edge of the Kitchen Court.

"I can't talk now, Moon. I have to get medicine for Tai Tai."

Although Moon and Rulan were friends, each knew very well whom the other served. Each owed allegiance to one of the two rival mistresses of the house. As long as Rulan's mistress lived, she was Tai Tai, whose age and status as the mother of General Li accorded her first place among the women. Her daughter-in-law Meng, on the other hand, was First Lady, powerful because out of the three women in the house currently enjoying his favor, she was General Li's only official wife and the mother of Liang Mo, the heir. But Meng was still second in command. It was common for Chinese mothers to clash with their son's wives. The rank of Tai Tai was earned, not bestowed.

Years of humiliation as a daughter-in-law were necessary to put iron into a Tai Tai's soul. Yet in the Li household, the rivalry between the chief women was particularly divisive because there were so many women to feed the flames of envy and so few males to quarrel over. The general was an only child, and Meng herself had given birth to just one son.

Moon hoisted herself off the wall with a small groan. The morning was turning sultry, and already her round face was oily with sweat. Panting loudly, she undid the collar of her blue cotton smock, heaved a great sigh, and tottered over to Rulan on ludicrously tiny feet. Because her feet could barely hold up her weight, Moon leaned against walls, chairs, or other people whenever she could, for as a *mui tsai* or slave girl like Rulan, she was not allowed to sit in the presence of the family but always had to be at some pretense of work.

Now Moon put a fat hand on Rulan's shoulder and eased herself against the girl for support. Inadvertently, that touch awakened a painful memory in Rulan. Her body recalled the sensation of Wing leaning on her arm in their walks around the *chai tang* during Wing's long recovery. Rulan's heart ached with loneliness. There had been times in the past nine months when the loss of Wing so overwhelmed her that it dismantled her sense of duty. Alone on her cot, she sometimes put a hand out in sleep, thinking to touch the comforting warmth of Wing's body. At such times, when she grasped emptiness, it seemed that her life among the Lis was a path through utter darkness.

Moon's prattling brought her back to herself.

"Help me up to the stalls, then. I'm glad I found you. First Lady wants me to buy fruit in honor of Tai Tai's healing. And she wants to talk to you," Moon added in a breathless whisper.

Moon complained to Rulan incessantly about her bad stomach, her bad feet, and her bad dreams. But Moon also knew everything that went on in the household: which of General Li's concubines were feuding, what *mui tsai* had gotten pregnant and by whom, who was sick and who was only pretending and for what reason. She was always ready with her brand of homely advice, heavily laced with village superstition, obscenities, and the natural skepticism that came from two decades of service to rich women. Rulan liked Moon, despite her sharp tongue, because she was the only *mui tsai* in the house who had befriended Rulan. The other maids, all small, lily-foot girls from local villages who were ashamed of their peasant origins and vain of their tiny feet, mocked Rulan's height, sunburned skin, and big feet. They called her nicknames to her face: "Big Rushing Wind," "Duck Feet," and "Barbarian Girl."

For the first time in her life, Rulan felt self-conscious. The refined manners and precisely defined roles and rank in the great house made her feel crude and unschooled. Everywhere there were watching eyes and wagging tongues.

"First Lady won't tell you, of course, but she's bleeding outside her moon-cycle again. Her childbearing years are finished, I'm sure. So she'll need powders. Tell me what to buy to ease a woman at the end of the earth road."

"What does Physician Wu say?"

"I wanted to send for him but she refuses. She blames the melons I bought yesterday for making her bleed. She forgets that she bled two weeks ago, too. Anyway, what can that old lecher who pretends to be a doctor tell us? He comes in, takes her pulse, strokes her forehead— wishing it were her bottom—and points to his little ivory statue marked with the organs and meridians, asking impertinent questions: 'Does it feel moist and hot here?' 'Yes, fool, it always feels moist and hot there, unless you touch it!' 'Is there gas there?' 'Yes, so hold your nose!' Rulan, you're a woman. You are allowed to examine her. Women know women; men's knowledge of women goes no deeper than their yang!"

"Be serious, Moon," Rulan said through her laughter. "First Lady won't let me touch her either. You know she thinks I bewitched her son."

"Ah, First Lady knows Liang Mo came sniffing after you. Why do you think she gives him this unfortunate fat maid? So Liang Mo won't be tempted to fall in love again! Poor boy, he doesn't know what he's missing. But she doesn't have to know you're examining her. When you come with me, watch her carefully and check for signs."

Rulan shook Moon's arm loose with a grin, but Moon's soft hand grabbed her again. "If you won't prescribe for my lady, what about me? Last night, I dreamed that a toad as ugly as a long-nosed barbarian crept into Tai Tai's room, and not even big-foot you stopped him. I awoke sweating and ran to check outside. But there was no one. I am still so dizzy from fright that I couldn't swallow my morning rice. Was it a bad dream, or did you see the toad too?"

So Moon had seen the barbarian, Rulan realized. She was tempted to laugh off Moon's obvious ploy to extract information about the stranger at the gates and the Tai Tai's health, but any dream, no matter how foolish the dreamer, was not to be dismissed. And besides, Moon's dream confirmed Rulan's own feeling of dread. Something terrible was about to happen; she could feel, if not see, the signs.

Rulan tried to seem offhand. "There was a barbarian waiting to see the general just now, but he's gone."

Moon gasped dramatically. "Then I was right, as I told my lady. An omen! An ugly white devil at our door. You think it means that the master is dead? Maybe even now he lies bleeding in some filthy alley in that dung hole of Peking. What about the Old One? She always knows what's going on with her son. She's like you, a witch, because she looks in her mirror and sees the dying. Tell me, did she have a dream too?"

"I don't know what she dreamed," snapped Rulan. "Tai Tai slept alone last night."

Moon gasped again and covered her heart. In a voice overlain with pity she declared, "You fought with her! Poor thing, is that why she dismissed you?"

"Why do you always think the worst?" Rulan laughed. "If I didn't know what an honest turtle you are, I would think you had been waiting on the wall just to ambush me with ten thousand questions. Maybe First Lady put you up to it," she said with a mischievous grin. "Tai Tai knows you spy for her daughter-in-law."

Suddenly Moon became grave and immensely solicitous about the old woman's health. It was hard for Rulan not to soften to the affable fat maid, whose motives were so easy to read. And there was so much to learn from Moon's unguarded talk. With Moon's sweaty arm locked around hers, Rulan moved at a fraction of her usual pace. But she gleaned a great deal of new information—more than she gave away about the Tai Tai, she was sure.

The women walked along the wall in silence. Then Moon sighed. "If only I were as smart as you, I could protect my lady as well as you do the Old One. First Lady is sick with worry."

"About what?" sniffed Rulan. She was craning her neck for the wizened old herb vendor with the headband. "Tai Tai has recovered. There's no need to plan a funeral now."

"No, no," Moon protested evenly. "It's Liang Mo's future she's desperate to settle. I've seen it happen before in big houses. Poor boys can sweat it out in the fields, but not the sons of rich men. As soon as the beard comes in, the young men begin to pine. They quit their studies, make calf-eyes at the youngest concubines, and hide from their fathers. All they want to do is play naughty games with the maids."

Rulan steeled herself for a new onslaught of intrusive questions. Rulan had come to the Lis innocent of a man's touch, but like most of her sisters in the society, she had been only technically a virgin. Wing, who had initiated her into love play, had been ardent and skillful. Because of her, Rulan knew all the secrets of how to give and receive pleasure. Remembering the "stone girls" among the sisters who could not bear to be touched by men because of the remembered brutality of husbands, fathers, uncles, or brothers, Rulan had been surprised to find that sex with a man, especially one whom she could not refuse, could be so enjoyable. She remembered the question she had long ago posed to Wing. After having slept with Liang Mo, Rulan now knew the answer. As far as a man's jade stalk was concerned, Rulan preferred it to anything else. But unlike most maids with their masters, Rulan did not fall in love with Liang Mo. She kept her promise to Wing. She let him enjoy her body and enjoyed his in return, but did not relinquish her heart. What she felt for him was tender pity, because Liang Mo, a rich man's son, was as needy as any orphan child abandoned on the road. Raised by servants and tutors, fought over by his mother and grandmother, ignored by his father, Liang Mo was a frightened, girlish youth, a "eunuch" to his friends until Rulan had made him feel a man. When a jealous First Lady separated them and punished her, Rulan left Liang Mo with little regret.

"Listen, Moon, I come from the village. I don't know about rich young men. I couldn't help it if Young Master sought me out. He doesn't anymore; First Lady made sure of that."

"Ah, my lady's beating still makes you mad, *hai ma*? She slaps all her maids, even her husband's whores if the master spends too much time with them. That's what good mistresses do to give themselves face, although Tai Tai disapproves. You're still mad? You miss him? And Moon knows how he misses you! He walks around limp all over, except for one place. But let a pretty girl come his way and his ungrateful stalk shrivels up. Poor boy, to be a shy sister in a family of randy warriors. But not with you! You're Hakka. You don't look like us. You're as big as a man. It makes his jade stalk feel like an explorer, *hai ma*? First Lady thinks you gave him a love potion to make him wilt with the others. No, my lady has had enough of scandal. She wants him to settle down."

"You mean marry?"

Moon put her chubby finger to her lips. "She would beat me if she knew I told—"

"What about Tai Tai? She hasn't approved—"

"Oh, but when the Old One sees this jewel, she'll give her consent."

"But the Tai Tai has her own plans."

"I tell you, Rulan, the girl is as beautiful as an imperial courtesan. Such skin! Such eyes! A willow waist. And a face like an almond seed. And forget all that—she's rich enough to save this bankrupt family!" Moon rolled her eyes into her head. "The size of the dowry alone would make most men stiff for a whole year."

Rulan was unable to stem her curiosity. "Is the family from around here?"

Moon looked around and whispered, "It's Old Wang, the salt merchant from Canton."

Rulan blurted out, "Tai Tai hates him! She curses Wang for causing her husband's heart to stop when he stole the old gentleman's salt license. How can First Lady even think of marrying Young Master to the family's enemy? Tai Tai would never—Liang Mo would never—"

"Money," Moon said with an impatient sigh. "You Hakka never see the obvious. Wang has more silver bars than the emperor. And the girl is his third granddaughter, his darling. Besides, how do you know what Liang Mo would do?" Moon asked slyly. "I thought you aren't his sweetheart anymore."

"I'm not," declared Rulan stoutly, "I mean, I never was. Liang Mo can marry whomever he wants. But he would never go behind Tai Tai's back. In this house her word is law."

Moon shook her head. "In this house, the master's word is law. And my lady knows all the best pillow tricks to get the general to agree. Where does the master sleep most nights when he's home? Not with the girls he bought for pleasure, but with First Lady, the mother of his son! Third Lady and Fourth Lady, for all their whorish ways from the Willow World, are no match for my lady. They are silly and boring and whelp daughters. But my lady makes herself as changeable as the moon. Mark what I say, in a year or two, the master will send those whores back to their village along with their whining daughters. First Lady knows her husband better than he knows himself. She knows us all. She sees that Liang Mo pines for you. Yes, yes, don't glare at me. Why do you think she's so anxious for him to marry? Maybe she wants to get him away from you. She's afraid he'll use up his juice on you. This family of scholars doesn't want to breed mongrel sons."

Laughing and panting, Moon steered Rulan into the thick of the peddlars. Rulan reminded herself that Moon was totally loyal to First Lady and would never have spoken so candidly about this matter if Meng had not sanctioned it. The general's wife must have intended the Tai Tai to know about the marriage preparations. But what was her motive? To shock the old woman into a relapse? It was, nevertheless, something that demanded the Tai Tai's immediate intercession despite that risk, because the Old One was as concerned as Meng about Liang Mo's well-being and was making her own plans for her grandson's future—one that certainly did not include union with the enemy of her dead husband.

■   ■   ■

The Kitchen Court was flanked on one side by a long porch with a green tile roof. In this alcove, food for the family was chopped and cooked over open-air charcoal braziers in huge round-bottomed pans. Against the walls of the cooking shed stood three mound-shaped clay ovens, each large enough to roast a whole pig. To the south stood the high outer walls and the massive iron gate in which was built the office of the house steward. In the center of the yard was a fountain for the animals and cook pots. From that point, the spring ran down a short spillway of granite into a tunnel under the walls and down to the river. There was drought that year, so the slopes of the rocky riverbed poked through the sluggish gray waters. On the western side were storage sheds and the washhouse, and behind that, hidden from view, the drying yard. Stables, which were dug into the granite cliff, ran parallel to the western wall for two hundred feet.

As the women passed the smoky kitchen alcove, they heard the steward arguing with the head cook.

"I sent you three crocks of good oil last month. Not a copper more goes for oil! If you waste, you use your own money." The steward's pale face was mottled with rage.

"You bought the wrong oil, turtle dung!" the cook replied. "Can't you taste the difference? The same for meat. I say pork, you get me horsemeat! Don't lie! You think I don't know?"

"That's good meat! I got a good price. You're the cook—chop it up so it tastes like pork. You fix it up good, nobody knows the difference!"

"I know. Tai Tai, she always knows. Horsemeat stinks like the sweaty white devil in the yard outside! You, you have no nose, no tongue for what tastes good. You get me what I want. I don't care the price. Tai Tai commands."

"Not anymore. First Lady says save money. No more whiskey and quail for the Old Lady," said the steward.

"There are sick people in this family. You think I can make magic for them out of the dung you buy?" Spying Rulan, the cook appealed. "Rulan, tell this dry turd what Tai Tai has to have."

"Whiskey to thicken the blood. Wild ginseng from Manchuria."

The steward's eyes bulged at the sight of Rulan. "Ask for Gold Essence or Jade Essence or powdered mother-of-pearl!" he screeched. "Who says you have the right to order me? Rotten egg, roll away! You wouldn't know how to purge a bloated pig of stones."

"My medicines cured the mistress. Do you mock what saved Tai Tai?"

"Not medicines. Hakka poisons! Witchery! You're the one who corrupted Young Master. Now all he does is play *wei chi* games and bring young boys into his rooms to drink this family's wine and eat for free. I hope his bride is rich, for this house has no money to pay for the presents Young Master gives his pretty boys. I ask First Lady, she says ask Tai Tai. Tai Tai says, don't bother me, I'm sick. I ask First Lady again, she says don't buy. Don't buy? This family is too spoiled to change its ways. They eat and spend, eat and spend. Buy with what? The master sends no silver. The tenants have rotten food to sell. The yamen takes the emperor's cut of rice first. What is left after that for rent, the peasants say? So everybody eats. Everybody spends. Everybody blames me!"

"Liar," the cook shouted. "I caught you red-handed. You know where the money goes, Rulan? With my own eyes I saw a river bandit pull his filthy barge up and go into this one's door. This dog smokes the mistress's money up like a rich man!"

The steward raised a fist at the cook. But the cook had already grabbed two cleavers and held them up inches away from the steward's red nose. "See how he attacks me, Rulan. Tell the mistress to send him back to his pigsty village. He robs this family."

"There's the robber," yelled the steward, backing carefully away while pointing to Rulan, who had disentangled herself from Moon and taken a fighting posture, with knees loose and hands open. "There's the spy. I ask you, what is a big-foot Hakka doing in this house in the first place? Where did she come from? Why is she here? I don't believe an ignorant Hakka can be a spirit-woman. She watches me! She accuses me, but she spends Tai Tai's money as freely as a Canton whore." He pointed a long fingernail at Rulan. "Everybody knows who will be blamed when Tai Tai dies. First Lady is watching you, mud hen. I have her word—"

Suddenly he stopped, for Moon had laid a fat arm on his shoulder. He turned away, brushing her off, and aimed an awkward kick at two crouching cook boys. He was sweating profusely, for in truth, he did fear what the old mistress might do to him if she found out that he had squeezed a little too much from the villagers' rents to pay off the Tanka opium dealer.

Moon made a quick motion with her fingers to indicate that the steward had finally lost his mind. "He's afraid of you because he knows you are Tai Tai's spy. Aiya, don't deny that you report his dealings in the market to her. That's why he doesn't want you in the kitchen when he buys from the farmers."

"He's a thief, so he tries to blame me for his bad conscience," replied Rulan, forcing herself to exhale slowly, to drive out the anger poisoning her body.

"They're all thieves." Moon shrugged. "Why should this one be different?" She waddled contentedly into the crowd of merchants and called over her shoulder, "Wait for me, remember. First Lady has something to ask you."

Rulan turned back to Second Cook, who was chopping cabbage for the midmorning noodles. She marveled that the brown, skinny man could be a cook, for there was nothing oily or well-fed about him as with all the other cooks. But he was as talented with a cleaver as a jeweler working ivory with a fine-pointed file. He could bone a duck from the inside, stuff it with sweet rice, cut it in pieces, and put it together as if it were whole and ready to fly. His father, First Cook, had fed the family throughout the lucky years before the old gentleman's disgrace. Even in these lean times, Second Cook was so loyal to the Tai Tai that he could not pronounce the daughter-in-law's name without spitting on the ground.

"Early morning, Uncle," called Rulan ruefully, using the honorific that the man's age and status among the servants warranted. "How are your piles?"

"Same as always. All the time bad," he snapped without looking up from the sawed-off tree trunk that served as a chopping board. "I see you made magic. The old lady lives again. Her rice bowl came back last night empty. What about something for these rock-hard bowels of mine?" His knife flew scant inches from his fingers, slicing white turnips into a line of thin ribbons. "I cannot eat, and when I do, something bitter comes up."

Rulan palpated his chest and found soft bulges over his heart and down his flanks. He wheezed and belched loudly but allowed her to examine him. His breath was musty but not sour, indicating that there was no deep-seated disease. When she held his wrist, she felt his pulse beat wiry and deep. "Your anger is entering the lungs and belly," she warned. "I can give you *huo ma* seeds crushed in tea to drink."

"Oho, you naughty girl, you want to kill me? I'm an old man, not a goat! I won't swallow that witch's brew. I heard it makes you hungry for women. Not me. Give it to the master on his next visit home. I feed one hunger, that's all."

"No, Uncle," Rulan laughed. "That only happens when you breathe the smoke from the burning leaves. And I wouldn't let you anyway. Only priests and storytellers use the *huo ma* smoke when they want to cross over to the spirit world without leaving their bodies." She challenged him, "So you defend me to the steward but you're afraid to take my medicine yourself! Then try northern wheat and sesame seeds for a day or two."

"Devils take Manchu wheat. In a day or two I'll be bloated as a pig."

A pot clattered to the tile floor and Second Cook whirled on the small cook boy. "Cut your head, monkey. Be careful with my cook pot or I'll send you to the long-noses. They eat Han children's eyeballs, you know." Looking a bit sick, the boy went back to picking the feathers and straw from the congealed mass of dried spittle which would later be boiled into a savory soup for the family's dinner.

"What will you make when Young Master's in-laws come to visit?" Rulan asked innocently.

Second Cook slammed his cleaver into the breastbone of a chicken, dividing it neatly at the center. "I'll make a stuffed turd flavored with the five poisons!" he shouted over the *rat-tat-tat* of his cleaver. "All barbarian gods slay me if I cook for Wang. He killed the old master!"

"Then it's to be his granddaughter, *hai ma*?" whispered Rulan.

"That's what the fat maid told the girl who sweeps the floor. And I believe it, for First Lady loves the feel of silver bars more than her husband's jade stalk."

"Have they exchanged charts?"

"Not yet. First Lady is too smart for that. But the fat one claims the girl is especially rare. First Lady has a painting of her. If so, then Young Master is lost, for he will fall in love with any pretty girl who will not have him. You know how long First Lady has looked for someone to make her son act like a man. The go-between might as well set a price."

That was disturbing news to Rulan, not because she was jealous over Liang Mo but because negotiations had proceeded further than Moon had allowed. The exchange of genealogical charts was one of the crucial "six rituals" in a gentry wedding and was tantamount to a declaration of intent between families to join their lines. Liang Mo could dally—or try to—with as many maids and boys as he wished, with his mother's tacit consent. But marriage was a different thing. It was a family matter, a bond between houses, with money paid for a bride who brought a dowry and relinquished her ancestors forever in exchange for her husband's. A wedding involved not just two people but countless generations, including the dead and the unborn.

"No, no," continued Second Cook. "First Lady could not pull off that trick alone. While she lives, the Old One would never put her thumbmark to a letter of promise to the Wangs." He raised his eyes to Rulan.

"Why worry?" she asked. "Tai Tai will not cross the Yellow Springs this time."

"But she is old, old. In time First Lady will have her way. She has already asked the wind-and-water sage to find the best place for the old lady's grave. If the general were here, his mother would make him chastise his wife and son so that this family's name would not be thrown in a cesspool."

"Tai Tai is strong. Don't give up hope, Uncle. I promise to keep her alive."

"Haugh!" he wheezed, rubbing his distended belly. "Go on, you make my blood red-hot. Get out of here. You hold up breakfast for half the house. Here, eat this." He fished a gizzard out of a simmering broth of red soy and held it out with chopsticks.

Rulan allowed herself to be fed the choice tidbit from the hand of the vitriolic old man and then left the steaming, fragrant cooking shed to resume her search for the herb vendor.

But she could not hear his high, clear bell; and nowhere did she see either the vendor or his huge triple-hinged wooden case. When fully opened, it revealed an amazingly complete pharmacopoeia of powdered roots, ground leaves, and animal organs, each carefully labeled and stored in bottles tucked into pockets sewn into the sides of the case. Because the herb vendor was as dirty and disreputable as his stall was immaculate, Rulan could not believe he had prepared the drugs himself. Perhaps he just hawked them for another, more exacting soul. He was a bitter-humored old man, as dry as the grass he sold. He was never friendly in the nine months that Rulan had dealt with him. But he was meticulous in his prescriptions, questioning her thoroughly about her patient's condition. His knowledge of the herbal remedies was more extensive than her own, and Rulan suspected that he did a thriving business in the village streets and lanes, treating the aches and pains of the poor.

The herb man usually set up his wares in front of the first clay oven. But this morning, there was only a small boy sitting against the warm door, holding a plump, short-legged dog he was selling as a table delicacy. Finally, Rulan spied the old man squatting well apart from the noisy throng on the side of the gate farthest from the steward's door. He seemed to be fast asleep, because his cloth-wrapped head was nodding between his bare legs. His bell lay mute in the dust.

Rulan crossed the courtyard swiftly. "I nearly missed you, Uncle," she called.

"These bones are slow. I've walked a long way," he muttered gruffly to the dirt. His medicine box lay closed before his knobby knees.

"I need gardenia fruit and wild ginseng," she said briskly. "My mistress complains of dizziness and nightmares, although the fever and palpitations are gone and the rash is fading." It had been her practice to draw the traveling pharmacist into a diagnosis of her patient so he could help her with the proper prescription.

The old man dug his ear with his little finger and watched a farmer with a basket of mangoes hurrying by.

"Something to drive away a lingering fire in the kidneys. Or what else would you give an old lady fighting off the last stages of deficient kidney yin?"

But the herb man only scanned the courtyard slowly with eyes that were mere slits beneath hairless lids.

"Come, come, let's get down to business," Rulan said.

"Yes, I have everything. Look here—" He opened his box a crack and beckoned Rulan. As she bent down, he brought his face close and said in a low voice, "Yang, your father, greets you. Hear this: 'The ox bones say, spring rain falls in the north. The farmer's daughter celebrates with a speckled hen.' "

Rulan jerked upright, nearly knocking the vendor off his haunches. She had bought from his stall weekly for months, but never had she suspected that he was a spy. In her astonishment, Rulan could not collect herself enough to translate the coded message.

"Wait!" she whispered, her knees like jelly. "Is that all? Where is the messenger from the Orchids? Why do you bring this news?"

Hastily he began folding up his box.

"Wait, Uncle. My medicines. Please!" She grabbed his stiff arm, while a small dark fear grew inside her like an evil mushroom. Her father had been watching her in secret the whole time! He didn't trust her! While she reported to a sister, he had been judging, measuring her worth through the herb vendor's eyes. Why did he send such a terrible message? Why use such an emissary? Had there been a falling out between the Orchids and the God Worshipers?

The old man spat out a curse and pulled out a bottle whose contents he spilled into a dirty envelope. "Now let me go," he pleaded gruffly, pushing the paper into her hand.

"Not yet. I want to know why you have been spying on me," she said, holding tightly to his arm. "Who put you up to it?"

"Are you crazy, girl? Let me go. People are looking."

"I don't care. Doesn't my father trust me? What did you tell the God Worshipers about me?"

"Nothing, truly. Nothing at all. What was there to tell?" The old man twisted in her grasp, but Rulan's fingers gripped him like a vise.

"I know how spies work now. You made something up so they'd pay money. You told the God Worshipers something you thought they wanted to hear. Why else would my father tell me to 'celebrate with the speckled hen'?"

"Aaiiee!" he groaned. "You're breaking my arm." He squirmed and tried to hit her, but she held him tighter. A boy with a broad shelf of teeth craned his neck above a basket of sugarcane to watch them.

"Tell me what you said, or I call the steward."

"We're both under orders. Our leaders have an agreement. These Li will send us to the magistrate in chains if they find out. Let me go," he whined.

"If you try to run," Rulan said in a low voice, "I'll call 'thief' and the steward will have the porters seize you. And then I'll swear that you tried to steal my bracelets. What did you tell them?"

"Nothing, I swear by your holy mother. I only told them which powders you bought."

"You knew everything about her illness. You knew that the Tai Tai was getting better."

"Yes—aaiiee, aaiiee," he groaned as Rulan grabbed him with her other hand behind the neck and below the ears, the way Iron Fist had taught her.

"What else? There's more."

"All right. I told them you'd sunk claws into the lazy grandson, and he was going to make you his concubine."

Rulan was so astonished that she released the vendor. "Why did you make up that lie?"

"Who is the liar?" he said as he rubbed his neck. "The fat maid told me, the one who buys powders for her mistress's stomachaches. She said the general's lady was going to make you concubine just to have peace with her son. Curse your loins, traitor. You betray your own kind to rut with the emperor's pampered dogs."

"Lies!" Rulan said under her breath. There must be a mistake. Maybe her father was only testing her. Maybe the vendor was not sent by her father but was an enemy, someone to lead her astray. But no, the code words were unmistakably the ones she and her father had agreed on the night before she'd left the community of women.

She envisioned that her father had whispered the command into the ear of a messenger in the camp of the charcoal-carriers at Thistle Mountain. Thus it had passed from ragged brother to brother, across rocky hills and deep gorges along the secret network of the God Worshipers and the Triads, until his words, repeated by the vendor in her own ear, echoed like thunder over the great house on the river. *Ox bones* meant "an emergency order to be carried out immediately." *Spring rain falls in the north,* meant that "a battle was to be fought in the north." She was the *farmer's daughter*. The *speckled hen* was the Tai Tai. *Celebrate* meant "to kill."

The sun glanced off Rulan's astonished face and set the copper coins afire in her open hand.

"Stupid girl," the bell-doctor hissed in disgust. "You are only an instrument, nothing more. We know General Li is going to be sent to command the emperor's army in Kwangsi. If the old lady dies, he will have to come home to bury her, and then as a doglike follower of the demon Confucius, he will have to stay home and mourn for three years, as Confucius has decreed. In this fashion the emperor loses the only general worth more than a pig's turd in his whole army. Who will the emperor put in his place? A fat Manchu from Peking who doesn't know the difference between a God Worshiper and a paddy farmer! And that gives us time to grow, to organize, to attack, to cut a road to the Forbidden City. This much I'll do for you: brew oblivion with this." The vendor pushed another envelope into Rulan's hands. "A death is ordered—hers or yours. You know the penalty for breaking faith."

Rulan peered into the second envelope and saw what she most feared—the dried remains of a plant with purplish branches, round furry fruit with small thorns, and white bell-like petals as thin as insect wings. Trumpet flower, a deadly poison.

She looked around. People everywhere were watching her and the old vendor. She had to act. "Don't cheat me, you turtle!" she cried. "I paid you twelve, but not a copper more! Now go!" She held out a few coins, feeling scores of curious eyes on her, but he scampered away, flinging his box onto his back.

"Honor your father, or rot in the last level of hell, Manchu dog's whore," he hissed.

Thinking of the frail old woman whom she and her mother had served, Rulan felt sick with indecision. "If I am the weapon by which my sisters will topple the empire," she prayed, "Kwan Yin save me, for I am not a warrior after all."

At that moment Moon appeared at her side and wheezed jovially into Rulan's ear, "Good. Kick the smelly stick out, I say. He cheated me too. Two coins he charged for a pinch of sour grass! He's the type who strokes your bottom when you bend to sniff his bottles. Come with me. First Lady wants to talk to you, and you can take these pomegranates up to your old lady."

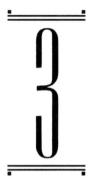

Moon seemed not to notice Rulan's distraction as they shuffled through winding paths and corridors, past the gardens and halls of the concubines, the minor relatives, and other hangers-on to the spacious chambers of the general's wife.

The rooms where Meng, the First Lady of the house, lived took up an entire wing of the second terrace. The central beam and cornices were carved with intertwining dragons to deter evil wind spirits from alighting on the roof. Inside the broad portico, which faced directly over the curve of the river, a round keyhole door opened into a large garden. Built around this patch of green were fifteen large rooms for Meng's household, and off to one side, a meeting hall for the general's use whenever he was at home. Her sitting room at the rear of the complex was exquisitely furnished. But Rulan noticed neither the translucent porcelain jars perched on dainty mahogany stands, nor the paintings of legendary beauties on old cloth. All she saw was the woman clad in brilliant silks behind a large embroidery frame.

Slender as a reed, Meng appeared much larger because of her quick tongue and authoritative manner. Meng's dark hair was piled high on her head in city fashion. Two tendrils of hair curled loosely at each ear, creating a look of studied disarray. Her married-lady's skirt was pale pink over a tunic of lavender satin, and her earrings were perfect teardrops of rare white jade. Meng did not look up until Moon dropped a string bag of fruit on a barrel-shaped porcelain stool.

"Tai Tai likes pomegranates. I hope you got them with small seeds this time," she said evenly.

"This miserable person did," Moon answered, "and at a good price. That wet-nosed boy came down three coppers!"

"Go then and leave us alone."

Sighing loudly, Moon shuffled into the next room with her bag of fruit.

"Stand there in the sun, Rulan, so I can see you," First Lady said.

Rulan took a step forward and found herself blinking in the harsh white light.

"Now," came Meng's silken voice out of the glare. "Tell me how our Tai Tai fares."

Rulan shut her eyes and tried to make her mind sharp, for she knew this was the enemy's lair. "She grows stronger every day, First Lady. Kwan Yin answers our prayers."

"It seems that you too are an answer to prayer. Physician Wu gave her little chance to live. But she is a remarkable old woman. Not many escape death at her age."

"She fights hard."

"So do I—when there is something worth fighting for. I dare say, so do you. You have a powerful influence on those you touch."

Ah, Rulan thought, so it was about poor Liang Mo after all. "First Lady," she began cautiously, "I am not as strong an individual as you give me credit for. In fact, my head is full of uncertainties."

"Interesting. You used the word *individual*. It must be how the Hakka raise their daughters, for none of us Punti ever use it. I doubt if Moon even knows the word. My maids rarely use *I*, certainly not with me. They hide behind *we, one,* and even vaguer references to their *miserable persons*. But you, for all your uncertainties, call yourself an individual. Truly an individual bears watching, because single-mindedness can change the course of rivers, *hai ma?*"

"I don't know what to say," replied Rulan, preparing for an attack. "I meant nothing special."

"Then the word is all the more revealing. I tell you individuals are dangerous because they do not put family first. Individuals will destroy this Land of Flowers because they overthrow custom for their own selfish ends. Even I, First Lady, as selfish as I am said to be, am totally devoted to this family."

Rulan decided then to bring the matter to a head. First Lady was mistaken if she thought Rulan could be bullied forever. Everything seemed unimportant next to the death Yang had charged her with. She looked directly into her opponent's eyes, a calculated rudeness. "Why talk to me to so politely? Slap me and complain to the Tai Tai like last time," Rulan said.

"Your bad manners illustrate all too well the point that I am making," came Meng's answer. "Self-centeredness tries to alter reality from its own narrow perspective. Like trying to move heaven with a small stick. You are entirely wrong, as well as impertinent, of course." She slipped an ivory filigree fan from her sleeve and spread the stiff white fronds apart with her fingertips.

"Then sell me and forget my impertinence."

Meng snapped her fan shut, and Rulan felt as if she had just been slapped. "Do not bait me! I told you that everything I do is for this family. I live for our ancestors and our unborn generations. You are correct. I beat you because you were a distraction to my son. I had to show him—and your mistress—that he needed to change. Liang Mo was not studying for the exams. He was reading pillow books in order to rut with you. He was not following his father's instructions about the proper behavior of a gentleman. I thought I had put an end to his infatuation for good, but I find that he wants you even now. If he does not quit his schoolboy pining and pass the provincial examination on his own, this family is finished. It cost us eight hundred silver taels spread among a dozen officials to buy him his first rank so that he could skip the examinations. The price was low only because they were his father's and grandfather's friends. But his is an irregular rank, and if he has no ability, he will not make his way. Everything depends on him, you see. We cannot count on the new emperor, for who knows which way the Dragon's favor blows? This family's wealth is rooted in taxes, salt, and silk. But Fan, our rent collector, says that the villages are impoverished by flood and famine, and Hung, the Hakka madman, is scaring our farmers out of the fields. How many tenants have already run away to make their fortunes in the Fragrant Tree Islands of Hawaii because of Hung's threats? We are thousands of silver taels poorer than when Liang Mo was born. You are Tai Tai's favorite. I want you to stay. But I will tolerate no more distractions."

"I have done nothing. What do you want from me?" Looking down at the floor to hide her indignation, Rulan saw First Lady's tiny shoes peeking out from the lavender underskirt like the noses of two black mice.

"Only what you want yourself. I want you to be Liang Mo's concubine."

"What? You said I am a distraction!"

"Surely you didn't believe him when he spoke of marrying you?"

Rulan shook her head firmly.

"Ah, then he did speak to you. But I believe him. As long as you fill his eyes, he isn't free to do his duty."

"First Lady," Rulan said, breathing hard. "Please understand me. I am saying that I never dreamed, never planned—that I do not want to be a concubine." Surely this could not be, Rulan thought. She was sent to be a spy, a woman apart. Now she was being sucked into the vortex of family and political intrigue, when all she wanted was to run back to Wing's protective arms.

Meng looked up at the tall girl. These Hakka faces, she mused. So bold and unmannerly in their irritating habit of staring. So broad and open, yet so difficult to read. Or was the inscrutability a mark of the Loi mother who had sunk her talons into the Tai Tai years ago? Her eyes traced the long line of Rulan's arms, noted the swell of breasts and hips, the bare white ankles and big feet in cheap cotton shoes. The girl would look ridiculous in thin skirts, First Lady decided—there was too much flesh on her. But Rulan was clearly made for dropping babies. "There may be bargaining power behind your insistence, I cannot tell," she said to Rulan. "Whether I believe you or not, or whether you desire it or not, the offer remains. I want you as Liang Mo's concubine."

"Why now?" Rulan flushed with the memory of the beating she had endured at Meng's hands and of the maids' laughter. Liang Mo was no match for his mother; she could not expect support from that quarter if First Lady's anger flared up again. And the Tai Tai, in her weakened condition, had no power to protect her.

"Because circumstances have changed. Liang Mo studies less without you than with you. I want him to marry, and he is unwilling, unless he has you as well. And so I need you to bind him to me."

"Then simply command him to marry."

"What I am planning needs his compliance, because as the favorite of Tai Tai, he alone may have a chance of making her agree to what I know is best for him. And there is something else. The bride is only thirteen years old and her grandfather's pet. Old Wang insists that she is too young and too precious to him to let go just now. He claims to want our family to take her in, but lately he has been complaining that he will miss her too much."

"Who is she?"

"That is not your concern. But to prove the seriousness of my offer, I will tell you. Mei Yuk, the youngest granddaughter of Old Wang. They say she is quite beautiful, which is why Old Wang spoils her so."

"Then let Young Master take another maid until the bargain is sealed."

"No. Because every groom, every cook boy knows about the girls he sneaks into his chamber, and it is not good for the servants to laugh at us. And because the girl's family is rich and would not like their darling promised to a"—a smile flickered on Meng's painted lips as she chose her next word—"a wastrel. But a concubine from the house— especially one who is grateful to be raised up—would be acceptable. Now I have told you all."

"First Lady is very generous to this poor person," said Rulan, still full of confusion, trying not to let her words entrap her. "But this poor person knows that the girls are sent, not invited. Liang Mo is chaste and upright in his dealings with women."

"Chaste?" Meng drew the silken syllable out. "You are even more subtle than I. *Chaste* does have a more pleasing sound than *lover of boys,* does it not? We understand each other. That is why I desire you as his concubine. To keep him a manly man. You know that no marriage is final until it is consummated."

Rulan was shocked into silence. So it was Liang Mo's reputation she was being invited to save! Meng had tried to counter the gossip about Liang Mo's homosexuality with evidence of his licentiousness, for rumors of his impotence with women must have spread beyond the walls of the house. Rulan was not offended by Liang Mo's occasional dalliance with boys; she recognized that loneliness more than anything drew him to his own kind. But the gossip might poison his acceptability as a suitable marriage partner and deny the family the bridal dowry it desperately needed.

"Why me when he can have any other?" Rulan blurted out, still shaken by the unexpected offer. She had enjoyed Liang Mo's lovemaking but she never thought their liaison would go this far. What would Wing think if she heard about this arrangement?

Meng sighed. "Because I have given him the choice of every kitchen slave and house maid and singsong girl that comes into our district, and he rejects them all—for other amusements. But he has always wanted you. And because you are, as you say, an 'individual' and can make choices. Whether you dreamed it or not, you know the advantages that being a member of this family brings. You did not object to his attentions before. Come now, you are hardly a 'poor person.' You are a free agent even though you have no dowry, no family to make a marriage for you. Where else will you go? Back to that house for spinsters? You will accept this offer because, like me, you look to the future and see that it is in your best interests. And you Hakka are shrewd. You smell a good bargain, especially when it comes without conditions."

"And if I refuse?"

"A slave girl is lucky to have chances to rise. This one will not come again."

"I have Tai Tai's protection!"

"As long as she lives, although you are foolish to put your trust in her. I was surprised she never said a word when I whipped you. But herbs and prayers will not keep her alive forever. Don't forget: I will be Tai Tai soon."

"The life of a concubine is precarious."

"Far less precarious than that of a disobedient slave."

"A concubine can be discarded when her husband gets tired of her, and her children can be snatched away."

"Think, Rulan! A concubine has the master's ear at the most receptive moments, and you are a most persuasive individual. Whom do we cherish in this house as the greatest ancestor? Oh, our great ancestor, Old Li, of course, and he had one wife and four concubines. But the last was The Concubine. From her loins this whole family springs. I am offering you nothing less than the chance to be a civilized person instead of a slave."

Rulan shook her head. Surely Meng was toying with her, tempting her to overreach herself, so that another beating or reprimand might be administered.

"I have drawn up the articles," Meng persisted. "They are most generous to you. Remember that we paid a sum of money to your foster mother in the girls' house. You sold yourself, and so there is only yourself to fear and to reward. A sum of money will be held in trust for you to use as you wish. But I promise that even if you're banished from Liang Mo's bed, we will not let you starve. Your children, should you have any, will remain here, of course." Meng drew a sheet of paper out of a drawer in the table beside her. "I have already put my husband's chop to it. You only have to make your thumbmark. You could have your rooms prepared in Liang Mo's wing whenever you wish."

"I would like more time to think," Rulan said slowly. Her tongue was thick and her mind sluggish. How did the herb vendor know of Meng's offer? she wondered. Why had Moon told him, of all people? How could she prove to Wing or Ma Tsu Po that this was not something she had plotted and schemed for?

"Not too much time, I hope. My husband needs to be informed."

"Of me?" Rulan asked.

"Yes, and of the ongoing arrangements with the Wangs."

"Tai Tai will never consent to either."

"Then you will help me persuade her. Of your acceptability first.

The other will follow in due time, for my son, once he is satisfied that he has you, will of course comply with my wishes. His father too. In these matters, men know that women are most often right. And you are the best person to plead the case to Tai Tai because again you have a bedside ear."

"And if Tai Tai still refuses?"

"She owes her life to you. How could she not be moved by your words? Why wouldn't she want to bind you to our family, to Liang Mo, her favorite? But if she refuses, well, Tai Tai will not live forever. Put your mark here, and I will send a copy to my husband for his approval."

Rulan bowed. "First Lady is very generous," was all she said. Rulan had no doubt that the terms of the contract would be exceedingly rich and that in agreeing, she would be hastening Tai Tai's death, for the old lady would make herself ill with rage and jealousy. If Rulan put her thumbmark to the document, First Lady, as mother-in-law, would so hold the articles over her that her new life of wealth and privilege as a daughter of the house would be more circumscribed than the narrow path she had trod as a slave. Meng's strategy was risky because she was planning for the long range. She wanted silver for the unborn generations. The Wangs were sullied by their merchant origins and hence disparaged by old scholar-gentry families like the Lis, but the Wangs held the purse strings of Kwangtung. Old Wang controlled the buying and selling of salt—and opium—in the whole of south China. By allying her husband's family with the Wangs, First Lady intended to save her beloved house from slow dissolution. The empire was disintegrating and only silver, she believed, would shore up the ruins. If, that is, she could convince the Wangs that the scion of the Lis was not a dessicated stalk but a manly man who had seed enough to waste before his bride was brought to bed. A concubine with sons would be proof to the Wangs of Liang Mo's virility and a valuable weapon against the bride's influence once she was installed in the house.

"We will speak again in a day or two. You can be of immense help to this family, but I will not wait forever. Moon!" First Lady called sharply. "Bring Tai Tai's present. I hope that pomegranates will not affect her adversely. They say deficient kidney yin so completely exhausts the blood and bowels that a relapse is a constant danger."

Moon appeared with the string bag stuffed with the shiny-skinned rosy-yellow fruit and handfuls of red lichees from the tree in First Lady's garden.

"This miserable person is glad not to carry this to the Upper House," she grumbled. "It weighs as much as a small pig."

Rulan took the bag and turned toward the round door.

"Let me know if there is any change in Tai Tai's condition. There are so many false springs in the course of kidney fever. One never knows." Meng bent her smoothly oiled head over the embroidery frame and picked up her needle.

Shaken and confused, Rulan strode up the winding path through hidden copses of plum and plantain to the oldest part of the mansion on the uppermost terrace, where the old woman lived. Now and then, Rulan's long feet slipped in their cheap cotton shoes on the wet stones. But each time she nearly fell, her body steadied itself instinctively.

Through an overhanging fringe of fern, Rulan glimpsed the gray robe of an approaching watchman. "Coming, coming," he sang out to forewarn ghosts lurking in the late morning shadows of the Upper House, the favorite haunt of household spirits. Automatically, Rulan slowed her gait into small half-steps and drew her head and shoulders into the bent, acquiescent posture of the *mui tsai*. The guard started when he saw Rulan's long shadow cross his path and brandished his cudgel. But after Rulan called out a greeting in a lilting voice, he grunted and passed on.

The second gong rang in the Kitchen Court signaling the slaves to serve the morning meal. The clamor of the ragtag marketplace faded slowly away. Rulan imagined her beloved mistress lying at that moment in the great wide bed, silently, courageously summoning her frail body to one more day of life. Even more than the medicine and prayers, Rulan concluded, the old lady's implacable will had vanquished death. Sliding perilously on the wet stones, Rulan doubled her pace up the rocky path to the Tai Tai's rooms, trusting in the strength and suppleness of her feet. There was no going back now. She could not, would not kill the woman whom she had worked so hard to save. Ailan had served the Old One faithfully; surely she would want her daughter to do the same. Her father and sisters had sent her to preserve the old lady's life, and she had. What they asked now of her was too cruel. If duty to her father and sisters prescribed one road and love another, Rulan would choose the way of love. If a death was required, it would have to be her own. She was a healer, not an assassin.

The Tai Tai sat stiffly at a small table, picking with silver chopsticks at several small dishes of dried fish and pickled vegetables. A steaming bowl of the thick rice soup called congee lay untouched before her. Light falling through the latticed windows scattered patterns of shining lace across the ebony floor. The air was thick with the cloying smells of camphor and crushed rose petals tied up in muslin bags around the bed to ward off night spirits.

"Tai Tai," Rulan called breathlessly as she burst through the door.

"One night at liberty and you forget your old mother," Madame Li said sourly as she dipped a spoon into the bowl and touched her dry lips to the viscous soup. Her mouth was as wrinkled as a purse cinched tight.

"I would have come sooner except that First Lady summoned me. She sends this fruit in honor of your 'second spring.' "

Madame Li made an elaborate pretense of ignoring the bag Rulan laid on the table. "I might have died waiting for you," she grumbled, thrusting her spoon at Rulan. She examined Rulan like a suspicious old owl.

Rulan leaned over to blow on the soup while stirring it with the spoon. Sighing, the old woman grabbed the utensil and began to eat noisily.

"Tea!" Madame Li demanded when the bowl was scraped clean.

Rulan poured out the tea from the porcelain pot warming in a straw basket, adding a stewed lemon from a covered dish.

After touching her lips to the tea, the mistress leaned back and announced hoarsely, "I am not deceived by my daughter-in-law's gift. I know disrespect even when it dresses up as piety. She is afraid now that I am well. This fruit gives her guilt away." Rulan's practiced eye took in the remaining traces of the old woman's illness, especially the purple rash on her cheeks that had so frightened the household. Only Rulan had entered the bedroom without fear. "In a while, I want you to bring her here," Madame Li continued. "Today I am going to set my house in order. I've been forgetting my duty too long." She belched softly and rubbed her neck. "Aiya, I hurt all over. My neck is still sore from waiting for you. Give me the needles now."

Rulan picked up the old woman in her arms and carried her back to the bed. Madame Li was as light as a child and her dry, hot skin burned through the gauze pajamas. She was breathing in shallow, short gasps. Rulan pulled the garments from the skinny shoulders and legs. When Madame Li was naked except for shoes and stockings, she curled herself around a hard pillow like a worm in a cocoon. In seconds, she was snoring. Rulan felt a wave of pity for the helpless old woman.

With the Tai Tai asleep, it was safe for Rulan to use *chi gung,* the heat from her hands. She had allowed the Tai Tai to think that needling alone had brought her out of feverish coma; in truth, it was *chi gung*—done as a last resort and always in secret—that had accomplished the healing. Educated folk such as the Lis considered *chi gung* village superstition. The danger to Rulan was not from Madame Li, who trusted folk medicine, but from First Lady, who would have welcomed any excuse to thrust Rulan out the door. There was one other reason why Rulan was loath to use her healing hands. The little she had learned from her mother and Physician Sung had shown her that there were no sure recipes, no predictable results. Every time the healing fire surged out of her hands, Rulan remembered that the heat had been unable to rouse her brother and mother out of the sleep of death. Lately, she had come to doubt her art, and she was sure she must be the weakest of spirit-women.

Rulan kneaded the cold air and prepared herself for the first shocking filaments of warmth that pulsed between her fingertips. Then she touched the fingers of one hand to the old woman's spine; arthritis had left the backbone knobby and twisted with odd outgrowths of bone. Rulan placed the fingers of her other hand on the soft bulges at the neck and felt the heat rush down the Tai Tai's gnarled backbone, up her own arm, and into her chest. She held her hands steady for long minutes, willing the heat to travel the circuit of sinew and bone, and feeling the force of her *chi* scorch her chest and swell her heart with fire. Madame Li whimpered in her sleep. With a sigh, Rulan lowered her hands, and the harsh throbbing in her chest stopped. Gently, she rubbed her patient's reddened flesh until the knotty muscles relaxed.

Growing tired, she turned with relief to her needles and to the simple matter of eliminating pain. This, at least, was healing that had method; she could touch and see results. Although Rulan had memorized Physician Sung's complicated charts and measurements locating the points along the meridians of the body where needles were inserted, she preferred to diagnose with only her eyes, nose, fingers, and intuition.

In this house, there was no need to economize with homemade needles out of porcelain shards. Now she kept a store of fifty gold needles in diverse shapes, stuck into balls of wax. She chose one needle as fine as a hair and another longer one and wiped each with a clean rag dipped in scalding tea. Rulan's fingers quickly found the swollen and distended lumps in the Tai Tai's muscles that signaled a blockage along a meridian. At first, because Madam Li's flesh was riddled with lumps, Rulan had decided not to needle each tender spot but to search out the primary source of pain. She had found it after days of searching, a nearly invisible scar at the base of the old woman's spine hidden by the twisted bones on the back. Probing the scar had caused the old woman intense agony. When Rulan had asked Madame Li for the cause of the scar, the mistress remembered a boil in her youth that had been drained several times.

Rulan preferred to work without the "dream potion" of hemp and wine, so that her mistress's response would be true. Now she lay her fingernail lightly at the tip of the scar, on the place where energy and blood converged. With her other hand she guided a long needle with her fingernail and pushed it into the skin to a depth of one *tsun,* the length of one joint of her middle finger.

The Tai Tai awoke with a start.

"It hurts?" Rulan asked her.

"*Ah shi.* Oh yes," the Tai Tai repeated. "*Ah shi.*"

The shorter needle was placed at the top of the spine between the shoulder blades. Pain in one part of the body, Rulan observed, was often triggered by sensitivity in another area of the body, so this needle tapped the primary point of the meridian that governed the length of the spine. She pushed down until the needle seemed to stick. Quickly then she twirled both needles up and down, seeing with satisfaction the grimace that came over the Tai Tai's face.

"It hurts more?"

"*Ah shi,*" the old woman breathed. "Oh yes."

"How else does it feel?"

"Hot. Like hot water coming up my back," the old woman muttered sleepily.

"Good." Rulan twirled the needles again and again, to clear the blockage and restore the normal path of *chi,* or energy, down the meridian of the Tai Tai's spine. It was not a cure, for nothing could repair the damaged bone and muscle; it was only a temporary relief from pain. After a half hour of twirling and reinserting the needles, when the Tai Tai moaned that she could stand no more heat, Rulan swiftly pulled out the needles. The Tai Tai sat up with a groan.

"Good medicine," she declared, swinging her elbows back and forth and twisting her neck. "I am as strong as a farm girl for the space of—how long, Daughter? It doesn't matter, I want to forget until I feel like an old woman again. Come, fix me up."

Madame Li walked unaided from the bed to a small dressing table on which stood an old brass mirror in the Shouchou style. Everything about her seemed different, brighter, younger. She dropped gracefully onto the low stool, keeping her spine straight and supple. Chattering instructions, Madame Li watched as Rulan unwrapped the long leg bindings of her mistress's bound feet. If touched, the mutilated stumps still pained the mistress, so Rulan drew the dampened cloth with particular care through the cleft between the three remaining toes and the horny heel, which had, in childhood, been forced together by breaking the instep. Madame Li was vain of her feet, for so well had they been bound as a girl that each could easily slip inside a teacup, the ideal-size "golden lily." Kneeling, Rulan expertly massaged the shortened Achilles tendon, the collapsed bones, and weakened leg muscles, then rewrapped each gnarled hoof with clean bandages and tied on black cotton bed shoes.

Madame Li sighed contentedly and leaned over to lift the heavy lid of the dressing table. The lid of the table concealed a cosmetics box, which a clever artisan had carved into the image of the terraced house of the Lis. The box swung open into five shelves holding an array of cosmetics and jewels: snuff bottles containing opium and tobacco; tiny bottles of jasmine- and ginger-scented oils; a small porcelain rouge pot; conch-shell combs, combs of horn inlaid with mother-of-pearl, ivory combs, and combs of sweet sandalwood from the Fragrant Tree Islands; cloisonné hairpins tipped with gold; tiny ear spoons of carved ivory; earrings, necklaces, and other bits of finery collected over the years by generations of Li women.

After passing a damp sponge over a hard ball of lead dust and rice flour, Rulan began to wipe long white lines on the Tai Tai's upturned face. The damp powder set Madame Li coughing; instantly she was old again. Rulan held the mistress's head over a big brass spittoon until the spasm had passed, then wiped the spittle from the wrinkled lips. Madame Li was breathing hard, and Rulan worried that if the old woman took to her bed again, disappointment might bring on fever. She patted the fine powder over the sallow skin so that the remnants of the purple rash would not show.

I will not let you die, Rulan vowed silently. The image of a whirling ball of flame burned at the back of her mind. Rulan's little finger trembled slightly as it drew a small red mouth on the Tai Tai's dry lips, while Madame Li's eyes, dark in their hollow sockets, searched the depths of the ancient mirror.

The mirror was haunted. Family talk story claimed that it was a love gift from the First Ancestor to the Concubine for the sons she had given him. The back was what made it unique; a talented artist had etched it in such a way that the design changed when the mirror was held at different angles. If one gazed at it directly, one saw two lovers seated chastely beside a spring. Tilted slightly, however, it showed the woman seated astride the man, naked except for her small stockinged feet, which he held aloft in the palms of his hands. Madame Li believed that the ancient brass mirror had the power to bring those who had seen demons back to their senses. And she also believed that the mirror contained one of the two souls of every Tai Tai who possessed it. Thus the ghosts of past generations were present in the mirror to caution and advise the living mistress of the house. Rulan wondered if the mirror ghosts had warned the Tai Tai about her.

Suddenly, Madame Li pulled Rulan's head down close to hers and inspected her intensely. Rulan knelt while the small hot hands stroked her hair and cheeks. Madame Li's skin was as dry and opaque as rice paper. Rulan put her hand on the Tai Tai's wrist and felt the pulse beating thin and fast, a sign that the fever burned low but deep.

"Aiya, you're no beauty, Daughter," the Tai Tai rasped, tilting Rulan's chin into the light. "I don't know what Liang Mo sees in you, unless he has more judgment than I give him credit for. Your face is round. Even your eyes are round. You're too tall. A man would feel like a child with you."

"You flatter me too much," Rulan said with a laugh.

"But what is beauty to you? You have character and strength, and that is more precious to one of your station. Unless First Lady has turned your head with gold!"

"I have big feet. I am a horror," replied Rulan with a shaky smile.

"Why worry about feet? Manchu ladies have feet like boats and think themselves finer than we. Go, go," Madame Li ordered affectionately. "Fix me up like a vain princess. I want to see my daughter-in-law's expression when she sees me as plump and rosy as a girl."

Rulan opened the top of the red leather clothes box and selected a dawn-gray married-lady's skirt from the pile. There were at least twenty of them in the box, each cut and sewn to lie flat without ironing.

"Character and strength, I say, are more important for a slave than a pretty face and small feet. It's different for people like me. I was judged a beauty. It took my husband five years to discover I could make a poem as well as he." Madame Li stood while Rulan pulled up the white silk underpants around her bony flanks. "How I wish I could blend your strong 'earth' with Liang Mo's weak 'water,' " she added pensively. Madame Li stepped awkwardly into the skirt Rulan held out. When she noticed Rulan's embarrassment, she burst out laughing. "What? You've lived with me so long, wiping my mouth and bottom, and you are ashamed before your old mother? Silly girl!"

"Tai Tai, you misjudge me. My 'earth' is common indeed. Too common for something as fine as water. Water may be passive, but it is not weak. Isn't water the vital element of this house?" Rulan fastened a green belt around Madam Li's waist and folded the smooth waistband of the skirt over the buckle.

"You needn't defend Liang Mo. He is not half the man his grandfather was. Oh yes, his degree is the best we can buy, and even that is irregular because we had to buy it in another district where the granaries were empty and the quota of scholars still open. But some things we cannot do for him. And his abilities—well, they need to be proven. Yet he is our only boy, our only hope. He needs a woman of character and strength. For that, you needn't be ashamed. When a young gentleman takes a bondmaid to bed, it's an honor to her. And he gains strength from her yin. Ha! I remember what a girlish child he was before I intervened. Still hiding behind his mother's skirts—until you took him under yours." The tunic slid over her head and hid her toothless smile. "So I was glad when he noticed you. From that day on, he began to be a man. He stopped playing naughty games with his worthless friends. He began to study, I recall, and listen when I gave him advice. No wonder his mother beat you. She fears Liang Mo's preference for common earth, as you call yourself. And so she planned an occasion to punish you. By chastising you, she thought to force me into relinquishing my hold over Liang Mo. I admit I was beaten that time," said Madame Li softly to the far wall. "When my son ordered a truce between us, I decided not to interfere. Kwan Yin forgive me, I set aside my obligation to protect the child of Ailan, the faithful *mui tsai* of my first years as mistress of this house. But who prevailed in the end? Character and strength, as I say. She shamed the whole house that day. Even Liang Mo turned against her. Now we have her where we want." Madame Li grabbed Rulan's arm and slid herself onto a porcelain barrel stool.

The old woman's confession disarmed Rulan. It was rare for a mistress to open her heart to a slave. Slaves were beaten to restore an owner's face and preserve harmony in the house as much as to put an end to bad behavior. The incident had begun as a simple slap from First Lady for an imagined slight, although all parties knew it had to do with Rulan's loyalty to the Tai Tai. Then because Rulan did not wail and beg for mercy, she had been stripped of her trousers and made to bend over a table while Meng whipped her with a thin bamboo, lecturing her all the while in the proper duty of slaves. Rulan had not cried out once; pain in the service of the society would make her strong. She reminded herself to be as Wing would: unemotional and unyielding. She also knew it was part of the price for protecting the Tai Tai, the true object of First Lady's fury.

Now it seemed that Rulan's loyalty to the Tai Tai had born fruit—the Tai Tai was opening her heart to her! Rulan wanted to embrace the frail old woman and unburden all to her—the vow she had taken as a spy, the contract First Lady had offered.

"Have you ever hoped that I would one day match Liang Mo with you—permanently?" The small eyes studied Rulan's face.

Rulan tried to keep her voice gay. "Tai Tai, you are too giddy."

"You never hoped? It's a good plan. First Lady is barren now. Second Lady's unborn child perished with her. And the Third and Fourth only whelp girls. But you Hakka farm girls are built for dropping sons. And sons are what this tired house needs. The Moon Princess and the Herd Boy—in reverse. Instead of the princess marrying a peasant, the prince raises up a farm girl. It's a common fable to beguile any slave."

"I am unworthy."

"Prettily said. But you could easily play me against my daughter-in-law. I have told you many secrets and it would be to your advantage to use them to better your station."

Rulan shook her head firmly.

"Come, come, Rulan," snapped the old woman with an impatient wave of her hand. "What did my daughter-in-law offer you this morning? A permanent place in my grandson's bed? I am not so ill or old to fail to see behind her clever gesture of friendship to a maid she despises. She needs allies now that I have risen from my sickbed—why not steal mine? Give Tai Tai respect. Tai Tai always knows."

Rulan was amazed and relieved that the mistress had guessed what happened in First Lady's chambers. "This miserable girl is too accustomed to old-fashioned ways. She would be ashamed to serve First Lady. That is why she is happiest with you." The words came easily for they were true.

"Yes, you are a simple girl, a good girl. For a *mui tsai* to rise above her station is unnatural. And of course, Meng would never let Liang Mo keep you for long. Look at the girls my son installs in the house, all whores from the Willow World, cleverly put forth by my son's First Lady. In a brothel, the girls shine like jewels. Bring them here, they seem gaudy and cheap next to the First. Their crudeness embarrasses him. Meng is kind, so kind. 'All they lack is training. Leave them to me,' she tells him. Don't believe her hollow talk. What other tales did she spin to hasten my journey across the Yellow Springs?"

Rulan took a deep breath. "Moon confessed that First Lady has invited a go-between from the Wang family to arrange a marriage with one of their granddaughters. First Lady knows you will stop the negotiations, and she wanted me to tell you that a wedding is in your interest because Old Wang's fortune will boost Liang Mo's career."

"Demon!" The word shattered the intimacy of the moment. "Which of Old Wang's whores is proposed?"

"The one they call Mei Yuk, Beautiful Jade." Rulan plunged on. "First Lady is preparing to exchange charts."

The mistress's hands trembled slightly in her lap. "So it is true! I have heard of the girl Mei Yuk," she told Rulan. "The old man dotes on her, the only pretty granddaughter—the rest are fat like him—and she pets and flirts with him like a whore. Who knows what lechery goes on in that evil house? She is spoiled, vain, with all the trappings of an actress, and not one grain of breeding such as our girls from scholars' families have by nature. Meng stabs me with the same knife that killed my husband! If my son will be a party to his wife's plans to join the virtuous ghosts of this house to the ghosts of pig sellers and bandits, he will feel my wrath." She raised her skinny arm high. "General or not, this old mother will beat him with the large bamboo."

The woman's anger at her celebrated son took Rulan by surprise. It was entirely within Madame Li's right to beat the general, although the beating would be more symbolic than real and, therefore, more humiliating. Even if the beating killed him, the courts would support the mother, not the general, for unfiliality was a crime worse than murder. Madame Li had always dealt more harshly with her son than with her maids. Consequently, her control over him was stronger than most gentry mothers'.

The general had never refused a command from his mother. Mother and son, it was said, were soul mates. Although her son was uncommonly respectful and continued to seek his mother's advice in political matters, Madame Li regretted that Li was a passionate and hence untrustworthy man. His sexual attachment to his wives and to First Lady above all far exceeded the "conjugal companionship" proper for a Confucian gentleman. Madame Li feared that if forced to choose one day between mother and wife, the general would accede to the kind of appeals that only First Lady could make. He loved and needed women's yin too much. This weakness, Madame Li regretted, was also in Liang Mo's character.

"When I first got the kidney fever, how respectful Meng was," the old woman wheezed. Her small eyes were rheumy and dim, shot through with blood, as if a powerful fire had suddenly been banked. "She came every day to measure my progress toward death. She sent the fat maid with greasy cakes to upset my stomach. Now she thinks she can use my son against me. She sent her doctor, for even in my fever I remember his high hat and stringy beard. He quoted to me from the sages, made me point on that silly naked statue to where I hurt. Then he went away, I suppose, to drink tea in her apartments. I ordered First Lady to send for your mother, for no one here knows the old ways of healing with prayers and potions. I was ignored. So I sent my servant to bring Ailan here. My old healer was dead. But, like a miracle, you came. My daughter-in-law called you a witch and passed vicious tales. But Liang Mo saw you and came to me. And then she was jealous and afraid when you beguiled him with peasant yin and tales of peasant heroes. While I lay dying, she rejoiced and began to lay her snares."

Rulan was annoyed that Liang Mo had confessed their intimate talk about village life and peasant rebels to both mother and grandmother. Although she enjoyed his body well enough, it was the chance to convert a rich man to the cause of her sisters that made her answer his nightly summons. And after she discovered that Liang Mo loved the stories of female warriors and village lore, she began to warm to his sympathies for the people. When she was with Liang Mo, she made herself believe that she was singing the old ballads with Harmony and Tsai Yen and Wing in the great hall. Rulan was cheered to discover that Madame Li was not angered, as First Lady was, by

Liang Mo's desire to help the poor. Only First Lady made the old woman shake with anger and indignation.

"But I will overrule her." The thin voice cracked with emotion. "I am still Tai Tai in this house. Liang Mo is mine to direct. You," she said deliberately, "will be my weapon against her. You must draw Liang Mo back to your bed. Banish any thought of the Wang slut from his mind. Peasant yin and peasant wisdom is a necessary medicine for spoiled young men these days. The Concubine was a peasant. My grandmother too, and it was her blood that saved the Lis in a wicked age. When I saw you, so tall, the image of your dear mother, you were all I prayed for. In you, I saw how the strength of the people might revive this tired family so that the house of Li might lead the Land of Flowers to new peace and prosperity."

Rulan's spirit soared. Here was the confirmation of her innermost hopes: the mistress was a sister to all the oppressed! If Rulan made her father understand this, then surely he would rescind the fatal order. It would be a simple matter of relaying this information to the messenger that the Orchids sent. She was due at the morning market in just two more days. Ma Tsu Po would be merciful; she would understand and intervene for the Tai Tai. Yang must be made to know that the mother of a great general was more useful to them alive than dead, for living, she might influence the general's allegiance. Rulan wanted to shout for joy.

"So I say, First Lady is a whore for gold. What else would the offspring of a minor scholar know? Our house's heritage is ashes to her." The old woman began to wail and tear at her hair. "Aaiiee! This house is ruined if Liang Mo marries her. Help me, Daughter, or we are undone!"

Tears started in Rulan's eyes. She knelt to grasp the thin hands and, finding them icy, warmed them between her breasts. She would send a message to her father. But not before guiding her beloved Tai Tai with a secret hand. Her father was wrong to believe that a healer could so easily turn and slay her patient.

"Tai Tai," she promised, "I will be your hands and feet."

After a long silence, Madame Li withdrew her hands and replied slowly. "Remember your promise then. You cannot serve two mistresses."

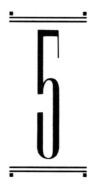

omeone coughed outside the open door. After a pause, in strode a pale, slender youth of twenty dressed in a blue vest over gray pantaloons. He clapped his hands and bowed twice from the waist, smiling broadly.

"Tai Tai," he declared, obviously moved to see his grandmother. "So you are well. I came in hope that what my mother told me this morning was true. I expected to find you in bed, but instead you and Rulan are sporting like two young girls who have not cut their front hair."

"Never listen at doors, Liang Mo, and you will not be disappointed in your expectations." Madame Li's stern words belied the tenderness of her glance.

"Ah, Tai Tai, don't scold me now," he replied unctuously. "I prayed every day before the Kwan Yin in the willow garden for your recovery. You know I could not live without you to guide me."

"I think you might survive very well, Liang Mo. How long has it been since you were in that chair? One month, two?"

"It was not my idea to stay away," he protested.

"Ah, the doting mother," said the Tai Tai. "So it was she who sent you now."

"No. She doesn't know—" He cleared his throat. "Scold me if you like for my bad manners. You are well—that is my only concern.

Now say you have missed your grandson who allows you to beat him mercilessly at the *wei chi* board. Or I shall sell myself to the Fragrant Tree Islands like a poor farmer. Then who will you have to gossip with?"

Madame Li burst out laughing. "Flatterer. Rascal boy. How I have missed you. Pull that chair close so I can see your face. Have you eaten? Did your mother remember to make you rice with peanuts last week at the summer Dragon Boat feast?"

Liang Mo arranged himself carefully before the old woman. Not once had he glanced at Rulan, although her scent was as sharp as new grass in the sick and sour room. For her sake, he told himself, he had not tried to bring her back into his bed. He could not bear it if she were beaten again. Now he remembered the heat the tall peasant girl had once wrapped around him.

"So you have come," Madame Li said softly, reaching over to stroke the youth's cheek. "But how pale you are." He was more handsome than his grandfather at that age, she observed, although he had inherited the old gentleman's tendency to fat. She acknowledged with some satisfaction that the youth's delicate skin came from her side; yet she could not ignore the glassy eyes that hinted at the opium hunger typical of the youths of his class. She also observed with distaste that he had his mother's affectations regarding clothes. His shiny blue vest was of summer silk, decorated with a flight of doves spreading their wings over a background of white clouds—the height of fashion for a playboy in the provincial capital but far too ostentatious for a young scholar in the country. His head was neatly shaved, and the long dark hair at the back of the crown was tightly braided into a queue.

"And you, Tai Tai, are as giddy as a young girl!" he replied with a laugh.

"I will die soon," she answered sternly, "but not before I do my duty."

"Then you will do your duty for many years—thanks to Rulan . . ." His voice trailed off. Finally, he allowed his eyes to rest on the slave girl standing behind his grandmother. Rulan met his eyes so boldly that he glanced away, embarrassed by the unexpected surge of warmth in his loins. Unlike the birdlike women of his own class, whose fulsome attentions frightened him, Rulan had never coddled, teased, or praised him. Neither his family's status nor the power of Liang Mo's position in the household moved her. She had been his first woman, he remembered proudly; because of her, he had abandoned his young hangers-on in the Willow World, had even thrown away his pipe, for the loving seemed more intense without the drug. Did Rulan disapprove of the boys or the dirt? If so, she had never told him directly. Although he confessed everything to her, she was still a mystery to him. Even at the height of passion, her joy was her own. The only time she showed emotion was when she recited village tales of peasant heroes and warrior women. Then tears would steal from under her long lashes. She made him believe that he could be a hero, a leader of the people. No one in the parade of pretty girls his mother sent to his room, no one in the company of beardless boys who knew him in the Willow World aroused him as Rulan had.

"Indeed," said the old woman sharply, following Liang Mo's eyes. "Rulan has fed me poisonous stews and told me tales about a Herd Girl who captured a Moon Prince and stole his golden sword." She chuckled when Liang Mo blushed at the ribald twist on the well-known fable. "It is well that you came. I have something to show you. Stay, Rulan. Fix my hair while my grandson and I talk story."

With long slow strokes of the comb, Rulan loosened the braids from Madame Li's sparse locks. She was determined not to encourage Liang Mo by responding to his lovesick glances. She had to sort out the conflicting claims the Tai Tai and First Lady were making.

Rulan combed the gray hair into a thin veil that hid Madame Li's face. In her illness, the Tai Tai had abandoned the matron's knot and insisted on wearing her hair coiled in two braids above the ears like a virgin. The affectation had not gone unnoticed in First Lady's quarters. It was this that she privately mocked in her comment about the old woman's "second spring." Rulan found the style awkward because so much of the Tai Tai's hair had fallen out during the fever. None of it had grown back, so Rulan saved the strands from her own comb and fashioned a set of false locks to fill out Madame Li's braids. Despite the fact that the two fake coils of hair above her ears were incongruously black, the finished coiffure pleased the old woman.

"Some say that long life is hard for a woman," the Tai Tai intoned through the mask of hair. "Her beauty is gone, her children leave her, and she is a stranger in her son's house. But a good household is so ordered that a virtuous widow does not lose respect. The old lean on the young, but the young learn wisdom from the old."

Liang Mo settled into the chair with a tired shake of his shoulders and prepared himself for a lengthy peroration on filial piety. He stole glances at Rulan, who was mixing cold water with shavings of hair jelly in a bowl.

The female ritual of hairdressing fascinated him. When Rulan lifted her arms to comb out the gray hair, her bodice opened, revealing a shapely breast. Rulan was agitated, he concluded with satisfaction. Her face was flushed. Traces of perspiration shone on her upper lip. He noticed that several strands of hair had worked loose from her long braid and clung to her damp skin. Liang Mo was sure Rulan was thinking of him.

"We are a great and ancient house," Madame Li was saying, amused by his distraction. "Our family has served emperors for a hundred generations. Why do the Lis survive when other houses fall down? We keep our vigor by our devotion to the old ways. We keep respect between the generations. We study the old books and do not let our minds grow slack with indulgence as is common in these times when merchants pretend to ape princes."

"It is sadly so," Liang Mo nodded, lowering his eyes. He saw that Rulan had stepped out of her cloth shoes to bend lower to her mistress—or, Liang Mo thought, to provoke him. The long bones of her arches were as delicate as ridges of carved ivory. Whenever she rose on the balls of her naked feet, he felt as if she were treading on his lungs and heart.

"Liang Mo, you are far too frivolous."

"Tai Tai," he replied gently, struggling to keep his mind on his words, "you know I devote myself wholly to my books. I think of nothing but passing the provincial examinations. In two years, when I have won my degree, you will be proud. And I won't be satisfied until I am an imperial scholar like my grandfather!"

The Tai Tai frowned. "You claim to be a true book-reading man, but you also like rare dishes, fine clothes, and the company of idle youths from low merchant families who smoke opium to ease the pain in their bellies from too much food and drink."

Liang Mo was blushing. "Tai Tai," he said with feigned bravado. "You never objected before when I took my pleasure."

"Merchant pleasures," sniffed the Tai Tai.

"Even Grandfather, before he died, smoked opium to relieve his distress. It makes me sleep better, and as for the other, well, I am not a monk," he whispered, trying not to look at Rulan.

"Perhaps you are, for they share your tastes—" She wrinkled her nose and burst out laughing. "Rascal boy, I don't care who you take to bed. No, I worry about the low company you keep. Merchants' sons, I hear, who are too happy to indulge an innocent scholar in all the vices he cannot afford. You love money too well!"

"Tai Tai," he said with a shaky smile, "I admit that I envy my friends' money. But they have an energy that we old families seem to lack. This is a new age. Merchants rule. The old order of emperor, scholar, warrior, peasant, and merchant no longer reflects the actual measure of power in the realm. Now that the barbarian has broken down our doors, the tradesman's role must be redefined. And the peasant's too—the rebellion of the God Worshipers is another sign that the old order is passing. The emperor would do well to give ear to the people's complaints."

"How learned you have become. I believe you study in your mother's school, for you can 'redefine' so easily the ancient relationships in whatever fashion suits you. Perhaps that is how you justify marrying Merchant Wang's filthy money—so you can grasp with your own hands the reins of this new age!"

"No, no," Liang Mo spluttered. "I swear, I never—"

Madame Li pinioned her grandson with her red-rimmed eyes. "I have heard that there are plans for a wedding. Plans that have been kept secret from me. Have I disappointed you by not dying?"

"Tai Tai, it was not my intention—" Liang Mo was nearly weeping with chagrin.

"I realize that you are compromised, Liang Mo, because you are filial to your mother in a way that she is not filial to me. But every Tai Tai, while she lives, has the last word in these matters. That is a law that neither you nor she may redefine. And I will not have you mixing our blood with that family of pig sellers!"

"Nothing is promised! I swear!"

"Is the exchange of charts nothing? Don't be a fool. When the letters are sent, we are obligated. The old man would sue us if we broke off negotiations. Perhaps that is even his intention, for he knows I would never consent. Did your scheming mother think of that? The villain would trap this family with his own flesh and blood!"

"But charts have not been exchanged!" he protested, thoroughly perplexed. At least he believed that his mother had not gone that far with the Wangs.

"Nor will they be while I speak for this house. I will tell your mother that all interviews must cease." Madame Li saw with satisfaction that Liang Mo did not try to defend his mother.

In truth, he was actually glad for his grandmother's intervention. He had gone along with his mother's secret plan to link him with the Wangs, because it was always easier not to resist her. Although at first he had been unwilling to marry, after his mother promised him Rulan as a concubine, he decided he would not mind the vast fortune the Wang girl would bring into his family. Besides, the Wang girl's portrait showed her to be a beauty, with a face like an almond seed, small pouting lips, and feathery eyebrows. He had indulged himself in several days of pleasant and lascivious dreaming about the two women, enhanced by a particularly pure cache of opium, until his mother and the go-between filled his ears with a careful profile of Wang Mei Yuk's most annoying attributes. The girl, she said, was a paragon of womanhood, skilled at embroidery, making tea, and knowing the proper rites and dishes and gifts for the proper seasons. She could manage a large household and please an old-fashioned mother-in-law, and already she bored him. Undoubtedly she already possessed the dreary attitude of every well-bred virgin who became a wife—jealousy of a husband's time and attention.

Rulan, on the other hand, was never boring. With her, he never needed the stupor of the pipe to be aroused, as he did with the girls his mother sent. In her arms, he felt himself a conquerer, every inch a man.

Sometimes, in the sadness after love, he would confide his fear of his warrior father, and she would make him read to her from his father's letters. "How can you fear a man who makes mistakes in the field?" she would say, and point out how the general might have deployed his men better in his skirmishes with bandits and rebels. She seemed to have a sixth sense about how peasant warriors thought and moved. And she pressed him for information about the celebrated general.

Liang Mo was proud that it was General Li, among all the Han advisers, who had proposed hiring barbarian mercenaries to train the emperor's troops to use cannon, rifles, and western military tactics. "Use the enemy's evil against him," Li had counseled. No one at court had listened, except a young eunuch without much influence named An-te-hai. But Liang Mo was certain, as he told Rulan, that one day his father's ideas would bear fruit.

Madame Li's eyes had an unnatural sparkle. "Your mother may speak to my son, but she does not speak for him. Rulan, go to the cabinet and bring me what you find in the drawer."

Rulan stepped to the low, canopied bed and opened the drawer of the chest beside it. A letter-roll lay inside. Rulan almost cried out in surprise. Where did it come from? There was nothing that passed through the Tai Tai's door in the last nine months that she had not seen or touched. So this was the source of Moon's dream, Rulan realized. The fat maid was no fool. Nor was the Tai Tai, who had slept alone in order to keep a secret rendezvous with a messenger from her son. Grasping the document, Rulan let her finger slip so that the scroll unrolled in her hand. The letter was written in "grass script," which was easier and faster to write than official script and therefore reserved for private correspondence. The characters were vigorous and masculine, and written in haste. The Tai Tai snatched it out of her hand and thrust it at Liang Mo.

"Read that. My eyes are bad. You will find it instructive, I believe. Rulan, raise the shutters so my grandson can see."

"It's my father's seal," Liang Mo said with a catch in his voice. As distant and untouchable as the emperor himself, the general had little direct impact on his son's life except to inculcate fear. He exerted a massive, tidal force from a great distance that oppressed Liang Mo and held him in thrall. Liang Mo could not remember his father ever holding him or playing games with him. He remembered only the servants hammering gongs and singing out his father's achievements as he came through the door on a rare visit home. Or the great man sailing upriver to his next post on a military boat, with drums beating and official flags flying.

White sun flooded the sickroom. With a practiced eye, Rulan scanned the room. Everything was in order, except for a large scroll painting that hung askew on the wall. She flipped it back into place as she passed. Behind the scroll, Madame Li had once divulged, was a hidden passage leading outside the mansion.

"Read aloud," Madame Li instructed. "It may help clarify your duty to me and place your mother's attempts to marry you off in better perspective."

Liang Mo spread the scroll on his lap with one hand and read in a voice higher than usual, following the curved pictographs down the scroll with the point of a polished fingernail.

> Venerated Mother:
> It is written that a son should stand by the bedside of a sick parent. Therefore the distance between Peking and Kwangtung is the measure of my transgression. Only my duty to the emperor prevents me from rushing to you. Even yet, say the word, and I will return at once. For the moment, I give you my son and wife to comfort you. Meng's letters are full of solicitude. I am pleased that she has learned to trust your counsel and that you are consulting together about my son's wedding.

"She has not said a word to me about this," Madame Li said venomously. "Now, mark this! See how she lies to your father, and what little opinion he has of her reasoning."

As Liang Mo read, the pale stalk of his neck became streaked with red.

Yet I can hardly believe that a girl from the Wang family has won
your assent so easily. I cannot forget that Old Wang is your
adversary. And I fear that my wife may have misunderstood your
counsel, which, in your weakened condition, may not have been made
clear to her.

"Did you wonder, Rulan," the Tai Tai said, "how I was so prescient?
It is lucky for you that you told me the truth. Go on, Liang Mo," she
said sternly.

In matters of marriage, it is wise for men to listen to women.
However, because this marriage involves the well-being of all the
souls of our family, I must intrude. First Lady intends by this union
to complete the circle of salt production and distribution and bring it
under one family head. She believes that one day Liang Mo may
inherit this entire enterprise—by what force of character, I do not
know. You need not ask my opinion of the talent manifest in that
pampered son of mine. Had I been home to tend to his discipline and
education, we might not have to grovel before merchants to gain
through marriage what any young man of ability might win through
honorable study and diligence.

You are the head of the household, and this union must win your
assent, or not go forth at all.

Liang Mo kept his eyes on the letter. Rulan felt his shame and wondered why the Tai Tai was subjecting her favorite to such humiliation.
Doubtless, she intended to teach the youth a lesson—but what?

The old woman perched like a small, proud bird on her stool.
"Continue," Madame Li ordered with a brisk nod of her head.

I must also seek your wisdom about another matter—the rebellion.
In the Forbidden City, the princes discuss the uprising of the Hakka
God Worshipers in our southern provinces as if unruly boys were chasing pigs through the alleys. But in Chin Tien, no one laughs. Since
early summer, our inept viceroy has been appealing to Peking for
more aid. All his efforts only enflamed the people. Doesn't he know
that the entire south will explode if he calls in the imperial soldiers?

Though I risk my reputation and perhaps my life, I have sent a
letter to the new Hsien Feng emperor through the eunuch An-te-hai
requesting an audience with the Dragon. I intend to offer my
services. The emperor is young; his advisers among the princes do
not favor me. Except for this eunuch, I have no one at court to

protect me. Yet unless I take this risk, my prospects for advance-
ment are slim.

And to further spice the stew, one more poison. Two months ago,
while on bivouac with my men in Kwangsi, I received an appeal from
a headman of the God Worshipers. He promises the surrender of
ten thousand rebels under his command—half their army—if I will
take up their cause and seek amnesty for the Hakka people with the
new emperor. This Yang, a former charcoal-carrier, says he will deal
with no other man but me. Restitution of lands lost through taxes is
what Yang seeks for his people—and peace under heaven, of
course—with my guidance and leadership. I have not replied.

Rulan nearly gasped aloud at the mention of her father's name. Now
she saw why her father wanted Madame Li killed! The God Worshipers had waited two months for the general's reply. And when none
came, they decided that he had rejected the offer and was preparing to
move against them. What could they do to foil the most ruthless and
brilliant general in the south? Send orders through their spy to his
mother's nurse to kill the sick old woman. At her death, the general
would be required by Confucian custom to leave the battlefield to go
home and mourn for three years—time enough for the God Worshipers to grow strong.

Liang Mo read with advancing excitement, while his grandmother
watched him coldly. Rulan's fingers trembled as they plaited the gray
hair.

Fate, you see, arranges everything. For once, my guards inter-
cepted the enemy spy on the camp's periphery. But having no
intelligence, they killed him and brought me his leg—nicely tattooed
with Triad symbols, to which was strapped Yang's letter. So I had
no way to return my reply had I wished to.

What should a man trapped at a crossroads between enemies do?
Sue for peace and carry Yang's message to the Dragon whose head
is clouded with opium smoke? Sue for war and take my chances,
with Hakka troops in front of me and the viceroy at my rear?

You have guided me through more traps than the gods have
devised for men. My heart is with the people, for the people—as the
sage says—are the heart of heaven. Advise me as you would the boy
that I once was.

The crying of a servant's child three courts below could be heard in the
silence as Liang Mo rolled up the scroll and placed it in his grandmoth-

er's hands. Madame Li tucked it into the drawer of her makeup table. Rulan wanted to weep herself—for joy! Here was the way to save both her Tai Tai and her father. With Rulan's persuasion, the Tai Tai could advise her son to accept Yang's surrender. Rulan would carry the message to her father herself. What tales she would tell Wing when her mission was over and the story of her father's heroism known. All she needed was more time to shape the Tai Tai's natural inclinations into a plan of action. Yang must have ordered the Tai Tai's death as a last resort. But Li was a dutiful son. If the Tai Tai, with information from Rulan, ordered him to meet with Rulan's father, an agreement could be worked out between the imperial army and the rebels. Rulan felt as if history was being drawn through her like silk thread through a needle's eye. She could help heal a nation!

Liang Mo was torn between exhilaration at his father's importance in the events that were shaping the kingdom, and shame at the low opinion in which his father held him. Most of all, he felt amazement that his grandmother's judgment was so valued. The letter revealed a man he hardly knew. A man, not a god! Perhaps even a son of small abilities could please such a man. "Tai Tai," he said, "Father writes Mother about what the women in town wear or what dishes they give him. To you, he entrusts his life!"

"And what would you have me advise?"

The words spilled out eagerly from his mouth. "I say we can learn from the courage of the rebels. This Land of Flowers is so weak that the barbarians do with us as they will. If my father negotiates a peace and brings the rebels back under the emperor's protection, this family's glory will live forever." Liang Mo stood up in agitation and began to move in an unconscious imitation of his tutor who came every day to teach him the analects, the books containing the wisdom of Confucius. He clasped his hands behind his back, took small steps in one direction, and then turned on his heel on an antithetical thought.

"But if only they hadn't taken the messenger's life! If only a message could be sent to Yang." His eyes found Rulan's and met approval there.

Rulan set down the comb and the pot of pomade carefully on the dressing table, for she could no longer concentrate on the mistress's hair. Her blood was afire. To think that the Tai Tai, who knew nothing of the world beyond the outer courts, might midwife the birth of a renewed empire! Rulan began to plan how to help the Tai Tai begin.

Liang Mo turned abruptly to his grandmother, anxious to see if she approved of his counsel.

"Well, Liang Mo," she nodded, "you have spoken like a sage. I see no reason why you couldn't reason your way through the hurdles of the eight-legged essay"—the youth brightened at her words—"if you had the wit to know what was asked of you. I was not soliciting your opinion about how to advise your father. I know enough to do my duty there. No, I wanted your reaction about your mother's scheme to marry you off to the grandchild of our enemy. What was your role in leading him to believe I would consent?"

"I am a fool," was his sheepish reply. "How could I think of advising my father or you? I cannot even guide myself. I did not know my mother had written about this marriage."

Madame Li caressed the table with the flat of her hand, caressed it again, and touched the old brass mirror. "To go behind Tai Tai's back," she crooned softly. "Vicious. Unfilial."

"I will do what you decide. It is absurd of course to talk of marriage with the Wangs when my father is in such a precarious position."

"I agree. The Wangs' influence over the viceroy has made them enemies among the leading families of Canton. An alliance with them would taint us. Your mother should know your feelings, of course."

"But I—I'm not sure how to tell her!"

"Leave it to me. She still lives under my roof, and I am Tai Tai here. Now that you and your father show respect to me, all is well."

"Wait, Tai Tai," blurted out Liang Mo. "I still have so much to tell him. If I could help him, I would count my stupid life worthwhile."

"Listen to me, Young Master," interrupted Rulan boldly. "I know how it can be done." She patted the Tai Tai on the shoulder.

"You?" said Liang Mo, incredulous. "What do you know about these things?"

Rulan began to invent a story that she hoped would convince both grandmother and grandson without implicating her sisters. "In my dormitory, there were many Hakka women with menfolk among the God Worshipers. I heard one worthy woman speak of Charcoal-Carrier Yang. She bragged that she had a relative marching with him." Rulan smiled inwardly at how shocked Liang Mo and the Tai Tai would be to learn that the "worthy Hakka woman" was herself.

"Why, this is extraordinary! Do you think this woman could get a message to Yang?" Liang Mo asked.

"I am certain she can," declared Rulan.

"Who is she? What is her name?" he demanded officiously.

"I do not know her given name, because in the girls' house we take new names, Young Master," Rulan lied.

"Isn't this good fortune, Tai Tai?" Liang Mo exulted. "We'll make this woman tell Yang that his messenger was accidentally killed and that another meeting must take place. If a truce is made with Yang, Hung will be forced to lay down his sword too. Rulan, come with me to find your friend. Then I will personally carry Tai Tai's reply to my father in Peking. Perhaps he might take me along when he brings Yang's proposition before the emperor—" Liang Mo caught himself short. "Is this pleasing to you, Tai Tai?"

Madame Li was turning a snuff bottle around in her hands, studying the rearing dragons cut into the red coral. "Why, I agree with all you say, Liang Mo." She smiled. "Who else could we trust with such dangerous information except a member of the family? Make your preparations while I write a letter to your father. Rulan, stay here. I am not done dressing."

"Then I'll tell the steward to prepare two litters right away. And food! We'll need money, and oh, so many things. I've never been to Peking." Liang Mo bowed hastily and strode out the door, as proud as a young cadet.

Rulan remained silent, although she wanted to shout in triumph and throw her arms around the old woman who had, in one instant, made her father's long-sought Kingdom of Great Peace possible on earth and freed her and her father from a bloody fate. Instead, her fingers tucked a strand of hair into the mistress's tight coils.

"How do you come to know relatives of these rebels so well, Daughter? Do they value a woman's opinion so much?"

"Yes, oh yes, Tai Tai."

Madame Li nodded and smiled, as if she had known all along. "My grandson has yet to show a man's wisdom," said the Tai Tai slowly. "He needs schooling, though not from books, as I once believed. Perhaps a sniff of war will stiffen Liang Mo's spine and clear his head of idle dreams."

"But there will be no war!" Rulan replied with assurance. "The God Worshipers will surrender to General Li."

"Of course there will be war. It is only a matter of time before the Hakka and the Triads rise up in Kwangtung. Do you think you can turn the river from the sea?"

"But my—Charcoal-carrier Yang wants peace!" protested Rulan, startled by the unexpected turn in the conversation. "The general can open the emperor's heart to the plight of his suffering children."

Madame Li fixed Rulan with a look of stern rebuke. "You could not possibly believe that desperate ploy by the villainous mule Yang to tempt my son into treason! He was not asking for peace. He was asking for my son to lead his doomed rebellion. If you were persuaded by such falsehood, you are as simple as Liang Mo himself. Or is it that you choose not to see? Perhaps sympathy for your own kind has distorted your understanding. Or perhaps you are trying to distort mine! Do you imagine that the Hakka rabble truly wants to return to the land before they drink the last drop of every civilized person's blood? No, your people are wanderers by nature. And what land do they have to return to anyway? It is either burned, drought-leached, and unplanted or in the hands of braver men who will not give it up. No, no, I say. Hakka are only peasants, and peasants are part of the *tao* of every age. They may be stupid and heartless, but they know when their bellies are empty. And when the great belly of the people goes unfed for three years and when taxes rise and the levees go unrepaired, there is always war!"

Rulan could not believe she had so misjudged the Tai Tai. "But war is surely a sign that heaven has withdrawn its mandate from the emperor. And if so, the people have the right to shake the throne."

"Take care, Daughter. That talk is treasonous. Hunger and strife are a peasant's fate."

"An individual can always change fate!" Rulan replied in confusion.

"Aiya, Rulan! No one can change fate! Who has a choice in the matter?"

Rulan was horrified that the Tai Tai had no understanding of the people at all. "The Hakka people fight only for food and land."

"And would you have lawlessness go unpunished? Heaven would fall to earth if the rebels who have slain priests and civilized families, sacked temples, and burned the good idols were not punished. The law applies to Hakka and Punti alike. And you want my son to abet your tribe in their drive toward chaos! Merely entertaining an application from the bandits, with their obvious hint that they would 'serve him,' makes my son guilty of treachery, in conscience if not in fact. Yang is trying to entrap him with visions of the Dragon Throne! It's an old ploy; every warlord has dreamed of sitting there—Hung himself covets it! And yet for each man who seized it, there were ten thousand others whose head crowned a stake. This Yang does not want my son on his side, as my dim-witted grandson supposes. He wants my son to cut his own throat. No, no. To seek peace with the rebels is treason. My son would be cut off. Lost. Our house thrown down this cliff. Our tree burned to the root. No, I say. Heaven may take back its mandate from the throne, but this family does its duty to the end. How else can the pattern be preserved? The Tao Kuang emperor dies, his son takes his place. And his son after that. Even if the whole dynasty is toppled, another dynasty will rise, and the loyalty of the Lis will win us a place in the new order. So I say there must be war!"

"Tai Tai," Rulan said, uncomprehending, "you told Liang Mo to carry your letter advising a truce—"

"Indeed, I shall send a letter telling my son to meet the charcoal-carrying dogs. But not to aid them. To invite them to talk, and then to take their heads." Madame Li's small eyes glowed like fiery coals in the pale cadaverous head. "You have tried to train Liang Mo like a cricket to sing your song. He is full of nonsense about 'the people.' But this is a kingdom of dragons, tigers, and powerful spirits—no mere peasant can change these forces! Liang Mo judged rightly only in this: he needs to leave these courts to escape his mother's influence and be delivered to his father to become a man." Madame Li scratched her dry cheek with her long fingernail. "The letter I will write will tell my son that duty to the emperor requires that he destroy all enemies of the throne, and that duty to me requires that he discipline his wife and turn a weakling son into a gentleman worthy of respect."

"Tai Tai—" pleaded Rulan.

"Enough! Until now I believed that all you did for Liang Mo was strengthen him. Now I see that you have filled his head with unaccept-able ideas. His romantic attachment to peasants is first among them. That idea will be scourged out of him in battle. How long will he think that the ragged farmer who charges at his eyes with a stick is a noble creature? In war he will see how close to the heart of heaven the people are when heaven lets them die like dung flies."

"I don't believe you! You love the people! You were my mother's friend. Your own grandmother was a peasant."

"Yes, and how grateful she was that her husband lifted her up out of the mud! He was only a scribe, but he was loyal. And how did he die? Protecting the granaries of the great-grandfather of this house! And who killed him? Peasants. Hunger marchers. I was only five years old, but I can still hear them roar, still see them swarm like locusts over the walls of our house. My grandmother and I hid on a ledge halfway down the well. And after they were done killing and stealing and smashing and stuffing our food into their bellies, we alone were left. Two days later, neighbors came and heard our cries and pulled us both up on the bucket rope. I saw my father and grandfather hacked to pieces like meat for the table and my mother hanging from a beam in our own house—hanging not by a rope, but by her own intestines. We put the pieces of the bodies together and buried them with our bare hands. Were it not for the good master Li whom my grandfather served, we too would have perished. But he brought my grandmother and me into this house, and here I met my husband, his third son, who became master when his brothers were cursed with early deaths. Here I bore a son who will do no less for his master, the emperor, than my grandfather for his. This is honor. This is duty. Peasants do not know this; only those pure of blood know what it truly means to be Han."

"But why let the innocent perish when there could be an end to the bloodshed? It was our dream in the commune to bring peace to the land and rights to women."

"Neither the Loi nor the Hakka teach their daughters to mind their tongues," the old woman said sadly. "You condemn yourself, Daughter. I perceive that you have a life that is unknown to me. I gave myself into your hands, trusted you to safeguard my life with your mother's medicines and prayers, but you have preserved it for reasons of your own, not loyalty to me. Perhaps *you* are a spy for the Hakka traitors. I regret that my daughter-in-law showed better judgment than I. She saw your bad influence on my grandson when my eyes were blinded with sympathy for the daughter of a loyal slave. Well, Liang Mo must be sent away, and so must you!"

"Where?" whispered Rulan.

"Not back to that house of women rebels. You too must learn to obey," declared Madame Li. "To accept fate. To accept the unacceptable, if need be. I may turn you over to the magistrate for prosecution as a spy. Or you might yet find a place on our land, though never again in this house or my chambers. Give Tai Tai respect. Resist, and—who knows?" Madame Li surveyed Rulan's ravaged face coldly.

Rulan did not know what to do or say. Her impulsive nature had made her see only what she wanted, and as a result, she had failed everyone who trusted her. How could she have imagined that the Tai Tai loved her when the old woman was only bent on securing power within the family? What Rulan had assumed was tender compassion was only the Tai Tai's physical weakness. The healer's gentle heart had overwhelmed the warrior's clear-eyed reason.

"You will obey me," the Tai Tai said. "This family will not allow insurrection to fester in our house or on our lands. We will take back our lease from those unnatural women you call 'sisters.' As for this Yang, his head will soon be separated from his shoulders after I advise my son to burn out the rebels in Kwangsi."

When Rulan began to protest, the Tai Tai signaled her to silence.

"Your mother has trained you badly, Daughter," the Tai Tai scolded.

"Ailan failed to teach you that a slave's only reason for being is to carry out the will of her mistress. Look here, look here. You have forgotten my jewels! Get the ruby earrings, there in the cabinet," she commanded.

Rulan stood paralyzed with horror at what she had brought upon her sisters and her father.

"Get them now!" Madame Li shouted.

After a moment, the old woman took the jewels that Rulan held out to her. Frowning into the depths of the burnished mirror, Madame Li lifted one, then another bright earring to her sallow cheek. Satisfied, she handed Rulan back the earrings, a pair of rubies raised like lotus blossoms on a circlet of small diamonds.

"What should this wretched person do in her life, Tai Tai?" sobbed Rulan, utterly undone by the hopelessness of her position. "How can such a miserable person ever find the way?" She pushed the ends of the gold wires through her mistress's lobes. Heavy jewelry had slackened the holes over the years and the ruby earrings now swung off center.

"Never resist duty, Daughter," came the stern reply. "Nothing else is a surer guide." Madame Li turned her oiled head from side to side to admire in the oval mirror the shiny coils of gray hair interwoven with Rulan's dark locks. The rubies flamed against her bloodless cheeks. She grimaced. "Aiya, I hurt all over. Hurry up and finish, then give me the needles." Stretching her swollen fingers, she reached into the cabinet and handed Rulan an ornament for the hair.

With trembling hands, Rulan moved the mistress's head forward and brushed up a few loose strands that had fallen down at the neck. The old woman's skin was clammy where Rulan's fingers touched. Rulan pulled a few strands of hair to hide the places where the pink scalp peeked through.

"Your hands are cold, Daughter," chided the old woman. "Tell Second Cook to give you black chicken stewed in ginseng."

"Thank you, Tai Tai. You are always kind to this miserable person." For a moment, Rulan hesitated, her heart warring with her head, but there was no point in waiting; her duty was clear. Again, Rulan brushed up the hair away from the neck and put the sharp jeweled needle at the forbidden point behind the ear where the brain was not covered by bone. The shaft entered with surprising ease, penetrating to the depth of four *tsun* before sticking fast.

"Ah yes," sighed Madame Li. The flesh of her neck shivered.

The smooth gray head with its incongruous black braids fell forward, struck the side of the cosmetics box, and sent it spilling across the floor. The Shouchou mirror tottered and fell, ringing like a gong.

The old woman's head lay tilted on the table to one side. Her small dark eyes were open, her lips caught in a half-smile. Placing a finger at the edge of the long pin, Rulan jiggled the unyielding shaft to free it. The merest trace of blood and fluid remained, as if the flesh did not want to let the jewel go. Rulan wiped the pin with the inside of her shirt and tossed it among the scattered combs and necklaces and broken bottles.

Feeling a terrible iciness creep over her heart, Rulan stumbled into the sunny courtyard where the ancestral spring welled up from a bed of rough rock.

"Aaiiee!" she wailed, blinded by tears. "Come quickly. Tai Tai has had a stroke!" The lie caught in her throat. As the servants came running, she thought of the peasants encircling her at the well, of the raiders breaking into the dormitory.

Again, she had killed her mother.

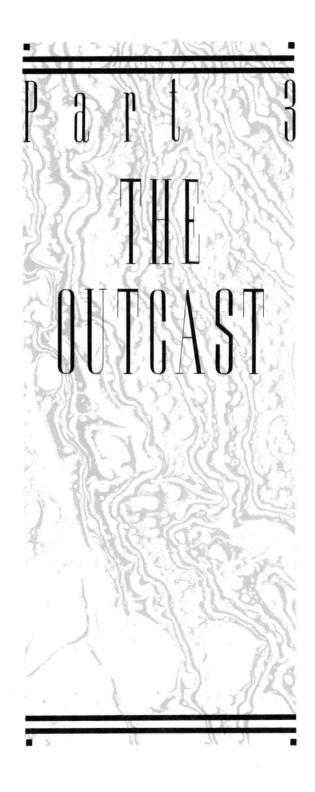

Part 3

THE
OUTCAST

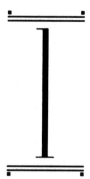

On Ting Village, Kwangtung Province, 1851

Mist rose off the paddies to the waists of the women. Whenever they bent to insert the slender green rice shoots into the flooded silt, they disappeared from view.

Ghosts dancing, Pao An thought, slowing his feet on the treadle of the water lift in order to catch his breath. The transformation of the short-legged, heavy-thighed farm wives in the spring ritual of planting never failed to fill him with awe and desire.

Twice each year, the homebound Punti women of On Ting village came out to the fields for the crucial and terribly brief period of planting. Watching the women work the land, Pao An saw in them an elemental beauty that was harmonious with the black earth, the white fog, and the slate-flat flooded fields. He was of marrying age but too poor to buy a wife, so the women were all the more desirable and unreal.

Sounds of the morning drifted over the wet earth: oxen lowing, men yelling across the fields, sea gulls screeching in from Hong Kong Bay. Pao An felt a surge of tenderness for the people, the creatures of soil and sky, and the stubborn land—half earth, half water. This tiny span along the lower Pearl River, which generations of the Chen clan had planted, tilled, harvested, and eventually fertilized with their own bodies, was all the world he knew.

A sweet, light drizzle called "plum rain" had blessed the first day of planting. From his perch on a paddle wheel atop a four-foot dike beside a canal, Pao An scanned the mist-shrouded river plain as it curved like the lip of a smiling dragon between the prominence of Cloud Head Mountain and the great turn in the Pearl River. Even at this early hour, sampans, junks, single-masted merchant ships, and the double-striped sails of government salt traders were negotiating the tricky currents up to the provincial capital of Canton or down to Hong Kong, the mosquito-infested island peopled by the white devils, who were poisoning the Land of Flowers by infecting merchants and officials, soldiers, and peasants with a gut-wrenching hunger for opium.

Between the levee and the rice fields, a narrow dirt road ran for one mile and disappeared into the cooperative mulberry groves. Rice was for the belly; silk was for cash. For years, the delta had produced too little rice and too much silk, so the price of silk was less than the cost of producing it. On Ting, however, was a fortunate village; bribes kept their taxes low and no more than a half-dozen girls and one revered elder had died the previous winter. More happily, the early omens for the new planting season were promising. There might yet be ample rice for the first time in years, if the summer monsoon came on schedule and if it blew with sufficient strength.

Pao An wiped his brow. Across the narrow canal San Kwei, the headman, and Fan, General Li's leech-faced rent collector, were sloshing past on horses.

"Aiya! There's my cousin's adopted son," the headman declared to the collector. "Fit for nothing but pumping water. My cousin bankrupted himself to buy a place on the ancestors' tablets for the ugly giant. I made him give back half his acres to the clan collective for the taint he brought into our line. This time next year, my cousin's last patch of land will be mine, and either that bag of bones will be dead and I'll inherit, or he'll default on his loan. Then the land goes back to a true Chen once again, not a 'legless crab' of an orphan like him."

"Keep climbing, Monkey," the collector snorted to Pao An over his shoulder as they rode away. "Maybe you'll get to heaven."

The collector's sarcastic reference to Tripitaka, the antic Monkey God, who had tricked his way into heaven and created chaos among the gods, stung. Turtles sucking mud, Pao An thought bitterly. I'll get to heaven and turn it upside down, just like Monkey. He spat angrily in their direction.

Pao An climbed off the water lift to catch his breath and stretched his arms to let the rain melt away his anger. The mechanism he worked was crudely fashioned of bamboo buckets, ropes, and rough wooden slats; it was like running upon an endless treadmill. Every step he took hoisted a hollowed section of giant bamboo sloshing with brown water from the canal along a rope incline to the top of the dike. At the peak of the incline, the train of buckets turned over and dumped water down a chute into the paddies.

At sixteen, he was already the biggest man in the Chen clan village of On Ting. Even bent beneath a shoulder yoke, he stood a full head taller than his bandy-legged cousin Pang, who was pedaling a water lift nearby. Pang had dubbed him "Manchu," a cruel insult considering the peasants' hatred of their Tartar oppressors and Pao An's precarious position in the clan, for Pao An was an orphan, a "legless crab," and the only outsider in a single-surname village where every man claimed descent from a common ancestor named Chen. Hot tempered and sensitive about his low status, Pao An permitted no one but Pang to insult him. Inseparable since childhood, they had tumbled in the dirt as rowdy boys, harassed the village schoolteacher, and shared turnips in starving times, although Pao An balked at Pang's habit of squandering precious coppers on black dirt. Now Pang had dared Pao An to join the outlawed Red Turban Society as the solution to his lack of money and position and to his grinding anger at those who pushed down his beloved adoptive father, Li Yu.

Was anger really as futile as his father, a former scholar, claimed? Li Yu, who had plucked Pao An as a baby from a field of burning cane, had always taught Pao An to forgive the soldiers who had burned his son's ancestral village. Li Yu's way was the "low way" of *tao,* the water way, the way of least resistance. A wise man, counseled Li Yu, does not disturb the course of events, lest he complicate circumstance and ensnare himself in misfortune. Li Yu's model in all things was water, which seeks the lowest level and in so doing wears down mountains. Maybe I'm unwise, Pao An reflected, but isn't my way also the way of water? The way of flood and storm! Remembering his father's gentle admonition to do all things "slowly, smoothly," Pao An laughed out loud, climbed back on the lift and began a furious pedaling action that made the old apparatus groan and the line of bamboo buckets jump and spatter brown water over the crest of the dike. All he could do in life, Pao An told himself angrily, was to pit human muscle against earth and water and the immense weight of clan tradition until they overcame him.

"Climb, Monkey, climb!" he yelled to Pang half a dozen paces away. "Let's flood this whole plain before noon! Faster! Faster! We'll storm heaven like warriors of the Monkey God!"

Pang hooted his acceptance of the challenge, and the two youths began a wild race against each other and the unending spill of water.

Rising and falling, the women continued with infinite patience inch by inch across the floodplain, their bodies moving to the rhythm of an ancient planting song.

They came on horses. Men as tall as giants and as ugly as demons with bodies of silver and gold. Who had ever seen so many? the small boy wondered. They threw torches into the fields and turned the cane from green to red.

Run, run! his mother said. He heard the aunts' screams, high and long like chickens slaughtered for the pot. The giants threw torches into the houses along the lane.

The boy's head was spinning with the noise of the aunts and the horses and the searing closeness of the flames. His nose was full of smoke. When he tried to talk, the words came out thick and silent and black.

The uncles thrust sharpened sticks at the horses' bellies. The horses rode over the uncles, trampling them into the red earth. The giants laughed so hard that the tassels on their pointed hats danced crazily.

His grandmother snatched him up. The boy tried to squirm away because her breath was sour, and she was weeping into his ear. But she clutched him tight around his belly, and ran bump, bump, bump through the lanes. The uncles, aunts, and cousins were fast asleep on the ground. Second Uncle lay with his face in the mud.

Get up or you will get all dirty! the boy called to Second Uncle. A black dog was sniffing Uncle's bloody hair.

His father ran past with a sharpened stick. Where is Mother? he yelled. The boy pointed behind them.

Where is she? Father yelled again, as if he did not understand.

A sound as deep as thunder came toward them. The horses, tall as mountains, filled the narrow lane from side to side. The men mounted on them were like clouds dressed in bright light. How they shone!

Run! his father shouted and rushed at the giants with his stick.

Grandmother darted from the alley between the two huts into another lane. A crowd of giants were there with their horses tethered nearby. Two were dragging Youngest Aunt along the ground. They pulled her like grandmother did when she tried to break the heartbone of a chicken. Another man stood between Auntie's legs with his pants around his ankles. The boy laughed. Auntie cried out to grandmother. Grandmother ran. How fast she could run! She went into the cane fields where he was never allowed to play. There were snakes in there.

Grandmother, he gasped. Had she forgotten about the snakes?

But she covered his mouth with her hand and squatted in a muddy ditch. Her eyes were red and wild, like the eyes of the horses. The smoke and the thunder and the screaming went on for a long time. He fell asleep against his grandmother's shoulder. The cane leaves made a thick green canopy above their heads.

When he awoke, black smoke was choking his lungs, and Grandmother was asleep. He could hear the burning cane stalks crashing down around them. Heat singed his throat.

Get up, Grandmother, he begged. She was sitting in the water. She still held him but her hands were cold. He could see the fire now through the dark veil of razor-sharp leaves. He wriggled out of her grasp.

Grandmother, I'm afraid, he told her. He tried to pull her arm, but she fell over in a heap. A fiery stalk crashed inches away from his grandmother's head and the small boy suddenly found his hiding place engulfed in flame.

With a cry, the boy leapt through the fire and ran through the burning cane, calling for his father.

Pao An woke with a start to see Li Yu's lined face bent over him. "Sorry, Father, I overslept again. I should get water boiling for you," he said. Pao An smelled smoke from the small coal brazier and wished that he had remembered to take a few leaves from the common kitchen at the boys' house to make his father tea. The unmarried youths and husbands whose wives were unclean from childbirth stayed in the large bachelors' dormitory supported by the clan. Pao An liked the noise, the camaraderie, and the gambling, although he returned most nights to sleep in the same bed with Li Yu. The old man's arthritic legs and back needed the warmth of his son's strong body, and he depended on Pao An to help him through his *tai chi* exercises, which he performed each morning, despite the pain.

"You were dreaming again," observed Li Yu.

"No, no. I stayed up too late," Pao An replied groggily. He had spent the night gambling for coppers in the boys' house, for which Li Yu always patiently rebuked him. Pao An would argue, never successfully, that he was smart, intuitive, very lucky—and rarely lost. He maintained too that gambling was his sole means to raise money to pay their debts. Li Yu would not be drawn into an argument about chance; any thinking man, he pointed out, could see that the odds eventually balanced out. Instead, he maintained that gambling was an evil in itself, and thus ought to be avoided if one was to grow toward perfection. It contributed to the corruption and impoverishment of the young men Pao An counted as friends, and surely that was not just.

"I'm ashamed I am not a better son, Father," Pao An said, remembering the headman's jokes. What pained Pao An even more than the land Li Yu had given up to San Kwei to buy the foundling a place on the clan rolls was Li Yu's loss of status. Without land, Li Yu had no influence, and hence had given up his claim to the position of head-man, which San Kwei had seized.

"Don't worry about me. You work hard. You need your sleep. Get dressed quickly now. I'm going out to the square to talk with the other old men who can't sleep. I've left hot water for you."

Pao An slipped his shirt over his head and pulled up his second pair of trousers, which he used for field work. He went outside to urinate, came back to rinse his mouth with hot water, and swallowed a few mouthfuls more. He would eat later, at midmorning with Li Yu, and this time he resolved to be back early so he could cook rice for the man to whom he owed so much. He dipped his fingers in the hot water and wiped his eyes, as if this simple act could cleanse the evil phantoms from his memory. Pao An was the only one of his clan to escape the government soldiers who had put his village to the torch for failing to pay taxes. The nightmare still hung around him, although the screams of the dying and the crackling of the flames had faded. As always, to dispel the last shreds of the bad dream, he made himself say the despised name over and over, a litany that never failed to fill his being with an all-consuming and righteous anger. Li. General Li, who owned most of the land on which On Ting stood. General Li, who as a young commander had led the troop of soldiers into Pao An's home village. General Li, who had slain his mother, father, and grandmother and now could casually ruin the kindly stranger who had plucked a fright-ened child out of a burning cane field and raised him as his own son. General Li, whom Pao An stood ready to risk everything to destroy.

The sun had just thrust itself up into a corner of the night sky when the great gong outside the Hall of Ancestors, where all the clan records and spirit tablets were kept, echoed through the lanes. Soon, bone-stiff men ambled to the steps of the hall rubbing their sleepy eyes with thick fingers. Already, a few old men were sitting on the steps of the porch of the hall trading stories and sucking the sap from sections of cut sugarcane. Pao An spied Li Yu among the group and went to join Pang and two other companions from the boys' house.

The Hall of Ancestors was the center of village life, the symbol of the ties of blood and obligation that had turned three uprooted families from central China into a vast southern clan that occupied an entire village. A hundred generations ago, their *Tai Kung* or founding ances-tor had followed the conquering soldiers of the new empire of Chin as far as the monsoon coast of the South China Sea and had hacked through jungle and rain forest to this lush river plain. The name of the *Tai Kung* and that of every male descendant were set down in the tablets safeguarded in the hall. At its doors, the dead were honored with offerings and prayers, wrongdoers flogged or paraded in the wooden collar called the cangue, and the "Sixteen Maxims" declaimed twice a month by officials from the yamen, the county seat.

The hall was the largest building in the village, the only one with a proper foundation cut from the granite quarry in the hills. The crown of the roof had a carved center beam that thrust up sharply at each end so that demons would not be tempted to alight there. The timbers were ancient and still solid, but the red paint that should have proclaimed it a house of joy as well as veneration was badly faded and chipped. In these last desperate years of drought, flood, and anarchy, the Chens had begun to call the Hall of Ancestors by a different name: the Lodge of Sorrows. It looked the part. Three crumbling sandstone steps led up to a decrepit porch overhung with a roof of broken clay tiles.

Scowling, the headman yelled for silence before introducing the collector, a guest in his house the night before. San Kwei strutted back and forth along the wide veranda where traveling storytellers performed, proudly self-conscious of the collector's approving eye. San Kwei's method of introducing any new enterprise was to harangue his kinsmen until someone was finally shamed into doing the work. The villagers, on their part, gave a grudging ear to the man's rude oratory, because San Kwei had steered On Ting through many natural disasters and political entanglements while leaders of other villages had erred, often fatally. San Kwei knew intuitively when to bribe an official and when to resist, when to yield to a band of marauders and when to brandish pikes and hoes. And he had a sixth sense about when the river would rise or shrink from its banks and which levee needed to be fortified with more dirt. The villagers admired, but did not love San Kwei, who was a moody, irascible man. No one had learned to predict when his round, jowly face, as brown and cracked as a basket weaver's thumb, would contort with rage or explode in laughter.

He stalked the veranda in pantaloons and cotton vest like a stubby Tartar general urging his reluctant troops to the kill. "You men from River Lane. You go to Mountain Field. The field needs to be cleared of stones. They seem to sprout there overnight." He stroked his short peppery beard and laughed gruffly at his own joke, orchestrating an answering murmur of laughter from the old men behind him. "All you men from Bamboo Lane and Brown Sugar Lane, we need you to pump water into the two empty fields along the levees. I promise you, if we get the last rice field cut in three days so that the seed for the second crop can be put down, everybody will be working his own plot next week. The rest of you, get your sickles into the common ground. Pile the stalks on the threshing yard for the women. Tomorrow when they finish winnowing, you can bag the grains and put them into the storehouse so I can count which sack goes for taxes and which we can keep to sell. Remember our duty," he said with a pious bow in the collector's direction. "General Li takes first from our hand, the emperor second, the yamen third, and we are last." He paused to glare at the rows of sleepy faces before unexpectedly baring his teeth in a broad grin. "But this year, I guarantee no belly goes without rice and we will make a profit on mulberry leaves. I personally burned joss sticks to our *Tai Kung* and he promised us a big crop! Everybody work hard."

The crowd began to break up at San Kwei's typical closing phrase, but this time he called them sternly back to attention.

"Now listen, you! We need a gang of men with strong backs to carry stone. The damn wood has rotted out of the central sluice gate, and the last flood tore away the foundation. Now I say, we need six or seven young bulls to cut stone and carry it down from the quarry to the canal. Step forward. Six or seven.

"What? Are there only girls here? Shall I call out the old women to do the job? Where are the bachelors who haven't been riding wives all night?" San Kwei waved his finger at the crowd of silent men, his jowls shaking, and scolded, "Don't hold up the planting!" The headman's gaze traveled over the mass of faces and suddenly stopped. "Aiya, my cousin's adopted son over there." He raised his voice so all could hear and directed his words to Li Yu, who was squatting against the sunny side of a building with two other old men. "That lame crab sleeps late and gambles early so he never has the energy to work my fields or volunteer for this village. Don't rush, don't run, Pao An. We'll hold the sun for you, and the monsoon too. You and your father hardly turn a spade in my field. Do I see you offering to carry rock? No!"

Before San Kwei could begin to rant at Li Yu, Pao An quickly stepped forward. "You are right, Uncle. I'll lead a work team." Pao An's anger at the insult to his father made the words sound like a challenge.

"Ha!" the headman sputtered. " 'Lead.' You couldn't lead a turtle to a pond. Hurry up, who else then? Quickly—who?"

When the men continued to scan the sky, the headman stamped his foot and yelled, "You husbands get your women out to the assigned fields. Pao An, I order you to finish the job by noon. I hold you responsible. That's what you get for bragging. Now everybody go! What are you waiting for—a decree from General Li?"

Pao An made a polite bow, but when he raised his head and saw San Kwei's mocking grin, his temper flared. Turning to hide his angry face, Pao An caught his three companions sneaking away into the fields. "Pang! Stay!"

"Your Tai Tai's gulley!" Pang yelled over his shoulder as the other boys guffawed. "You aren't going to crack my spine. Besides, I want to see the headman flog you when you fail."

"I make you a wager. I bet I can carry the weight of two and still beat you eunuchs to the sluice gate."

"Then you have to start down last," one boy demanded sullenly; he knew Pao An's strength but couldn't resist the wager.

"Agreed."

"Four cash each. Winner take all!" Pang added, his small eyes beginning to dance. "I'll be as rich as an opium pirate."

ao An set off across the rice fields at a furious pace,
making the others run to keep up. At the summit of the
ridge, the youths collapsed in the dirt, punching and cursing each other
good-naturedly and swallowing deep gulps of sweet air. Pao An dragged
himself to his feet and gazed back over the fields he had just crossed.

Below him lay the entire circumference of his world—the islands of
alluvial soil afloat in the Pearl River as it coursed through rocky
shallows before turning south to Hong Kong and the crescent-shaped
mouth of the South China Sea. As far as he could see, checkerboard
fields were laid end to end against each other, broken by canals, ponds,
hills, and dense clusters of buildings where the villagers lived. Most of
the villages were of reddish-brown brick, like the village of On Ting.
There lived the Punti, whether wealthy, like the Lis, or poor like the
Chens, who had come fleeing a famine in central China centuries
before. A scattering of rustic white buildings, more hovels than houses,
poked out humbly now and then from the waterlogged plain or
perched precariously on the arid, inaccessible foothills. These were the
villages of the Hakka, descendants of a second Han incursion from
central China, and even poorer than the poorest Punti. The Punti and
Hakka traveled the same roads and canals, set their market stalls side
by side, but they spoke different tongues, ate different foods, and
would not hesitate to kill the other if a boundary was breached or an
insult given.

Who, looking at the beauty of the land, thought Pao An, would be foolish enough to care for the squalid villages that marred the landscape? Beyond the villages, the view was breathtaking: the plain was crisscrossed with branching waterways on which slow-moving sampans and crude rafts vied with each other for every inch of brown water. To the east, terraced fields cut a narrow green stairway over low yellow hills. The countryside was long denuded of trees except for a thick grove of banyan south of the village haunted by a vengeful *kuei* who coveted girl babies. A marshy promontory at the edge of the grove jutted like a woman's hip into the river. That part of the land was owned by the Lis, who had built a shrine around a white, egg-shaped rock that was considered good magic for infertile women. Along its narrow margin, a dirt road ran north to Canton, the provincial capital, past the cliff-clinging mansion of General Li. If he squinted, Pao An could make out the rugged mountain over the curve of the river into which the huge country house was dug. All the Chens lived in the shadow of that house. If luck was with them, General Li would ignore them; if luck ran out, and they could not pay their taxes or rents, General Li would snuff them out. Few escaped the reach of the general's family. Only Li Yu had slipped the noose and gone to Canton to study, until famine had caused the Chen clan to cut off his stipend. In the end, the perennial misfortune that dogged the poor had ensnared Li Yu as well and brought him back to On Ting and under General Li's hand to suffer.

Li Yu was the only son of On Ting to venture to Canton. No one in Pao An's generation had ever strolled its narrow streets, even to beg. Pao An looked down on the delta and vowed that he would be the first of his peers to do so. For what was On Ting that he should love it so? Only a collection of mud huts surrounded by a low wall of dirt, overrun one year in three by the very waters that nourished it. Only a collection of battling relatives—all ill-fed, ignorant, and tied to a small span of dirt by a line of ancestors as long as a rope around an ox's neck. Pao An knew that his impious thoughts arose out of defeat, for San Kwei, he admitted, was right. Pao An did not belong, was not clan, and had no claim to his own name. It was grafted onto him by his father's love.

And what was the Land of Flowers but On Ting writ large? A land of the dead governed by the living in their ancestors' names. Even its officials, from the new emperor to the lowest civil servant, were rotten to the core. Li Yu had once alleged mildly that the examinations by which leaders were picked were frauds; and the young men who had escaped the last corvée whispered that the once-formidable imperial army was no more than a legalized band of bandits. The Chens distrusted everyone, believed in nothing—except the graves and tablets of their ancestors, which they kept with tender devotion. Purity of blood was the tenet on which this orthodoxy rested. Sons were treasures because they were the living link to the fathers in the land beyond the Yellow Springs. Girls were "guests" in their fathers' house, expensive to feed and eventually lost through marriage to outsiders. In such a rigid system, Pao An was an impurity in the pure seed of the clan.

After he reached the quarry, Pao An drove his tired body on, splitting the blue-gray slate with an iron bit and wedge. He ignored the chatter of the others, content to spend his anger on the massive rock face. They, in turn, were content to leave the work to him. He wielded an ancient cutting tool, a thick bamboo pole fitted with an iron point. Skillfully, he loosened the shale in flat platter-size sheets, then stopped to load each basket with rock.

Pang's baskets were first. Pao An lifted the yoke onto his friend's bony shoulders and placed a firm kick to Pang's buttocks to send him down the mountain. Then he quickly filled the other baskets so that Pang's lead was no more than a few paces. He loaded his own baskets more carefully to make sure that each was exactly equal in weight. He had not been as scrupulous with the others'. Balance, his father taught him, was the key to controlling the twin forces in the universe. That was why he had dominated his dark mood by breaking rock before trying to lift it. The secret of strength, Li Yu said, came from matching one's *chi,* the vital energy moving through the five precious organs. *Chi* was at the heart of *tai chi chuan,* the cosmic dance, the ancient art of shadowboxing. Li Yu had taught his adopted son the dance from the moment he brought him home. Each evening father and son would practice the patterned motions of rising, falling, bending, and lifting that had been refined by practitioners of *tai chi chuan* over the centuries. Li Yu claimed that the dance helped to loosen an old man's stiffening bones and to discipline a young man's fire. While they danced, Li Yu explained that each rounded movement of the hands and body reproduced yin and yang, the contending but harmonious forces in nature. Pao An, softly pummeling the air, wished that he was learning the more deadly martial arts that derived from the dance. He longed to feel the crack of his fists against his enemies' bones.

Pao An breathed deeply, cleansing his lungs of dead air and his mind of hatred or revenge. Then he braced his legs on the crumbling shale and hoisted the yoke onto his shoulders with a single graceful movement. He regarded the slow descent of the river to the sea, the movement of the clouds inland, and the flight of birds across the white porcelain dome of the sky and waited for the world to shift. Quickly, he caught the moment, felt the axis of power surge in his gut, and with a firm stride, started down to the crumbling irrigation ditch, two miles away.

He passed Pang struggling with his tilted yoke at the base of the mountain. With two-thirds of a mile to go, Pao An was far ahead of the others. As he nimbly traversed the small dikes separating the rice paddies and measured the progress of the threshers, he noticed that the harvesters had not yet touched the paddy on his right, which showed a bristling of green stalks waving above the flat expanse of silvery water. To his left, an emaciated old man was leveling the ground with a bullock who pulled a heavy wooden sledge weighted with stones.

The earth had been lightly soaked, and the flanks of both man and bull were stained black with mud. As Pao An drew nearer, the water buffalo lunged and seemed to trip. It got awkwardly to its feet, then balked again, as if an invisible hand were strangling it. The old man slapped the bullock's haunches and ran around to tickle its ear, but the beast stood stock-still. Only Pao An saw what beast and man could not: a spur of rock had caught the back end of the sledge. Its ribs heaving like a bellows, the bullock craned its gaunt neck and moaned, trying to hook its horns into the old man whenever he came too close.

A perfect picture of this village, Pao An thought ruefully. Starving man and starving beast, turning their frustration on each other. He watched the man hobble comically back and forth, first pushing the sledge, then pleading with the bull, to no avail. Then the man shrugged his shoulders in a gesture of pain and resignation that was all too familiar. At once, Pao An forgot the race, dropped his yoke, and ran down to stop the man.

"Father!" he yelled frantically. "Stand back. Watch his horns!"

"Aiya? Who calls? Pao An?"

A decrepit scarecrow stood before Pao An. Li Yu was naked except for ragged trousers rolled up above his knees. Pao An grabbed the reins from his father's hands, forgetting good manners. "Who made you do this, Father? Plowing is not for you. You were assigned to cut rice shoots, *hai ma?*"

"This is your uncle's new field. When I went to the shed for the cutting, he sent me here to grade this for tomorrow. This bullock was the last one in the stable—so we have been sowing our disharmony since dawn. We do not understand each other, this bull and I."

"Curse my uncle! Can't you see he wants to hurt you? Ah, Father, this bullock is bad and the sledge is stuck. Let me free it!" Pao An ran around the beast and lifted the heavy sledge over the sharp rock.

Li Yu shuffled behind his son, noticing with pride the ease with which the youth lifted the sledge. "Foolish boy," he scolded affectionately, "you'll tip the stones that way or break your neck." He lifted one skinny arm and made an awkward two-handed gesture in the air. "Do all things with fluid lines. One at a time. First one stone, then the next." Shakily, he picked up a rock that had tumbled out and found that he needed both hands to hold it. Li Yu was barely five feet tall, small even by Kwangtung standards. His long scholar's fingers had been broken by farm labor, and now they were swollen at the joints by arthritis.

"Ho haw! Move you!" Li Yu shouted at the bullock, but when the beast still refused to move, he threw up his hands. "It is useless for me to force him." He turned to regard the bull dreamily, as if it were an old friend rather than a belligerent adversary. Suddenly Li Yu's legs collapsed, and he fell against the animal. When Pao An snatched his father out of the way of the stamping hooves, he discovered that the old man was as light as a sheaf of rice stalks and burning with fever.

Suspicion began to nag at Pao An. Moving inside the radius of the swinging horns, he groped along the stiff harness and found what he had feared. A nail had cut through the strap and dug itself into the animal's neck. He pulled out the nail, loosened the halter, and yanked the reins hard. The beast moved backward, stumbled, and fell on its haunches on the sledge like a broken lady too tired to walk on her lily feet. Li Yu stepped toward the bull.

"Be careful, Father," said Pao An. "The beast is either sick or crazy. Someone gave you a bad harness. Who?"

Li Yu said nothing.

Pao An's rage flared. He slammed down his fist on the handle of the sledge.

Suddenly, from the direction of the village, San Kwei and the collector cantered in on their mounts, spattering mud in all directions. San Kwei leapt off his mount and sloshed through the wet grime, shaking his fist at Li Yu and glaring at Pao An. "Can't you make this old wreck work for you? Why can't you do a single job I give you? Give me that stick!" He snatched the driving rod from Li Yu's hand and prodded the dazed animal in the ribs. "My cousin has no damn sense for beasts," he declared to the collector smugly. "And no wonder. You have to show them command!" He began to beat the animal hard about the neck and haunches until it shifted and got unsteadily to its feet.

"Perhaps you should command your cousin in the same fashion so he might learn," the collector said drily.

"Sorry, Cousin," said Li Yu. "You're quite right. I have no understanding of animals." As he spoke, he looked steadily at his son's clenched hands.

"Then get out of the way. You're distracting him. Pao An, get in front and make the bullock charge you. Maybe your ugly face can get him to move."

Pao An could barely contain his anger at the headman's insults and at the darker mischief he suspected San Kwei had arranged. He wished that Li Yu would not constrain him with downcast eyes and measured words. Li Yu's passivity hid a spirit stronger than iron; yet Pao An had never seen Li Yu display a trace of fire to San Kwei, whose jealousy over Li Yu's past prowess as a scholar had festered over the years. Pao An suffered for his father, although he had to admit that every altercation with San Kwei seemed to enhance Li Yu's dignity.

While San Kwei ranted, Pang and the others hurried along the dike, laughing and calling disaster on Pao An's head while staggering under their uneven loads. "Hui, Manchu! The headman's caught you by your sack now!"

Pao An gritted his teeth. May the Thunder God strike the headman and this fat bloodsucking demon, he swore. May their bones be ground to powder. They had beaten him again!

The headman heard neither Pang's rude words nor saw Pao An's anger, so intent was he on punishing the exhausted bullock. Sweat lathered the animal's shrunken flanks, and he hooked blindly right and left, bleating, still without moving. His long pink tongue lolled in his mouth, and foam flecked his snout and washboard ribs.

"Forgive me, Cousin," Li Yu said pleasantly, "but knowing nothing as I do of animals, it seems to me that this bullock is sick."

The collector gave a shrill whoop that sounded more like a hyena than a man.

"Eh?" The headman whirled about to see where the sound came from. The beast tossed his head unexpectedly and raked San Kwei's forearm with a horn.

"Aaiiee!" A track of blood welled up along the headman's arm. "You sack of bones, I fix you." He charged behind the bullock and thrust the stick under its tail. The animal bucked, roared, twisted toward his assailant, and then fell forward awkwardly into the mud. Again and again, San Kwei jammed the point of the stick into the fallen animal, who struggled to regain his footing. Then the sledge jerked and sent San Kwei toppling backward into the mud.

At that, the collector's horse reared up in blind panic, his front legs flailing the air.

"Aaiiee!" The collector hung on to the saddle horn. "Help me!"

Pao An saw his chance. He ran up and grabbed the reins, and while appearing to calm the horse, kicked the beast in the scrotum instead. The horse streaked across the muddy field, with the collector screaming in terror on its back. A hundred yards away, he tumbled to the ground. Pao An had already turned back solicitously to San Kwei.

"This pig shit bullock has cut me once before," San Kwei yelled at Pao An. "Last time with his hoof. I should have gelded him that time if he were not gelded already!" He climbed up on the sledge again with a murderous look, drew back his elbow, and stuck the point of the stick in the bull's anus.

Pao An grabbed his arm before San Kwei lunged. "You've punished him enough, Uncle. Look what has happened to our honored master, the collector. The bullock frightened his horse and now the horse has thrown him."

"Eh? What do you say?" San Kwei shook the bloodlust from his head.

"Ride over and see if he broke his neck. Quickly or General Li may punish our village. Go, I'll take care of the bullock."

"You don't know how to handle animals," San Kwei began again, unnerved. "Your mischief nearly cost me an arm, and if the collector's dead, you're to blame. Not me! Don't you know this one is vicious, blind in one eye. He hooks to his blind side." Realizing he had said too much, he railed louder in pretended outrage. He pushed his pug face into Li Yu's, his straggly beard quivering. "I hold you responsible, Cousin. You made him angry and distracted me when he hooked. If he dies, you pay. On New Year's when the accounts are settled, you pay your back rent and the full cost of the bull."

Li Yu held out empty hands, unmoved. "Empty my bowl, Cousin. You only bring me closer to the Way."

San Kwei stopped ranting and mounted his horse with a look of profound contempt. "You're a fool."

"No man is a fool if he can greet death like a friend."

"Then be glad I'm not a fool. If I throw you off my land, you'll drown like a dog in his own vomit. Greet that. You need me. You pay me respect, or I'll plow your carcass into the mud. Who will burn incense for you then? That lame crab there?"

With a touch softer than a moth's wing, Li Yu held Pao An back. San Kwei dug his heels into his horse and galloped to where the collector was stumbling, covered with mud, and holding his injured ribs.

"One day, Father, I'll stick his head on a stake before your door."

Like most Punti fathers, Li Yu rarely touched his son. Now he covered Pao An's mouth with one hand. "I should beat you for such disrespect. You do not know what you say. Everything depends on that rude, low man. What has come over you? Go, get water for this poor creature."

Pao An helped his father to sit on the sledge and went for water. Coating the outside of his conical straw hat with clay, he filled its ample interior with water from the canal. Then he held his hat for the stunned and bloodied beast. The small red eyes watched through a white film, but the bullock drank and after a moment struggled to its feet.

"I'll take him back to the stalls," said Li Yu. "His days are numbered anyway. There is nothing for you to fear. Your uncle has used up his anger at me for today."

"Let me take the bullock, Father."

"No, you made Uncle a vow to carry stone. Everybody heard. Do not shame me. Do what you promised."

"Then remember to walk on his right side, Father. He is afraid of what he can't see. Uncle knew that."

"Then Uncle forgot."

Li Yu led the bullock slowly, painfully away. Pao An went back to the dike, lifted his yoke, and found the path to the sluice gate. His heart felt ready to explode, and he prayed to Kwan Kung, the God of War, that his hands and feet might be ready when the time was right. Sweat dripped down his dirty cheeks, not tears, not tears. Shame, he thought, unmanly shame.

Watching Li Yu lead the sick animal away, Pao An began to weep for them both, the old man and the bull.

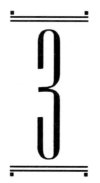

San Kwei had his revenge. Like every village in the Land of Flowers, On Ting was periodically obliged to send a number of able-bodied men to keep dikes, levees, and public roads in repair. The headman knew how to take care of troublesome youths. He assigned Pao An and Pang to double duty on a county corvée—a labor gang—to serve the time that four men would have typically shared: four months in all. For Pao An, it was a double punishment, not only because the labor was cruel and backbreaking but because Li Yu would have to till their small plot alone, thus sentencing them both to another year of food shortage because of the impossibility of paying off their debt to San Kwei. Pao An was afraid to leave his father, but Li Yu explained that four months out of the headman's reach would cool Pao An's temper and San Kwei's resentment.

Pao An spent the first week hauling rock and digging trenches to drain ponds and flood basins and carrying brick to repair levee walls. He and Pang slept in a lean-to without blankets and ate cold rice flavored with fish paste, but the labor that was meant to grind them down only fanned their rebellious spirits. They found other youths like themselves, wild, discontent, impatient, who were also being punished for impious behavior by clan elders or local magistrates.

After the first week, when the corvée guards had sneaked off to the river to smoke their nightly cache of black dirt, and the corvée workers were eating in the cook tent, a dark, sullen youth from the Mau village put down his empty rice bowl in the dirt and arranged his chopsticks to form a triangle across his bowl. Pang recognized the sign, a Triad symbol, and caught the forked fingers Mau flashed to the others.

"Red Turban meeting tonight," Pang whispered self-importantly in Pao An's ear.

"Not me. I'm a filial son," one young man replied nervously. "My father would cut out my heart and tongue if he finds out."

The skinny Mau boy frowned in disgust. "Filial! You mean scared. We need true men of Han, not girls who piss at the sight of blood."

"I take on any big-bellied Manchu," Pang declared, with a sharp jab at Pao An's shoulder.

"Pah," grunted the boy named Mau. "Every child is brave if the enemy is far away. Can you cut the neck of your landlord? Or better yet, your headman? They are our real enemies because they do the will of the Manchu demons. We need men who aren't afraid to turn heaven and earth upside down."

In the silence, Pao An's cheeks began to burn.

After the second week, a new leader was posted to the corvée—Fan, General Li's rent collector. The general had suggested Fan's name to provincial officials who were only too glad to promote a local man to the post in order to save their own resources and men for other tasks. Complicity between state officials and local gentry was the typical means of governing, but the unfairness of a system that rewarded leeches such as the collector enraged and depressed Pao An. In the past weeks, he had observed that the inequities he and Li Yu suffered at the hands of their clansmen were spread throughout the county and, he supposed, throughout the empire: the entire tax system was corrupt. The wealthy scholars of the gentry class paid not more but less tax by law, because it was assumed that the superior man earned the reward of enriching himself. Pao An was grimly amused that most of the gang's efforts were spent repairing the levees abutting General Li's fields and dredging the filth from Li's fishponds and irrigation ditches, labor at which Li's own peasants would have balked. The Lis owned acres of mulberry groves and several silk factories in the foothills and thus controlled the prices for leaves, worms, flats, thread, cloth, and bolts in Kwangtung Province. Gradually, they had swallowed up most of the clan-owned mulberry groves in nearby counties as well.

At twilight one evening of the third week, the men of the corvée dragged long shadows in the dust as they returned to the crude lean-tos set up for them one mile away from Abundant Spring Mountain, the general's great house overlooking the Pearl River. Bone weary, glad to escape the dank fields and channels and the night spirits that inhabited them, they came to where the lights burned against the edges of the outer darkness. Those with opium hunger drifted off to the tents of the corvée guards, who bartered their cache for whatever a man had to sell. Some stopped to drink from the well where a wandering Taoist priest told fortunes during the day.

Pao An alone lingered in the wet fields waist deep in water, scooping the silt from the bottom of one of the general's fishponds. He stayed, not because he liked the foul, debilitating work, but because he hated to leave any job half-done. The effluvia he was scooping out of the bed of the pond—a mixture of cocoons, insect and fish droppings, and human waste—would be poured over the mulberry plants in the fields as fertilizer.

Normally he liked the outside work of the silk industry, which was the typical province of men—catching fish in the ponds, pruning the trees, picking the young mulberry leaves for the worms' food. In his home village, women did the inside work of tending the worm flats and drawing off the cocoon thread. But this part of the cycle, dredging the fishponds for fertilizer, was particularly loathsome. Filthy from the neck down, he was determined to finish that evening so that he couldn't be reassigned to the same place by the collector.

Sure that his stomach would rebel at food after the day's long labor in the cesspool, he had given up his ration of rice to Pang. Besides, he was too excited to eat: that night, the long-awaited meeting of the Red Turban Society, a local sect of the Triads, was to occur. The Mau boy had promised to take the On Ting youths to the secret meeting in a warehouse approximately a mile and a half away. They had pooled their last dirty coins to bribe the night guards into letting them sneak off, although nothing would have awakened the guards from their opium torpor. The regional leader of the Triads was expected, and Mau explained to Pao An how great an honor it would be to be inducted by his hands.

The camp was already dark when Pao An climbed the footpath into the clearing in the mulberry grove. Through a light veil of rain, he watched the spirit lamps wink on in the main cook tent, signaling the dinner hour. Fuel was too scarce to waste on light, so as soon as the buckets of rice and vegetables were consumed and the laborers went to their lean-tos to fall into exhausted sleep, the lamps were snuffed out. Pao An stopped at the well, stripped, and threw a bucket of water over his body. Shadowy forms loomed on the walls of the cook tent. The water was so cold that it made him gasp, but he emptied bucket after bucket over his head while scraping the oily filth out of his hair and off his limbs. Snatches of gutteral invective came his way. He could smell the sweet, cloying smoke from the guards' pipes, which were pinpricks of fire on the dark edge of the river.

Pao An could barely make out the shadows of corvée guards as they squatted on the ground, but he could feel their eyes measuring his worth and availability. A man called out an invitation in an opium-coarsened voice while the others laughed. Pao An bit his lip to keep from cursing the gods for turning fools like these into dragons, while strong youths like himself were kicked aside like dirt. He rinsed out his trousers and pulled them on soaking wet. Trembling from the cold bath, he hurried into the cook tent and stepped around Pang, who was squatting on the earthen floor with a bowl pushed against his open mouth, chopsticks furiously shoveling in rice. Pang ignored him, so he staggered to their lean-to and collapsed on his wooden pallet.

He closed his eyes and imagined himself in the boys' house in On Ting. Most boys in On Ting spent the years between puberty and marriage separated from clan girls, whom they could not marry. They were under the care and supervision of the elders until they married a girl from another clan and returned to their fathers' houses. There was no such woman in all the world for him, he thought bitterly. Not even an ugly one. He would never be able to afford a wife unless she came to him dowryless and of her own free will.

The next thing he knew, someone was shaking him awake. Pang's pug face thrust itself through the gloom. Pao An arose, still groggy, and followed Pang past the row of lean-tos filled with snoring men, past the tent where the guards lay in an opium trance. Now there were half a dozen of them—the Mau boy, Pang, and a few other frightened youths. The moon was stealing like a bandit through a thick blanket of clouds as they hurried stealthily across the mulberry groves to a big warehouse.

The door opened a crack at Mau's knock.

"Where were you born?" came a gruff whisper.

"Under a peach tree in the Vermilion Garden," growled Mau in return.

"Why is your tunic so worn?"

"It was passed down by the Five Ancestors."

A hand reached out and pulled them into the cavernous room.

A hundred men, mostly youths under twenty, were squatting on their haunches yelling out bets and insults in a room lit by smoky torches. The local leader, who was seated with others around a wooden table, rose with a frown to admonish Mau for his tardiness. They whispered together and Mau returned, his teeth a pale ribbon of light in his dark face. Yes, he grinned at Pao An, One-Clean-Sweep, the regional director, was present that night to induct Pao An and the others into the cell. Pang began to babble loudly until Mau clamped a rough hand over his mouth and pointed.

One-Clean-Sweep was a sniveling stick, Pao An decided, more like a beggar than a leader of men. Even his name, "One-Clean-Sweep," was misleading: it did not denote the viciousness of the man's sword arm but referred to a homemade salve of "fly poison grass" used for ringworm, leg ulcers, insect bites, and maggoty sores. Mau whispered that the leader was an itinerant herb vendor and occasional bell-doctor. And One-Clean-Sweep looked the part: bare-chested, old, thin as a hoe, he squatted on his haunches in the dirt and nodded as if he were asleep. But when he raised his head to speak to the local leader, his whining, high-pitched voice carried over the cacophony in the warehouse.

There was a round of introductions, bows, and high-minded speeches until Mau was called up to present One-Clean-Sweep to the assembly. The old man stepped up on an overturned wooden rice bin so that all could see him. Torches stuck in wall stanchions sent shifting waves of light across the gloom.

"If I had fished for a grandfather carp and caught that one, I would throw him back in," Pang whispered.

"Hush," said the Mau boy. He pointed to his own head and then to the old man's own red turban. "I heard he cut his pigtail, like the God Worshipers."

Except for the uninitiated, the Red Turbans wore a red cloth wrapped around their head; none had gone so far as to cut off the queue, for to do so was to make one's rebelliousness visible to all. Pao An squinted at the regional leader's headband, a curious affair with five red loops dangling from the cloth, and decided from the bulge at the back that Mau was wrong.

"Cell leaders, young men, Red Turbans all," the herb vendor began in a wheezing voice. "We are here tonight for a planting—" A fit of coughing nearly knocked the old man off his makeshift podium. Pao An shifted his feet to keep from smiling. One-Clean-Sweep painstakingly rolled up one leg of his dirty trousers past his knobby knee, leaving the other to dangle incongruously around the ankle, and began again. It had, Pao An realized, some sort of symbolic meaning. "I say again, we are here to transplant tender shoots into a great field of revolution."

There was an answering sigh of assent in the crowd. Mau shook his fist and shouted the slogan of the rebels, "Kill the Ching emperor, restore the Ming!" The old man's head snapped up and all the muscles of his leathery body tensed.

"Kill? Kill?" he growled. "Oh, my impatient young brother, but we are peaceful, simple men. We are here to plant, not to kill. We are here to sow. We are here to warm the silkworm still curled in its blind sleep." He lowered his head and paused so long that Pao An wondered if the old man were dozing. The room breathed with him. One-Clean-Sweep raised his head dreamily and leaned over the edge of his make-shift platform. His finger shot out like an arrow, singling out first one man, then another, while he whispered, "Heaven will bring the harvest."

Suddenly, the finger found Pao An. The youth's skin prickled as if an icy wind had suddenly swept into the crowded warehouse.

"Look at my hand," the old man growled, and held out an open palm. He spread wide his short, stubby fingers, and slowly turned the palm up to the dark, smoke-filled rafters. "Empty. It carries no weapon— and even the last grain of rice has been stolen out of it. The hand of the people is empty, and yet the demons are demanding more. In Kwangsi, after a drought, a whole district was put to the sword because the people hung the tax collector who was extorting five times more than customary from them. The hand of the people is empty! I have stood in the courtyard of Li, the wicked general, and watched a daughter of Han defile herself with the son of that rotten house. The hand is empty . . . but wait! In Chin Tien village at Thistle Mountain, thousands are gathering under our brother, Hung Hsiu Chuan. Thousands are leaving their homes to follow him. And the pig that squats on the throne is sending out the demon imps to slay these good, brave sisters and brothers. And why? When the hand of the people is empty! I have seen with my own eyes strong Punti sons sold like pigs to the barbarians overseas, seen with my own eyes long lines of them pulling the rice barges on the Grand Canal northward into the insatiable maw of the Manchu dogs. While the stomach and the mouth and the hand of the people are empty—but look now! The empty hand is the hand of Heaven."

He closed his fingers one by one to make a fist, then swung it in the air so that it seemed to give new flame to the torches behind him. With one swift motion, he brought it down like a falling ax into the palm of his other hand. And instantly, there was a sea of fists pommeling the air and a great roar from the crowd.

One-Clean-Sweep held his fist above his head and bellowed, "What do we need of daggers and swords? Each finger is a dagger! Each hand is a sword! Like a fist, we are one!"

As one, the men shouted back his words.

"I am a Turban," he exulted.

"Turban!" they cried back.

"I am one with my brothers."

"My brothers!"

"I am ready to die."

"To die!"

"Kill the Ching! Bring back the Ming!"

And again they echoed him.

He leaped down from the rice bin, "Bring the initiates forth."

Pao An, Pang, and a half dozen others pressed forward, pushed by many hands. Faceless men pulled off the boys' shirts so that they all stood half-naked, clad only in loincloths, in a semicircle around an awesome apparition. Pao An gasped at the transformation of One-Clean-Sweep. The old man had put on a long red robe marked with curious signs in black ink. Three of them Pao An recognized from temple decorations as the symbolic markings on Buddha's foot—a fish; an angular, twisted knot; and a swastika enclosed in a circle. The old man blazed forth in the darkness like a god sprung out of fire. He held his arm outstretched, with the second and last fingers extended like the horns of a dragon over the heads of the men.

"Are you ready to do the will of Heaven?"

The youths nodded.

"Are you willing to die that the brothers may live?"

Again, they nodded.

"Will you swear to defend this family, obey your leaders as you do your father, and on pain of death never reveal the law, the command, the secret signs, or the names of any of your brothers? Swear!"

They swore.

"Will you open your doors to your brothers, give them the last grain from your bowl? Swear!"

"I swear," whispered Pao An. Thirty-three more times he swore.

"Bow down."

All of them knelt on the floor in the position of extreme kowtow, and knocked their heads on the dirt.

"Then may you be struck by five thunderbolts, speared by ten thousand daggers, your sons and daughters swept into the mouth of Hell if you break the oaths." He held the finger of his left hand straight up toward the ceiling and pointed the finger of his right hand toward the floor. Slowly, the right hand moved over the heads of the prostrate men and touched his heart. "Rise now, brothers, and die."

Pao An was the first to die. His heart was beating with fury, fear, joy as two men led him to the rice bin where One-Clean-Sweep had stood moments before. Now it was covered with a red cloth and held a mirror, some rusty scales, and an abacus, by which Pao An knew that his virtues would be examined and measured. He was bent backward, his head pulled back to expose the neck. The torches crackled and the light wavered. Then One-Clean-Sweep knelt on his one bare knee in the dust and pulled a knife from his belt.

"Know death," One-Clean-Sweep intoned, and brought the blade down as slowly as a falling star. It blinded Pao An with its light. It seemed to sing to him of war and fire and the death chants of a mighty race of heroes. He felt warm where he wet himself.

The blade nicked his throat; One-Clean-Sweep took a cup and caught the dark drops of blood that flowed from the wound and poured it into a bowl.

Then the two who held him pulled his loincloth aside while One-Clean-Sweep pressed on Pao An's thigh the sign of a snake etched in red ink with needles. They tied up his queue around his head, wrapped his head in a red rag, and made him travel the circuit of the warehouse on his knees. They led him through the "mountain of knives," a heap of dirt studded with sharp rocks; "the red flower pavilion," a makeshift curtain of tattered red cloth; a bamboo hoop called the "circle of heaven and earth"; a "fiery furnace" of burning joss paper; a muddy trail of "shifting stones." When he tottered across the rough strips of wood called the "two-planked bridge," they tied his hands behind his back and dragged him to the rice bin. One-Clean-Sweep held out a small cup balanced on the blade of a machete. Pao An dipped his tongue into the cup. It tasted as thick and warm as a heady rich wine, his own blood mixed with the blood of his brothers.

The brothers roared their approval when Pao An lifted his head, his mouth stained red from the cup. One-Clean-Sweep plunged a burning joss stick into the bloody cup and held the smoky taper aloft, and Pao An knew that his life would be thus snuffed out if he broke the oaths he had taken that night.

At last he belonged.

After serving four months, Pao An and Pang were released from the corvée back to On Ting, secretly swearing eternal fealty to their new brother, Mau. Early summer was slowly yielding to the variegated days of a transitional season, neither hazy and hot, nor windy and wet monsoon.

Pao An and Pang were set to work stripping leaves with their hands in a small communal plot in the marshland near the banyan grove. Pao An worked furiously, partly because he was nervous and partly to take up the slack for the slow-moving Pang, who had a hangover from a black-dirt dream the night before. Pang now needed one pipe in the morning simply to stop his head from throbbing, but the result was that he often could not work. By midmorning, however, Pang had crawled out of his lethargy and the two had fallen into an easy work rhythm. In another two hours, they had filled four baskets apiece—much less than they would have if Pang had been whole. Pao An poured the leaves into two long conical carrying baskets that hung from shoulder height to the ground; then he tied the strap around Pang's head and he and Pang started off to the nearby silk farms at Sun Tien Di a couple of miles to the south. Because the day was particularly fine, Pao An chose the scenic road across the fallow end of the paddies that paralleled the river before turning toward the banyan grove and the market town beyond.

Although it was the longer route to Sun Tien Di, Pang did not protest; he was growing bored and irritated with the labor and welcomed the chance to dawdle and talk story and wished he had a pipeful of dirt to smoke along the way.

The sun was at its acme in the heavens. The last of the morning fog had burnt off, and the brown hills stood with fresh-washed clarity against the pale yellow sky. As they walked, the watery green fields slipped slowly by. Behind the youths, a line of harvesters had marched to the extreme edge of the field. It was the time of day when exhaustion begins its long, slow creep into the body. Pang was growing more edgy and unstable. The drug craving was coming over him.

Southwest along the levee road, a cloud of dust was rising. On the soft breeze came the distant whisper of a flute, a sharp answering clang, and muffled voices chanting rhythmically. Pao An squinted against the sun and saw a dark column of men and horses winding slowly toward them.

"Cymbals?" asked Pang in bewilderment. "It must be a funeral, *hai ma?*"

Pao An felt a rush of excitement. He churned his legs harder under the weight of the heavy load.

"A procession that long means a rich man, maybe a minister of the first or second degree," said Pang. "The only one that big is General Li from Abundant Spring Mountain. Second Uncle heard he lost his heart for fighting after his mother died last year. Maybe he followed the old lady to the Yellow Springs." Pang's small black eyes were dancing.

Pang's casual mention of the general's possible death filled Pao An with mixed emotions. He wished Li dead, but wanted to be the one to kill him. He helped Pang hide their baskets in a ditch at the side of the road. They climbed up the muddy bank and broke into a run, swerving onto a narrow path through the marsh. Then they jogged up a small slope and stepped up onto the levee road. The procession was three hundred yards away, shimmering in the dust and heat. Masked dancers leapt toward them like phantom tigers. A lone flute pleaded shrilly with an angry cymbal. Other reeds joined in the discordant chorus while the cymbals clanged and raucous male laughter cut through the din.

"Oh ho! Not a funeral—a wedding!" Pang guffawed. "But what big-foot girl gets to wed on the morning of a workday?"

Pao An's curiosity mounted. "That's no village girl's wedding. There must be at least two hundred marchers. The family's too rich to come from a farming village." He felt his spirits rising at the chance to glimpse a high-born virgin passing above the heads of the crowd in her bridal litter. Weddings were a highlight of village life. Even in On Ting, where existence was marginal, parents vied with those of other, equally poor villages to provide as much music, food, and rented finery as their meager fortunes would allow. Pao An and Pang had followed many a village girl to her husband's door, and Pang was considered a master at reducing a girl to embarrassed tears at the bride-teasing while the drunken husband looked helplessly on. But neither of them had ever seen a rich girl's processional before.

On the other side of the levee road, thick-trunked banyan trees filled an acre of land, projecting into the river. Pao An climbed a large lemon tree with Pang scrambling up after him. The tree grew at a crazy angle out of the paddy side of the marsh, but it gave a good view of the road.

In moments, the procession was upon them. The marchers snaked by in a swaying column of drums, flutes, and crashing cymbals. First came two horsemen, each holding an immense pole from which floated a long red banner. One banner bore the name "Wang," the other "Li." Pang cheered as the name flags passed. The officers scrutinized him warily from the backs of their prancing mounts.

"The two big families," Pang chuckled, making an obscene coupling gesture with his fingers.

At the sight of the Li flag and the road lined with Li soldiers, Pao An felt his stomach twist with anger. And what if the general himself should ride by? If he had a knife with him, he'd leap down and shove the blade into the throat of the murderer of his clan.

Behind the banner carriers came two more riders. Pao An recognized the one nearest their tree as Fan, the rent collector, who was accompanying the bride as the groom's emissary and had exchanged his pale robes for bright red. Fan looked at Pao An with a sneer of recognition and pointed him out to the other rider, a dignified young man wearing the robes and insignia of a provincial magistrate. In his left hand the magistrate held a banner of red felt marked with signs to deflect evil spirits and bad luck from the bride. This was a task the bride's brother usually performed. To have a magistrate play this familial role demonstrated the power of the bride's family in official circles.

Fan's presence at the head of the procession turned Pao An's blood cold. It was like finding a snake in a basket of eggs. Pao An's eyes nervously followed the sinister Fan and the magistrate down the dirt road. The horses moved like the feet of dragon dancers, beating the fine dust into puffs of exploding powder while the name flags curled and snapped in the rising wind.

In the riders' wake, barefoot boys in black pajamas marched by with huge conical lanterns lit from within by burning candles. They floated above the procession like accompanying angels. Each lantern was stamped with the "double-hey" linked ideogram of connubial joy. Giggling, the smallest servant boys poked each other with rented umbrellas and cardboard pikes, playing at war.

"That's good, generals," Pang crowed. And the boys strutted bow-legged like warrior-kings, savoring the applause.

After the boys had danced beyond the tree, fifty stern-faced Han guards wearing Li insignia draped over their chests and carrying muzzle-loading muskets came into view. A thick pigtail trailed from every helmet like the long black tail of a horse. Under the embroidered breastplates, they wore jackets of bark pulp, which made them sweat profusely.

Then the flutists and cymbalists stepped forth like stiff-legged geese in their green uniforms and red-tasseled hats, followed by drummers with castanets and barrel drums. The *dok-dok-dok* of their tympany raised Pao An's pulse and caused Pang to shout louder to make himself heard.

Pang waved madly at one musician on the outside line. "Hui, you boy! Who's the girl causing all this noise? Does she live around here?"

"Not from this ugly mud flat. She's from Canton! Old Wang, the salt merchant, marries off his third granddaughter today. Since the old man is superstitious he sent her from her aunt's house downriver instead of Canton. The miser couldn't stand a bad luck loss from his own house," the boy yelled over the drumming, taking the grandeur of the procession as his own.

No girl, rich or poor, the youths knew, could be married directly out of her own house or luck would drain away from her family. "A smart man. A careful man. Tell Wang, the God of Wealth, when you see him next that Farmer Pang would gladly sit at his knee and learn wisdom," Pang cried. Suddenly a wild thought seemed to seize Pang. "Aaiiee!" he yelled. "She must be ugly, her feet the size of mulberry baskets, if her grandfather needs muskets to prod the groom to bed!"

A flutist retorted, "I take the ugliest Canton whore and match her against the prettiest girl in your village any day!"

"Ha! I hear Canton girls have hairy legs like oceanic barbarians and squawk like ducks," Pang shouted to Pao An. He erupted in high-pitched duck sounds while moving his hands as if to fan his face like a shy lady.

Pao An watched Pang anxiously, studying the unnatural effects of the opium-hunger on his cousin, and for a while forgot about the musicians as they hammered on their barrel drums and swung their flutes.

Pang rubbed his hands together lewdly. "Tell the grandfather, if he needs a guard for this girl, I'm trustworthy."

The drummer yelled back, enjoying the joke, "You would be, too. Old Wang gelds his houseboys, like the emperor!"

Pang howled and grabbed his crotch in pretended pain; he somersaulted backward off his limb and nimbly landed on his feet to the immense amusement of the musicians. The young drummer pounded his stick in glee and roared at the impromptu acrobatics.

Hard on the musicians' heels came masked acrobats, who cavorted on the road for their audience of two. Pang tried to imitate their handsprings and backbends, but all he got for his efforts was a tumble in the dirt.

Next marched a dozen overweight priests in dusty saffron robes, each chanting the Buddhist prothalamion and sweating from the unaccustomed rigor of their journey.

"Hui! Reverend Masters! Put your hands behind your backs. I'll give you something," Pang shouted, with a wink to Pao An, for priests were known to covet money pressed on them at weddings and funerals, to make their vow of poverty easier to bear.

When the priests ignored him, Pang waddled alongside their train, holding his arms in a circle in front as if he had a bulging belly and putting on a pious face.

"You better watch yourself, Dead Boy," Pao An warned. "They lock you in the cangue if you mock priests." He imagined Pang's round face stuck like a gourd atop the forty-pound cangue, which brought shame as well as punishment to the evildoer—the image was ghastly.

" 'Dead Boy' yourself! I want to see what the bride looks like." Pang marched beside the contingent of marching priests, who swung their steaming censers at him to chase away the taint of his presence along the road.

Then Pao An looked up and yelled, for behind the priests he saw what Pang could not: the bridal palanquin festooned with flowers and hanging lanterns.

The palanquin was a carved mahogany box the size of a large cupboard, crowned with a pointed roof and decorated with red tassels and mother-of-pearl. Inside there was room for only one person to sit on a cushioned bench; sliding doors and heavy red curtains hid small windows from which the rider could peer without being seen. The ride was as precarious as a trip on stormy waters, but every person of consequence in China was carried, gladly sacrificing comfort for status. Officials and rich landowners were carried because their wealth and learning decreed that they need not exert themselves in walking. Gentry women were carried because they could neither be seen by the vulgar crowd nor go very far on their tiny lily feet. But any bride, of whatever class, had to be carried to her husband's door, for it was bad luck for the family that took her in if her feet touched the ground on her nuptial journey.

The marriage chair followed the last of the sweating, murmuring priests. Its bearers strutted with one arm akimbo and the other clutching their poles, proud to be carrying a virgin bride who was, moreover, granddaughter to the richest man in the southern provinces.

"Hui! Goddess lady! Stick your head out your mountain tower! Pang, the warrior, wants to see your face. Let's see if a hairy Canton girl is worth this commotion!" Pang trotted beside the sedan chair, ignoring the curses and kicks of the bearers and proud of his own audacity.

Pao An leapt off the tree and grabbed Pang's arm. "Do you want to feel the cangue, Dead Boy?" he hissed.

"Not me!" Pang said defiantly. "I want to feel her golden lilies!"

Just then, the carved window opened and the curtains were parted by a small hand. Gold and jade glowed on the thin white fingers. A girl's frightened face, powdered stark white, appeared in the window— the perfectly oval, "watermelon seed" face of the classic Han beauty. She had removed her heavy veil because of the heat and now looked out at them in utter confusion. Her headdress of hanging flowers, pearls, ribbons, and embroidered tassels shimmered with her quavering. Beneath the headdress and the elaborately coiled coiffure were small pouting lips painted crimson, crescent brows drawn as fine as willow leaves with a single stroke, and kohl-darkened eyes, brilliant and filled with fear.

"What do you want?" the girl asked.

The youths stumbled along beside her litter, struck dumb but unable to take their eyes off the bride's face. Never had they seen such a face! Her lynx eyes looked blankly at Pao An, who had flushed crimson.

"A fox-spirit," gasped Pang.

"Fox-spirit?" she said, and turned her head round, as if expecting a ghost to materialize out of the churning dust. Slowly, her eyes began to focus, and she seemed to see for the first time the two paddy boys alongside her chair. "I was sleeping, dreaming," she told them, "and you woke me, you frightened me. I was dreaming my husband had fangs like a dog. But a dream can't hurt you, can it?" she asked in a shaky voice.

Pao An thought her the most beautiful creature he had ever seen. Her words were like wind chimes, each syllable clear, soaring, unbearably high. The simplicity of her manner, despite her elaborate dress, made her more a child than a woman about to be wed. Suddenly she covered her mouth with her long red sleeve and giggled. "Perhaps I'm dreaming now." she said to herself. "Nothing's real, everything is changing." Frightened, she quickly ducked back into the palanquin, letting the curtain fall. They heard her talking to herself in her high-pitched voice as the bearers carried her swiftly away.

"A she-devil," said Pang softly, knocking his head to throw off the girl's spell. Pao An gazed after the retreating chair, transfixed.

Fan rode up so sharply that the flank of his mount crashed into Pao An, knocking him down. Iron-shod hooves stamped around Pao An's outstretched legs. "Get your dirty eyes out of here, village lice!" He spat and swung a short ceremonial sword at them. "I know your headman. He'll peel your skin off when he finds out how you defiled this wedding parade. Get your bad luck eyes out of here." He spurred his mount forward, leaving Pao An sprawled in the dirt.

The dazed Pang pulled Pao An up and brushed him off as the procession disappeared in a cloud of dust, music, and droning voices.

"Aiya! Say I'm dreaming. Say that was a demon parade that a heavenly wind whirled away," Pang moaned.

"I don't think so, Cousin," Pao An whispered. "She was real." Fox-spirit! his heart cried out. Pao An knew many tales of fox-spirits: Red Jade, who climbed the garden wall into Scholar Hsiang's bedroom and so ignited his desire that he abandoned his wife, child, and reputation to follow her; Miss Jen, who lost her heart to a wastrel and was eaten by dogs. Li Yu said that the fox was a woman named Tzu who, for her insatiable lust, was transformed into a cunning and beautiful beast. But her supernatural powers also allowed her to turn herself at will into a lovely maiden who brought innocent men to ruin. All the stories warned of the punishments inflicted on mortals who succumbed to the fox. Yet it was also said that no imperial courtesan knew half the pillow tricks of a fox-spirit.

No such woman as this bride existed in On Ting. Village girls were moonfaced and loud, their skin roughened by sun and hard work. The bride was rare white jade, with bones so delicate one would fear crushing her.

"She scares me," Pang declared, for once unable to make a joke. "That face, white like death. I'd take a black barbarian girl from the Fragrant Tree Islands before her."

Pao An had no words to tell Pang how that face burned in his vitals. One look from the bride had made him feel the full force of desire. He had to have her, although he knew it was impossible, for the distance between them was unbridgeable, spanning generations of ironbound tradition. They were as different as a mud hovel surrounded by barking dogs and a high-walled courtyard alive with the music of running water. The thought that she was going into his enemy's house to bear sons with the name Li made him sick with envy and loss.

The riders at the head of the parade disappeared between the banyan grove and the marshland at the point where a long section of the road rose up into a high, narrow causeway above the low-lying floodplain. Since no more than two men could walk abreast on the causeway, the procession slowed. The litter bearers had to move with particular caution, because any misstep would send the heavy palanquin hurtling down into the marshland on one side or into the overgrown banyan grove on the other.

Pang, whose hunger for dirt had returned, was pushing Pao An impatiently back along the road toward the distant patch of reeds where they had hidden their baskets, when, over the waning noise of flutes, came the explosion of firecrackers. Pao An looked up. Not firecrackers. Short, single bursts, like guns firing. Pang hunkered down on the road like a frightened animal. Pao An ran a few paces in the direction of the procession just in time to see the line break apart and men in gay costume running wildly in all directions. Some leapt off the levee road into the marsh, others staggered through the disordered ranks of the startled guardsmen. The horses reared and whinnied. There was a moment of silence, then a single chant: *Sha, sha, sha.* "Kill, kill, kill." And screams. The young drummer who had laughed with the youths along the road fled in their direction. Suddenly he shivered and fell forward like a tree. Two arrows stuck out of his back.

"Bandits!" screamed Pang and ran up to drag Pao An into the safety of the reeds.

"Wait!" said Pao An, struggling free.

"Run! This isn't our fight!"

Another volley of shots rang out, and Pang pulled the startled Pao An down with him into the cover of tall grass just inside the banyan grove. Blue-clad men in the trees were shooting down on the trapped caravan. In vain the terrified bearers tried to move their burden out of the way of falling arrows, but finding their path blocked on all sides, they dropped the litter and jumped off the causeway into the marsh. The bride's frightened cries came from behind the curtains of the palanquin, which had toppled over on its side. Farther down the narrow road, Fan shouted to the guards over screams and gunfire. The guards at the front and rear of the train tried to push their way into the unprotected center of the caravan, but they were sealed off from the attack by the priests, acrobats, and musicians stampeding wildly in all directions.

The arrows drove the rear guards into retreat, leaving the litter defenseless. When Fan ordered a group of General Li's guards to surround the litter, they leapt off the causeway into the marshes and ran away. Seeing them flee, Fan lost all his courage and stumbled after them.

"Coward!" the magistrate shouted in disgust. "General Li will hear of this!" He beat at the scattering soldiers with a bridal banner trying to force them back toward the banyan grove, while spurring his mount toward the bride, who was hurling curses at the escaping guards. One of Li's guardsmen rallied the remaining men to defend the bride, but before he could raise his musket, an arrow pierced his throat and knocked him backward. With a painful effort, he rose on his knees and pulled the arrow out with both hands. A red wave poured over his forearms as he gazed at his bloody hands in dismay. When the rest of the guards saw their comrade fall, they lost their courage and began to run, only to be cut down by a dozen bandits who ran out of the woods under a volley of arrows. Dressed in blue pajamas with long braids flying out from their cone-shaped straw hats, the bandits looked like any paddy-laborer in the county. Pao An wondered whether some farmers had wandered into the fray by mistake.

A high-pitched scream took Pao An by surprise. Two bandits were dragging the bride out of the litter. "They've stolen the bride!" he cried to Pang.

Sha, sha, sha. "Kill, kill, kill!" the chant droned.

"Aiya, my father. Take me home," mumbled Pang, his face in the dirt. "I'm scared. Where's my mulberry baskets? Hui, where you going?"

"I've got to help."

"Help who? The bandits don't need us."

"No. The girl."

"How are you going to help?" Pang whimpered through mud-caked lips. "Help your cousin run home! Help save him for his sons! You got a musket in your pants? Aiya! You do—the fox-girl caught you by your yang, Dead Boy."

Pao An crawled up the bank, but Pang grabbed him by the ankle. With a rough kick, Pao An broke loose and slipped through the reeds.

Pang lowered his face into the dirt. "Oh my father," he moaned. He got up slowly on his haunches, looked around in dread, and crawled after his friend.

Pao An pushed his way through the underbrush, keeping his body low and watching for bandits. All through the grove, the chant echoed. Dark shapes darted across the dappled light. He crouched in a tangle of roots near the egg-shaped rock barely daring to breathe. The thieves, he realized, were few, no more than two dozen armed with knives, crossbows, and a few muskets. They had relied on surprise to overcome the heavily armed guards, and now the panicked soldiers would be wary of entering the grove. They wouldn't risk themselves to save the life of a mere merchant's daughter.

Out of the corner of his eye, Pao An saw a sudden movement and a flash of red. No more than forty paces away, two bandits were dragging the struggling, kicking bride past the egg-shaped rock. Her dress was thrown over her head, revealing slim legs tangled under a thin underskirt.

"A devil!" one bandit cried. He loosened his grasp and slapped her covered head. The muffled screams grew louder.

"Keep her quiet," hissed his tall, dark-browed companion. "I'll call back the others. We have what we want. Now we can launch the boats." He darted ahead, swerving around an outcrop of stone, and vaulted over roots and fallen vines.

As soon as the big bandit vanished, the girl began to squirm so violently that her lone captor tripped over one of the running roots of a banyan tree, releasing his hold. The girl landed heavily on her side. Still dazed from the fall, she pulled her skirt away from her face and screamed curses at her kidnapper.

"Such filth from that pretty mouth," he growled, crawling forward and jerking back the fallen coils of her long hair. He hit her in the face with the flat of his hand. "Not what you're used to from the likes of us. You're used to doing the slapping, *hai ma*?" He pulled her head back hard and saw the blood streaming from her nose and mouth.

"Not so pretty now, Young Mistress," he said to the sobbing girl. "But still better than what I'm used to. If we had a little time now, I wouldn't have to wait in line later." With his knife, he ripped the seam of her thin white pantaloons. Laughing deep in his throat, he tried to grab her again, when a blow to his back sent him sprawling in the dirt.

Before the villian could turn around, Pao An had twisted the bandit's long braid around his neck like a garrote and yanked it tight. When the man began to gurgle, Pao An shoved his knee into the arched spine and pulled so hard that the queue was buried in the swollen folds of the man's neck. There was a sharp crack like the breaking of dry bamboo. The man flopped over like a fish. Pao An rolled the dead bandit to one side, trying not to look at the mottled purple face. He had just killed a man! Mau had said one's first killing was always the worst. Mau was wrong, Pao An decided. The dead bandit wasn't even human to him. He felt only relief at having freed an innocent from the hands of a crazed animal. He rushed up to the dazed girl, who was lying behind a screen of willow leaves. Kneeling, he wiped the blood off her face with the torn flap of her satin bodice and blew gently again and again on her eyes and mouth to bring her back to life. Fox-spirit, his heart called out in fear and longing.

"You found me. You always find me," she whispered. Her tongue licked her bloody lips, and when she opened her eyes, an expression of childish surprise came over her face.

"What, Lady?"

"We mustn't play like this, even in the cover of the willow leaves. Willow is a bad woman. Mama calls her 'mischief maker.' "

"Hush, Young Mistress. The bandits are everywhere." He covered her lips with his hands, and she pressed herself into his arms. Up close, he could see that she was even younger than she first appeared.

"Bandits. I like that game. Grandfather is a bandit. Come sleep with me. Touch me like you do. Old One. Bandit." Gently she bit his fingers and giggled. Inside her torn bodice, a jade pendant carved in the shape of twin peaches hung between the small, pale mounds of her breasts. She turned a smooth, untroubled face into the soft part of his neck. Slowly, her hand moved down his bare chest. Desire, like an uncontrollable sickness, passed from his throat to his vitals and down to his loins. His eyes were heavy and his head was heavy, and he felt nothing but the scalding line her fingers traveled. Light, slanting through the canopy of long leaves, seemed to grow deep inside him.

"What are you doing?" she screamed. "Don't be hateful. Leave me alone. Why do you always come around to bother me?"

He came suddenly awake. Men were moving at the edge of the grove. Shouts and whistles came their way.

"Mama says not to let you play with me. It's not proper. I'm going to tell her you came into my room again!" She pushed him away and tried to run, but he pulled her down.

A crackling of twigs. The bandit leader burst into the grove. He whistled softly, looking around, then frowned at the sight of his comrade, his eyebrows making a black slash across his wide forehead. Quickly he swiveled and spied Pao An and the girl.

"The farm boy in the tree," he rasped. "And he has snared the crimson bird." He drew out his knife and circled around the small shrine toward them, ducking around the egg-shaped stone and under the leaves of the banyan.

Pao An's fingers felt along the base of the banyan root and found the dead man's knife.

"What are you doing here? Leave her. Run back to your village," said the bandit as he circled near. His eyes narrowed under the broad ridge of bone. "Brother," he said deliberately, raising his hand and placing it against his shoulder, three fingers pointing straight across.

Pao An gaped at the sign! "No," replied Pao An, swallowing his panic at confronting not a simple bandit, as he assumed, but a Triad, although this giant looked nothing at all like the skinny Mau or the tubercular One-Clean-Sweep. "Brother or no brother, I won't let you take her!" The knife glinted in his hand.

The burly Triad looked up in amazement. "What's this? You would fight a brother for this slut? See my hands? As hard as iron. I can snap your neck like a chicken. My fingers know magic too. Watch me pluck your heart out, like so—" He held his hand out and slowly rearranged his fingers so that the second and the last finger pointed straight at Pao An's chest. Like the horns of a dragon, thought Pao An, who wondered where he had seen the gesture before. Then the man made a quick two-handed movement that set Pao An's heart jerking like a dying fish. Now Pao An remembered. One-Clean-Sweep had made such a sign with his fingers. And that time, too, his heart had nearly jumped out of his chest.

Pao An ignored the searing pain. "Then use your magic to bring your comrade back to life," he taunted the bandit. When the Triad hesitated, Pao An moved closer to the girl.

The Triad feinted to the right. At the same time, Pao An leapt forward and brought his blade up. Only a hand as fast as Pao An's could have stopped the thrust. And Pao An, equally deft, caught the bandit's hand that aimed his own knife at Pao An's throat. Forehead to forehead, blade to blade, the two men grappled like two stags with antlers entwined.

For an eternity, neither seemed to move. Pao An found his strength failing under the bigger man's relentless pressure. With the Triad's hand touching his throat, Pao An felt his grasp slipping. The pain in his chest was like a snake gnawing at his heart, so he twisted desperately and sank his teeth into the thick hand. The knife fell, but the big arms held him fast. Grasping Pao An's arm, the Triad bent it back until Pao An dropped his knife. He pushed Pao An to the ground and grabbed his neck below the ears. Pinpoints of light exploded in the corners of Pao An's eyes. All sensation fled. In the distance, Pao An heard shouts and musket fire, and the numbness in his body became a pleasing warmth.

"I should kill you for breaking faith. But you are just another naive recruit. And you're right, my magic is no good today," the Triad said. "Two times I cast the yarrow stalks. Two times I asked the question, 'Is this the proper day?' The eight diagrams were clear: 'The superior man acts at the proper time.' But am I the superior man? Or General Li? Or you? Tell me what business is it of yours if Li bleeds a little or loses his bride-price? Doesn't he tax and flog you unjustly? Why do you thwart our plan?"

Pao An's life was ebbing away. He was ashamed that the frightened girl sprawled in the dirt should witness his defeat.

"Today all must band together, farmer, bandit, magistrate, to take what is ours. You should be helping us throw off the beardless weakling on the throne and put back one of our own kind, a proper Han like the first Ming ruler. We can build a kingdom of peace and bring back the age of gold. And load our pockets with the stuff."

The girl had risen and crept behind the men. Without warning, she hit the bandit in the head with a stone she held in her fist. When he raised both hands to ward off the next blow, Pao An rolled away, dazed and gasping for air while the world tilted and spun. The girl struck again, this time missing the Triad's head and hitting his hands. Frustrated, she snatched the knife that the bandit had dropped and rushed at him. She managed to cut the palms of his outstretched hands and pressed closer still, flailing wildly as the bandit tried to regain his balance. She gave him a dozen more slashes, which he parried by using his forearm like a sword, before he finally struck her a blow that tossed her against a tree.

As if from under water, Pao An saw the Triad step toward him. Then the big man paused and listened to the sound of the guards thrashing in the underbrush. Sighing, he said, "Take her. She's bad luck anyway. You've poured pig dung on our plans, you and that dancing lout friend of yours. I give you your life, my Triad brother. That's more than her bloodsucking father-in-law will do. Go home, live if you can, hide today's shame from the brothers you betrayed, and tell your children that you owe your life to Iron Fist, commander in the Red Turban brotherhood and once a farmer like you. If knowledge catches up with your strength one day, come find me in Thistle Mountain."

A bullet shattered the edge of the egg-shaped stone. Iron Fist whirled and ran for the river. "Smash the officials!" he yelled.

His breath searing his bruised throat, Pao An staggered painfully to his feet. Who was his enemy, who was his friend? In less than an hour, the tight, small world of paddies and fishponds had vanished and a new one of violence and intrigue had arisen in its place.

A small hand slid over his shoulder. The girl's eyes had lost their dazed look. Now she remembered what she had said and done.

"If you betray me, I am lost." Her anxious eyes searched the battered face of the young man and traveled over the dirty, bruised body.

Pao An saw that he revolted her. But before he could run away in shame, her legs buckled, and he caught her around the waist. He smelled her blood and sweat and the sandalwood musk of her hair. The perfect oval of her face with its kohl-darkened eyelids and small swollen lips were tilted up to him like an offering. How he longed to press his lips against the tiny pulse that beat in the hollow of her neck.

A peasant knows desire, but cannot afford it, for love is a luxury granted only to men rich enough to keep a special woman for pleasure. Love, the village elders said, creates havoc within a family, where duty, not desire should reign. Love confuses the order by which families contract to prolong their line. It poisons the harmony of a household and sends fissures into the rock of filial piety. It is an intolerable force, willful, egocentric, and therefore destructive because self must never be asserted above family. Pao An had never before felt such an emotion. Love came to him like an immense and incomprehensible sadness, a burning ache in his vitals.

Suddenly, Pao An remembered Pang, whom he had lost in the melee. He got painfully to his feet, holding the senseless girl in his arms, and plunged into the banyan grove, calling Pang's name. Hastening to the river's edge, Pao An saw the marks of a dozen small boats in the sand. At the far side of the river, a toylike flotilla was moving south toward the sea—a small fleet of Tanka fishing boats rigged with ragged straw coverings—bearing the Triad raiders swiftly away.

He lay the girl down on the grass and began to run up and down the beach shouting for Pang to come out from his hiding place. Then he spied a loincloth-clad rump stuck high into the air among the low reeds.

He waited for Pang to spring up and roar, but when Pang didn't move, Pao An stepped over a log, grasped the loincloth, and pulled. A dozen small jagged mouths, like the marks left by leeches, gaped on Pang's broad back. The grass he lay in was black with blood.

Part 4

BRIDE AND CONCUBINE GENERAL AND SLAVE

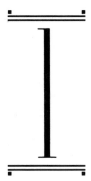

Abundant Spring Mountain, 1851

General Li sat on a small stone bench behind the sacred spring of the Concubine, airing his favorite bird. Mist swept through the air like an iridescent veil. The long slanting light of the late afternoon and the tranquil dance of the waters were a balm to his restless spirit.

Many gentlemen kept birds, and it was the task of trusted servants to sit for hours in utter silence while the birds drew *chi* or new vitality from the setting sun. During the year of enforced rest after his mother's passing, the general had taken on this task himself. He liked to think that he had trained himself like a bird, shut himself up within the cage of his ancestral dwelling to learn again the lesson of patience forced on him in childhood by his mother. "Through disciplined thought, one marshals resources," she had preached to him. What a cranky old general she had been. He laughed—in death she was disciplining him still.

The general was a slim, swarthy man of nearly forty who moved with the muscular grace of a trained boxer. Although his rank and the occasion entitled him to elaborate costume, he wore only a simple gown in keeping with the first year of deep mourning paid to a dead mother. Caught in the vicious power struggle among the princes, eunuchs, and generals in Peking at the young emperor's ascent to the throne, Li had used his mother's death as an excuse to retreat from danger with grace and tact. But retreat was not the general's way.

At first the maddeningly slow pace of rural life had grated on Li. Gradually, however, he realized that the same scheming that dominated court life was rampant in his own home. Soon he had trained himself to dance within the narrow space his family allowed him. He read again from Sun Tzu's *Art of War,* practiced calligraphy, wrote poems, strolled with his wife in their secluded garden, and savored the taut, young bodies of his two concubines. And he pushed up his daily regimen of *tai chi chuan* from one to two hours, lest leisure lose him his edge.

Now he pressed his face against the cage and stuck his tongue between the bamboo slats. The bird nodded, cocked its head, and darted forward to steal the sesame seed from the general's tongue. It was only a common songbird, not the fabled firebird of the south that the general had always coveted, but it had a charm of its own. He laughed and leaned back to watch the tiny feathered creature hop and turn in the narrow confines of the cage. It seemed to Li that the bird was describing in three dimensions, as surely as a black ink brush, the character for "equanimity."

Li had come to the spring, to the source of his line and his fortune, to escape the frenetic activity of the courtyards below where there were women arguing, men laughing too loud, the coming and going of tradesmen, coolies, musicians, and slaves, all preparing for the arrival of the bride and her grandfather. No one had noticed when the general quit the mob for the Upper Terrace, where the cages were kept in a special aerie.

On the morrow, his only son's three-day wedding feast would begin. Three days of excruciating politeness and posturing before the officials, magistrates, landlords, and ladies who had envied and hated his family for generations; three nights of enduring his concubines' quarrels over who should precede the other at table and in his bed; three days and nights of watching Old Wang stuff himself with dainties and wondering which servants he was bribing to be spies. Endless laughter, gossip, and explosive intrigue—all conducted on a note of strained hilarity because of the years of enmity between the two families that no wedding could sweep away.

It had amused him to allow his First Lady, Meng, whose longing for the dowry was as obvious as a cat mewing for milk, to plead the Wang girl's case. By first rejecting it, then gradually allowing himself to be persuaded, he had put Meng eternally in his debt. For such a large consideration, she did not dare to trouble him for inconsiderable ones.

Therefore, he had bought himself peace from her incessant importunities and won, in addition, the chance to turn Old Wang from a foe into a supplicant.

Li had paid far more than his family could afford for the bride gift, but Wang had ceded a fortune for the ages by giving Li half his government licenses for the transportation and distribution of salt for the dowry. In the long run, these were worth a hundred times more than any gift of silver or land and were of untold political value—for he who controlled the roads and tolls and canals controlled the routes of war and a spy network of porters and boatmen that stretched from one end of the empire to the other.

The actual transfer of the licenses would take place over a three-year period, and the general would have to be wary of Old Wang every step of the way to see that the bargain was fulfilled. What advantage in the match had Wang perceived that Li had missed? If Wang hoped to undermine his enemy's clan by weakening it from within—for who made a better spy than a daughter trained in the art of dissembling?—Li was prepared for such treachery. In fact, the peril in which the match placed the Lis excited the general. In battle, Li always sought a place in the front line where disaster loomed on every side, for he believed that danger could always be turned to advantage by a superior man.

His hexagram was *Kan*—the perilous pit. Whenever the general tossed the yarrow stalks, invariably the sign turned up at one point or another. The two trigrams, above and below, suggested "water," "pit," and "danger." It held within its alternative structures both the possibility of great jeopardy and supreme fortune. The general regarded the sign as a personal challenge: if a superior man, in accordance with the symbol, maintained his integrity despite the pit that yawned below, despite enormous temptations to falter or quit, that man would win everything before him. And so it was that Li lay his course and did not worry about the dangers on either side.

He wondered at Liang Mo's inability to see the advantage of a marriage with the Wangs. Li found his son maddeningly naive, particularly about the motives of those closest to him. Liang Mo had even confided ingenuously that his Hakka concubine, Rulan, had contacts with the Taiping rebels through her nunnery. An investigation not only proved that the nunnery was a women's society in league with the Triads but that the women paid rent to the Li family. The general had moved swiftly and ruthlessly to discipline his unruly tenants. He would have done the same to his son's concubine, who was undoubtedly a spy, except that Liang Mo had fashioned a foolish attachment to her. And the girl herself had a curious charm. Her grief for his dead

mother seemed genuine enough. She grew wan and pale, refused to eat
or leave her bed, and would have quietly slipped into oblivion were it
not for Liang Mo, who threatened to kill himself if she preceded him
in death. What did Rulan feel for his weakling son that would make
her put aside her grief to allay his? Surely it was pity, not the fear and
respect that such a vibrant woman might feel for a manlier man. There
was something odd and secret about Rulan that excited him. She was
another perilous pit!

Would sleeping with a spirit-woman be like leaping into fire?

His lips curved into a smile under the black mustache as the small
bird before him pecked at seeds and ruffled its feathers. The general
pursed his lips and whistled long and low, never taking his eyes off the
tiny creature. The bird stopped and listened intently to the flutelike
music.

From Li's perch on Abundant Spring Mountain surrounded by old
graves, the rebellion seemed far, far away. Yet, as he had predicted,
the viceroy's stupid intervention had transformed the God Worshipers
from a small aberrant religious band into an army of angry peasants
numbering over thirty thousand. They called themselves Taiping,
Warriors of Great Peace. What galled Li most was that the fat viceroy
of Kwangtung who oversaw the military operation in Kwangsi against
the Taiping appeared to bask as much in the new emperor's favor as in
the old. There would be little chance of the general's supplanting his
rival as long as the viceroy enjoyed the support of the Dragon Throne.

Not for long, he predicted. The viceroy was destined to fail. The
Hakka infidels were more ambitious, or at least luckier, than the rebels
Li had encountered in the past. Yang, the charcoal-carrier who had
extended Li an invitation to join the rebellion, had succeeded without
him.

And if the empire were to fall to the Taiping rebels in a mighty
conflagration, Li was not deceived—as his mother had been—by the
softheaded dictum: family persists, though empires fall. He shook his
head over the old woman's simple tenacity to that sentimental principle of Confucian rectitude. No family was impervious to the irrational
fluctuations of dynasties! Even a family as ancient as the Lis could
vanish in the space of a thunderclap. It took constant vigilance to
prevail in the world.

Look how his own vigilance had paid off. Just that morning, the
long-awaited letter from the Hsien Feng emperor excusing Li from the
obligation of two more years of deep mourning had come. The opium-
dazed profligate had invited the general to accept the position of
second in command to Deputy Military Governor Wulantai, a Man-

chu. It was not first place, not what he had hoped—but patience, he told the bird, who hopped right and left and scolded him like an old lady. The new emperor must still be paying off debts to others. In his nomination, Li sensed the shadowy hand of the eunuch An-te-hai, who was putting friends such as the general in strategic places so that as he succeeded the old chief eunuch, his web would already be spun throughout the empire.

In only a little while, Li chided the impatient bird, the emperor would come begging. Then the real prize for which he had schemed and plotted would be in his grasp—not commander of the Han armies, not even Han adviser, for those were merely necessary steps along the way. No, he wanted to be known as slayer of the Manchu barbarians, father of his people. Emperor! The first Han to sit on the Dragon Throne since the Ming.

The little black bird hopped and turned, hopped and turned, and cocked first one, then the other eye at the general. Li turned his own dark head from side to side, imitating the bird's quizzical look, before the bird finally ended the game by breaking into a throaty song that sounded like bubbles breaking over rocks.

The general laughed softly and reclined on the grass to catch the slanting rays of the sun. He thought of the firebird, the vermilion sparrow of legend, which had never been snared. This ugly little bird was not what he coveted, but it would do for now. "I should compose a poem to you," he said contentedly to the bird, "but I am empty."

He remembered his mother on the flower-strewn catafalque that had awaited his return. The heat had been unbearable, and the stench had overwhelmed the flowers. He had done all that was right, all that was proper as a filial son. He had counted out the food offerings and libations of wine among the closest kin; led the white-clad women in the forty-nine days of fasting and lamentation; followed the coffin on foot, unshaved, his queue untied, tottering between two servants who held him by the elbows. The procession had measured half a mile, as befitted the wife of a Hanlin scholar and mother of a general, and had taken every spare copper in the family treasury.

Now the world was calling him back. Soon he would be free of this house, especially of this weakling son who could not see the obvious advantage of a Wang for a bride. If left alone, Liang Mo would lie abed with his concubine and postpone the day of marriage forever.

Had his mother known Rulan was a Golden Orchid? Never mind, the old lady was dead, and just as well, for she would never have relished the excitement of keeping a beautiful and dangerous woman in their midst, just as she never would have permitted an alliance with her husband's old enemy, despite the obvious fact that it was a perfect union.

"Ah," he said to the bird, "war is less hazardous than family life."

Feeling his *chi* grow more agitated by his thoughts, the general rose and took up the cage.

"What do you signify, Sleek Feathers? Are you a slave in a cage? Or does your song make you free? Are you I? Some cipher? A written character in three dimensions—or maybe even yourself?"

Annoyed by the movement of the cage, the bird chirped angrily, and the general laughed.

Meng preened as her husband watched her from the peacock chair. Her colors were gorgeous: blue and red and gold, apple green jade, ivory skin, ebony hair still without a trace of gray. She sat before her mirror as he had seen her so many times before, ordering her maid to turn the shimmering fabric just this way or that. Meng could still excite her husband, because she knew that artifice and staging were the real wellsprings of ardor. Next to birds, Li loved to watch women. There were so many similarities: their vanity, their bright plumage, their caged existence, and their anxious twittering and pecking.

"You're making me nervous, Liang Mo's father! After wasting a whole day hiding with your bird, how can you sit there like a cat licking its chin when there is so much to do?"

"Because I am assured that you have thought of everything."

"With the bride's entourage hours late? My poor mother was right—one is never prepared enough for a wedding."

"Or marriage."

"You men, what do you need to prepare for, except someone else to indulge you?"

"My point exactly. That's why I can sit here like a cat licking its chin."

Meng made a perfectly artificial moue and shook her head so that her hair shimmered like black water down her smooth back. Nude from the waist up, with her hair undone, she was trying on gown after gown. Beneath the diaphanous skirt, her legs were as slim as a girl's. He was amused by her attempt to arouse him: Meng was a master of such games, and whenever she sensed that he was growing bored, she would place a new slave girl, a *mui tsai*, in his path. He would take his pleasure and inevitably return to his wife, who, unlike his slow-witted Third and his frivolous Fourth, was always new and endlessly entertaining. Now Meng was twisting her lithe body this way and that, pretending displeasure with each dress that her fat maid brought.

"Rulan!" she called. "I am all asweat!"

Liang Mo's concubine peered in at the door and returned with a perfume-soaked towel. Meng stood up on her tiny silk-shod feet and lifted her arms. She was perfectly smooth and hairless, even in the hollow under her arms; even, he knew, to the fine, soft skin on her cleft. He thought back to past lovers and tried to remember what it was like to possess a woman with a less-than-perfect body, one who was not so fastidious over hair and sweat as his wife. Two or three vivid memories reminded him that the imperfections of the flesh had often helped to stir it. There had been dozens of actresses and maids, often another friend's wife or daughter, and, when he was young, women taken in the heat of a raid while the blood of their men was still on his hands. But even those were women of the same sort—all supple flesh and limbs, yielding out of calculation or fear. Had there ever been a girl as tall and broad shouldered as the one beside Meng? There was no trace of softness in Rulan. Her arms were long and sinewy, which made him think incongruously of a warrior's bow. He suspected that they could as easily kill as embrace—a talent that would befit a spy, he thought, although in his experience women sent as spies were traps baited with softer, more honeyed flesh.

Meng leaned back her head to let Rulan wipe the hollow of her neck and the ridge of bone between her small breasts. The Hakka girl's fingers were unusually long and fine. When the general looked down, he saw that she had stepped out of her cloth slippers: the sight of her bare feet stirred him in a way that Meng's nakedness had not. He had seen big feet before, but Rulan's were not calloused and dirty like a peasant woman's; rather, the bones were as delicate as her fingers and the flesh as smooth as the skin on the underside of her arms—not white but peach-gold. The sight of her unbound feet was both horrifying and intensely erotic.

His eyes traveled the length of his son's concubine. Rulan was wearing a high-necked dress of light green polished cotton, finer than what most maids wore, although not as elaborately decorated as the silk garments Meng wore. He guessed that it was an old robe of Moon's made over to fit Rulan, for it came only to her ankles and gaped open between the buttons of the bodice. Rulan leaned to wipe the curve of Meng's waist, and he caught a glimpse of a full breast tipped with rose.

She was stroking a salve over Meng's pale arms. Her face was turned toward his. Was this poisonous Orchid calculating how to kill him with an incantation? he wondered. As if she had read the general's thoughts, Rulan looked up over Meng's bare back and caught the heat in his eyes. Li saw with a start that her eyes were round, not almond shaped, and with a fringe of long lashes that cast shadows on her cheeks. The aberration was fascinating! Beneath the trappings of respectability, she was a creature still untamed. Her hair, too thick for the matron's knot, was secured in one braid down her back. She wore no paint, but her color was so vivid that the fashionably powdered Meng looked pallid by comparison. Meng, he realized, was using the rawboned girl as a foil for her own delicacy. Did Rulan mind being paraded like a mule in his wife's charade? He raised his teacup in a half-mocking toast to the comely savage within his walls.

Meng nodded demurely, taking the compliment as her own, while the girl's face remained unreadable. Li was disappointed to discover that Rulan was not afraid of him at all.

He rose from the peacock chair and walked past Rulan to gaze down through the moon window of his wife's room at the Third Terrace where the Wang party was awaiting their darling's arrival. With Old Wang perched like a carrion bird in his midst, Li had begun to feel a grinding unease: Wang's bestowal of his granddaughter seemed all the more ominous. The girl's picture showed her to be beautiful, but perhaps that was merely the artist's lie. What if there was a defect hidden under the sleek porcelain glaze? A slow-witted wife was not uncommon. Or a termagant, a shrew, or worse, a barren womb. Li discarded the thoughts; he was becoming as paranoid as a woman these days.

The general comforted himself with the fact that nothing had changed in their bargaining positions. Wang wanted exactly what Li did: control over the complete circle of the salt trade from the salt pans to the individual consumer. Wang held the better part, the transportation and sale, part of which he would cede to Li as Mei Yuk's dowry; whereas Li, under government license, still held the sources, the salt pans that Wang had failed to extort from Li's father. The general surmised that Lam, the young magistrate who advised Old Wang, and who was escorting the bride on her marriage journey, provided additional surety that the terms of the contract would be met. Wang had been a favorite of the dead emperor. It would stand to reason that the young eunuchs and princes who counseled the Hsien Feng emperor hoped to cut Wang down to size. All the more important for Wang to secure his trade through marriage.

Moon rushed in with her hair in her face and her arms filled with yet another pile of dresses.

"Don't dash about! Are all the lanterns lit in the hall?" Meng asked her servant.

"Yes, Lady. I could see the light from your terrace," Moon gasped.

"Liang Mo—is he dressed?" came Meng's muffled voice through a snowy camisole.

"Hours ago, Tai Tai," Rulan said. "I dressed him myself."

Li thought her voice surprisingly well bred, as low and smooth as running water. He strolled back to his wife and eased himself into the peacock chair with a sigh.

"He wasn't drinking yet, was he, Rulan?" Meng asked anxiously.

Rulan shook her head. "He will not embarrass you."

"Then that," General Li said drily, "will be a notable first, worth recording in the clan record." He watched the mother and the concubine respond: the first with angry reproach, the latter with cool detachment, like one who is only mildly surprised by the bad behavior of a neighbor's child.

A crash and angry shouts from the gate made Moon glance out the window. What she saw made her stagger back on her tiny feet. "Aaiiee! Aaiiee! Bandits!"

The general jumped to his feet and pushed the wailing maid aside. He saw guards scuffling with ragged intruders at the gates, heard the servants' wailing, the guards' angry curses. He ran to the terrace with the half-dressed Meng tottering behind.

"What is it, Liang Mo's father? Tell me!" she cried at his elbow.

Below them shone the Great Hall, lit by hundreds of red candles. And below that the Kitchen Court. Suddenly, the gates swung outward to admit a staggering column of soldiers, priests, and musicians into the yard. As the splintered sedan burst through the line of frantic servants, Meng screamed and fell back in a faint against him; the general stopped long enough to lower her into the arms of a sobbing Moon. Then he raced down through the terraced gardens into the Kitchen Court in time to see one of the palanquin bearers collapse in the dust. And the bride stepped out of her covered chair—over the bloody body of the man who had borne her on his shoulders. She was filthy; her headdress and veil were missing, her hair tangled and matted, and her face exposed for any stranger to see. She had tied a flap of her dress over her naked breast.

It was a scene from a terrible nightmare: a death procession lit by crackling torches and torn lanterns.

Behind him, he heard Rulan snapping out instructions to the servants for bandages and medicine, and the answering scurry of the maids and houseboys.

"What happened?" Li yelled.

"Ambush!" The wide, flat face of his collector Fan pushed rudely into his. Fan began to babble about his own innocence and his courageous resistance and a peasant boy who had been a lookout on the road for the bandits. Li listened impatiently, knowing too well Fan's tendency toward self-preservation, then dismissed him and politely demanded an explanation from Lam, the magistrate who acted as Wang's surrogate in the procession. Lam was a coolly precise man, careful not to say too much. He offered the barest details and no opinions whatsoever. Even without Fan's embellishments, the tale told by Lam was fairly sordid. Clearly, kidnap and ransom had been the objective of the ambush, for the attack was too coincidental and prolonged to be the work of half-starved bandits who picked their victims at random. The objective was the girl. And the kidnapping had been thwarted by a simple farmer, according to Magistrate Lam. Listening to the official's controlled presentation, Li felt the earth shift under the foundations of the house his ancestors had sunk into the rock. The magistrate was ever so carefully constructing a case for the culpability of the Lis for not protecting the bride. A dark panic was rising in Li's gut at the realization that the grand alliance with the Wangs was fast coming undone—lawsuits—the vanished dowry—

Rulan came up and spoke quietly, her face level with his. "I'll take the girl to my rooms. Her legs and arms are scratched and her nose might be broken, but I do not think she is seriously hurt." Rulan leaned closer to the general and whispered, "She says she was not forced. I'll find out."

"Yes, exactly right," he nodded, grateful for the girl's calm efficiency. "Take her quickly then," he growled. "Clean her up before her grandfather sees her." With the return of self-control came the familiar rush of battle fever. He was at war again, and it felt good to be with strong comrades—until he remembered that Rulan's loyalty to the family was still not proven.

Just after Li dismissed the wounded guards and entertainers with promises of reparations and sent servants to pay off the families of the dead, Old Wang arrived on a litter borne by his hangers-on, and the brawl began.

"My precious . . . my precious," he said, panting. "The child is lost, and who will save her? I demand full payment! No less, no less."

"Calm yourself," Li snapped. "Your granddaughter is not lost. She is upstairs. My son's concubine is taking care of her."

The old man's mouth clamped shut. Li thought the merchant seemed more shocked than relieved.

"It is true," Magistrate Lam said rapidly. "The girl is inside the house. We were attacked by bandits on Li property, but we beat back their attack."

"Aaiiee!" sputtered Wang, who had managed to find his voice. "I blame you and your deceitful guards. If the child is hurt, I'll sue. Yes, yes, take heed, Magistrate, I'll sue! If she was ravished, I'll appeal to the viceroy. She was on Li land, you said it yourself, protected by Li soldiers—"

"She's not been harmed, and now she is in appropriate hands," Li answered. "My son's Second is a healer."

Merchant Wang's hysterical threats disgusted the general. Wang was known for his noise and bullying nature; Li had never considered it more than ill-bred blustering, but now he saw it was a conscious act to throw his opponents off guard.

"Let me remind you," Li said, "that a woman belongs to the house of her father until she reaches her husband's door. If the girl has been soiled, who then is the wronged party? No one will accuse us of injustice if we refuse to take your family's bad luck under our roof. Tell the viceroy that. And we in turn will tell the good families of our province that the granddaughter of Wang was spoiled by bandits."

"He slanders my family!" Wang swore and threatened the general with lawsuits and bloodletting for not protecting his darling with sufficient troops "on lands supposedly under your control." Now the fat merchant's voice was crude and loud, and his nails slashed the air like knives.

"Ah, but perhaps the girl ought not to have been sent out of her aunt's house into the countryside where bandits lurk instead of coming down by barge with the rest of you. Perhaps it is her family's fault for clinging to the old-fashioned notion that taking a girl directly out of her house might precipitate a loss of money," retorted the general.

"This would not have happened on Wang land!" the huge merchant raged.

"Nor did it happen on Li land," replied the general in a silken voice, "although I have a few tenants in the area. It was most assuredly not within Li walls. Nothing is firm. We have not been delivered a dowry, although we have paid a bride-price. So no one can blame us for turning away damaged goods. And no one can blame us if we sue for the return of our part of the contract and additional damages, *hai ma,* Magistrate?"

Lam made a clucking noise with his tongue and looked sidelong at Wang, whose face had gone as white as the pearls hanging around the folds of his neck. "Where is she? Where is my precious? Take me to my rooms. I demand that you bring her to me," the old man cried. He climbed into his litter and shouted at his sweating bearers to carry him back up the cliffside.

Lam bowed apologetically to Li and followed the merchant up to the Third Terrace.

General Li saw by the old man's consternation that his barbs had hit home. Whether rape had taken place or no, the suspicion was there. Good families would perceive the girl as soiled, and the old scholar families Wang so desperately longed to impress would have more reason to turn their backs on him. Wang was a social climber to whom face meant everything. He would undoubtedly pay to have his "precious" taken in quietly by the Lis. Li could barely contain his elation at feeling the pendulum of fate swing back in his direction. Once more on the thin rope of chance, he had swung across a chasm.

Li decided to send for the peasant boy who had been a witness to the attack on the girl on the chance that he might know something that would be helpful. It would also be necessary in case of lawsuit to establish that the attack was made not on Li lands but on the land owned in common by independent villagers. Li would insist that the magistrate go too. Lam was clearly Wang's ally, and it would be dangerous to have them plotting together within his walls. Divide the enemy; that was the first rule of encounter. And there was the immediate problem of the girl. He must see what Rulan had discovered before Wang and his women spoke to the bride.

The general ran up a dark secondary path to avoid the curious guests streaming down to the Kitchen Court from their rooms in the Lower House and sprinted to the wing on the Second Terrace where Liang Mo lived.

The rooms were ablaze with lights, but only one small *mui tsai* was in the sitting room to bow him through to the interior of Liang Mo's chambers. The tiny girl shook her head when Li asked for Liang Mo. But she knew where the bride was. Trembling, she took him to the rear of Liang Mo's sleeping quarters where a half-dozen maids were whispering outside a doorway hidden behind a thick curtain. "Out, out! All of you!" he shouted. The maids rushed past him in a swish of flowing skirts.

He pulled aside the curtain slowly and saw Rulan sitting on the bed by the reclining girl. She was crooning softly while brushing the girl's hair from her white forehead. "Poor girl. No one wants you. Sleep, sleep. I once knew a girl like you, a girl with orchids in her hair—"

"How is she?" Li demanded gruffly.

Rulan stood up and covered the girl with an embroidered quilt.

"She's exhausted but unhurt. I put opium in her tea to make her sleep."

"Have you examined her?" the general demanded.

Rulan nodded, frowning.

He saw her whole body tighten as if girding itself for unpleasantness. "Was she raped?"

"No!" Embarrassed, she cleared her throat and repeated more softly this time, "No."

"You're sure!"

Rulan nodded. "Her lower garments were ripped, but there were no marks on her jade gate and no evidence that a man might leave."

"Good! Old Wang cannot claim rape and accuse my men of not defending her! And I have strong enough reason to throw the slut out." He decided that her loyalty should not go unrewarded. "Well done, Daughter!"

Rulan did not return Li's smile. "She means nothing to you, does she?"

The statement was made so directly that it took the general aback. "Why, of course not," he blurted. "A girl is only a girl."

"Begging your pardon, Father, this small person could be the mother of your line."

The general was not used to being rebuked. "And why should you be concerned about the one who would replace you?" he bristled.

"I am not at all concerned about my place. I care only about those who hurt and are treated unjustly," she replied.

"Guard your tongue. There is no place in this house for a disrespectful woman!" he said severely.

The general's threat had no effect on Rulan. "But how does it serve your purpose to turn this girl out?" she continued stubbornly. "You will lose the dowry, which you have not received, and the bride-price which you have paid. And the Wangs will make a fat profit, take back the girl, and laugh at this house as well."

He quit the room without acknowledging Rulan's scrupulously subservient bow.

In the Great Hall, a horde of guests was trading gossip and sneaking looks at the wedding gifts. Li directed them firmly back to the guest rooms and instructed a servant to send up hot wine and small dishes to distract them. Then he sent a messenger to Wang.

Fifteen minutes later, someone came—not the grandfather but Wang's principal wife. The old woman came unadorned and unpainted and alone, without daughters or servants. As soon as she saw Li, she knelt on the polished floor. She crawled to his chair, pulling her hair loose with her fingers and abasing herself before him, a man outside the family.

Wang's wife was a skinny old woman, the very opposite of her gross husband. "Forgive this miserable slave, Elder Brother," she wailed, though her cold, hard eyes belied the begging words. "Show this slave compassion. Do not drag our good name before strangers. If our worthless daughter has been defiled, it is not your fault but some angry god has turned against us. We cannot set our shame in your house. Give us our own girl back, and we will take the miserable child home this very night."

Li was astonished by the woman's abject behavior. Why would Wang, who never passed up a chance to haggle and barter, send a woman to bargain for him? Suddenly, he laughed out loud. Rulan had understood Wang's merchant logic perfectly! The wife was a tool, and her pleading for her "precious child" a subterfuge. Wang did not mind losing face—as traders, the Wangs had never known respect. Nor did he care about the girl except as an item for barter. The issue was money, pure and simple: the dowry, the trade routes, the salt pans. Wang would reason that if the Lis kept the bride after the kidnap attempt, they would rightfully claim the dowry. But he would also fear that they might sue to retrieve the bride-price, just as any common merchant would sue if he received damaged goods. Sly trader that Wang was, he did not want to risk losing both. So he would take back his goods and fight to retain what Li had already paid, pleading broken contract.

"Dear Sister-in-law," Li said kindly. "Be assured that I am not one of those old-fashioned men who believes that if a bride's foot brushes the ground on the way to her husband's house she brings misfortune to her groom. My son's concubine is a healer. She examined your daughter and found no evidence of dishonor. I will hold back my wrath for her sake by honoring my bargain with the house of Wang."

"You do us too much honor. We cannot accept it," the old woman protested furiously.

Li was all righteous severity. "Why do you doubt us, Sister-in-law? This family holds its honor dearer than mere gold. We would never turn your daughter aside, but declare that she is our daughter from this time forth."

The old woman, stunned into angry silence, could do nothing but knock her forehead again and again to the cold floor.

Storm above, pit below—and still, the superior man will win, thought

Li. Inwardly, he rejoiced at how his mother would have given her eyes just to see, at the last moment before darkness, her enemies licking the dust of her halls.

The next day, the wedding went forth—to the astonishment of the guests and both families—like a stone hurtling blindly downhill. The bride was in such a state of paralysis that she needed her ladies to help her move and sit and stand; the groom looked as if he were witnessing his own death. The young concubine, who should have been angry at her loss of place, was an island of calm among the embarrassed and uneasy company. At the ceremony, she supported the groom's tearful mother on her arm. And the general surveyed his ravaged household with the same grim detachment that he had watched so many battles run their course from the high ground—not counting the carnage or the shame around him, but only the victory he knew was at hand.

On Ting Village, Kwantung Province, 1851

When the first shots rained down on the bridal procession and echoed across the rice fields, the villagers of On Ting dropped their bundles of leaves and rice stalks and fled in terror to their homes. There was no time to send the women and children to the mountain caves, so San Kwei, the headman, ordered wagons drawn up around the lodge for protection. The boys unhitched the oxen and whipped them through the gates, while the men seized axes, hoes, and pikes and raced onto the crumbled earthworks. All felt the ancient fear—bandits! Every armed band, whether emperor's troop, Triad party, or aimless horde, did to a village what soldiers did to women in war.

San Kwei scurried to the storehouse for his ancient flintlock, panting with anger and frustration. Silently, he damned the gods for the new threat. Why me? he raged at the heavens. And why now, when the planting looked so good? His first responsibility was clear. The genealogies had to be protected even if the whole clan perished. After making sure that the tablets were safely buried beneath the stairs of the Hall of Ancestors, he turned to the task of protecting the living. Running to the ramparts, he prayed that the marauders wouldn't come before his men were ready.

Then a lone horse and rider came pounding up the road. San Kwei saw with relief that it was Collector Fan, come in person to allay the village's fears. "Hui!" the headman called and felt his smile freeze as Fan, hatless and stained from head to toe with blood and mud, reined in the panting horse a few paces past where the headman stood and waited in icy silence for the rest of the procession to pass.

Bad luck to lose a friend, San Kwei told himself, and clutched his musket as the bridal train limped on to Abundant Spring Mountain. He counted bleeding guards, one richly decorated palanquin with broken poles and doors, and a corpse in blue satin slung across a saddle. Then came a dour young man in the formal regalia of a magistrate holding two ripped and broken name flags, one emblazoned with the character "Li" and the emperor's insignia and the other standard with the name "Wang." Terrified priests, weeping acrobats, and musicians stumbled after.

San Kwei's quick mind began to click the broken pieces of the procession together until they fit like a wall of mah jong tiles. The wedding banners had given him the first clue to the importance of the parade passing before him: Li and Wang, two of the most prominent families in the province. Bitterly, he cursed the ill wind that had blown Li's future daughter-in-law to the edge of his precious village. His luck, despite the prayers to brave gods, had turned inescapably sour.

Looking up with dread, he saw Pao An approaching with a rope around his neck and the body of Pang slung across his shoulders, yanked along by a soldier on a horse.

Magistrate Lam ordered San Kwei to gather the dead from the road and hold Pao An prisoner until he returned to question him. His first responsibility was to get the luckless bride to Abundant Spring Mountain. San Kwei saw his opportunity to rid himself of the orphan who was a constant thorn in his side and humiliate his cousin Li Yu, whom he had always envied and despised.

Pao An was tried before a council of clan elders that very afternoon. The offense was "unfiliality" for having implicated On Ting in the raid on the bridal party and thus exposed the village to the wrath of its landlord, General Li, and to that of Li's powerful new in-law, Merchant Wang of Canton.

Before the sentencing, Li Yu had rushed into the gathering and begun slapping his son's face. "Give him to me! I'll punish him. Unfilial! Disrespectful!" But even this calculated show of discipline did not save Pao An from the wrath of the headman.

"What is your verdict?" shouted San Kwei.

"Guilty!" the elders cried as one.

"Death," declared San Kwei, and inwardly smiled to see that the sentence he pronounced met no opposition except from Li Yu, whose lamentations he ignored. Emboldened by the ugly mood of the council, San Kwei saw how the punishment of the son could be visited on the father as well. His jealousy of Li Yu's degree had festered for years; now, in one night, he could be rid of the only two in the village who would not bend.

"And what of the man who brought this lame crab into our midst?" demanded San Kwei. The uneasy faces of the elders told the headman that he must tread delicately in this matter, for despite what Pao An had done, Li Yu was an honored member of the clan. San Kwei's pug face hardened. "I say strike Li Yu's name from the tablets. We do not know him."

The elders began to babble in confusion.

"Exile!" San Kwei commanded. His chin was thrust out belligerently as if daring anyone to defy him.

"Exile!" the elders echoed shamefacedly. It was a dreadful punishment, for it meant that Li Yu's ghost would be forever homeless.

Li Yu was given one night to gather what he could carry before being thrust out to beg on the road. All his goods were declared forfeit to the man whose land he and his son rented, San Kwei. The wooden tablets bearing the names of Li Yu and his adopted son were dug up from their hiding place beneath the stairs of the Hall of Ancestors and burned.

The villagers kicked and beat Pao An until he lost consciousness, then dragged him into the square and thrust his head through the cangue, a square collar of wood the size of a wagon wheel. Strong hands nailed down the crossbraces to lock the grotesque portable pillory around Pao An's neck.

San Kwei brushed Pao An's offenses on a large sheet of paper and tacked it to the front of the cangue. It read, "This seditious stranger defiled our gates. We of On Ting do not know him." After dragging the youth through the lanes so that the old folk and the small children could witness his shame, they beat him with bamboo sticks until he again passed out. Then they tied his legs to a stake set in the ground outside the gate.

Pao An came to, briefly, at dusk when the paddies emptied and the young men with whom he had worked, played, and gambled filed through the village gate. The men made two silent streams on either side of him. Pao An lay in the dirt, listening to the thunder echoing over the foothills, the cangue strangling him, his back and chest crisscrossed with cuts from the bamboo scourging. He was dead to them, a *kuei*, a demon from which they averted their eyes. Pao An could barely breathe because of the cangue and the dust and blood filling his mouth. By nightfall, he had maneuvered himself into a sitting position, with the weight of the collar resting on the stake between his feet. The pain in his ribs, groin, and head was unbearable; yet the realization that he had brought his father exile was worse.

When he was sure no one could hear him, not even the guards watching uneasily from the shadow of the gate, Pao An began to weep. He tasted ten thousand bitternesses on his tongue. He cursed the fox-spirit for coming his way, cursed the Triads who killed Pang, and prayed that Kwan Kung, the God of War, would hurl a bolt of fire from heaven to consume him.

Around midnight, exhausted, Pao An heard footsteps.

"Who is it?" he called nervously. Two young men from the village militia pushed Li Yu ahead of them. They carried pikes to prod him.

"A no-name man." Li Yu walked slowly through the shadows carrying a blue bowl, a stick, and a small string bag.

"You aren't allowed to talk to him. No one can," one of the guards said.

"My name has been removed from clan rolls. I am no one, now. So excuse me, please stand aside, while I talk to my son."

Ashamed, the two men who had known Li Yu all their lives moved away.

Li Yu put down the bag and tenderly touched the back of Pao An's neck where the cangue had cut a deep wound. "My son," he said softly.

"How can I ever raise my eyes to you again, Father?"

"There's a boy's vanity for you. 'Ever' and 'never' belong to the Void, not to man. Do you think you are the first to plummet a thousand miles in one fall? We have little time left now. Lift your head for me." He had brought rice gruel in the bowl.

"I cannot eat."

"Are you my obedient son?"

Pao An said nothing.

"Open your mouth."

It hurt Pao An to lift his head, so Li Yu knelt to pour the warm congee into his son's mouth, while cradling the battered head in his arms. When the bowl was empty, Li Yu set it down on the ground, squatted on his haunches, and regarded the youth tenderly. "You are Triad?"

Pao An's head sagged. "Forgive—"

"Forgive? Forgive what? I know that whatever you did, you did for me. I know that without your saying so."

"Father, I am nothing. It was stupid to think I could change my fate. Stupid to presume—"

"Fate conspires with the gods to entrap us all. It was fate that made the money run out for my studies on the eve of the higher examinations and the clan call me back to the fields. But to the compliant, fate is kind. A man of *tao* knows that wisdom lies in weakness. He knows that nothing is weaker than water, yet water wears down the highest mountains. Nothing is lower than the ocean, yet it swallows great rivers. My master taught me to take strength from knowing we are nothing, for nothingness is the source of all things." He smiled. "I am going now."

"I cannot bear it!"

"I do not reject you, Pao An. But tomorrow you must not have a sick old man around your neck like a wooden collar. I seek my own death, not yours. They have pillaged our house, but I need nothing but this bowl for begging. They turned their backs as I walked down the street, but like master, I will make the whole universe my home."

"Forgive—" but the rest of Pao An's words was swallowed up in tears.

"I do not blame you, Pao An, my son, my friend. I bless you for helping me find my fate. I have loved you more than anyone, more than my dead wife or my dead children or my master, the sage from Fukien who taught me." He leaned closer. "Listen. You chose me. After my wife and children were snatched from me in the plague, I wandered for days gathering up the courage to throw myself into the river. And finally when I went to report their deaths and found my wife's home village afire, I wandered among the dead hoping a passing soldier would ride up to slay me. But the murderers had gone. Then I heard a cry among the smoking cane. It was you, red and fat, already fighting with the world. You had fought your way out of your burned clothing and were running naked, shouting angrily for your father. My dead sons and daughter were the children of my loins. But you are the child of my heart, my dragon's pearl, waiting for me in the burning cane. You were a son fallen out of the stars for me. I loved you because you were an open mouth, a starving belly, and as alone as I. At first I told myself that I wanted a living son to chant my praises when I was dead. That was vanity. What I needed was a companion in the dark days in this world, not for the next. And you have given me all I desired, even now. If this is the end, I cut you free of all duty to me and this evil place. And if you live, my son, don't choose my way. For who am I but an old tortoise dragging through the mud, seeking the low way, the way of water? You are wholly other, a tiger, pure yang. Like a tiger, you will struggle all your life against gods and men." Li Yu brought out the iron bit Pao An used to crack slate and slipped it into his son's hand. "Here, my strong son, my heart, and my liver," he whispered. "Quarry your fate with this. It is all I have to leave you."

"Father," Pao An begged, scarcely feeling the cold metal. "I cannot bear to be without you. Who will show me the way?"

"Make your own way. Only after tasting bitterness can one become a superior man. Who was the founder of this clan but a man cast off his lands, dishonored in his own time but revered in ours? If you live—and you will—be such a man!"

Li Yu stood and straightened the robe that billowed about his thin haunches. Pao An realized it was the student's robe that had lain in his father's clothes box for thirty years, untouched. The gray cloth was shiny and threadbare, and now too long for his father's shrunken body.

"Go on then, old man," one of the guards commanded.

"Father!" Pao An cried.

The old man stepped slowly toward the river. Pao An tried to crawl after him, but the rope brought him up short. Only the cangue kept him from falling through the earth into a netherworld.

At the Hour of the Dog, before dawn broke over the river, a small train of men and horses wound slowly out of the foothills. Hand-held torches cast long, pale fingers of light through the darkness. As soon as the two guards saw the men, they yelled across the ramparts to rouse the clan. In moments, the gong in the Hall of Ancestors was ringing, and the bamboo clappers were echoing the alarm.

Pao An dropped the bit he had worked between the latched halves of the cangue and pushed it into the dirt with his heel. Using all the strength in his fingers, Pao An had managed to chip part of the wood away and dislodge two of the five nails that held the collar together. Too late. He prayed that the soldiers or bandits would kill him quickly.

Near the gate a shot rang out, and a child began to scream. San Kwei came running to the gate, cursing his luck.

"What now? I should have strangled you in the night," Pao An heard San Kwei call.

Twenty paces from where Pao An lay staked in the shadows, the lamps stopped, and a harsh, mocking voice called out, "Loyal people of On Ting, my master General Li greets you. My master seeks the farmer called Chen Pao An."

"Ho, strangers," returned San Kwei cautiously. "He's no son of ours. We stuck his head in a wooden collar and put him there by the gate. Take him and be gone." He recognized Collector Fan's cruel voice. He hoped the man he had stuffed with so many bribes would play along with him now.

The torches came together until the pinpoints of light became one.

Two men dismounted and leaned over Pao An. One, he saw, was Fan. He pulled up Pao An's head by the queue and studied his bloodied face. In the dark Pao An did not recognize the other, slighter man who motioned to a servant to cut his tether. Pao An tottered to his feet, the cangue still bending him in half.

"Can you believe, Magistrate Lam, that this beaten dog is the bride's champion?" Fan laughed.

"Go get the headman to pry that thing off," Lam said to Pao An's guard.

Pao An studied the magistrate. He was about thirty, dressed in a riding suit of dark polished cotton. He had the pale, somber mien that came from years of poring over thick manuscripts in a scholar's cubicle. The only thing he wore to denote his official status was a high-brimmed black cap crowned with a button of gold. His eyes were anxious and, Pao An concluded, kind.

The magistrate bent to read the filthy paper, splattered with the prisoner's blood, that was nailed to the front of the cangue and raised an eyebrow. " 'Seditious stranger.' This place, which does not know you, sees fit to judge you. Come, unlock your tongue and explain."

"Why would you take a criminal's word?" said Pao An in a voice thick with pain and grief.

"Because I have not decided whether you are a criminal yet," Lam replied. He took out an ivory fan from his sleeve and began to fan himself while studying the man in the cangue. Lam was surprised to find in Pao An traces of his own passionate, rebellious younger brother. The resemblance was not so much in the configuration of the features, or even in the muscular arms, but in the unruly passions that brought eyes, lips, and hands to life.

At that moment, San Kwei burst through the gate, trailed by a crowd of wary elders.

"Early morning," San Kwei said curtly to Fan. "I never expected such a quick return. The bodies of your dead soldiers are in the temple already washed by the women and prayed over by our priests. As you see, I kept my word and held this demon for you to question," he said briskly, then turned to face the slight figure in a black hat tipped with gold. Instantly, San Kwei prostrated himself before Lam in the dirt and felt his stomach turn over.

"Forgive me, Great Sir, I didn't notice you there. You are so young for a magistrate. Beg your pardon, Great Sir, I don't mean to offend." Stumbling to his feet, San Kwei decided to make a show of firmness. "Take this dog-piss stranger and cut his throat with our compliments. You see, Great Sir, we suspect he is in league with the Triads. Naturally, we do not know him. The other one's body is with the pigs, may the gods strangle his ghost. But this stranger is to blame. I mean to break him so our other youths will not follow his bad example. No traitors in On Ting, we are all loyal here, all proud to wear the braid. Ask me anything, I'll tell you."

"Since you claim you do not know him," Lam said wryly, "I suspect you have nothing to say. Our inquiry concerns firsthand witnesses alone and begins with this boy."

San Kwei's mouth went dry at the prospect of Pao An closeted with a magistrate. What lies would he tell? Worse—what truths! There were enough unpaid taxes and hidden storage sheds of rice to send every man in the village into exile—and to sentence its headman to a traitor's death of a thousand cuts.

"Why do you think this criminal knows anything at all?" he protested. "He is dull witted and mean. Anyone here can tell you."

"Then he is not a seditious stranger, as the sign would have us believe," said Lam. The ivory fan stirred the dank air.

San Kwei began to sputter.

"Well, never mind," said the magistrate mildly. "I cannot stay. General Li wants to question this man himself. The bride told me this man saved her life—but the general's collector thinks he might be an accomplice of the bandits. Perhaps there are things about this village I should know, Headman."

San Kwei was speechless. Had Fan betrayed him?

"In any case," Lam continued, "I am making this boy my responsibility, not yours. I will bring him to the general myself. Unlock the collar, if you please. I want to talk to him as we ride, and this collar constricts the throat."

"But Great Sir, he's too dangerous." San Kwei appealed indirectly to Fan for confirmation, but he walked away to talk to the soldiers.

"Headman!" said Lam, and snapped his fan shut.

San Kwei motioned to two youths to pry apart the wooden crossbeams that held the cangue together. The cangue fell off with a clatter, and Pao An straightened slowly, rubbing his bruised arms. An angry red band ran around his neck and his ankles bled where the thongs had cut him.

"I'm free," he said unhappily to no one in particular.

"That remains to be seen, Farmer Chen," said Lam, noticing how the headman jumped back and the two young farmers moved uneasily out of Pao An's range. "Are you a hero or a traitor? No one I have heard so far seems to agree."

"Out of chaos, every man makes something," Pao An's broken voice rasped.

"A peasant who spouts philosophy. Do you know Lao Tzu, boy? 'When the people are so sure of their opinion,' said Lao, 'why am I alone confused?' "

"Begging your pardon, Great Sir," interjected San Kwei, dancing from one foot to another, "what does philosophy have to do with this criminal, *hai ma*? Can you play music to an ox? If you take him to the wedding, watch out he doesn't cut anyone's throat. Better yet, leave him with us. This clan knows how to deal with troublemakers."

"But every clan must deal in due course with me," Lam said pointedly. "My responsibility covers all of this county, so clans and troublemakers are entirely within my jurisdiction."

The headman's mouth opened, but San Kwei could think of nothing to say.

"We were talking," continued Lam to Pao An, "about the different landscapes men see."

"I am an unlearned man, sir. In all my life I have seen no other landscape but this village and these fields—except in my dreams."

"Such landscapes have inspired many men. I find your unlearned words most evocative. We will talk as we ride back to the wedding. Can you ride, Farmer Chen?"

"Only a bullock."

"Come then. You'll find a horse easier to straddle than an ox, but harder to direct." He called down to a servant. "Give Farmer Chen your mount. I fear he's too worn for walking."

Before the young magistrate could mount, the headman grabbed his sleeve.

"Great Sir, I swear you have a loyal village in On Ting. We're taxed heavily, but On Ting always pays its due. Even in these last five years, the emperor's loyal servants paid in copper cash and rice, although your agents' rates were two times higher than the official rate for copper against silver; we starved our own sons and daughters. If there was ever any discrepancy, it must have occurred in the administration." He said this pointedly to Fan, now seated on horseback beside the magistrate.

"I have heard reports about your honesty, Headman," said Lam smoothly, nodding in Fan's direction.

"Great Sir, you are too kind," answered San Kwei. The bastard has betrayed me, he thought.

Pao An's blood-caked lips curved into a smile. Mounted awkwardly on his horse, he looked down into the flushed face of San Kwei. "I'll be back in time to pay my father's debts. May his ghost keep watch over your house until then."

Led by Lam, the cortege wheeled around and turned back toward the foothills.

"To wherever," Pao An said to himself, reeling wildly on the horse's back. "To my fate. Father, I will find you," he promised.

San Kwei stood in the dust of the procession. "Aaiiee, Kwan Kung smite my enemies," he cried. "That new judge is a filthy Hakka, I swear! I saw how he smiled at that dealer of dog piss, Fan! I better buy my grave suit." He spat abundantly in the dirt and bellowed to his kinfolk. "Get your lazy women moving. You want the rice to plant itself? Aaiiee! A filthy Hakka come to judge us! Oh Kwan Kung, I'm already dead!"

Bouncing painfully in his saddle, Pao An glanced back over his shoulder and felt an unexpected rush of panic. On Ting was just a cluster of dirty brick hovels rapidly disappearing from view. Yet it was the only home he knew. But as the foothills rose from the green, waterlogged paddies like sleeping dragons, his broken spirit began to lift. He was loosed from the cangue as his father had foretold and sent by fate into the house of Li, his enemy. And if fate was kind enough, he would appease the angry ghosts of his kin and kill General Li. He would bring Li Yu back to honor, and he would see the beautiful girl again.

Seeing Pao An wince when his horse jumped across a rut in the road, Lam slowed his mount until the others had gone ahead and he and Pao An were moving at the same pace.

"Fan tells me you are a troublemaker. Are you also a kidnapper and bandit chieftain?" the magistrate said affably, leaning over his saddle.

"No," Pao An replied, his own voice even and unafraid. "But the bandit chief introduced himself to me when we fought." Pao An guessed it was to be a long interrogation. He determined to answer everything directly and truthfully. "He called himself Iron Fist. He had me by the throat. He could have killed me, but he relented. He said, 'Iron Fist gives you back your life.' " Pao An glanced at his inquisitor, but Lam was staring straight ahead.

"Brazen, wasn't he? Too poetic a gesture for a mere bandit. A Triad, without question. Even his name is poetic, although a bit crude. Obviously a name he chose, not a milk name or a school name. . . . Was he hurt?"

"Oh no, Sir. I was like a child to him. I couldn't even hold him when we grappled. I still don't understand why he let me go. He could have easily crushed me."

"And what did he look like, this so-called Iron Fist?"

"Tall. With hands as big as a man's head. No queue, so his front hair was long, but not like a woman. Like a warrior from the Ming."

The young magistrate raised one dark eyebrow at the mention of Iron Fist's hair, and Pao An was struck by another thought.

"Aiya, his brows were thick, a mark across his forehead—like yours. His voice was soft—like yours. Until he shouted."

"What did he shout?" asked Lam mildly.

" 'Smash the officials!' "

"Indeed!" Lam replied. He wondered if his younger brother Iron Fist truly intended to smash him. They were brothers in blood and brothers by Triad oath. But he also knew that his brother was jealous of his degrees and his office, jealous of the money and hope poured into him as the one chosen by the clan to be a scholar. He wondered if his brother would be true to any oath—or if gold and power would be his goals, as they were for Wang and other ruthless, hungry men in the Triad brotherhood.

For a moment, Pao An saw the magistrate's imperturbability waver. Then Lam cantered to the front of the train, spurring on his men to a more rapid pace.

As they galloped over the crest of the mountain and looked down into a valley boiling with fog, Pao An came face-to-face with the terrifying expanse of earth, sky, and water that lay beyond his village. It looked to him like a nest of ghosts seething in hell.

Chin Tien Village, Kwangsi Province

The predawn mist rose like the breath of a dragon from the wet earth. Charcoal-carrier Yang laughed silently as he sat—small, erect, and unmoving—on the huge platform set on a knoll outside the village of Chin Tien. He was watching Hung pray over the assembled faithful, who knelt in the bare, brown meadow below. The God Worshipers were celebrating a triple happiness: their first great victory over government troops; Hung's thirty-seventh birthday; and Hung's, Pawnbroker Wei's, and Scholar Feng's safe return from the neighboring district of Ping Nan, where they had been on an "evangelistic mission of recruitment." That was the official story that Yang and his new barbarian adviser "Man-da-li" had concocted to save Hung's face.

"Spirit show," sniffed Yang as Hung raised his hands to the heavens and shouted over the heads of the multitude. All his days Yang had struggled with gifted people such as Hung and his wife Ailan who possessed such power, and because they could summon spirits with their fingers or with the power of their tongue, they had always bested him. Until now.

The other leaders were there on the platform beside him: Hung's faction—Pawnbroker Wei and Scholar Feng. Yang's own people—Farmer Hsiao; Shih Ta Kai, who, despite his youth, could command men twice his age; and Mandley. The air crackled with a tension that the prayers of the faithful could not dispel. Eight months ago, Yang and Hung had fought, and the community had split in two.

It happened this way: in a move to check Yang's mounting power, Hung had demanded Yang's daughter as concubine, just as he had taken daughters from all the other leaders as a token of filiality. Yang had refused, reminding Hung that Rulan served a more useful purpose as a spy in the house of Li. Whereupon Wei had advised that the girl should simply let the old lady die in order to draw the general from the battlefield, and then come to take her place as Hung's bride. Again Yang had refused and quit the meeting angrily with all his train.

The breach between Hung and Yang moved swiftly from private disagreement to public enmity. Lackeys in one faction took to berating their rivals. There was pushing and shoving in the drill yard, and blood was spilled in the market areas.

Then one night, Yang fell sick after eating in Hung's house. Back in his own tent, he vomited blood, screamed that his throat was on fire and his stomach filled with burning stones. Soon he fell unconscious. Roving bands of God Worshipers turned the camp into an uproar. As the policemen of the camp, the tough Hakka porters and miners under Yang's command owned most of the weapons and made no secret that they were intent on revenge for their leader's sickness. When Yang's men tried to storm Hung's farmhouse, Hung fled with Scholar Feng and Pawnbroker Wei to Ping Nan, expecting most of the people to follow after. Only a quarter of the God Worshipers did.

The rest waited anxiously for Yang to emerge from his sickness. Pus came out of his ears, blood and bile with his stools. In his delirium, Yang called out to his dead wife to save him. Perhaps in some mysterious way she had, for in the second month of his illness, the barbarian Mandley came to the camp claiming that Yang's daughter had sent him. Yang's people said that the barbarian was a messenger from God to bring their leader back from death. When Mandley prayed over Yang, the sick man opened his eyes. Sensing that only Yang's iron will kept him from death, Mandley began to read the Old Testament to him in Chinese. I have found my David, Mandley said to himself in exultation, for he recognized that only a brilliant leader could inspire such loyalty among the men. Surely, he thought, his encounter with the girl in the house of Li had been an act of providence.

Mandley would not leave Yang's side. His prayers were fierce and specific: "Lord, do not let thy gallant servant Yang slip too soon from his people into death." He shouted the prophecies of Jeremiah and Isaiah over the sick man, as if the prophets' fiery words would quicken the inert body.

In the sixth month of Yang's illness, the viceroy's army moved against the warring factions and launched an attack on both camps.

At the news that provincial troops were massing against them, Yang whispered through burned vocal chords to Mandley, now his closest companion.

"Hung is in danger!" he rasped.

"Worry about yourself! Let the heretic go!" Mandley said angrily.

"No," Yang gasped. "Hung makes us more than a crowd of bandits. We need him. I control the army—he cannot win over me—but he is our symbol to the masses."

"Leave him! It's too dangerous."

Yang's choking laugh was awful. "I won't take rice with him anymore."

"He'll turn the people against you. His eloquence is his weapon."

"Yes, yes," said Yang. "But I will be prepared. I'll be eloquent too. You teach me."

With Mandley's help, Yang rose from his sickbed and led his men to break the cordon of government troops that were strangling Hung's camp in Ping Nan. Having saved Hung from death, Yang wrested from him the private agreement that henceforth there would be only one community of the faithful over which Hung would retain priestly power and over which he, Yang, would exercise full military and administrative command.

Now as Hung finished his prayer, Yang glanced out of the corner of his eyes at the odd yet already indispensible protector Rulan had sent him. The barbarian was a creature of contradictions—big as a bear yet gentle, a priest who bore arms. Through Mandley's influence Yang had obtained guns and powder—a pitifully scanty hoard but enough to bedevil a few local militia, from whom his men had stolen more powder and guns. Man-da-li was Rulan's most valuable gift, Yang believed. More precious than the information she had sent about the general's household. After he had awoken from sickness to defeat the troops and triumph over Hung, he'd inquired about her welfare, but in the months of turmoil and schism no one had been in communication with the Orchids. Finally, Yang had sent a man to the *chai tang* to investigate. He found that the stockade had been burned to the ground and the women slain. "Bandits came one night. Burned them all out," the villagers told him, "and good riddance to those immoral women." When Yang sent a spy to Li's house, he learned that the Tai Tai had died, the general had come home to mourn—and Rulan had become the concubine of the general's son.

"It is done," Yang said grimly. He reasoned that with her sisters dead and after months of silence from him, Rulan must have believed herself abandoned and had accepted the offer to marry a rich man. "I have put her at too much risk already," he confessed to Mandley, who begged him to bring the girl to Chin Tien. "May the High God grant her sons," Yang said. But his heart and liver were like lead. Now he had no one.

Yang did not let private tribulation hobble his actions for long. Soon he had found a way to turn mourning into purpose. He used Mandley to strengthen his hand against Hung. Eventually, Mandley's Bible proved more powerful than the few guns he commandeered. Mandley's knowledge of the "black book" gave Yang credence among the believers and made Hung fear him. Seeing this, Mandley advised Yang to buy a printing press to turn out Bibles in Chinese so that Hung's claim to revelation would not be exclusive. Eventually, some might see how errant Hung's interpretation of Scripture was.

That morning Yang had placed the first copy of the new translation, the book of Genesis, on a rope around his neck.

"A Protestant does not wear talismans," Mandley had protested when Yang insisted that he wear one too.

"But a barbarian sitting on a platform in front of a horde of fanatical God Worshipers might find it has protective virtues," Yang had insisted.

Mandley wiped the sweat from around his collar, which felt as tight as a noose, and regretted that he had jettisoned his loose Chinese pajamas for a western frock coat and pants. The air, heavy with humidity, seemed to threaten thunder and poisonous winds. Earlier, he had scanned the thousands pouring into the little valley—God Worshipers and Triad hangers-on, true believers, half-believers, opportunists, spies, hungry mouths—all as easily stirred by an exhortation to murder as a vision of promise; Mandley agreed to wear the Bible. He hung it on a rope around his neck, where it lay over his dark coat like a warrior's breastplate.

After Hung's prayer came long speeches that made the masses restive. Finally, Hung rose to give his birthday blessing and to make a declaration about the new alignments of power established among his followers. He stepped to the lip of the platform and raised his hands in the air to the thunderous cries of the brothers and sisters.

"I declare Taiping Tien Kuo, the Kingdom of Great Peace," he told them, and described to them the new dispensation that their victory over government troops at Chin Tien had made possible.

"From now on, we are no longer simple men and women but holy soldiers of the Kingdom of Great Peace. No longer God Worshipers but warriors of Taiping!"

"Taiping!" the brothers and sisters shouted in one voice.

Yang's heart sank at Hung's spellbinding effect on the crowd. Yang had bested Hung politically, but Hung still ruled the hearts of the people through his visionary gifts and brilliant oratory. Even the Miao savages, who had joined to put rice in their bellies and whose temples and priests had been slaughtered by Hung's guards, cheered Hung's words. Yang rued the gullibility of men. If he aspired to be Moses, he dared not keep this treacherous Aaron as a mouthpiece too long.

Mandley stepped forward to lead the chieftains in prayer, signifying the end of the convocation. Suddenly, a huge hand yanked him back.

"Tell them that I have a proclamation too—from Heaven," declared Yang hoarsely.

Mandley looked down at his friend in surprise. "Not now!" he cried. "You're not prepared. What will you say?"

"With his words Hung did more than our arrows and pikes at Chin Tien. If I am to lead the people, I must use words too."

"But Hung is an orator by profession, while you do not know what words to use or how to make your voice heard."

"I will prophesy," Yang insisted.

As he watched Yang approach Hung, Mandley noted with alarm the bizarre contrast they made on the dais; Hung with his leonine good looks and flashing eyes towered over the ugly, emaciated Yang. As soon as Yang spoke, the people would turn away from him; he was no match for Hung in either appearance or oratory.

Hung was amused at Yang's temerity. Did this illiterate peasant actually think he could speak before the people?

"Brothers and sisters. I have something to testify." Yang's voice, whistling in his burned throat, was a hollow echo compared to the golden voice of the Younger Son.

At the front of the crowd, Hung's men tittered at Yang's crude village accent and unnatural hoarseness. They had been humiliated at having to be rescued by the troops of a crude charcoal-carrier and were spoiling for revenge. "What gives Yang the right to speak?" came the rude whispers. "Does he have a degree? Can he even read?"

Yang coughed and began again in a voice that was only slightly stronger than before. "It is said that an ox cannot make music. I am a simple, untutored man." The people at the edge of the crowd stirred uneasily, and Yang realized that they could not hear him. In minutes, they would begin to sneak away.

Ashamed for their master, Yang's men cast murderous looks at the smirking guards around Hung.

Hung raised a hand to quell the jeers. "Listen to your general. Give him respect as you did God's Younger Son!" Hung lowered his voice. "Speak, then, if you can," he told Yang.

Fear was gnawing at Yang's vitals. Why had he placed himself in this position? Lights and colors began to swim before his eyes. The memory of long, bitter years of subjugation at the hands of more glib and gifted men made him angry, dizzy, and sick all at once.

"Be silent!" yelled a warrior in Scholar Feng's train to Yang. Quickly, the refrain swept through Hung's and Feng's troops.

Yang stretched his neck and gave a single mad shout, more an animal's cry than a man's, that burst open the scarred pipes of his throat. He staggered and fell, spitting blood. With the laughter of Hung's guards echoing in his ears, Mandley tried to drag Yang off the platform, but Yang threw off Mandley's arm and cried out once more. And suddenly, a great voice boomed out of him. Not his old voice, the crude, coarse voice of Yang, the charcoal-carrier, but a voice like a clanging gong that rang across the valley. "For Zion's sake, I will not hold my peace—I will not rest, until the righteous go forth as the sun!"

Hung fell back as if struck by lightning.

Mandley was amazed. Yang was speaking the words of Jeremiah, taking the prophet's eloquence as his own. Before Hung could challenge Yang, Mandley leapt forward and shouted, "Hear the voice of God, O my people, as spoken by His prophet!"

"The Voice of God," wailed a frightened woman.

Yang pointed his finger at Hung and cried in a voice that made the most stalwart soldier shiver. "I have set watchmen upon thy walls, which shall never hold their peace by day or night!" Hung threw his long tunic over his head. Yang pointed to the ashen-faced Feng and shouted, "I have set watchmen over you, saying, 'Hearken to the sound of the trumpet.' But they said, 'He will not hearken.'" His finger swept the trembling multitude. "Your burnt offerings are not acceptable, nor your sacrifices sweet to me! Repent!"

One by one, the brothers and sisters fell on the ground like stalks of grain flayed by the wind until every man, woman, and child lay with his face in the dust.

For an hour, the words of Jeremiah thundered out of the mouth of Yang, the charcoal-carrier, and swept the prostrate multitude like a wind out of heaven. When he bid them rise, they could not stand as warriors but staggered as if bruised by the force of his words.

Yang lifted his arms to heaven and shouted for silence. Not a breath stirred. "Thus saith the Lord: 'Behold a people cometh from the north country, and a great nation shall be raised from the sides of the earth! Their voice roareth like the sea! They ride upon horses, set in array as men for war.' "

When the people had done with weeping and cheering, Yang dropped his voice. His whisper carried to the far corners of the crowd: "The spirit of the Lord is upon me. He hath sent me to bind up the brokenhearted, to proclaim liberty to the captives, and healing to the sick. Thus saith the Lord: 'I will take you to a calm valley where your flocks shall lie down, for you are the people that have sought me.' "

"Amen!" they cried as one.

"Kneel down," boomed Yang. And they fell to their knees in the dust. "Remember the Younger Son, who covets your love. Pay respect to the Elder Son, and Taiping Tien Kuo, the Kingdom of Great Peace, will be yours!"

Yang made the people swear obedience to Hung before dismissing them. But as they went away, the brothers and sisters began to ask each other: Who is greater, Yang or Hung? Hadn't Yang triumphed over death and descended from Heaven even as Hung had after his forty-day struggle with the serpent *Ku*? If Hung was God's Younger Son, brother of Jesus, what then was Yang? Was he not the Voice of God, the Father himself come down to speak with the faithful?

Hung, Feng, and Wei went quickly to the farmhouse where Hung barricaded himself in an upper room with his wives while the others talked in quiet, strained voices far into the night.

The barbarian stayed with Yang to watch and pray. "You spoke as Jeremiah, but they heard only the Voice of God, not His intermediary," observed Mandley. With Yang's newfound power he could guide the Taiping to the gates of General Li's mansion or to the Dragon Throne itself.

Yang nodded. "They knelt down to me. My words made them do it! Blasphemy, *hai ma*? Shall I correct them?"

Mandley thought for a long moment. His Christian conscience said yes, but he shook his head.

Abundant Spring Mountain

The dead Tai Tai's ghost seemed to haunt the house of Li. She was a blackbird that dove at Rulan's head in the Kitchen Court. A flight of bats, kiting back and forth, back and forth beneath the moon.

But the union the Old One had labeled a disaster rolled on. After the marriage feast came the bride-teasing ceremony, usually a time of ribald sport where friends of the groom good-naturedly mock the bride. But this promised to be a dismal, dust-and-ashes affair, the jokes dry in every mouth and shame on every face.

"Let her go now," Rulan had pleaded with the general. "She's exhausted and still half in shock."

But when Li proposed to skip the ritual entirely, the girl's grand-mother insisted that it go on as proof of the bride's virtue. It was apparent to Li that Wang's women were trying to throw the cloth of ritual and custom over an alliance that had begun so unpleasantly. Yet his curiosity was piqued—how would the girl acquit herself before the guests?

The bride appeared as confused as a woman made stupid by drink. She showed little sign of underlying grace or modesty. When one young man told a most obscene story about a girl who seduced an aged scholar, she took off her shoe and threw it, cursing, at the youth's head.

"My precious," Old Wang kept crooning drunkenly to no one in particular. "My darling girl. Tomorrow she will no longer be ours!"

Li counted up his winnings smugly. The girl. The boats, the caravans, the donkey trains. All no longer Wang's.

"Ah, you must die to us. You must bleed for us. My darling, my eternal young one," keened the merchant.

And after Wang had been carried back to his rooms by his bearers and the bachelors had slouched out of the bridal chamber—some so drunk that they had vomited on the stones and had to be lain in makeshift pallets in the servants' hall—the bridal couple was put to bed. The contract between two houses who hated and needed each other was to be sealed by the breaking of a maidenhead.

Li bowed the last tipsy uncle into the guest wing, dismissed the exhausted servants, and crawled into bed beside his rigidly awake wife. When Meng tried to speak, the general commanded her to silence. His nerves were taut and jangled, his body too tense for sleep. After a time spent tossing, Li shuffled out in his slippers to look at the moon, but just as he set foot in the garden, the moon slipped behind a cloud. He went down then to the Kitchen Court for a bun and a calming tea, and found the mountains of food left over from the feast had been spirited away by a hundred gluttonous hands, for it was a custom at rural weddings for guests to claim the leavings for "servants" left at home—an excuse to sneak yet another meal out of the host.

Annoyed and impatient, Li searched the cupboards and found a small stack of dried cuttlefish tied with string. He began to tear at the leathery meat with his teeth. It came off in papery strips, filling his mouth with a mossy sweetness that made his throat catch in delight. This was what he ate in the field when his horse took him too far from the cook tents. He grabbed another piece and strode past the stable yards. The horses blew and stamped in their stalls at the smell of his passing.

The guard at the gate was startled out of his wine-laden sleep by the sight of the master chewing on a handful of dried fish like an idle boy. Li motioned to the guard to open the gate and strolled past the crouching lions onto the dark jetty. For a long while, he stood at the edge of the pier listening to the river. The sound of the waves carried whispers of war from far upstream: blood, smoke, the cries of the dying. Victory was not yet his. He had only gained the high ground.

Deeply unsettled, he turned back through the gates and began the long slow climb to his rooms. The moon had drifted beyond the thick covering of clouds, lighting the empty courts with silvery ghosts. His feet swept aside the dry, red husks of firecrackers that swirled across the cobblestones in the night wind. The fish had left a cloying after-taste in his mouth, and now his head began to ache from the toasts he had drunk throughout the thirteen-course feast. There was still an hour or so before cockcrow. At dawn, the old women would inspect the bridal silk, a piece of white cloth laid on the sheets. The public ritual of viewing the blood-kissed silk would be proof of the bride's chastity and the groom's potency. Never, the general concluded with bitter irony, were two virtues more perilously placed than in the persons of Li Liang Mo and Wang Mei Yuk.

On the path to the Second Terrace where Liang Mo and his bride slept, Li heard a brisk footfall on the gravel. The noise was too quick and light for the tread of the nightwatch. It sounded like the swift, sure footsteps of a thief. Out of habit, he slowed his breathing and stepped into the shadow of a willow tree. She had almost passed before he saw her: a tall woman in a dress the color of the night sky.

"Stop!" he said, stepping out from under the tree.

The woman pushed something up her sleeve and took a fighting stance to face him. She flicked the long hair off her shoulder with a twist of her head. The sharp bones of her face were illumined by moonlight.

"You! Why are you wandering the house?" he said in surprise.

Rulan's head dipped in a perfunctory bow. "I'm on an errand for Liang Mo. And you, Father?"

The question annoyed him. "Liang Mo should be lying with his bride!"

"So he is. I'm bringing a salve for my sister." She made no move to show what she had hidden in her garment.

"Saddle soap for the new mare?" He laughed, embarrassed by his lapse of decorum. What was it about Rulan that made him forget his dignity? He sighed, remembering that she might be a spy and not an ally. She was a daughter-in-law, not a free woman. One who survived at his pleasure and therefore was not worth his concern.

"She's only a girl," Rulan reminded him.

"Yes, yes!" he said, remembering their earlier heated exchange when the bride had just come. Suddenly he felt weary and ashamed. The wedding had been a sordid business from start to finish. Now a fourteen-year-old girl was the wax into which his family's chop was to be impressed forever.

"I will take you up," he said firmly. He tried to mask his attraction to her with a show of anger, but his voice sounded tired and hoarse. "There are priests and musicians wandering about. It is not seemly for you to go alone."

"You need not trouble yourself with this humble person." Coming from Rulan's lips, the subservient words sounded like a challenge.

"Come," he commanded, encircling the firm muscle of her arm. His fingers inadvertently touched the softer flesh near her breast. She stiffened and clutched her left sleeve with her right hand but did not draw away. They walked together in silence through the perfume of climbing honeysuckle. Her breathing was unlabored, her stride as long as his, and she did not lean against him as a woman with bound feet would have done.

At the moon gate of the bridal chamber, Liang Mo rushed out the door in his sleeping clothes.

"Rulan?" he panted.

"Yes, and your father."

Liang Mo froze. "Father—I—please don't—" blurted out Liang Mo.

The general's anger rose at the sight of his son's ashen face, but before he could lash out at Liang Mo, Rulan had drawn him through the door of her own apartment.

Rulan's sitting room was almost empty of furnishings; there were four high-backed teak chairs, a small table, and wooden medicine cases with narrow drawers set against the walls. There was also a loom, but it was bare of thread. The second room held only a bed and a small round side table. The general thought it looked more like a barracks than the room of a concubine in a great house. She hates this house, he decided. She makes her room like a girls' dormitory in a poor village.

"I should have heeded my Tai Tai. This marriage is a disaster," Liang Mo groaned. He scratched the sweaty dome of his shaved head.

"Where is your wife?" the general demanded.

"In there. Sleeping." Liang Mo made a face. "She's mad, like the old man."

"Have you made her your wife yet?"

Liang Mo burst into tears. "I can't—she screamed. After that, I couldn't—"

Li's hand ached to strike his son. "Show me."

Numbly, Liang Mo led the way through Rulan's apartment through a door that passed from the rear of her rooms into his.

"Over there," Liang Mo whispered. He pointed among the smashed winecups and torn bedclothes to where Mei Yuk lay on the floor wrapped in a blue silk wall hanging, fast asleep. Her red wedding gown was wadded up under her head. Her painted face was streaked with tears, and the crimson from her lips had smeared over her chin.

"She said I sickened her. She said she would sooner kill herself than have me touch her. Then she snatched up her hairpins and held them to her heart. I went to my writing table and wrote some letters, and gradually she stopped crying. I tried to read, but I couldn't see the characters. Finally she fell asleep."

"You failed me," Li said harshly to his tearful son. "You have only an hour. The deed must be done by then." The general moved grimly toward the sleeping girl and bent to pick her up.

Liang Mo's eyes opened wide. "No, Father, please!" he cried.

"Eh?" said the general. One look at Liang Mo's horrified face made his anger blaze even higher. "Impious idiot! Do you think I am capable of such a thing?" He realized that he was a stranger to his son, who saw him as an obdurate, violent man, capable of immense cruelty in the service of the family. He himself had purposely fashioned such an image in his dealings with his son. Still, it made him angry. Why was it that everything his son did made him angry? "Well then, jealous bridegroom, you pick her up. Put her back on the bed."

Liang Mo's face had turned an ugly, mottled red. He lifted up the girl awkwardly and rolled her onto the bed so that her thin arms and legs splayed out across the sheets. Then he unbuttoned his shirt slowly, his face averted from Rulan. "Father— What if she starts screaming again?"

"The dowry is signed. You can beat her, cast her out," snapped the general. "But first you have to take her. Besides," he added gruffly, intending his words for the tall woman beside his son, "women like a little roughness. It makes the closing sweeter. My soldiers would think it all in a day's fighting."

"I am not a soldier," declared Liang Mo primly.

The general slapped his son's face. "You are not a man!" he hissed.

"Father," Rulan said swiftly. "If you make Liang Mo force her, she will hate him. This house needs sons, and a cold womb will not help her bear. There is a better way."

Li showed his disgust for his son with a contemptuous wave of his hand. "Show me," he said, relinquishing the battle to her.

Rulan took out a small vial from her sleeve. "Pig's blood from the cook shed," she explained. She went over to the sleeping girl and searched through the bedclothes until she found the piece of white silk. Quickly, Rulan daubed the blood on the conjugal cloth and placed it carefully under the bride's slender hips.

The general bit back an exclamation. The concubine was clever as well as fearless. She had played her part perfectly, far better than the groom or the master of the house.

Once outside the garden, the general glanced back through the moon gate and saw Liang Mo weeping in Rulan's arms. Li knew then that he should kill her, for she had made herself essential in his house: she knew its guilty secrets, nursed its private tribulations. What was she after? He yearned to know, for his son—and for himself.

He went to his rooms, undressed quickly, and slipped into bed again beside his sleeping wife. Impatiently, he rolled her shift up to her neck and put his hand on her small breast. Meng groaned and tried to push him away, but he was already fully aroused. He pulled her knees apart with rough hands to make her ready. Groggily, Meng lifted her hips to meet him. He began to probe her, first with slow, measured strokes, then faster, holding her tiny feet aloft in the palms of his hands. But even as he felt his face pucker and the heat gathering in his loins, he felt no joy at the anticipated release, only a mounting anger at his wife's false cries of ecstasy and her dry welcome.

Before breakfast, he hastened to Liang Mo's wing to meet the Wang women who would inspect, as was their right, the conjugal silk to see that their daughter had been properly inducted into wifehood by her husband. He was not surprised to see Magistrate Lam leading the party of old women.

"How gratifying to witness your concern for our son and daughter, Magistrate," said the general.

"Unusual, but not unprecedented," Lam replied. "Wang has asked me to accompany his ladies to the marriage bed to see that the contract of marriage has been consummated and the proof of blood is on the marriage silk, as law demands."

The young magistrate sets forth his case concisely, Li thought with grudging admiration; he makes acceptable even a last indecent attempt by Wang, his benefactor, to besmirch his own kin. But I have out-flanked Wang again. "I am sure my son and daughter-in-law are everything we suspect they are—and have rewarded us with what we desire," he told Lam with finality. And led him into the bridal chamber with a mocking smile.

General Li rose at dawn from the warm fragrance of his bed and walked into the cool morning air. A *jing wei* bird flew out of a tree and skimmed over the pond, disturbing the image of the sky in the water. He looked down and saw that the hem of his gown was wet with dew. And what did it matter if one's skirts were wet, he asked himself, recalling the words of the poet Tao Yuan Ming, as long as one gained one's heart's desire?

Four days had passed since Liang Mo's wedding night, and disaster had not come. Wang had moved his forces with ruthless abandon, and the general had checked him at every turn. Li had escaped the watery pit and leapt to victory. The day before, Wang and his train had left for Canton like a line of people abandoning a city. Magistrate Lam had asked to stay behind to oversee the proper transfer of licenses to the agreed-upon salt routes. The general suspected that Lam would introduce the next battle with the Wangs. It would be a lifelong struggle to stunt the growth of the poisonous flower from the house of Wang who now inhabited his garden.

Li found his new daughter-in-law impossible to read. She had been through a terrible shock, to be sure, but he had quickly discerned that hysteria was a practiced strategy she used to manipulate others. Mei Yuk had begged an audience to plead for the life of the prisoner, so he had decided to deny it. He now dealt with the girl only through his wife or Rulan. According to Meng, Mei Yuk's tantrums had stopped when no one except Rulan bothered to listen to the girl's prattle about how the peasant had saved her life.

Maybe it was better that the groom loved his concubine and hated his wife, for if there were rotten sons from the Wangs, there would also be healthy ones to challenge them. The general willed the image of his son's concubine to the edge of his mind. He would not let the placid mood of the morning be marred by the unruly winds of doubt and desire.

The moment was so beautiful, so self-sufficient, that if he were a singing man, he felt that he might break into song. He glanced back into the room and saw that the girl his wife had sent with his bathwater still slept. Meng had sensed his dissatisfaction at their last lovemaking and had placed the girl in his path as a gift. It amused him that his wife's crude attempts to arouse him, whether with her own body or another's, always worked, although sometimes it pleased him more to deny himself pleasure and her the triumph of believing she could control him.

Such crude devices, he acknowledged, worked with others as well. Men were not complex creatures. A woman, a string of coins, a cup of wine always had predictable results. The effects might differ from man to man, but were always predictable, and once you knew how a man reacted to women, money, and wine, you knew the man. General Li knew his own weaknesses. Money and wine were not among them. So he was thankful that the only one who procured for him, who could yank his reins in this way, was Meng. And if, on these occasions, she had something to extort, it was usually something he was prepared to give, because he knew that Meng viewed her welfare as inseparable from his.

After the clouds and rain and an exquisite, short sleep, he felt the need to cleanse his spirit, to catch the essence of the morning.

Without warning, the tall, shapely image of Rulan floated before him and shattered his composure.

Food, he told himself quickly. Think of Second Cook slamming dishes and pots while the rest of the house is still asleep. Think of the Kitchen Court—the pots, the steam, the ten thousand scents, the rush, the regimentation, and the clatter, so like the army. So many sweating men striving to jump to the next grade. Slop boy looking to wash cabbages, cabbage boy looking to slice pork, knife boy looking to fold dumplings—and all aspiring to supplant the toothless old man whose nimble fingers gave the disparate raw elements the final alchemical union in the fire.

Li rubbed his bare chest, reveling in the tautness of his muscles. Not the kitchen; the stables, he decided, as the *jing wei* bird called to its mate overhead. What better way to prolong the voluptuous mood of the morning than to exercise in tandem with his favorite mounts while the sun slanted over the wall.

By the time the general reached the stable yard, the hands were walking his favorite gray. The animal, smelling his master, did a small delighted dance to shake out the stiffness brought about by the overnight confinement. Li leapt on the wall, nodding to the grooms who led the horses out two by two from the warren of narrow stalls dug into the base of the cliff. With the Concubine's pagoda looming above him on one side and the river breaking below him on the other, Li positioned himself on a low wall separating the stable yard from the Kitchen Court and adjusted the pressure of his feet so that the weight of his body was perfectly balanced on the rough stones.

He closed his eyes and felt his spine tugging gently upward, felt it slowly straighten as if someone were softly pulling on an invisible string attached to the top of his head. He felt his neck and arms relax; the muscles of his face grow slack. The steam rising from the nostrils of his horses, the pink-and-white pagoda, the foam-flecked river—all had become elements in a painted backdrop waiting for him to begin the transcendent dance. He filled his lungs slowly while pondering his next move against Old Wang. The fat merchant had pressed far more money and gifts on his hosts than they had given to him. Calling attention to his wealth and the Lis' penury was Wang's way of evening up the score. Li savored the memory of his victory for an instant, then released it with the stale air in his lungs in a single, long exhalation that cleansed his whole being. Concentrating on the axle of power deep in his gut, he swung into the first set of *tai chi chuan*.

Even before he lifted his foot, so completely had Li shaped the gestures in his mind that the river of movement had the inevitability of an afterthought. "Let the mind, not the muscles lead," Li reminded himself, pleased that his body and his mind were one, as Cheng San Feng's treatise on the "effortless art" directed. Long ago, *tai chi chuan* had sprung from a set of exercises called five animals play, which was designed to promote digestion, circulation, and absorption of food and increase resistance to disease. Each movement had its complement, and so he stepped right and then left, turned and lifted, lifted and turned. Now he was a tiger slouching, a deer springing, now a bear, a monkey, a bird. His gestures were as round and rhythmical as the waves washing over the rocks below. Sensation broke into layers—he was at once a being of pure air, and a creature of sullen earth moving heavily against an invisible current. His skin seemed to taste the morning on all its surfaces; he savored the tiny wisps of air brushing the hair on his chest, moving mote by mote over his face. Sweat stood out on his skin like pearls. The horses circled the yard, pounding the ground with their iron hooves, yet he knew them only as fellow creatures who for this moment had matched their pulse to his: to-gether, they moved within the *tao,* the subtle way of wind and water, of breath overcoming bone, of winning by having nothing to win.

He did not know when he began to be aware of the man in the box by the wall.

The box in which the prisoner crouched was no higher than a man's knees, and narrow enough so that he could not sit or lie down. The prisoner was unusually large, judging from the way his hunched form filled the trunk-size prison. The general thought he saw the man's head turn to watch him. Suddenly self-conscious, Li felt his hold over the moment slip away. A hand crept out from behind the bars. Li was sure now that the prisoner's eyes were following him. Was he being mocked or stalked by a vicious tiger in a cage? How long had it been? Three days? Four? Most men died in three, but this man still moved and breathed. He had meant to interrogate the prisoner, but in the rush of the wedding events, he'd forgotten all about the prisoner until Lam had asked the evening before if the man were dead. It brought to mind Merchant Wang's loud insistence that the peasant die a painful death. Their interest in his quick dispatch aroused the general's curiosity.

Li decided that because fate had delivered an enemy into his hands, he should at least learn something about this particular specimen. It was astounding that anyone could survive four days of hell in the box when most animals, let alone men, would have died from the cramps, heat, and lack of food and water. How had the creature avoided the inevitable pain that made most men insensible within hours?

Li circled slowly into the movement called carry the dragon over the mountain, brought the gesture back into a graceful antithesis, and smiled. *Tai chi,* of course. What exquisite control the man must have.

After watching a while, Li became convinced that the man hunched in the box like an animal in a trap was indeed moving his muscles in the pattern of Li's dance. And one thing more. Marks in the dirt showed that the box had been toppled over. Somehow the man had managed to push the box over on its side in order to take the pressure off his bent legs. Perhaps at night, Li concluded, when no one was looking. He must be a strong as well as a patient animal, for in the morning, he would push the box upright again. A master of the effortless art. The thought excited him.

"*Sssssss.*" Li pushed a small stream of air through clenched teeth. Slowly, he raised one leg, moved it in an arc before planting it on the edge of the stone wall, and balancing bowlegged with arms akimbo.

He performed the final movements of the sequence with particular care, piqued by the knowledge that an expert was judging his style. He lowered his forearm in a gesture recalling a green sapling swaying in the wind and finished the movement with the arm at his side, elbow, wrist, and fingers gently curved. He would plan his entire morning around this caged animal, instead of around his bird.

He motioned for one of the stable hands to bring him a towel to wipe the sweat away. "The man in the box is strong, *hai ma?*"

"I'm stronger, Lord," the boy said stoutly. He had just gotten the first growth of manhood and was proud.

"So I see," the general said, rubbing his face with the thick cloth.

"He would have died a long time ago, if your son's Second, the lady doctor, had not been feeding him. I lost my bet because of her. I said he would die on the third day."

"What did you lose?"

"A copper, Master."

"Here's two coppers for you then," the general said, searching in the small bag he carried at his waist. "A strong boy like you should be able to carry it." Li never quibbled about paying for good information. And it was always wise to train a spy in such a way that he did not know he was being groomed. "Ah," he muttered, "both my son's women. One is crazy and the other is probably a spy with tender mercies—why are they interested in him? We must take this tiger out of his cage to see if he bites."

■   ■   ■

The general, his son, and the magistrate sat around a small round table outside the vase-shaped door of a pavilion on the Second Terrace, so surrounded by rockery and trees that it seemed unconnected with the other parts of the great house. Inside the hall, there were small cabinets curtained with gauze where, in years past, men in long robes and gold-buttoned hats went often to read and write poetry, to smoke the water pipe, to drink tea, and to meditate on virtue and obedience, error and law. No official had come to visit the cubicles in decades, and the garden had long gone to seed. But the south corner, which was overhung with pine branches and trellises trailing wild honeysuckle, had become a favorite place for Meng and her ladies to sew and gossip. Since his homecoming, the general had preempted the glade for "official business" but really because he preferred these dusty courts and their soothing aroma of old books and decayed lily ponds to his own newly painted chambers. A flight of small stone steps led from the garden to a shallow pond, from which rose a tiny Kwan Yin of terra-cotta lifting one crumbling hand in benediction. It was here at the water's edge that Li greeted Lam and Liang Mo.

Li had decided that the time was ripe to begin Liang Mo's training. It would be interesting, he speculated, to bring the pampered champion of the peasantry face-to-face with the real thing. Li suspected that the encounter would teach Liang Mo a lesson. The youth needed toughening. The general was still furious at Liang Mo for his weakness on the wedding night and still annoyed at his son's stupid romantic scheme of a year ago to aid the Hakka rebels.

He surmised that Rulan, the Golden Orchid, was the source of Liang Mo's delusions. What a puzzle she was! By all accounts, the girl was fanatically loyal to his mother: she had coddled and humored the old woman when no one else would, nursed her through sickness, and mourned her far more than her own kin.

Yet after the events of the last days, Li was less concerned about Rulan's loyalty; women spies were easily turned, and she had proven herself true again and again. It was common for spies to fall in love with the subjects they were sent to seduce. And because she was now a permanent member of his house, it would be a challenge for him to reeducate her—along with his thickheaded son. Again, he wondered how she could bear such a youth!

At Li's instruction, two servants dragged Pao An into the garden and threw him at the men's feet. Lam continued to extol the beauty of the cassia trees while Li protested the compliment. Only Liang Mo stared at the man lying facedown in the dirt.

"Give him a drink," Li ordered, pointing to the pot of now tepid tea on the table.

The servants lifted Pao An up and pried open his mouth and hastily emptied the pot. Pao An swallowed greedily without opening his eyes. Suddenly, he shuddered and vomited into the dirt. The servants recoiled and dropped Pao An, whose head rolled forward into the filth. Liang Mo looked away in horror.

"Put him there," Li directed.

Grimacing at the stench, the servants picked up Pao An once more. Pao An tried to lift his knees as they dragged him across the yard, but the effort to walk was fruitless. The men propped him up against a stone bench like a battered doll.

An idea popped into Li's head, and he held it a moment, studying the intricate possibilities. "Liang Mo," he barked, "send for your second wife, the healer. I do not wish this dog to die quite yet." General Li watched as his son gave the order. Liang Mo was visibly upset by the wretched man before him.

Li turned with a smile to Lam, who was reciting Tao Chien's drinking song, "The Green Pine Grows in the Eastern Garden," and shaking his shoulders to the rhythm of the words. If one scraped away the filth, Li thought, while tapping his fingers in time to Lam's voice, the man was a remarkable specimen: broad shoulders, narrow hips, and long limbs. He was quite sick, of course, sicker since he had been fed, and he was obviously wasted from the ordeal in the box. It would be interesting to see what rapport Rulan had forged with the prisoner— and on whose account.

Li noticed that even as they talked, the man was stretching his muscles imperceptibly without moving his body. He is uncoiling himself before our eyes, Li marveled. Perhaps he might spring up and strike us all. Li uncrossed his legs and dropped his arms into a defensive posture as he heard the shift in rhythm that signaled the ending of Lam's song: "Why should I tie myself to this worldly bondage?" Lam sang. Because, Li thought, we do not know how cruelly we may be bound in the next.

"Tell me, Magistrate," Li said to Lam, "how do you propose to dispense with the criminal?"

Lam's voice dropped quickly into the cadences of everyday speech. "However it pleases you, although with such incendiary characters it is best done quickly."

"But surely we should squeeze what we can out of him," Li ventured.

"I am not sure if this rotten lemon is worth squeezing," Lam opined. "He must be small trash, for his fellow robbers did not hesitate to leave him when they failed to kidnap your daughter-in-law. His conduct is so atrocious that I can make an exception and kill him now instead of waiting until autumn for the emperor's official time to punish capital crimes. Cut off the head and throw him into the river. Leave it to me. I keep a man who helps me chastise thieves. He makes a clean cut."

"I am grateful for your help," said Li. "But whichever way he dies, the question remains—what does he know? Holding this case for autumn for the emperor's review has some merit. Although a stubborn man might go to his death with secrets, an intelligent one might retain life by his openness."

The general intended his words as a rope for the bandit, who had no other lifeline left. He also observed that Lam's remarks, while failing to frighten the criminal, had made an impact on Liang Mo.

Something in the garden was making Liang Mo's eyes water. "Why all this talk of cutting heads? Mei Yuk says he saved her from the bandits," said Liang Mo. "Send the poor man home."

"Look at the creature," said the general to Lam, ignoring his son. "Even under his own excrement, he stinks of the paddies. As big as a tiger, but hardly a hero. Since when do farmers come to the aid of their betters?"

"You turn your wrath on a weakling, Father," said Liang Mo shakily.

"Ah, the passionate bridegroom," General Li observed. "Less defensive of his wife's honor than the honor of thieves."

Liang Mo turned white.

The general was astounded at his son's naïveté. Liang Mo believed in the peasant's innocence! "My curiosity is aroused, Magistrate. I want to know the name of his Triad commander."

Lam raised an eyebrow. "It seems impossible that this paddy boy would be in league with Triads—bandits perhaps."

"There are men who say Merchant Wang is Triad—so why not this peasant? The bandits gave all the signs of being highly organized, Collector Fan told me. He distinctly heard them cry out for the restoration of the Ming."

"As does every starving village boy who steals a handful of rice at the neighboring market," Lam replied. "I have discovered they are mere thieves."

"This boy is from a pigsty village I own that never pays its rents in full. Such villages are rank with Triad corruption."

"Then let me take him back to his village, and I will set his head upon the gate."

Li shook his head, intrigued by Lam's obdurate prosecution of the peasant. "I have made this salt marriage. My enemies seem to want to prevent so strong an alliance. I want to know why. This boy is my only link."

Lam's face was utterly unresponsive.

"What do you mean 'salt marriage'?" interjected Liang Mo.

The general gave an exasperated sigh.

Lam turned with great patience to Liang Mo. "In joining with the Wangs, your family now controls every bridge, road, and inland waterway in the richest part of the Land of Flowers. That includes the routes of the salt boats."

"And more," snapped the general. "Every porter who packs on his back or in his wheelbarrow the salt the bargemen haul on the water, every merchant who buys and sells the salt that the coolies carry. Some say that 'he who controls the salt monopolies controls the empire.' Men like our estimable Merchant Wang and his cohorts, the Yang Chou salt merchants, who sit astride the Grand Canal—they are among the most powerful men in the Middle Kingdom. Their hand grasps the leg of the throne itself. A man of courage and conviction could use that army of bearers for many purposes, *hai ma,* Magistrate?"

"It is possible," Lam said.

Liang Mo looked fearfully from the general to Lam, unable to grasp the implications of his father's lecture. In the middle of the silence came a strangled sound.

"Opium," Pao An rasped. He fixed his swollen eyes on General Li.

The general turned his head in surprise. "Here is an erudite pupil."

"Opium—Tanka pirates—Triad—" Pao An slowly said.

"You cannot mean the loyal Tanka," said Lam quietly.

"I'm sure he does not mean the 'loyal' Tanka," replied the general. "There are so few. Didn't the bandits who attacked my daughter-in-law's bridal train escape on the barges of the rat-men? And everyone knows the Tanka have joined the Triads."

"There are no traitorous Tanka in my district," protested Lam. "No opium traded. My people know the punishment for smuggling." For the first time that morning, Lam's composure was shaken.

"Tanka have no district," whispered Pao An.

"And for every salt boat, they have two to carry dirt. A floating kingdom to build alongside the one I am claiming by dowry. That must make the merchants of opium nervous. I have made clear my hatred for the filth—from the foreign filth who bring it, to the rat filth who carry it, to the dead filth who smoke it. The Tanka have good reason not to want this marriage of salt."

"Not the Tanka," insisted Lam. "They know how harshly I deal with opium peddlers!"

"Well, deal harshly with this one. Fan, my rent collector, claims that the boy is one of their black dirt disciples. So, Boy, what of these water rat allies of yours. Did they make a pact with the Triads? Do you intend to put a knife between my ribs?"

Pao An opened his lips to reveal a mouth blackened by dried blood. His lips tried to form a word, but opened instead in a silent scream. Yes, he longed to shout, I want to drive one into your heart.

"How awful," gasped Liang Mo.

"Go interpret for us," said Li in disgust. "Go listen to the voice of the people."

Pao An stared at the general with hot eyes. Death would be a small price to pay for killing the man who had slain his family. Hatred for Li had given him the courage to survive his ordeal in the box. But as yet, his legs and arms, even his voice did not obey him. He was a prisoner still. A beetle crawled out of one of the legs of his pants. It struggled for a moment, its antennae shaking, then moved back into the grime. In helpless anger, Pao An tried to raise his hand to crush it, but the hand would not move. He saw that Liang Mo was trying to hold back his robe so it would not brush against Pao An.

Rulan entered the garden as Liang Mo was about to address Pao An.

The general pointed an accusing finger in her direction. "I understand that we have you to thank for keeping the prisoner alive while he was in the box!"

Ignoring Liang Mo's shocked face, Rulan nodded. "Yes, Father. I gave him food and medicine. There have been too many deaths already."

"If I ask you to save him, will you kill him to spite me?" asked the general harshly.

Rulan answered boldly. "He'll fight to live because he wants to find his father. He spoke of him several times while delirious in the box."

"It's true," Lam added. "That is all he talked about on the ride here. The old man was exiled by the clan. Surely he planned the bandit raid and the clan feared he would bring disaster on their heads."

It pained Pao An to hear the young magistrate's treacherous words. But he was too sick to fight back.

Li eased himself against the stiff teakwood chair, pleased that he had finally found the key to this tiger. Here was a man so gloriously simple that he might have leapt out of the pages of an old chronicle. A man who sought neither women, wine, nor money. A filial son!

"You are alone, Boy," he said. "Your brothers have thrown you aside like slop. I kill traitors, but I admire filial sons. Tell me about the river men. Tell me the name of your Triad leader, and I will not put you back in the box."

"This is not the work of Triads," Lam insisted. "Not in my district."

Li ignored the magistrate and added slowly, "One name. And I will help you find your father."

A hard lump formed in Pao An's throat. He swallowed it and tasted bile. Fate had made the enemy Li into his ally against the young magistrate, who wanted him dead. He only vaguely remembered the tall girl from the time she had brought rice gruel when he was dying of hunger and thirst. He had thought her kind, but she was their spy too, listening from the shadows for his secrets so she could report them to these smug and callous monsters. They were all watching him, waiting to pick the secrets from his skull, and now they wanted to know what internal fires were rising toward combustion, as if he, the beetle who had crawled out of a dung heap, could tell them. Very well. He would keep his face better than the young lord who was so obviously an opium-weakened fool. He would tell his tormentor lies mixed with half-truths that would lead him astray. That would buy time enough to heal. Time to gather strength. And if by some miracle, he was left alive when Abundant Spring Mountain was ashes and dust, perhaps he would take up with Iron Fist after all and search for his father. He would never be the lackey of gentry leeches again.

"Quickly, your leader," growled the general. "If your father is alive, I can find him."

"The Triads," Pao An said bitterly. "They catch fools like me the way they haul fish with twine. I met the leader—"

"What did he look like? What did he promise you? Gold? A small-foot woman with soft hands? Enough dirt to make you a king in your village?" pressed Li.

Pao An closed his eyes. "A kingdom of peace where all men are brothers." He laughed. Suddenly, it seemed that there was a gong sounding in his ears. The wall had begun to sink like quicksand behind him.

"He has fainted," observed the general. "Rulan, make sure he does not die. If we can win him to us, he might be a useful tool against the rats along the river. Go," he said curtly to his son. "Take her home."

Liang Mo rose, obviously relieved at the dismissal.

Leaning across the table, Li made a graceful gesture for Lam to remain. "How curious it is," he remarked to the magistrate, "that so many have an interest in this criminal—even you."

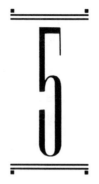

Pao An awoke in dark, luminescent space. A sweet, low sound, like laughter rising or water sliding over rocks, echoed in his ears. He thought he heard Pang's raucous voice over the sounds of the river. Pang, he called back softly. And then he remembered Pang's ruined body in the reeds; he remembered Li Yu walking toward the river, the weight of the cangue on his own neck and knees, the agonizing thirst in the box.

Surely I have died, he told himself. But when he moved his legs, he found them free and extended, sore but without the mind-bending pain that had nearly killed him in the box. He sat up and touched a hand to his face like a blind man, then to the rest of his body. How strange to feel the stubborn fact of one's own flesh, he thought. What joy! He opened his arms as if to fly and his right hand caught on a veil of silk. Sweeping it aside, he discovered that he was lying in a canopied bed in a large room. The windows were open. The murmuring of a fountain filled his ears. A moon in the shape of a golden bowl floated in the sky.

I can escape, he whispered. But when he swung his feet to the ground and stood up, the humming in his ears became a roar and the floor a living, writhing creature. Much later, two cool, strong hands lifted him back to the bed. The scent of her was as fresh as new grass.

She gave him something bitter to drink, and in moments he was drifting in a current of sweet, pure song.

Pao An awoke again in twilight to the sound of running water. The same day? The next? Again he tried to rise, but more slowly and stepped carefully across the floor toward a large round window. Peering out on tiptoe, he saw a walled garden, a willow tree, and a fountain. A breeze stirred the filigreed branches of the tree and teased his face with the fragrance of honeysuckle. He wondered if he could scale the walls in his present condition and decided to wait.

As his eyes gradually accommodated to the dim light, he began to explore the room. The heavy door was bolted from outside, but surely this was no prison. It was larger than Li Yu's entire house, and empty except for the bed and a few chairs. Sharp lemony odors came from jars and wooden boxes stacked against the door.

The sound of feet scraping the gravel outside sent him tottering back to the bed. The heavy door creaked open, and a tall, well-dressed woman carrying an oil lamp moved toward him in a corona of light. From beneath his lashes, he saw that it was the woman who had fed him in the box and who had appeared briefly in the garden. Pretending sleep, he felt her bend over him. Her fingers touched his bare knee, traveled up his thigh. She spoke softly to herself in a dialect that he at first did not recognize.

He strained with all his being to say nothing.

"Good," she said softly, sensing that he heard, and kneaded the swollen tendon of his leg. "The inflammation has gone down. You're very lucky. Not many people survive such punishment."

Pao An sat up, embarrassed to have the girl touch him so intimately. "It was you who saved me from the box," he said, dipping his head in an awkward gesture of thanks. You who told about my father, he accused silently. Although she had spoken the local Punti dialect perfectly, the words she had first uttered were, he now realized, unmistakably Hakka, and he wondered what business a Hakka had with a Punti family as prominent as the Lis, when Hakka and Punti despised each other. Looking down his body, he saw for the first time that he had been washed clean, and that someone had changed his loincloth. Then he remembered the mark on his leg.

The girl's face betrayed no emotion. She unwrapped a parcel and laid its contents out on the floor. There were several kinds of cold buns, a jar of warm tea, and three oranges—better than he had eaten in the village on holiday.

"I thought this might be the hour you'd awaken. Now you will be hungry, but eat little and very slowly. Take tea. A piece of orange at first. Later, a bun or two if you can keep it down. I brought three kinds—coconut, black sugar, and red pork."

He grabbed a bun and broke it open. The sugary aroma from the thick, dark filling made him nauseous, and he put it back, after wiping the thick black syrup from his fingers.

While the famished man sipped his tea, Rulan lingered, watching her patient. She told herself that as a healer, she had a right to be pleased. But there was something more about him that excited her. Was it his strength? His tenacity? Rulan knew that most men in his condition died. Once she might have used *chi gung* to heal him. But with the Tai Tai's death, the healing fire had vanished, leaving her hands as icy as her heart. A fitting punishment, she told herself, for one who had used her arts to kill. She had given up the secret exercises; she was only an herb-woman now, her powers limited to mixing broths, manipulating needles—and offering up half-hearted prayers to the goddess who no longer listened.

Needles. Herbs. Incantations. Which had wrought the miracle? When she had first seen him in his cage, he'd looked more like a wounded animal than a man: his lips were split open and the muscles of his legs, arms, and stomach rippled with spasms from being bent so long in the box. The servants had taken bets on the hour of his death. She had stirred a pinch of powdered rhinoceros horn—an antidote for fever and infection—into a bowl of strong broth wheedled from Second Cook and held it before his face. He shook his head, but she let the smells assail his nostrils until finally he opened his mouth to take a spoonful.

Her confrontation with the general in the garden had earned her a small victory: the general had placed the prisoner in her care, not in his son's. She wondered why Li would so humiliate Liang Mo, although she was glad to be a healer once again. And the man needed her arts, for his legs and stomach were grossly distended and the infection gone inward. White moss coated his tongue, and his pulse was low and slippery, hardly discernible to her fingers. It was curiously like the disease that some women get if they take their husband's stalk too soon after childbirth. So Rulan had taken fire-cooling herbs to cleanse and drive the heat from the reddened skin. For the internal fire, she had made a poultice of gardenia, jasmine, and gentian blossoms mixed with abalone shell. She had applied the healing mixture four times a day, and waited for him to die.

She saw him die the first night he was placed in her care. With a small cry, his ghost flew out of his mouth. Knowing that ghosts travel only in straight lines, Rulan had leapt to slam shut the door directly opposite the bed. Then she remembered the window and jumped up on a chair to pull the paper shutters closed so the ghost had no means of escape. The sick man quivered, and Rulan knew that the ghost was hovering in midair, loath to leave the body. As much for herself as for the sick one, Rulan began an incantation. The man sighed. There was an answering whisper as the ghost sank back into the inert flesh. After that, he seemed stronger, and the poisons were quickly expunged.

Bereft of the healing fire, she had fought off the pain with needles, and the invisible demons with herbs and snatches of old songs. But she could not drive out the she-demon that repeatedly invaded his dreams. He had stretched tumescent in his delirium, his hands struggling to catch hold of an invisible shape and crying "Fox-spirit!" She inadvertently told Mei Yuk about the demon, because the girl always pleaded to know everything about the boy, especially what he said in his sleep.

"Be ashamed," Rulan chided. "You are a married woman."

"Then talk to me!" Mei Yuk pouted. "You don't pay attention to me. No one does. No one likes me. That boy is the only person who has shown me one grain of kindness since I left my auntie's house in that bad luck procession! I'll tell my Kung Kung."

"Your grandfather has gone home. Remember? You said good-bye to him."

"He said he'd be back to claim me one day, the liar."

The girl's impious, unbridled behavior shocked Rulan. Yet she refused to join the maids who laughed among themselves about the "illness" that kept bride and groom apart at night. Moon had hinted to Meng that the bride was possessed and took as confirmation the fact that only the "witch" Rulan could make the girl behave.

What convinced Rulan that there was a genuinely tender side to Mei Yuk was the girl's grief for the sick man.

"Second Sister," she pleaded to Rulan, "I am ashamed of how this family treats the boy. Let me see him. Only then will I know that he has not suffered for me."

Finally, Rulan relented and took Mei Yuk with her to help administer medicines. The girl proved clumsy and too easily distracted, her eyes wandering always from the herb jars to the face and body of the unconscious youth.

Liang Mo zealously questioned Rulan daily about the prisoner. But something stopped her from telling more than she had to. She related his dream talk about his father to Liang Mo, who dutifully reported it to the general. But she did not tell Liang Mo about the youth's dream of the fox-spirit or about the mark his thigh. She had seen a similar tattoo in the Orchid compound on a Triad horse trainer who had cut his leg. After seeing this same mark on the youth's leg, she had begun to feel the stirring of old sympathies that the Tai Tai's death had nearly destroyed. Knowing that if the mark was observed, the general would doubtless kill the youth, she needled his skin with red dye and made the symbol into a strawberry-colored birthmark.

The snatches of news about the Taiping community terrified her: the viceroy's provincial army had surrounded the Taiping families at Thistle Mountain. The Taiping warriors had broken through the lines and were being chased farther north into Kwangsi. She dared not believe that her father and the Orchids had abandoned her in their struggle to found a new kingdom for the people. For the past year, she had lived in constant fear of discovery; lying next to Liang Mo, she was afraid she might cry out in dreams and reveal the horrible thing that she had done. Sometimes in the midst of making love to him, she saw the Tai Tai's face forming on the ceiling, and she cringed in his embrace; he, feeling more powerful, would plunge harder. She felt like a stone sinking into a bottomless pool. She could not forget the feeling of soft resistance when the gold pin pierced the old woman's flesh.

But the sight of the man's tattoo induced an unexpected rush of fond memories—Wing chanting the saga of the warrior maiden Fa Mulan, the exhilaration of guiding a galloping horse by the pressure of her knees, and the good, loose feeling in her limbs when she and Iron Fist grappled in the dirt. She thought constantly of the youth who had saved Mei Yuk. Was he a spy? Or an ignorant boy who had stumbled into the brotherhood? Was he one for the people? Even when he was still in the box, she had seen that he was as handsome as Mei Yuk described. And now that he was awake and truly himself, she was not disappointed. He was tall and dark, with a broad forehead, a well-chiseled mouth, and strong chin. He was surprisingly grave and solemn considering the anger that flowed through him, blocking the *chi* force and making his pulse race even when asleep; he was also capable of civilized behavior, for he ate slowly, despite enormous hunger, and turned away from her while eating to disguise his shaking hands.

"Is the general going to execute me?" he had demanded finally, looking up from the crumbs of his meal.

"I don't know," Rulan admitted. "The master sent the magistrate away. He says no man could have survived so long in the box unless his heart was pure." What could she tell him—that after healing him, she would have to turn him over to the general for more interrogation? That very morning, she had overheard Liang Mo talking with his father. The general, angry at Liang Mo for something he did not name, had refused Liang Mo's request to let the prisoner go. The general had shouted that he would bend his son into a soldier, that Liang Mo must compel the peasant to tell all he knew about the Triad-Tanka partnership that was festering in his district. If Liang Mo failed, the peasant boy would be beheaded under military law while Liang Mo himself read the Sixteen Maxims to the assembled crowd.

The boy raised one eyebrow. "Then I am his prisoner still," he said to Rulan.

"No, no, you are a guest." She laughed, disguising the dread that lay at the back of her mind. "But don't try to run off. You're still weak and the medicine is mind confusing. You wouldn't get far. Rest some more." She left him sipping the now tepid tea.

Two days later, Rulan brought Mei Yuk again. The girl had begged so piteously to see her "savior" that Rulan relented to keep her quiet. The maids were calling Mei Yuk a "screaming woman," one of those wild, unmannerly brides who threw decorum aside and attacked her husband's family rather than submit to a despised mother-in-law. Mei Yuk's insolence had already produced two unhappy results: Meng treated her new daughter-in-law like a windblown pestilence. And Liang Mo had still not visited Mei Yuk's bed.

Mei Yuk seemed delighted to see the boy. She clapped her hands and bombarded him with chatter, as if he were an old friend. Pao An, on his part, was too abashed to speak. Fearing that her patient would wither entirely under Mei Yuk's barrage of words, Rulan tried to draw the girl's attention to the more mundane matters of nursing. But when Mei Yuk insisted on helping to press the poultice on his legs and stomach, his whole body turned red under her small, awkward hands. Then, to his horror, his member grew large and stood out under the thin loincloth.

Mei Yuk covered her face with her sleeve and giggled. Pao An shut his eyes tightly, praying that his body would not betray him again. This time when Rulan gave him the cup of bitter liquid, he drank it down gratefully, knowing that it would take him quickly into oblivion.

∎   ∎   ∎

That evening, Rulan came alone.

"Who are you?" he growled as she set a basket of food and the oil lamp on the floor.

Rulan told him her name, but he was looking with longing at the door and did not hear her. His head hurt and his tongue was as sluggish as a fish in a fetid pool.

"If the mother-in-law knew of this morning's visit, Young Mistress would be beaten." She had not intended to scold, but the realization that he preferred Mei Yuk wounded her.

Pao An nodded, crestfallen. He understood too what the young woman had left out—that her own punishment would be worse.

"What is your name? What is your village?" Rulan asked.

"I have none," he said simply.

"Someone named you and raised you up," she accused him. "Nobody drowned you like a girl-child, or smothered you, or put you out on the road to starve." She knew it was not decent for her to talk so freely to a man outside the family, but something about him made her abandon caution. "You speak the local Punti dialect, so you must live around here. You don't look Punti, though. You are far too tall. Are your parents tall? What is your clan?"

"I have no clan," he said, wilting a little from her questions. "Hakka, Punti, this or that village, the names mean nothing."

"You must have a clan," she asserted, "or a place where your name is written down. Or where your family's bones are buried. All men do. Otherwise, how does a man know who he is?"

"I am no one. I belong nowhere."

"I found your Triad mark. I know you belong to something."

Pao An glanced fearfully down at his thigh. "You told the general," he said flatly.

"No, I disguised it with my needles. I have sympathies that the general does not share and those too have to be disguised. Do you have a wife?"

Wary of her, he shook his head now. If the girl knew so much about him, would he be forced to be her friend?

"A sweetheart? A girl from the village?" she insisted. She was being rude, but she had to know.

He replied harshly, "A no-name man like me has no prospects. What girl would want to marry a man who doesn't know who he is? No girl in the world would be so foolish!"

"Some women don't care about names! A girl could give him her own! Or choose one for him!"

He stared at her with astonishment, and Rulan blushed. Had she really said those immodest words? Well, she was not ashamed to say them, she told herself. He was different from anyone else in the house, different from anyone she had known in the village. She felt herself opening to this tall stranger. If he belonged nowhere, he did not seem to care, as if being an outcast was not grounds for shame but a path he had chosen to walk with courage. She wanted to touch him, shake him, thump his shoulder like a comrade, but held back, because this was not from any desire to heal. Instead, unmindful of her long skirts, she sat down on the tile floor inside the golden circle cast by the lamp.

Her questions were making him uncomfortable, so when Pao An saw the girl sit down as if to prolong the exchange, he bristled. "You needn't pay attention to this beggar."

"My lord ordered me here—" said Rulan. "He is a scholar and doesn't know village dialect, so I speak for him to the people."

Pao An looked puzzled. "You're not a maid?"

"Not now."

"You're a wife? You're Hakka!"

Suddenly, she was overcome with shyness. "My lord asked for me. And his mother thought I would make him study better, so she drew up a contract of concubinage. My people are dead. I had nowhere else to go."

Rulan was surprised to see the man's expression turn sour at the mention of her connection with Liang Mo.

"And the small one?" he said without looking at her. "The one who came this morning?"

"She is my husband's First Lady," she replied, feeling a stab of sorrow at the yearning in his face. "She is above me, although she is only fourteen."

"How many wives does one man need?" he blurted out, envying the youth in the garden. His heart ached for the Wang girl whose husband didn't know jade from rough quarry stone. "A poor man is lucky to have one to start his fire."

"Not many maids become concubines. A poor girl without parents takes her luck where she can." She decided sorrowfully that if he preferred young rich girls perhaps he could not be trusted.

Pao An nodded politely, and Rulan saw with alarm that he also distrusted her.

He took a pear from the basket and bit into the hard, sour fruit. She was not like a girl from the village at all, he decided. This one knew ambition, the politics of the women's courts. He put himself on guard against her, for since she had discovered his mark and disguised it, she might want something from him. "I have seen your husband," Pao An said, unable to hide his jealousy of Liang Mo. "Time will not bring the son out of the father's shadow."

Rulan felt as if he had rejected her too. "Then you measure him unfairly. You don't know how hard it is to be the general's son," she declared heatedly. "My father-in-law comes when he pleases, orders his son's life from afar. And never with words of praise—only rebukes and demands. What can any son do but obey? If he dies from obeying, they put him down in the annals as a filial son and sing his praises at Ching Ming, the Festival of the Dead. I pity all sons."

"No, no. Pity fathers with sons." Pao An's voice was low and tight.

"Ah, I forgot that you are a dutiful son," she retorted, happy that her words had finally found their mark. Hadn't she suffered as much for a father? Rulan reproached herself angrily for trying to wound one as vulnerable as he, even as the scornful words left her lips. "Doubtless your father can reward you for your sacrifice."

Pao An looked down at his hands. "He has nothing. He studied for the examinations, but victory eluded him. He tried to farm, but nothing grew. When he lost his family to cholera and found me in a burned-out village—" Pao An swallowed the words he was about to say about the man who had laid waste that village. "My father gave away his land and his position in the clan to adopt me. Because of his education he could have been headman, but he gave up that chance when he took me."

"Does he beat you because you spoiled his chances? Does he blame you because he failed?" She wanted to hurt him for criticizing the very weakness in Liang Mo she had tried to ignore. She wanted him to look up and see her, really see her, as he did Mei Yuk. "Isn't that what fathers do to make their sons succeed?"

" 'Success' and 'failure' are empty words to my father. He is too tenderhearted to beat an ox in the field. Once in the starving time, I trapped a bird and brought it home to eat. He healed its wing and set it free. That time we ate clay and whatever we could beg from the neighbors."

Silence fell between them. Rulan watched Pao An staring into the shadows and knew he was peopling the room with beloved ghosts. Suddenly, she was ashamed. Here was no enemy, but someone snatched out of his place and station, like herself, for who knew what purpose and what design. She sighed. "I've known men like him—their kindness makes them as weak as children."

"Not at all. He is the strongest man I know. He knows the way."

Pao An answered her unspoken question by tracing a river through the air with his hands.

"The way of wind and water," he repeated, plucking out an invisible current with his fingers. "He taught me the dance, since I have no interest in books and he has no hands for the plow, and it was something we both could share." He reached out as if to grasp something, but his hands closed on emptiness, so he moved them before his face in a heartrending gesture of loss. Rulan wondered what she would do if he began to cry, but instead his head rolled forward to catch the thrust of his hands, and then his whole body lunged and dipped, lifted itself on its knees in time to sounds of sadness and longing.

> He was sold to Southern barbarians, ever farther
> south they took him,
> Because he resisted, they nailed him to boards;
> in agony, he spent his years,
> In a pit, ten years, without a message from his
> home in the Central Plain,
> Only in dreams did he see his dear friend; they
> spoke not a word.

"That's the song of Chung Hsiang among the southern barbarians," whispered Rulan. "My husband read it to me out of the old books." But what was quaint and sad in Liang Mo's song had suddenly become as real as her parting with Wing. When this man sang, the words tore like knives at her breast. She was stunned by the grace of his affliction, and by the fact that a peasant knew the old poems.

"All the while I was caged," continued Pao An, rising from the bed and kneeling before her on the cold tiles, "I heard my father sing this song. He sang in bed, when he was too sick to plant; he sang when he walked down the road away from me with his begging bowl. Could I do less, when he suffered more? In the box, I took up his song." He began to rock like a man at sea. The muscles of his back and shoulders rippled; the tendons of his legs stretched and stood out like ropes. He was acting out his imprisonment as she had seen traveling acrobats and actors pantomime the old stories in the movements of the dance.

"No one heard?"

"No one heard," he confirmed. "At night, I sang to myself and no one heard. I danced and no one saw." He rolled on his side. And Rulan saw the prison box turned over in the dust of the stable yard. He rocked and with a tremendous effort seemed to draw himself back upright. "Chung Hsiang was nailed to the boards by his feet, caged so that he could not turn the smallest part of his body; his feet oozed blood and pus from where the nails had been driven in. With his eyes he followed the birds as they soared away. But whither could he fly, his body bound by a cage?"

"Poor man," echoed Rulan, her eyes wet. "Whither could he fly?"

His hands stopped in midair, and he looked at the girl as if seeing her for the first time. "Ah," he said warmly. "Chung Hsiang was saved by his friend, Pao An. My father loved the tale because it is about friendship, the only true bond of the heart, the only love that survives calamity and death. Finding a true friend, he told me, is as difficult as scraping the moon from the surface of a pond. For the ten years that Chung Hsiang was a captive in barbarian wastes, Pao An toiled to save up the ransom for his friend. Waking or sleeping, his thoughts were only of Chung Hsiang, so that there was no room in his heart for his wife."

"That is the part I cannot bear. I like only the ending," said Rulan, brushing away her tears. When last had she allowed herself to think of Wing? And what torment might her sisters have suffered so that they left her without word or promise?

He nodded, and went on to shape a new pattern, whose round, rhythmical movements signaled joy rather than grief. "The ending. When Chung Hsiang was brought to him, his friend Pao An beheld him as though he were his own flesh and blood. As soon as they laid eyes on each other, they fell on each other's shoulders and wept."

The man and the woman were kneeling face-to-face, not too far apart to touch. The girl's body rocked gently, in sympathy with the man's more violent rhythm. She raised her hands, wanting to touch him, and suddenly, the old heat crackled in her fingertips. And just as suddenly, her hands were cold again. She sighed and dropped them, afraid that she might kill him too, this strange new friend.

"The friend lost all in redeeming Chung Hsiang from captivity. The friend died," said Rulan, barely breathing, praying that the moment would not slip away. "It's a dreadful story. Not happy. Not just."

His words seemed to come from a far place. "Holding hands daily does not prove affection. Only in calamity will one know who is true. Lovers share wine, meat, and the same bed, but when misfortune calls, they are enemies. Only friendship of the heart survives."

"What has this to do with a father?" Rulan asked softly, in order not to break the spell.

"He is more than a father. He is my friend," came the reply, and his fists swung out through the air like eagles rising. "He plucked me from the burning field and traded his birthright for me. He called me his dragon's pearl, his friend. He named me Pao An.''

She leaned forward, forgetting that her hands were cold and that she was a woman who belonged to another man. She smelled the fragrance of the cheek that she had bathed and laid her head on his shoulder. "Pao An," she whispered, warmed by his name.

The moment was long. She felt the emotion change, slowly, sweetly. When he held her a trifle closer, she clutched him tightly, then loosed herself and went away.

"Stay," begged Liang Mo.

Rulan came back into his embrace. And as she did she realized that she was thinking about Pao An—not Liang Mo, not Wing.

It was a hot, airless afternoon two months after Liang Mo's wedding day. The humidity weighed so heavily on the household that even the cicadas were too wet with heat to sing. Rulan listened to the droning of Meng's servant girls just beyond the walls of the little garden where Liang Mo liked to take pleasure with her. There was a hush, followed by a peal of rude laughter from Moon. Rulan knew they were talking about her because the sound of Liang Mo's lovemaking could not go unheard. Nothing went unreported in these courts where servants' eyes were everywhere, where ears listened behind doors and walls, and gossip was as thick as the flies in late summer.

The Triad youth named Pao An was still confined to one room and a small adjacent courtyard in the servants' quarters just above the Kitchen Court. She saw him twice a day, and although she sensed his jealousy of Liang Mo, he had come to trust her so wholly that she could have gotten anything out of him—even a confession about the tattoo—had she not grown so attached to him. Because he seemed so vulnerable, she had been determined to protect him from the Lis. Fortunately Mei Yuk appeared to have lost interest in Pao An completely, although he still looked with calf eyes at the door. Rulan was relieved that the general too had forgotten Pao An in the excitement of receiving a letter, stamped with the Deputy Military Governor's chop, that summoned him to Canton to oversee the mobilization of the provincial troops for an attack on the Taiping-held city of Yung An. Li had put Liang Mo in charge of interrogating Pao An while he was away and demanded weekly reports be sent to him. The general was so strong, Rulan began to worry that her father's ragged troops could not possibly defeat General Li and the full might of the provincial army.

Her father, Wing, Ma Tsu Po, she had heard nothing from any of them since—Since I killed the Tai Tai, she reminded herself. She forced herself to write the awful characters on the dark walls of her mind in order to acknowledge her terrible deed. Why had they abandoned her? Why did they leave her alone with her despair and her memories?

Somewhere there was a war going on. Somewhere men lay staring with wide, unseeing eyes at the pitiless sky. Somewhere women cried for their lost children while their houses crumbled in flames. But here she lay with Liang Mo in a garden hung with star fruit and gardenias. She told herself that she was not a useless toy in a rich man's house, but someone sent by fate to nurse Liang Mo toward maturity, and now to heal yet another broken bird. She would do her duty to them all as expiation for the Tai Tai, whose ghost always seemed to follow her.

Liang Mo groaned and put his bare leg over hers.

"Don't," she said. "Your leg is heavy." But he nestled closer into her back, despite the heat, pressing his nose against her neck. The dagger-shaped leaves of an overhanging willow brushed against her face. Inside a web. Inside a cage—of lies and plots and futile plans, she thought.

When she was sure Liang Mo slept, Rulan took his hand from her breast. There was a soft sucking sound as her back separated from his chest. Still flushed from their last lovemaking, he rolled face up on the grass, snoring gently. A fine stubble had begun to darken his pale cheeks. Ordinarily a fastidious and passive lover, he seemed since his wedding to seek Rulan with a desperate urgency, as if to prove in the arms of his concubine what he could not in the arms of his wife.

Rulan gathered up the garments Liang Mo had flung into the bushes and dressed slowly.

Outwardly, she was one with the Lis. She fixed their bruises, stomach pains, and imaginary headaches, changed their bandages, put their slightest needs and whims above her own. Yet she did not love them. Secretly, each day of the month, she drank a decoction of the crushed roots of blood tonic lily, single-foot lotus, and eight-cornered lotus mixed into a cup of cold water. The thick, cold brew made her gag, but she would not bear a child that would bind her forever to the Lis. She still clung to the hope that she was an "individual," destined for fire and the clash of arms, as Ailan had predicted.

Ever since she had become a concubine, she had felt as gray and cold as river ice. Sometimes the Tai Tai appeared in her dreams as a hungry bird; sometimes the ghost loomed in the shape of a shadow or a pattern on the bark of a tree or the water stains on a stucco wall. The image lingered, never marring or spoiling her thoughts but always and ominously there, like a sore that would not heal. Rather than resenting the fact that she was the Lis' creature, with far less freedom as a lady than as a slave, she was content to sink into the monotony of domestic routine. She was content to forget, do her duty, and survive—until Pao An came to lift her heavy spirits, to warm her with his courage.

Rulan closed the gate of the garden and listened for the bolt's drop inside. As she walked to Mei Yuk's rooms, which adjoined Liang Mo's and hers, a rush of frigid air on her cheek signaled the passing of a familiar ghost—the Tai Tai's spirit. Rulan detected no malicious purpose—unless the ghost was waiting to take revenge when Rulan least expected it.

On the eve of the general's departure for Canton, the mood of the house was oppressive. All around her, Rulan read the luckless signs. That very morning, a starving man had thrust a bundle of rags into the steward's hands. It was a girl child, nearly dead from hunger. When the steward gave it back angrily, the father ran to the edge of the dock and tossed the child into the river, cursing the name of Li.

"I have a conundrum," Mei Yuk said as Rulan stepped up on the veranda outside the girl's sleeping room. "Guess, Rulan!"

Rulan was barely listening; she was thinking about Pao An and the next phase of his treatment. She had decided to ask Second Cook for a bowl of the strong broth made from chicken feet and innards that was kept boiling on the stove to make fine gravies. The broth was an excellent tonic to help build up his blood.

"Listen, Rulan," Mei Yuk giggled, "it goes like this:

Solid earth, yet soft as cloud
Sometimes humble, sometimes proud
Lowly peasant, upright scholar,
Father of nations, to woman I bow.
Who am I now?

"What?" Rulan asked absentmindedly.

"You're not listening to me! I want you to pay attention to me. No one pays attention to me."

"I'm sorry, Mei Mei," Rulan said, addressing her as a child. "Say your riddle again."

"I won't. I won't. And now you've wasted a perfectly good conundrum. I made it up about that boy, Pao An! Now it's not amusing! How I hate this place. There's nothing to do here, and everyone is so old and dull! I want to go see the opera as I used to in Canton! I want a storyteller!"

"This is your house now, Mei Mei."

"I hate this house. I am a Wang, not a Li."

"If Liang Mo's mother hears you say that, she will beat you until you cannot stand!"

"I don't care. I'll make her sorry. I'll die. Oh, Rulan, my mother-in-law does not like me. Even you are my enemy because you seduce my husband so he won't come to me. I have no friends. Only that farm boy likes me. When I went to him his yang stuck out!" Mei Yuk brightened. "Does he ask about me?"

"Be ashamed! Liang Mo would disown you if he heard such talk," Rulan reprimanded, feeling a twinge of guilt herself.

But Mei Yuk would not be chastened. "The peasant boy saved my life. I should die for him, for he is my true husband, unlike this false one here who hates me." Mei Yuk blew her nose into a handkerchief she kept tucked in her sleeve.

"Cut your head and tongue! Do you want to be a dead woman?" Rulan cried, truly horrified. "Liang Mo is your husband, and you owe him respect!"

"I respect him as much as I do my Kung Kung, who is a demon. And I won't tell you why! Please! I want to see the farm boy again. Let me go with you tonight." The girl touched a corner of the handkerchief delicately to one painted eyebrow.

"No, I won't! You mustn't show yourself to strangers, Mei Yuk," Rulan said firmly. "You are a married woman now."

"I am a prisoner in my own house! I'd rather be a low-caste concubine like you. At least I could walk to the stables and the kitchen and see things!" She began to pout. "I hope the dirty boy dies. Then I will pine for him until I perish. And everyone will be sorry for ignoring me, and Liang Mo will be sorry and desire me, but it will be too late."

Rulan hastened her off the veranda where she might be heard, and tried to turn Mei Yuk's attention to the new western clock Liang Mo had ordered from Canton.

A small dark blot on a ribbon of brown water in an infinite expanse of blue.

Pao An was poling a barge laden with mulberry leaves up the muddy canal. The sky had the hard flat glint of metal, and the air was so close he could scarcely breathe.

Get up, he shouted to Pang, who was sprawled at his feet, grinning up at the clouds. There was so much he wanted to say, but Pao An's words were swallowed up in the blankness of the sky.

Only a little farther, he yelled to Pang. A tower touching the clouds. A bed for each of us. Food from a sorceress's hand. Everything so vast and smelling so clean. Get up! Help me push this boat along.

Pang laughed. The hundred red mouths on Pang's body laughed too. Wider and wider they grinned until there was no Pang, no boat, no sky —only a roaring maw into which the small dark figure of his father was falling, falling.

The click of the outside bolt pulled Pao An up from the abyss. He turned toward the door, groggy and thick tongued from Rulan's medicine.

Sweet night air poured in, a sibilance of silk, and suddenly the fox-spirit was in his bed.

"What impudence," she breathed. "The door isn't even locked," she lied, "and here you lie unclothed. Are you cold? Are you dead? Let me cover you up," she said.

She had placed a spell on him so that he could not move. His jagged breathing thundered in the silence of the room, and he thought his head and heart would burst. But the *kuei* was panting even harder. His head began to spin, whether from the medicine or her perfume he could not tell.

"I washed you. I touched you here—here—there."

"Fox-spirit," he began, but the *kuei* had taken away his will. His rough fingers caught on the thin cloth, groping blindly until they found her face. Where else had he known the same smooth cheek, the sweetly pointed chin? Dizzy with the powdery smell of her, he put a hand to her hungry mouth, and she bit his fingers, one by one.

The fox-spirit laughed again, more languorously now, as her fingers brushed a river of fire down his heaving chest and hard belly. His manhood leapt into her tiny hand, while her mouth found a secret place beneath his ear. There was a whisper of silk sliding to the floor, and suddenly she was naked and burning hot. Her limbs squirmed around him, strangling him, drawing him into her depths. Then, uttering small, sharp cries like an incantation, she clasped him so tightly that he could not breathe or move or see, and lifted him swiftly into a cloud of driving thunder and pelting rain.

Had it been a dream? he asked himself the next day. It was too impossible to be real. Pao An pushed the awful, wonderful hope from his mind. But still, her heavy perfume lingered on his body and overpowered the lemon-scent of Rulan's herbs in the hot, small room.

When Rulan came at midday with food and found his door un-latched, she feared Pao An had escaped. But she found him working in the garden, scrubbing the moss from the walkway that led to the ancient fountain. At first she worried he was too weak to be working, but all week he was a perfect patient. And when he met with Liang Mo at the end of the week, Rulan saw how Pao An let him have small pieces of information for his father. The general, Pao An had correctly guessed, was like a cat who enjoyed the hunt more than he enjoyed the kill. So the intelligent prey prolonged the game.

Rulan awoke with a start. She studied the darkness, her heart racing and her ears pricked for the noise that had disturbed her sleep and invaded her dreams. But all she heard was Liang Mo's breathing.

Then it came again: a soft footfall, a whispering of cloth against leg outside in the garden, as if someone were taking one careful step at a time to avoid being heard. The way an assassin walked. Rulan's mind flooded with violent images—the attack on the commune, her mother, the fire—

Impossible, she told herself. This is Abundant Spring Mountain, the fortress of General Li, a powerful man. But Li was a man with many enemies, and the assassination of the wives and sons of powerful men inside their own walls was a common enough occurrence in these chaotic times. The Triads, it was said, trained special squads for such assignments.

She was about to raise the alarm, when another thought made the cry die in her throat. Many nights she had lain in bed listening to the Tai Tai's ghost call out to her. Perhaps this sound was only the Old

One's ghost wandering the house, hungry for revenge—but no, she decided. This was a warm being passing by, one that did not come for her. Could it be a guard trying to steal a precious vase or hanging? Or a maid sneaking out to meet her sweetheart? Lest anyone think her foolish for crying out, Rulan determined to investigate.

Carefully, so as not to disturb Liang Mo, she rose from the bed, pulled on a loose night robe over her nakedness, and tiptoed barefoot into the garden to confront whatever prowled outside. The ground was cold against her feet, and she stepped noiselessly through the moon gate and along the low wall that enclosed the Second Terrace of the house.

She stooped under a fanlike branch of a willow tree and waited for another sound; her heart beat wildly. And then she heard the patter of hurried footsteps far below on the steps that led to the maze of winding courtyards and secret gardens at the rear of the house. The intruder must have known the layout of the house, for he now moved with deliberation and speed. Not an aimless thief, but an assassin!

The footsteps died away. Still, Rulan resisted crying out, unable to pinpoint the reason for her unease. And then in an instant, Rulan knew what was dreadfully wrong. Meng's sleeping quarters lay on the other side of the wing where she and Liang Mo slept. The intruder was headed in the wrong direction—unless the assassin never intended to slay the absent general's wife. Unless a Triad assassin had come for a Triad informer—to silence him.

She began running with long, swift strides down to the part of the house where Pao An slept. Frantically, she tried to visualize the path to Pao An's room in the darkness, picking out the stones and holes and swift turnings before they could trip her. She took the steep, narrow way down to the servants' quarters on the terrace above the Kitchen Court in order not to alert the intruder, praying that she was not too late.

The guard outside Pao An's gate was gone. The gate swung open on a rusty hinge. Had the guard been bribed? The torch that normally burned in the stanchion beside the gate was cold. Rulan plucked it out of its stand for a weapon. Her breath was hot in her chest. She heard a small, choked gasp become a feral grunt. Truly afraid now, Rulan crept through the gate to the small round window above Pao An's bed. The oil lamp that burned inside was dim, but still bright enough to illuminate a faint shadow moving behind the paper window. The shadow slowly descended.

Rulan raced to the door, kicked it open, and leapt into the room with the burned-out torch raised like a cudgel.

Mei Yuk looked up from where she crouched over Pao An on the bed. Her pale white body gleamed in the flickering light of the oil lamp. The girl's face was swollen with desire, and her hair hung loose over her small bare breasts. Seeing Rulan, she rolled off the youth and scrambled into the bedclothes, trying to pull the rough blanket around herself.

"It's not her fault," Pao An exclaimed when he recognized Rulan. He stood up to shield Mei Yuk, but remembering his own nakedness, sat back down on the bed.

And then Mei Yuk was weeping. "Oh Sister, I swear by Kwan Yin, he tried to force me, but nothing happened. Thank goodness you came in time!"

Rulan recognized the surprise and confusion on Pao An's face. A terrible anger came over her, and she raised her hand to strike Mei Yuk, whose foolishness threatened to destroy them all. But then she saw Pao An put a gentle, protective arm around Mei Yuk to shield her from the blow. That simple gesture of intimacy and possession made Rulan as weak as if he had struck her. She dropped her hand and turned away.

When Rulan spoke, she could not control her tears. "What have you done?" she asked Mei Yuk, although in her heart she spoke to Pao An.

Mei Yuk was sobbing. "Oh, Sister, don't punish me. It isn't fair that you have our husband's love when I am above you. It isn't fair that I am so lonely in this house, that no one listens to me."

Pao An tried to draw Mei Yuk closer, but she squirmed away from him.

"I'm to blame," he said. "When she came to me before, I thought she was a fox-spirit. I should have known. I should have sent her away."

"This is not the first time?" Rulan asked quietly. She told herself that she did not care, that nothing either of them said or did could touch her. Before Mei Yuk could protest, Rulan demanded harshly, "Did you bribe the guard?" She had to know if anyone in the servants' wing suspected.

"No!" Mei Yuk answered. The girl was beginning to realize the enormity of her indiscretion, and her fingers shook as she pulled her loose hair back into a matron's knot. "He sneaks away to drink in the Kitchen Court. I noticed that the first night."

In the uncomfortable silence that followed, the lovers rose and began to put on their clothes. They did not look at each other as they dressed, but Rulan studied them both, unmoved by their nakedness, as a nurse looks on the wounded. I should hate them, she thought, and cursed herself, because even now, when they had defiled themselves and betrayed her friendship, all she could see was their weakness and their need and their shame.

"You must go," she told Pao An. "You will ruin her. Go now, before the first gong sounds."

Pao An swallowed and nodded.

"Then you won't tell," Mei Yuk cried. "Oh Sister, how good you are to me!"

"I did not intend to make you unhappy," Rulan said painfully to Mei Yuk. "I have done nothing to woo Liang Mo away. Whatever he does to us is his right. And you must do your part. You are to be the mother of his line, so eventually, he will warm to you. Until that day, you must act the proper wife, faithful and obedient. If you want to live, swear!"

"I will. I promise, I will," the girl said fervently.

"Lady—" ventured Pao An to Mei Yuk, dismayed by the finality of her last words. But Mei Yuk was putting the pins into her hair and had turned her back on him.

"I know a place in the Upper Terrace," announced Rulan briskly. "Great houses always have escape tunnels in case hunger marchers storm the walls. On the First Terrace, there is a hole cut through the cliff to the other side of the mountain. Tai Tai showed it to me once."

The first gong sounded. Pao An drew a tired hand across his face. He felt old and dirty, and his tongue was thick in his mouth, as if he had been drugged. Part of him yearned to escape this house of death; part of him felt he would die if he were forced to leave Mei Yuk. "Please," he begged Rulan, "give me a moment with her."

"Are you mad?" declared Rulan. "The gong has just rung. The guards will be about soon."

"Please," he mumbled, shamefaced but stubborn.

"You put us all in danger!" she cried.

"One minute only!" he pleaded.

Rulan felt her head spinning. Just when she thought he could not hurt her anymore, he had found another way to wound. "Do what you wish," she whispered.

Pao An reached for Mei Yuk before she could scurry after Rulan.

I should die, Rulan told herself as she pulled the door fast. She hardly heard the clamor from the Kitchen Court where the sleepy cooks were screaming at the cook boys to light the fires for water.

My heart betrays me in ten thousand ways, she thought. Yes, I have lived too long and grown stupid.

Mei Yuk's eyes shifted from side to side, searching for danger. She would not let him embrace her. Her face was again the ivory mask he had seen on the road: too white to be real, too beautiful to be his.

"Good-bye, Lady," he said finally, too abashed to play at lover's games with her.

Slowly, reluctantly, she turned her face up to him. "Where will you go?" she asked.

The word came to his lips automatically, although until that moment, he had not considered it. "Canton."

"Canton! Oh, take me too. I hate this ugly prison of a house. I want to hear the gongs from the temple and the Muslims crying from their prayer tower. I want to see the acrobats and the storytellers with their sticks." The beautiful mask had cracked and twisted as if she were about to spit. "I wish I were a cap on your head, a slipper on your foot. I'd walk with you through the dust of a thousand miles to see the white walls of Canton again!"

Pao An almost wept for her.

"Help me," she whispered, leaning on him.

"Yes, oh yes," he answered.

"Go to my Kung Kung's house. Tell him to break his covenant with these Lis and take me back—No, don't tell him that or he will be angry. Tell him that my husband is a eunuch and that poor Mei Mei is dying of unhappiness. A marriage can be annulled if your husband is a eunuch. Tell him I don't know what my Kung Kung wants me to do here. Beg him to send for me before they kill me."

"I don't think he will see a man like me."

Mei Yuk yanked at the earring on her left lobe until it came off in her hand. It was red jade in the shape of a teardrop. "Here, give him this," she said, and hooked the jewel to the inside of his shirt. Then she smiled, showing white pointed teeth and looked up through her lashes at him. "You do this for me?"

He bowed, not as a servant but as a lover come to plead his case.

Her words came in a rush. "I knew," she told him. "You are my protector. You'll do anything I say." She pressed herself against him and laughed softly. "You called me 'fox-spirit,' remember? Be good to me, and the fox-spirit will come to you again, I promise!" She slipped away.

He was lost once more—as he had been in the grove where he first found her with the bandit—but now he had a promise. And an impossible hope.

"It's growing light out," Rulan said. "You must hurry!"

She seemed angry and hurt, although Pao An told himself that he had done nothing to offend her. The jewel burned against his chest.

Quickly he followed her to the First Terrace. The rooms were kept shuttered and dark, for not even the maids would go where the Tai Tai's angry ghost lurked. They passed behind the shrine in the Tai Tai's garden and went directly into the dead woman's deserted chambers. Leaning together, they pushed against the heavy door of the sleeping room. Suddenly it gave way, and they were inside the rank bedchamber in a cloud of swirling dust motes. Mildewy bedclothes were stacked on the chairs. The hangings were streaked with water stains where the rains had seeped through the cracks in the ceiling. Mice scurried across the wooden floor, once dark and fine, now hidden under more than a year of dust.

Are you here, old woman? Rulan asked silently. But the ghost was gone.

Rulan found the scroll painting that hid the escape passage. "Help me," she called to Pao An. The two of them lifted the scroll. Her fingers crept along the wall, desperately seeking a break in the mortar. "I've found it," she said in relief. There was a narrow door, barely wide enough for Pao An to slip through. Behind it, a flight of stairs led down into darkness. What secrets had passed through this ancient tunnel?

"Hurry!" ordered Rulan. She urged him toward the narrow opening.

"My dearest friend, come with me!" he replied impulsively, having caught a glimpse of her desolation and misunderstanding its cause. "We will be comrades together."

And again, she felt how easily this man could wound her. "No!" she told him curtly, although her heart rebelled against the word. More than anything she wanted to follow him out the tunnel, for there was nothing to keep her in Abundant Spring Mountain. Not love and not duty, for she had long been abandoned by the father and sisters who claimed to cherish her.

"You and I are dug out of the same paddy. You're nothing to these people. They will use you and throw you out when they are done. Come now. Run away!"

"No!" She would never go with Pao An, who took her out of pity; she would stay with Liang Mo, who took her out of love. "Go, leave me alone," she said, and pushed him through the door. She wanted to forget that she too was an unfaithful wife, in spirit if not in the flesh, and that she burned—still burned—for Pao An's touch.

Alone in the darkness, he heard the door scrape closed. Rulan's footsteps grew fainter; soon there was only silence above him. Without her, Pao An felt unaccountably bereft. He groped along the walls. Chattering lizards slithered over his fingers, and the smell of decay clogged his nostrils. Finally, he saw a dim thread of light. He stumbled toward it and, reaching out to grasp it, found something blocking his way. He pushed hard, and the rotten wood of an ancient door collapsed. Pale light burst into the tunnel, making him blink. He crawled into the gray light of dawn on the mountain on which the house was built. Under his feet, he felt the rush of an underground stream, and from the foot of the mountain far below, he heard the faint cries of tradesmen and coolies calling to the servants at the gates of Abundant Spring Mountain.

For the first time in his life, he was free.

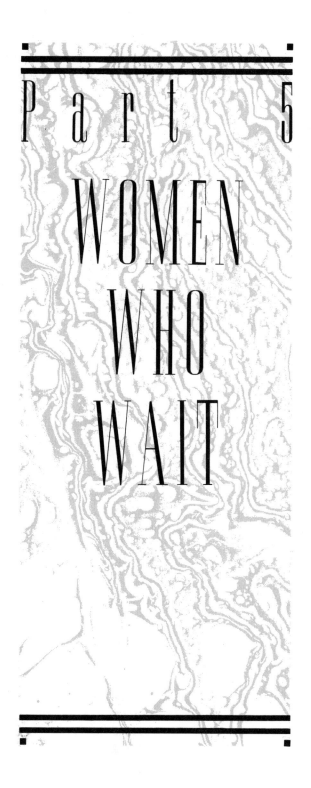

Part 5

WOMEN WHO WAIT

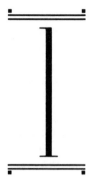

Abundant Spring Mountain, 1851

The harvest moon glinted through the clouds like a fat gold coin wrapped in a silk handkerchief. All the women and children had gathered in the gardens of the Upper House to eat, gossip, and gaze at the symbol of yin, the imprint of woman on the night sky. A line of charcoal braziers glowed in the darkness, radiating islands of warmth in the cold air.

The autumn moon festival was the one holiday whose rituals belonged to women alone, so despite the painful gout to which she had succumbed after the wedding, Meng, the new Tai Tai, had supervised everything, from the fresh grooming of the garden to the baking of moon cakes. Pastries and plates of the five ritual fruits were placed on an altar set up on the porch outside her rooms. Then on the fifteenth day of the eighth month of the lunar calendar, she rose from her sickbed to join the other women in the joyful sport of moon watching. Although the night sky was whipped with streaming clouds, every woman in the great house from kitchen maid to Meng as well as all the aunts, cousins, and nieces from surrounding villages had gathered at the tables set up under flickering paper lanterns—all the women, except one.

Rulan, Meng, and Moon stood together in uneasy silence on the bridge as the light, silvery voices of the women mingled with the water of the spring that flowed beneath their feet.

How strange, Rulan thought, that Meng, who hated her, had come to depend on her daily, just as the old Tai Tai had. Gazing into the depths of the spray, Rulan thought she saw something move. She looked harder, and suddenly the dead Tai Tai's face appeared out of the mist. Rulan closed her eyes to will the frightening image away. In the Golden Orchid Society, this was called practicing the art of the fleeting. Ma Tsu Po claimed that those who had mastered it could survive torture by concentrating on the interstices between waves of pain; she had led a group of sisters into attaining trances so deep that they could prick themselves with knives and never bleed. Yet even though the heat in her hands had vanished and her power as a spirit-woman faded, Rulan could never close her mind to pain—except her own. Instead, she had learned to divide her mind into many rooms and to shut the door to each except the one she was in—the room of passing. It was the only way she could endure the emptiness of her life after Pao An had gone.

It had been two months since she sent him down the tunnel. Mei Yuk had never whispered a word to Rulan about the shameful scene in Pao An's room. Their mutual secret made both women uneasy with one another. Rulan avoided Mei Yuk, and the girl grew more sullen and withdrawn.

"What's the good of a woman's festival if there are no men to exclude?" Meng grumbled.

"Give the master one more week at Yung An, and he'll ride back with the head of Demon Hung on his pike, I guarantee. How long does it take half a million stalwart lions to grind the bones of thirty thousand rebels into dust?" asked Moon with a wave of her chubby hand.

Meng wiped her brow delicately with the tip of her sleeve. "His letters leave me uneasy. I have bad dreams."

"Is anything amiss?" asked Rulan quickly.

"No. His last letter was full of idle chatter about how well the Manchu generals eat. But the men are down to a half-bowl of rice a day. Supplies are running low—except for opium, which the boatmen sell."

"What else is there to do in war but smoke dirt! The general has been there barely a month, but he is a patient man!" declared Moon. "He'll starve them out."

Meng looked at Moon critically. "Father patient? He quotes his favorite sage, Sun Tzu, the warrior, who said, 'Waiting is a waste of life and time.' Father will wait only if it brings a worthwhile reward."

Moon's tiny eyes disappeared as her broad face crinkled into a huge grin. "Reward! Aiya, don't worry, Mother. At the Moon Festival, all are rewarded for waiting. When I was a skinny young bride my husband used to wait all night for me," Moon chuckled. "I was always the last one back from the temple. By then, my man was as randy as a rooster in a hen house. What ardor from that stick of a paddy farmer's son. You'd have thought I was the Moon Goddess instead of just plain Moon." She laughed ruefully for her lost years. "A pity he died. A pity I was barren."

The gay, brittle banter had turned maudlin. "This rebellion is going to make more widows," Meng said. She coughed and glanced up at Rulan. "I intend to get drunk tonight. I don't care what evil it does to my skin or my feet. I am an ugly old woman."

"You are as beautiful as you ever were, Mother," Moon soothed. "Shall I get the last boy in the stable or the one cook in the kitchen to prove it?"

"Cut your tongue," snapped Meng. "I am surrounded with loose-lipped whores and sullen witches." She pushed Moon's soft arms away and tottered toward the tables laden with festival food.

"Eat what you want tonight, Mother. Rulan advises it," Moon called sweetly. "The war is far away, Father is safe, no blood is shed. Leave tomorrow for tomorrow."

Rulan helped Moon across the gravel courtyard to the round tables. Tinkling voices chorused a greeting. The Third and Fourth Ladies bustled up to Meng, desperate to please. Meng looked them over critically, spoke sharply to the Fourth, whose face fell, and took the Third Lady's fan. "Where is Liang Mo's lazy Number One?" she snapped at Rulan, as she stirred the air with the peacock feathers.

"She was complaining of stomachache when I left her," replied Rulan, trying to sound gay. "She promised to join us later."

"Sick four times this week!" grumbled Meng. "How convenient. She falls ill whenever her old mother summons her." Meng called out a greeting to an old woman and waved her fan at the maids, signaling them to serve the festival foods.

The moon rolled out from behind a cloud, and suddenly the court-yard was bathed in silver light. All the ladies clapped their hands and pointed at the bright disk floating in the heavens. Two who could play plucked a love song on the moon harp.

"Look! I see a rabbit under a cassia tree."

"A three-legged toad."

"No, a moon-maiden with big feet grinding out the elixir of life. Rulan, how did you fly up there?" Moon laughed agreeably at her own joke as she helped the Third and Fourth Ladies ease Meng into a chair. Settling her vast bulk on a tiny porcelain barrel stool, Moon sighed with ecstasy as a servant placed a steaming dish of water snails in front of her. She hoisted a small brown snail to her mouth with chopsticks and began to suck the meat noisily from the shell.

"Eat," she commanded her mistress. "Rulan, put some on Mother's plate." Meng waved Rulan's chopsticks aside and reached for the cruet of hot wine. The Third and Fourth Ladies and their *mui tsai* took seats farthest away from Meng and began to whisper among themselves.

After the snails came a salad of raw fish, a dish of freshwater carp steamed in savory sauce, and, finally, the sweet rich pastries shaped like a full moon. Meng had eaten nothing and drunk far more than anyone else. Already giddy, she ordered the Third and Fourth Ladies to serve the round cakes. The two concubines exclaimed when they broke open their pastries and found Meng's surprise—a salted duck's egg yolk at the heart of each cake, an expensive treat. Meng called out to Rulan, "Take the rest to your lazy sister. Tell her not to bother to send one back. I already know the name of the tyrant she intends to overthrow."

All ears were instantly alert to the venom in Meng's voice. Centuries ago, messages signaling the people to kill their Mongol oppressors were secretly concealed in autumn moon cakes. Mei Yuk's and Meng's dislike of each other was so obvious now that no one could pretend to ignore it.

"Well?" said Meng sharply. "Go quickly, Rulan, or I will think that you serve two mistresses."

Greatly perturbed at the danger Mei Yuk's behavior had put them both in, Rulan rose with the plate of cakes and threaded her way through the tables. As soon as she reached the edge of the courtyard, she heard a burst of loud laughter behind her, and an answering sally from Moon.

She found Mei Yuk in a half-stupor with a glowing pipe in her mouth. "Ah, my husband's bed warmer. Why do you come to my cold rooms?" the girl said sleepily.

"Foolish girl! Who gives you that poison? I'll have the slave skinned."

"You'll kill me too. Good. I feel sick all the time."

"Dirt does that, Mei Mei."

"Dirt is the only thing that makes the sick feeling go away." Mei Yuk sat up on her bed and threw down the pipe on a table, where a miniature charcoal brazier rested.

"Eat, then," Rulan told the girl, placing a plate of moon cakes before her. She gathered up the pipe and the half-covered ceramic box of raw opium and threw them into the waste bucket. Then she dumped the smouldering embers out of the brazier.

Mei Yuk whimpered and fell back on the bed.

Pondering how she would advise Mei Yuk, who seemed oblivious to the danger of her position, Rulan broke a cake in half and handed it to the girl. At the sight of the oozing yolk, Mei Yuk turned white and ran to a basin in the corner of the room.

When the girl's retching had ceased, Rulan helped her back into bed and wiped Mei Yuk's face with a towel.

"When did you last eat? Dirt takes away hunger."

"I don't know, Sister," Mei Yuk groaned. "Oh, I am so sick. The pain comes, then stops, then comes again. I have nothing more to throw up, but still my stomach is so sore."

Rulan leaned down to knead the stomach. She looked in the girl's eyes and felt her pulse in her wrist. Then she felt Mei Yuk's small hard breasts.

"Aaiiee," said the girl crossly. "What are you doing? You are making them hurt more."

Rulan cupped her hand under the pointed chin, forcing Mei Yuk to look up at her. "Mei Mei," Rulan said, aghast at her discovery. "You are with child."

Mei Yuk's eyes grew fearful. "No, no. It's just this opium and country food that makes me vomit."

"Has Liang Mo ever come to you?" Rulan asked.

Mei Yuk's chin quivered. "You know he hasn't." Her face puckered up in dismay. "Oh, Sister. I am undone."

For a moment Rulan's own stomach twisted painfully. "Has there been anyone since Pao An?"

"No, I swear. Don't leave me," cried Mei Yuk piteously, clawing at Rulan's dress. "You brought him. You're to blame. Oh, oh," Mei Yuk gasped, seeing Rulan recoil. "Oh, Sister, no! Don't look at me with such scorn! You took Liang Mo away from me. Why shouldn't I take away the boy you want! Oh! Where are you going, Sister?"

Rulan was pulling her skirt out of Mei Yuk's strong fingers, as if the girl's touch had defiled it. She felt outraged for herself and for Pao An, who adored this stupid, vain, malicious child.

Mei Yuk's eyes narrowed. "Then I will tell Liang Mo that you lured me into the boy's bed. Our husband will beat me and send me back to my grandfather's house. But he will kill you!"

"No, it is you he will punish," replied Rulan, sick at heart.

"You side with a paddy boy against me, First Lady in this house? You peasants always stick together! What about me? Your duty is to protect me!" cried Mei Yuk, tearing at the cloth. "We could say that he forced me—or would that be worse for me?"

"This time I cannot fix things up, Mei Mei," said Rulan, without disguising her revulsion.

"Then I swear I will kill it! You are a spirit-woman. Give me something to drink. Cast it out like you cast out devils. Or I will take silver chopsticks and pluck out the peanut—"

"You vicious, spoiled girl! What are you saying? Kwan Yin forbids me to do such an evil thing. Is that what you did before? When they brought you in, scratched and bleeding from the bandit attack, I felt pity for you. And after I examined you, I knew that you had been opened by a man. I thought then, poor girl, you are like my sisters Harmony and Wing, who were abused by their fathers and uncles. I tried to protect you from the Lis and Wangs so that they would not throw you out, but now I know. You were not forced, you already had a lover, before you came here, young as you were. Didn't you? Didn't you!" said Rulan.

"You knew?" Mei Yuk said, white with shock.

"Yes."

"Forgive me, Sister," Mei Yuk begged. "You are my only friend."

"Who was he? Someone in your father's household?"

"I can never tell. I swore. Don't make me think of it. Don't." Weeping bitterly, she threw herself at Rulan's feet.

"Get up," Rulan said. "With all the trouble you've been in, why did you go looking for more?"

"I didn't mean to. Really. It is just that I hear Liang Mo laughing every night in your room, and it makes me so sad. I went to the peasant boy because I was lonely."

The girl's tears had washed away the thick paint from her face. Rulan wondered how Pao An could desire her so.

"I know I am just another tile for my grandfather to play against this family. He calls me his darling, but do you think he would pay a copper of ransom if the bandits had soiled me? 'In doing business, one seeks only profits,' he says. For myself alone, I am nothing." Mei Yuk raked her nails through her hair. "Oh, oh, Kwan Yin forgive me, I am evil. I do not deserve to live. Tonight I will plug up this family's well!"

There was not a single true note in anything Mei Yuk did or said, Rulan observed sadly. The tears, the pleas, the confession of guilt, the vows of sisterhood—everything about Mei Yuk, from her arched eyebrows to her mincing walk, was false. And yet men would always believe her because she seemed small and helpless. There would always be someone stronger to coddle her and clean up the mess she had made.

"I will help," Rulan said. "Not for your sake, but for the innocent life you carry." And for you, Pao An, my foolish friend, she told herself sadly. I will midwife your child; I will see your child is reared in wealth and luxury.

Rulan took a teacup from the tray and smashed it on the floor. And after commanding Mei Yuk to sit on the bed and drop her robe, Rulan drew long scratches on Mei Yuk's back and shoulders. Then she carefully coached the girl in what to say to Liang Mo.

Late that night Rulan found Liang Mo impatiently waiting for her. He had been with his new tutor in the afternoon, and he was exhilarated by the responsibility thrust on him as head of the house in his father's absence, and bursting with new schemes for building up the family fortune. He already had decided to manage the salt routes that had come with Mei Yuk's dowry after the first of the licenses had been turned over by Old Wang.

"Think of it, Rulan. I am going to open an office in Yang Chou where the rich salt merchants live. With Old Wang's influence in the capital, I'm sure we will be able to gain a share of the transport on the Grand Canal. What do people need in time of war or peace? Salt! All the old families in the south would buy from us, I know—"

"Yang Chou, indeed. You are the only son. Think of your sick mother who needs you. Your father would never approve!" Rulan chided him.

"Does he care about me?" Liang Mo declared hotly. "I begged him to take me to Yung An to fight the rebels, and he laughed! So here I sit, wasting my youth and strength. Nothing will come to me unless I seize it myself. After all, Mei Yuk's money is mine to use. I am the husband. If he objects, well then—you and I will run away!"

He had been drinking *mao tai* from a porcelain cup and was already quite drunk and eager to make love. Rulan prepared one more drink for him and laced it with a strong soporific. Then she drew him to the bed where they played the slapping game that he liked, and she told him erotic tales until Liang Mo passed out.

"What am I doing here?" he asked late the next morning, rubbing his eyes.

Mei Yuk was sitting at her dressing table combing her hair. "Shall I come back to bed, Husband?" she asked nervously, pulling the long strands as taut as wires.

"Where is Rulan?" Liang Mo demanded peevishly. "When did I come to you."

"Don't you remember, Husband?" Mei Yuk replied in a querulous voice. "You pushed your way into my room, dragging Rulan. You were very amorous. You made scratches on my back, see? And look what you did to my room!" She pointed to where discarded clothes lay strewn across tables and chairs. A pillow book lay open to the page where the lover and his lady, assisted by a second woman, were entwined in the position called the monkey moans and clasps the tree.

Liang Mo scowled and heaved his bare legs off the bed. "Where is Rulan then? She knows I do not like to wake up without her," he muttered, then groaned. "I need something for this headache."

Mei Yuk dropped her comb and ran to him, swallowing her fear and playing her role just as Rulan had coached her. "Oh, are you tired, Husband? You were a galloping horse last night. Nine times you touched me up to the Palace of the Child, until I had to beg you to stop!" She leaned against his back and began to massage his neck.

Liang Mo sighed irritably and let her pommel his shoulders. He felt her draw her robe apart so her small breasts pressed against his bare back. How clumsy the girl was. And how obvious. When Rulan massaged him, her fingers instantly found the knots in his muscles and drew the soreness magically away, making him more eager for love. But then Mei Yuk hardly knew him. Poor girl, he realized; she must undoubtedly be afraid of him. His skin began to burn where her soft flesh touched. He hoped he hadn't been too violent. She was a virgin, after all.

"Come, let me look at you," he said gruffly. He pulled off Mei Yuk's robe and examined the body of his bride for the first time. Her shoulders were scratched, and the tiny rise of her sex looked swollen. She was a child really, her petals barely unfolded, but a pretty child nevertheless. Had he really been such a brute? It pleased him that the girl thought him a strong, passionate man. "Did I hurt you?"

"Nothing you do could hurt me, Husband. How manly you were! You cannot know how you thrilled me."

Liang Mo touched her roughly on a budding breast.

Throughout the cold, rainy winter and a dismal spring, the house seemed as still as the breathless pause before lightning. Every day on the horizon, gray clouds gathered as thick and billowing as smoke.

And yet, Rulan observed wryly, Liang Mo and Mei Yuk were at play, drinking, sweating through the exertions of sex and telling silly riddles. When Mei Yuk's belly began to grow, she stopped vomiting, and Liang Mo began to vomit in her place. It was comical. When he was not with his bride, Liang Mo was strutting through the wineshops, bragging about the child who was not his. Mei Yuk indulged him in his old craving for opium. Soon, Liang Mo had abandoned his books and had given himself over to dirt and the whims of his child-wife.

As for Meng, she was beginning to look drawn and sick, as if being a grandmother was more cause for pain than joy. Meng spent long hours gazing into the dead Tai Tai's mirror searching for her lost beauty—or reading her family's future in its depths.

Yung An, Kwangsi Province, 1852

"Look, Man-da-li!" Yang's arms described a huge arc. "Like ants attacking a dead ox—and we're the ox." Yang's sardonic laughter cut through the early morning silence. To-day, Yang was dressed like the rest of the holy soldiers, in metal fittings over a leather breastpiece, without the gaudier trappings that Taiping kings usually wore.

Mandley looked out over the valley to the mountains from the eastern tower of Yung An. Half a million imperial soldiers in red-and-blue uniforms, armed with cannon and muskets, were encamped around the city. Inside the city walls, thirty thousand Taiping men, women, and children, armed with pikes, swords, bows and arrows, and a dwindling supply of explosives waited.

"Afraid, my friend?" asked Yang, who moved up to stand at Mandley's side.

"Terrified."

"Ha, ha, ha!" Yang roared. "A sensible answer. If a man doesn't lose a little of his urine in a situation like this, more than his kidneys are bad. Your Book better be right or those ants will feast on you—and me."

Mandley swallowed a lump in his throat and began to recite by way of answer. "Therefore, thus says the Lord concerning the king of Assyria, 'He shall not come to this city, or shoot an arrow there;

neither shall he come before it with a shield, nor throw up a mound against it. By the way that he came, by the same he shall return, and he shall not come to this city,' declares the Lord. 'For I will defend this city to save it for My own sake and for My servant David's sake.' " He had been reciting the same passage at meetings of the five newly promoted Taiping kings throughout the seven months of the siege, while the imperial troops grew from one hundred thousand to five hundred thousand. These words from the book of Isaiah, he hoped desperately, might prove more effective than the few hundred muskets and antiquated gingalls he had wheedled from British and American traders. The westerners were not averse to doing business; they just didn't want to get caught backing the wrong side.

Yang seemed to sense his trepidation. "Aiya! The best weapon of all—the Word of God, which cuts sharper than a sword. The Word of God, which bequeaths to us a plan."

Mandley nodded, wondering if he was hearing authentic words of faith or motivational propaganda. Yang never ceased to surprise him. Sometimes when Yang spoke to the assembled masses, Mandley could swear he was an Old Testament prophet set down in China. At other times, he was convinced that the wily charcoal-carrier was simply manipulating words and concepts he barely understood. But there was no denying that with his newfound eloquence Yang had acquired tremendous personal power. Mandley had sensed the same strength in Yang's daughter in their brief encounter at Abundant Spring Mountain. Physically, father and daughter were opposites. Yang was short, monkey faced and bowlegged, with powerful arms and a huge head, whereas the girl he remembered in the general's house was as tall and graceful in form as an ancient Greek huntress. Yet both had command. It pained him to think of that vibrant creature as "property" of the same cruel general whose troops stood outside the Yung An walls, waiting to slay them all.

"The spies say that General Li commands the imps lying between us and the mountains. Is that true?" Mandley asked.

Yang looked down at the imperial army and nodded. "How God works for the good of all. Li ignored my overtures for peace made in a moment of weakness when I doubted our cause. Now it will be my pleasure to kill him as we push through."

Yang rarely spoke about his daughter, yet Mandley often wondered if Yang thought his ambition had been too high. Losing a daughter of that quality would crush a weaker man. "Do you ever think of Rulan?" he said.

"Yes—and of her mother."

Screwing up his courage, Mandley continued, "Do you consider this worth that sacrifice?"

Only Yang's eyes betrayed his pain. "Who chooses what God sets before us? We chase after treasures only dimly perceived and discover in the chasing a river of pain. When I heard what General Li had done to the Golden Orchids, I wished Hung's poison had killed me. I wanted only to go down to my grave. Then when I learned Rulan was still alive in Li's house and had not tried to escape, I felt she must have come to prefer the life of a rich woman behind walls. So be it, I said. She has suffered enough. And then that one tall Orchid who fled to us—Wing, who leads the horsewomen under the direction of Hung's sister—set my eye on anger and revenge, just as you set down the fiery words from the Book in my heart. From that time, I knew my enemies—the one within these walls and the one outside. Why should I lie down like a sick bull and let that enemy, who snatched from me all that I love, take my life through weakness? I vowed revenge on Li, but not on his son. If I take the general's life, I do my daughter a service. Her husband will inherit, and she will be lady in a great house."

Good, Mandley thought. With Yang's righteous anger fueling the Taiping, the wrath of the Lord might yet prevail against overwhelming odds, especially because God Himself had granted them a plan. Mandley had discovered it in a passage in II Samuel. The small band of Israelites under the young King David had been challenged by thousands of Philistines who had spread themselves across the valley of Rephaim. Forsaking his stronghold, David had defied conventional military strategy and gone out to attack superior forces on the plain. And he said, "As waters break out, The Lord has broken out against my enemies." That day, the Lord burst through the enemy like a raging flood. And David smote the enemy from Gibeon to Gezer.

"The Lord will go before us to strike the enemy down!" Mandley declared.

Yang chuckled. "Never will the banner generals believe that thirty thousand peasants would come out to fight five hundred thousand of the emperor's forces, *hai ma?*"

Mandley grinned. "Precisely. We won't fight. We'll run!"

"Yes, yes," said Yang, pointing to where the imperial troops were wheeling a huge cannon into place. "Punch a hole through there, the weakest part of the line. Those opium eaters will never be able to load the guns in time. Then we run fast, fast, like the renegade David, and an army as huge as this one will go mad. Leader will crash into leader, and each one will point the blame."

"Do you really think we have a chance?"

Yang nodded impatiently. "You see how the imperial army has blockaded the north and south gates? We'll fool them. We'll run out the three small gates on the east wall. And we'll run, not toward the plain, but to the mountains! Only a single stream of people can pass through, never that whole ocean of imps."

Mandley squinted in the direction of Yang's pointing finger. The path up the mountain was rocky and narrow. If they could break through the enemy lines and reach the heights, they could hide in the fog, in the trees, in the ravines. *If* they could break through and reach the heights. If not, the imperial troops would catch them on the plain and slaughter them like chickens. He looked down at Yang's face, as wrinkled and wizened as an ape's, at the fleshy mouth out of which thundered the awesome words of Jeremiah, which the brothers and sisters took to be the Voice of God. Was it sin to mimic a prophet? Perhaps. Perhaps Yang was not exactly David, yet David, too, was but a precursor of the True King, just as the Taipings fought for the day still to come, when the True Faith would rule. And how else was one supposed to transform the heathen if the heathen saw no need to be reformed? By fire and sword and the Word of God, which cut sharper than steel! In the by-and-by, the Law would be superseded by grace, but the preparatory stage of imperfect kingship would have to come before the Kingship of Christ. And the way would be made clear by Yang, His stalwart general, for Hung was flawed, Mandley had discovered. Hung was a Saul, whose growing madness proved that the Lord had cursed his kingship. God's favor had instead fallen on Yang, whose faith was more ardent and whose command over men more sure. And Mandley, like the prophet Samuel, would make this David a king.

A contingent of brothers and sisters marched up on the tower to relieve the exhausted night guard. They looked frightened and young as they took in the huge panoply of arms and men spread out before them. To give them courage, Yang raised his arms over the thousands of tiny cook fires that stood out against the velvet darkness. "And the children shall pass through unharmed," he shouted to the antlike hordes.

"Amen," intoned Mandley, wishing he had been able to purchase the thirty cannons that a German broker had almost released into his hands.

Hung, the Heavenly King, was kicking his newest concubine. The small of his back ached and sweat trickled behind his ears.

The girl screamed and held her arms around her abdomen as she rolled on the floor trying to avoid his feet.

"Rotten egg," he swore, stumbling. He was growing tired and the pounding in his head was louder than a hundred gongs. "I don't want you," he screamed. "I asked for the girl, not you. I call, but she will not answer. My soul is not meant for you. Who allowed you to steal the holy essence from me? You are a *kuei* sent from the King of Hell to bear a demon child with my face!"

Hung was sealed up in this town called Yung An, "Everlasting Peace," and he had no peace at all. He was losing control of his own movement to a nobody. A carrier of charcoal. Because of that evil man, the glory of the new kingdom ushered in at Yung An was dimmed. It mattered little that he, Hung, was now Heavenly King of Taiping Tien Kuo. It was a grand title, but one with little meaning, for he, on Yang's orders, had had to redefine his position to the faithful. Only God and Elder Brother Jesus were truly holy and supreme. He, Hung, was not holy, not supreme, only a man like the other five, who were now made kings to keep the peace among the warring factions. Yang was the Eastern King, general of the central army, commander-in-chief of the Taiping force. The faithful Scholar Feng, Southern King, and Pawnbroker Wei, Northern King, had been appointed to curb Yang's power, but Hung feared that both kings lacked the influence to block the ambitions of the Eastern King and his lackeys, Farmer Hsiao, Western King; the upstart Shih Ta Kai, Assistant King; and Mandley, the barbarian adviser. If he, Hung, was the rising sun, then Yang, the commander of the Taiping armies and the Voice of God, was blocking his light. Yang had convinced the other kings, even Wei, that he alone could get the brothers and sisters out of Yung An alive. Hadn't he done the same at Chin Tien in Thistle Mountain when the odds were against them? Hung hated Yang. But Hung hated dying more. He had no choice but to trust Yang a little longer.

Hung gave his concubine a final, desultory kick.

Niang Niang, the Heavenly Queen, tried to soothe Hung with kisses and pull him away from the poor girl whose misfortune it was to conceive a child without Hung's permission. She managed to lead him back to the bed where the other girls lay, but Hung was trembling with frustration and could not respond to their obedient caresses.

The meeting of the council had been a disaster for Hung. He and Wei had argued that they should wait out the Manchu army's siege. There was still a little food, enough for him and his wives at least. Surely the soldiers outside the gates with their half a million mouths and empty bellies and opium hunger would eventually deplete the land and vanish. And in the midst of the meeting, Yang had stunned them all by being seized with the Holy Spirit once again. He rolled his eyes into his head, and miraculously, God the Father's voice thundered out of Yang's mouth. But when Scholar Feng suggested to the council that Yang was playacting, Yang, in his terrible God voice, pointed his finger at Hung. "I am displeased in the Younger Son," he thundered. And he ordered the kings to cut the rations of their wives and concubines for the long siege. Hung dared not raise his voice against Yang. Then Yang went out on the tower and exhorted the troops to resist the "imps and demons of the eight banners." His head shaking with rage, Yang declared God's great anger against the Taiping warriors if they refused to bloody their hands. "Haven't these beasts enslaved you, ravished your daughters, forced vulgar habits on you? Are you not ashamed for having suffered all this? How can you still call yourselves men?" He offered a great reward for anyone who brought him the head of the "Tartar dog who sits on the Dragon Throne." All trembled before the Voice of God.

The memory of that humiliation before the council and this new trouble with the unfortunate woman who had conceived his child made Hung weep. Niang Niang, his queen, wept too out of sympathy for her lord. She took hot cloths and wiped the sweat and spittle tenderly from her husband's face. Eventually, his great rage evaporated, and he gathered the stunned and bloody concubine to his breast, kissing her bruises and declaring her blessed among women, his "darling moon."

But it was Yang's daughter he wanted. The girl who had broken the snake's back was the only woman fit to rule beside him in the empire to come. She was the Bride, his Chosen One who would complete him. Through her, he would subdue the demons outside his kingdom and within as well. For once the girl was his, Hung would control her upstart father through the only thing in the world he loved.

Forbidden City, Peking, 1852

The general knew most of the ways that men could die. He had witnessed them. Had ordered them. The disgrace always cut the deepest. To die by this callow young emperor who had acquired neither the grand style nor the great victories of his predecessors—and who had chosen the reign title Hsien Feng, "Universal Plenty," when the cycle of nature was so obviously proving otherwise—to die by such a one . . . the thought made the general furious. The fire in the line of the Tartar conquerer Nurhachi had long been snuffed out by the time the young emperor ascended the Dragon Throne; what remained was something rotten. Rotten too were the swaggering Manchu generals in Peking who sported the uniforms of the eight banners but were more adept at aping Han manners than taming a horse or bending a bow. To be snuffed out by this rotten stalk. The shame.

Li had been lodged outside the yellow crenulated walls of the Forbidden City in a warren of buildings reserved for foreign tributaries and visiting officials. The winds blowing off the Gobi sent dust as fine as mist through the broad avenues of Peking, scorching Li's throat and lungs. Peking in the first months of the lunar new year was gray, cold, unpleasant; Li missed his native mountain with its surfeit of bright flowers and soft, humid air. Above his narrow window slit, the golden roofs of the palace soared on painted red columns above the dusty city, a gorgeous dragon absorbed in its own useless beauty and cut off from the great shadowy empire it was meant to serve. Squinting his eyes against the hazy yellow light filled with thousands of swirling dust motes, he studied the tiny ceramic objects hanging off the tiled roofs of gold: mythical beasts and one lone man, the effigy of the hated tyrant Prince Min, who had been hanged by his enemies from a rooftop until he died. Was it pure chance that he was assigned this room, directly facing the twisted body of Prince Min? An omen—if one believed in such things.

Because of the disaster at Yung An, Li knew that he was not a guest, as the eunuchs pretended, but a prisoner. His own guards and servants had been taken away and a palace sentry stationed in the small court-yard outside his door. And although he was given clean clothes, a parade of lavish dishes, and all the books and papers he requested, it was clear that his movements were being carefully watched. The silent, soft-fleshed eunuchs in cone-shaped hats and brilliant long skirts always managed to slip past when he practiced the dance at dawn. These were undoubtedly spies sent by the grand councillor, who hated Li, or by An-te-hai, who might be cutting his losses among his former allies. The dour, raw-boned Manchu girl who stoked the fire under the low brick bed was undoubtedly sent to watch him too. Like all the women who served in the palace, she had been chosen for her physical charms—to suit the Manchu taste. Yet every time she glided through his room on high-heeled "boat shoes," her dark hair pulled tight over the incongruous, wide-winged wooden slab and the narrow slash of rouge gleaming like a drop of blood on her lower lip, his flesh crawled. These Manchu women were like huge birds of prey sent to watch him die.

So the general slept little, ate only pure white rice and scalding tea, which could not disguise the taste of poison, and sent no messages to his allies in the south. And he waited. For two days, he threw himself into the most strenuous *tai chi chuan* sequences he remembered and sketched complicated battle plans that he immediately threw into the fire. Discipline, he hoped, would purge his mind and body of the poisons of fear. He wondered whether Wulantai, his commander, had been summoned, for he had not seen a single officer, Han or Manchu, accompanying him to Peking.

Li's room faced the U-shaped Meridian Gate, which was surmounted by five pavilions and surrounded by a moat. Peking, the city of shadows, was as impenetrable as the empire itself, a labyrinth of palaces, gardens, moats, and temples in the general shape of three rectangles, each inside the other. The outer wall enclosed the city itself;

the second rectangle was the red-walled Imperial City, which lay between the northern, or Tartar, and the southern, or Han, sectors. The central rectangle, the "Great Within" or Forbidden City, was the palace where the young emperor, his women and those of his dead father lived. Under the Manchu, the citadel had become like the conquerers themselves: remote, gorgeous, and overburdened with ritual and pomp. Because no man except the emperor and his sons was allowed inside the four gates after nightfall, the emperor's intimate needs were served by five thousand castrati, drawn from the criminal classes, the more clever and ruthless of whom had amassed huge fortunes from the squeeze exacted from tradesmen, princes, diplomats, and particularly from the imperial concubines, for no one passed into the august presence without having first run the gauntlet of putty-faced eunuchs guarding every door. Above the lowest eunuch slop boy were the "ordinary eunuchs," who carried heaters and umbrellas, transmitted imperial orders, tended the palace pets, polished the old brasses, safeguarded the imperial seals, made medicines, and cleaned the water clocks. Above them were the eunuch supervisors of the ninth to the third rank, who ordered and maintained the robes, furs, weapons, and enormous quantities of foodstuffs consumed in the palace, recorded the names of visitors, guards, and academicians, and served the emperor's family. Highest of all was An-te-hai, who on his ascension to chief eunuch of the Presence had been promoted to the second rank, higher than any cut man had ever been placed. Walls and more walls. And behind the last wall, on a throne of mother-of-pearl inlaid with twisting dragons, sat the young emperor himself, the sacred and imperial Face, the northern polestar toward which millions of lesser lights in the kingdom turned in homage.

At noon on the second day, as the general was performing the final movements of the sequence called grasp the bird's tail, he heard the maid cough. Li lifted his left hand up, as if clutching a bird's neck, and moved his right hand slowly downward to smooth the invisible plumage from an imaginary tail. Someone shifted behind him; pivoting gracefully on his right heel, letting his left hand fall to his side, he turned his body to face a tall, spectral man in a ruby-tipped cap and peacock feather. The general's breath slid out in a long exhalation. Sweating profusely, he felt as if he were in the paroxysms of love—or death.

An-te-hai was sleeker, better fed than Li remembered; beneath the black coat trimmed with ermine he wore a gown of blue embroidered satin. His long, narrow eyes slowly swept the courtyard for spies.

Then he made a quick gesture with his head, and the girl slipped out of the courtyard.

The eunuch dipped his head in a graceful salute that fell short of a bow. "You have rested well, I hear, General. We are pleased," he murmured. "At dawn tomorrow, you are summoned into the Presence. We will take you in."

Li marveled at the amazing softness of An-te-hai's voice. "Thank you. This miserable person would not want to discredit himself by getting lost," replied the general, unsettled by the eunuch's new and pointed use of the royal we to denote his intimacy with the emperor. As he bent from the waist with his hands resting on his knees, a lower bow than the one he had been given, Li tried to dominate his blinding panic. If Li was named in the investigation of the imperial army's defeat at Yung An, An-te-hai's presence meant that there was still a chance for Li to save himself. That is, if he knew what squeeze the eunuch wanted. But Li had nothing to give! Again, the perilous pit yawned beneath him.

"There will, of course, be others summoned besides yourself. After the heralds have given the morning orders, I will take you into the Lesser Throne Room." The chief eunuch's eyes were narrow slits between swollen lids. "We have set aside part of the morning to discuss the rebellion with you. There is so much to learn from our loyal Han generals," he purred.

So his death was decided, thought Li.

"If you have questions?" ventured the eunuch.

"None," Li replied blandly, surprised by his own calm. "I will gladly await the emperor's pleasure. I have learned patience in the field."

"Good, good," said the eunuch softly. The smile stopped short of his hooded eyes. "The field. Of course, he will want to know all about that. Like most cloistered youths, the emperor finds the jangle and trappings of war endlessly intriguing. Still, the brillance of the Ten Thousand Years allows him to comprehend the essence of battle strategy in an instant. Be mindful of this. I know how you Han love to embroider on happenstance," said An-te-hai with a slippery smile. It was a warning to Li to be discreet about the letters and promises that had passed between them.

After the eunuch left, the anxiety that he had held in check made Li suddenly sag with fatigue. He was sure now that he would be made to share in the disgrace of the Manchu leader of the siege, Wulantai, who had had the bad fortune to live after being wounded in the skirmish with the fleeing rebels. In the hard comfort of his brick bed, Li's mind went over the siege, as it had a thousand times before—the months of waiting for the rebels to starve. Then in a single, unbelievably swift move, the Taiping had charged out of the city. Not to the river or the plains but into the mountains, a strategy that all military wisdom declared wrong.

Except that it worked. An astonishing escape, from the race into the misty hills to the final, awful rout as the government troops, many of them northerners in ungainly long gowns and boots, tried to follow the fleeing Taiping families. The big-foot Hakka women ran as fast as their men. The Taiping had secretly mined the fields and bridges, so they fled in the midst of powder and smoke and noise. Luck was against the imperial troops from the first: the cannon got stuck in the wet earth, and fire raged out of control in the camps. And once the Taiping got above the narrow passes, they rained down rocks and arrows on the frightened soldiers. As the bodies clogged the path, the Taiping sprang, naked and barefoot, upon the soldiers and pushed them off the cliffs. It was a brilliant strategy, by a master of guile, stealth—and explosives. The hand of Yang, the charcoal-carrier, was everywhere.

Li knew what had gone wrong from the moment he arrived at Yung An. The Manchu commanders were soft, and the foot soldiers opium weakened and afraid. How did one say that and not appear a coward or a traitor before one's superiors? Friendship with the chief eunuch stopped short of a defeat; An-te-hai would simply find another Han favorite to push. The emperor sent a silk cord after some "consultations," an invitation to the recipient to hang himself. One accepted with gratitude, for the alternatives were the public shame of decapitation or the private agony of the "thousand cuts."

The grim-faced Manchu girl came to lay out his evening meal. Five dishes: shrimp cunningly arranged on rare, out-of-season vegetables in the shape of a flower; spiced mutton; fried duck eggs studded with bits of glutinous bird spittle; red-cooked tripe and lung; and sea cucumbers glazed to look like glistening fruit. The food was beautiful without substance, showy without taste, elaborate without nourishment. The maid moved slowly, as if charged with a weighty burden, and Li noticed that she was painted and doused with a cloying perfume. He wondered if he dare make her taste the food and decided that she was measuring his worth for whomever had bought her. He picked up his chopsticks and filled his bowl without relish. As he ate, he watched the girl.

She appeared as tall as Rulan, but whereas his son's concubine was clean limbed and supple, the Manchu girl was merely gross. When she bent over to straighten the bedclothes, her robe fell open, revealing pendulous breasts tipped with rouge. This was what royal concubines did to pique their lord's jaded appetite. Because Li said nothing, she smiled and sat heavily on the bed, rolled down her stockings and hitched her underskirt past her brown, bare thighs to her waist.

The quilts were cold and the girl long gone by the time Li finally rose to light the oil lamp and throw more coal beneath the platform of the brick bed. He had intended to absorb her yin-essence without expending his own vital force, as a personal demonstration of self-control. Yet at the last moment, he lost all reserve and expelled both his seed and, to his surprise, a burst of tears. His heart flooded with shame. And then she asked for money, which further denigrated the moment. He paid her and slipped into a profound sadness. How absurd life was. How futile the striving. It was not that he feared dying. What he felt was a sense of needless loss, of humiliating capitulation to an unworthy foe.

In the dim lamplight, he lay down again and thought of Meng's slim, impeccable whiteness. She would be so dramatic in bereavement. Virtuous widowhood and total power over Abundant Spring Mountain would be hers—if his lands were not confiscated. Perhaps it was he, not Liang Mo, who would bring the line to an end, as his mother's fortune-tellers had predicted. He remembered how Yang's laughter had echoed through the gorges when Li's troops were too stuck in the mud to follow. The shame.

The general had been waiting in the dark for hours when a young eunuch dressed in green came at dawn to summon him. The eunuch boy held the mirror as Li shaved his forehead and face by torchlight, braided his queue neatly, washed himself in scented water, and clipped his mustache. He put on the black robe adorned with his insignias and the gold-buttoned hat of the military official of the ninth degree. He had earned his own rank through study and bloody striving on the battlefield, and although his honors were not nearly as glorious as his father's—a Hanlin scholar—they were honorably won and worthy of respect.

Outside in the gray half-light of dawn, the procession was already amassing under the snapping torches. He breathed in the clean, astringent smells of fire and paraffin. The Forbidden City was a giant hive, for, like a ruler bee surrounded by drones, the emperor was never alone; a walk in the garden was accompanied by the water-bearing eunuchs, the food-bearing eunuchs, the commode-bearing eunuch, and the eunuch of ceremonies and rites; when the emperor bedded down, there were concubines to warm his sheets and soft eunuch hands to tuck him in. Each night, those same hands carried a chosen concubine in a fur-lined cloak through the huge, cold courts and placed her naked at the foot of the imperial bed, her hair brushing the floor, until the Ten Thousand Years invited her under his quilt. There were eunuch guards outside his door should his dreams trouble him. And every dawn, the councillors and princes, the Han officials of the court, and dignitaries from other lands came to behold his brilliance, which, like that of the sun, could quicken or destroy.

All this took place in utter darkness, because the emperor was the sun, and the sun had not yet risen.

In the flickering torchlight, Li saw men he had served with in the field. All ignored him, for they knew he was there to report on the Yung An disaster. His eunuch guide led him to the head of the procession. Wulantai was already there in full regalia, though bereft of his sword, as Li was, for weapons were forbidden before the Presence; Wulantai's dark, long face was gray and unshaved, as if his wounds still pained him. His hollow eyes brightened feverishly when he saw Li. He limped over to Li and grabbed him by the shoulder. Others nearby turned away.

"You're here, eh? Look, we got to stick together. Who could have guessed, who could have known that those shit-kicking coal-carriers would try to break out!" His hands shook, and he talked too loud.

"We should have guessed," Li said stoically.

"Don't try to save your hide at my expense," Wulantai hissed. "I'll bury you, Han man. I have friends who will swear that you gave the order for the advance—"

"Get hold of yourself," Li retorted.

"Yes, yes," Wulantai said, his face crumbling. Driven back and forth like a leaf in a storm, he was half-dead from illness and fear, and ready now to fall at Li's feet to beseech his aid.

A eunuch carrying a lighted torch came up to stand beside them. At that moment, the west Flowery Gate swung wide. The Seal of Heaven was opened again for another day. The parade of military officials moved forward under the direction of the green-clad eunuchs; next came the civil servants, then the laborers, until the great yard was filled with the representatives of the people, five or six thousand, filing in between the torches to behold a single man. Line upon line they stood, rank upon rank, the design known only to those shadowy half-men, whose mission in life was to sort out the differences between one person and the next.

As the bells sounded and the crier whined, all prostrated themselves on the cobblestones while out of the gates came three eunuchs walking sideways with their arms churning the air and calling out to the crowd to make way. They were followed by the brilliant jeweled palanquin of the emperor. The litter was lowered, and down stepped a small man, clothed in heavy garments of bright yellow.

The youth spoke, but no one heard. The message, which had already been drafted by eunuch scribes, was echoed softly through the crowd by more criers. The emperor came to the edge of the platform and gestured in the direction from which he came.

Even Li was awed. For an instant, he saw beyond the tubercular youth he despised to the spirit of the man who occupied the throne. Here was God-on-earth, glittering like the sun. Seeing him circle out of the gate, Li knew why peasants and princes, even his fierce mother, had chosen to place their faith on whatever stranger sat on the Dragon Throne: with the sun in place, hunger, chaos, and despair were only illusion; order in the universe prevailed. Li had destroyed that order. The emperor's armies had been defeated by rabble; the face of the sun was dimmed.

At that moment the cold, yellow eye of heaven broke through the gray clouds in the eastern sky. Gongs crashed, the criers chanted. "Kneel! Kowtow! Again kowtow! A third time kowtow! Rise!" Again the gongs and criers sounded, and the people knelt to knock their foreheads three more times before rising. And again once more.

Then the emperor turned away his face, and the massive gates closed behind the last green-clad eunuch; bereft of the glorious vision, the crowd slowly melted away.

Somehow the eunuchs found him. Li was pushed through the gate into a passage of great length running between two blood red walls. Ushered into the Hall of Military Prowess, he waited with other military officials until his name was called. From there he stepped into a sedan chair whose bearers carried him swiftly across the tiny bridges that arced like crossbows over the arrow-shaped Golden Stream into the heart of the palace. Peering out from behind the tapestries, Li saw that everything was dying of age: the stones were eaten away by time, the wooden doors were crumbling and dusty; the squint-eyed lion dogs that guarded the doors were streaked yellow from the rains of countless seasons. As the bare feet of the bearers slapped the marble floors, Li passed hundreds of tiny courts inhabited by white-haired eunuchs, who cultivated birds or flowers under the eyes of the cruel, grinning faces of mythical beasts.

In the next section, they came on row after row of open corridors lined with potted trees. High above the brick walkways and lotus pools, Li saw small rooms hung with curtains of billowing gauze behind which moved shapely shadows. He wondered if these were the forgotten women of the palace, those who had been chosen for the old emperor's bed and never summoned. A breeze stirred the perfumed air and brought with it the unmistakable chords of a moon harp and the lilting strains of an old song. A woman was singing in a sweet, low voice, as rich and pliant as velvet. The eunuch bearers slowed of their own accord, as enchanted as Li with the siren call of the hidden singer. The song seemed to follow them. Or were they following the song? And suddenly Li saw the singer—a Manchu girl dressed in a violet gown seated on an outcrop of stone in a grotto tucked into a space off the passageway. She was still in her teens, far too young for a forgotten concubine—unless she was one newly chosen for the young emperor's bed. She had escaped her eunuch guard to venture into the forbidden warren beyond the Inner Palace.

The girl raised her head, and, although she betrayed no trace of emotion, Li felt her disappointment keenly. She expected another.

It was not simply her beauty that made Li stare, but the aura of sensuality that hung about her like a heavy perfume. She had placed herself astride his path with as much purpose as her grandmothers who had galloped over the steppes to meet their savage lovers. What do the rules of this place have to do with me? she seemed to sing. She wore a purple orchid in her hair, a real one, not the cunningly painted artificial flowers that Manchu women favored.

When her long fingers brushed the strings of the moon harp that lay across her lap, Li felt as if he had been caressed most intimately. Here was one who would not stay hidden for long, he decided. She would find a clever eunuch to advance her cause. Once in the Dragon's bed, the lady with the orchid would spin a web that would ensnare an empire.

The bearers picked up speed, and the sound of the harp was quickly lost in the soft padding of the eunuchs' bare feet as they carried Li through a maze of hidden passages that turned and twisted alarmingly. At the next turn, the bearers stopped, and Li was conducted into a palace chair of red satin slung on the shoulders of two imperial bearers, ushered through the Gate of Supreme Harmony, and carried up a set of marble stairs to a raised terrace of white marble. Then he was left in a small, sumptuous chamber with more guards, until he saw a familiar figure approach.

An-te-hai clapped his hands. The guards exited, and An-te-hai turned and scratched at the door of the Lesser Throne Room.

The youth was seated on a divan covered with yellow silk. He was younger than Liang Mo, as slight as a woman, dressed in a pointed red hat and a loose robe of yellow silk embroidered with the imperial dragon. Through the incense haze, Li saw a crowd of eunuchs in gold-buttoned hats, and on the side of the throne, two officials of the realm were seated on stools, their peacock feathers rising from their caps like the plumage of ghostly birds.

Li stretched facedown on the thick rug and touched his head to the ground the prescribed nine times in sets of three, rising briefly after the third bow.

"Rise, General, rise," came the languid voice of the boy-king. He gestured to the eunuch of rites, a short, fat man beside him. "Let our loyal servant seat himself."

As Li was brushing the dust from his trousers, there was a rustle at the door. Wulantai came in behind the young eunuch guard and threw himself awkwardly into a kowtow. The ritual does not become any of them, observed Li wryly. The Manchu are too big and clumsy for our small, hard chairs and dainty tables. The room was far more suited to the compact bodies of Han, like himself, and the one obviously Han councillor near the throne. Under the ceiling of entwined dragons and phoenixes, the Manchu seemed the outsiders, and he the one who truly belonged.

Besides Li, Wulantai, and the emperor, there were ten others in the room. The cold-eyed Han mandarin who pretended not to notice Li; a tall Manchu prince; three scribes; the eunuch of rites, who had placed an octagonal stool before Li; three young eunuchs clad in green; and the chief eunuch.

The boy on the throne flicked his finger toward the eunuch of rites, who took up a paper and began to read in a voice as sweet as a virgin's. "His majesty, in the course of overseeing the welfare of his children in the right and proper order, has determined to discover the cause of the defeat of the imperial army at the hands of the rebels in Yung An. Therefore, he has called before him the head of the grand council and dear and trusted friends of the throne." The eunuch read the names of those present, among them: Prince Su Shun, Councillor Chi, Commander Wulantai, and General Li.

Li recognized the prince as the emperor's cousin, the boon companion of his profligate youth. Was Prince Su Shun setting himself up as imperial adviser as well? A glance at the tight-lipped Han mandarin showed the general that his guess was not off the mark.

There was no denying the effect of the young Manchu prince's powerful personality in the throne room. Su Shun was thickset and tall, with a long, high-cheekboned face that might have been handsome in the first flush of adolescence but was now pockmarked and sallow from overindulgence. It was he who made the first bold, flat statement to Wulantai. "Defeat has dogged the heels of our imperial armies of late."

"Fate," replied Wulantai weakly. "Who could have predicted? Who could have foreseen?"

"Talk like one of us, not a Han," retorted Su Shun, pointing a long fingernail at the Manchu general's frightened face. "I have little patience for circumlocution. Say the truth clearly. You were unprepared."

"No, no," Wulantai muttered. "It could not be helped. If I had not been hurt . . . well . . ."

Li looked up from the pattern of scrolls on the thick blue-and-white carpet and met the flat, black eyes of Councillor Chi.

"Forgive me, Commander," sighed the Councillor, "but I still do not know how you were wounded. I understand that you had no arrow wounds. No gunpowder burns. The court doctors claimed that the internal bleeding . . ." He let the last words hang in the air.

"An ambush. Treacherous, cowardly rebel dogs," shot back Wulantai. He rubbed his abdomen as if in pain.

The emperor scratched his left knee and instantly the chief eunuch was kneeling before him, adjusting the footstool.

Su Shun rocked back and forth on the thick columns of his legs, his peacock feather bobbing. "You were unprepared! The facts do not lie!"

"Wait, Sir!" Wulantai replied. "These Hakka are not ordinary men. I swear they are demons. I heard their prayers and incantations behind the walls. They spoke to strange gods, none I've ever heard of. Even their women are demons. They climbed up the mountains as easily as goats. They don't bind their feet or tie up their hair like respectable women."

Councillor Chi showed opium-stained teeth. "Hakka women are devoid of shame or decorum."

Encouraged by the mandarin's assent, Wulantai continued. "See? They're not like any Han we're used to. They're as stern as priests. They don't sell their daughters, fancy that! They pool their money, even with people of a rival clan. They don't smoke dirt!" He leaned forward to the emperor and said in a conspiratorial manner, "They don't even pillow! Can you imagine? Although who would want to pillow their women? It would be like pillowing a man."

There was a flicker behind the chief eunuch's hooded eyes.

"The women," continued Wulantai, warming to his tale, "ride horses and shoot arrows and plant explosives. Uncivilized! Maybe the men carry water and bear the children. Yes, families are upside down with those demons. Next time I'll catch a devil-woman for you and bring her back as a gift."

The ends of Su Shun's long mustache were trembling. "My great-grandmother could ride and shoot the crossbow. I wager yours did too. But poor women, they were so uncivilized. Leave talking about trivial matters. I want to know how you were wounded and who these Taiping are. A tribe? A clan? A secret society? Is this another White Lotus uprising? Is that why they cut off their queues—to bedevil my poor cousin as soon as he ascends the throne?"

Wulantai shrugged evasively. "They are Han and untrustworthy by nature. They call us barbarians behind our backs, but turn away, and they slit our throats."

"We Han are not fit to rule ourselves," interrupted Councillor Chi mildly but for General Li's benefit. "History bears this out. In all the dynasties, the most corrupt, the most cruel kings have been Han."

"My sentiments exactly, Sir," growled Wulantai. "And as soon as I am healed and get back on the field, I will make the demons pay for cutting off their queues."

The emperor made a soft, hesitant sound like a shy girl protesting a compliment. "And why should you have another chance to fail?"

The silence was so deep that Li could hear a bead of water fall from the water clock.

"Let us venture to suggest that the brave commander take a rest," the emperor added quietly.

"Well said," echoed Su Shun. "We will choose someone who knows these crazy Hakka well. A Han man. But who? That worthy man from Hunan, Scholar Tseng Kuo Fan, is my choice. He is hard and incorruptible, utterly loyal to the throne. Or perhaps we should consider a military man—"

"We beg the emperor's indulgence," interrupted Councillor Chi, "but the world has not known a warrior's heart like a stalwart Manchu. Your kind is far more capable of leading Han troops than a Han man."

"Ha!" said the prince with a disparaging grimace. "How you Han love each other!"

"We shall decide on our own," piped the emperor. "But let us return to the matter at hand. What happened at Yung An? We are still confused."

An-te-hai slid his eyes toward the general. The emperor began again with more warmth. "Let us ask our brave Han general, Li, to explain. Why is it that the rebels got away?"

Councillor Chi opened his mouth to protest, but the youth waved him into silence.

"They followed the first tenet of warfare, Highness," said Li. "Do the unexpected and you will win."

"A bandit ploy," fumed Wulantai.

"Begging your pardon," replied Li politely, "not bandits but Sun Tzu. He says, 'All warfare is based on deception.' And again, he says, 'When most strong, pretend incapacity. When active, inactivity.' The rebels fooled us."

"But not you, eh, Li? You're a soldier who can read. I grant you can read these crazy Taiping too," guffawed Prince Su Shun.

General Li bowed by way of answer.

The chief eunuch's lips moved imperceptibly near the emperor's cheek. The emperor nodded at Li to continue.

"Sun Tzu says again, 'The wise general moves so swiftly he cannot be overtaken. He conducts a war of movement.' We were outmaneuvered," Li added gravely.

The emperor curled into the yellow chair as if settling down for a story.

Li went on cautiously. "Sun Tzu describes the 'heavenly cracks.' This is where the mountain gorges are narrow. 'When one man defends a narrow mountain defile, which is like sheep's intestines, or the door of a doghouse, he can withstand ten thousand.' "

Wulantai's voice seemed to come from the bottom of a well. "It was pouring rain. We could not see. The way was so narrow that two men could not walk shoulder to shoulder . . ."

"Again, I ask, how were you wounded?" said Su Shun sharply.

"An accident," croaked Wulantai.

The emperor stifled a yawn. "You have not answered the prince's question," he said petulantly. "How were you wounded?" Slowly his eyes moved to General Li.

"From a fall," Li replied in the silence. "Yang of the rebels led him off in one direction and the commander slipped in the mud and fell off a precipice." Li exhaled slowly. He felt a dark pit yawn beneath him. He had said what had to be said. Shame and death would shortly follow; the certainty made him almost happy. He wondered how the head must feel cut off from the body, whether one continued to think and feel for a while before the light was extinguished forever.

The emperor began to giggle, then to laugh, his mouth uncovered. Councillor Chi smiled. Wulantai laughed as if he were out of his head with drink. The prince and An-te-hai continued to study General Li.

That night, Wulantai was sent out of Peking in disgrace. Li was given a message stamped with the seal of the Imperial Council and rolled in yellow silk. The edict excused him from further service in the field and invited him to accept the Celestial Commission as the new viceroy of Kwangtung and Kwangsi.

Abundant Spring Mountain, 1852

ulan was making Four Things Soup, a yin tonic for women. The rest of the house was asleep, but because she now lived in the storeroom where Pao An's sickbed had stood, she felt free to use the midnight hours for her own work. Out of guilt, Liang Mo had allowed Rulan to do whatever she pleased, in this case, to build a small cook shed next to the storeroom for drying herbs to be pounded into healing powders.

Making medicine was a precise, meticulous art that commanded all her attention and made her forget her loneliness for a time. The herbs had to be weighed and measured and the water heated to the right temperature to produce a liquid with the proper thickness or color. And yet there was an element of unpredictability to the preparation of the medicines, for one could never quite trust the heat of the pan or the purity of the herbs. The plants themselves produced varying results depending on the quality of the soil, the season they were picked, and the amount of time they were kept. Only the best healers could make the medicine come out the same each time. Rulan had had many batches fail; yet she was refining her technique, and there were fewer and fewer medicine gourds she had to throw away.

Every day she concentrated on the thing at hand. She did not want to think about the past. She did not want to put names to the angry ghosts that were invading her dreams once again. Occasionally she heard word about the war. The Taiping had escaped the siege at Yung An and were marching northeast through Hunan Province. Did her father still walk among them? Wing and her sisters—did they live? Did Pao An ever think of her? Or were his dreams invaded by a fox-spirit rubbing against him, belly dragging on the ground heavy with his seed?

The yin tonic she was making to build up Mei Yuk's blood was her own recipe. Mei Yuk, who had grown as fat as a pigeon, refused to take the standard medicine for pregnancy because she found it bitter. So Rulan had created new recipes using *tang kuei* root, the herb that cured women's ills: she put *tang kuei* into chicken soup to make a fortifying broth and fed it to Mei Yuk until the girl complained of being treated like a baby. Then Rulan had the idea of steaming the *tang kuei* and other herbs with a handful of red dates; the viscous syrup delighted Mei Yuk, who drank a cupful eagerly every day. Rulan did this for the child, not the child's mother. And for Pao An.

She no longer prayed to Kwan Yin because the goddess had turned her face away. Rulan felt soiled, tainted before the goddess, unworthy of her sisters' love or trust. She thought herself an evil thing whose prayers were an abomination to the goddess.

To guard against sadness, she made her world small with routine. She would not walk if she could stand still, or stand if she could sit, or sit if she could sleep. She tried not to think—so she would not be lonely. She resisted beginnings.

By contrast, the house of Li was frenetic with beginnings. General Li and his closest advisers were in Canton preparing for his ceremony of installation as viceroy. If Mei Yuk's baby was a boy, the women of the house would make the journey to Canton for the investiture, and show themselves before the first families of Canton. With its line ensured, the house of Li would rise gloriously from the ashes of its former shame.

Rulan told herself she was happy without the burden of caring for Liang Mo or Mei Yuk. Mei Yuk refused to listen to Rulan's warnings to abstain from sex. Liang Mo was no better; he allowed Mei Yuk to stuff herself with sweets and humored her when she refused to eat the duck eggs that Second Cook had steamed into a custard. Nor would she take the infusion of stove ashes and gingerroot for the intermittent nausea that plagued her throughout the pregnancy. Instead, she complained that the vomiting made her crave the "cold" foods normally forbidden to pregnant women, and gorged on hami melons, which made her bleed. When Rulan pointed out that the rich food was causing an imbalance of yin that would weaken her after labor when the bones opened up, Mei Yuk screamed that she needed no advice from a jealous, barren woman. Just as suddenly, in fear and shame, she would beg Rulan's pardon.

Rulan made Liang Mo tend his fretful wife, since Mei Yuk would not let the maids come near her. He had stopped coming to Rulan at Mei Yuk's urging, guiltily claiming that he dared not refuse the girl in her condition. Rulan also suspected that he did not like the somber person she had become and preferred playing the child with his child-like wife. Because Mei Yuk took up all his time, he dropped his studies, and Meng, too enervated by her illness to protest, did not interfere. So husband and wife stayed in bed most of the day, quarreling and eating, playing games, smoking dirt, and reading pillow books, for as her belly grew, so did Mei Yuk's ardor.

Rulan warned Liang Mo about the dangers of sex as the time of delivery drew near, especially because Mei Yuk continued to bleed at her moon time, but Mei Yuk cried that Rulan was trying to steal Liang Mo away. Nor could Liang Mo bear to part from Mei Yuk; her pregnancy had piqued his appetite for unusual sensations. But whenever she watched Mei Yuk, Rulan was troubled by the girl's gait and by the way her belly hung. The girl's hips were far too narrow, and the baby was growing dangerously large.

Grind the herbs, Rulan told herself. She held a pinch up to her nose and sniffed the dry, acerbic fragrance.

She was steaming a whole *tang kuei* root for herself after making a new batch of red syrup for the women of the house when Liang Mo ran into the room.

"Come quick," he cried. "The child is coming. Mei Yuk is in frightful pain."

Rulan brushed the hair out of her eyes. "It's too early. Night pains come often for a first child. Go back and rub her stomach, and the soreness will go away."

"I did that," he protested. "But nothing is helping. And when I felt around, the sheets were wet. A man should not have to know these things. Please—"

An alarm sounded in Rulan's head, so she quickly snuffed out the fire under the pot and hastened with Liang Mo to the bedroom they had once shared. There she found Mei Yuk biting on a towel with the bedclothes rumpled around her bare loins. She seemed a child herself except for her swollen belly, which stuck out like a melon.

Rulan pressed her hand on Mei Yuk's stomach and felt the womb clutch. The bedclothes were damp and slightly bloody. "Your water has broken," Rulan said. "The child will come soon."

"But you said not for weeks!" whimpered Mei Yuk. "You lied to me! This is not the right time."

Of course it's not the right time, Rulan wanted to shout back. Because the child was conceived weeks before your husband touched you! She quelled the urge to slap Mei Yuk. "Sometimes the first one comes early—especially when the mother is so small," she explained for Liang Mo's benefit.

He was making small incoherent noises of sympathy, when a contraction made Mei Yuk scream and lift her hips in terror.

"Oh, oh," she moaned. "I am in the grip of a demon. Kwan Yin help me, I'm going to die."

Liang Mo looked as if he might faint.

"Please wait outside, Husband," Rulan ordered. Liang Mo fled gratefully.

Mei Yuk's screams had wakened the maids and now two of them were shivering by the bedside in their nightdresses. Rulan sent them out for hot wine and towels, and then she ran to get her medicine gourds.

All Rulan's worst fears were being realized. As if fulfilling the promise that all things happened in this house out of phase with nature and propriety, Mei Yuk's child refused to be born. Liang Mo occasionally poked his face in the door, but then Mei Yuk's purple face would erupt in screams and curses, sending him running.

So violent were Mei Yuk's contractions that Rulan had to hold the girl's shoulders down on the bed until each spasm subsided. She tried to show Mei Yuk how to ride the pain as one might ride the crest of a wave, but the girl was too frightened to hear.

"Scream!" Rulan commanded. "The more you scream, the better it will be for the child."

A veil seemed to grow over Mei Yuk's eyes. "I hate this child," she gasped. "I am being punished for my sin. Kwan Yin curse you, you made me have this demon-child. Witch-woman, you refused me the medicine to kill the child so I would suffer and die. You want to take my husband away!"

Despite the enmity that had arisen between them over Pao An and Liang Mo, the two women had kept the secret of Mei Yuk's pregnancy and Pao An's escape. Secrets were the food of great houses, and women were trained in them from birth. But if Mei Yuk grew delirious, Rulan feared she would let something slip, thus jeopardizing Pao An's unborn child. She pinched the girl hard on her cheek and whispered in Mei Yuk's ear, so that the maids couldn't hear. "Don't say such things again, Mei Mei. Or I will send the ghost bird to pluck out your soul. You know what a witch-woman can do. Would you have the ghost bird kill you?"

Mei Yuk's lips opened in a silent scream.

"A ghost bird has breasts like a woman and a face like a woman. And a huge mouth to suck out the souls of women who hate their unborn babies. Never tell our husband what you or I know, or the bird will pluck out your heart from your breast. Listen, the bird comes for you even now." Rulan opened her mouth and screamed. So loud and unearthly was the sound that in the next room, Liang Mo began to wail in terror, convinced that Mei Yuk had died. But then he heard Mei Yuk's shrill cries threaded like beads on Rulan's softer moaning. Liang Mo put his head under a cushion so he could not hear; but in the Kitchen Court, the maids nodded in approval at the familiar, rhythmic sounds of childbirth as Rulan taught Mei Yuk how to scream as a woman in labor should.

During the brief intervals between pains, Mei Yuk would lapse into a twilight sleep. Then Liang Mo would tiptoe into the room, and he and Rulan would stare without speaking at the tiny, birdlike girl who had changed both their lives.

For an entire day, the pains were strong and unremitting, but the baby would not descend, and Mei Yuk grew steadily weaker. Rulan discovered that the child was set to come out buttocks first. Yet there was still a small chance that the child might turn and descend headfirst into the canal. She would wait and see. In the meantime, she had nothing for pain except opium, of course. But Rulan hated the evil drug.

Then she remembered the dried petals of the trumpet flower that the old bell-doctor had given her. She had discovered them after the Tai Tai's death. Rulan had never used the deadly plant before and did not know how much to give. A little would help quiet the pain, but if she gave too much, Mei Yuk and the child would surely perish.

By nightfall, Mei Yuk's contractions were stronger and closer together, but the baby had still not turned and Mei Yuk was losing the strength to fight the pain.

"Liang Mo, come," Rulan commanded.

He entered a room filled with the steamy-sweet smell of medicine and sweat.

"Hold her," Rulan said. "I have to turn the baby. If that fails, I will have to cut."

"Get the *mui tsai!* I am a man. I don't belong here," Liang Mo said.

"She will die if you do not help. And the maids are too frightened to be of use. No one else can do this but you. Besides, you are the father and must bear the responsibility for her suffering."

She showed Liang Mo how to hold Mei Yuk's hands above her head and to pin her shoulders against the quilts.

"Don't let go," Rulan warned. "And don't listen to what she says. Women say anything when they are in pain."

Liang Mo nodded, without understanding.

Rulan took a pinch of trumpet flower leaves from the packet the herb vendor had given her and stirred the herbs into a small porcelain pot of hot wine. Then she put the spigot of the wine pot into Mei Yuk's mouth and let the medicine drip between the girl's parched lips, praying that the girl would not reveal anything in her delirium. Mei Yuk's lips closed over the spout like a child's around a teat.

Rulan pulled the bedclothes away from Mei Yuk, exposing the girl's thighs. Liang Mo put his face into Mei Yuk's shoulder so he need not look. The girl's sex was as distended as a wound. Rulan greased her hand with clean plant oil, made her fingers into a point, and reached in for the child. Mei Yuk screamed as if she were being stabbed to death, then fainted. The child's taut, slippery hipbone eluded Rulan's grasp. She pinched and the child stirred and moved.

Liang Mo let loose a nonsensical stream of syllables that sounded like the cry of a marsh bird to its mate. Again Rulan pulled at the slippery creature caught in Mei Yuk's womb, but the child was stuck fast. With her other hand, Rulan pressed down on Mei Yuk's stomach, until, incredibly, the child somersaulted in the cavity of its mother's body. From Mei Yuk's open mouth came a deathly groan.

"Now," Rulan called to Liang Mo. "I have the head. Hold her fast."

Liang Mo's litany grew louder and higher until he was shrieking in Mei Yuk's ear. Mei Yuk, half-conscious, was drawing in shuddering gasps of air.

Then there was a shoulder, and suddenly, the child slipped out as easily as a seed bursts from a pod. Rulan gathered the child dangling in its coils to her breast, reached into its throat with one finger and pulled out the plug of white mucus. The child sucked in air and began a tremendous complaint.

Rulan broke a cup and with the clean edges cut the cord in two and lay the child on its mother's breast. Then she took a towel and tenderly wiped the infant clean. He was red faced and broad shouldered, with a shock of wet black hair. A boy.

"A girl is born," declared Rulan to fool the unkind ghosts. "Bad luck for this poor house."

Liang Mo was crying. "No more, I promise, Mei Mei. I didn't know it was like this."

The child squirmed on Mei Yuk's bare belly, but the girl turned her head away with a grimace. "Away, away!" she moaned, as if the child were a piece of excrescence.

Revolted by Mei Yuk's response, Rulan gave it instead into Liang Mo's trembling hands. "Here, take your son. And remember how its mother suffered for you." Then she turned back to Mei Yuk.

Mei Yuk's belly was dangerously soft. The placenta had not been expelled. She kneaded the belly and a stream of blood issued, but nothing happened. So she did what Ailan used to do in such cases. She turned Mei Yuk's head to the side so she would not swallow her tongue, and put her finger down Mei Yuk's throat until the girl gagged and began a dry vomit. The contractions forced the placenta out at once.

Rulan buried the placenta in the garden to distract the ghosts. "Such a pity," she said aloud again. "A girl child and it died." The words made her feel bereft and empty, as if she had indeed placed a dead child into the ground.

Much later, when Mei Yuk was sleeping, Liang Mo came into Rulan's herb room. He had given his son into the hands of a wet nurse whose milk already flowed copiously at his cries.

"Will the next time be like this?" he asked, unable to disguise his joy and fear. Liang Mo's hair was slicked down with sweat, and he looked as if he had been pulled half-drowned from a river.

"The first time is always the hardest," Rulan replied. "If you had not helped, she would have died."

"Yes," Liang Mo said proudly. "Look what Mei Mei did to me." He showed Rulan where Mei Yuk's nails had left deep, red half-moons on his arms. "Did you ever hear such screaming before? Who would have known that such a small person could make such fat sons!"

"Be firm with her then," Rulan said, relieved that things were finally finished between them. Liang Mo would never take her back into his bed now. He was a father, and henceforth would choose his women by their fecundity. To him, Rulan would be a woman for healing, not for pleasure. He would cherish her like a revered aunt. "Your mother is not well," she told Liang Mo, "so you must order the red eggs and roast pig to be sent to all the neighbors to announce the child. Now you can have no secrets from Mei Yuk. She cannot bathe for a month, or too much yin will enter her bones and cause her pain later on. She must lie and not sit, again for a month, at least until we leave for Canton. And you must not make her cry or her eyes will be weakened. And no matter how much you or she desire it, you must not touch each other. Yes, yes, I know it is hard, but it is up to you. The month must be observed before you start another son."

Liang Mo blushed and ducked his head in grudging assent. She remembered that that was how he always reacted to an order he disliked—one he had no intention of following.

The next day Meng came, leaning on Moon's arm like an old woman. She saw the child and approved. And after the prescribed month, the baby was given a feast and brought into the Great Hall with all the relatives assembled.

Rulan took the child to where Meng sat in a straight-backed mahogany chair. The polished seat beside her was empty, except for a black official's cap with a ruby button and peacock feather, a reminder of the general's new promotion to mandarin of the first degree with the right to be carried by twelve bearers, and of his constant vigilance over his house.

"Now will this house live for a thousand years," Meng whispered fiercely as she took the child.

The child began to cry, as loud and as lustily as any peasant infant. Rulan's heart melted at the sound. May Pao An's line live for a thousand years, she prayed silently to the goddess she dared not name.

Canton

"Careful with her, idiots. Dogs. Go gently. My lady is not a duck to stuff inside a pot." Moon flapped her small, plump hands at the porters, who were lifting Meng into the mule cart at the head of the line. The sun was just crowning the hills to the east. The family was going by mule cart to the viceroy's installation in Canton, instead of by the safer, speedier barge because Meng was terrified of drowning. The drivers, all members of General Li's Yung An troops pressed into domestic service, were squatting around an earthen jar near the gates and complaining in loud whispers.

"Look at the belly of this animal! Do you think he has the juice to go all the way to Canton? Can he outrun arrows if we're attacked? Give me my pike. Give me a battalion of able men."

"Yes, yes," said one who hobbled about on a wooden leg. "But what can you do, old friend? Carrying ladies is still better than a begging bowl."

"But not as safe, *hai ma*? I'd gamble a bucket of salt against this old beast's farts that we get killed on this journey."

"The general has a plan," said one.

"Better than what he had at Yung An, I hope," the mutilated man protested.

"Cut your head and tongue, fool," said an old soldier. "Look how his plan worked out for him. He's viceroy, not a general anymore. No more sleeping in a cold cot. Warm beds and a dozen concubines."

"I don't like his plans. The last one got me a Taiping arrow in the buttocks," another man whined. The others, having witnessed the occasion, guffawed. "And the people are complaining that he will turn the ceremony of taking office into a conscription for new recruits. They say he plans to raise the salt tax to buy weapons."

"And stuff his pockets too, since he and Grandfather Wang control the salt trade," the one with the wooden leg said as he cinched up the harness on a snorting mule.

"Curb your tongues!" the old soldier hissed. "I'm not even going to stand near you. I don't want to watch them cut you into small pieces."

For a while no one spoke. "Aiya," said a thin, tall driver as he threw a basket of linen into the cart. "My old mother still thinks I'm fighting the Taiping. She would throw dirt on her head if she saw me carrying women's clothes."

Moon, overhearing the talk, waddled over to hit the driver behind the ear with her fan. "Ungrateful! I'll tell your old mother myself where you are. You're right here, stealing this family's silver."

The driver hopped and nearly lost a sandal, to the amusement of his friends. "What good is silver when you're dead? If I were you, Auntie, I'd pretend a bellyache and beg my lady to leave me home! We're soldiers. We carry weapons, not laundry. If you think putting on beggars' rags will protect you from bandits and hunger marchers, I hope you have no children," he retorted, but Moon had already limped out of earshot.

Rulan came out with a jug of hot tea, which she poured into the earthen jar outside the gate. The bearers crowded around, dipping the cups she handed them into the thick brew. Rulan talked freely with the drivers and peered into each cart to see if there were enough blue cotton cushions for the women.

"Ride with me, sweetheart. The other mules are slow," whispered the porter with the wooden leg. When he leaned over to Rulan, she smelled the sour stench of cheap wine.

"Cut your head and tongue," puffed Moon, coming around the gate with bundles of glutinous rice wrapped in ti leaves for the journey. "Watch how you talk to Second Lady. Be ashamed!"

The man slapped his face in embarrassment, and Rulan laughed out loud, her red lips parted wide, like a country girl's. She was glad to be out of the cage that had kept her a prisoner for two years. Even the air outside the walls of Abundant Spring Mountain smelled sweeter than that within. To go to Canton was an unbelievable adventure—and an opportunity for escape! There was, she remembered, a nunnery in Canton that the Orchids sent old women to. She would find a way to get word to her sisters.

"Wait," she said to the bearer and made a show of comparing carts. "Your mule has sores in his mouth. You must stop jerking the bit." She paused and added, "I'll load my medicine gourds into your cart. The other animals look sickly." The man's face cracked open in a toothy grin.

Mei Yuk came walking very slowly out of the gate between two giggling maids. She glowered and cursed when Rulan came to lift her into her cart. Mei Yuk was furious. She had completed the one-month postpartum period closeted in her rooms, as custom demanded of a new mother. But Mei Yuk could neither bathe nor wash her hair nor eat the sweet, sticky foods she loved. So she had railed at Liang Mo, claiming that he didn't love her now that she was dirty and smelly and that he was only looking for excuses to take up with Rulan again.

Not once had she mentioned Pao An's name to Rulan. Mei Yuk bragged constantly about her child, made elaborate comparisons between the baby and Liang Mo, although the child looked nothing like the Lis. Only Rulan noticed how Mei Yuk shrank from him. And the infant, as if sensing his mother's aversion, squirmed like a fish on the rare occasions that Mei Yuk took him in her arms. Liang Mo and the wet nurse cared for him, while Mei Yuk complained about her sore breasts and women's parts and about the lack of service in the country and how in her grandfather's house there were a dozen *mui tsai* for every young mother.

"You should be happy, Mei Mei," Rulan said to Mei Yuk. "You're going home for a visit. It's what you've always wanted."

"I feel like a turned-out whore in these smelly rags! How selfish of Liang Mo's father to make me leave my son just to watch them put a viceroy's hat on his head! What if I did not have an adequate wet nurse? What then? He would let my son starve to feed his vanity! And I know my breasts will hurt the whole time because I am still making milk."

Mei Yuk's pretended concern for her son, Rulan knew, was only another excuse to avoid going. Rulan could not understand why.

"The medicine I gave you will stop that. And you know that you cannot bring the boy because of bandits."

"I said I don't want to go. No one hears me!"

"That's absurd. Your family is there," replied Rulan with impatience. "You always said you were homesick!"

Mei Yuk shivered. "I don't want to see Kung Kung," she whispered.

"Why?" Rulan asked.

"Why, why! That's why! Don't be impertinent," Mei Yuk retorted. She settled herself down on the pillows like a hen shaking her bottom into a nest.

From her cart at the head of the train, Meng watched her daughter-in-law with ill-disguised contempt. Meng had counted heavily on Mei Yuk and Rulan to divide her son's loyalty, so that she herself would still be the ruling party, as was proper for a Tai Tai. But the sharp-tongued girl had exiled both mother and concubine from Liang Mo's affections. How the old Tai Tai would have laughed at the outcome of all Meng's carefully laid plans!

Meng silently cursed along with the bearers as they hoisted Moon up beside her. There was little room in the cart, and Moon took most of it, forcing Meng up against the boards. Meng cursed every stone of the new pagoda in Canton that her husband was building to commemorate his dead mother's virtue. How ironic that the Tai Tai would be honored with the money that the hated daughter-in-law had brought. How ironic that the old woman had foreseen the agony that was hers.

"This rocking journey over the foothills and along the river roads will probably kill me," she told Moon, "if bandits don't. I know I'm going to die in a ditch, not in my own bed."

Already Meng's tiny feet were crippled from gout and her eyes weakened from a fever that burned incessantly. A part of her was ecstatic over the birth of a grandson, but a grandson also meant that she was old, like the hated Tai Tai, and that was an insupportable thought. A grandmother? Grandmothers were ugly, unwelcome in a man's bed. Sick grandmothers in particular, for it seemed that her health had begun to fail the moment her mother-in-law had died, and with the death, a pall cast over her marriage. Meng had mistakenly thought herself triumphant when the Third and Fourth were sent back to their families. She was wrong. She suspected that in this, as in other things, the general had allowed her to be his instrument. After his promotion, when things ought to have been most glorious between her and her husband, he seemed not to need her. He no longer allowed her to arrange his life, his women, or his pleasures. He kept his own counsel in Canton; he undoubtedly chose his own bedmates, for he was a lusty man and could never go without a woman for long. His letters from Canton were kind—and revealed nothing. What was to stop him from installing a new woman in the viceroy's mansion, someone beautiful, ambitious, young enough to bear sons? The more Meng thought about this, the more she was convinced that the old woman's ghost was trying to kill her by stealing away her husband's love.

The journey to Canton took four days, not two, because one cart broke its axle. Meng's stomach was cold; her bones were cold. She saw heads hanging in the limbs of the trees. The party ran out of food. Mei Yuk cried for her baby, claiming that her grandfather would want to see him—but that she would never, never let her Kung Kung have him.

At last they came up to the south bank of the Pearl to the ferry landings that carried people across to the northern bank and the white-walled city. In the ferocious heat, the river lay as flat, lifeless, and gray as a dead eel on a bed of shimmering sand. Yet Meng was still cold.

General Li met them with an immense entourage at the gate of the city. Resplendent as an image on an altar, he wore a stiff blue gown embroidered with purple and green, and a hat with the ruby button and peacock feather of his new rank; gold gleamed on his breastplate and cascaded down his sleeves. Servants ran before him to announce his titles; two others followed with umbrellas, and two more carried banners proclaiming his status as viceroy-to-be. Meng, in her fevered state, shrank from her husband as if he were a glittering stranger or some deity dropped down from the skies.

Because so many mandarins had assembled in the viceroy's house for the installation, there was room only for Meng, Moon, and Liang Mo. Mei Yuk, Rulan, and the guards and servants from Abundant Spring Mountain were sent to the house of Wang, a vast compound spilling over both sides of a narrow street that paralleled the river.

Rulan found that Wang's mansion was laid out in a totally haphazard way. The servants' wings abutted the master's quarters. A beautiful rock garden, ideal for meditation, flanked the kitchen on one side; pigs rooted in their pens on the other. The gardens were overgrown with costly plantings; banyan trees, untended for years, had sent snakelike roots underneath the open patios, causing long ruptures in the cobble-stones. Geckos ran squeaking over the walls and floors. And over everything hung the fetid stench of the polluted river, which pervaded the rooms, the food, the grounds, even the clothes of the servants. It reminded Rulan of a pond clogged with fish droppings.

The servants stared sullenly at the tall Hakka girl dressed like a fine Punti lady. For her part, Rulan was surprised that the Wangs, about whom Mei Yuk had boasted for months, treated their daughter with cold disdain. Their greeting was elaborate, formal, precisely correct, yet totally lacking in warmth or conviction. The grandmother espe-cially seemed to treat the girl like a well-connected stranger who had wandered into their midst, not a daughter who had married a viceroy's son. Once they were installed, no girl cousins, sisters, or aunts crossed the lane to pepper Mei Yuk with questions about her husband and baby. No elder brothers came to pay fond courtesies. Even her mother stayed away.

"They're jealous of my good luck," sniffed Mei Yuk. "Especially the old lady. She always hated me for being pretty, Kung Kung's favorite." But Rulan sensed that their coldness went beyond the typical disparagement of married daughters by families who were only too glad to get rid of an extra mouth, for Mei Yuk had married gloriously and produced a son. No, if there was ill will against the girl, it was a grudge of long standing that her promotion had only brought to the fore.

Mei Yuk, Rulan, and their serving girls were given a suite of rooms away from the main wing.

Servants brought bowls of hot water for the women to wash off the grime of travel. Once refreshed, they fell into a deep sleep from which they did not awaken until after the dinner hour. They asked for rice but were told that the kitchens were closed, as they always were at sunset. Anyone who did not eat had to make do for themselves. Mei Yuk complained so bitterly that Rulan, accompanied by one of the servant girls, went to the kitchen herself for food. She found the cooks and kitchen boys squatting on their haunches in the dark, passing around a glowing opium pipe. Already, their heads and shoulders were sagging with the drug. Inside the cook sheds, Rulan found stacks of dirty bowls and cups, and dozens of dishes brought back from Wang's table untasted. Mice scurried into the crevices of the walls at her approach. Rulan searched through the leavings for cold rice and a few pieces of boiled chicken that had escaped the ravages of the rodents and put them carefully into the cleanest dishes she could find. Then she sent the servant girl back to Mei Yuk with the food.

On the way back, Rulan spied a small group of men in peasant pajamas talking furtively on their way from Old Wang's quarters. They hurried away at her approach, as if she, not they, were the interloper. A hundred hungry eyes seemed to watch from the shadows. There was so much abundance in the house that everything smelled half-rotten. Overall was an atmosphere of oppression and lethargy.

Outside the walls she could hear the noisy exhalation of the huge city—a sound unlike anything she had ever heard in her life. Not clean and natural, like women calling to their children or men to other men, but heavy and threatening, like the river rising, intercut with sounds that were only vaguely human: anger, weeping, and pain-choked screams. Rulan shivered and retreated to the small stucco house. There the voice of the city was less pronounced, although the sighing of the waves beyond the wall seemed no less disturbing.

The next day, after a breakfast of congee accompanied by nine lavish seafood dishes—too much for them to eat—Mei Yuk was sent for by her mother. While she was gone, Rulan wandered through the neighboring courts. The oppressiveness in the house, Rulan decided, could only be attributed to its master, Merchant Wang. Everyone in the compound seemed to be languishing under his heavy hand. It was not a matter of respect or awe, but outright fear, as when a superior bears down viciously and unpredictably on those below. As Rulan walked from court to court, no one greeted her. The *mui tsai* were pinched and furtive, like the mice that feasted on the spoiled food at night or the geckos that scurried in the shadows. She knew that Wang kept many concubines, but they were nowhere to be seen.

What Rulan did see in the course of her stroll were more serving maids and men cuffed or slapped for not working, looking idle, or whispering than in a week at Abundant Spring Mountain under the tightfisted steward. She passed one court around noon where a serving girl of eight years old was being beaten on the palm with a bamboo rod for dropping a teacup. As she came around a corner, a huge, rawboned gardener was slapping a boy on the side of the head for some offense. The boy was either too frightened or too hurt to cry. He sat quietly where he had fallen, the blood running down his chin, until he was told to get up. Then he went back to trimming a flowering bush. Rulan gave him a handkerchief for his chin as she passed and touched his shoulder, but he cringed.

Mei Yuk came back from her visit in a pout and went into the bedroom to lie down.

"What is wrong, Mei Mei?" Rulan asked.

"My grandfather wants to see us this afternoon," was all she said. Then she put a pillow over her head and went to sleep, complaining about her stomach.

Later in the day, Rulan woke Mei Yuk and went with her to her grandfather's apartments. The two boys who led them fled as soon as they reached his door.

Wang's rooms were in a back section of the compound, in a small stucco house closed off to the rest of the mansion by a moat filled with dark water. The rear walls were high enough to serve as a fortress against thieves or pirates on the river. It was a house within a house, a sanctuary so isolated that its inhabitant could not be surprised by land or sea. Rulan found that the garden outside his private walls, like the one outside her room, was surprisingly orderly and bright—except for one corner where poisonous specimens grew and a twisted tree dropped hundreds of small round fruit called longan, or dragon's eye, on the ground, where they were left to spoil. It was the most complete pharmacological garden she had ever seen. Hundreds of medicinal plants and herbs grew there, dozens that she did not even recognize. She plucked several leaves and smelled the sap—this one she dimly remembered as pearl-under-the-leaf for its strong, biting scent and tiny globular capsules under each leaf; another spilled a thick, familiar, tea-colored nectar from its stem and smelled like rancid fish—"stinkroot, for snakebite" she could hear her mother say. One section of the garden behind a high fence held at least a hundred poisonous plants, each growing in its own clay pot. Beehives stood along one side of the house near a small pen of live deer. They were being raised for their antlers, a basic ingredient in longevity powder. This ancient one, whom the Tai Tai called a "seller of pigs," is a secret alchemist, Rulan told herself. And here is the vault from which the venom pours. Rulan had a vision of Wang sitting at the center of this vast web casting out thread after thread to entrap people to serve him.

Mei Yuk was visibly nervous as Old Wang's personal servant led them from the veranda into a shadowy anteroom encircled by huge porcelain jars of great antiquity.

Legends about Merchant Wang abounded. Rulan had heard that he was the son of a river pirate, the offspring of a prostitute, the by-blow of a Hanlin master. In fact, Mei Yuk claimed that he was a country wine maker's son who had brought his father's rice wine to town in a wheelbarrow as a child and later stayed to organize first the independent carters, then the wine seller's guilds, the intercity porters, and finally the convoys of salt and opium. Because he was uneducated and illiterate, he could hold no government position, but he held many officials—along with the Tanka boatmen and leaders of the beggars' guild—in the palm of his fat hand. He had prospered under every viceroy, commissioner, and magistrate for fifty years, miraculously escaping censure and execution, a nearly impossible feat for any man of influence of such great age. It was said that his friends were everywhere: in the Triad bands, at the emperor's elbow—even in the imperial bed. The deputy chief eunuch smoked Wang's opium and supplied it to the Dragon himself, who smoked it to aid his digestion. Another customer was a young Manchu military officer who, it was said, was the secret lover of the emperor's new favorite in the harem, a girl from the Yehonala clan named Orchid. All these great ones filled Wang's hands with silver and their lungs with Wang's smoke.

The "auntie" who came to usher them in was pretty and younger than Mei Yuk. She was heavily painted and provocatively dressed.

"I don't know this one," Mei Yuk said petulantly. "He has a new one and when he tires of her, he sends her back to the Willow World or the country." Mei Yuk commented acidly on the girl's appearance as they followed the concubine through a series of rooms to a larger one in the back. The dark room had a smoky smell—not of opium, but of joss sticks stuck into pots filled with sand, as if the space was used for prayer. The red pillars that held up the roof were black from the sweet smoke.

Wang sat like a huge crab with his hands on his knees. A round brimless hat covered his head almost to his eyebrows; his sagging face was crosscut by a thousand fine wrinkles. Rulan had seen him only from afar at the wedding party in Abundant Spring Mountain. If he seemed huge then, in his own sanctum he was immense. The sides of his belly rested on the two arms of his mahogany chair, which was inlaid with mother-of-pearl. He could have been fifty, or sixty, or eighty. His outer robe was black, the inner vest and skirt sky blue, and around his neck hung a long necklace of red and black jade, each piece the size of a quail's egg. He was clean shaven, eschewing the long mustaches favored by wealthy men of his age. His lips were thin and turned in over toothless gums. But when he spoke, his voice was surprisingly strong and youthful.

"Mei Mei. Granddaughter, come." He held out his large, loose arms, and at that signal, she ran and buried her face in his lap.

From the moment she lifted her face to his, Mei Yuk's nervousness disappeared. "Why didn't you call me before? You're bad to your Mei Mei when her heart was breaking for Kung Kung," she pouted.

"You have been away a long time."

"Yes, and how I have missed all the good things here. Why did you send this worthless person to that pigpen of a house in the country?"

Rulan had dropped to her knees and touched her head to the ground when she had come in. He had not yet noticed her or asked her to rise from her kneeling position. From her crouch, she watched his hand move over Mei Yuk's hair, stopping to play with her earlobe while the girl talked. The gesture seemed extraordinarily indecent. She felt, rather than saw, his small eyes move away from Mei Yuk and come to rest on her.

He laughed indulgently at Mei Yuk's prattle and pushed her onto a little settee. Mei Yuk leaned her head against the arm of his chair and continued to scold him coquettishly.

"Kung Kung is angry with me. I know he will not give me anything nice to take back to that awful place."

He grunted, pleased at Mei Yuk's avowal that no place was as good as his own.

"And I have made you a glorious grandson and given this family great face!"

"Not my great-grandson," he reminded her. "Not Wang's but Li's."

Mei Yuk pouted. "Kung Kung has sold me to another house. He has forgotten his favorite granddaughter."

"Yes, and I lost on that transaction," he said, "your husband's father brought back a viceroy's hat from battle. It seems I must kowtow to you, now that your husband's house is rising and you are the mother of sons. I thought to put an extra pair of eyes and hands in the house of Li. But what has it gained me? Instead, Li has installed one of his own in my house to listen and watch, one who forgets too easily who she is." His voice was deep and churlish, laden with malice. Mei Yuk jerked her head up to look at him, but he pulled her back by the earlobe and made her lean against the arm of his chair again. Rulan saw that Mei Yuk's mouth had gone suddenly dry. Mei Yuk licked her lips and couldn't speak. The old man sat, saying nothing. He looked up at the rafters of the house, still stroking Mei Yuk's hair. After a while he asked the ceiling, "Who is this girl you brought with you?"

"It's Rulan, my husband's second. You asked to see her."

"Yes, and now I have seen her."

Rulan took this, finally, as a sign to rise.

Wang squinted at her. "I can see you are good for my little Mei Mei. Come, give me your hands." He held his own out in a gesture of benign acceptance. Rulan reluctantly put her hands into his. They were smooth, cold, and very dry, like the skin of a snake. His fingers barely moved, but she felt them palpating hers imperceptibly. He whispered to Mei Yuk, but Rulan shivered as she saw him glance quickly at her out of the corners of his eyes. Suddenly she felt a spark of warmth surge out of her hands. He looked up at the slant of sunlight and released her hand, and while murmuring to Mei Yuk, rubbed his hands together like a cook rolling rice balls.

This is the enemy, Rulan said to herself. A thief of *chi*. Her hands had turned to ice.

"How may this miserable granddaughter serve you, Kung Kung?" Mei Yuk said at last, her voice rising flirtatiously.

"You may leave."

Mei Yuk rose quickly, grabbed Rulan's arm and began to pull her out of the room.

"I would like a word with your husband's second," he added.

Rulan tried to cover her aversion with downcast eyes.

"Oh, that silly girl has nothing to say," blurted out Mei Yuk, clearly terrified. "She is an unreliable person, Kung Kung. Her father is Hakka, her mother was Loi. She's not one of us, she doesn't know a thing."

"Go," he whispered.

After Mei Yuk had fled, the old man put a tip of a plump finger into the rim of his collar.

"It's good to sweat, *hai ma*?" he said in village Cantonese. "Sit, sit, sit there." He pointed to a small porcelain stool near his feet.

Rulan eased herself onto the barrel stool, moving it slightly away from Wang's reach.

"Forgive an old man. I like to look at the pretty and the young."

Rulan raised her eyes to meet his small, milky ones, which were swimming with an emotion she could not read.

"I have heard about you and your arts. You kept the old Tai Tai alive!"

"Kwan Yin favored me."

"Kwan Yin? Ah, but you also learned from your mother, a great physician among the Loi, an herbalist and a healer with hands. Yes, I have heard about her."

Rulan's mind reeled. How did he know? Who could have told him about the healing hands? "My mother taught me much, but I don't have her gift."

"I have an herb garden and a pen of deer for their antlers. And back there," he pointed, "I have an apothecary room. You see, like your mother, I too am a modest dabbler in the medicinal arts. Please, you are welcome to use my herbs, my animals, my garden."

Rulan wondered if Wang was ill, for he seemed on the verge of collapse, although his face was smooth and oily, and the malevolent force that emanated from him was incredibly strong.

"You are a good girl. I have a gift for you." On the table next to him was a small cloisonné box. "Take, take."

Rulan opened the box gingerly and found a stone of opaline jade, perfectly egg shaped and as yellow as amber.

"A dragon's eye," he said, "a piece hatched from the one true stone! It could be worth more than everything I own—or worth nothing at all. There is immortality in it—or wasted time. All that is required are the hands to use it. Hands with healing fire. Take it."

"No," she said, and thrust the box back at him.

"I can give you anything," he whispered. "What do you want? Tell Kung Kung."

"I want nothing," Rulan replied.

"Many people desire nothing. I make a business out of supplying them with nothing—in opium, or in the body of another. I can give you nothing—if you desire it."

"I'm not afraid of you. You can kill me, but you cannot force me."

"Who said anything about force? Why would I kill you, Rulan, Daughter—Little Quail?" When he spoke her milk name, Rulan caught her breath. Although he moved not at all, she felt as if he were winding her up in a thread.

"How do you know my name? Who told you?" she said.

"You have the wrong idea. I come by that knowledge in a very innocent way. I have not divined it. I am a merchant. I buy and sell what men desire. Do you want to know who you are and how I know what you are?"

Rulan felt her head nod, as if another will had moved it.

"Well, that's a beginning. There was a boy here. He came into my house with an earring from that small, ugly noise, my granddaughter. 'She longs for you and this house,' he said. 'She wants to leave Abundant Spring Mountain. Please bring her home.' Imagine! He didn't run away to sell that earring, which was worth more than his whole village, no doubt. He put it in my hand and pleaded for a mere girl!"

Rulan could barely stammer. "Where is he now?"

"That boy is dead." Out of the corner of his eye, he saw Rulan's head knocked back by the force of his words. "So there is something I can give you. You desire that boy," Wang said with satisfaction.

"He's alive then," she whispered.

"Yes, but he doesn't have to be."

Rulan faced him boldly, praying she was right. "He's not here. I'd feel it if he were."

"No, but I can lay my hand on him. I've kept him on a string, the way boys do crickets."

"What has he to do with you?"

Wang lifted his fat shoulders. He looked annoyed. "Fate arranges all things. Fate threw this boy into the middle of a game I was arranging. I feared that he might see a pattern that might be inconvenient for my colleagues. I was worried that Li might learn something from him— but thanks to you, he escaped." He shifted his position and smiled. "You can help him escape again!"

Once more, Rulan felt Old Wang's net tighten about her. She shook her head, denying the malevolence that crept over her and closing her mind to the memory of Pao An trapped in the box.

"It's true. It's true." Wang laughed, as if reading her thoughts. "No one escapes me. When he came here, of his own accord, I thought him brazen enough to warrant a doubly painful death. But the presumptuous beggar told me such intriguing stories, about my worthless granddaughter, about you, and about my old enemy Li. I figured that anyone who hates my enemy as much as this dumb ox would be valuable to me. And now that I find he is valuable to you too, his value rises even more."

"Leave him alone," Rulan demanded.

"You cannot have what you desire without paying the proper price," he admonished. "I must have something for my trouble. I can let him go, or I can let you go, not both."

"What do you want from me?"

"Aiya, Little Quail, I want your warmth, the heat you hold in your hands. I cannot do this for myself. I need your arts. But you are a stubborn girl. If I try to force you, I know your *chi* won't flow. So I must persuade you to give me freely what you do not want to give. I must create an excuse for you. I must allow you to give yourself pardon. If you think you are saving that miserable boy, then you will willingly give me what I want."

"You would steal the life from me!"

"No, no, I would give you the means to replenish that fire. Your *chi* merely sparks the flame. Here, for one who has that spark, is the fuel that burns forever!" He held out the dragon's eye to her.

She shuddered. "I won't take it."

His thin lips widened in an indulgent smile, as if she were a recalcitrant child. "Come play with the little bauble. Your Kung Kung gives you pardon. Pardon for killing that old crow who roosted too long on Abundant Spring Mountain." He laid the stone in his lap and gestured lasciviously. "Come, hold it in your hands and make the eye open for me. Help your Kung Kung see eternity!"

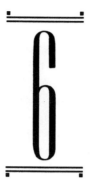

Pearl River

Thirty miles northwest of Tiger Gate, a salt boat flying the red-and-gold flags of Merchant Wang fought against the current toward Canton. The half-ton of salt in the hold made the pole-men groan as they pushed the boat through the yellow waters.

Pao An stood in the bow with the young Tanka captain, whose face split into a bucktoothed grin. "Not long now to Canton, my friend. It's full of rot like me but we make the place run."

Although hundreds of small boats clogged the waterway, the captain easily guided his ship through the maze of nets and sharp poles that would have brought a less skillful sailor to grief. Looking upstream to the five-story red pagoda that loomed over the river, the boatman was content. The breeze and the tide ran in his favor; his boat was moving more swiftly than it had for two days. He swatted his youngest son on his bare bottom and sent the child squealing under a ragged tarp where his wives and daughters crouched.

Pao An squinted into the wind, enjoying the taste of the brackish spray on his lips and the company of the rough Tanka men. The months he had spent on the canals and waterways with the Tanka were in some ways the happiest in his life. He blessed Merchant Wang for sending him to these simple folk, who asked nothing but that he earn his keep. The clean air, the hard work, the plain food had made the pain and humiliation he had endured in the house of Li fade. Pao An felt himself whole, revivified, a man once more. Only the lingering memory of the two women he had left in Abundant Spring Mountain disturbed his newfound equanimity.

"An honest man like you is a rare commodity," Merchant Wang had told him after accepting Mei Yuk's token. "Most men would have sold this jade earring and wasted the money on dirt or women."

Pao An had tried to make Wang understand his true motives. "Your granddaughter was very good to me—" he had stammered, astonished at the force of his emotion, before lapsing into silence, so fearful was he of endangering Mei Yuk's reputation.

Wang had been extraordinarily patient and kind. He had taken Pao An across a moat through his private herb garden, past a pen of tame deer, and into a small house where they could talk without being heard. Gradually, Pao An found himself telling Merchant Wang everything—the annihilation of his clan by General Li, his life with Li Yu in On Ting, his expulsion from the village after the attack on the bridal procession.

"Good boy, good boy," the merchant had said. "I can trust you because there is bad blood between the Lis and my house too." He beckoned Pao An close. "I confess my secret fear—don't betray me, now! I believe Li sent those bandits against my granddaughter to shame me. He meant to bring suit against me for his bride money. But you, brave fellow, put his plans to rout! I will find a way to bring my darling back. Trust me!" Pao An felt uneasy despite Wang's assurances. Wang was too confiding for a canny merchant.

"Now tell me," Wang said kindly. "What can Kung Kung give you as reward for taking care of my darling in that evil place?"

"Help me find my father!" Pao An blurted out. If the trader was in a generous mood, one had better take advantage.

There was no better way, Wang avowed, to search for a missing relative than by boat. Li Yu was sure to be traveling along the river where the Taoist monasteries lay. So Wang had given Pao An a job on one of his salt boats. Pao An had tracked every inch of the waterways that snaked through the delta; he had questioned toll officials, headmen in each village, and every group of landless peasants fleeing north to join the Taiping in Kwangsi in the vain hope that they had seen his father. Sometimes Wang sent him messages via the boatmen; on two occasions he had sent strings of coppers. The last message had come just two days ago from a ten-year-old boy who had leaped aboard their boat from a huge, one-eyed junk.

"Kung Kung says, you come to Canton now," the boy said. "He has a job for you."

Pao An doubted that Wang had found some information about his father. More likely, the "job" Wang had in mind had something to do with the news that was being passed from boatman to boatman: the old viceroy had been removed and General Li lifted out of disgrace and appointed in his stead. The people in the city and on the water were incensed over Li's promotion. Boatman called to boatman to whisper the rumor that the Triads were paying the guilds of beggars, wine sellers, porters, actors, and artisans to start a riot over the increase in the salt tax that would go to finance Li's provincial army. Pao An's dearest wish was that Wang would send him to slip a knife into the new viceroy as he was donning his hat and robes of office.

In Canton, there was also a chance of seeing Mei Yuk. His desire for her had intensified over the long months of waiting on the river. Sometimes he thought he would risk going back to Abundant Spring Mountain simply to hold her in his arms again. Just as suddenly, the image of Rulan, slim as a reed and suffused with light, would rise in his mind. He desired them both but in contradictory, immensely confusing ways. Mei Yuk was a fever in his blood, and Rulan a draft of cool water. When they came to him in dreams, Mei Yuk was always beckoning and running away, whereas Rulan was always walking at his side.

The captain's voice brought him back to the present. "Curse that pockmarked emperor for appointing Li. It's the Dragon's way of grinding us down all the more. The emperor alters tradition to allow Li to serve in his own province because he knows that Li will squeeze all the old families who debased his father. I hear the stealing has already started. Li is using tax money to finance a pagoda to honor his dead mother!" The boatman hawked and spat into the river.

Pao An frowned. "Li will burn us out, sell us to the emperor, and feast on our bones. Even you who have no home will not escape."

"This is why I hate your General Li," affirmed the Tanka. "If he has his way, he will close the doors of the city, keep Canton locked up tight, and scatter my boats. But the doors cannot stay closed for long. Besides, the city has other appetites, which my boats feed." He patted the bag of raw opium under his tunic.

Pao An grunted uncomfortably, remembering the day the opium was won. They had sailed to Hong Kong Bay below the Brogue Forts and picked up opium from a "scuttling crab," one of the fast, cannon-mounted, square-rigged lorchas that took on opium from the British ships while they were still out in the sea routes beyond Hong Kong. On the way up through the delta, they had stopped briefly to steal a shipment of salt, which General Li's salt pan workers had set aside for just that purpose, and had sold most of their opium cache to the laborers there. Pao An had no pangs of guilt stealing from Li, but he did not relish corrupting Li's men with dirt.

The Tanka saw Pao An's distaste. "Salt is better, my friend! No shame in salt. And it's a good living, especially when the opium boats don't come. Pick up a little here, a little there, carry it along duty free, tax free. The only trouble with salt is that it's heavy. Opium is easier to carry, easier to hide. No one ever broke their backs smuggling opium. Anyone, even a Han paddy mucker like you, can smuggle enough opium in his loincloth to eat for a month. But salt is a different matter. It takes a clever merchant or a Tanka to smuggle salt. Salt smuggling is our national duty. Why else were the Rat People made?" He gave a raucous laugh.

"How does salt pay?" Pao An asked, his interest piqued.

"Fabulous. Fabulous. Just look at my riches," the youth roared again, sweeping his hand about the cluttered, filthy scow. "It's the safest, most risk-free job a man could want. Less dangerous than a court eunuch—you keep your testicles as long as you can keep your head."

"You prefer salt to opium?" said Pao An in amused disbelief.

"Look here, don't you know anything?" the Tanka scolded. "Everyone needs salt, right? Everyone, whether they eat rice in the south or noodles in the north, needs a pinch of white on week-old meat so it doesn't stink. The emperors figured that out centuries ago. So the emperor says, you paddy muckers can have what grows on the ground, but I own what's under it—gold, tin, and salt from mines and wells. Why in southern Szechwan, they have wells three thousand feet deep, dug with iron-tipped bamboo. Down here in Kwangtung, we have salt pans. Ever see one of those salt flats turning all colors as the sun dries up the water?" He spat. "Beautiful and stinks too."

Pao An laughed into the wind, enjoying the story.

"Do as I do," the captain continued. "Steal it before you trade. I am a transporter like Merchant Wang. General Li holds the manufacturing rights in his salt pans on the coast. That's the reason for the old rivalry between the families. It's better to be a transporter; you make more money. Producers have to sell at the government's fixed rate. We get what the traffic will bear. It grieves our new viceroy so much that he made a marriage to get part of the routes from his rival in the bride's dowry. Except that Old Wang, who had already received the bride-price, set a trap to waylay the bride, claim rape, and demand to break the contract."

Pao An grinned and shook his head at the madness of the suggestion. "It was a Triad attack! I know because—it happened outside my village. And anyway, it doesn't make sense. Li would sue—"

The Tanka began to guffaw. "Old Wang cares nothing about suits! Nothing shames a merchant! And the suit would never come to trial because Wang owns every Canton official from Magistrate Lam up to his crony, the old viceroy. Aiya, Li is one viceroy he will not own. Mark my words, marriage or no marriage, there will be war between the two houses again soon!" The young captain leaned closer and whispered in Pao An's ear. "They say that Wang is the One, the leader of all the Triad clans in the south. Anyone he wants, he can buy—or force, it's the same thing to Wang. Anyone—"

"He runs the Red Turbans?" Pao An asked, still unwilling to believe.

"Yes, and the Yellow Handkerchiefs, and the Ring Gang, and the White Lotus—"

"Impossible! I know Wang," Pao An protested. "Even if he is the One, he would never do that to his granddaughter."

"Why not? The trick is to steal back goods so they can be sold again. It's done every day with salt, why not with granddaughters, who are worth a lot less?" The captain blew his nose with his fingers. "But something went wrong."

I am what went wrong, Pao An thought. "Not true, not true," he muttered to the young captain, while his mind clicked the pieces of Wang's plot into place, feeling instinctively the correctness of the fit.

"I have it from the lips of the fish," the Tanka confided. "A cousin of mine was in charge of ferrying the Triad men downriver by On Ting village." The captain glowered. "The girl is a slut, my cousin said. The grandmother caught the girl in bed with some man in her own house and wanted her out of the family. Wang is a merchant, remember? Send the Triads to kidnap the girl and demand ransom! That way you get double—bride-price and ransom—and no one finds out that the goods are bad."

Pao An lurched to his feet and smashed his fist against the board holding up the ragged tarpaulin. Then he dove into the swirling brown waters and swam alongside the boat, heedless of the shouts of the excited polemen, until he was too exhausted to think.

Canton

Except for the coronation of the emperor, there was no grander occasion than the investiture of a provincial viceroy. The women were allowed to watch the proceedings from a discreet distance behind a screen placed to the side of the podium in the Great Hall, a grand red-columned building in the middle of a busy square where district officials met and candidates gathered to take the examinations. Dignitaries and their hangers-on began assembling while it was still early, and by nine o'clock the hall was full. It was a solemn ceremony presided over by an imperial envoy and a contingent of princes and officials from Peking sent by the minister of rites. Landowners, scholars, yamen officials, magistrates, and prefects from the nearby districts had come to Canton out of duty and self-interest: a new viceroy meant a new network of spies, new offerings of bribes, new rivals for favors and appointments. A memorial from the emperor was read, gongs sounded, ceremonial kowtows made, and the hat and robes of office placed on the general. At that moment, Li became the most powerful man in southern China, governor of the provinces of Kwangtung and Kwangsi and of the barbarian wealth in Hong Kong.

Li received the tokens of office and the presents of the officials with the stiff dignity he had cultivated through hundreds of military parades. Later that evening he would go to the platform that had been erected in front of the hall and give a speech to the people that would put his new power to the test. He would proclaim his long-held dream: to create a private provincial army independent of the throne, led by Han men of his choice. A real army of stalwart fighting men, mercenaries if need be, not the opium-ridden weaklings who had been pressed into service by the former viceroy. He would warn the people of the threat posed by the Taiping in the northeast and the white barbarians in the south. Salvation would come via a strong local army. But all must help, all must sacrifice. Mothers must part with their sons, wives must relinquish their husbands—and all bear the burden of an additional tax. If he could convince the people to starve themselves still further so that an army could be appointed and equipped, that army could cut off the Taiping before they passed into Hunan. He must defeat the rebels on his own soil to redeem the only blot on his record, but he had to act quickly, decisively, before the Taiping marched entirely out of his territory into the provinces beyond.

Once out of his grasp, the rebels would become the problem of another official—perhaps Scholar Tseng Kuo Fan in Hunan, whose brilliance had already come to the attention of Chief Eunuch An-te-hai—for if the eunuch's favor passed to Tseng, greatness would slip forever from Li's grasp into that of a rival with talents and ambitions as great as his. Li had to raise money for his army quickly, and so he had decided on a salt tax that would hit every citizen. It would be steep but entirely necessary; moreover, it would not evoke the ire of the gentry because it was a tax on every head, not on their precious land. Then he would call on the landlords to enlist volunteers at a price higher than the imperial troops. At least two hundred thousand men. He knew just the place in Kwangsi to cut off Yang's battalions. In this way, he would redeem the debacle at Yung An and utterly destroy the upstart Yang and his mongrel horde.

Behind the women's screen, Meng watched her husband receive the accolades of the great men of the south. Mei Yuk peeked through a hole in the carved rosewood lattice and squealed at the sight of Liang Mo sitting self-importantly in the front row flanked by the scholar officials of Canton, some of whom she remembered from her childhood. They had been too good to enter the door of a mere merchant then. Now they would bow to her.

Rulan was sunk in silent despair behind the screen. She was remembering Wang's fat, oily face, and the thin, mirthless lips murmuring his terrible accusations. She was remembering Ailan's stories of evil alchemists who spent their lives searching for the elixir of immortality. She was recalling the gossip in the *chai tang* about Taoist priests and magicians who seduced young girls with promises of eternal beauty in exchange for their warmth. She had dismissed these stories as foolish tales to frighten girls into virtue and obedience. But now she had found an old one who practiced the very dark arts Ailan had warned her against. And she was powerless to stop him.

When she had run from Wang the day before, he had called after her, "I can wait! I have been waiting for years."

In panic and confusion, she'd fled into the courtyard outside his apartments where poisonous herbs and flowers gave up their vapors into the muggy air. But as she started across the narrow bridge, she saw a demon astride it, with one foot on each handrail, its mouth dripping blood. She defied it, saying, "What have you to do with me?" And held her head up as the monster aimed a black dart at her heart.

The creature drew back its arm.

Rulan walked slowly forward. But when she passed between the demon's legs, fully expecting to die, only an icy breath, as soft as a floating cobweb, brushed her neck.

That night, she lay awake in the room she shared with Mei Yuk, listening for the door, hearing soft noises at the window, watching ghostly shadows stream across the wall. Wang did not come for her. But the Tai Tai came. No longer bowed by age, the old woman's ghost was as nimble and crafty as a monkey. It leaped through the window, ran across the floor chattering obscenities, and jumped to the top of a cupboard, where it hurled invectives at Rulan. "Murderer!" it screamed. "I say that all whom you love will perish. Throats slit, guts spilled, spiked with iron, split with wood, cut with wire, starved of food, branded, buried: every one you love will die." Cackling with glee, the ghost split apart like a chestnut in the fire.

Rulan barely heard the general recite the oath of office; her head was filled with Wang's words and the Tai Tai's curses. Wang knew about the Tai Tai's murder! And he held Pao An's life in the hollow of his hand. Again she was the helpless tool of a cruel man. Why should she care for Pao An? she asked herself. He did not desire her; he loved the little dissembler, Mei Yuk, who glowed in the reflected glory of her father-in-law and husband.

The ceremony ended with the loud clamor of gongs and the explosion of firecrackers. The viceroy returned in triumph to his mansion on the shoulders of his bearers. Before him ran twelve runners to clear the road of people and to announce his many titles. Behind his palanquin marched two hundred soldiers.

Although the women were exhausted, there was little time to rest. A banquet was scheduled for the first families of Canton that evening, another public ceremony the following day; and in order to show that a great man could also be a dutiful son, the general had announced a second ceremony a few days hence to mark the construction of a seven-storied pagoda to his mother. The women were to take a chief role in this ritual, for a pagoda typically venerated a virtuous woman from an illustrious family. A contingent of gray-robed nuns had been hired to instruct the women on what to do and where they would stand. Servant girls, led by Moon, practiced holding name flags. Meng and Mei Yuk were shown how to proceed up a long flight of stairs to the dais set before the newly laid foundation of the pagoda itself, where the general and the head priestess would stand. Meng would carry fruit and buns to the temporary altar, a long low table covered with red silk, manned by Buddhist monks. Then Liang Mo, followed by Mei Yuk, would do obeisance to the spirit of the departed Tai Tai. The women would have to bare their faces before "outside" men—not the priests, who did not count, but officials of the capital city and Manchu officers. It was necessary, therefore, for the women to keep their faces downcast and expressionless to avoid shaming the family. At the rehearsal, all the maids, even Moon, managed the feat. The one who could not was Mei Yuk.

"If you make this family lose face, Mei Yuk," Meng scolded her daughter-in-law, "I will leave you in Canton." The women were in Meng's rooms dressing for the banquet following the investiture.

"Perhaps you think that would make me unhappy," the girl snapped before flouncing away.

Mei Yuk was aflutter with the excitement of appearing in a splendid new dress for so regal a gathering. She was a grown-up woman, a wife, and the mother of a son. And daughter-in-law to the new viceroy! Even her grandfather would have to bow low before Mei Yuk now.

Meng looked accusingly at Rulan. "Your sister has no shame!"

Rulan did not reply.

"Rulan!"

Rulan was watching a tree that hung over the wall of the viceroy's enclosure. "I see the Tai Tai's ghost glaring down at me from the top of that tree," she said dully. "How odd to see a ghost before twilight."

Meng went pale. "She's come to accuse me!"

Moon bustled officiously into the room, still dressed in her finery from the investiture. When she saw Meng's drawn face, Moon said, "What is it, Mother? Are you hungry? Are you sick?"

"The Old One's come back. Now at the final hour of our glory, she returns to undo our luck. So much does she hate me."

"We must call up the ghost and reason with her face-to-face," Moon declared. "It's the only way!"

"No," Rulan said warily, stirring herself. "Maybe she means no harm."

"She's up to her old tricks," Meng said. "Why else does a ghost appear?"

"Let Rulan do a seance, Mother! She's a spirit-woman. And the Tai Tai loves her," Moon insisted. "We can't go to the pagoda and bow to an angry ghost. What if she upsets the altar or makes one of us trip? What if she provokes the people to riot? They might even take back the viceroy's commission."

"Do it! Call up your old mistress, Rulan," ordered Meng.

"Ghosts, how exciting," Mei Yuk said, clapping her hands.

Rulan barely heard Moon and the others planning the seance around her. I have nothing to fear from ghosts, she reminded herself, for I have no power, no power at all.

Meng's bedroom at the back of the viceroy's residence was the largest in the women's wing, and because it was out of bounds to the men, Moon deemed it perfect for a seance. But Meng was moody and distraught; when a maid dropped a bowl of perfumed water on her skirt, Meng slapped the girl and tried to curse her own agitation away.

Rulan's thoughts were filled with violent premonition for the seance and the dedication to come. If a defiled person knelt before an altar, ill would fall upon the sinner. And there she was, a murderer, the poison festering in their midst. When the nuns in her village had poured pigs' blood over her altar, Kwan Yin had cursed the village, turned the thriving place into a wasteland. Why would the goddess protect Rulan now, when Rulan had violated her vows as a healer?

"Rulan, I need a powder and a massage," Meng called from the dressing table. "My head feels like a pomegranate ready to burst. I know I shall never survive this shame. It's the Tai Tai's last punishment on me." Meng gave a small, nervous laugh as if her own words frightened her.

"I have the powder here. I thought you might be in distress, Mother," Rulan said.

In the corner of the room, Mei Yuk had stripped down to her shift. Now she came up behind Meng and held up the dress she was to wear at the dedication, studying the stiff gold brocade lined with green satin in the brass mirror. "I don't like your mirror, Mother. It makes me look fat," she complained as she turned from side to side. "Rulan, are my eyebrows painted right? You made the curve crooked."

"Stupid girl. Get away," Meng scolded.

Mei Yuk began to pout.

"The curve is fine. And you are not fat. You've just had a child," Rulan said.

"Don't be tiresome. I know I am as fat as a cow. Liang Mo likes me fat, but if my baby weren't so perfect I don't think it would have been worth it. Look at me!" she pouted. "My face is still puffy. My breasts are like gourds. My bottom is as broad as a lily pad. My—"

"Enough!" Meng cried. "You are making my headache worse."

Mei Yuk turned away, stifling a loud sob. But Rulan saw that the girl was almost smiling. For in truth, Mei Yuk could barely contain her pleasure whenever she managed to shatter Meng's self-control. Producing a son had given Mei Yuk much more confidence; her place in the family was secure, especially now that she had set Liang Mo against his mother.

Meng was sitting with her head tilted forward. Rulan's heart lurched suddenly in her chest. Except for the sleek black helmet of hair, the angle of Meng's head and the curve of the thin shoulder were exactly like the Tai Tai's at the moment when the needle slipped behind her ear. With shaking hands, Rulan undid the bun at the nape of Meng's neck and began to massage Meng's scalp above the eyebrows and over the head to the base of the skull. Meng did not respond. Touching the knotted cords at the back of the neck, Rulan felt a great heat emanating from Meng's skin. Rulan kneaded the neck and shoulders with her fingers and felt Meng's muscles grow more taut and hard.

Rulan released her fingers with a sigh and put a camphor compress on Meng's forehead. As soon as Rulan's hands had left her, Meng sighed as if some great pain had been lifted from her head and shifted her white shoulders like a cat stretching. Rulan could see the thin blue veins beneath the translucent skin. How beautiful Meng used to be, Rulan thought sadly.

Meng's eyes were closed but her lips moved. "Out of the entire household, only I cannot be healed by you. Perhaps it is the Tai Tai's revenge to make me impervious to your magic."

Rulan felt tears sting her eyes at Meng's words. Inadvertently, she touched Meng's neck with her fingertips. Meng's eyes flew open, revealing naked terror. But in the next moment, the terror had vanished under Meng's self-control.

Moon's broad face appeared at the door. "A beggar in the courtyard is calling your name, Rulan. Bad luck! Shall I send the impertinent creature away?"

"No, no," exclaimed Rulan, grateful for the excuse to leave, though she wondered how a beggar would know her name. She fled from the oppressive room and the fear in Meng's eyes into the labyrinth of the viceregal mansion.

As night approached, the courtyard had filled with the soldiers, ministers, and slaves who had followed the great ones into the mansion after Viceroy Li's speech to the people, hoping for food and small gifts. It was a cloudless night with a full moon. Torches in sockets against the walls had been lit early. A few persistent common folk huddled in corners. Hundreds of the people had thrown rocks during the general's speech and trailed his procession in the street, overwhelming the guards and railing at his plan to raise taxes. There were others too who waited greedily to ask for favors if they joined his militia, in the expectation that after the inaugural day, the new viceroy would be beneficent.

As Rulan walked dejectedly across the courtyard, a figure covered in filthy rags stumbled across the stones toward Rulan. "Rulan," the beggar called.

A rock landed with deadly accuracy on the back of the cowl-covered head. "Aaiiee!" screamed a guard. "A leper inside!"

Rulan ran forward to put her body between the beggar and the guards. But the figure, more out of rage than pain, pushed her away and let loose a strangled, inhuman sound that sent the guards flying back into the courtyard. The hood fell back, revealing mutilated flesh. Once that face had belonged to a woman, for half the head was still covered with long black hair. The other half seemed to have been scalped. Red-and-yellow scars covered what had once been a face. One eye was gone; the lid, caving inward, flapped uncontrollably. The lips were red welts that grinned from ear to ear. The creature held up its fingerless hands to Rulan in supplication.

"Get stones. Bring torches. Burn out the disease!" cried the guards.

"Leave her!" Rulan yelled. "Move back, I say! I am a daughter in Viceroy Li's house. I'll take her away."

"These creatures are clever, Young Mistress," one of the bailiffs shouted, his shrill voice thick with loathing. "Because their flesh rots, they take pleasure in afflicting others. Be careful she doesn't smear her lips on you."

"Don't talk nonsense," Rulan said to the man. Although her own flesh crawled at the sight of the old woman, she kneeled down to examine her, for she knew that lepers suffered from other people as well as from their disease. And she could not turn away a petitioner. The woman must have heard that the viceroy's daughter-in-law was a a healer and had come seeking a cure.

The bailiff backed away with a shudder.

"Help me," Rulan called out. But he had gone.

Rulan knelt on the hard earth while the crowd drifted to the periphery of the courtyard. She gripped the woman by the shoulders and folded her into a sitting position against the courtyard fountain. Rulan steeled herself to open the filthy robes and touch the creature's flesh. She lifted the lid of the one good eye and studied the scars on the ruined face. "This woman is not a leper. She's just badly hurt," she said loudly.

The woman raised her battered fingers and made a series of rapid gestures in the air. Suddenly, Rulan found that she could not breathe. The world had shifted; now nothing seemed real.

"Daughter—" said the face that was not a face. And although the voice that whistled through split cheeks was not at all like the voice she remembered, Rulan knew at once that it was Ma Tsu Po.

With gentle, trembling hands, Rulan examined the mutilated woman. The broken bones had not healed. The breath was fetid, indicating that the injuries were internal and irreversible.

A dark hole opened. "Rulan. I knew I would find you."

"Who did this?" Rulan whispered, sick with apprehension.

"Soldiers. General Li. They came at night, a whole brigade." She grabbed Rulan's arm. "They burned the *chai tang* and slew the sisters. It was part of a campaign to crush the Triads in the county. General Li knew about our pact with the Triads and the Taiping—"

"All the sisters?" Rulan asked, praying that Wing was still alive.

"A few escaped."

"And Wing?"

"I don't know. I was left for dead when the soldiers finished with me." Ma Tsu Po's nails dug hard. "Who did you tell? The Old One? The young lord? Aaiiee, your mouth was opened. With gold? With love?"

"No!" she protested. Then she collapsed in misery, remembering what she had told Liang Mo. "Oh, Mother," Rulan whispered. "I have been betrayed."

"Aiya, Daughter." Ma Tsu Po's voice seemed to trail away. "Now Li has scattered the sisters to the winds. There is no peace, only war and deceit. Punti against Hakka, Triads against Manchu, Taiping against all. The old world is sick with hate. This Land of Flowers is killing its own children."

"Where are the survivors?" Rulan asked, not daring to hope.

Ma Tsu Po's voice echoed with a trace of its old steel. "Orchids from other houses have joined with the Taiping on their march. Kwan Yin is not dead. The sisters are not crushed. You must go to them and to your father. But first, kill the monster Li!"

"I cannot," sputtered Rulan, white-faced. "I cannot. I have killed for you already."

The mutilated face twisted horribly. "You owe us one more death to pay back the innocents who died for you," Ma Tsu Po's voice rasped. Ma Tsu Po leaned back and was quiet a long time. When she spoke again, her voice came out of a profound weariness. "Remember who you are, Daughter."

"I cannot take another life," Rulan replied, aghast at what the woman required of her.

"You refuse? For your loose tongue your sisters were dishonored in a dirty cellar and hacked to pieces. The place was burned so there would be no bodies. Even the soldiers were afraid to set fire to a holy place. But General Li ordered it done—for his amusement."

"No, no," Rulan moaned, putting her hands to her ears.

"Then I curse you," hissed the mutilated woman. "I curse you with death and sorrow and wandering."

Rulan put her hands over the fleshy folds of Ma Tsu Po's lips. "Holy Mother, pity me—"

"You ask for pity? Look at me!" The breath whistled through the ruined nose. Ma Tsu Po opened her dress and showed the terrible scar where a breast had been. "May Kwan Yin abandon you to those monsters if you fail in your duty to your sisters. Be a warrior or die a craven traitor. I made myself live only to tell you this. Now I have finished," she said. "Remember your vow as an Orchid. One heart, one sword. Remember—"

Rulan grabbed for her hand. Too late. Ma Tsu Po had taken something out of her rags and swallowed it.

"Daughter, Daughter," Ma Tsu Po murmured. "What things the gods allow—" She seemed to disappear inside her rags.

Rulan's body was wracked with a fit of trembling; she was as helpless as an infant struggling for breath. She touched Ma Tsu Po's face and saw the face of Wing and her other sisters. Dead. Rulan lay down over the lifeless form of the abbess and wept.

■   ■   ■

A guard lifted her up from the cobblestones and shouted for the soldiers to take the corpse away. Suddenly, Moon was at her side. "Where have you been?" Moon scolded. She pulled the dazed Rulan back to Meng's quarters, grumbling all the while. According to Moon, everything was ready for the seance: the sacrificial food, the wine, and even the makeshift altar to Kwan Yin.

Kwan Yin, repeated Rulan to herself. Kwan Yin, the Unmerciful.

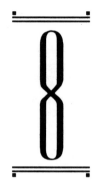

T hin trails of smoke rose from the joss sticks on the makeshift altar and mingled with the scent of sandalwood and stale cosmetics. Between the two red candles on the round table lay small bowls of sacrificial wine and rice, and the Shouchou mirror. It was Moon's idea to tempt the Tai Tai's ghost with something from its former life that it treasured. Recollecting the dead woman's enormous vanity, Meng agreed, although she could never look at the brass rondel without shuddering, for she was sure it harbored the old woman's angry ghost.

All the women had loosened their collars and seated themselves on stools placed in a circle on the tile floor. As the maids passed around cups of steaming tea and plates of sugared coconut, their voices rose along with their excitement and impatience. At the sight of the dazed Rulan pulled along by Moon, the chattering suddenly stopped.

"Here she is, Mother," exclaimed Moon, "and lucky for us, she's already half in a trance. I found her mumbling over a dead beggar."

The encounter with Ma Tsu Po had left Rulan disoriented, confused. She saw Moon's sweating face alight with expectation; Meng's naked fear; Mei Yuk's wild glee. Why did they want her to shake the ghosts loose? Didn't they hear, as she did, the angry spirits of a hundred Orchid sisters? The air was filled with their cries, accusations, and laments.

"Begin," Meng ordered.

Rulan knew by heart the ancient charms by which her mother had raised the dead. But because the weight of her sins seemed to grow more immense with every passing minute, she half-believed that she was safe; the ghosts would never obey. Still, to please the others, she forced herself to begin the opening ritual.

She stood in the circle of women and stamped her foot. She walked slowly around the circle, her arms held aloft, and when she completed the circuit, she made the Gesture of Departing and whirled once. She came around to the left and whirled again, then around once more to the right. She crouched like a cat, then collapsed into a cross-legged sitting position.

Her mouth opened and the words of the old Loi song fell automatically from her lips. Tears spilled from her eyes as she heard herself chant the Calling of the Dead. She sang in the queer, high-pitched voice that her mother used, while rocking her body and drumming on her knees for emphasis. The song was long. The sweet smoke burned her eyes and made her throat hoarse.

A wind blew into the window slit, flattening the flame of the red candles. The candles sputtered, and the women's tense faces were bathed for a moment in a garishly red glow. Rulan's song had turned savage.

She felt the vibration long before the others. It was in the floor, then in the small table that served as an altar. The table began to shake. The bowls of rice shivered; the teacups filled with the reddish brew spilled on the floor. The surface of the brass mirror glimmered and winked. There was the faintest fluttering deep within its depths. The tapping grew louder and louder; it filled the room with an unearthly cadence that drove on and on. It so thundered inside Rulan's head that she felt as if she were splitting in two. The table toppled over; the Shouchou mirror crashed like a gong to the floor. And at the sound, angry female ghosts leapt out of the void and into the room, swirling and crying for revenge.

Meng wailed, "The Old One comes. I am undone." The mirror had landed on its back, revealing the lovers in the enclosed bower of Abundant Spring Mountain. Rulan crawled over to the mirror like one crawling to a pool to drink. She leaned over the mirror. The golden surface of the mirror reflected the changing faces of the ghosts who inhabited it—lustful, angry, full of hate and terror. She felt herself being drawn into its depths . . .

A rushing sound gathered deep in Rulan's body and poured out from between her lips. An echo rolled into the room. Rulan's mouth opened wide.

"Daughter, Daughter," came a soft voice from between the unmoving lips. "I am here. But have a care." Ailan's voice was like a willow limb brushing against a paper window.

The smell of joss was as sweet and thick as blood. Rulan leapt straight into the air from a sitting position. She screamed and spat, now bending and unbending her body like a bow, now whirling on her toes. Her hair had come undone and fell around her. Suddenly, she sank down and spun on her stomach like a crab in the dust.

Again, her mouth opened wide, and this time a man's voice, low and unctuous, came forth: "Blood, vigorous new blood pulsing through my veins. Fresh air fills my lungs. I smell the incense, the wet earth. I can move as fast as any youth. Youth is mine. Vigor. Strong blood. Aiya, give me your heat!"

Mei Yuk screamed. It was Wang's voice.

Rulan rested on the floor with her face to the ground. When she lifted her head, an old woman seemed to stare out at them through a fringe of matted hair. She bared her teeth. "I smell her but I cannot see. I wander and wander. So tired. And always so hungry."

"Aaiiee," Moon wept. "The Tai Tai comes for me!"

"In the morning room, we women wind the hair into a knot and draw it up tight. Day after day, we wind the knot and fasten it with the long needle. In and out, in and out. Bent over the mirror, we see only the skin smooth as old ivory, trace the half-moon brow with a brush as fine as moths' wings. A girl stares into the mirror, my mirror. Daughter of pig sellers. Betrayed! Thou knowest this, Meng!"

"Forgive, Old One," Meng babbled. "I did not know what I was doing. I thought only of Liang Mo's happiness. You should see how happy he is, Tai Tai, with his new son—"

"The child is a bastard! The mother is a whore. The husband is a cuckold. The master of the house is a murderer. The woman of the house is a dying thing!" the voice intoned.

Mei Yuk shrieked and threw her skirt over her head. "Lies, filthy lies!"

"Aaiiee. I am undone. She wants my death. Forgive me, Tai Tai. Oh. Oh. Mercy, mercy, mercy. Kwan Yin, intercede for me." Meng was shaking uncontrollably.

"In the pale light of the oil lamp, our thoughts are only of our house. We put paint over the cheeks and lips. The rouge pot is nearly empty, our fingers dry and sore. Make the knot tighter, we say. Now make it fast. Thou knowest this, Meng."

"Forgive!" Meng begged. She watched the spiteful face with horror.

"You sent her. You! A girl with fire in her hands. Spy, snare, snake-daughter. Fingers, needles, like vipers' teeth. Lies from her lips, sweet words dripping death. See how the daughter of my bosom becomes the agent of my death. She takes up the jeweled pin. The needle sinks in as easily as a man's yang. The golden needle with the butterfly. Deep, deep into the soft, secret places. Our vain dreams go in and out, pale white moths that flutter aimlessly around a broken shell until they rise no more. I dreamed of dynasty, I inherited death! Aaiiee, my foolish daughter, the hunger marchers are upon us. The fires will overcome our house. You began the cycle of greed and despair! Thou knowest this, Meng!"

Meng had covered her face with her white hands.

"Hurry, hurry before she comes again with her golden needle. Catch her. Stop her. The daughter of death comes next for thy husband! The healer is a killer, the nurse is a spy. The woman you gave to your son is a demon." Rulan began to rake her face with fingers not her own.

Mei Yuk tried to get up and run, but her strength had drained away.

The voice of the Tai Tai became as stern as a judge's. "Death for a death. All must die, even you, Daughter!" The spirit that inhabited Rulan's body threw out her arms in wide arcs, whirling ever more wildly, as if sowing the seeds of death in her wake.

One by one, the women fell like yarrow stalks cast by the dark hand of fate. First the maids, then Moon and Mei Yuk, until only Meng was left still seated in the circle. She held out her hands to Rulan, pleading with the Tai Tai's ghost, as tears ran down her face. Her head shook from side to side denying the sentence that the avenging ghost, speaking out of Rulan's mouth, had pronounced on her family. Closer and closer Rulan came toward Meng, her hands raised above her head like an executioner's sword.

"Do you know who I am?" the Tai Tai's voice said.

Meng fell to the floor, her limbs splayed in all directions.

Rulan began to falter. Panting, she reached over Meng's inert body and took a red candle from the altar. She held it up to her face to examine its flickering light, which twisted and danced like the tongue of a snake.

The women awoke slowly, each fighting the sinking waters of forgetfulness and fear, to the roar of the world outside, a sound like that of a river overflowing its banks.

Moon got up on her hands and knees. She heard screams, crockery breaking, the crackle of flames, the shouts of angry guards punctuated by gunfire. She recognized the sounds instantly. "Riot!" she screamed.

Mei Yuk and the others roused themselves, Meng last of all.

"Husband, where are you?" Meng moaned as she crawled across the floor, oblivious to the thunderous din outside. She shivered with revulsion when she saw Rulan, who was staring into the flame of a candle held an inch from her eyes.

"I hear footsteps!" Moon cried; her small eyes were bright with foreboding. She tottered toward the doorway, but in seconds she was back, panting in terror. "Bandits running through the house! Triads!" she cried. "The guards and servants have fled! Quickly, or we are undone!" Grimly, Moon dragged Meng into the courtyard. The maids followed, whimpering in confusion.

Mei Yuk was desperately dabbing at her face, trying to fix her make-up and her ruined coiffure. "Wait for me!" she called, but the words became a scream as two men in peasant pajamas, their faces masked by head rags tied around their nose and mouth, burst through the door.

"Here they are—the granddaughter and the spirit-woman, taking tea while the house burns down," one panted. "Leave the old ones for the rabble."

Seeing that Rulan was in a trance, he approached her cautiously, as if he were afraid that she might cast a spell on him. But Rulan never moved; her eyes were locked on the candle in front of her nose. Hesitantly, he blew out the flame, and still Rulan neither moved nor spoke.

The other man knelt before Mei Yuk. "What?" he chuckled. "No greeting for an old friend, Little Bride?" With a jerk, he pulled down his mask.

Mei Yuk's eyes widened. But before she could cry out, the man had thrown her over his shoulder like a sack of rice and was running after his companion, who was halfway across the courtyard with Rulan in his arms.

Outside the gates, the small cannon boomed once, twice, three times, before the roar of the angry mob overcame it. With a crack louder than thunder, the gates of the viceroy's mansion gave way, and the citizens of Canton, led by the Triads, poured through the breach with fists, sticks, and an overwhelming hunger.

usk had fallen when the Tanka boat tied up at the outskirts of the city. Too late, Pao An feared, to catch a
glimpse of the palanquins of the viceroy's family as they were borne
through the streets. There was no way of knowing whether Mei Yuk
and Rulan were in Canton now. The city was steaming. Somewhere a
fire burned, for Pao An saw that the sky was glazed red.

He had decided to confront Wang with his perfidy. He had to know,
for Mei Yuk's sake, the truth about the raid. And he had to allay the
suspicion that Wang was playing him for a fool, for if Wang was
indeed the supreme leader of the Triads, he ought to be able to find out
where a certain beggar from On Ting had wandered. What if Wang
knew all along where Li Yu was?

Pao An hastened north through the city gates and into the Avenue of
Apothecaries which led to Viceroy Li's mansion. The street was desolate; no wheelbarrows or jostling vendors clogged the lane. No thin-
faced merchants peered out from the narrow stalls. The fire, Pao An
thought, remembering how city merchants banded together to fight
the deadly flames. As he darted farther up the lane, Pao An heard a
low, insistent murmur from the direction of the official buildings.
The groaning seemed to rise. Then he heard loud explosions, bursts
from a cannon. And screams.

Running now, he turned a corner and fell into a crowded avenue filled with flames and shouts. A roar came from behind the high walls where a row of wealthy families lived. There were howls of anguish and sounds of crockery smashing. At one corner, forty or more men were using a flagpole as a battering ram to smash down the door of a mansion, while servants threw down trash and stones on the heads of the mob. He ran by just as the invaders, having broken through, poured past the splintered gates with shrieks of triumph.

Pao An pushed his way through the mob toward the viceregal headquarters. An angry crowd had begun to form at the entrance of the viceroy's mansion, which was barred by a line of water carts swarming with frantic soldiers carrying wooden buckets. Already the living quarters in the rear were totally engulfed in flames.

Frantic at the possibility that Mei Yuk and Rulan might be trapped inside, Pao An started to push his way toward the burning mansion, but the guards shoved him aside, and suddenly, to his distress, he found himself borne along with the mob in the direction of the river. Bands of drunken youths were smashing the locked storefronts and grabbing whatever they could reach. When he tried to cry out, acrid smoke filled his lungs. The mob swarmed like locusts over the muck of the streets: carts and baskets, torn bedding, and broken crockery, spoiled food, and discarded finery. And still, he was carried helplessly along, like a pebble drawn out to sea by the tide. As the road turned, he saw Wang's compound straddling two sides of the street ahead. A cordon of red-turbaned Triads armed with pikes surrounded the gates on one side.

"Move on, move on!" the Triads shouted and prodded the crowd with their sharp sticks.

But the mob was not intimidated. The promise of booty from the wealthiest citizen of Canton had canceled their fear of the Triads. The gates of the mansion where Wang's wife and sons lived were the first to fall; part of the mob surged inside, leaving several hundred ragged men and women to pelt the Triads with sticks and sharp rocks. Some clambered over the walls with makeshift ladders. The gates of the second mansion buckled, giving way with a crack, and the mob surged forward over the fallen Triad guards.

Pao An pushed his way in as the first invaders were running out with arms filled with vases, chairs, joints of meat, sacks of rice. He had to find Wang! Ruthlessly, he shoved the looters in front of him aside, ignoring their wails and their twisting, flailing limbs. He remembered the tunnel in the house of Li at the summit of the mountain. The Wangs would have their secret exit in a similar spot in the heart of the mansion, except that the river, not the mountain, would be the escape route. And old Wang's rooms were in the rear of the compound at the river's edge, a perfect place for a getaway. Pao An doubled his speed, lashing out madly with his fists, thrusting aside the greed-crazed men and women who were ripping the brocade hangings from the beds and tearing the old paintings from the walls. He got lost in a winding, open corridor and had to double back over a many-angled bridge that led to a labyrinth of inner rooms and gardens. Finally, he spied the curved bridge and the pen of live deer near Wang's cottage. The mob had not yet found this secret section of the house.

The door of the cottage was wide open. Pao An crept through the smaller anteroom to the chamber at the back where he had met with the old man. A lone torch crackled in a wall stanchion. Hearing voices, Pao An hid himself in the shadows. Two women dressed in white were standing before Wang, who was stumbling around the room stuffing jewels, small bowls, and bric-a-brac into a bag and muttering distractedly to himself. Pao An recognized the smaller girl instantly. Mei Yuk!

"Everything is ruined," Wang said, panting. "The small distraction I planned with my brothers has overflowed its banks. Now Kung Kung and his girls must flee. It offends me that a merchant should be outwitted by the witless crowd! Still, a prudent man is always prepared for emergencies. Though my faithless wives desert me, my sons steal my treasure, my brothers fail, Kung Kung will triumph in the end. Kung Kung will sail with his two girls to the Isle of Immortality! A few moments to gather up my treasures—"

The tall girl was holding a golden ball in her outstretched hand.

"Get my box," the old man ordered Mei Yuk. He was running his hand distractedly over a tiny rosewood carving of a rampant horse. "Aiya, my beauty, how can I bear to leave you?" Quickly, he pushed the horse up his sleeve and stuffed a rope of delicately carved ivory prayer beads into the folds of his undergarments before grabbing the small box from Mei Yuk. He gestured toward the tall, silent woman. "Put it back. Quick, quick, before the rats come running."

The girl stood perfectly still.

"Put it here, Daughter," he said in a silken voice. "You," he ordered Mei Yuk rudely. "Go behind the painting and hold the door."

Mei Yuk began to cry. "I am not a *mui tsai* to order about, Kung Kung. And I'm frightened!"

Pao An strode into the room. "Mei Yuk," he called out. "Don't go with him!"

Recognizing Pao An, Mei Yuk cried out in joyful astonishment. But in seconds, the beautiful face had contorted in fear. "Oh, oh, Kung

Kung. I don't know this one," she shrieked, throwing her arms around Wang's neck. "He's one of them—one of the murderers who wrecked the viceroy's house! He followed me here. Stop him. Kill him!"

Wang pushed her roughly aside. "Away! Away!" he cried in annoyance.

The tall woman turned her head in Pao An's direction.

"Rulan!" he called in surprise. She had grown pale and thin, and seemed half-asleep. He called her name again, but although she looked directly at him, she seemed not to see or hear.

"Look here, look at me, Daughter," Wang cried to Rulan. "What do those two matter? Forget the boy! I will buy you another."

"Liang Mo! Husband!" Mei Yuk wailed, raking her fingers through her hair. "Aaiiee!" she screamed, and darted to the wall. There was the sound of ripping cloth as Mei Yuk tore away the hanging and stumbled through the hidden door, calling, "Husband, where are you?"

"Come!" Wang was trembling now, and his voice rose to a nervous, high-pitched whine. "Give me the eye!"

Rulan did not move.

Pao An could hear the frenzied deer galloping in their pens as greedy hands clawed at their flanks. The mob crashed through the outer court, overturning tables and chairs, and crying out at the treasures tucked in every alcove.

"Give the eye to me! Now!" Wang screamed. The small gilt box trembled on the tips of his jeweled fingersheaths.

Pao An watched in dreadful fascination as Rulan raised the golden ball over her head.

"Stop!" Wang squealed. "You must not!"

A strange light had come into Rulan's eyes. With one swift movement, she hurled the jewel to the tile floor, where it shattered like an egg.

Then Wang fell on the floor, howling like a woman who has lost her beloved. "Aaiiee!" He swept his hands wildly about in a mad effort to gather the broken pieces of jade that were rolling rapidly away.

Pao An pulled Wang back by the neck of his robes. "Where is my father!" he demanded. "Have you hidden him away to torment me?"

But Wang twisted out of his grasp and scrambled after the pieces of his ruined orb. Small exquisite treasures of ivory and delicate stone spilled out of the hidden places in Wang's clothes and were crushed under the fat merchant's knees. "Aaiiee!" he wept while scuttling like a wounded crab across the floor. "What have you done, Loi woman?"

Pao An heard the sound of bare feet thudding on the floor, the sharp, hungry cries of the approaching mob. He lifted Rulan into his arms and leaped for the door through which Mei Yuk had disappeared. But the girl had bolted it from the outside. Lowering his head like an ox then, he turned and charged the mob. They ignored him, thinking him one of them, a hunger marcher intent on robbery and rape. Their eyes were already fastened on their chosen prey. They surged past, their clubs and knives ready for the merchant holding his fat bejeweled fingers vainly aloft in the sign of the three.

Part 6
WARRIOR WOMAN

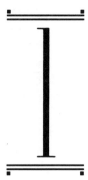

Kwangtung Province, Summer 1852

Pao An bore Rulan through the burning city to where the Tanka docked their boats. Rulan was mute, almost lifeless in his arms. When he spoke, he could not rouse her.

Most of the Tanka had taken to the waters as soon as the city had been set afire; the remaining junks and barges had been commandeered by those who had stolen enough to buy passage to flee. Pao An found a Tanka couple who owned a fishing boat and with a jade ring on Rulan's finger, he bought passage for three days. He had no idea where he wanted to go; in the vain hope that he might find Li Yu on the upper reaches of the delta, he made the Tanka take the route north along the Pak River. Then he hid with Rulan in the bottom of the boat and slept the sleep of the dead.

In the middle of the night she cried out, "Boy-Boy!"

Pao An started awake. "Who's Boy-Boy?" he whispered, thinking that she had regained her senses.

But Rulan was speaking from the middle of a dream. "You'll have rice wherever you go," she murmured.

"Hush," he said, cradling her in his arms.

"What things the gods allow," she moaned.

She has secrets too, he told himself. She has lost someone dear, as I have. They were both outcasts, and the world a great hole into which the things and people they loved were lost forever. Now, in the darkness of the hold, he faced the horror of Mei Yuk's words in Wang's chamber. The small sweet mouth that had vowed devotion had cursed him. He felt the hot, shameful tears sting his eyes. He was no different from the callow, foolish youths of legend who had leapt to their ruin by falling in love with fox-spirits. The tears seemed to ease his mood of bitterness and defeat, and he dozed for a while, completely spent, only to awake to the sounds of the boatman and his wife making love. Rulan lay in the curve of his arm fast asleep, and in spite of himself he became aroused.

Dog, cur, he thought. How can you take advantage of a sick woman? How can you think of taking this girl after making such a fool of yourself over her sister? It's your fate, he told himself, never to have a wife. Your punishment for trying to catch hold of an evil fox-spirit.

This time when he slept, he dreamed of Mei Yuk calling for his death and pointing a long finger at him that dripped with blood.

The next day he sat on the rail and watched the white clouds drifting across the pale yellow sky. What was he going to do now? Wang, who had employed him, was dead. Pao An had neither money nor trade— and now, he had a mad girl on his hands. He watched Rulan as she stared sightlessly into the distance. The Tanka would not eat with them because they thought Rulan was bewitched.

Within two days, when the Tanka family tied up at a small market town, Pao An had decided where to go. Many of the Tanka opium pirates who were being hunted by the barbarians for a head price had given up the marauders' life and gone north to join the Taiping. The Tanka wife told Pao An that the rebels took in women—any kind, no matter how degraded—whores, runaways, even crazy women. Pao An used some of Rulan's bracelets to buy provisions—string bags, two blankets, and a small bag of rice. With Rulan shuffling behind him like a dumb beast, he began to walk north. Sometimes she wandered off when he wasn't looking. Finally he found some vines, tied them around her waist and his own, and led her like a calf behind the carts and wheelbarrows that jostled against them on the rutted roads.

After a week on the road, they washed off the filth from their faces with river water and crept into a village to pick up bits of rotten vegetables left behind by the farmers in the marketplace. Pao An found placards nailed to the posts of the village gate offering one hundred pieces of silver for anyone who turned in suspicious vagabonds to the local authorities. Two dangerous rebels, a man and a woman, were mentioned by name: Chen Pao An and Yang Rulan. Their offenses were also listed: inciting a riot, murdering a loyal merchant of the city, and the viceroy's own wife. The seal was Viceroy Li's, and the witness against them was Li Mei Yuk, wife of the viceroy's son.

Pao An intended to sink into the sea of homeless who swelled the roads and canals after the salt riot. He bartered another of Rulan's bracelets for a string of coppers and some cold rice and boiled peanuts, and he fed Rulan with his fingers.

One night, dirty slips of paper filled with writing were passed from hand to hand among the refugees. One paper railed against the "demon imps" and called on all decent Han people to revolt; the strangest message described the glorious visions of Hung, the Taiping leader, on his ascent to heaven. But the one that caught Pao An's eye was an invitation to carpenters, soldiers, book-reading men, and doctors to march with the Taiping. This paper was stamped with a rectangular seal and signed by one who called himself the Eastern King of the Taiping.

Pao An memorized the message and the name, before passing the paper to a family of traveling jugglers. The Taiping had sprung out of their fortress in Kwangsi and were rumored to be marching into Hunan. He had to find them. Summer was ending in the highlands. He had to find the rebels before cold weather set in.

Half a day's journey from the Hunan border, on an evening when both were near collapse for want of food and sleep, they passed a cluster of rude hovels hidden in the rice paddies. A thin, tired-looking housewife came out of the yard rubbing her hands on her padded pants. Glassy eyed, Rulan shuffled past the woman with one hand tucked limply into Pao An's.

"A little rice, Auntie," Pao An begged. "I can work." The woman's big feet, and the fearless way she regarded him made him guess that she was Hakka.

The farm woman stared out of a flat, stolid-looking face, saying nothing. When they had almost passed around the corner of the hen house, she barked, "What's the matter with your woman?"

Pao An hoped that his instinct was right. They were still in Kwangtung, still within the viceroy's reach. If she were Hakka, his words might move her. If not, she would be one hundred silver coins richer. "She's lost her senses. The government troops came. Ran us off our land."

She shouted out a command. Two grimy boys came running out of the house and pulled Pao An and Rulan into the kitchen. In minutes, their mother was blowing a small fire of dried grass and dung to life in a clay oven. She served a meal of rice and bitter greens seasoned with chicken fat, and in honor of the guests, two duck eggs, which had been preserved in limy clay for several months. The frugal housewife carefully cut the eggs into thin slivers. Unshelled, the albumen of the egg was a translucent black, and the yolk an iridescent blue-green, like the inside of a black opal. They each took a dab of the egg on the end of their chopsticks, taking care not to drop a bit of the precious, soft yolk where the mellow taste of the egg was concentrated. The black egg was scraped on the tongue, tenderly savored, before finally being wolfed down with a mouthful of hot rice. The children ceased their chatter, concentrating on the savory egg, and Pao An wondered how many times they had eaten as well as this.

The house had three small rooms where boxes and baskets of seed were stored and the family slept. A few chickens scratched in a small yard in the back. Although the Hakka wife asked no questions, Pao An told her that he was a farmer from the delta driven off the land by government troops. She gave them a straw mat and helped Pao An make a rude bed in the shed outside. Rulan was already sleeping when he came back from washing his hands and feet at the community well.

There was a new pot of tea on the stove when he returned. The Hakka wife poured out a bowlful and banged it on the table, beckoning him to sit down. Her sons were wrapped up in blankets around the sputtering coal stove, fast asleep.

"My husband died on a corvée. They said he broke his back hauling stones," she said softly. "But a man from another village came by later. The soldiers played a game with him because he was very strong. They bet that he could carry more stone than a mule and made him run a race. He collapsed, and the ones that lost the bet refused to pick him up." She was on her knees now, poking a stick into the dying coals of the stove. After a while, she asked, "Where do you go?"

"North," replied Pao An vaguely.

"Taiping long-hairs there."

Pao An grunted.

The woman spoke as if in a dream. "They say that the rebels cut soldiers out of paper and breathe on them. The paper turns into fierce warriors who cannot be defeated. After the enemy heads are counted, the rebels breathe again on the soldiers and when they are changed back into paper, the soldiers are packed away in boxes. That's why they don't need food or powder to win. You believe that?"

Pao An grunted again.

"I believe," she whispered. "Their spirits are everywhere, even here." She gestured around the smoke-filled room. "Their spirits are so strong, anyone can change paper into real men. Even me. If I had scissors and paper, I would make a battalion to collect ten thousand heads." She picked up his emptied cup, tossed out the dregs into the coals, and watched the wet tea leaves sizzle and disappear. "Pretty soon I go north too," she whispered.

He stayed a month and did her husband's work, bringing in the crop of rice. But two extra mouths strained her resources. Pao An told her they had to go.

"When you find the long-hairs, ask Hung for a healing for your wife," she said slowly. "I give you my husband's pants. Yours have bloodstains. Tomorrow I take your woman's dress and color it black with see leong fiber. It's not decent for her to go around with blood in the front. And the cloth gives you both away to the viceroy's soldiers. A good Hakka girl should not be wearing such fine stuff anyway."

Before leaving the next day, Pao An gave the woman his last copper. She gave him two lumps of cold rice wrapped in ti leaves and the last of the duck eggs.

"There was a girl in our village once like your woman. She was possessed by a ghost after being raped by the old viceroy's soldiers. She killed herself. I pray your woman will be healed."

After crossing the border, they climbed the hills to beg coppers and bits of food from farmers hoeing in terraced tea fields. They slept huddled in ditches. One night Pao An found a hole in a flood wall, which he lined with straw for a makeshift shelter. Rulan put her head against his shoulder and slept. Again she talked in her sleep.

"Wing. Hold me. I have no one."

"Yes," he answered. He felt like her brother, her protector against the angry wind.

"I'm cold."

He covered her as best he could with the flap of his coat.

Suddenly she called his name. "Pao An. Friend." Hearing her speak his name, he felt sadness wash over him like cold rain. Between them they had not one inch of land, not one living friend. He began to caress her. Soon, his touch had grown more ardent and more intimate. But when he lifted the hem of her skirt to stroke her thighs, her body became rigid, and she began to cry.

Suddenly, he had a vision of himself making love to a weeping woman against a wall with the wind blowing and the dust swirling around them. He pulled down her dress and clutched her tightly in his arms, hating himself.

But his caresses had awakened something in Rulan. For the first time her mind, wandering in darkness, found a path. She felt the warmth of his body, the strong sinews of his arms.

"Friend," she said again, unable to say more.

"I will be your friend," he said. And wrapped his tattered coat more closely about them both.

They climbed north on foot from village to village until they reached the high passes in the Nan Ling mountains on the border of Kwangtung and Hunan. The narrow roads leading through the gorges were jammed with families fleeing, itinerant soldiers, and long lines of coolies and mule trains making the long trek out of the ravaged southern cities into the rich rice lands of the interior. No one noticed the ragged man and woman amid the thousands on the road.

Soon they were only a few days behind the rebels. There were signs everywhere of the Taiping's passing. Each small boat and barge on the Hsiang River seemed to be poling north. Those villages lying in the wake of the Taiping exodus were empty, stripped of goods, animals, and people; families had packed their belongings, boarded up their houses, and traded their land for cash.

Two nights before they reached the outposts of the rebel line around Chang Sha, Pao An made a rude lean-to of sticks on the flat, open expanse of paddy fields where dozens of Hakka refugee families were encamped and built a fire out of leaves and ox droppings.

They had eaten a handful of rice gathered grain by grain on scattered fields along the way and had drunk hot water mixed with fragrant leaves. The Hakka were huddled in groups singing the strange songs that had thrilled and perplexed Pao An, songs about the one great God, Elder Brother Jesus, God's first Son, and another son who made "demons and devils hide out of fear of his light." This latter son he construed to be the leader of the Taiping, Hung Hsiu Chuan, who called himself by the title Heavenly King.

Pao An stirred up the fire with a stick and cleared his throat nervously. He had fallen into the habit of talking aloud to Rulan and not expecting an answer. Staring into the flames, he said to her, "You know we must go to separate camps when we reach the Taiping. I can't take care of you any longer. I worry about people thinking you're crazy, although I know you're not. You are just quiet. I respect a quiet person. My father was a quiet person, as I told you. When I'd come banging into our house as a child, he would say, 'Typhoon is blowing.' Then he'd laugh. I liked to lean my head against his knees while he read his books. But I'd make him annoyed with all my wiggling. 'Get away, Master Mongoose,' he'd say. Was your father like that? I heard the guards say in the house of Li that your mother was a great spirit-woman. I think such people must be quiet to commune with ghosts, not full of twitches and jitters and impatient questions to make the spirits uneasy. I have no gift at all. Well, maybe for gambling and fighting. But not for spirits. All I can do is jump and run, swing my arms in the air. Was your mother quiet then, or—"

"Yes."

"Oh," he said, embarrassed that his prattle had awakened a real response.

"Quiet in her heart."

The tension he felt was so great that he had to stand up. He shook out his legs, rocked back and forth to unkink his spine from the effort of sitting so long. "Like you?" he said finally.

"My heart is not quiet. It is dead."

"Oh, don't say that," he said, falling to his knees by her side. "I—forgive me—I've held you all night in the cold. I felt your heart beating. Do not say your heart is dead. You are—you have been a good companion."

Moron, he chastised himself. Now that she could talk, he had lost all speech. How he longed to sleep with his face turned against hers, feeling her breath against his cheek. But he feared that she would see him as he was: a no-name boy. Speech had made her a person again. He could not hold her without her assent. And if he confessed his feelings, she might come to hate him as Mei Yuk had. He could not bear it if she did.

They watched the fire hiss and spit and slowly die. Finally he pulled his blanket to the opposite side of the warm embers.

The next day, looking down from the terraced fields, they saw the triangular yellow flags of the Taiping army, which was spread out on both banks of the Hsiang River near Chang Sha. A small boy who was fishing for crabs in a canal pointed the way to the women's column.

"You are too thin. Tell the Taiping women to give you meat," Pao An told her, feeling like a foolish old uncle. He wanted to take her in his arms and tell her that he loved her, but her reticence frightened him.

"I can take care of myself now," Rulan said.

Stung by her rebuke, he forced himself to continue. "The Taiping keep men and women separate. We may not meet again—so take this," Pao An said. He held out one of the blankets that had covered them on their long journey together. Their hands touched. Unable to stop himself, he pulled her close and buried his face in the soft fall of her hair. But her arms did not go around him.

"I'm afraid," she said tonelessly, loosening his hold.

"Don't be afraid," he whispered. "I'll take care—you'll be safe. The women will—"

"Pao An," she said seriously. "I'm cold inside. I am not the woman for you. You need someone who is alive."

Pao An murmured a protest, knowing that she meant Mei Yuk. He longed to tell her that he wanted her, not Mei Yuk, but he was ashamed and he could not.

"Then you must wait until I am alive again." She touched his rough, unshaven cheek and wondered why she had no tears to shed. "You were kind to me. I'll remember that. Kindness is better than love, sometimes."

He watched her as she walked down the rutted, rocky path, until she disappeared around the bend of the road.

Rulan was dizzy from hunger. The lookout had told her that the Women's Camp was over the next hill. Yet she had passed three hills, and there was still so sign of anyone. Already she missed Pao An. A small hope stirred in her: if he could find Yang, her father might make a match between them if the laws separating the men from the women were ever revoked. She sighed at the impossibility of the wish. She was a stone girl, a woman with a bad fate destined never to have a man. Hearing Pao An unburden his heart to her the night before, loving him all the while, she still would never yield to him if he desired Mei Yuk.

Up high where the dark pine forest ended, there was smoke blowing through the wet trees and horses coming slowly downhill. The animals and their riders moved like ghosts through the smoke and the low-lying clouds. As the dark shapes drew near, Rulan saw that the riders had long hair, which streamed behind them in the rising wind. They rode on and on, until they were level with the road. She could hear the thudding of the horses' hooves and the shouts of the riders, their voices light as rainwater. As they came close, she saw that the riders were women in red jackets. A tall girl sitting bareback astride a dark brown horse, holding reins made of rope, was in the lead. She had red lips and white teeth, and she was laughing like the others and calling out to them without bothering to cover her mouth.

Rulan stood in the middle of the road clutching the blanket to her head. Like a peasant woman, she thought: stupid, dull. While the horsewomen flowed around her, taking no notice, she looked up at them, thinking them so beautiful and alive. Perhaps she was a ghost they could not see. Their voices rang in her ears like pipes and drums.

And still she could neither speak nor move; she was a dead tree lodged in a river. So they passed her by; the horses' hooves cut moon cake molds in the wet, black soil.

"You, Sister," sang out the last rider in Hakka dialect. "If you have come to enlist, the Women's Camp is around the next turn. Go down into the valley by the stream."

They left her standing in the road weeping. "Sister," they called her. She had come home.

Hunan Province, Fall 1852

The valley breathed great clouds of smoke like a waking dragon. Looking down from the heights, Rulan saw for the first time the vast river of humanity that was the Taiping nation. It stretched along the floor of the river valley, mile upon mile, as far as the eye could see. She smelled the sharp scent of burning pine and saw that the army had paused on its relentless drive north; thousands of campfires were burning on the peaks and ridges and on both banks of the Hsiang River at the western edge of the city of Chang Sha. Just below her, a clear fast-running stream curved down the terraced mountain through a wide meadow to a beach of bleached stones at the bend of the river. Thousands of red-jacketed people were encamped there, and she saw that every one was a woman. She heard the women calling to each other, their laughter rising high and clear like bells, without the answering clamor of men's voices. Some were running races on the meadow or throwing javelins. Those nearest her were washing clothes in the stream or bent over the cook fires. But the ones that caught Rulan's attention were the women mounted on small ponies with tall bows slung over their shoulders who guarded the edges of the camp.

Rulan was directed to a long line of disheveled women leading up to the tent where the battalion's "mother" lived. The newcomers all had pinched, hungry faces like hers. Most of the women had big feet, although some tottered on golden lilies swathed in filthy shoes and bloody bandages.

"Where you from, the Willow World?" asked a rat-faced girl, elbowing an older companion who was so covered with dried mud that the color of her garments was indiscernible. Both women had brass ear hoops, dark skin, and hair as dirty and matted as the nest of a burrowing animal. They were Miao. Han women avoided them.

"I'm not a prostitute, I'm a healer. Well, I used to be one," Rulan said, too exhausted to think of a retort.

"Are you really?" asked a woman standing behind Rulan. Long lines of pain were etched on her brow and her face was as gray as ashes. "I keep bleeding. Fourteen days now. Do you have *tang kuei* root?"

"I don't have anything. I came without my gourds and needles. But I promise I will find something for you tomorrow."

"She's lying. She's no healer," said the thin Miao girl viciously, reaching out to grab Rulan's skirt. "Only some kind of mandarin's big-foot whore. Here, feel this! Rough cloth like you and I wear is not good enough for this one. Probably her house was overrun, and she crawled off to seek protection here. But there's no room for gentry pigs in this place." She pulled a pointed stick out of the bodice of her pajamas and jabbed it in Rulan's direction.

But the stick was immediately snatched away by a tall, big-boned woman who had come out unannounced from the tent. The woman's jacket was of plain cotton, but clean, unlike the others in line, and dyed a bright red. Her long black hair fell past her shoulders to the backs of her thighs. She looked no older than Rulan but carried herself with the authority of a general.

"No bickering here. We are warriors, not fishwives. We have no time for the kind of stupid talk that goes on around the village well. Everyone is equal in this place," she added pointedly to the angry Miao. "Each of us is sister to the other. If you are not willing to die to save the life of your sister, leave now!" No one moved or breathed. Even the sharp-tongued Miao girl looked chastened. The leader took the stick and broke it easily across her knee. "All weapons must be checked. We will issue you new ones and teach you how to use them. First you wash, get new clothes, then you eat."

"Follow us," said a woman with a round, pockmarked face, and headed for the cooking fires.

For the first time in weeks, Rulan would sleep with real food in her belly. It was not much: half a bowl of rice, a cabbage leaf floating in pork broth seasoned with wild gingerroot. At her campfire of five were the two Miao women. The leader, Rulan guessed, had put them all together purposely to test them. The rat-faced girl wolfed down her food, barely taking time to swallow. A few minutes later she began to vomit.

"We haven't eaten in a week," the older woman said to Rulan while sipping very slowly from her own bowl.

Rulan ate the stringy cabbage, mashed up the rice with her homemade wooden chopsticks, and carried the bowl over to the emaciated Miao girl who was retching over a moss-covered stone. In the flickering light of the fire, the half-starved woman was hardly distinguishable from the shadow of the tree beside her.

"I'm not an infant. I don't need you to chew my food," the girl said bitterly, wiping her mouth with the back of a hand.

"Come, eat, Sister. Tomorrow I'll find some herbs that will help you keep down rice. Slowly, now."

"Whatever you say, Sister," the girl retorted sarcastically, but she did not refuse the food.

Their hearth leader, an experienced warrior assigned to teach them the rules of the camp, ordered them to opposite sides of the fire.

In the morning, Rulan and the women around the campfire were directed to the riverbank, where they were given a crude soap of lye and ashes and ordered to strip and wash themselves. Rulan threw her torn dress into a fire. It blazed higher, fed by the other verminous rags the recruits had worn into camp.

Then her group of five women were herded, naked and shivering, into the frigid river as horsewomen rode past on the riverbanks, tossing their long hair and laughing at them. Steam rose from the river and draped the white bodies of the women in a fine mist. Soon the bathers had lost their shyness and were laughing like children and splashing icy water on each other as the months of hardship were washed away. Rulan let herself drift along with the current until she was a few hundred feet away from the others. From the corner of one eye, she saw a tall rider cantering on the riverbank alone. The woman seemed to move as one with the horse, both rider and mount pressing their faces into the breeze, their muscles rippling. The rider's strong arms were bronzed by the sun, and she carried a long pike as easily as a woman behind walls carries a fan. Moving behind a tree, she came up within scant yards of Rulan, while flicking the heavy mane of her hair off her neck with an impatient gesture.

Rulan cried out and dashed toward the rider, her legs churning the water into foam and her arms flailing wildly. The horse reared up; the rider brandished her pike with a high-pitched warrior's cry. Water streamed off Rulan's pale body like strings of pearls.

"Wing!" she called, weeping like a lost child who has just been found. "It's me!"

Wing took Rulan into her own tent. She looked after her, fed her special foods, and made sure that her duties were few and easy.

After the first shock of seeing Rulan, Wing's emotions had seesawed from elation to loathing and every emotion in between. Was this the girl she loved, she asked herself, or a traitor who had caused the destruction of the Golden Orchids? Wing examined Rulan's story from every angle until she saw that the girl's guilt and distress were real. Ma Tsu Po had not been wise to send Rulan out as a spy, Wing concluded. Rulan was much too simple and innocent; naturally she had become an unwitting accomplice to Viceroy Li's plan to stamp out all opposition groups in the province.

"Oh, my sisters! They are all dead because of me," Rulan said sorrowfully.

"Hush," Wing said, taking Rulan in her arms and wiping away her tears. "The whole world is on fire. You are not responsible."

But Wing was too protective, and Rulan soon chafed under the special treatment. In time they began to fight.

"You treat me like a man's woman. I'm a warrior as good as you," Rulan protested.

"I'm a Taiping captain now. You're a new recruit. You'll go through the same training process as anyone else," Wing commanded.

"You know I can ride! Long ago I beat you in a race!"

"I am the elder sister here. You owe me respect," Wing commanded.

Rulan begged, demanded, and wept, but Wing would not let her join the horsewomen. It was too dangerous, she declared. The siege of Chang Sha was costing the Taiping time and many lives, and there were rumors that the women might be made to fight alongside the men. Wing ordered Rulan to stay in camp, away from the eyes of men and the spies of the Taiping kings. It was no secret that Hung was searching for a celestial bride, a woman to complete his transformation from earthly to heavenly being. The wives he accumulated, the strange elixirs he obtained from Wei to prolong his ardor, the poems he chanted at morning worship meetings in the Women's Camp confirmed this obsession, she told Rulan. Wing noticed how Hung enjoyed parading before the women like a gaudy peacock, his eyes alighting now and then on a comely recruit. Wing was afraid, too, of Yang, for Rulan's father was locked in a power struggle with Hung over the command of the movement. Wing did not want Rulan to be caught up in the rivalry between the ambitious kings and be taken from her once more, and she persuaded Rulan that the time was not at hand to reveal herself to Yang.

"Any big-foot girl can learn to ride, but only you know how to mix the right herbs, put the needles in the proper place—you're more precious to me than a dozen riders." Wing's voice dropped to a passionate whisper. "You're precious to Kwan Yin, who is still our holy sister no matter what Hung and the kings say about demons from the old days!"

"I want to be a warrior, Wing. I have grown sick and soft in the house of Li. I won't hide anymore. I won't be a *mui tsai,* yours or anyone else's," Rulan declared.

"You are not my *mui tsai!*" Wing protested. "You are my sister! But you will surely be Hung's *mui tsai* if you go running about the camps with the horsewomen."

"Hung is looking for a pretty face, not a warrior," Rulan replied wearily. "With so many women in camp, why would he be attracted to me?"

"I am elder sister here," Wing repeated. "Duty is duty. Yours is to obey."

"When the Tai Tai talked about duty, I thought her cruel because my eyes were blinded by love. But now I see that my duty is to avenge my sisters. To do all this, I have to prove to myself that I can meet death face-to-face, as a warrior, not a spy. I want the chance to turn the world upside down, to rid it of leeches like Wang and Li, so that the meek might rule the strong."

"Death is not a game that girls play to while away a lazy afternoon," Wing answered her. "No one wants to die. The first man I slew begged for his life. I was standing ten paces from him with a bow. He threw the knife at me and missed. Then he started to cry. I shot him in the chest. I stood there gasping for breath, while his lungs filled up with blood."

"I'm not a stranger to death, Wing. People die in great houses just as they do in battle. How can I make you understand how important this is to me! I've been a spy too long. Let me be a warrior like you!"

Wing's voice was shrill with frustration. "If you show yourself, your father will take you from me. You'll be bartered like trash by the kings."

"Why, you're jealous!" Rulan said, astounded. "You're no better than Liang Mo or the viceroy. You would keep me a concubine forever."

Wing's face had turned bright red. "I tell you this," Wing said angrily. "If the Younger Son desires you, he will pick your soul apart like a carrion bird. Then no one, not even your father, for all his power, will be able to get you out of Hung's harem."

"Women have rights here. My sisters would never make me go to Hung against my will." Rulan paused and added uncertainly, "And my father is a king—"

"Hung is God-on-earth. The sisters would never go against his wishes," said Wing angrily. "And your father commands the army, not the peoples' hearts. How well did he protect you in the house of Li?"

Rulan refused to be shaken by Wing's jibe. "I don't need him. I can protect myself!" she declared. "I'm not the little girl you trained to take Tsai Yen's place. I'm not someone white and soft to keep by your campfire like a jewel to be cherished in secret. I know men's weaknesses when they pretend to pet your cheek or offer you gifts or when they open to a woman in love—oh!"

"Whore!" Wing sputtered.

"Maybe I am," Rulan said belligerently, "if being a whore means that I enjoy the caresses of men as much as I do yours. Maybe more! If that makes me too filthy to ride with you and your chaste horse-women, then you do not deserve to be called Golden Orchid because I became a whore for you."

Wing looked stricken.

"You don't trust me," Rulan accused her, furious. She grabbed Wing by the ends of her vest. "We are the last two sisters from Ma Tsu Po's hearth. If you and I don't keep faith—"

"Don't lie to me about keeping faith! I've watched you for weeks looking over the hill to the Men's Camp when the gong sounds for prayer. I've seen you run like a slop girl when the courier comes with news of the last assault at Chang Sha. You would deny me in a minute if that ox of a farmer bellowed your name."

"I'm leaving your fire!" Rulan raged, sick inside, because what Wing said was true. Her heart yearned for Pao An.

In the days following her argument with Wing, Rulan scrubbed pots, carried water, and washed menstrual rags. She fumed and cursed her ill luck. But she put aside her original intention to seek out her father. It was the memory of Pao An, not Wing's fears, that kept her from entering the Men's Camp. She pictured Pao An carrying a pike in some Taiping general's train, and told herself that she was better off without him. Why had she allowed herself to be stirred by a man stupid enough to love the vapid, treacherous Mei Yuk?

A few days later, when Rulan was drying clothes on the stones of the river with the other novices, Wing and her riders came back with a captured horse—a white stallion with a black mane and tail taken in a raid on a local landlord. Rulan nearly dropped the wet load in her hands at the sight of the horse. There was so much pride in the way it held its head in the noose, like a warrior who had chosen to sacrifice himself for some great cause.

"Devil-steed," Wing called the horse. She was convinced that the creature was a harbinger of death. "Look at the color!" she warned. "White, like a mourning robe."

But Rulan loved him. Secretly, she named him Cloud, for he thundered across the land like a gray-white nimbus full of angry foreboding. What she saw in the horse was what she desperately wanted. She wanted to be as free as he was to rampage at will. She wanted to ride on his back over the edge of the earth. She wanted to fling aside duty and tradition and to pour all her life's passion into a single transcendent race.

Wing put the horse in a pen with others, but he bit and kicked them and tried to mate with the unwilling mares. They built a pen just for him, and for the next week, Wing hand-fed him greens and grain—and was bitten three times for her trouble. At the beginning of the second week, she went into the corral to rope him, and he nearly trampled her. Three women threw ropes around his neck and held his head down while Wing mounted him. The horse bucked her off. She tied his legs and blindfolded him, and still he threw her. Then she beat him with a stick before limping angrily away.

That evening Rulan took wild carrots and tossed them over the fence to the horse, but he would not eat.

The next morning, the best rider in camp, the belligerent Miao woman, rode the horse for a minute before he bucked her off and came back to kick her in the ribs. When Rulan offered to treat her, she declined, more politely than Rulan believed possible. The woman, who had christened herself Heavenly Glory, no longer cursed and fought and spat: she had shed her reviled Miao past and was transformed into an inspired devotee of Hung.

"Tomorrow morning, when the cooks kill the ducks, butcher him too," declared Wing. "We're short of meat."

Rulan spent the night making poultices, which others carried in to Heavenly Glory, whose two lower ribs had been smashed by the angry hooves. When the camp was asleep, Rulan went quietly to the horse's pen, opened the gate, and walked away. The horse snorted softly and slowly cantered through the open gate. She watched him gallop toward the hills, his pale hide gleaming in the moonlight.

Wing was furious. She blamed the watch, who had fallen asleep at the fire, but she knew who had set the horse free. Rulan was sentenced to more scrubbing, more washing.

Rulan performed her onerous chores without complaint. She was well aware that the other women, jealous of her relationship to Wing, called her "Soft Meat" and "Punti whore." She knew too that they were watching to see if she could hold up to punishment.

Curiously, the madness she had experienced on the road and the harsh regimen at camp helped to cleanse her soul of guilt. She had walked far beyond the ghost-filled courts of the Lis. There were no more conflicting loyalties to muddle her. Anger flared with a clean, pure flame, revealing her purpose and her enemies clearly. She had come into the tents of the rebels to destroy the viceroy and those of his class, whom she blamed for the Orchids' massacre and the oppression of the people. She had decided to take Hung as her leader, madman or no, for only a madman could unite the desperate and downtrodden from all provinces into a mighty army. Only a being who conversed with heaven and spoke with tongues of fire could make men and women of common earth see visions and dream dreams.

She had no idea what to do about her father. He was close enough so that she could walk to him. But she still didn't know if she wanted to see him. He had made her a living sacrifice to his ambitions. And then he had abandoned her again.

Patience, Rulan told herself as she scrubbed the women's stockings and plucked the feathers off the skinny ducks the horsewomen brought back from their raids. Patience.

One afternoon while the exhausted novices were sleeping, she bartered with an older horsewoman for a small bow. The horsewoman had thought it an uneven trade: an ancient, scarred short bow, which looked more like a toy than a weapon, for several sessions of pain-relieving massage. But Rulan knew that the bow was a treasure, for it fit a woman's hand better than the long and ungainly Manchu bow that the horsewomen carried. Rulan wrapped the bow in dry moss and hid it from the others in her bedroll.

Now when Wing led the line of women riders to the hunt or on a raiding party, Rulan did not sit with the other novices to gossip or to memorize the versified edicts Hung sent daily into their camp. Instead, she practiced firing homemade arrows into a target on a grassy knoll where none could see.

Two days after she had let Cloud go, Rulan found horse tracks in a high meadow cut by a mountain stream. She was a thousand feet above the Hsiang River valley in which the besieged city of Chang Sha lay a few miles to the north. No horse soldiers passed, and there were no wild horses in this region. She was certain it was Cloud. Then she discovered the place where he slept, a small cave in an outcrop of rock. The spoor was still fresh at the edge of the water where he had stopped to drink.

With Wing's permission, Rulan chose twenty novices and taught them how to forage for plants and how to make needles out of broken crockery. She taught them all that Ailan and Physician Sung had taught her—except for healing with hands. She had lost pleasure in healing. Ma Tsu Po's malediction had burned the last vestige of tenderness from her soul.

Under Rulan's tutelage, the recruits combed the hills for plants and insects to dry for medicine. The land in Hunan was much richer than the parched fields of her native Kwangsi, and the pickings overflowed their baskets. The women brought back philodendron for lung ailments, cinnabar root for snakebite, dandelion for stomachache, and wild leeks for worms. Rulan showed them where to dig into the banks of small streams or into the trunks of rotted trees for centipedes, which could be dried and dropped into boiling water to cure scrofula. They caught crickets in the tall grass and baked them in the fire for the small-feet women whose golden lilies swelled up on the long march. On the grassy slopes beside the lakes, they found buttercup and honeysuckle, wild asters and violets, which they dried and preserved for fevers and infection.

When dandelions were plentiful, she made the women search out the young buds. These the novices kept for themselves. Fried in chicken fat with the bitter dandelion leaves, the buds tasted like meat, which the Taiping women seldom ate. Wild chrysanthemum they kept for making poultices for open wounds; occasionally, when the fighting was fierce, Yang sent for women archers on their small wild ponies to reinforce the men.

Late one afternoon, when Rulan was roaming the hills alone for a place to fire her bow in secret, a strange sound assaulted her ears. It came again. Unearthly, inhuman. A *kuei,* she thought. The Tai Tai.

The sound came again, one note, high and shrill, which broke apart without warning into breathless quavers like spirits sobbing. Rulan began to run.

The horse had raced into a high meadow in the saddle of a mountain where a stream became stagnant. He had slipped and fallen into the mud and was sunk up to his chest in the swamp. He was almost unrecognizable: mud had turned his pale coat the color of ink. He whinnied and thrashed, working himself deeper into the slime.

Throwing down her arrows and bow, she tried to run to him, but the muck gripped her ankles, and she was forced back on the hard ground. Looking around frantically for a rope, she saw a tree overhung with long tendrils. She pulled down a mass of vines, hastily stripped off the leaves, and wove four strands into a crude rope.

It took several tosses to get the rope over his head. He shook his neck weakly when the noose tightened, but it held fast. Then she dug her heels into the dirt and pulled, called him tender names, urged him on. Her arms felt as if they were being pulled from their sockets. Yet her voice seemed to convince the horse that she was helping him. He began to strain when she pulled, and relax when she paused. She brought pine boughs, which she stomped into a fragile foothold in the mire. She sweated and strained, as filthy as he, tasting dust and insects; still, she pulled.

Hours later, after a mighty tug, he lurched free! While he lay on his side on the ground, panting hard, she crawled over to him. Gently, she caressed the ridges above his red-rimmed eyes.

"You are mine," she told him.

She spent the next three days tending and feeding the horse. When he was clean again, she pulled herself on his back. On the third day she rode him into camp where Wing greeted her with weeping and prayers.

The next morning, she and Cloud rode in the train of the horsewomen.

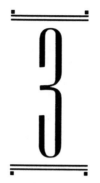

When Rulan mounted Cloud in the morning, he always did an arrogant little dance, like a warrior-prince strutting before the foe. On his back, she felt proud and purposeful, a scourge of the High God of the Taiping, overturning the old order of the ages, as a rider with a pole knocks over pottery in a market run by thieves. On Cloud she outran every other horse in the women's brigade. Although armed, the women's battalions did not directly engage the enemy, for Yang refused to put women on the front line of battle. Instead, they guarded the stragglers in the line of march against spies and snipers, and rode every day as messengers from one part of the immense sprawling chain of people to the other. Once riding in the rear guard, Rulan came to an overlook above the Hsiang River valley. Below her, the green plain curved toward the east a full seven miles, and as far as she could see, the valley surrounding Chang Sha was filled with the winding columns of God Worshipers—men on one side of the river, women on the other.

On scouting patrols, Rulan and Cloud invariably surged into the lead. Wing, who had command, would point her blue beribboned standard after the pale horse and its rider, and the red-jacketed warrior maidens would gallop after Rulan, a river of flame scorching the wet brown earth, flying their long hair like dark pennants. Tall and bronzed, Rulan appeared to the other horsewomen as the incarnation of the warrior maiden Fa Mulan risen out of the ashes of the Golden Orchids. Every one of them coveted Rulan's skill and grace.

Because of Hung's order of chastity among the holy soldiers, the two women could never be lovers, only comrades-in-arms. Besides, Rulan had changed toward Wing. At night, lying side by side, they whispered like an old couple reflecting on the enormous changes in their lives.

"Hung is growing strange," Wing said. "I saw him up close for the first time in months when I was standing with his sister Jiao at morning prayers. After insisting on putting his feet exactly where the sun fell, he began to whisper nonsense: 'You moons are moons forever. My sun shall warm you. In my light you shall glow eternally.' Jiao was bowing, bending, swooning as he spoke. His other women too. That little Miao girl who calls herself Heavenly Glory was dizzy with love. Am I the odd one? The women look at this man and see heaven. I see someone limp, white, soft like the pastries they make in rich houses."

"Don't underestimate him," Rulan demurred. "My mother predicted that he would bring death and fire to this Land of Flowers."

"You talk like Heavenly Glory."

"I do not love him," Rulan replied slowly. "But I admire him for the power that he wields over the people. If I could, I would help him turn this whole land upside down."

"You'll perish trying to tame him," Wing warned.

"My mother tamed the Younger Son. She tamed my father too. I wonder what she would say if she saw them together, these two angry men. Yet when I think of what they could do, I burn too! Women walking freely in the world, even taking examinations. Peasants owning the land on which they were born!"

"I did not know that your mother preached of a woman's revolution!" said Wing wryly.

"She did not. She believed in things so old that their time comes round again. She said that long ago women shared authority with men, and everyone worshiped a First Mother."

"Don't let Hung or your father hear that!"

"How Ailan of the Loi would laugh if she heard that her renegade husband, who scorned all gods and demons, now speaks for God the Father." Rulan's voice was small and wistful. "He was always ready with his fists, not his tongue. In our village they called him Lead Donkey after the loudest mule at the head of the charcoal wagons. How Mother would laugh to behold the proud Eastern King."

"Hush," Wing said, pointing to the other women curled up in their bed pallets around the fire. "Hung's spies are everywhere—"

"Why do you fear Hung? What does it matter if I am revealed as Yang's daughter?" Rulan rose on one elbow. "I do not think he is evil. He unleashes the people the way a typhoon unleashes the wind. If such a being destroys anything, it will be the old and corrupt. No one is safe, not the poor man who hides in a hovel nor the powerful who hide behind high gates. Everyone is caught in the wind from heaven. I am part of the wind. So are you! Wing," she whispered with a catch in her throat, "I want to ride that wind. I want to sweep the country-side clean, burn out the old, build everything new." She reached out in the darkness and grasped Wing's hand.

"You kept your vow, but were you tempted to give away your heart?" came the thread of a whisper.

"I could have, but he didn't want me," replied Rulan softly.

Wing's fingers gripped Rulan's so tightly that Rulan's eyes smarted from the pain. "I don't care," came her fierce reply. More wistfully, she asked, "What is he called?"

"Pao An. His father chose the name from a story about a faithful friend."

"I am your faithful friend," Wing said.

"And we will ride the heavenly wind to freedom," replied Rulan.

Wing was one of twenty-five captains who reported directly to Hung's sister, Jiao, at her camp just outside the walls of Chang Sha. Since Yang directed the Taiping's movements and personally commanded the cen-tral army which guarded Hung, all messages passed through him. Lacking access to the immense spy system Yang had organized among the men's troops, Hung had come to count on the women's corps for information and for carrying his poems and memorials on swift horses to the Triad spies in the villages for dissemination throughout the empire. He showered the women with lofty titles—conveyer of heav-enly decrees and heavenly annunciators—and led them in ecstatic prayer.

Women had always preferred Hung to the crude, ungainly Yang, for Hung was a man of eloquence, charm, and beauty according to many. He was broad shouldered and well formed and especially vain about his hair, which had red highlights. The women claimed it glowed in the sun like flame. He wore his hair as long as a lion's mane and grew his beard down to his chest.

Because the daughters of Wei, the Northern King, and the now dead kings Feng and Hsiao, were leaders in the women's troops, Hung set them apart in a newly formed elite corps charged with guarding his own person and his growing number of wives. He dressed them in yellow, the emperor's color, which he had usurped as his own. Because they were free to move about in both Women's and Men's Camps, this corps was invaluable to him as spies.

Wing's heart froze the day Jaio asked each of her captains to send the best of their warriors to fill up the remaining places in Hung's personal guard. Wing sent the youngest and prettiest of the horsewomen, hoping he would be satisfied.

On patrol, Wing's women riders were constantly vigilant against ambush as they scouted the green hills above the huge encirclement of Taiping foot soldiers in the valley below. Tension throughout the Taiping armies was high because nothing they did seemed to break the walls or the will of Chang Sha's defenders.

One day, as the horsewomen rode far inland to patrol the southern flank, they stopped on a rocky ridge cut by a small stream to rest and water their horses. Below was an old trade route. The maidens sipped from a canal with cupped hands, some wetting their red head rags and opening their tunics to wipe off the sweat and grime. Rulan shook the dust from her hair and waited for the others to finish before drinking her fill. Wing slipped up silently behind her and wrapped her arm around Rulan's waist; they leaned against each other, exhausted but content. They had ridden over twenty miles since midmorning to guard the women's column against the Manchu imps rumored to be in the area.

Rulan's practiced eye was measuring the injury of a horse who had just gone lame, when a bright flash of metal behind the grove caught her attention. She squinted hard and saw in the distance a column of men pulling a line of tarpaulin-covered carts. Two hundred heavily armed soldiers walked alongside the convoy.

Wing's eyes had found them too.

"Can they see us?" asked Rulan.

Wing shook her head. Her nostrils flared, her dark eyes danced. "Look closely. When the men stumble, the soldiers prod them with lances. That means they are farmers forced to cart rice to the imps' camp."

Rulan hesitated and pointed suddenly. "A rice train would not be so heavily guarded. They carry something more precious. Something to make the guards curse and look over their shoulders in fear."

"Ammunition," declared Wing. "Gunpowder. Ten carts. Enough for the brothers to mine the walls of Chang Sha!"

At Wing's low whistle, the heads of the women and horses came up instantly. She signaled with her arm, and the riders led the horses behind a stand of trees.

"What should we do?" Rulan asked.

"Send a rider to Shih Ta Kai, who commands the southern flank. Tell him where the train is headed. There are too many for us to attack. We'll have to let this one go."

"But we need the powder! Listen, Wing. I think I know how we could capture it," Rulan told her.

"I don't want to hear it."

Heavenly Glory hovered excitedly by their side.

"That road will take them down to the place we passed a half hour ago," Rulan said. "Remember the earth slide grown over with grass? The road below is wet there. They should be climbing uphill at that point. If we wait for them at the top of the slide, we could surprise them. The farmers will be tired from the climb. They won't stay to fight."

"But the soldiers have guns. We have nothing except bows—and not enough of those."

"If we shot fire-arrows into those wagons—"

Wing cried out in alarm. "It is too dangerous!"

"I'm not afraid," Heavenly Glory interrupted eagerly. "I welcome an honorable death." The Miao girl prayed morning and night and was always in the first row when Hung came to lead them in worship.

Rulan ignored the girl. "If we leave now, we can be there an hour before them."

"Impossible!" Wing retorted.

"They may have guns, but we will have the advantage of surprise."

"How?"

"We'll take the high ground and station our warriors above the slide where the rocks and boulders are still loose. We'll start another land-slide and block their way."

"So they turn and swat us like flies!"

"They are carrying powder," Rulan persisted. "We will carry flame. Do you think farmers or even conscripted soldiers will stay and defend burning powder wagons? If we can hit one wagon with fire-arrows, they will abandon the rest."

"If you can get to them before they explode."

"We can do it!" Heavenly Glory exulted. Her eyes were glowing in anticipation of battle.

Wing dismissed Heavenly Glory to be alone with Rulan. "Why do you want to die?" Wing asked at last.

"I have never felt so alive as now. On my horse, I am invincible!"

"You are not," said Wing.

"It will be over in minutes. The farmers will run at the first volley. We'll use up all our arrows to make the soldiers think there is a battalion on the hill above them. Please, Wing, we cannot let them have that ammunition."

Wing was an able captain. She knew their needs. There was a chance of success, although a slim one. Against her will, she nodded. "But at the first sign of trouble, I call a retreat. I will not lose you again."

Rulan ran to Cloud, signaling the others with her hands. The women swung up, each pressing her hand into the neck of her pony to ensure silence. Cautiously, Wing led the troop out of the grove. Good-luck crickets were singing in the tall grass as the horses' hooves trod on the soft earth.

They had almost two hours to prepare before the convoy came into view. The women pried loose the pile of rock, started several small coal fires in which their arrows, tied with rags, were left to smolder, and set up a hiding place in the brush at the top of the ridge. Eventually, they heard the soldiers cursing and the farmers groaning and the wagons creaking uphill through the mud. When the train was beneath them, Wing gave a yell, high and shrill, like the cry of a wild crane swooping out of the sky. The echo of twenty-five voices melted into a single savage chorus. The wooden braces that held the large boulders were released. Slowly the top stones tipped, rolled, crashed into other stones, until a wave of dirt and rock cascaded downhill. The screams began even before the slide hit; the forward carts and their guards were buried under a pile of rubble. Then the road was blocked and all movement ground to a halt.

While confusion reigned below, the women let fly the flame-tipped arrows. The farmers screamed, dropped the ropes, and ran madly for the woods. Cursing the fleeing peasants, the soldiers unslung their guns and were peppering the ridge of the hill at the unseen enemy in the brush above. It was clear that firearms were new to them, for there was much shouting amid the *pop-pop-pop* of aimless fire. Soldiers in the rear wagons had taken up the ropes and were desperately trying to turn the wagons around.

"Block the retreat. Aim for the last two wagons!" Wing shouted.

A stream of blazing arrows arched across the sky. All fell short, for the last wagons were out of range.

Heavenly Glory ran along the top of the ridge firing arrows down on the heads of the soldiers. A few arrows stuck in the wagons, but the soldiers broke them off or beat out the flames. The women cast down torches too, but these bounced on the rocks far short of the tarpaulin-covered wagons.

"They're getting away!" an agonized Rulan shouted. Deaf to Wing's angry protests, she snatched up four burning brands from the fire and raced to where Cloud was tied. The horse reared up at the sight of the burning sticks, but she calmed him with soothing noises and leaped on his back.

"Stop her!" Wing cried.

Rulan burst out of cover into the open, sliding down the hill ahead of the train, praying that the soldiers' attention was concentrated on the last wagons. She knew the danger: she would have to rely on luck and speed to get past the line of imps huddled behind the wagons and boulders. If she could throw her torches into the wagons at the rear, there would be no escape for the train. The gunpowder would be theirs.

She was on the road when the first soldier saw her.

"That one, that one!" he cried.

Cloud spurted ahead behind the first wagon of the train, which was covered in dirt and rock up to its axles. He leapt to avoid the crumbling slopes, while Rulan crouched over his neck, the burning brands held high. Now all the soldiers had seen her. Bullets ricocheted off the fallen rock scant feet from Cloud's trembling flanks.

She swept past the second and third wagons. Cloud charged ahead and ran right over the head of a soldier hiding behind the fourth wagon.

The leader whooped, "A long-hair woman. They have no men. And no guns! Take her!" He was bleeding from an arrow that had stuck in the top of his boot and laughing like a madman.

Two men sprang out to grab Cloud's reins. Rulan smashed one in the face with the torches, and he fell back, holding his eyes and screaming. But the other man held tight. He avoided Cloud's gnashing teeth and grabbed Rulan's trousers to pull her down. Suddenly, out of nowhere, Heavenly Glory was behind him with a long knife.

"For the Younger Son!" she shouted, panting from her race downhill, and thrust once, twice, with the blade. In moments Rulan passed the sixth and seventh wagons.

The last carts had been turned around, and the soldiers were pulling them frantically downhill. The wagons began to pick up speed. Rulan raced past two more wagons just as the last wagon hurtled out of reach. She turned her attention to the tenth wagon, which was tottering on a rickety wheel. There were four soldiers pulling it, but only one had a gun. He dropped the line and took aim. Swiftly, Rulan pulled Cloud to the right just as a bullet whizzed past her head. The wagon was jammed with kegs of black powder and boxes of ammunition, enough to arm an entire Taiping battalion. Just as the soldier raised his gun again, she threw the torches on the floor of the wagon where powder had spilled from a cracked keg and dug her heels into Cloud's flanks.

The man screamed and dropped his gun. Soldiers scattered in all directions. Ten seconds later, the first barrel exploded. Burning sticks and fiery debris rained down on Rulan and Cloud as they galloped through the underbrush. Some of the flaming ash landed in her hair, and Rulan had to beat out the sparks with her hands as she rode. A second explosion went off. A little more, a little more, she whispered in Cloud's ear, fixing her eye on a rock shelf scant yards beyond. Just as she rounded the outcrop of stone, a third explosion, greater than the other two, roared through the valley on a rush of wind.

Rulan shouted with joy as she felt the old world shudder and split open. Then she spurred Cloud on, faster and faster up the hill toward her comrades.

The horsewomen counted up the spoils: they had captured five wagons of gunpowder, rifles, and ammunition, and destroyed five others. Three sisters had been killed; another six, Heavenly Glory among them, were wounded. The Miao girl had been struck by a piece of splintered wood when the wagons exploded, which left a gash four inches long from her left eye to her chin and punctured her cheek clear through.

Twenty-five women had vanquished two hundred seasoned imperial soldiers. Now the women tied the bodies of the captain and his lieutenant to their own mounts and dragged the men in the dust as proof of their victory, while their beloved dead lay over the horses like fallen heroes.

Jiao, the general of the women's army, came herself to commend Wing's warriors. She announced that she would send a letter that very day to her brother Hung, extolling their bravery.

Jiao could not help but notice the tall, golden-skinned Hakka girl, who had turned the tide of battle in the sisters' favor. She was struck by the girl's proud bearing and requested her for Hung's elite corps. Wing told Jiao that the Hakka girl, whose camp name was White Horse Woman, was a troublemaker. The real hero, Wing declared, was the Miao girl named Heavenly Glory, who, despite her wounds, glowed like a bride under Jiao's scrutiny.

Jiao was annoyed by Wing's reluctance to give up the Hakka girl.

She asked Wing pointedly at morning worship to name White Horse Woman to Hung's elite guard.

Again, Wing demurred. She complained that her troops had already lost three women in battle and could not stand to lose another. Besides, she insisted, the girl was unseasoned in her belief, and not as pure of heart as Heavenly Glory.

But that excuse was absurd, Jiao argued, for wouldn't any believer grow stronger from sitting at the foot of the Younger Son and caring for his holy person? And wouldn't any woman welcome Hung's praise and attention—and his holy seed in her womb?

Wing procrastinated, avoided Jiao, missed morning worship. Finally, responding to a written command to send another warrior from her troop, she sent Heavenly Glory, who departed singing hymns, her wounded face radiant with joy.

Wing's reluctance to release White Horse Woman piqued Jiao's curiosity. Was the girl a relative that Wing was protecting—or a lover? If so, both would have to be reported. The penalty set by Hung for such transgressions was death.

And where, Jiao asked herself, had she seen such bold, black eyes before?

Border of Hupeh Province, Winter 1852

"What are you reading?" Yang demanded. His horse stood perfectly still in the bright shimmering cold, its sides moving like a bellows, its nose puffing steam.

He and Mandley had dismounted for a moment to rest among a grove of spindly orange trees. The sun fell futilely through its branches stripped bare by winter and the masses that had preceded them. Even the leaves had gone to make poultices for gangrenous feet or to flavor rancid meat.

Mandley had taken a worn leather journal out of his saddlebags and was squinting at the crabbed writing.

"I'm reading about you," Mandley said. "How you broke the siege at Yung An and put Li to flight. Then how you drove us like cattle through Kwangsi Province to besiege Kuei Lin."

"I'm a bastard ass and cattle driver, all right. But I lost Kuei Lin, even after blasting those damn walls for a month." Yang frowned in an effort to hide the fact that Mandley's gruff praise pleased him. They were battle comrades now, and Yang was delighted to see how tough and hard his barbarian adviser had grown during the months on the open road. Now Mandley sat as easily in the saddle as any other Taiping warrior. Except for his bright blue eyes peering out under the broad brim of his hat, he might have passed for a grizzled Han patriarch from the countryside.

"So what do your chicken tracks say?"

"I'm making notes of our march," Mandley answered. "You'll want a record someday."

"Only if I win. If I lose, somebody else will write the words down. Besides, I don't read. And even a civilized man couldn't make sense of that scratching you barbarians do, so what good will your work be?" He tried to pretend nonchalance, but for all his bluff manner, Yang was intrigued to think of himself as a man worthy to be put into a book. "Go ahead, read some," Yang said airily.

Mandley scowled over his notations. Ever since his arrival at Thistle Mountain, he had kept a lengthy weekly summary as well as smaller entries for each day. He flipped back some pages and read now from the longer account.

"In the year of our Lord, 1851, the followers of Hung Hsiu Chuan encamped at Chin Tien and marched back and forth to Tung Hsiang and the village of Mo."

"That's the old-fashioned way," Yang corrected him. "You mean the first year of the Taiping rule, according to the new calendar the Council of Kings agreed on in Yung An."

Mandley nodded, humoring him. "Yes, yes, I can change that later," he said and began reading again. "From Chin Tien, where they declared a new dynasty, they moved west to Wu Hsuan, north to Hsiang Chou, and then to Hsin Hsu, which they put to the torch. They moved east again to Kuan Tsun where they scored a great victory, then to Teng Hsien and from there to the city of Yung An, which they captured—"

Yang was shaking his head. "Put down that the cowards opened the gates for us! Put down that the damned mandarins paid us in silver for the privilege of converting to our cause—"

Mandley waved Yang impatiently aside. "Let me finish. At Yung An, they tarried from September to April of 1852, besieged by the emperor's soldiers. It was there that the people ran out of food and powder. But because the Heavenly Father had charged their hearts, they broke through the siege and gained a great victory, though their rear guard sustained grievous losses—" He looked up to see Yang laughing quietly to himself.

"No offense, my friend, but there's so little color or poetry in your language! That's why you long-noses will never become civilized. Everything is numbers and dry sticks in your language. Now a civilized man first of all so paints his characters that there is beauty and balance in what you see on the page. Then he doesn't throw dust and ashes all over a victory like Yung An." Yang closed his eyes tightly, thinking hard. "A civilized man would write, 'The great and mighty Eastern King plunged his iron columns through the soft noodle guts of the demon imps.' Such civilized words as that! And mind you I'm not a poet like Su Tung Po, but I make an educated barbarian like yourself taste like donkey's piss compared to plum wine!"

Mandley laughed and made a few energetic scratches with his pen. "How's this then? They encamped for one month among the green mountains outside Kuei Lin, the major city of northern Kwangsi. But so evil were the demon-inspired inhabitants that the virtuous blades of the Taiping could not pierce their walls. Enemies lay on every side: evil landlords, magistrates, fearful merchants, even brother peasants who did not understand the great mission on which they were embarked. So the mighty Eastern King, shining like the sun at noon, turned away from the large cities and the tall mountains rising out of the river like jade hairpins and journeyed instead into the hilly regions along the border."

Yang glowered. "How come you waste this elegant poetry on my defeats? You shame me to future generations! Get on to something I won."

"Wait, wait!" Mandley's pen assiduously tracked across the rough paper. "Ah, here then. The subtle Eastern King next captured the town of Chuan Chou. It was there that the Taiping warriors sustained a grievous blow. Scholar Feng, Southern King and the dearest comrade-in-arms of Hung, was hit by a cannonball and died from the wound."

"May God the Father bless the eye that sighted and the hand that touched the fuse of that cannon. He saved me from another draft of poison one day!"

"Hung so mourned the sacrifice of his friend that his family and comrades feared for his health. So painful was the loss of the Southern King that Hung demanded the Council of Kings suspend its authority until he could nominate another leader."

Yang slapped his knee with delight. "He tried. He tried to elevate Wei, King of the Northern Pigs, to offset my power. But I won that round. Wei will never be anything but a whipping boy for Triad scum like the fat bastard Wang in Canton, may the High God strangle his ghost."

"I still don't believe that Merchant Wang could be headman of the southern Triads. He was friends with barb—the British and American traders in Hong Kong," Mandley added.

"Salt, black dirt, prostitution, magic potions and spells, and guns— all the things that the Triads sell, Wang provided. Every fool that joined the brotherhood to overthrow the Manchu became a laborer in his store. Pawnbroker Wei was a friend of long standing, Wang's major conduit of dirt east of Canton."

"Wei would never deal in opium! He would lose his head!" Mandley objected. The one thing Mandley admired Hung for was his harsh stand against opium smoking.

"Who knows what the Northern King did before he became a true believer? Even I, as righteous as I am now, was a profligate smoker and seller of dirt in years gone by. But after he became a king, our brother Wei kept up his lucrative alliance with Wang. He turned from procuring dirt to procuring potions, magic, stones, and elixirs of longevity."

"Abominable!" Mandley declared, grimacing at the allegation. He found Wei's connection to pagan witchcraft more repugnant than any suspected connection to dirt. "This proves once again the folly of men who seek immortality in this world and reject the saving blood of Christ Jesus for the eternal life to come. Hung will have to know of Wei's treachery!"

"Ah, my barbarian friend, don't talk too loudly, for the Younger Son of God himself claims his flesh is immortal, although he must have doubts because his hair is falling out in back. It was for him that brother Wei traded in charms and powders with the worm-eaten Wang."

Mandley suppressed an oath under his breath. Just when he thought he knew these people, something they said or did shocked him utterly. Even Yang, for all his courage and protestations of faith—

"As you say, it is an abomination," Yang said soothingly. "Go on with your book about me," he urged.

Mandley tried to collect his thoughts. Only half-listening to his own words, he began to read again. "Hung, in grief over Scholar Feng's death, took to his sickbed while a dispute arose in the council. Finally a new oath of fealty was sworn among the remaining kings and the Taiping journeyed through the wilderness of Kwangsi where they encountered stubborn resistance from the gentry. Many of the original inner circle of Hakka hillmen were slain, and the Taiping were compelled to abandon the water route along the Hsiang River for the mountain trail along the Hunan border."

Yang scratched his hairy chin thoughtfully. "Best thing that ever happened. While Hung was crying like an old lady in his pallet that this was the beginning of the end, I realized that staying away from the cities on the river and marching through the hill country would bring the peasants to our side. Isn't that where poverty is greatest? Isn't that where there have been a hundred uprisings in the last decade?" His excitement rekindled by the force of memory, Yang began to shake his head in glee. "Put that in your account. Don't write, 'They went here, they went there.' Write, 'The Eastern King knew what he was doing!' " Yang declared.

Mandley ignored Yang's outburst and droned on in his most pedestrian manner. "They turned north to the provincial capital of Chang Sha. For two months, the Taiping hammered at the gates of the city, but it was God's will that the city be spared, and so the rebels moved on."

"Aaiiee! I swear you are a devil of a writer! No matter what I do, it sounds like I'm fleeing from battle. I will surely make you my official historian when I come to power. That way the fall of our dynasty will be recorded in advance, and scholars won't have to waste any time thinking about it years later."

Mandley read on. "Beyond Chang Sha, over the plains and lakes of Hunan, the great rivers joined the Yangtze in Lake Tung Ting. From thence, flowing northeast the Yangtze became a mighty thoroughfare through the heartland of the nation."

"Don't tell me about Chang Sha! I lost my comrade Hsiao there. I got dysentery there!"

Mandley read on to provoke him more. "Chang Sha lay on the right bank of the Hsiang River, surrounded by endless rice fields and mountains rich in cinnabar and soapstone. For two months, the Taiping armies had battered the high rectangular walls of the city with cannon. The charcoal-carriers, with the help of local coal miners who were experts at digging tunnels, mined the nine gates with explosives—to no avail. Chang Sha was the second city in Hunan to repel the invaders. Yang sent spies into the city who reported that the scholar Tseng Kuo Fan had fortified the city and trained its guards so well that the city dwellers were prepared to hold out for months."

"I was right to pull out," said Yang, suddenly serious. "After Hsiao's death, we couldn't stand to lose more leaders. Mark my words. This Scholar Tseng is more dangerous than Viceroy Li because Tseng is an old-fashioned man, the kind that believes the emperor can do no wrong. That kind can't be bribed or bullied. Li, on the other hand, doesn't care who he fights or what he fights for, as long as he wins. Besides, with the Triads rioting in Canton, Li is going to be occupied for a long time. May the High God destroy him with a thousand cuts and preserve my daughter."

Mandley closed his book and glared at Yang. They had quarreled repeatedly over Rulan. "Shouldn't you take her out of Li's house and bring her with you now?"

"She's safer with Li," Yang insisted, his wide mouth set in a stubborn line. "Here she makes me vulnerable to Hung. I'd rather fight on one front. Scholar Tseng will be opponent enough. Worse for us when the emperor wakes up out of his opium dream one day, as he must, and sets that straitlaced Hunanese on our tail." He rose and dusted off his clothes. "Aiya, it's time for us to 'flee' again, Man-da-li. Write this down in your little book. 'The Eastern King paused for a winter orange in the shade of an orangeless tree and seeing his shadow tremble, decided to abandon the siege of the unfortunate tree to search for an easier fruit to pluck.' "

"In western writing, that would be called a mixed metaphor," Mandley declared, annoyed at Yang's maddening habit of veering away from an uncomfortable subject.

"In the Land of Flowers," Yang roared, "that is not called poetry at all. Just a charcoal-carrier's ravings." He remounted, spurred his horse, and raced across the cold, dry fields, followed by a pensive Mandley.

In the valley were three hundred thousand men, women, and children marching in two columns.

That night when they had made camp, Yang invited Mandley to share his evening rice. The other kings dined like mandarins on the march, but Yang ate the same food as his men: rice and soup from the common pot, now and than a slice from a tough rooster commandeered from a passing farmhouse. Sausages, buns, and rich sauces, he would say, turned hard in the stomach the next day in the saddle. And he refused to be carried in a litter, as Hung was. "A horse can dodge a cannonball better than a slow-moving palanquin," he said, referring to the way Scholar Feng had met his death.

After dinner, he and Mandley sat down on the hard ground to smoke Yang's pleasant-smelling tobacco and to read the Bible, which had become Yang's book of war.

"Read me that part where Joshua is at the Jordan River," Yang said.

Mandley carefully translated the words into Chinese while Yang listened raptly, nodding after each verse.

When the recital was over, Yang grew pensive. "You know the easiest way to pass over a river dry-shod like those exiles following Moses? Float downriver! Outrun the armies that the emperor is sending north to stop us."

Mandley shook his head at the impossibility of the task. "We'd have to build the boats first."

"The High God will provide us with good boats. I just have to figure out a way to steal them."

Mandley started. "What do you mean 'steal'?"

Yang grinned. "My spies tell me that there is a fleet of boats, five thousand of them, tied up in Yo Chou on the north bank of Lake Tung Ting."

"But Yo Chou is a Manchu garrison. It controls access to the lower Yangtze. It's the door to Hupeh Province and all that lies downriver. The Manchu will defend it to the last man!" Mandley declared. "It will be twice as hard to take as Chang Sha."

Yang smiled. "There you go with Chang Sha again. Write this down in your book. 'The wise and swiftly moving Eastern King prophesied, saying, "The High God is beneficent," and Yang caught himself a net full of Lake Tung Ting shrimp.' " He took a long drag on his pipe and watched the excitement rise in the face of his friend.

Avidly Mandley flipped eagerly from Exodus to the Book of Revelation. " 'Jerusalem shall be a city without walls, because of the multitude of men and cattle within it. For I, saith the Lord, will be a wall of fire around her and I will be the glory in her midst.' " Then he put into words the suspicion he had been harboring for weeks. "You have found a Jerusalem for us!"

"Yes, yes," Yang admitted, happy that Mandley had known all along that this prophet would not let his people wander as long in the wilderness as Moses had. He told Mandley that the Han had a place akin to the Heavenly Jerusalem called the Blessed Isle, which lay in a great gulf into which poured the torrents of spring floods. There were palaces of gold with pillars of white jade, birds with white feathers roosting in trees laden with the fruit of immortality.

This time Mandley did not turn to the Book to ask his question. "Where is it?"

Yang emptied the cold ashes from his pipe and used the long end of it to draw a map in the dirt, gouging out rivers, mountains, and walled cities with quick jabs. Then he stabbed the stem deep into the ground, where a thin trail meant to be the Hsiang River fed into the wider dirt trough of the Yangtze. "Nanking, the ancient capital of the southern dynasty, the heart of the 'water country.' A place of altars. This is where the Ming emperors are buried. This is where we Taiping will bury the Manchu. If we catch our little shrimp in Lake Tung Ting, we will tame the Yangtze and ride to Nanking on its waters. We will make our enemy, the river, a servant. From it, we will command the inland waterways and can carry the fire of heaven north, south, and west across the Land of Flowers."

Mandley sucked in his breath, seeing the brilliance of Yang's plan—a rebel capital, the heart of a new China, built on the ruins of the ancient one, the old city of heroes, from which to found a new dynasty of God's chosen—a true Han city to rival Peking, the barbarian Tartar capital.

The Men's Camp

P ao An had expected to be challenged at the entrance to the Men's Camp, but there was no security at all. With so many recruits arriving daily, there was no practical way to sort out spies. Nor did the Taiping seem to care, for they expected spies to come and be converted. From all over the Land of Flowers, people came flowing to them like thousands of small streams into a mighty river. The Taiping accepted them all.

The day he had left Rulan was the loneliest of his life. He no longer yearned for Mei Yuk; the girl had proven as false as her grandfather, a figment of his foolish dreams. Only Rulan was real. He had her to thank for helping him take the final step into rebellion. Because of her, he knew what he wanted—not riches, not even revenge for injury. He wanted to build a new world.

What shocked Pao An most about the rebels was their hair. The Land of Flowers was, by order of the Manchu, a nation of bald pates and smoothly shaven faces, with wagging queues at the back of the head to honor the horse, the animal revered by the Manchu. But everywhere Pao An turned in the Men's Camp, he saw mustaches, curling beards, and dark locks tumbling over sunburned foreheads. Most men wore their hair in a thick braid which they tied around their heads. Wound over the braid was a red bandanna secured by a fantastic knot over the left ear. Some of the younger men eschewed the turban for a long red cord, which they braided into their pigtail. When the cord was wrapped around the head, the red tassel hung down over the ear like a tiny flag.

And the colors of their clothes! Not the dark monochrome of the lower classes, but all the gaudy, proud hues of a pheasant cock. Over a red jacket and black pants, the men wore vests of blue or green, white or violet. Once he saw a man in a bright yellow vest with a yellow cap descending from a gold palanquin and discovered that the rider was a Taiping king. Despite the odd raiment, Pao An found the rebels excitingly familiar, for underneath their brilliant dress and shaggy hair, the Taiping were like himself—without land or family, yet brash and proud and full of hope.

Again, he found himself joined with the Triads, for whole bands of them had taken up with the Taiping. After the Canton salt riots and the deaths of such Triad leaders as Wang, many of the Tanka pirates and the Triad captains suddenly found the delta area too dangerous. Viceroy Li had embarked on a campaign to burn the Triads out of the province, and so the most venturesome of the brotherhood headed north to join the Taiping. Pao An remembered that the Triads had twice brought him close to ruin. Once when Iron Fist had nearly throttled him, and again when Wang had made him an unwitting pawn in his game with Li. If he found Mau or One-Clean-Sweep or Iron Fist, would he be able to put aside his anger and hatred, and call them brother?

When Pao An came into the Men's Camp, he was herded with a hundred other weary men to the recruitment station. An officer wearing a white vest was seated at a table in the open air, talking to a young farmer and his family.

The farmer had the air of a dog who had been beaten. He looked over his shoulder as he talked, like a criminal waiting for the ax. When asked why he had come, he pointed to his flat belly, adding nervously that his village had been burned by the imps to prevent the rebels from gathering food as they marched.

The sergeant spat. "You have arms and legs. Why didn't you fight back?"

The man exchanged startled looks with his wife.

"Who is this one?" barked the sergeant, pointing rudely at the woman.

Pao An decided that the soldier was not really angry, just a sergeant who enjoyed his office.

"My foolish woman and her two lazy sons," the man mumbled.

"Good, good. She'll do well in the women's column. You'll stay here with me."

"Oh, oh," the man said, afraid to disagree.

Weeping, the wife pulled the boys close as if trying to hide them in her rags.

"Don't worry," the soldier said gruffly. "They'll be fed."

"But we have been together since we were children. She is so small, she cannot get along without me."

"You are brother and sister now," the recruitment officer retorted. "An army on the move cannot stop every other day for a woman to drop a child. And after plowing his woman all night, what soldier can jump up at the morning gong and do exercises? Put husband and wife together and it undermines all discipline and devotion. When the demon imps come pouring in on us, are you going to charge them at my order or run to look for your sons? Each father is going to defend his own, *hai ma?*"

"Yes," the man admitted, trying not to see his young wife's desolation.

"So we got to split you up," the sergeant continued. "The boys go to the Children's Brigade, the sister to the Women's Camp. They have their own set of leaders and officers, a bunch of old aunties to yell at them and keep them in line—nothing worse than a mother-in-law. Everybody works more that way. So we are not going to have any rebellion in the ranks, *hai ma?* No sneaking off to meet your sister at night!"

The man nodded, hollow eyed, as his wife and sons were taken away.

"Forget her, Brother. When we reach the Holy City, every man will have a hundred wives—"

But the young farmer did not seem to hear.

Because of Pao An's size, he was sent to a unit that fought with long wooden pikes topped with a sharp iron blade. Within a week, Pao An was made sergeant of his own squad of twenty-five men.

Because the only requirement for leadership was strength, Pao An qualified. All that the Taiping asked in return for food and weapons was that each new warrior pledge allegiance to the Taiping creed. This posed no problem of conscience for men and women like Pao An who came with empty bellies. He was given three weeks to learn the tenets: the Lord's Prayer, and the "Ten Heavenly Rules," which set aside a holy day called the Sabbath and exhorted the warriors to be filial to their kings, to avoid murder, adultery, and all related evils such as evil thoughts, evil glances, evil songs, and evil deeds such as smoking dirt.

Everyone worked, because the Taiping was a nation on the move.

The military units were organized by trades: miners became sappers who made bombs and tunneled under city walls. Tinsmiths made weapons. Boatmen became transport specialists. Triad leaders who had worked as pawnbrokers in the cities became captains of spies. Scholars became scribes and information officers, turning out hundreds of announcements and translations of the Holy Book for the Taiping printing presses in a war of words aimed at the uncommitted villages and cities that lay in their path. The announcements ranged from hymns and prayers and lyric praising Hung's first ascent to heaven, to promises of earthly and heavenly reward, to threats of extinction if the invitation of conversion was ignored.

All was change, for thousands were arriving every day. By his sixth week, Pao An felt like a veteran. In the unsuccessful siege of Chang Sha, he had been wounded twice. Once while in the rear guard that fought off the imps, who had pursued the Taiping when they retreated. That engagement had nearly cost him his life when a musket ball grazed his neck. Afterward, he was made a captain, the head of 625 pikemen, in the central army of Yang, the Eastern King.

These events happened so quickly that he had little time to inquire about Rulan. When he tried, his questions were turned away with the same curt response: "Forget about women until the Kingdom of Great Peace is won."

Still, he worried constantly about Rulan, for she had been near exhaustion at the time of their parting. How he missed her. There was no one in the world except Li Yu with whom he had talked so intimately. Even if she had been mute at the time, he was certain that she understood his heart. He knew now the depth of his passion for Rulan, for it was not at all like what he had felt for Mei Yuk. The fox-spirit had made him sick with self-hatred and longing. With Rulan he felt deep contentment, a conviction that he belonged. Pao An laughed ruefully at his predicament. Even if Rulan lived and declared her love, the Taiping would have separated them. One way or another, he seemed destined to be alone.

Pao An's commander was Eng, a tough, toothless Hakka hillsman who had served with Yang at Thistle Mountain. Eng had lost some teeth when an arrow had hit him in the mouth, splitting his upper lip like a hare's. Over the years of fighting, Eng's face had become a grotesque mask of scars and burned flesh, and he joked that only a blind woman would be willing to have him. But the sappers and pikemen so revered him that any derisive word by warriors serving another king was deemed just cause for a fight, despite the death sentence for brawling. Although he was bandy-legged, foul mouthed, and less than five feet tall, Eng was as fearless as a tiger. In every battle for a key city, it was Eng who showed the miners where to dig long tunnels under the very feet of the imperial troops. It was Eng who led the select platoon of "tunnel rats" to plant explosives under the wall—a black flag mission, one that required the men to fight to the death, for they had to crawl with live charges through tunnels barely wide enough for a child to stand upright. If the charges exploded prematurely, not only would the squad be blown to bits, but the enemy would be alerted and would attack immediately. Still, Eng always brought his squad back from the steaming tunnels in time for them to listen to the explosions and to cheer the pikemen as they poured into the holes in the broken walls.

Because he was so short, General Eng appreciated size. All his captains were a foot taller than he. There was additional reason for picking giants: it took a big man to handle the twelve-foot pike or the halberd, a huge iron ax fastened to a long bamboo by rawhide thongs. For an army that was continually on the move, the pikemen were its earthworks and its fortifications, a movable redoubt. Perhaps no one appreciated the value of the army on the move more than Eng, as the leader of its pike formations, the army's slowest-moving unit.

"You, Chen," he called to Pao An one day. "Tell me your background. Someone told me you had lived with the Tanka rat people on the river. So if you tolerated the stink, you must know a thing or two about handling a boat!"

Eng whistled when he talked because of his split lip, and Pao An found it hard to keep a straight face. "Yes," he said in his most respectful manner. "I sailed with them on the Pearl and in Hong Kong Bay when the British barbarians had put a price on every honest sailor's head."

Eng prodded Pao An's stomach with his forefinger. He squeezed Pao An's biceps. "Do you know how to paddle? Could you row a heavy boat in swift current?"

"Of course."

"At night?"

"Yes."

"Carrying several hundred pounds of cargo?"

"I suppose."

"Under fire of forty-six cannons?"

Eng watched Pao An's growing consternation and burst out laughing. "With a hot poker up your ass?"

Pao An lapsed into uncomfortable silence.

"Good. I want some Han man I can trust to go with these Tanka pirates. The King of Charcoal—known to most fools as the Voice of God the Father, but known to me as Yang, a fool of fools who drank too much when he led the mule train—has decided to capture the whole transport clan that's tied up just downriver from the garrison in Yo Chou. That way we can have a navy as stupid as our army. Then we can float down the Yangtze like princes instead of walking like the honorable beggars we are. Personally, I hate water. My stomach turns upside down looking at a lily pad floating on a pond. Did the High God make us fish with scales and fins? But we are going to get us a fleet or kill a few of you stupid volunteers in the process."

Volunteer? said Pao An to himself, feeling a certain weakness in his knees.

"Move, you," barked Eng. "Don't keep the Voice of God waiting."

Only Eng in the entire Taiping army could say what he had said about Yang, for he knew Yang in the years before Hung had come to tell the Hakka of Kwangsi about the glories of heaven.

Pao An was afraid of the Eastern King. Yang was said to be the cruelest of the Taiping leaders. It was he who made the most dreaded of Taiping laws. When the black banner is raised, follow wherever it goes unto death, for he who runs in battle will be killed. Yang meant it. Three farmers who ran during Pao An's first engagement had been decapitated on the spot and their heads stuck on pikes at the entrance to the Men's Camp as a warning to others. Pao An himself had felt like running when the banner men charged his pike block. That he had stayed he attributed more to cowardice than bravery; he was ashamed to let the others see him run. And he feared what Yang might do. Yang's presence was felt everywhere in the army. But no one doubted his success at making the unpredictable work on the field of battle.

As for Yang's speaking as the Voice of God, Pao An, who was not a believer, felt as Eng did: it was merely a way of controlling the credulous. The meeting Eng took him to was attended by a thousand holy soldiers, mostly Tanka boatmen and a few cannoneers. Yang addressed them from a rock outside the Tanka camp. A barbarian with a devilishly red beard loomed over Yang. The great general himself was hardly an imposing figure. He was as short as Pao An's old friend Pang, with the huge hands of a charcoal-carrier. His face was blackened by the sun, and he looked more like an ape than a great general of over half a million men and women. Only his dress was awe inspiring. He wore a long robe of bright yellow and a high peaked red cap edged in gold.

But when he spoke, his great voice took Pao An by surprise: everyone in the hollow could easily hear him.

"Who's a boatman here?" he shouted. A roar went up from the

Tanka. "Listen, Brothers! I have a great task for you. I am going to make you fishers of men."

The assembly laughed nervously; they knew that he was speaking in the language of the Great Book and were not in the mood for a sermon.

Yang did not disappoint them. "What the Manchu dogs took from you, I am going to give you back. Who wants a boat?" The men shouted their delight. "I will give you boats. I will give you breezes. I will give you back your face!" The men were cheering, bloodthirsty, ready for a brawl. "We are going to take the Hsia clan who are hiding from us at the docks at Yo Chou. We will throw a net over their fishing fleet. Here is our chance to humiliate the imps before the entire world. The provincial commander-in-chief is a Manchu dog named Po-le-kung-wu. He has come to Yo Chou to take charge personally, vowing he will show what cowards Taiping soldiers are when they face real imperial troops. And he has brought an imp battalion with him to fortify the garrison.

"But our friend Iron Fist has fortified us as well. He's contacted the local Triads and river people like yourselves to assist us. Once we blockade the fisher fleet, they will roll out cannon downriver so that the fleet will be bottled up completely. There are rich stores of gunpowder, rifles, ammunition, and no end of food supplies in the garrison waiting for us. Who here is hungry?"

The Tanka roared because their bellies were empty; the army had been moving so quickly there had been little time to fill the canteens with supplies from conquered towns.

"General Eng will lead your expedition. He knows my plan. We cannot fail because the High God ordains it. Once we capture the five thousand boats of the lake fleet in Yo Chou, we will sail down the Yangtze like kings to claim our holy city—where Hakka and Punti, Tanka, Miao, and Loi will be one people, all Han heroes, equal in the eyes of the High God. May He be adored."

The thought was a new one for the clannish sailors, who cherished their separateness. They were hesitant to cheer again.

"Equal in the eyes of the High God, I say! So Tanka may own land as well as boats, hold office, buy salt licenses, become leaders of the nation."

There was a roar of startled approval.

"Who is a coward here? Who wants to die on land?"

The Tanka hooted their derision.

"Let us take back what is ours!"

In spite of himself, Pao An felt excitement rising in his chest. So this was Yang, a powerful motivator of men, able to sway the rabble by giving back to them their secret dreams. Pao An could taste the victory that was not yet theirs.

In minutes, Eng had gathered the men into units. Only Pao An's unit was not called.

"What do you want us to do?" Pao An called to Eng.

"Not 'us,' paddy boy Chen. You!" declared a faintly familiar voice. Pao An turned around to see a beetle-browed giant of a man dressed in the uniform of a Taiping commander. It was Iron Fist, the bandit he had wrestled in the woods outside his village.

"He says he knows you," Eng laughed. "He says he used to rock you when you were a child."

Pao An was shaking with fury. He saw again in his mind Pang's body with the holes torn by bullets. "I won't take orders from him," he declared. "This man is a murderer. He's not fit to be in charge of anything." The laughter stopped.

"Listen, Chen," General Eng said. "You two don't like each other and I don't give a dog's turd why. What a man was before counts for nothing. Here, everyone starts new. I was a thief and a smuggler myself. That's done. Now I'm Taiping. And if a man who was a mandarin doesn't obey my orders, I have him bound up in wire, and I cut off little pieces of his flesh until he dies. Iron Fist has proven his loyalty to us. He has commanded the Triads and Tanka. And now I say that in this mission you do what he says. Otherwise—" Eng made a slicing motion with his finger.

"Choose someone else. We shouldn't send a paddy boy out in a boat," Iron Fist spat out. "He couldn't catch a carp swimming in a bucket."

"Who do we send, half a dozen of these little Tanka rats?" Eng asked. "There isn't one of them strong enough to row the line we plan to lay. And I don't trust them. All water rats swim together. These pirates might tip off the fisher clan for a price and send them running to the emperor, *hai ma?*"

"I threw a net over your plans once, Iron Fist, and I can catch the fisher people just as easily," Pao An said, his pride growing with his anger. Now it was Iron Fist's turn to fume.

"Come, come. No time for schoolboy rivalries here. We need you on this expedition," Eng said.

Between the headlands lay two miles of open water with tricky currents where the Yangtze drained Lake Tung Ting. From the western

bank, Eng and Pao An watched the Hsia clan move their boats in and
out of the harbor of Yo Chou on the opposite shore. The city, a rich
trading center, offered the main entry to the lake and the Yangtze
River, which flowed out its other end. Beyond were the rich agricul-
tural lands of Hupeh Province. The garrison at Yo Chou held an
immense quantity of grain, explosives, cannon, and ammunition—and
protected five thousand fishing vessels. Normally the Hsia clan fished
in family groups, but the warfare in the area had brought the clan
together from the nearby rivers and canals, a thousand Hsia families
along with others who sought protection. Some boats were armed
with small guns which stuck out of the curved awnings of straw. By
nightfall, the boats would be anchored downriver out of the dangers of
wind and Taiping attack on the lake.

Eng watched the movement and grunted to Pao An. "Tonight we
put the cork in their bottle, *hai ma,* Chen?"

Pao An nodded. He hoped he was equal to the task. It was his
assignment to row a small boat across the lake between the headlands,
playing out a line fixed with bobbers. When he reached it, where Iron
Fist and his soldiers were hidden, they would pull in the line and attach
it to a large winch turned by five oxen. The line, in turn, was attached
to an iron chain. If all went well, the iron chain, which floated on
small buoys, would close off access to the lake. Tung Ting would
become a Taiping sea. The chain had been forged link by link by
Taiping smithies working day and night for seven days. There were
six links to a foot, nearly 70,000 links in all.

Pao An looked out over the black water. Five thousand boats
twinkling with burning braziers lay idling along the long, broad river.
The flotilla looked like a mirror city reflecting the city above.

Is it possible to catch two cities in a net? Pao An wondered.

Eng was in charge of loading Pao An's boat. It was filled to the
gunwales with the line, which had been fitted with small cork floats so
that it would not sink to the bottom. Six of the Tankas helped push
him into the water, where the boat sank to within scant inches of the
rail.

"Look you, Chen," said General Eng. "Don't slow down out there.
We don't have much time before daylight to reel the chain across. I
don't care if you have to crap in your pants. Keep rowing."

"She's so low, she's going to be hard to move," Pao An told him.
"The wind's blowing straight downriver."

"I don't care if a typhoon is blowing. If you overturn this boat, you
better not swim to shore. Drown yourself, because if I get you, you
will wish you were fish food. This is our only chance to net these

boats that old Mule Head Yang wants so badly. The imps are right behind us, and the clan is switching harbors tomorrow."

"I'll do my best."

"Your best had better be good enough. Row fast. The moon's behind a cloud now. If it comes out, they might see you. There's two miles of open water here, and you've got just enough line, so if you go crooked you're going to come up short. In that case, strangle yourself with the last foot. I don't want to see your ugly face again."

Pao An nodded.

"It's time! Row, you no-name boy." The little general was trembling with suppressed energy.

"Yes."

"You got three hours. That's all."

Eng gave the signal, and the launching crew pushed Pao An off. He stroked awkwardly at first. The boat floundered. He stroked again, pulling with all his strength. The oars broke water and splashed. He heard Eng curse and the Tanka boatmen laugh. Finally, he straightened out, found his rhythm, and began to pull. His arms tensed with the strain. The rope jerked over the side, hopping into the water, as each little bobber bumped over the rail.

It took an eternity for the boat to feel lighter, but midway across the lake a breeze began to blow against him, driving him toward the anchored fleet. The boat tipped; water rushed in. He was sure he had been blown off course. From time to time, he heard the sentries on the fishing boats calling to one another. Now the garrison loomed above. If they saw him, he'd be cut down in a minute by strong youths unencumbered by a mile of jute cord.

A night bird swept across the water and circled back, trying to decide if Pao An were edible. When it called out mournfully to him, he almost dropped a paddle. Would the sentries see him moving in the moonlight?

With every stroke, his arms ached; the wind seemed to get stronger, the current faster, the water choppier. It was worse than carrying stone or pulling a plow with his own back. The minutes dragged into hours, hours seemed like days of torture. He began to see visions: Rulan stumbling against him. Rulan sleeping. He was sure he would never see her or Li Yu again. Soon the sun would rise and he would be an easy target for the fishermen's guns.

After two and a half hours of rowing against the wind and the current, Pao An came in sight of the dark shore on the other side. He saw that he was off course by a quarter of a mile. The line would be too short. He had failed.

There was the splash of a paddle and a dark shape looming in the water from the opposite shore. Pao An's muscles tightened. A voice cried out, low, gruff, familiar.

"Hey you, paddy boy," growled Iron Fist. "I've come to give you back your life again. Take hold of this rope and tie up. I thought you'd be off course and would need more line, so I had some waiting on the other side."

Pao An was too exhausted to offer thanks. He hated being indebted to Pang's murderer.

There was just enough line to reach the team that was anxiously waiting at the winch. Iron Fist got the oxen moving immediately.

Dawn was breaking across the gray waters when the first of the Hsia boats were raising sail to catch the early morning breeze. By then, the chain was stretched tightly across the mouth of the river, and the Taiping cannon were rolled into place on either shore.

"Send the elders of the city and of the Hsia clan this message," Eng told his Tanka emissary. "My cannons start firing when the sun reaches its zenith. Tell them they cannot escape downriver because more Taiping cannon are in place below Yo Chou. They must tell me before then if they want to become the holy sailors of the Kingdom of Great Peace or be eaten by the fishes they have harassed for so many years."

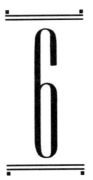

Wu Chang, Hupeh Province, 1853

"Don't cough, don't fidget! You're in a civilized house, not a Kwangtung mud flat," Eng barked.

The Eastern King's scribe squinted at Pao An, whose body completely filled the doorway of the main hall of an official's house occupied by Yang's people after the fall of Wu Chang. Pao An felt like a small delta boy the first time he enters a city.

Another lackey hurried up, his long robes sweeping the floor. He was dressed like a mandarin, not a Taiping warrior, and Pao An was amazed at the luxury that was beginning to creep into the Taiping, even at its lowest levels.

"Congratulations, General Eng," the servant said, his embroidered sleeves brushing the ground. "You scored a great victory at Yo Chou."

The stubby general shoved Pao An forward. "Not me. This is the strong back that gave us five thousand boats," he lisped. "He strung a fishnet for us across the lake. After that, it was easy to get the fisherfolk to accept the High God's commandments, especially once they saw my cannon lined up on the bank." He laughed, remembering the speediness of their conversion. "Is the Eastern King here? I think this dumb Kwangtung farm boy ought to get a promotion for his rowing. And big and clumsy as he is, he was the one who just led fifty soldiers into Wu Chang when we blew up the walls the other day."

"Excellent. Excellent. God be adored," the man said. "The Eastern King is closeted with—"

Eng guffawed. "What's her name? He has so many flowers now I lose track."

"No, no. He's with the sage from across the sea. The barbarian is quite sick," he replied. "The Eastern King has left word not to be disturbed, yet I think that seeing you will be better medicine than what the Wu Chang doctors have been pouring down the foreigner's gullet."

The three men picked their way through the ransacked rooms of the former county magistrate's mansion up a narrow staircase to the upper floor. The huge wing at the rear had been made into Yang's living quarters. Scribes were cataloging the wall hangings, furniture, porcelains, and assigning them to baskets and chests. It was rumored that Yang had five concubines now, although no official consort to take the place of the dead wife he still honored.

Pao An's knees shook with apprehension. He preferred anyplace, even the front line of battle, to the formidable Yang's sanctum. Yang had succeeded where no other peasant rebel in the last three hundred years had: he had welded over half a million warring souls into a single fighting force. He had done this through bullying, cruelty, and a gift for calling down the Voice of God whenever the people weakened. Everyone knew Yang's penalty for failing to charge when the black flag was raised or for sneaking a puff of dirt or for lying with a woman: decapitation. That so few broke his commandments spoke of the fear and respect with which the men held their commander. Yang could be mercilessly legalistic in the enforcement of religious or regimental regulations—but they knew him to be just. Yang had also decreed that no commoner should be harmed, no women raped when a city was taken, and he enforced that law with as much rigor as the feared black flag dictum.

Two canopied beds had been shoved to opposite sides of the room. On one lay the Eastern King in full regalia, his headdress askew. The bed was piled high with pillows, maps, discarded clothes. In the middle sat Yang himself and a fresh-faced Hakka girl dressed in a thin chemise who was wiping his face with a hot towel. The girl was laughing softly in his ear; Yang, however, was neither interested nor aroused, but was speaking earnestly to a man half-hidden in a mass of quilts on the other bed.

Pao An prostrated himself on the floor in a full kowtow. Eng remained standing.

Yang perked up immediately at the sight of his old friend. "Eng, you illegitimate son, did you doubt what I told Hung to avoid his useless councils? Prayer meetings, poetry-writing sessions, household linen inventories, wife-disciplining tribunals, and other revolutionary activities kept me away! You thought it was me who was ailing, and you came to watch me die, *hai ma?*"

"No, no. I hear how you work night and day for our cause, so I came to help," said Eng, leering at the girl through his one good eye.

Yang laughed gruffly. "This one rubs, that one fans, the other chews my food for me and puts it in my mouth like women do with a baby. I don't even have to shake myself when I stand up to piss. Also I get no damn peace." He swatted the girl's rump as she swayed out of the room.

"Sit," Yang said. "And tell that fool to pull his face out of the dirt. Looking at his backside reminds me of the Younger Son crying to Heaven about his unworthiness. He claims that his odes are winning us victories. And you probably thought that it was your cannon and gunpowder, and all those lads with pikes!" He grinned at the man on the other bed. "Show my friend respect."

Feeling Eng's foot jab his backside, Pao An got up sheepishly and found himself gawking at the man lying in the bed at the opposite wall.

The barbarian's skin was not red, as stories about barbarians alleged, but as brown as a Han peasant's, with dark hollows under his eyes. He had a long scholar's face, eyes of a truly repugnant hue, and bushy sideburns of an unbelievably garish golden-red that came down past his ears before soaring under a nose of rhinoceros proportions. Although he was clearly ill, he was dressed as if he were ready to walk outdoors. His Chinese-style jacket was lined with fur and sported pouches of cloth from which bulged a strange assortment of items: bits of paper, a comb, Han writing brushes, a leatherbound book, and old handkerchiefs. Pao An, who had never seen such pockets, thought the pouches ingenious, although ugly.

"General Eng," the barbarian called out in a hoarse voice. "What other victory have you won for us?"

Pao An was so shocked that a barbarian could speak fluent Cantonese that he didn't hear Eng's reply. All three men seemed to be on terms of easy intimacy. But how could anyone stand to look at such a frightful apparition? thought Pao An. Although the foreigner had taught the Eastern King clever battle strategies out of the Great Book, he was still a "white ghost," a creature barely human. Pao An bowed low to hide his revulsion.

Eng seemed to have forgotten Pao An in his excitement at meeting his old friend. He cleaned off the dust from a porcelain taboret, brought it near Yang's bed, and sat down without being invited. "Is it true that Hung has bells rung every time he takes a shit?" he asked companionably.

"It's true," Yang said, laughing.

"And when he washes his face, seven maids must stand by so he can wipe his ugly snout with seven different fresh towels?"

Yang grunted his assent.

"And when the Younger Son cuts his fingernails, they must be incinerated on the altar?"

"That I have not heard. You must have spies in his harem. So why did you come here? To spy on me?"

"No, I came to collect a debt."

"Aiya," Yang smirked. "Old friends, old debts. You came to see what you can steal."

"No, no. I'm not a robber. I do your dirty work, remember? The robber and plotter is your brother Wei, the Northern King, who is still a filthy pawnbroker no matter how many titles he has. His tent is a pawnshop where spies come to barter. He tells lies to Hung about you. He makes deals with the Triads in your own camp against you. He—"

"Oh, don't you think I know all these things?"

"No. You don't know how to take care of yourself. You need me to protect you from kings as well as imps. You tolerate too much deceit. It will mean a knife in your ribs one day."

Yang shook his head, resigned. "Wei abets Hung's madness. He fills Hung's head with fears about insects, snakes, fox-spirits, girls who suck the soul from his body. Then Wei, with tears in his eyes, prays that Hung not dream of demons and hordes of flying insects, and leaves Hung sleepless with terror."

Mandley tried to talk, but his words were drowned out in a fit of coughing.

"Listen, I didn't come to collect a debt for myself," said Eng. "This young bull here is the one I told you about. He captured you a navy. I think you ought to make him a colonel because he's a good southern ox like you and me."

"Did you do all that by yourself?" Yang asked Pao An.

"No, King, this miserable person only rowed the boat with the rope. General Eng and the cannoneers did the rest. Then your loyal

Tanka boatmen seized the boats." Pao An left out Iron Fist's name, and Eng did not correct him.

Yang nodded in approval. "You praise your men. Good. I will make you a colonel. Man-da-li, write it up. Put my dragon seal on it. Sign it with my grandest title: *chien sui,* One Thousand Years. Let it be done."

The barbarian lifted his head and showed huge yellow teeth. Pao An was appalled until he realized that the barbarian was smiling, not grimacing in pain.

"You don't look so good, my friend," Eng told Mandley. "Send away your girls, Eastern King, and I'll come and cook for you both. I'll boil chicken feet with ginger. Put his bowels back in order."

"It's not my bowels. It's my throat, my chest." Mandley groaned.

"Maybe it's the same poison that Hung gave me back in Chin Tien," Yang said with a worried frown. "He knows that Man-da-li is the source of my prophesying. That power gives me status almost equal to Hung's. Almost!"

Eng laid a hand on Mandley's knee. "Drink only water you boil yourself. Throw intruders like myself out. Don't talk. Banish the Eastern King's girls so you are not tempted." Eng laughed at the barbarian's discomfort. "Aiya, you white devils are as finicky as virgins. What about doctors?"

"He's got twenty doctors from our newly conquered city of Wu Chang," Yang fumed. "They all promised to make him as hard as a stallion again. A useless and dangerous thing for any Taiping soldier, as I reminded them. I threatened to cut off their heads for their unholy words. Each one gives him a different medicine. He'll die of their cures before the sickness takes him. If he had a spirit-woman like my old wife, he would have been out of this bed a week ago."

Eng, who had known Ailan, grunted his assent. "Aiya, we live in an enlightened age. Who among the sisters remembers the old chants and cures?"

"King," interjected Pao An, "I know a woman." Instantly, he regretted his outburst. No one had invited him to speak, and after Yang's diatribe against Mandley's doctors, he shouldn't have mentioned that he knew any woman at all, for Yang was ruthless in enforcing the separation of the sexes.

"Who's that?" Yang demanded over Mandley's hoarse protests.

"Excuse my bad manners, King. I should not presume—"

"Speak up!" Eng barked, his split lip trembling.

"A young Hakka woman who healed me," Pao An replied, swallowing his fear. "She was in Viceroy Li's household when I met her in Canton. We came across Hunan together." Pao An could not interpret the rush of emotions that passed rapidly over Yang's face.

"Is she alive? Is she here?" Yang cried.

Pao An nodded, fully aware of the awful risk of admitting any affection for a woman. He paused and made his decision to chance everything in order to see her again. "Her name is Rulan, and she is the best of her kind," he declared.

Yang crawled out of bed, his face paler than the sick man's. He grasped the youth's shoulders like a man drowning.

Secretly, Rulan had begun to hope her father would discover her presence in the Women's Camp. So when the summons from him came, she could not disguise her excitement from Wing. The time she had spent traveling with the Taiping had finally opened her eyes to her father's gifts. She saw that Yang was responsible for the victories the Taiping soldiers were winning; she heard the women speak of his courage and brilliance in the field. Surely she had misjudged him; her father's concerns were too vast and complicated for a girl like her to understand. How then could she reproach him for ordering the Tai Tai's death if that death had in some way secured the freedom of the entire Taiping nation?

Frantic with anxiety, Wing warned Rulan of the dangers in the Eastern King's household.

"Hung orders us to put aside family relationships," Rulan assured Wing. "I'm no longer a daughter but a holy soldier, a colonel in the women's regiment. My father and I meet as warriors."

"Don't be naive. None of the kings can be trusted. Their lives are all treachery and deceit."

Rulan put aside Wing's warnings, yet as soon as she came to Yang's headquarters, the unwieldy past began to seep through her restraints. Would he be stern and unloving now that he was king? Would he rebuke her for hiding so long in the Women's Camp? Her anxiety turned to joy when she saw Pao An, wearing colonel's insignia, at the gate to greet her. She saw his happiness at seeing her—and recognized, too, his undisguised admiration, even desire. Proudly, she realized that her regimen as a warrior had changed her—she was tanned and hard, her hair hung loose and free and she walked with a warrior's stride. Then she remembered that he had looked that way at Mei Yuk—and the joy in her died.

"I told the Eastern King about you," he said by way of greeting.

Rulan acknowledged his words with a formal salute.

His eyes widened when he saw her colonel's insignia. "I missed you," he added. "You were so weak when we parted—"

"I am strong now." She was playing at being regal and controlled, and she tried not to see the pleading in his eyes.

Yang was waiting for her in an inner room, pacing. His small, square frame was draped in a scarlet robe with a yellow border. The last time they had met, he had been wearing beggar's rags.

It was like stepping back into another time. Her father was a king. Yet still her father. She remembered him on the earthen floor of their hut nuzzling Boy-Boy's bare belly with his nose and blowing in the infant's face to make him laugh.

The Eastern King opened his arms to his daughter, and suddenly Rulan was eleven years old and running forward to be taken up in her father's embrace.

"And so you have come," he whispered into her hair, his voice breaking. "I knew I would find you, although I was too full of sin to hope." He smelled her cheek as parents do to an especially beloved child. "Little Quail," he murmured.

Neither noticed when Pao An slipped away.

The barbarian who shared Yang's rooms was the very one she had met in Abundant Spring Mountain. Rulan felt as if she had stumbled into a place where the remnants of the past were collected and reused, the way women in great houses bring out a particular plate again and again for ceremonial occasions. The run-down mansion that her father and his retinue now occupied even resembled the commune of the Golden Orchids. There were barns and stables and outbuildings and groves, although the trees were orange, not mulberry. She half expected her sisters to spring out of the ground and come running toward her, resurrected like creatures of legend out of the ancient soil.

Rulan sensed that her father had a mission in mind for her. But she would not obey him this time if his orders were again to kill against her will. So Yang's request to heal the foreigner, who had become the source of his authority among the holy soldiers, was a command she welcomed.

She put her ear to Mandley's chest. The soft bubbling in his breathing meant that his lungs were afflicted. She wiped his feverish forehead, felt the pulse beating fast and weakly on his thin wrist. He seemed like a candle snuffed out; she could not believe that this was the ungainly giant whose anger had so terrified the steward and housemaids in the house of Li. The problem seemed more allergic in nature than disease borne, probably a foreigner's natural intolerance of the dust and the filth of a strange countryside—or perhaps poison, as her father had suggested. Physician Sung at the *chai tang* had taught her that the leaf of either the maidenhair fern or the ginkgo tree was the best remedy for lung ailments. She sent back to her band of herb gatherers for the third-strength extract of ginkgo leaf. When she had prepared the infusion, the barbarian drank it down wearily.

Rulan's past was singing to her once again in a new set of discordant rhythms. Even Pao An, whom she had steeled herself against loving, had become part of the strange pattern of her life as a warrior woman. She swore she would not open herself up to him, as she had in the mansion of the Lis. But when she heard Pao An joking with the guard outside the door of Mandley's sickroom, her heart began to race and her cheeks flushed at his nearness.

The Younger Son was lying naked on a divan while his woman bathed him, and because no moment must be idle, he was also composing a poem. The poem would become an edict for deportment, a law within his house. It would prescribe movement and direction for his wives and serving girls, and thereby impose order on a disreputable and fallen world. Only by tightly circumscribing the movements of his ladies could he create a semblance of heaven within his immediate sphere. And if perfect order was achieved, it would necessarily follow that the Taiping nation would be ordered as well, for the part was an echo, a shadow, a mirror of the whole.

Thus he must keep his mind always active, always alert to the chaos and foul substances lurking just beyond his sight. The empire he was creating was not made by hands or deeds, as the false prophet Yang, who was busily stealing glory from him, proclaimed, but rather by the sacred rituals of Hung's own mind as manifested in the proper ordering of his bodily functions. How would the winds blow and the rains fall and the rivers flow if his digestion and elimination were disordered? The hours of eating and partaking of drink must therefore be perfectly balanced with sleep and relaxation, so that the seasons might be balanced as well. He needed to keep his person and his habitation clean so that the empire would be pure and would last until he was taken up into heaven to reign with God the Father and Elder Brother Jesus. And if his empire were to last ten thousand years, he must keep perfect order on earth, and the key to that was—

"Your sister says that Yang has found his daughter," whispered Pawnbroker Wei at his ear.

"Impossible! She is locked behind the walls of Viceroy Li's house," Hung replied.

"She is a warrior among Jiao's own women. Jiao let the girl slip away. See how your own sister fails you? Now Yang has her guarded in his own house. She is restoring the barbarian to life." Wei had come close enough that the bath girls would not hear. He watched with pleasure as Hung began to twitch. "She is here," Wei repeated, his voice insistent and spiteful. "The one that killed my brother Wang and stole his dragon's eye."

"Wang is drowning in hell," Hung declared. Discomfited by Wei's accusations, he could seize only that one certainty. "He thought to live forever, but he is drowning in hell."

Wei waved the bath girls away from the divan. "Yes, my brother Wang is suffering eternal damnation because he tried to cheat you out of the secret of eternal life. But the girl who knows the secret is here!"

Hung closed his eyes and tossed his head from side to side.

"Now Yang will use her against you. He will try to make himself greater than you. He will have the barbarian with his Book and the girl with her magic."

Tears spilled down Hung's bearded cheeks. He got up from his couch and began to kick and slap his maids. "Disobedient! You do not clean me as I was clean in Heaven. Go!" he shrieked. When the women had run from the room, he turned to Wei. "Help me, help me," he begged.

At the New Year, Pawnbroker Wei sent presents to Yang's ladies. Among them was a green and gold snake for Rulan fashioned of circles of jade strung ingeniously together. When Rulan opened the box, she started at the sight of the coiled serpent and fell back into Mandley's arms. For a moment, he held her close.

Pao An was attending Yang at the time. Mandley could not help but notice Pao An's steely repression give way to jealousy at the sight of the inadvertent embrace. But the look that Rulan gave the peasant warrior on disengaging herself from Mandley's arms was what pierced Mandley to the core. She desired him too! This realization made his heart ache even as he held her.

Rulan picked the snake up carefully. It was actually a necklace so cunningly made that the tail fastened into its teeth. The fangs were ivory and hollow; a small drop of amber liquid gleamed at the tip.

Deftly, Pao An snatched it out of her hand and threw it on the table, where it shivered like a living serpent. "Poison!" he exclaimed. "If you had scratched your finger fastening it—"

Mandley thought that the catch in Pao An's voice betrayed a depth of feeling surprising in so simple a peasant. He wished he had been the one to discover the poison.

Rulan gave a ringing laugh. "Why should the Northern King want to kill me? I barely know him."

Yang beckoned them closer and told them about the battles among the rival kings for power and the growing eccentricities of Hung. He ended with a stern warning to his daughter.

Rulan replied, "When I was my mother's child, the world was an eddying stream of spirits. I saw ghosts wherever my mother pointed. Now I have gained a warrior's understanding." She nodded at Mandley. "I have learned from Man-da-li that there are no such things are *kuei*. I know that men and not demons stir the currents of fate." Suddenly, she shivered. "Yet at times, I would rather live in my mother's world, for men are more devious than ghosts."

At Yang's orders, Mandley had been giving Rulan English lessons twice a day in his room. They were virtually the only man and woman, except for the kings and their wives, who could meet without fear of reprisals. Mandley felt himself falling more and more under the girl's spell. He was excruciatingly conscious of his open and unmade bed, of her shape, her face, the smell of her skin and hair. The heat she brought into his room . . .

He set her to reading from Deuteronomy, partly to instruct her and partly to enjoy the sweet, low sound of her voice. At one point, she stumbled over a lengthy description of the cities in the east set aside by Moses as places of refuge for murderers.

Mandley urged her to skip the place names. "You Han cannot wind your tongue around a Hebrew word or an English phrase," he cautioned.

Tossing her hair defiantly, Rulan made him say each name slowly so she could repeat it. "Bezer in the wilderness," "Ramoth in Gilead,"

"Golan in Bashan," and the other names until she was satisfied with her accent. "Now that I can say the names, tell me what they mean," she demanded.

Mandley sighed and read the passage through again. How alike they are, he thought, Yang and his daughter. He wondered what archaism from the Old Testament would next take their fancy. What does Yang perceive in the endless lists of Old Testament laws or Rulan in this catalog of trivial place names? he asked himself. They were sanctuaries, he told her. Places of refuge for the outcast.

Rulan persisted. "What does that mean, 'a homicide who kills without intent and with no previous enmity?' "

Mandley told her that it meant those who had not harbored malice in their hearts or planned murder could go to these places and be cleansed, for "this was the law, as given by the prophet Moses."

Rulan's eyes closed. For a moment, Mandley wondered what he might do if she offered herself to him. "I am searching for such a city," she whispered. She was so close that he could see the sheen of sweat on her upper lip.

"You are so beautiful to me," he told her, not bothering to disguise his yearning.

Rulan looked up in surprise.

"Has no one ever said that to you before?"

She frowned and shook her head. "Men have desired me, which is most curious because I am not beautiful. This troubles me because people seem to see in me what I do not see in myself. I do not understand this." She began to falter. "For whenever I think of my past life, when I think of Rulan, I think of an outcast, an unworthy thing."

Terribly moved by her confession, he said, "Rulan, we've all been chosen for something beyond ourselves. Look at me! I hate war, yet here I am, a man of God, adviser to an infamous rebel. But I am sure that God has a purpose for me in this madness, as He has for you."

"Would a barbarian god accept what Han gods abhor? No, Manda-li, I cannot admit any god into my life. Or any man."

Her sad, bitter words left him speechless.

"I have something else to tell you," she whispered, "because you are my brother. I have been dreaming about my death. You know I am meant to die by fire, as my mother foretold."

"You mustn't talk this way! You cannot know the hour of your death."

"It will be by fire," she insisted. "My mother died that way too."

"Then I will guard you from the fire," he told her tenderly.

"This is war, Man-da-li. And one is taken standing by another's side."

"Then give me a place in your heart," he begged. "I'll guard you from there."

When he took her in his arms, she did not move away, for she desperately needed the comfort of a friend. But Rulan knew that this gentle man with the ghastly tigerish face was not the one to alter the moment of her dying. Or turn a stone girl back to flesh.

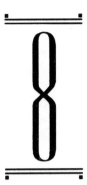

Yangtze River, Anhwei Province, 1853

"What's the count?" Eng barked. Having taken all the inhabitants of Wu Chang as conscripts and captured the provincial capital of Anking, they had been engaged for two days in taking the census of the entire army. Owing to the tight organization by fives and twenty-fives, the number was amazingly accurate.

"Seven hundred and fifty thousand holy soldiers, counting the newly enlisted brothers and sisters of Wu Chang, Kiu Kiang, and An King," replied Pao An.

"We're strong as a typhoon now," Eng said. "We blow down everything before us."

Yang demurred. "Never rely on strength alone. When you are strong, that is the time for guile. Use your enemy's fear and weakness against him. What is the next obstacle in our path?"

Shih Ta Kai answered, "The imperial garrison on Tung Liang Shan Island. We know the imps are low on gunpowder. How can we best exploit that situation?"

Yang turned his gaze from one commander to the other and waited. Iron Fist and half a dozen other generals wilted under the silent inquisition until the irrepressible Eng spoke.

"Bring up all our cannon on the lead boats. Maneuver into two lines, divide their fire. Circle the imps and blast that garbage pile off the island!" Eng shouted.

"That way we present two neat lines of targets, like ducklings following their mother," Iron Fist sneered. But no one had another suggestion.

"General Eng's plan is better if you reverse it," Pao An ventured at last. "We collect our own garbage pile first, burn it with their gunpowder, then bring our cannon up last."

"What does that mean," Eng scowled, annoyed that his underling had corrected him.

"All of you," Yang commanded, "kowtow to General Chen, who has just saved your life. You first, Eng!"

Thoroughly perplexed, Eng bobbed his head irritably.

But Iron Fist saw the genius in the plan and the look he gave Pao An was one of pure envy and surprise.

Pao An and Iron Fist were appointed by Shih Ta Kai to lead the attack. Sailing under the banner of the Assistant King Shih, leader of the land forces, Pao An would guide in seven hundred boats filled with mud and garbage toward Tung Liang Shan Island. Each boat was "armed" with tree trunks painted to resemble cannon. Iron Fist commanded the real gunboats, which were to be held in reserve until Pao An's fleet of decoys had drawn off the fire.

Iron Fist warned Pao An as the decoy boats set sail, "Keep your head low, Farmer Chen. I need you alive to wrestle again!"

"Maybe a cannonball will send you to the Yellow Springs before you get the chance," Pao An shouted back.

Iron Fist laughed loud and long. "You will not get rid of me with a wish."

At the great bend in the river, Pao An pulled his fleet into a single line. Yang had given him the oldest, most dilapidated boats in the fleet, each one steered by a single man, each man a master sailor and skillful swimmer.

The defenders of the fort had been hearing reports for two weeks about the huge Taiping flotilla. They had finished the last of their stores of rice and had hoarded their precious gunpowder for the attack that was sure to come. As soon as the ships rounded the turn in the river and came into view, the imp forces bombarded the decoy boats with every gun in their artillery. Pao An survived the inferno on the water by clinging to the side of his burning scow, which sank just across the river from the island. From that vantage point, he was able to watch the perfect completion of his plan, for just as the last fiery decoy hissed beneath the waters of the Yangtze, a thousand warships of the Taiping fleet under Iron Fist's command, with an expanded fleet of nearly twenty thousand troop boats behind them, rounded the curve of the river flying the yellow flags of the Kingdom of Great Peace. Iron Fist's cannon opened fire. The cheers died in the throats of the imperial soldiers, and they fled the citadel.

Rulan was waiting on shore astride her stallion with five hundred horsewomen. With a graceful leap, she dismounted and walked up to Pao An as he emerged from the river, dripping wet, black from the smoke and smelling of garbage and gunpowder. Before them all, unmindful of her father's laws, she embraced him.

From his canopied chair on the deck of a dragon boat in the center of the river, the Younger Son of God scanned the columns of women drawn up like bright seraphim. He watched the girl descend like an angel and cross the dark earth to where the wet, dirty warrior had dragged himself. He watched her embrace him shamelessly before the holy soldiers, and he was filled with jealousy and doubt. *Ku* reared up out of the depths of the dark, watery pity and coiled again around his heart.

He called for Wei, the Northern King, and went to his cabin to weep for the woman whom his greatest rival, the Eastern King, withheld from him.

The Yangtze, which snaked wide, flat and fast-running through the rich, populous region of Anhwei Province, became the Taiping royal road. Yang and his retinue rode an ancient boat with tattered quilted sails used to haul salt and smuggle opium; Hung and his wives occupied an immense barge carved in the shape of a dragon and hung with banners of yellow silk. Because there were no more imps left to plague him, Yang was able to rest aboard his vessel and plan for the future of his nation. Hung sent Yang his poems, visions, and ecstatic proclamations. Yang, Mandley, and Rulan began to reshape Hung's wild ideas into the practical regulations, edicts, and policies that Yang had formulated during the long march to Nanking.

Yang enjoined Mandley to draft a series of provisions that would be the basis for the Kingdom of Great Peace once their wandering was over. "The problem is that the people still don't know what to do when we reach the Holy City, or how we will rebuild this Land of Flowers once Peking is won," he grumbled to Mandley. "We need to fix my primitive utterances into proper words, the kind a mandarin can understand, or the history books will laugh at us. I talk, Manda-li, you clean it up, put it into proper language. Get book-reading men, those with ambition, to help you. Put what I tell you into the form of a letter. Call it by some lofty title; call it 'The Declaration of

Rights and Responsibilities!' And then we command—no, we *ask*—Hung to put his dragon and phoenix chop to it. No one can accuse me of taking away his face. We will send this letter to the emperor and to the barbarian kings across the sea to show them that we are not peasants but civilized men."

Under his crude exterior, the tough, wily charcoal-carrier was a philosopher-king: he had taken all the experiences of the march—every hardship and failure, every hard-won victory, every half-teasing conversation with Mandley about America—and fashioned a plan for turning the huge army into the most progressive nation in the East! This was the reason for Yang's fascination with the Book of Leviticus, Mandley realized. Yang had been drafting in his head the laws that would create a holy nation. Emboldened by the challenge of building a theocracy like Calvin's Geneva or Moses' Israel, Mandley whittled Yang's ideas for reform into eleven precepts, spare and sharp, totally un-Chinese in both shape and content and couched in epistle form to Hung. Yang was planning to make treaties with foreign nations—something the emperor had done only under duress. Yang also proposed establishing a business tax, building up a navy, declaring uncultivated areas public domain, and opening them up for farming and mining, building railroads, and welcoming foreign immigration.

When Mandley read the final draft to Rulan, she grimaced to show her disapproval.

"What's wrong?" he asked in surprise.

"There's something left out."

"What?"

"We women were promised a place in the Heavenly Kingdom," Rulan declared. "This letter makes no mention of us."

"It goes without saying that brothers and sisters are one," said Mandley, obviously ill at ease. "The Eastern King is not making a special case of either."

Rulan's temper flared. Mandley sometimes reasoned as deviously as a Han man. "Special cases are everywhere! We are equal to the brothers but live in separate camps, fight in different brigades, are the last to climb the walls. The women long to lie next to their men, but we are told to wait until the Holy City is won before husbands and wives can live together or lovers marry. Meanwhile, the kings take into their bed whichever girl catches their eye."

She noticed Mandley's embarrassment and marveled that a grown man should be so squeamish about sex. Even his desire for her, which she found inoffensive, seemed to frighten him.

He shrugged. "What can I do?"

"Use your power over my father. Make him change the rules to give women more freedom and responsibility."

"He listens to no one—except God the Father," he added lamely.

"He listens to you!"

"You suggest something, then," Mandley said, stung by her criticism. "When he made you head over his women, he gave you the right to speak before him."

She paused, savoring the moment. Here was the opportunity for which Ma Tsu Po had planned and dreamed. "In the matter of women, all the promises made to the Orchids long ago—schools, examinations, offices—should go into the proposal."

Mandley's brush flew up and down the page. He read the sentences back to her. " 'Although the Land of Flowers has many people, our women have never been able to perform any services. We should build girls' schools, give government examinations to women scholars, and open offices to women—' "

"Ah, one thing more," Rulan interjected. "Unbind the feet."

Mandley murmured his approval and added a line of black marks. "Anything else?"

"Write that the Kingdom of Great Peace should promote a 'manly spirit' in women. When men and women become useful, nothing can stop our country from being strong," said Rulan earnestly.

When the letter was done, Mandley put a title on the document with a flourish, The Declaration of Twelve Rights and Responsibilities. Then he lay his brush across the ink stone, while Rulan clapped her hands like a child and kissed his cheek.

But Hung would not sign it.

The mood aboard the Eastern King's salt boat plunged from jubilation to anger. Wei was whispering that the document was a plot by Yang to steal the love of the people away from the Younger Son.

Yang would agree neither to rescind his document nor to revise it. "It's good the way it is. Anything else would make us laughingstocks!" Yang fumed. " 'Coolie kings!' That's what the emperor calls us! And that's what we will be to the world unless we can prove we can talk and think better than the Dragon!"

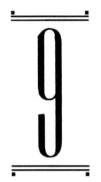

he crackle of a hundred night fires filled the air. Rulan watched Pao An from under her lashes. He was cleaning his rifle and seemed oblivious of the press of men and the buzz of conversation around them. She watched in fascination as he broke open the barrel with the careful deliberation of a peasant cracking open a precious egg and began rubbing the mechanism with a rag soaked in oil. His long fingers, calloused from pike fighting, seemed to know instinctively every orifice, curve, and depression of the new weapon, which every Taiping commander had learned to use. She, Mandley, and Pao An were seated around a campfire, waiting for Eng and Iron Fist to return from a meeting with a messenger from Hung. Rulan had been genuinely delighted to see her old teacher again, although she could not understand why Iron Fist had appeared so coldly remote. He had claimed barely to remember Ma Tsu Po and the Orchids and seemed unmoved at her account of their deaths.

They were a curious and tense group: the barbarian adviser, the giant pikeman, and the Eastern King's daughter. Mandley and Pao An sat glumly at opposite sides of the fire and spoke little to each other.

Two hundred holy soldiers had set out in three columns under Eng, Pao An, and Iron Fist to sweep the southern banks of the river clean of enemy snipers, the last obstacle between the Taiping and the citadel of

Nanking. Yang had told the three generals to "march around and scare the imps, but don't waste time fighting."

When she had heard that Wing's women were riding as scouts for the campaign, Rulan demanded to go too. After a terrible row, Yang finally agreed to let his daughter ride—but with the men. He put Mandley in charge of her safety and made the missionary promise to spirit Rulan away at the first sign of attack. Once the boats and tents disappeared in the distance, however, Rulan insisted that she and Mandley ride at the head of the column with Eng and Iron Fist and Pao An. She seemed giddy, almost drunk with freedom and hungry for a taste of danger.

As they rode through the small villages, the sight of the golden-skinned warrior woman astride a white stallion moved the uncommitted folk more than the flood of Taiping memorials and copies of the Book. All through the countryside, the people decorated themselves in yellow in honor of their passing: women and children waved anything yellow they could find—rags, paper, bits of ribbon or string. Yellow kites streamed from the rooftops and bare branches of trees. Yellow, the imperial color, long forbidden to the people, had become the symbol of the inevitability of the people's triumph: to Rulan, the way to Nanking now seemed paved with gold.

Amid the sweaty crush of men, Rulan was conscious only of Pao An, although it was Mandley who walked in the dust beside Cloud, who shook her awake each morning, who read to her each night out of the Book, and who argued points of doctrine with her. When she asked the barbarian why he bothered, he replied, "To win your soul."

It was Mandley who sat beside her at the campfire now, as if to guard her from the dark, unsmiling young man on the opposite side. Mandley's open journal lay on his knees, and he was writing in the script that went backward like a crab across the page, from left to right. He used a hollow duck's quill instead of a proper brush, and formed each letter with a uniform thinness without the subtle shadings and gradations of a brush. Rulan liked these strange, sharply etched marks because they reminded her of the scratches on ox bones that her mother used to make.

Mandley taught Rulan every night, no matter how exhausted they were from the march or from battle. She now recognized the twenty-six characters of the barbarian alphabet. When he had first introduced her to the language, she had marveled at how few characters there were—unlike the thousands of separate Chinese ideographs. How could a language be built on such a puny foundation? she wondered. When he told her that the characters stood not for ideas but for sounds, her mind leaped at the notion. She wanted to know immediately what the sounds were and how they fit together to make sense, but he suddenly became shy and would not translate. She guessed he was writing about her . . . as if his naked desire weren't evident.

It was even stranger to experience the collective passion of all the men in camp. To them, she was "White Horse Woman," the legendary Fa Mulan come alive. Even the toothless Eng devoured her with his good eye when she rose from her dusty blankets, sleepy and disheveled, her throat parched for morning tea. She pulled his beard and called him grandpa. Only Pao An held himself aloof from her. Had he forgotten the days of her madness when the two of them slept beneath the same ragged blankets, and he fed her rice with his fingers? Did he so discount the danger she had courted when she embraced him before all the warriors? Now on the nights when they spoke around the campfire, Pao An was as correct with her as an elder brother. Their talk was of arms and maneuvers and rations and the murderously ambitious counts and dukes who had sprung up overnight in the train of the rival kings. Her position as Yang's daughter lay like a sword between them.

The meeting between Eng, Iron Fist, and the messenger from Hung's council had broken up with some rancor. Eng came to Rulan's campfire with his sword drawn and squatted on his haunches next to Pao An.

"Great triumphs by our illustrious Hung." Eng beat his short sword on his thigh like a storyteller picking up the rhythm of his tale with his staff. "Hung's two older brothers have poured dung over the Eastern King's reputation among the followers of Shih Ta Kai. The priests are squabbling like fishwives. Hung's 'moons' are fighting in the boat he calls a palace. Bah! No wonder he refuses to sign the Declaration of Rights and Responsibilities with such women in his house. Someone should pour hot water on that pit of vipers. And our brave Triad general with the Fist of Shit tells me to be careful, go slow, don't anger Hung with another victory now because Pawnbroker Wei's army must have the honor of clearing the way to Nanking. Aaiiee," he said ruefully to Pao An. "You do not know how lucky you are to be here with me away from the great ones."

"Assuredly," retorted Pao An. "To be here with you, to hear your sweet voice instead of lying on pillows and listening to the silvery tongues of ten concubines. My fortune is great."

Ill at ease over the mention of the sexual excesses of the Taiping leaders, Mandley steered the conversation to matters of war, particularly the problem that had been worrying him for some time. "I heard that Scholar Tseng is building several hundred ships to make a navy," he said darkly.

"When did a poet ever command?" Eng scoffed. "He's cut the necks of too many Triads and boatmen when he was cleaning house in Chang Sha. The fisherfolk and canal workers are for us. The Tanka fly our flags. None of Tseng's shit-eating Hunan farmers know how to sail."

"Sail?" Pao An retorted. "They have to make the boats first. Where will he learn to build them—from a book?"

"It can be done," Mandley said with some heat. "If a charcoal-carrier can command a holy nation, a scholar can make a navy. Compare Tseng to Hung and you will see in every instance how Tseng triumphed where Hung faltered. Instead of failing the examinations, he came in first. He made friends with the old emperor and when the Tao Kuang died, he shifted his friendship to the right eunuchs, princes, and harem concubines. He's every bit as smart as the Eastern King, only without our commander's faith or scruples. Need sailors? He bribes the people who sail our boats, the lake fishermen. I grant you that the idea for his militia he stole from the Eastern King! He picks poor farmers, whole clans if he can, who are only too grateful to be chosen, and makes them swear to serve a single officer as sons do a father. One family fighting under a single flag, like us. And his rules are the same as the ones the Eastern King enforces: no wine, no opium, no rape, no gambling. The difference is Tseng pays them top wages and Confucius, not God Almighty, is their king. The Hunanese peasants follow him to their deaths because he tells them they are fighting for the old ways against us. I warrant that in one year, he will have his navy and an army of toughs to rival the holy soldiers."

Pao An shook his turbaned head indignantly. "But Tseng does not have White Horse Woman to lead his ruffians. With Rulan before us, we will crack the walls of Nanking before Scholar Tseng can throw together his pile of leaking boards!"

Rulan barely heard Mandley's reply as the quarrel subsided into gruff syllables. A wisp of smoke from the fire had passed before her, blurring all the bodies except one: the dark, muscular man sitting beyond the leaping flames. She saw the small lines at the corners of Pao An's eyes (when had those appeared?), the curling hairs of his black beard, the full lips trembling from the effort of suppressing the anger that always threatened to wreck his composure. Her eyes traced the scars along his throat, lingered at the flutter of pulse above the ridge of bone, and came to rest at the trace of pale skin where the brown flesh disappeared into the sweat-stained tunic. So it has begun again, she thought with a shock, feeling the familiar melting in her loins. The heat. The yearning. Just when she most needed to be as cold and hard as a spear to bring the Kingdom of Great Peace into being. Help me, she begged whatever god might hear. Make me a stone girl again or else I will go mad.

Her face burned when she saw that Pao An was watching her. He desired her too!

Mandley saw the silent exchange between them. In a burst of sudden anger, he asked Pao An in a voice that was low and tight, "What do you now prefer to kill with, Chen—the gun or the pike?"

"This," replied Pao An slowly, fingering the gun with distaste, "is a weapon for the squeamish. A touch of my finger and the head of some man far away explodes like an overripe melon. I don't have to touch him or to look into his face. I don't even sweat. You barbarians deal out death so coldly. We Han prefer a more artful way of killing, like the thousand cuts. It is slow, but it greatly involves the killer and his victim." The smile he gave Mandley made Rulan afraid. "Yet, since I have always been a coward in battle, I guess the gun will be my way too."

"It had better be your way or the imps will shoot off your testicles before you get near them with your rusty blade," Eng said, laughing uproariously. He was old-fashioned in everything except the technology of war.

Mandley's face was bright red underneath the grizzled beard. "If there is one thing you Han can learn from the West," he challenged Pao An, "it is to be more efficient. One of our sages gave us a saying, Time and tide wait for no man. I was surprised to find that there is no equivalent among you proverb-spouting men of Han."

"Oh. But you are wrong. We Hakka have a saying," Rulan interjected brightly. She tried to make her manner lighthearted. " 'Time is a man.' Women say that when they are rushing to make meals, or draw water, or clean the steps before their men come home from the fields. Women know that time is an endless circle, except when you men hurry us."

"And you? Do you hurry for any man, Rulan?" Mandley asked, almost angrily.

"I don't have a man."

"You had one in Abundant Spring Mountain," Pao An accused and then immediately hung his head.

In the embarrassed silence that followed, Rulan rose. "It's late. I should go."

"No, stay," Mandley pleaded, glowering at Pao An.

"Aiya," Eng said. "Stay. Don't let this big stupid rush you. Damn you, Chen, for suggesting the name of that one testicle, Viceroy Li. You poured water on a fine discussion of Han and barbarian ways."

"I'm sorry," Pao An mumbled.

"If a woman could choose a man to hurry her, she could do no better than General Chen Pao An, hero of Yo Chou," Rulan said with great deliberateness.

The men were silent.

Rulan drowned her desire for Pao An by arguing with him in council. Against Pao An's and Eng's protests, she suggested that the Taiping slow their march to Nanking in order to appease Hung and Wei. This made her the inadvertent ally of Iron Fist.

"Let's smash down the walls of Nanking ourselves. Who needs the main columns?" Eng shouted, enraged.

"The Eastern King has agreed to this," Iron Fist declared. "He is willing to let Wei be first into Nanking if it pleases Hung." Iron Fist argued that they ought to go slower and leave fortifications at key points lest their offensive fail and the Taiping be forced to retreat.

"Retreat?" Pao An fumed. "Since when are we imitating the strategy of the Manchu devils?"

Rulan wondered why, with the promise of victory so close, betrayal of her warrior resolve had come from an unexpected source—her own body. So long a cold, unfeeling thing, the perfect instrument for revenge, her body breathed new fire whenever Pao An came near, hungering for connection even as her mind embraced chastity and self-denial. First lay waste Nanking and Peking, the twin cities of pride, she told herself. After the Kingdom of Great Peace is established on earth and the people made free, there would be time for a man, time for her own happiness.

In the close quarters of the camp she shared with Eng, Mandley, and Pao An, Rulan could not make a completely private toilet. Once or twice, Mandley had chanced on her while she was dressing. It was the closest he had ever been to a woman, and soon he came to think it was the most natural thing in the world to have her around. But he was also deeply unsettled that the eyes of other men were on her, too. Her attraction for Pao An both wounded and puzzled him. Why would she prefer the untutored young commander to himself? He vowed to win her away from Pao An and tormented himself by imagining all sorts of past intimacies between them.

In his pallet at night, with Rulan sleeping at his elbow, Mandley concocted wild schemes to steal her away from China and spirit her back to America. She would be the evidence of his great triumph among the Taiping. His convert, his helpmate, his child in the Lord. He had taught her to read and write English; he would teach her to love him. He would show her off in Richmond and Savannah to the Board of Missions. There would be speaking tours for the ladies of the churches—how they would quake at her stories of battlefield conversions!

Pao An dreamed too. Of a woman straight and tall as a pagoda, with flashing eyes and teeth, sun-bronzed skin, and hair that flowed like a dark river over her shoulders.

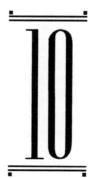

ng had been heaping scorn on his fellow officers: the string of easy victories had made them as soft as the imps, he said. And when Mandley protested that intelligence and not muscle was the mark of a true soldier, Rulan had tied her long hair into a braid and gaily challenged Mandley to wrestle.

Mandley had protested that it wasn't decorous for a man to fight a woman because their strength was unequal and he might hurt her.

"Ha." Iron Fist laughed. "This lady will cook you up a dish of barnyard dirt and push your face in it."

"Mandley, you shock me! Didn't we draft the Twelve Rights and Responsibilities together? Didn't we agree that women and men would walk side by side?" Rulan said, grinning mischievously.

"Walk yes, wrestle no!" he shot back. He was chagrined that she would actually put their proposals to the test in this unorthodox and public way. "Perhaps Hung knows the extent to which women would go if he endorses those principles," Mandley grumbled. "That is why he is refusing to sign them."

Rulan merely laughed and shook her finger playfully at him. "Do not mock me with Hung's prejudices. For my part, I will only pit my weakness against your strength. Let us see who stands firm."

When the impromptu match was called, Iron Fist went about boasting that he had once taught Yang's daughter to fight with open hands.

Pao An was incensed anew at the Triad's uncanny involvement in every important drama of his life and with every woman he'd loved. He was sure that despite Iron Fist's protestations of faith to the High God, the Triad was a creature of opportunity, turning this way and that, according to how he perceived the current of power to be flowing.

A circle had been drawn in the dirt, and Eng stood in the center of it, holding his gun. "When I fire this thing, fight! The first one to fall loses. If you go out of the circle, you lose!" The gun went off accidentally while he was still talking, and Eng jumped back in alarm.

Reluctantly, Mandley grabbed Rulan's forearm, and she pushed his hand away as if she were brushing off a mosquito.

"That's no hold. Grip me tighter," she said.

Mandley put his arms around her, too embarrassed to squeeze. She twisted free in an instant. Pao An stood to the side, grinning from ear to ear.

Rulan flicked her long braid over her shoulder. "Make like a monkey grasping the tree," she teased, acting out her meaning for him. But no matter what he did, she slipped through his arms. Again and again, he tried and failed to hold her; it was like catching the wind in a net.

"Hit me," she dared then, her eyes dancing.

Mandley had boxed as a boy. It was the one thing that had pleased his drunken father.

Rulan was standing up, facing him, making herself an easy target. Her tunic had slipped open and he could see the hollow between her breasts where sweat beaded.

"Aim for my belly!" she cried.

Mandley closed his eyes and doubled his fist. "What a strange way to court a woman," he said to himself. He had seen Pao An's eye on him and felt all the more ridiculous.

Unbelievably, his fist hit empty air. He opened his eyes and struck again. But her belly seemed to slide away. He lunged for her, and again, nothing. He aimed and swung, panting now, but she vanished from the place before, without ever leaving the circle in the dirt.

After ten minutes, Mandley was awash in sweat and frustration. Rulan had barely begun to perspire. She parried or eluded every one of his thrusts. Finally, she took his feet out from beneath him with a graceful sweep of her leg, and he plopped down on the ground, his mouth dry, his throat tight, and sweat dripping off his matted hair into the dirt. She fell on her hands and knees, close enough to kiss him.

"Such is the weakness of women," she said, laughing, leaning down to him.

He willed her close and shook the drops of sweat from his hair. The moment was so intimate that he felt his heart ache with the joy of her. "Rulan," he said, savoring her name on his tongue. "You are a miracle."

"She was my pupil!" Iron Fist bragged.

"No miracle, it's *chi*. You have it too," she told Mandley.

He rolled his eyes. They had argued about this before. "I thought *chi* had left you."

"This is the *chi* that is commonplace, nothing more than one needs to live and move around. I think a woman is better than a man at wrestling because *chi* conquers through weakness. A strong man like you can be defeated by using that strength against you. If I had my healing fire back, I could knock you senseless. In the old days, there were *chi gung* masters who could leap higher than a house, or turn their bodies into air, or heal without touching, simply by raising the palm, so—"

Seeing Mandley's expression, Rulan bristled. "You do not believe me!"

Mandley's breath exploded in a burst of laughter. "It's not part of my barbarian experience."

"But you could not hold me! Can you doubt that?"

"No." He shook his head. "But there must be evil in this *chi*. Anything that deadens the mind, that makes the body move despite—or against—one's God-given reason and will would be without conscience, which is the seed of divinity planted within."

"Then what about my father's trances? What about Hung, when he speaks the sounds of the high heaven? You call my father the Voice of God, the Wind of Heaven, the Holy Spirit. I call it *chi*—"

Without warning, Pao An stood between them. "You are too smart, Teacher. Everything must pass through your head. You barbarians have to prove everything, doubt everything. Let me show you about *chi*." He reached down and pulled Rulan to her feet. "Come, try me."

After arranging Rulan's palm on his, he raised them to chest level. Rulan seemed uncharacteristically demure.

"But you know me," she said softly.

The word sounded shockingly biblical to Mandley. This was what he could not accept about the East: the unclear borders between spirit and flesh, passion caught within ritual and magic.

Slowly, Pao An moved his hands back and forth, as if pumping heat into hers. She held back at first, as a woman would, and then began to push against him with all her might. He broke the hold and moved his hand low to the ground, and in the same instant, she adjusted the pressure and position of her hands and her stance to match his. Push, pull, high, low. She caught and held every thrust, seeming to collapse, then pushing back with a smooth, graceful twist of hips, knees, and hands that made him sway in the opposite direction. Back and forth they moved within the circle drawn in the dust, then faster and faster, their hands together, panting now, moving expertly against and with each other in a fluid antagonism. One seemed to know instinctively how the other would move. She broke the hold and aimed a punch at his midsection. Pao An writhed away with so much grace that he seemed to roll in slow motion. Pao An was obviously the stronger, but he was not holding back, as Mandley had, out of mistaken concern for Rulan's weakness. Pao An caught her hands again and they swayed together, hip to hip, so close now that one could not tell which hand, which leg it was that rose and fell.

They had attracted a large crowd of onlookers. Soldiers always appreciated an exhibition of push-hands boxing, and this one, between a man and a woman, was extraordinary. Eng bounced around on his haunches close to them, shouting encouragement to Rulan, while Iron Fist muttered derisive disclaimers about Pao An's masculinity.

"Aaiiee!" exclaimed Eng, when a blow from Pao An toppled Rulan in the dirt. He had to be restrained from going after his own friend.

Mandley didn't know if it was a dance, a combat—or the paroxysms of love. "Aaiiee!" he echoed softly. It was the first time he had uttered that familiar Han epithet of sorrow and loss in all the years he had lived in China. He felt himself already an old man.

To give her honor, Pao An fought as long as her strength held out, and when he had finally beat her, he took off his embroidered headband, shook his braid free, and placed the red cloth in her hands.

That night Pao An couldn't sleep. He went out to look at the moon from a rocky promontory near their camp.

She came so quietly he didn't hear her.

"Rulan," he said to the sky.

"Yes," she answered him. She had tied his red headband around her neck.

He turned to her, as if her name had been a prayer that made her materialize. "Are you real?"

"Once when you were ill, you asked me that."

He pulled her close and felt how easily her body molded to his.

How slowly he began with her! She was surprised by his tenderness.

She watched the stars turn in the heavens. The Spinning Maid moved above the bough of the cypress while he was still discovering her.

And he made her discover herself. There was a hand flowered with fingers. There was a bone beneath the flesh like a white stone under a smooth curve of water. There was an eye fluttering like a hiding bird. And there a place where she ended—and there a place where she began. There were islands in her, and mountains. Her body was a kingdom she had never explored.

And when the Cowherd had turned under the bough of the cypress, and the Spinning Maid was hidden from view, he taught her about time. She had been moving in circles, like water whirling down toward the center of the earth, but then he began to rise up in a straight line, like a kite carried on the wind. And he began to bargain with her, the way the wind plays games with water. And he began and she began. And he began to hurry her. And she said to him with the softness of flesh, hurry me. Oh hurry me, hurry me.

And she rode a white cloud over the edge of the world.

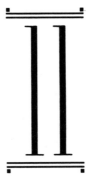

With the area around Nanking swept clean of spies and snipers, Eng, Pao An, and Iron Fist led their men back to the flotilla. Iron Fist's attitude toward Pao An seemed to have changed. He left off sneering and even sent Pao An two horses—which were promptly returned. And he spoke with renewed affection to his old pupil, flattering Rulan and commending her on her fighting skills.

Iron Fist's warmth made Rulan more suspicious than his former coldness. It was hard for her to believe that this man had played as pivotal a role in Pao An's life as in her own. She knew that coincidence was the mark of fate, so she avoided Iron Fist because he had been a harbinger of death in the past. Besides, she could not tell whom he served. Was he her father's spy in Wei's camp, or Wei's spy in her father's, or merely satisfying his own devious ends?

The two hundred warriors returned from their mission on the southern bank without further incident, and the generals went to confer with the kings for the final assault on Nanking.

Yang's cabin was rank with the sour-sweet stench of raw opium cakes, which had soaked into the wood of the drafty old salt boat. His ship was half the size of the dragon boat, where Hung traveled in splendor with his wives, sycophants, and retainers, but it was the hub of activity in the long flotilla. The two nine-foot rectangular flags signaling Yang's kingship floated proudly above the tattered quilted sails. If the dragon boat was the symbol of the holy soldiers' glory, Yang's mean vessel was the symbol of their bloody striving. The cabin barely accommodated Yang, his women, Mandley, Rulan, and six or seven of his trusted generals. But none of the hundreds of warriors who flocked to the salt boat to pay court to the Eastern King seemed to mind the cramped and humble quarters.

More often than not in those heady days as the Taiping nation floated unopposed the last few miles to Nanking, politics rather than warfare occupied the attention of Yang's inner circle. What was Wei doing in his secret meetings with Hung? Was the most powerful of the pirate-generals still loyal to Yang or had he pledged his swift "scrambling dragons"—the opium-running craft he had stolen in Hong Kong—to Yang's rival Wei? What information had been brought by the forward scouts on the northern bank that had been reported to one king and not the other?

For Rulan and Pao An, the days on the water before the invasion of Nanking were filled with danger, excitement, and unparalleled joy. They saw each other only in the company of others during the day. Yet Rulan was not so foolish as to believe that the passion that had sprung up between them on the long march might go unnoticed. She suspected from Mandley's melancholy that the barbarian guessed at her liaison with Pao An, but she believed that his loyalty would move him to compassion—and discretion.

Loving was impossible in the close confines of the boat; it was enough for her to be near Pao An, to talk to him out of some pretense of duty. A glance from the corner of his long eyes, a certain catch in his voice, the way his calloused hands caressed a rough table would call up for her vivid reminders of their stolen night together. In her happiness, Rulan allowed herself to dream of some future life with him, especially of the day when the empire was won and the brothers and sisters allowed to seek each other in marriage, as her father had promised.

For Yang, dealing with Hung was more trying than fighting the imps. Having rejected the Twelve Rights and Responsibilities, Hung now refused to countersign any of Yang's edicts. While Yang did not need Hung's assent to deal with the army, protocol demanded Hung's seal on all legislation governing the social aspects of Taiping life. By ignoring Yang's messages, Hung had effectively halted all plans for establishing a permanent community. Yang worried that the million Taiping sojourners would arrive at Nanking with no plan for their stay. There would be more chaos when the march ended than at any time on their long, bloody journey from Thistle Mountain. Where would each person live? Should families be brought back together immediately? What jobs would people pursue, and how would those jobs be assigned? There were a million questions for a million people, and only the Eastern King seemed to care how these might be addressed.

Hung ignored Yang's appeals for drafting plans for their journey's end. He sent back fulsome but guarded replies to Yang's impatient queries, while making elaborate excuses about why he could not meet with Yang in person. Instead he sent emissaries—his fawning older brothers and his sister Jiao, who remonstrated with Rulan for "stealing away" from the women's corps. And the Northern King Wei launched yet another campaign of innuendo against Yang, saying that the Eastern King was putting himself higher than Hung. Wei had taken to calling Yang's ecstatic speech the "screeching of a blind owl," claiming that he, not Yang, was the only king capable of translating Hung's visions into law.

Yang dismissed Wei as an "effeminate weakling," but Eng argued that Wei, as a pawnbroker, could not be discounted. Throughout history, pawnbrokers were fronts for secret societies and hence were master manipulators of men. Wei was more dangerous than Hung, Eng warned. Hadn't he once tried to poison Rulan? But Yang turned aside his old friend's warnings with a joke.

One morning, as Yang's coterie gathered in his cabin, Iron Fist and a small retinue hailed the watch to announce that they were coming aboard.

"The Northern King called on me," Iron Fist said after polite greetings were exchanged.

Yang waved a gnarled hand to dismiss the guards who had been handing around bowls of steaming yellow tea. "What does Wei want that he has convinced Hung to demand of me?"

"A bargain," replied Iron Fist.

The group moved closer around the table as they always did when the talk shifted to Wei or Hung.

"I have discovered that when Wei holds one hand open, his other hand makes a fist," Eng stated, illustrating his words. "The blow follows the gift."

"You worry too much, Brother," admonished Yang. "The army is ours. That makes Wei no threat."

"The Triads are yours too," Iron Fist assured Yang.

"Loyal to me or to Wei?"

"Loyal to *me*," Iron Fist replied evenly. "And I am loyal to you."

Pao An made a rude noise, which made Iron Fist scowl.

"Wei was a pawnbroker who stole whatever he could, even the farms of honest men," Eng accused. "He was the banker of the Red Turbans, to which I believe you belonged!"

Iron Fist's smile was without warmth. "Then I suppose you know that General Chen was also my brother in the Turbans."

"I took the oath and bore the tattoo," Pao An admitted. "Now I am a Taiping general, and if this one calls me 'brother,' then I strike my name from whatever foul tablets he claims as clan."

Iron Fist swallowed his anger with an effort and began again. It seemed to Rulan that he was addressing her, although he kept his eyes on Pao An. "I meant you no embarrassment in mentioning our past association. We are all new men, washed clean by faith. What does it matter what we once were? Murderers, liars, fornicators. We are now chaste and of one intent. Is that not so, White Horse Woman? You, as a former sister of the Golden Orchids, know how one may use an older loyalty to strengthen a new one. So I say to you that the Triads are loyal to the Eastern King!"

"When I am strong, they serve. When I appeal to their better nature with laws, they run," Yang said reproachfully. "How many men ran away when I ordered necks cut if they broke the rules? Prayers before meals, no wine or opium, no women, no looting. They called me cruel! Me, who have only their heavenly souls in mind! Do you deny that some of your brothers went over to the imps for the looting and rape? Tell me your business. What did Wei and the Younger Son say?"

Iron Fist's eyes darted toward Rulan. "You have power over the army, King. Power that the Younger Son bestowed on you by making you commander-in-chief. But soon the long march will end."

Mandley nodded vigorously. He and Yang had labored hard for the day when the empire was won, and Yang would no longer be needed as commander-in-chief. One could not be a Nazarite and wander forever, Yang liked to say. Witness the example of Samson, who was blinded by desire and enslaved by pride. One had to prepare for the time when the brothers and sisters would return to a softer life and build families and homes.

"The Younger Son is thinking of that day," continued Iron Fist. "Wei told me that Hung will give you command over the civil government just as he has granted you authority over military matters. Hung invites you to put into practice your design of a Holy City for Nanking, particularly your plans for land redistribution and guilds and treasure. He will sign the Declaration of Rights and Responsibilities. Moreover, he will bestow upon you the title Nine Thousand Years."

Rulan, who had been unconsciously holding her breath, gave a cry of triumph. Eng swore, and Mandley swallowed his shock. Only Hung was addressed as *Wan Sui,* Ten Thousand Years, the emperor's honorific. Hung was offering the unthinkable—to raise Yang to near divine status and hence to diminish his own power.

"Then we would have to call the Younger Son another name," replied Yang with perfect sincerity. "Ten Thousand Thousand Years, perhaps, to do justice to his glory."

Iron Fist made a deprecating gesture and continued. "He told Wei that he is tired of governing. He wants to live inside the walls, to plan for the Heavenly Kingdom, and to proclaim his divine revelations."

"Fascinating," Mandley said, wiping away the sweat that had suddenly gathered on his forehead. "He seems to be suggesting something like the shogunate in Japan. One all-powerful political and military leader would carry out the emperor's will. Of course, in actuality, the shogun rules. It's an unprecedented opportunity, Eastern King—"

"For turtle dung fools!" Eng stormed. "It's a trap! If the Eastern King accepts, he is guilty of raising himself too high—Nine Thousand Years means he covets Hung's place. Hung is trying to goad you into treason, so he can turn the other kings against you!"

"Quiet, old friend. Hear our brother out. Nothing is given for free. He wants something in return," Yang observed dispassionately. "Something that would cost me dearly to give."

All heads swung in Iron Fist's direction.

Iron Fist drew himself up and announced, "He wants Rulan to ride ahead of his palanquin when he enters Nanking. He wants her as head of his bodyguard and as his celestial bride. He wants to marry her."

"Marry?" Mandley choked on the word.

A shout from Yang brought Pao An up short, just as he was about to strike Iron Fist. Yang had risen from his seat, his cheeks trembling, his face suffused with blood. "You tell Pawnbroker Wei that the Eastern King does not sell his daughter!" A look of anguish passed between him and Rulan, for he had, of course, sold her once before.

"Of course the Eastern King cannot sell his daughter!" Mandley sputtered. "To do so would be construed by the foreign powers as a sign of barbarism. We have left that evil custom behind when we made the resolution to honor women."

Iron Fist and Pao An had squared off like two bulls snorting and pawing, ready to charge.

"Wait!" Rulan shouted. She suspected that Iron Fist was baiting Pao An, the most hot tempered of Yang's generals, into pushing Yang into an all-out rebellion against Hung. "What else does he want from me?"

Yang shot back brusquely, "This does not concern you, Daughter. I have already decided. Hung wants to unman me. Tell him I refuse the offer."

Iron Fist dominated his blinding anger with effort. "He will honor Rulan above all his other women. He will make her chancelloress over the women officials in his house, over all the women generals, except for Jiao, his own sister. He says she is the Key to Heaven, the one thing necessary to complete the prophecy he has spoken with his own lips—that a special woman will open the gates of paradise for him. He will not make Nanking his capital unless she comes to him willingly."

"Oh, that is how he means to subvert my plans," Yang declared. He pounded his fist on the table and made the heavy crockery jump. "A trap with two jaws—pride and position! If I give him Rulan and accept the title Nine Thousand Years, he sets the other kings upon me. If I refuse him Rulan, he will not claim Nanking as our holy city. And if he turns our weary troops toward Peking, we will be defeated. Our people are tired, hungry, deprived of clan. We have been marching two years. They will not move north with goodwill when Nanking is ours for the taking. And the Dragon will defend his homelands more vigorously than these regions. We will lose everything if we go to Peking!"

"Precisely," Iron Fist interjected darkly. "A hundred of his odes have praised a woman as the key. He believes Rulan is that woman. The army already believes it. The men will follow her anywhere. If she will not open the gates of Nanking then that must not be the intended city, and he will direct our feet northwest to Peking."

"The imps and Scholar Tseng's shit-eaters will be waiting for us on top of every hill we have to pass," Eng declared. He held his head in his hands, the long red tassel shaking incongruously with every movement of his head.

Rulan had been quietly listening while the men shouted. She was amazed at how little fear she had. Instead, she heard her mother's dying words, "To defeat him, give him what he most desires."

A strange peace had descended on her now that she had decided to heed her mother and run to her fate instead of waiting for it to overtake her. Consenting, she observed, made one free. "I will go," she said quietly.

There was a howl of pain from her father. "I'll not risk you again!" Yang cried.

"I'll kill you if you try to take her away!" Pao An declared to Iron Fist through clenched teeth.

Rulan found herself shouting over the din. "How can brother fight brother? We would lose everything we have marched and fought for!"

"But Hung will have your father in his power if he holds you hostage in his harem," Mandley cried in agony. "That will defeat everything we've fought for too."

"Will he guarantee my father the title Nine Thousand Years and sign the Rights and Responsibilities?" she challenged Iron Fist.

"He has sworn to do so," Iron Fist avowed.

"Unfilial! Disrespectful!" Yang shouted angrily at his daughter.

"Then I go into the tiger's den willingly and with a warrior's heart," Rulan declared.

"This is barbaric," Mandley stammered, frantic at the drift the argument was taking.

"Please—" Yang whispered.

"Tell my father that Jael and Esther did no less than I intend," Rulan said stubbornly to Mandley.

"You must not do this," Mandley shouted, but Rulan had already taken off her bracelet and given it to Iron Fist as a token of her acceptance.

After the others had taken their leave, Yang sat alone in the stinking hold of the salt boat as the sounds of the morning rose around him: hungry gulls screaming for breakfast scraps, women scolding, and the splash of night soil thrown into the river.

Suddenly, he laughed out loud. It had come to him in an instant how everything could be made right.

He had a plan. Didn't he always have a plan?

After the capture of their city and their men, hundreds
of Wu Chang women had hurled themselves off the
Taiping boats into the Yangtze, preferring death to conversion; those
who remained were a sullen, desperate lot. Wing strengthened discipline among her squads, ordered worship and taught classes, appointed
sentries, and called up whole brigades for sanitation and for care of the
sick. And their numbers were soon swollen by more women from Kiu
Kiang and An King. There were thousands of nursing mothers and
infants, unmarried girls and widows, and, until they were ten, boys as
well. There were also the aged and infirm of both sexes who needed
medical care and who could not march with the male battalions.

Wing was quick to make known her impatience with her duties as
leader of the captive women. "Let one of the Younger Son's guard,
who knows doctrine, take over for me," she proposed to Jiao. "Let
Heavenly Glory preach."

"She accompanies my brother now," Jiao said.

"But you know that my tongue is too thick for preaching. And
besides, I don't know what to tell them. These women were pushed
out of their homes, their sons snatched away into the Boy's Guard,
their husbands vanished into that endless pile of floating barracks. No
wonder so many drowned themselves as we sailed away from Wu

Chang. They believe they are only being kept alive to become the soldiers' playthings. They don't believe anything I say!"

"Be careful, Sister," Jiao replied. "Not to love doctrine is to demean the Younger Son. If you cannot preach, teach them the Lord's Prayer and the Ten Heavenly Rules, so they can follow the Younger Son's ritual every day. Promise them a beating if they refuse to memorize the laws of the road and the marching formation."

"Lily-foot women can't march!"

"They'll learn," replied Jiao grimly.

Reluctantly Wing agreed because she knew that the Taiping were being overwhelmed more by their victories than their defeats. As a nation without a home, they were drowning in their own vast and unruly numbers. And the Women's Camp was the most unruly of all. The Taiping had come so fast by land and water that the food and ammunition taken from Yo Chou and Wu Chang were already depleted. The women's column numbered over three hundred thousand.

One Sabbath, after delivering the jewels taken from the conscripts to the holy treasury, Wing received a message from Rulan to meet secretly outside the city gates at An King, near the burial grounds where the heads of the Manchu were stuck on pikes. The city had been occupied after being attacked for just a week.

As Wing approached on horseback, she smelled the acrid smoke of the fires where the bodies of the righteous Taiping had been burned. Because enemy dead were left to rot in the open for the dogs and jackals, partially eaten carcasses were strewn everywhere. The grisly setting began to weaken Wing's resolve. This might easily be a trick laid by Jiao, she thought. Maybe Jiao planned to assassinate her in this desolate boneyard. Then she saw Cloud pawing the soft earth on a little knoll, and her fears subsided.

Wing found Rulan seated on an ancient U-shaped crypt, dressed in the plain blue vest and red jacket of a common horsewoman. She carried two short swords stuck into her sash, as did Wing, and wore her hair unbound.

When Wing dismounted, Rulan embraced her warmly, ignoring the older woman's reticence.

"I shouldn't be here," Wing said stiffly. "Jiao hates you more than she hates me. It won't do either of us any good to be seen together."

"Who is going to see us?" Rulan laughed. "The dead?" She sat back down on the granite cenotaph and motioned to Wing to sit beside her.

"I see you on your knees praying next to Jiao at the morning convocations. I hear you bellowing the songs Hung writes for us. And I wonder about you," said Rulan archly. "Have you become a believer?"

"No, but I have learned discretion," Wing told her. "When giants fight, small people are crushed between them. Jiao mistrusts me because of you and is waiting for me to stumble. One fall, one—and I am undone."

"But you are under my father's protection."

Wing's laugh was bitter. "Can he protect me from an arrow let loose by accident on the practice yard? Can he taste my food before I lift it to my mouth?" Her face was pale and frightened. "I have been ready for some time to join my sisters across the Yellow Springs."

"Good," Rulan declared through clenched teeth. "I too am ready!"

Wing was taken aback. "You? I thought you were happy with—with—General Chen."

Rulan's face was suddenly still. "Is it so apparent that I love him?" Cloud shifted uneasily at his mistress's agitation.

"Everyone knows!" Wing said angrily over the horse's complaint.

"No, not everyone," she stumbled, suddenly ashamed. "But I know. I've always known."

"Then you have no more cause to grieve. I have agreed to become Hung's celestial bride. He wants me to lead the bodyguard into Nanking."

Wing grabbed Rulan's hands. "You must not! I won't let you."

"I told you I was looking for a warrior's death. I will lead Hung into Nanking and take my place in his harem. He will sign the Twelve Rights and Responsibilities giving all women freedom. The Kingdom of Great Peace will be real. And after that, when my father has been named Nine Thousand Years and Hung is shut up in his palace, I will kill myself as a sacrifice to Kwan Yin to give the restless souls of my sisters and the old woman I killed some peace."

A small starved dog came sniffing out of the ruins searching for food. Seeing the women, it began to howl with hunger.

"Please don't go to him," said Wing wanly.

Rulan sighed. She was only seventeen, and already she felt old and tired. "I have no mother, sisters, or aunts to dress me for my wedding. I want you to decorate me. I need your strength, Wing. This is my last chance to wash my guilt away."

"What about me? Did you ever think of me?"

"You have the women of Wu Chang," Rulan said. "And there is Li. Destroy the murderer of our sisters."

"I don't care about the others. I don't care about Li. If you die, I want to die too."

Rulan shook her head. "Wing, oh Wing," she said sorrowfully, and leaned her head on Wing's broad shoulder. Wing sat as if turned to stone.

"Sometimes the annunciator of heavenly decrees reads the songs of King David to us," Wing said softly. She reached up to caress Rulan's long hair. "I feel like him, running and hiding in holes, surrounded by spies, rumors, evil tongues. How I long to stop. I tell these Wu Chang recruits, 'Soon we will find our Heavenly City, soon you will take your children home and sleep with your man again.' But I don't believe it. I am a girl on a water lift trying to drain the ocean. I want an end to the hiding and the yearning and the dying. I would welcome death—with you."

Rulan said nothing.

"We will make a new pact, you and I," said Wing fiercely. "I will dress you myself for Hung's bed. I will make plans to destroy the viceroy. But you must make me a promise," Wing said.

"Another?" Rulan protested sadly.

"That you will not die before me."

"I cannot promise that."

Wing pulled out the knife from her sash and held the tip pointed upward at the base of her throat. "We stand on holy ground. Promise."

The brightness of Wing's eyes told Rulan that Wing was beyond caring. "All right, but you must stop loving me. Otherwise, I cannot trust you."

Wing looked as if something had been ripped from her. She clutched Rulan's hand and kissed it, then threw it angrily aside. "I am too hungry to fast and too depressed to pray," she said before putting her knife away.

They mounted their ponies and rode awhile in silence until they skirted a small lake on which a single duck was idling. The green-headed mallard swam fast, dove deep, exploded from the water and the reeds, and disappeared into the sky. Spurring her horse into the shallow end of the lake, Wing drove the duck into the backwater and set a trap in the rushes, and the two women sat in uneasy silence to wait. Eventually, the duck fell into her trap. Wing grabbed it as it was stretching its neck to bite and swung it around in a circle until the neck snapped. She gutted it swiftly with her knife and tossed the offal over her shoulder into the lake.

Their pact had turned them into strangers. Each felt the new breach between them and tried to hide her growing agitation in a flurry of words. Rulan complained that they had no pot to cook the bird. Wing retorted that she was no soldier if she didn't know how to make "beggar's duck." She searched along the lakeshore, and when she had found a place where the mud was mixed with a clay, she plastered the duck with the wet earth. Then she pushed it into the fire Rulan had made of twigs and horse droppings.

After an hour, when the clay had baked dry, Wing rolled the gray shell out of the fire. Taking a clean stone, she rapped it twice. The clay burst open in a cloud of steam. Feathers and skin came off with the clay, leaving just the dark edible flesh.

"Aiya," cried Wing, gingerly pulling the hot flesh from the bones with her fingers. "We should toast death with a cup of hot wine right now."

A man stepped out from the gathering darkness.

They had lain their weapons aside to eat. Wing grabbed a burning stick from the fire and lunged at the intruder.

"Pao An!" cried Rulan.

Wing's flaming brand stopped inches from his eyes.

"Forgive me, General Wing," Pao An said. "I heard that a woman on a white horse rode this way. I had to make sure it was Rulan." Pao An found it hard to believe that this was the same girl he had wrestled and loved only days before. That girl, unencumbered by duty, was sunburned and strong, with a gay beribboned pigtail and flashing eyes and teeth. The one who had promised herself to Hung was pale as death; her unbound hair hung like a dark veil around her melancholy face.

Sadly, Rulan approached Pao An and beckoned to Wing. "Come, Wing, greet my friend. We are all warriors meant for death here."

It was such a strange request, yet made so commandingly that Wing came up to them, and Pao An embraced them both. The one he knew least, the one who once wished for his death, wet him with her tears.

Then they sat down to eat together one last time.

That evening, as the oil lamps in the thousands of junks and barges winked on, Iron Fist hastened to Wei's vessel with a message stamped with Yang's chop and bloody thumbmark. Overjoyed at Yang's capitulation, Wei went himself by torchlight to Hung's dragon boat and gave the letter to a conveyer, who placed it into the slim, white hands of the annunciator of heavenly decrees, who in turn gave the paper to Niang Niang, the Heavenly Queen. But because the queen was unschooled and uncomfortable with court protocol, she importuned Wei to accompany her when she delivered the message to Hung, her sovereign husband. By noon the next day, the news had reached all the other minor kings, generals, and officials on their boats that negotiations were under way for the betrothal of the Younger Son to Rulan, daughter of the Eastern King and chancelloress in the Kingdom of Great Peace.

The City of Taiping, Anhwei Province,
March 1853

The ceremony of betrothal took place the following afternoon in the metropolitan hall of the city just outside Nanking called by prophetic coincidence, Taiping. The city had only lately been captured, and because of its name, Hung ordered the brothers and sisters neither to raze the buildings nor to invade the citizens' homes. A round table was turned into a makeshift altar and draped with a red cloth embroidered with a dragon and a phoenix intertwined. Rulan waited with Wing in a large anteroom concealed behind a red curtain for Hung to enter with Wei and her father. Like all Taiping women, she wore no cosmetics. Her only ornament was a necklace of ancient gold coins, a gift from Hung, which hung over her red embroidered gown to her waist.

What would he look like now, this man whose fate was linked with hers? In six years, she had seen him only from afar during official convocations. There was nothing to connect that brilliantly garbed figure with the long-haired stranger with incandescent eyes who had greeted her like a lover in the Hakka Village Hall. Women loved him, yes; but did he love them back? The women of his entourage were a dour, plain lot. All Taiping women were discouraged from wearing jewelry or painting their faces, but because they did not work in the open or ride horses or do strenuous exercise, Hung's women seemed like shadows next to the other, more robust sisters. Rulan noticed that the women were draped in dark veils and wore long dresses the color of night. Only Jiao seemed to carry herself with pride.

Arrogance, Wing called it. "You see who you put yourself under?" Wing whispered with a worried frown. "In the harem, that one will be ten times worse than the First Wife. And you will have to see that crazy Miao girl we sent away."

"Heavenly Glory doesn't look happy," Rulan observed. Indeed, the Miao girl with the scarred face was clearly miserable. Rulan wondered guiltily if the scar prevented Hung from loving the girl.

There was a ripple of excitement among the women. Heavenly Glory's face lit up with joy as the object of her veneration entered the hall at its eastern end, like the sun rising. Hung wore a long, old-fashioned robe of brilliant yellow that hung down to his embroidered boots. A high peaked yellow hood decorated with twin dragons and twin phoenixes hid the coils of his braid. He was fatter than she remembered, and his beard seemed more red since it had been allowed to grow. He held a scepter of heavy gold encrusted with precious stones. Next to their husband, Hung's women faded even more. It was a brilliant stroke by one whose genius lay in creating visual drama. One sun shone; all else was darkness.

Hung seemed distracted and dreamy. He took tea from the women but forgot to drink, and he murmured to himself when the assembly knelt at the sound of the gong to the light that streamed from the doorway. The priest led them in the Lord's Prayer. Hung did not protest when Yang ordered his women to wait behind the red curtain while the terms of the contract were set. Wei stayed to speak for Hung; Mandley stayed to record the agreement for Yang.

Behind the red curtain, the ladies of Hung's household were silent and resentful. Heavenly Glory and Jiao did not acknowledge Rulan, and Rulan was made aware that they were jealous of her necklace and red dress.

Then the golden gong, which was stolen from a temple in Wu Chang, sounded, and with one accord Hung's ladies rushed to answer their husband's summons.

Rulan entered the room just as the annunciator of heavenly decrees read the long genealogy that ended with the marriage contract:

"Hear this. Yang, the Eastern King and Voice of God, by his wife Ailan of the Loi, has a daughter, Rulan. She is now seventeen years old. Since her mother is dead and her former contract of concubinage to the heir of the house of Li was not sanctified by Heaven, the Eastern King is happy to give her to the Younger Son of God as his celestial bride.

"The kings have agreed on the following conditions. As bride-price, the Younger Son will pay to the family of his wife ten thousand taels of silver, five thousand bolts of silk, and two thousand cakes.

"In addition, the Ten Thousand Years agrees to give the Eastern King dominion over the holy army and the heavenly court, and likewise over the six ministries of heaven, earth, spring, summer, autumn, and winter. His new title will be Nine Thousand Years."

A humming sound, like the murmuring of angry pigeons, rose from Hung's women.

The annunciator continued. "In turn, the Eastern King agrees that his daughter is not a kidnapped child of suspicious origin; that she is indeed her mother's daughter, skilled in the arts of midwifery, herbal medicine, wrestling, horsemanship, and archery; and that she is heir to the titles and benefits of a chancelloress.

"An auspicious day will be selected by the Eastern King's priests for the wedding."

When the two kings had pricked their wrists and imprinted their chops in their own blood, the golden gong sounded again, and all present knelt and said, *"Wan Sui!"* "Ten Thousand Years!"

Then the betrothal gifts were announced: a necklace of ancient gold coins from the groom and a jar made of rare white jade containing raw ginseng from the bride.

In the silence, Hung beckoned to Rulan. He touched the necklace of gold coins around her neck and spoke to her as if he and she were lovers alone:

"Thou. Thou art the key," he said.

Rulan felt an overpowering wave of revulsion. Hung was still a handsome man, but his beauty no longer moved her. His eyes traveled over her body hungrily, and she was reminded of Wang, the fat and greedy merchant in Canton. She could not stop herself from shaking.

"You thought it was your mother who lifted me out of the coils of the snake," he continued, "but I tell you truly, it was your heel which broke the back of *Ku.*"

"I have no magic," she whispered, appalled.

He opened the jar of ginseng that she had given him, sniffed at it, and closed it again, obviously disappointed. "You know herbs and plants. Don't deny that you also know the recipe for the elixir of eternity."

Rulan was aghast. When Hung caught her hand in his and began to rub it lasciviously, she remembered that Wang had done the same. "I am only a woman," she protested, pulling her hand away. Her flesh crawled at the thought that he would touch her more intimately before the night was over.

He looked at her with naked desire, then doubt. Then suspicion.

The last act of the ritual was the prayer poem to be offered up by Hung. "Worship God!" he intoned, and the assembly fell to their knees facing the bright golden figure. On yellow paper, he brushed the prayer of betrothal on a piece of paper and handed it to the priest to read.

> Faithful in heart, in mind and face and with your
>   tongue,
> Faithful in deed, in body and clothed in brilliance.
> Sixfold faithful and singularly bright, serve your
>   Sovereign Husband—with
> Ceremony, glory, and happiness for ten thousand years!

The priest put the paper into an ornamental porcelain basin on the altar and set it on fire. The smoke coiled upward as a loud moaning suddenly filled the room. It seemed to come from everywhere, from the mouths of the women, from the rafters, from Yang, who fell on the floor as if dead. His lips did not move and yet a great voice came out of him like water surging out of a rock.

"Thou art my Son, in whom I am greatly displeased. Are you to defile thyself in the Spirit with the flesh I gave you for your earthly walk?"

"The Voice of the Father," screamed Heavenly Glory.

Yang tottered to his feet. His eyes rolled back into his head, his hands waved uncontrollably. "Will you commit incest in the flesh?" he chanted. "You are my Son after the Spirit. But this woman is my Daughter in the flesh. What is lawful in the Spirit is an abomination in the flesh. Truly she is thine intended. Truly, she is thy Celestial Bride. But hearken to what is required of thee."

Hung dared not lift up his eyes. "What must I do?" he mumbled into the dirt.

"On earth you may not touch her. On earth the Bridegroom may not know the Bride as a man knows a wife. On earth you may not kill her or look upon her with lust. The Celestial Bride is yours to enjoy in Heaven and in Heaven alone. I give her to you for rites and rituals, for feast days and for days of mourning. But she shall live in the house of her father, the Eastern King, until you have ascended into Heaven. If you disobey, you are not my Son. I revoke by my word your sonship. I will disinherit you on earth and in heaven—"

"Thy will be done, thy will be done," Hung whispered.

"I have spoken. God, the Father has spoken! Obey me, else I will cast you out into the wilderness of Sheol."

That night, on the dragon boat, Hung gnashed his teeth and tore his hair and beard. He slapped Heavenly Glory, screaming that he could not abide an ugly woman. When Jiao tried to stop him, he screamed and slapped her too. He told her that Wei must be ordered to commit suicide for his part in Yang's scheme. He swore that he would break the contract even if it meant calling down God's wrath on his own head. In one stroke, Yang had claimed civil and military powers over the Taiping nation, and wrested away the title that he, Hung, had so foolishly offered him as bait. With one hand, Yang had given his daughter and with the other placed her out of Hung's reach. Rulan was his and not his. A bride, and not a bride.

By midnight, Hung's fury had subsided. No, he told Jiao, he would let Wei live. The contract would be fulfilled. For what could not be commanded in the flesh could still be scarred in spirit, and what could not be governed in spirit could still be wounded in the flesh. He swore, by his own godhead, that he would be revenged on Yang's house.

Nanking, March 1853

anking, the old capital of the Ming emperors, sank under the waves of the holy warriors, as a rock is inundated by the relentless tide. Taiping soldiers under Pao An's command on the southeastern bank of the Yangtze stuck millions of bamboo spikes into the ground outside the city gate. At the same time General Eng's sappers dug ditches and tunnels beneath the city walls under cover of cannon fire. In six days, the entire Taiping army had encircled the city, the vast navy lay at anchor to the north, and an endless expanse of red-turbaned warriors stretched in orderly array to the horizon. On the twelfth night of the assault, hundreds of torch-bearing Taiping horsemen were seen galloping by the western wall. The frightened imperialists raced toward the western side to fire down at the horsemen, only to find that the Taiping cavalry were effigies made of paper. At that very moment, tunnels mined with gunpowder exploded on the northeast wall by the Ifeng gate.

When Rulan astride Cloud carried the black flag at the head of eighty thousand red-turbaned Taiping warriors, Pao An was at her side. Some of his men scrambled through the holes in the wall while more climbed the unprotected south wall with ropes and ladders and raced to the west side to open the gates for the pikemen. Once inside the city, three thousand holy soldiers, who had slipped into the Nanking monasteries disguised as Buddhist monks, set fire to the houses near the gates along the deserted parts of the wall—the signal to Yang that the Taiping had taken the outer city.

Thirteen days after the Taiping had come upon the city, Hung announced plans to cross the moat to enter Nanking. "The Bride has come," he said, "so that the Bridegroom may enter his mansion."

Rulan lifted her face into the wind to smell the smoky exhalation of the captured city. She had imagined Nanking as a towering formation of clouds and light peopled by a race of heroes, descendants of the first Ming emperors whose tombs were carved into the surrounding limestone hills. But Nanking, like all cities, was merely stone erected by human sweat. Once its thick sandstone walls had crumbled, and its ten gates had been breached, the people were no different from those who had wept and cried for mercy in Wu Chang and An King. In the hot, moist breath that the city exuded, Rulan could smell terror and defeat. This was the city ordained by her father to be the new home of the Taiping nation.

A gong sounded. Rulan turned back to Hung, who was standing beside his official palanquin wearing a gold diadem over his yellow cap and a yellow robe embroidered with nine dragons. Behind them rose the Golden Pearl Mountain, in whose shadows the dragon boat lay gently idling at the head of the vast flotilla of junks and barges that had borne a million warriors downriver. The southern bank of the river was crowded with red-turbaned foot soldiers and brilliant regimental flags. Rulan picked out the horsewomen, the Miao camp, the Children's Brigade, the women and men of Wu Chang, An King, Kiu Kiang, all the villages and cities they had taken wholly into their midst. These people carried only rice, oil, and salt—enough to sustain them for several days. Nothing remained to remind them of their former homes: not the family tablets nor the deeds nor the bits of jade or gold handed down by women through the generations, for all these had been given to the common treasury.

A gong sounded. And another and another. A river of humanity eight miles long stood along the southern bank of the Yangtze swathed in clouds of steam rising from the recent touch of rain on the hot earth. Silence spread like a lengthening shadow as the Taiping stood on the threshold of a new world.

Hung surveyed his kingdom: the clouds brought low to kiss the earth and the river. The multitude. The city spread out like a feast before him. As the echo of gongs died away, he felt holiness rising like a strong wine into his head. "Thus is heaven come down to earth!" he shouted. "Enter now its gates! Worship God!" commanded the Younger Son.

As one, the brothers on the right and the sisters on the left rose up and roared their love in a hymn of praise that Hung had written and taught them. Tens of thousands and hundreds of thousands.

Then Hung stretched out his arms and chanted the verses that the High God had whispered in his ear to console him during the bleak days when he had wandered Kwangtung alone.

> Those who believe are the sons and daughters of
>   Heaven.
> Whatever their origins, they come from Heaven.
> Wherever they travel, they go to Heaven.
> Theirs is the Empire of Heaven.

Two million arms reached out to the skies and shouted the measured response.

> No longer are we slaves of demons!
> Hung, the Younger Son, establishes a new
>   Empire.
> We are sons and daughters of the Most High.

The roar of the people ended; the gongs clashed three times, and all the Taiping prostrated themselves on the dirt.

A gong sounded and the people rose. Rulan leapt on Cloud's back and turned the horse toward Nanking. The red walls of the city sparkled in the cool light of dawn. A gong sounded and Hung's holy guard of thirty-six horsewomen led by Jiao and Heavenly Glory fell in behind Rulan. They wore yellow robes and carried yellow parasols to hide themselves from the sun. A gong sounded and sixteen pikemen in yellow caps and tunics lifted Hung's palanquin high. Trumpets blared, and the three kings riding yellow palanquins, each emblazoned with a single crane, fell in behind Hung. Next came the ladies of the kings mounted on horses led by servants, and then the officers on battle steeds.

Again the gongs sounded, signaling the advance, the horns gave the refrain and the echo was taken up by more instruments until the whole valley was filled with the martial music. A million brothers and sisters followed the kings and officials slowly down the southern bank of the Yangtze, past the devastated temples and mansions outside the city walls, across the bridge that spanned the twisting moat and through the blasted gates of Nanking.

Rulen led the people out of their exile in the wilderness into the holy city. And all the warriors followed behind her, chanting hymns and raising their voices in loud hallelujahs.

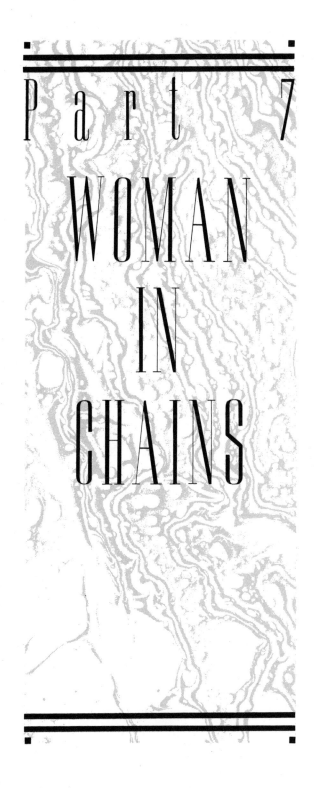

Part 7

WOMAN IN CHAINS

Canton, 1853

The fire she started will never be extinguished, not now, not by me, thought Viceroy Li. His spies said the Taiping, led by a girl on a white horse, had swept through four provinces and taken Nanking. In her wake, a dynasty is falling. More than that: the order of four thousand years is changing before my eyes, and I cannot discern the shape of what is being born.

Viceroy Li was sitting in his private chambers reviewing Liang Mo's transcript of Magistrate Lam's trial. Li ran his finger down the rows of tiny ideographs looking for errors, but the notes were clear and meticulously detailed, the phrasing precise, even elegant. Liang Mo coughed to conceal his relief and pleasure that his father's finger had no reason to pause, and Li scowled at his son, despising Liang Mo's effeminate gestures. Magistrate Lam, he remembered, was barely older than Liang Mo, but without his son's affectations. A youth of rare simplicity and intelligence, Lam was one who might even have been a friend, had he not served a different master. And here again was another victim of the warrior woman who had once been a slave within Li walls.

There was no way to save the young magistrate from execution, because Lam was a Triad, Merchant Wang's master spy. And Lam had a brother, Iron Fist, a general among the Taiping. Even if Lam were persuaded to turn against his secret society, he could not relinquish the ties of clan. So Lam's death was necessary, but still a waste of a talented man. The viceroy wished his son had half Lam's talent. But talented or not, Lam, the scholar-official and Triad rebel, the loyal Confucian and consummate traitor, had stumbled, and so would have to die. And Liang Mo, the gentry-dilettante, would live—for now. Until the revolution, the will of the people, rose up to threaten him too.

The viceroy put down the transcript and pulled at his long beard with both hands. In moments, Liang Mo was balancing a steaming bowl of tea gingerly on the tips of his long fingers. Li growled his acceptance and took the bowl between his palms. One ought not reduce such a complicated phenomenon as revolution to a single image; and yet, he thought, while noisily sipping the fragrant, perfectly brewed tea, all the troubles of the last years were perfectly summed up in the stubborn Hakka girl with unbound feet who had escaped from his house, his vengeance, his embrace. A servant, a daughter-in-law, a healer, a spy—a being that changed her outward shape, although her essence was always the same, like smoke from a single fire. Rulan. Revolution. Rulan. Like some ineffectual Confucian scholar, Li found himself trying to balance the violent and contradictory events of recent months in order to attain a numbness that he pretended was self-control.

"Is there anything else you require, Father?"

"Nothing," Li replied.

"Then I'll go home. Mei Yuk suffers in the summer from the mosquitoes and the heat."

"How is my daughter-in-law?" Li forced himself to be polite. He had never gotten over his distaste for Wang's granddaughter, although she had served her part in his plan to eliminate Wang's clan and the Triads that Wang secretly funded. Luckily, she had proven as fertile as all the Wang women and had given the Lis a son to ensure the generations. Whose son? he sometimes wondered.

"The child quickens nicely. A girl this time, her women say, though Mei Mei swears the vomiting means a boy."

"And my grandson?" Li had trouble with the word, "grandson." He sent the child long letters detailing matters of discipline and education, but he hated having the child in his presence.

"Good, good, Father. But the boy misses Abundant Spring Mountain, although I remind myself that here there are more servants to spoil him. And storytellers and swordsmen in the square—how he loves the swordsmen . . ." Liang Mo always warmed to a discussion of the child, whom he doted on to excess. But seeing his father's impatience, he fell silent.

"I must speak to you about the boy."

"If it's about his behavior at the banquet, the child meant no harm," Liang Mo replied. "He's only a baby, not used to sitting for so long."

Li shook his head. "I shouldn't have made you bring him to Canton. Tomorrow. We'll talk tomorrow."

Liang Mo slipped out with a frown. Was his father thinking of sending the boy back to Abundant Spring Mountain? If so, he would fight his father on this. He hated being separated from his son for more than a few hours. He delighted in the toddler's antics.

Liang Mo would have been relieved to discover that the child was the furthest thing from the viceroy's mind. Li was thinking about Rulan again. He did not intend her to take another victim from the Lis. That meant seeing clearly, as a superior man would. It demanded an unencumbered heart. He could not be snared if he had no weaknesses. He could not be entrapped if he desired nothing. After Meng's death in the riot in Canton, Li had taken the measure of his affection for his wife and decided that he had, at one time, been weak enough to love her. That weakness was healed when the rabble took her life. Now he took the measure of his affection for his son and grandson and decided to send them away to save them from assassins. As viceroy he had countless enemies. Now he was mistrusted by the great ones around the Dragon Throne who had settled their affections on Scholar Tseng from Hunan. Why had An-te-hai changed toward him? Was it the imperial concubine, who had taken a dislike to him? Who could ever be sure of what went on in the splendid isolation of the Forbidden City? An-te-hai and the Dragon used Li for trade, for gain, but would not trust him north of his vice regency in Kwangtung and Kwangsi with an army. Yet the emperor had recently invited Liang Mo to Peking to be an imperial scholar. Liang Mo, who had to have his degrees bought for him, was offered the consummate prize! No, Li could not allow the son to become bait in a snare meant to trap the father. He would send his son away because Liang Mo was a danger to the family, a reminder that the Lis had once harbored Revolution within their walls. A reminder that Liang Mo had made love to Revolution, as fools of legend made love to fox-spirits.

He would send the youth to the Fragrant Tree Islands, where barbarians bought the sandalwood that was made into music boxes and combs for the women of Han and into carvings for the Forbidden City. How could the emperor object if he sent Liang Mo to procure the scented wood that would deodorize his opium-sated escapades with his teenage whores? Li would hide Liang Mo away until the emperor wasted himself.

The viceroy could not afford to have his plans for a southern empire compromised by a fool.

To think that Rulan was the daughter of the Taiping Eastern King! If that information fell into the wrong hands, Li's own death would doubtless prove a diversion for the emperor, the concubine, Orchid, An-te-hai, and their new Han minion, Scholar Tseng. Li blamed himself for whatever disaster had grown like vipers' eggs in the cracks of his house. All the fault and folly was his because he had desired Rulan too much to kill her.

Had Lam been privy to the plan to bring Revolution into Li's house? Was Lam another head of the monster of rebellion Rulan had summoned out of its sleep? Lam would have a last chance to confess before he died. Li had decided on the method. The magistrate would be buried up to his neck in quicklime, which would be slaked with water. Properly done, it would take a week for the chemicals to dissolve skin, muscle, tendon, guts to the point of death. Then they would transcribe the screams issuing from the gaping mouth before stopping it up forever and burying the skeletal head. What was once a man would be nothing but a howl of pain. Lam would tell all that he knew not for the promise of life but of a quicker extermination.

Li reminded himself dispassionately that there had always been rebels like Lam. Rebels were an alternative to the official order, the world reversed, as in a mirror. Secret societies like the Triads were the left, the yin, the shadow. But the collective discontent of the people, the Rulan of the Age, had roused the Triads out of their futile quest to restore the Ming. The Rulan of the Age, a woman on a white horse, had galvanized petty bandits and ragged sects and brought them into the sun, the rightful realm of yang. The pattern was broken, the world turned inside out. Revolution was a woman who walked like a man, a servant who would not bow, a spy who could not be bought. Rulan.

All this Li had decided as he pieced together the evidence of the salt riot, as he sifted through the ashes of the house of Wang. He had beheaded many of the rioters who had been turned in by their own families. Some he had hung up on a scaffold until their lungs collapsed; the leaders he had sentenced to die by the thousand cuts. Li had gotten many confessions, but none that satisfied. Lam would supply the final answer to the unanswered question. Why Revolution?

It was this belief in something that puzzled him.

It was this belief in something that had created a Triad insurrection in all of south China. The Small Swords in Amoy and the Red Turbans in Hong Kong were aiming their forces against the very gates of Canton. Cut off the head, declared his friend, the magistrate of Amoy, and the body will surely die. But Li said no, the head was nothing. Burn out the heart, for it is the heart that believes. The Amoy magistrate had cut off the heads of twenty-five hundred Triad leaders in his city. Less than a year later, the magistrate of Amoy was killed in his bed. But Li began in the villages with the landless peasants: he cut off their feet; thence to the market towns, where he cut off the hands of the merchants; and next to the district cities, where the unemployed porters, traveling barbers, hot-water sellers, charcoal-carriers, and deserters and marauding boatmen were gathered into pens. He ran them through with stakes so that the point passed through the stomach and then the heart. He created a forest of stakes. One hundred thousand scarecrows, to be sure the south would be rid of birds of prey. Then he stacked the corpses into a mountain outside the walls of Canton and surrounded the walls with the severed heads. Li swept through Foshan, Hsi Nan, San Shui, Shun Te—all the towns ringing the capital, clearing out not the Triad elite—but the innocent throng whom the Triads could corrupt with belief.

And when the Triads came up to Canton on boats to mass against him, he invited the British barbarians, whom he hated, to break the blockade of Canton. "Use an enemy to kill an enemy" was the strategy. And the barbarians were more than willing because they needed to bring their ships up to Whampoa Island to load silks and tea and unload dirt. Seeing that they were no match for western ships and guns, the Triads withdrew their junks up the Pearl River. In the systematic slaughter of the Triads that followed, the city ran out of baskets to hold the severed heads; the executioners were forced to send the viceroy boxes of the rebels' right ears as proof that justice was done. In a few years after his swearing-in, Li would make Kwangtung clean, although an estimated million people would die on the stake or of famine or of disease in the ruin that followed the local uprisings.

Even at that moment, the Rulan of the Age was marching through the villages, her big feet spanning the rows. She was seen refusing to bow when his cortège passed through the slums of the city. She was observed spying in the kitchens of the houses of his officials.

The thing that surprised the viceroy was not the vehemence of his hatred for Rulan. He had manufactured that emotion often enough, as occasion demanded, to protect himself against weakness. What surprised him was that he still desired her. When he captured her, he would not kill her. Nor would he take her as a soldier would, at least not right away. What he wanted was to see her bow. He wanted . . . an apology. Yes, that was it. He wanted her to apologize for destroying his dream of an empire.

Nanking, April 1853

anking was hushed and gray. The parks and boulevards, the temples, stores, and narrow alleys were emptied of people. The surviving imperial soldiers were held captive with their women and children in the garrison in the Tartar section of the city. The ordinary Han had been left to their own devices and were hiding in temples and stores, monasteries, wells, trees, storehouses, and secret rooms in scholars' mansions, any corner they could find.

Yang sent criers through the city to announce the terms of the surrender. All Han were told to seek the safety of their homes and to affix on the doors of their dwellings a sign with the word *shun,* "obedience." Inside, three cups of tea were to be placed on the table as further proof of their acquiescence to their conquerors. Then he went with Pao An and Eng to the garrison to negotiate the terms of the truce with the captive Manchu officers.

As soon as she had thrown off her court robes, Rulan insisted on accompanying her father. An uneasy premonition was taking the edge off the joy of victory. The brothers and sisters were too nervous, their eyes too bright and hard. The psalms were shrieked at too high a pitch. She wondered what effect the years of abstinence would have on the brothers and sisters now that the enemy had been delivered into their hands.

The first day was like a dream. The holy soldiers went to the metropolitan buildings and took over the official residences.

The second day, the elders of the city were invited to do obeisance before Hung and the three remaining kings. The elders ignored the summons. So Yang sent messengers with red placards throughout the city. And this proclamation was made

> THE YOUNGER SON HAS RECEIVED THE MANDATE OF GOD TO SAVE THE PEOPLE OF THE WORLD. ALL MEN SHOULD TURN OBEDIENTLY TO THE YOUNGER SON, AND BY HIM WE WILL CONQUER THE RIVERS AND MOUNTAINS AND ENJOY HIS EMPIRE OF HEAVEN.

Then the Taiping troops went through the city, rounding up the Manchu and Han moneylenders, landlords, bailiffs, and judges.

"What will you do with them?" Rulan asked her father.

"The demons will be executed for defying us," he replied.

"How can you tell a demon from an innocent man?"

"They have oily skin from too much pampered living."

"Then I must be blind, for I cannot see it. I cannot even tell a Manchu from a Han when they dress alike."

"You look at the slope of the head. The Tartars strap their children to a board and press the back of the head to a bag of rice. The shape can't be hidden, even by a queue."

"So for the slope of their head they must die?"

"We cannot allow the enemy inside our walls, Daughter. They did not write 'obedience' on their doors."

"But if they swear obedience now?"

"They had their chance. How can we be sure of them?"

"We rule here. The city is ours. Can't we put an end to war and forgive those who opposed us?"

"As a healer, you know that the evil limb must be cut off, or else the whole will fester and die."

"When will there be an end to the bloodshed?"

"Rulan, these men are Manchu officials and soldiers. Hung has declared that all imps and demons must be killed to purify the city."

"And the women and children, are they dangerous to you too? Will you kill them in order to purify the city?"

Yang seemed to sink down into his enormous robes. Finally he nodded. "The women and children I will spare, for your sake."

Hung established his harem in the dead viceroy's mansion, a place far grander than Viceroy Li's in Canton. Yang had seized the metropolitan palace. The other kings occupied the mansions of the mandarins and rich merchants. Generals and colonels and captains were rousting citizens out of their houses and taking them for their own. The city was being divided into wards for each Taiping king, with each appointing counts and dukes and drafting plans for new palaces.

On the third day, the slaughter of the garrison defenders began, for Hung decreed that there was to be no compromise for Manchu demons.

Were those whom the demons married and fathered counted demons themselves? Rulan wondered. Surely not, for the cornerstone of the Taiping faith was the protection of the weak. Never had the innocent suffered. Except, she remembered, toward the end of the march when a few cities had stubbornly resisted. How many massacres had she put out of her mind and heart?

Rulan avoided the official gathering at the execution grounds and commandeered a compound for a makeshift hospital where the ill and wounded among the citizens would be treated.

The Kingdom of Great Peace became an Empire of Blood. Outside the city gates, the heads of Manchu soldiers were stuck on the pikes that the old women had sharpened on the boats; so many thousands of headless bodies clogged the Yangtze that the boats could not move forward or back.

On the fourth day, the holy soldiers set fire to the warehouse where the Han officials and any man who appeared to be Manchu were held captive. Then the Taiping warriors ran through the streets slaying anyone with a sloping head. As they slashed and thrust, the brothers and sisters chanted hymns to keep up their courage. Rulan rode Cloud through the streets, screaming at the soldiers to lay down their swords and go back to their barracks, but they were too giddy with bloodlust to listen. They rounded up the women and children of the dead officials, despite Yang's order to spare them; they dragged forth every woman found hiding in alleys, basements, on roofs, and in gardens. They tied them up and drove them with bamboo goads; some they killed and some they locked up in a Taoist temple. Then they threw rubbish in the temple yard, closed the gates, stacked broken furniture against the great doors, and set everything on fire.

Mandley broke into the council where Hung and the three kings were bargaining for the choicest neighborhoods and the finest houses. Yang had just demanded that the Porcelain Pagoda, one of the great wonders of the Land of Flowers, be included in his sector and had relinquished the government offices, the yamen, in the inner city to Hung for his new palace.

"Abomination!" Mandley shouted. He waved the Taiping Testament in one hand and two broken sticks in the other. "You kings proclaim peace and abjure murder. Yet your soldiers are killing innocents in the streets. Now that you have won your Heavenly City, will you pollute it with blood?"

The intrusion shattered Hung's concentration. "The City of God is not polluted by the blood of devils. It is purified," he said vaguely.

"Be realistic. Any imp we kill now is one less enemy to fight later," Yang said to Mandley.

"I am talking about women and children! Unarmed. Set afire like offerings on a pyre." Mandley's head rag had come undone and his long hair tumbled over his shoulders so that he looked like an angry prophet from the Book.

Yang kept his composure while shrewdly measuring the mood of the Younger Son. "This is our home, at least until we take Peking. We cannot have saboteurs hiding in every alley. But defenseless women are another matter—"

"As you say, they are only women and girl children." Wei shrugged, embarrassed by Mandley's squeamishness.

"They are not our kind," Hung said dreamily. He closed his eyes and began to rock back and forth in his chair. "A city must be rid of vermin to be made habitable. The Land of Flowers has suffered a plague of vermin. Now I will poison their holes, burn them out of the fields."

"And how will you open the door to Paradise without your Key?" demanded Mandley. "What will you do when your celestial bride is consumed in the flames?" He held up the sticks in his left hand. It was a broken Manchu short bow. "Rulan broke this over her knee. She climbed up over the wall to join the Manchu women and children. The officer who gave this to me said that the people were howling for torches and more tinder. He wasn't sure whether they know that White Horse Woman was inside or whether he could prevent them from setting the temple on fire."

"Go, go! Quickly!" Hung screamed to his guards. "Stop them from lighting torches!"

Yang had already run from the room. Mandley followed behind the frantic officials and scribes. What have I done? he kept asking himself. What have we become?

The temple had already collapsed in flames when Yang's and Mandley's palanquins arrived. Fifty holy soldiers under Pao An's command ran behind with shovels and buckets. They could hear the cries of the women and children above the hiss and crackle of the fire. The mob had dispersed at the sight of the Eastern King's yellow litter; only a few white-faced soldiers remained to greet him.

"Where is White Horse Woman?" Pao An demanded of a soldier.

The man pointed to the inferno helplessly. "She won't come out. There was nothing to be done."

"Put out the fire or I cut your necks!" Yang bellowed. "Quickly!" While Yang scolded the men into teams—some to carry sand and dig trenches, others to form a bucket brigade—Pao An ordered twenty men to hoist a fallen pillar and batter down the temple gates. He saw that Mandley had clambered over the top of the wall with a rope tied around his waist and was staring into the courtyard of the fiery temple, his face drained of blood.

Please, please, Mandley prayed silently, sick with the stench of burning flesh and dizzy from his climb. He made himself scan the faces of the screaming women in the only clearing that was not in flames. The temple had vanished: all was burning rubble and billowing black smoke. From the few women and children huddled there, Mandley guessed that many had already perished inside the building. He cried out in relief when he spotted Rulan, a small child astride her hip, pulling an old woman out of the way of a blazing idol that had toppled from its perch.

"Rulan, climb up!" Mandley yelled. He unwound the rope around his waist and dangled it along the wall.

"How many women can escape by that rope?" she called back. "I will not be a traitor to them. And I will not live with those who burn women and children."

"Your father has ordered the soldiers to put out the fire and let the women and children go free! Come out now."

"I stay till the door is open and the flames put out," she called back angrily. The girl child in her arms had begun to wail. "Take this orphan and give it to my father's women to raise." She tied the end of the rope to the child's waist and motioned Mandley to haul the screaming girl up the wall. She wanted to tell the barbarian not to grieve. It was not a bad death, to die by fire as Ailan had foretold.

But Rulan's time had not come. In minutes, Pao An's men had broken down the gates and dragged the women out. They dug trenches around the temple, threw sand into the fire, and went about the task of burying the dead.

Rulan won from her father the promise that the surviving women and children of Nanking would remain under her protection to be rehabilitated with the women conscripts from Wu Chang, An King, and Kiu Kiang, and taught trades so they could be useful members of the Empire of Heaven.

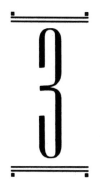

As the celestial bride, Rulan attended Hung on court occasions and at Sabbath worship, but she lived in the mansion that Yang set aside for himself in the quarter of the city graced by the Porcelain Pagoda, the famous landmark of Nanking. The former charcoal-carrier confided to Mandley that he intended to turn the tall, elegant obelisk into a memorial to Ailan. Yang had put the pagoda under his personal protection, guarded it from the rampaging soldiers, and had chosen the site of his dwelling for the view it offered of the gleaming white marvel.

With more than fifty refurbished buildings inside a new wall, Yang's palace was grander than Abundant Spring Mountain, eclipsed only by the palace where Hung lived in isolation with his eighty-eight "moons." No one but the women, his relatives, and one or two trusted officials now saw Hung face-to-face. He kept himself more isolated than the emperor in Peking, as if he feared pollution from the common rank of men and women. Hung's growing paranoia had dictated the layout of the new Nanking that the Taiping carpenters were hammering into place: the captured people were confined to the barren outskirts, while the holy soldiers and the Nanking literati, who were pressed into service as clerks, occupied the inner city, where the Tartars and the Ming emperors had lived.

Although she hated the ritual role of celestial bride, Rulan took seriously her promotion to chancelloress. She placed Wing in charge of the silk makers and organized other guilds of women. As the months went by, however, she found less and less pleasure inside the newly furnished mansion of the Eastern King. She was treated with the elaborate courtesies due the daughter of the most powerful man in Nanking. She had more wealth than Meng, more servants than Mei Yuk, and infinitely more power than the Tai Tai once had over the inhabitants of her house. But Rulan held this meaningless unless the Twelve Rights and Responsibilities she had helped her father and Mandley draft came to pass, for if she could somehow free herself from Hung, a new set of Taiping rules could offer hope for a life with Pao An. Yet Hung, once having signed the proposal, went back on his word. He did not oppose the reforms directly; he simply neglected to sign into law any of Yang's practical initiatives to redistribute land, to permit marriage, or to make treaties with foreign nations. And he would not set a date for Yang's coronation, as he had promised on the day of Rulan's betrothal.

Instead Hung pushed for an assault against Peking.

Yang thought it a disastrous plan. Although he could count on the support of thirty thousand bodyguards and soldiers in the field, the kings Wei and Shih were a constant threat. Iron Fist's Triads had finally made known their open allegiance to Wei and their jealousy of Eng's pikemen, who enjoyed Yang's special favor. If Yang showed signs of weakening, the kings and their factions would undoubtedly fall on him. Yang's strategy for keeping power had always been to pit his rivals against each other. This strategy had succeeded before, when he had used the alliance of kings at Chin Tien to offset the charismatic Hung. While Hung made costly mistakes in the open, Yang had grown strong in the shade. Now Hung, from behind the walls of his harem, began to weave a deadly network of spies in Nanking. It was fear for his own life that led Yang, at the height of his power, to embark on a shrewd but dangerous game: to use the ancient strategy of "moving the tigers away from the mountains" or sending the most troublesome kings away from the capital to fight the enemy. This was why he acquiesced, against his soldier's instincts, to Hung's insistence to push on without delay to Peking.

Yang divided the holy army into three parts: one unit was sent west under Shih Ta Kai's command along the Yangtze River. Two more units, the best of Yang's soldiers, were sent north under Eng and Pao An in a pincer movement to capture Peking. Wei was given the largest area to patrol—the capital, Chen Kiang, to the north, and the region immediately north of the Yangtze—which Wei put under Iron Fist's command.

The seasons progressed and Rulan yearned to be with Pao An in the field, because Nanking had become a prison to her. One night, she said to her father, "When I was fighting, I had no personal guard; I carried my own bow, and I was not afraid. And yet now that we have built a new empire, you send guards with me if I set foot outside these gates."

Yang's face was grim. "Hung covets what I love. You and this city."

"Leave the city to him. Come with me and join Pao An and the troops marching on Peking. You and I can turn the tide against the imps again," Rulan said.

"I will confess something." Yang drew his daughter close and whispered, for even in the sanctity of his own rooms, he feared Hung's spies. "I fear my desire for empire more than I fear Hung. Your mother told me once that my dream of a celestial city would kill me. I told her, 'Then I shall live forever because I will never enter its gates.' And she laughed, and said, 'But your heart is already in the celestial city, and the city knows it.' At the time I thought she was talking about my troubles with the magistrate. Now I think she was talking about my hunger for power, which disturbed the balance of nature. Truly, I am a man who has desired too much."

"Then call the troops back. Get rid of the lackeys that feed your desire. Forget about being crowned Nine Thousand Years. Come with me into the streets back to the people. We have a million warriors who want to put an end to war. They want land, jobs, their old life back."

"Yes," he agreed. "It is time to stop dreaming and start building homes." But he didn't call the troops back, and he still wanted to be higher than the other kings.

To take her mind off the absent Pao An, Rulan spent her hours with the "new sisters" from Wu Chang, An King, Kiu Kiang, and the survivors of the temple fire in Nanking, who were living with their children in a set of abandoned warehouses in the outer city.

The small-foot women were filthy from neglect and near starvation. Rulan was shocked to discover that they received less food than the beggars of Nanking and no medicine or salt. Rulan and Wing, accompanied by a convoy of horsewomen, brought rice and supplies and spent a week tending infected feet and malnutrition. Soon the children were scrambling happily up and down the ruins of the outer city, but there was little she could do for their homesick mothers. She decided that the only way to prevent mass suicides was to put the women to work. She had the idea of turning them into a women's society modeled after the *chai tang,* and so she divided them into families of five and set them to scrubbing floors and mending clothes. Rulan discovered that although the Wu Chang women could not march or fight or endure hardship, they were brilliant with needle and thread. When a family of weavers turned up among them, a plan began to take shape. She sent Wing's horsewomen to commandeer the mulberry groves in the suburbs and scour the countryside for worm farms. Within weeks the warehouses had become a silk factory, with mat-sheds for the worm flats and cocoons, lean-tos for the spinners, and a hive of rooms for the weavers and embroiderers. Rulan started them out making flags and banners, then uniforms. Soon they were getting orders from the officers for embroidered vests and boots, and the Taiping priests were submitting designs for altar cloths, caps, and robes.

Hung was heard to grumble to his wives that Rulan was more concerned with silkworms than she was with her ritual duties to him. For her part, Rulan found the worm sheds and embroidery rooms a welcome respite from Hung's dark, oppressive chambers where she was forced to spend several hours each day listening to the women read sacred odes to each other.

"This is like the old days," she told Wing.

"You're quite wrong," Wing said. "Nothing is the same."

Wing, certainly, was different. Off her horse, among these settled women, she looked old, disappointed, tired.

"Perhaps we will go campaigning once again," Rulan told her, for she still hoped that her father would find a way to let her join Pao An.

"You are Hung's celestial bride. You will never ride into battle again," Wing replied sadly.

In Nanking men and women were coming together unofficially to set up households. And Yang did not invoke the sanctions of the march against them. Rulan began to hope that her father, whose ascendancy over the Younger Son was now almost complete, would soon have enough power to annul her tie to Hung and to permit a liaison with Pao An when he returned from the northern campaign. At any moment, a message from Eng might announce the anticipated victory over the emperor, who had run away to his summer palace and left the capital to his generals to defend. Then Nanking would gird up for one final, victorious sweep to the Forbidden City. And in the glorious empire to come, her liaison with Hung would be a faint memory, and she and Pao An would never have to part.

Yet with the holy city springing back into vigorous new life, Yang inexplicably took sick. Those who saw him swore that he looked like a man with a body-wasting demon.

"I'm getting old, I can't throw off devils anymore," Yang whispered to Rulan with a wry smile. She was using all her knowledge of medicine, but could not seem to find the right herbal remedy. "That's the sum of it. You are like your mother. You never get sick, do you?"

Yang's eyes were so grotesquely swollen that the lashes were turned inward against his eyeballs. He screamed when she lifted his eyelids to examine the tissue beneath. There she discovered uneven layers of tiny hard sores, like granules of sand, "pepper sores," which she had often seen among the boys who dredged the fishponds or who dug latrines.

Yang was ashamed of his weakness and pain. "My strength was always in others. I could move people about better than I could move my own limbs. Big voice, full of orders. In myself now, I know I am weak."

She scraped her father's eyelids with a cuttlefish bone dipped in powdered *huang lian*. He did not complain or fight her treatment. After the pustules had been punctured, the lids were reduced to normal size. But even after she had bathed the eyes with human milk, the infection persisted.

"It is ironic, is it not, Daughter, that at the height of my power, I am as blind as an impotent beggar?"

Rulan was deeply bewildered. "Pepper sores" was a disease of poverty and filth. How could it attack the Eastern King in the pristine splendor of his new chambers? Everything he ate was prepared by his wives; everything that touched his body was carefully washed and locked away.

Why can't he see? Rulan wondered. My medicine is right.

She immersed herself in old books of herbal concoctions and rare medicines in the attempt to prove that any illness could be turned aside if one found the right antidote. She could not face the fact that her father was blind and dying.

It seemed to Rulan that her father's illness precipitated a wave of new disasters that threatened all that she had hoped would come to pass for her and Pao An. The newest reports from the northern front were horrific. After the first string of victories, the Taiping soldiers had been inundated by Mongol horsemen hired by the emperor; thousands more were killed in a flood. Yang's spies said that the troops attributed their ill fortune to the fact that Rulan had left the battlefield for a life within walls. The spies said that Pao An had been among those who survived the Mongolian ambush and the flood, but Rulan would not be comforted by the news. Awake and in her dreams, she seemed to hear him cry out to her over the noise and tumult of battle. She ceased to plan for a life with him. All she prayed for was his safe return.

One evening, Rulan slipped through the huge courtyard adjoining the women's dormitory. She could hear the noise and chatter from the dining hall where Yang's concubines were taking evening rice. Maids were bringing in plates of steaming food and vats of hot rice; more maids were carrying away empty platters, which they tucked into the crook of their arm into a petal-shaped pattern. She stepped into the room, but the sight of the women stuffing themselves on the hot food made her gorge rise. Tired and dirty after tending the sickroom, and exhausted from sleepless nights worrying about Yang and Pao An, she walked toward the bathhouse that lay beyond the dispensary.

Ahead of her, a slim figure was moving stealthily into the sickroom. When the girl looked back over her shoulder, Rulan recognized the young maid who brought the hot towels with which Yang's face and body were wiped every night.

Curious, Rulan edged toward the door and peeked in. The girl was bent over a pallet; her hands moved swiftly over the invalid's face.

In an instant, Rulan leapt into the room and flung the girl aside. The girl screamed and tried to stuff what looked like a rag under her shift, but Rulan pulled it away. The sick woman on the pallet, fully awake now, was crying out. Her sightless eyes were oozing pus, and her lids and cheeks were still red from the brisk rubbing.

"Shall I wipe your face with this towel?" Rulan asked the shuddering girl. "If it washes the Eastern King, it should please you too."

"No!" squealed the girl, twisting away.

"And how do you clean your lord's tongue scraper? By dipping it into a leper's sores? Or in a corpse's open mouth?"

The girl screamed, and Rulan pinioned her against a wall.

"Who paid you? You couldn't think this scheme up yourself."

The girl wailed and shook her head.

Rulan twisted the girl's braid around and around her hand until the girl began to sob.

"A woman, she didn't tell me her name. She promised to let me see my man."

"You are lying. What woman could fulfill that promise?"

The young woman began to moan. "Oh my husband, my husband!"

"Who?" Rulan demanded.

"One of the great ones—"

"Do you know what 'lighting the lamp' is?" Rulan asked. The girl gave a body-wrenching shudder. Hung had devised that sentence when a plot to open the gates of Nanking to the imperial forces had been discovered. He had ordered the traitors to be disemboweled, and their entrails set afire with burning tar and straw while they were still half-alive.

"What did she look like?" Rulan demanded.

"She was little. Dark. With a long scar down her left cheek."

In her shock, Rulan released her hold on the girl, who collapsed, moaning. "Aaiiee, I have killed us, Husband."

Rulan weighed the alternatives. She could give the girl to her father, who would undoubtedly have her killed. But no, Rulan decided, the best cure was to make the agent of illness turn the poison back on its source.

"What is your name?"

"Pearl Lily, Mistress," the woman sobbed.

"What you did was evil, but done out of fear and love of your husband. I will not report you this time."

The young woman wept and clung to Rulan's knees, calling her, "Kwan Yin, the Merciful Goddess," although it was forbidden to name a deity from the old days.

Rulan wondered if Hung would be as merciful to a "moon" who had failed in her duty.

Yang reacted with surprising calm to the news that Hung had tried to poison him yet again, as he had in Chin Tien. He said nothing to Hung; instead, he sent letters reminding Hung that the timetable for the reforms dictated by the Declaration of Twelve Rights was long overdue.

The pain and swelling in the Eastern King's eyes abated, but the blindness never wholly lifted. His energy returned. Nothing pleased him now. He yelled at the bath women that he was being boiled red and rubbed raw. As Mandley pored over maps of the northern campaign, Yang moved small red beans atop a table to simulate his troops. He spent hours with Mandley, who read aloud from the Psalms, a book which seemed to comfort Yang.

For the first time in months, Yang went out of his palace to review the city and to prove to Hung that he had escaped assassins a second time. Because his sight had only partially returned, Rulan rode with him as his eyes. She pointed out the disparity between the palaces where the kings and warriors lived and the misery of the captive residents and civilians who lived in the outer city and the desolate areas beyond the walls. She stopped the palanquins to ask the people on the streets and in the shops how they fared. And in that way, Yang learned which of his officials had gone over to Hung, for these were the ones who kept from him information about the shortages of oil, rice, salt, and gunpowder. She brought him to the women in the silk factory who despaired of ever living with their husbands again. This time, Yang listened and did not lecture them about sacrifices for the Heavenly Kingdom and the sanctity of warrior life.

The first two proclamations he drafted as his illness abated were these: He let five hundred women and children from Wu Chang and An King return to their homes in order to relieve the food shortages. And he repealed the law separating men and women into different camps and made it known that the brothers and sisters could marry.

But Peking did not fall.

Nanking, Late Summer 1856

A lone rider slipped through the gates of Nanking and limped into the Eastern King's palace.

In minutes, news of Pao An's arrival had reached the ears of the Eastern King. The annunciator dropped to her knees and knocked her forehead on the floor. "General Chen of the northern army," she panted.

Rulan started up from her chair and began to run for the Audience Hall. But Yang's voice stopped her. "Rulan, tell the watch to sound the gong twice!" he croaked with something of his old power. That was the signal for an emergency meeting of his household officials. He had sent Mandley with secret orders to the northern army to return as quickly as possible, for Iron Fist, without alerting the commander-in-chief, Yang, had moved Wei's troops within striking distance of Nanking. Suspecting trouble, Yang needed his most loyal and seasoned warriors around him; that is, if the best of them still survived. Yang had gambled on a swift victory in Peking on which he could ride to absolute power over the Taiping nation. But victory had eluded him. Now he was ill and alone in Nanking with only a skeleton guard to defend him against Hung and his personal militia.

"Quickly," he ordered Rulan. "Get me dressed!"

Barely able to control her excitement, Rulan flung a yellow court robe over Yang's sleeping clothes, put on the red hat bordered in yellow and embroidered with twin dragons and a lone phoenix, and called for her father's palanquin. Because his hair had been shaved, Yang's great head seemed to have shrunk under the ornate cap. Trembling, no heavier than a bundle of sticks, he leaned against her as she helped him into his litter.

The annunciator ran before Yang's chair, shouting his titles. At the door of the Audience Hall, her cry was picked up by another annunciator, who ordered the assembled crowd to kneel. Yang was borne into the cavernous chamber in his golden litter as the officials who managed his kitchens, palanquins, robes, books, oil, and salt and who oversaw his carpenters and his wives dropped to their knees as one, crying, *"Chien sui! Chien sui!* May you live a thousand years."

Yang squinted into the brightly lit room but saw only the shadowy shapes of the kneeling officials. He whispered to Rulan, who put her hands on his face and turned his head toward the tall bedraggled man standing in their midst.

Pao An was crouched over in a weary bow, and Rulan's heart nearly broke at his look of dejection and defeat.

It had been nearly four years since their stolen night on the long march to Nanking. How she longed to wipe the grime of battle from Pao An's face, to take on herself the weariness that sapped his spirit. But as he rose out of his kowtow, she was shocked to see neither sorrow nor longing on his face. Instead, the look he gave her was one of bitterness, even anger.

When the annunciator had read off Pao An's titles and regiment from the brass tag around his neck, and the information was recorded by the scribe, Yang beckoned him closer.

"Where is Eng and Man-da-li?"

Pao An's whole body sprang to attention. "Seven days behind with the troops."

"Why are they so slow?" Yang felt a terrible foreboding.

"A cannonball shattered Eng's leg. He sent me ahead with the message," Pao An said.

"The letter scroll you hold. Give it to me." Yang held out his hand.

Pao An gave a quizzical frown. "Man-da-li ordered me to memorize it in case of ambush."

Yang quickly drew his hand in as Pao An began to recite: "Eng says, 'When the Eastern King saw fit to take the Lady Rulan from us, the men lost courage. At Kai Feng, a rainstorm made the Yellow River flood its banks. Our stores were running out, and we kept losing to the imps because General Iron Fist had not established the supply lines to reach us as Wei, the Pawnbroker King, had promised. Therefore, I ordered the troops to push on to Peking. At Huai Ching, the imps sent Mongol troops, who rode small ponies and never seemed to tire. We pushed them back, and retreated as fast as we could to Chih Li Province. The Mongols waited until we were starving to strike again. By then we were within range of Peking. I built three wooden camp-sites and dug trenches, but they pounded us with cannon and muskets. I myself took a piece of a cannonball there. Know, old friend, that I would have struggled to the death but for your order to return. Now the barbarian and I and the others are crawling south through the mud and rain. Our legs are numb and our skin cracked, and many of the warriors have died of dysentery. But I would count our sufferings worthwhile if the High God holds you safely in His Hands.' "

Yang's dim eyes were now bright with tears. "My poor Eng," he said.

Pao An wanted to weep for Yang. This was a man, after all, not a god, not even a king. He saw finally why Rulan had led Yang to the chair. He thought of his own father, who had had to make his way alone without a son's strong arm to lean on. What are the battles worth, he wanted to cry out, if all they brought were death and suffering to the valiant, and bitter tears to a blind old man?

Rulan tormented herself with the suspicion that Pao An blamed her for the defeat of the northern army. He had implied that the holy soldiers' luck was taken away when Rulan exchanged her warrior's bow for a chancelloress's robe. So sure was she of his hatred that she did not seek him out. Instead, she shut herself up in a net of ritual. If it were true that she brought death to those she loved, then she would not allow Pao An to come close again. When Yang ordered Rulan to show Pao An the women's guild, she accepted the order with cold formality and took him to the weavers' factory that Wing managed. Wing embraced Pao An as a fellow warrior, and Rulan saw that the affection between them was real.

Pao An listened politely as Wing extolled the quality of the embroidery. But he heard only the pulsation of Rulan's breathing, the sweet, low tone of her voice.

After a time, Wing wandered away. Rulan and Pao An found themselves standing alone between the bolts of woven cloth stacked higher than a man's head.

"They say that Pawnbroker Wei has returned to the city to make peace with my father, now that Hung is finally giving him the title Nine Thousand Years."

"Why do you despise me?" Pao An interrupted.

She turned to him in surprise. "I thought you hated me."

"I don't hate you," he said, turning away. "I don't know who you are anymore."

She paled. "What do you mean?"

"How long were you mine? One night? I don't understand you. When I love, I love with my heart, my lungs, my guts. I made myself live through the horror of these years and endless campaigns because I could not survive without seeing you again. You do not love that way! You cherish your new power more than you do me!"

"You are the only man I have loved freely, with no other purpose or design."

"And what about Hung, who has made you a queen?" Pao An demanded. "Aren't you wearing a dress he gave you?" He stared with anger and disdain at the brilliant yellow silk embroidered with a white crane spreading its wings on a background of blue clouds.

"He is mad, evil." She shuddered. "His gifts and promises mean nothing. But there is no word to describe what you are to me, Pao An. Remember what you once told me? 'Only friendship of the heart survives.'"

"I would rather be your lover than your friend," he replied angrily.

She moved away from him. This was the hardest thing she had ever had to tell him. "My father is repealing the laws against marriage. Find another woman, Pao An. Marry her. Get sons and daughters from her."

His reserve shattered. He smashed his fist into a bale of silk. "You are taking everything from me, even hope!" he cried. "I cannot live with just the *idea* of Rulan!" His torment so grieved her that she put out her hand to touch him, and suddenly she found herself crushed in his arms. They held on to each other as if they were caught in a flood.

"Who am I now?" he whispered against her hair.

"Pao An," she replied. "The friend of my heart—" And when he murmured his disapproval, she said in surrender, "My only love."

After a while, she said against his lips. "If anyone reports us to Hung, you'll be killed."

"Let me die then," and he licked the tears from her cheeks. "I desire the daughter of the Eastern King. Though I miss the warrior woman with my red kerchief around her neck."

"We will be together," she promised fiercely.

Wing found them a sanctuary, a hiding place away from the prying eyes of palace spies, in a space between the walls of the silk warehouse.

When Pao An wrapped his arms around Rulan, his elbows almost scraped the sides of the narrow place. He declared his love for her in tender kisses, and she felt how his body shifted and tightened in their small space.

"This is how you kept alive in the box at Abundant Spring Mountain," she whispered in wonder.

He answered by moving his hips against hers. She could visualize the patterned gestures in her head and anticipate the flow of the sequence that his movements were suggesting. She felt her own body moving rhythmically, felt his strength pouring into her.

They lay down one atop the other, her legs entwined around his. Soon, the tiny room seemed big, too big.

By daybreak, they had half-forgotten that she was Hung's woman, or that he was a general without an army in a citadel menaced by warring kings. They slept with their faces pressed against each other, their limbs locked in love. And only when Wing scratched at the wall, signaling the approach of the women to the looms, did they return like strangers to the world of the living.

For a week, they crept out of their beds to meet at midnight. Rulan taught Pao An the Orchids' secret finger talk. And whenever they were with Yang and the officials in the Audience Hall, they would speak to each other silently, wishing the crowd away so they could lie down together in love.

A young woman who served Yang as chancelloress wandered into Rulan's room one night.

"How beautiful your new robe is," the girl exclaimed wistfully, while caressing the embroidered crane on the shiny yellow silk. "Would the weavers make one for me?"

"Take it," Rulan offered. She hated the robe because it reminded her of Hung, the giver.

"Oh, no!"

"You can have it, but you'll need to make it shorter, and take in the hips and shoulders," Rulan pointed out.

After the woman left her, Rulan lay in bed in a state of great excitement. She had decided to escape with Pao An out of the cage of Nanking, south to the Fragrant Tree Islands of Hawaii. The Younger Son had finally capitulated to Yang's final bid for complete power over the Taiping. The coronation was assured. Hung had made overtures of peace the day before, and Wei, from his camp outside the city, had sent costly gifts to Yang on his projected coronation. Rulan reasoned that after her father was crowned Nine Thousand Years, her mission would be finished. Mandley would stay to help Yang put into practice the new laws that would check Hung's power. She herself had had enough of blood and intrigue and duty to a people who did not warrant her sacrifice. She did not want an empire, only peace for herself and Pao An—and for their children. Thinking of how she would surprise Pao An with her plan when they met in a few hours, she slipped happily into a dreamless sleep.

The scream awakened her. Long and faraway, then ending in a bubbling sigh. At first, she thought that a woman was in labor. But there were more screams, each one threaded over the other. And gunfire. Rulan had sprung out of bed and was already feeling for her bow, before realizing that she was in her father's palace, not in the field. Every nerve of her body tingled with alarm.

There was no time to dress or to search for weapons. The screams were coming from the adjacent wing where Yang's women slept. She heard men's cries and the muffled sound of cloth-shod feet. "Kill the Nine Thousand Years," came the cry. "Praise, praise for the Younger Son."

Rulan stumbled into an open courtyard and found herself caught in a maelstrom of blood and fire. Where was her father? Behind a curtain of flame, men in red jackets were pulling Yang's women along the ground by their hair. Brother against sister. Heaven turned into hell.

They came after her like vultures on the wing. Fear made her feet fly faster. Down a passageway, through a small, secret garden and back again along another dark tunnel. She lost them in the halls she knew so well. She called her father's name, but her voice was drowned out by the women's screams and the men's wild cries.

"Kill the Nine Thousand Years!"

The slaughter was in every corner of the palace. Blood ran down the cobblestones and the front of the walls. She heard the swish of the sword as it cut downward, the screams of the women cut off suddenly.

"Yang's daughter. Take her!" A troop of women wearing Jiao's colors swarmed after her.

Rulan grabbed up a stool with a cry and held it before her like a shield.

                    •   ▪   •

In another corridor, Iron Fist and the Northern King Wei ran through the carnage like starved dogs closing in on a wounded tiger.

At first, Yang thought he was on the battlefield of Yung An. He felt the fear, tasted the sweat, smelled the smoke from the explosives. Run, he told himself. Break through the lines and escape! He came fully awake when he heard his concubines' screams. Lights swam vaguely before him. Cursing his clouded vision and the weakness of his arms, he took up the sword he kept by his head and pushed himself out of the room.

When Yang groped through a small passage, thinking to find a garden, he discovered that he had fled in a circle back to the fiery corridors outside his bedroom.

Iron Fist and Wei were waiting there with a dozen men.

Wei held his painted fan in front of his face against the stench of burning hair and flesh. "This is the day of the Younger Son. Vengeance is his!"

"Coward!" Yang shouted, lunging with his sword as Wei's men dragged off the women. "This is how you always fight! At the rear with the assassins."

"The girl is not with him," Iron Fist observed dispassionately. "She must be hiding." He gave the order to Wei's men and left quickly with Wei to comb the rooms and halls for Rulan.

Yang fought the attackers with the fury of an old bull, hooking to the right and left with his sword.

"I marched and starved with you," he bellowed. "I would give you land and freedom. What has your Younger Son ever given you but poems and empty promises and lies about a heaven he has never seen?"

Yang's arms were bleeding from a score of cuts. He staggered and fell. One of the soldiers knocked the sword from his hands.

Solemnly, the others approached. They were still afraid of him. One struck him tentatively with the flat side of a sword, as if testing the Voice of God's power.

Yang whirled around on the ground, his eyes wild, his hands raking the air. "Do you dare?" he cried. He tried to summon the great voice, but he had barely enough strength to breathe.

Braver now, the soldiers pricked him with their blades. They held his head by the hair, reviling him. One cut off his ears. Another hacked off his nose.

"Why do you do this?" he groaned, choking on his own blood. "I would have given you all—" Suddenly, he lifted his arms and called out his dead wife's name. At that instant, a sword cut through his neck.

Then they were piercing him through with their blades like children playing a game. When they were done with his body, they dragged him along the bloody cobblestones into the next room to show his captive wives. And then, because they had been killing for hours, and the blood and the women had stirred their senses, they put aside their weapons for a while to feel what it was like to put their seed into the wives of kings, before slaying them all.

When Pao An heard the shouts and gunfire, he raced out of his room in the men's wing. Six men charged him with halberds and pikes. One hit him a glancing blow on the head and another struck him in the stomach.

"Kill the Nine Thousand Years!" they cried as they ran away.

He came awake with his face in a pool of blood. Blood was oozing from a gaping wound in his side. Dimly, he remembered that his attackers had been brothers with long hair.

With each step through the ravaged pavilions, he felt pain shoot through him like shafts of lightning. He had neither musket nor sword, and still he pressed on to find Rulan. Corpses wearing the yellow and crimson of Yang's officers lay everywhere; here and there sprawled a dead soldier with Wei's colors. The ringing in Pao An's head turned to high-pitched howls. To disguise himself, he donned the vest and ornaments of one of Wei's fallen soldiers. The pain in his side made him want to vomit. He reeled and fell, then pulled himself up again. He staggered toward Yang's sleeping room and the women's wing beyond, calling Rulan's name.

Everything there too was in flames. Brothers and sisters lay together in death, as they had not done in life. Most were headless. The rest had slit throats or great wounds across their faces. Someone had thought to bring along baskets in which to stack the severed heads.

He recognized the charred doorway of Yang's hall and pushed with all his might against the clamorous press of Wei's men to the private quarters. He dragged himself into a room burned black. In the embers, dark pools glistened like tar. He saw the broken fans soaked in the clotting blood, the blood-spattered screens and wall hangings, a stack of red slippers, and in the middle of the room a mass of twisted bodies that had once been Yang and his women. Overcome with pain and anguish, he forced himself toward Rulan's room. More bodies lay heaped before the doorway. He looked into the faces of the dead maidens who had served Rulan. A spark of hope flared: had she escaped in time?

A glimmer of gold caught his eye.

On the floor behind the bed was the yellow dress with a white crane spreading its wings over a background of curling blue clouds that she had worn that day in Wing's warehouse. It was a body without a head, from which poured a scarlet river.

Kwangtung Province, 1857-1860

Viceroy Li sat alone on the veranda of his country house outside Canton feeding the monkeys that swung from the banyan trees. Pilgrims no longer climbed the bandit-ridden hills to the temples, and the temple monks who fed the monkeys were gone begging; so the starving creatures had come down from the hills closer and closer to the mansions that ringed the outer districts of Canton. Beggars everywhere, Li observed. Even in the trees.

A new manservant arrived with his morning congee. Li threw the last of the kumquats to a pitiful, nearly hairless creature hanging on a vine and wiped his hands on a towel. "Now I eat," Li told the monkey, who began to chatter its annoyance as Li wolfed down the hot gruel. The animal clambered up and down the vine, loudly beseeching. Something landed at the Viceroy's feet with a plop. Li looked down and laughed. A rotten fruit. Li went on eating, oblivious to the screeching in the trees and the shower of dry leaves that came from the small, twisting shape that bounced higher and higher in the umbrella-shaped tree.

"Go find your rascal Monkey God and wreak havoc in heaven," he told the little beast. "We have quite enough of it on earth already." From north to south, the Land of Flowers was at war with itself.

Li put down his bowl, leaned back in the bamboo chair, and closed his eyes to enjoy the small, hot breeze moving among the dagger-shaped leaves. There was a rustling sound, and a soft footfall on the bamboo mat behind him. "You are insatiable," he said in reproach.

"And you," came the quiet reply.

Li turned and found himself staring into the long dark eyes of the man who had brought his breakfast.

"Who are you?" he demanded.

"I brought you tea. I brought you congee. But it is not until I speak that you realize that you do not know me. How powerful words are when the people speak."

The viceroy tensed the muscles of his belly, readying himself for the blow, but the man continued to study him.

"You're the farmer I put in the box!" Li blurted out. Then he smiled in apology. "Excuse me, you are General Chen. Destiny and the Taiping Eastern King have favored you." Li's heart leaped with hope. Generals did not come to assassinate. He must have come with a message! Was there treachery among the kings? Or had Yang sent another overture like the one that had gone astray years ago? One of his birds in a bamboo cage on the limb of the tree trilled a note of pure exhilaration. That which I loosed from my hand comes back to me, thought the viceroy with a shiver of excitement he had not known since his days in battle. "What, no greeting for a former master?"

"I've lost the habit of bowing to imps and demons."

The viceroy studied the Taiping fanatic who had slain so many thousands of imperialists. The man looked awful: travel worn, dirty, probably sick. Then Li remembered that this one had a weakness: he was a filial son. "Aiya," Li said in mild reproach. "War has made you old and proud, General Chen. Sit. I will not cry out. Where is my man?"

"Sleeping. With a knife in his belly." Pao An ran his fingers through the stubble around his temple and ears. Although he had shaved off his beard and forelock with a stolen razor, he felt ugly and dirty, a feeling he had never known in the Taiping camp. "And you," he accused. "You are old too."

Li flinched. Did the bitterness and fatigue of the last years show so clearly? "Sit, sit. We can make a poem about which is worse, losing wars—or losing hair. But later. You have not come all this way for polite talk. How is your master, the Eastern King?"

"Imp army intelligence must be poor indeed. Yang is dead," Pao An declared angrily. "Murdered months ago."

"Aaiiee," said the viceroy softly. Fate, he told himself, as his hopes plummeted. He had been prepared to accept if Yang had invited him to oppose the Dragon Throne. This time he had an army. But if Yang was dead, then Scholar Tseng was ascendant in Peking. Would he ever get his feet out of the water pit?

"The Eastern King and all his generals and the officials and servants of his house. His wives and his daughter, Rulan, dead. Murdered by Hung." Pao An's voice rose in rage. "Had Yang and Rulan not been betrayed, they would have stamped you and your line to dust."

"So you have come to finish the job."

Pao An said nothing. He watched Li's face, his hands, his feet.

Fear seemed to clear Li's head. He saw that Pao An had not eaten or slept in days. Pao An would not have come so far alone, through imperial lines and bandit-held terrain, to kill for a fruitless purpose and a dead leader. Yield, yield, he cautioned himself, to mask a deeper design. His mind leaped over the water trap in pursuit of a sudden wild intuition. "If you had wanted to kill me, you could have already done so. That's what you wanted to show me by serving food, wasn't it?"

"Yes."

"You hate me?"

"I do."

"Compromise is made out of powerful inconsistencies. You hate and mistrust me but you will not kill me until your needs are satisfied. Is that right?"

"You reason better than you see."

"Let me go on. You loved Yang's daughter. You want revenge on the leader of the Taiping."

Pao An's icy control shattered. "Hung murdered her! Hung and Wei and Iron Fist!"

Li saw Rulan burning like a living flame. Would revolution ever truly die? "So you hate me and my house, but you hate the Taiping kings and this Iron Fist more. I know something about Iron Fist and his brother Lam who freed you from the cangue and brought you into my house."

"They were brothers?" Pao An said, unable to disguise his shock.

"Yes. Brothers in flesh and brothers of the Triad, both servants of Merchant Wang. See how far the circles in the water spread! But come, we need to reason together. You have enemies. So do I. What is your proposal?"

"I know how the Taiping fight and where they are strong. I know the good generals from the bad. I know that Scholar Tseng is gathering his Hunan braves for an assault on Nanking and the captured Taiping cities. You want to rise above him. If we join hands we can stroll to Nanking like children going to the well. I promise to win you every battle if you grant me the right to cut out Hung's heart and liver with my own hands."

"As I recall, you were willing to die for the people. What happened, General Chen, to turn you against your kind?"

Pao An's laugh was bitter. "I loved a woman who cherished the people even more than I—and they killed her. Now I am as cold as this blade," he said, tapping the knife shoved in the waistband of his cheap blue cotton trousers. He sighed deeply. "Aaiiee, I disgust myself, but I will not be dissuaded."

The viceroy replied with stern authority, as a father to a son. "Every man in the middle of his life is aghast at himself, which is merely another way of saying that he requires further instruction. That is why we Han have ethics to keep awareness of imperfection at bay, why the sage is our image of virtue, albeit an incomplete one. What men truly want is to stuff themselves with dainties, to shoot their seed, to indulge all whims. Civilized men in the middle of life discover they are always slaves of their worst passions. Those who live to old age learn to win because of it."

"Then you will let me lead the Kwangtung braves against Hung?"

"Yes. Unlike Master Hung, I do not expect you to be a believer. I will count on your desire for revenge, not your loyalty."

"Agreed. We will help each other until our enemies are destroyed. Then beware!"

"Such wisdom will bring rewards."

Pao An scowled. "I don't need any reward except Hung and his minion Iron Fist stuck like pigs on the end of my sword." He turned wrathfully to the viceroy. "But if I discover that you are lying to me—"

"I detest liars. The world is hard enough to decipher without liars changing the characters or the script." Inwardly Li wanted to shout with glee. Again he had triumphed where others might have failed. And he had turned an enemy, a general, no less, into a slave.

Pao An built Li's inadequate provincial militia into an army of fighting men. He put down Triad uprisings for the viceroy with brutal efficiency and stamped out feuds between Hakka and Punti villages without remorse. With every death he witnessed, he imagined the dying of Wei and Iron Fist and Hung at his own hands.

One day, in the summer of 1858, Li told Pao An of a letter he had received from the viceroy of Fukien. "The Taiping king Shih Ta Kai has broken from Hung and is plaguing Fukien. The viceroy there begs me to send men to fight alongside his own. I have no interest in helping this official, but I do not want Shih Ta Kai crossing the border into Kwangtung next. Take some men and go fight your old comrade in Fukien. It might do well for you to know Fukien better, since I may want to explore it one day for my own reasons."

"Send me to fight alongside Scholar Tseng," Pao An said eagerly. He was not used to such caution in a commander and found himself nervous and irascible in the viceroy's presence. "Tseng has sent his armies to encircle Nanking. Let someone else hold off the stray rebels running loose to other provinces. I want to be there when Nanking falls!"

"No, my friend," Li replied, pleased at how well Pao An's ambitions matched his own. "Nanking is still too strong, and you are too impatient for revenge. Impatience gives rise to error. Let Tseng beat on the city walls for a while and wear himself out. I will send you when the time is right—and when you have studied patience a little longer."

A year passed, and another. As Viceroy Li predicted, Nanking did not fall. And Pao An learned patience while winning glory for the viceroy by subduing Shih Ta Kai in battle after battle. Pao An saw with grim satisfaction that now the Taiping were bottled up in cities, while the imperialist forces and provincial troops roamed the countryside like hungry tigers.

Finally, when Pao An had chased the last band of rebels from the south, he strode unannounced into Li's presence in the viceroy's mansion in Canton. "Let me join Tseng now, and I promise in three months, I will win you glory," he demanded.

Li shook his head wearily. The viceroy seemed older, more careworn to Pao An. "You do not understand how civilized men think," Li told his general slowly. "Tseng is unwilling to share credit with me. He won't call for help unless he's in danger himself."

"But the time for victory is now," Pao An insisted. "The Taiping are sick of the kings. They see how Hung slays his own followers and how he has not distributed land as he has promised. That plan, Hung claims, was Yang's and not his own. The people see through the lie. The city will fall if we strike now. Otherwise, the opportunity is lost!"

"The opportunity may already be lost," the viceroy said sharply, betraying the frustration he had hoped to conceal. "You have been so successful in chasing out rebels that the timorous viceroy of Fukien feels threatened by your presence and has complained about you to the eunuchs. So Tseng is more than happy to oblige his friends and snatch away any advantage I might have won in Peking. You must be content to root out a few Triads for me this year."

"They cannot unman us," Pao An declared in disappointment and anger. "Let me go anyway."

"Use the time to look for your father," Li said gently. "I promise you will be there when Tseng tries to take the city. You will be strong when Nanking is ready to fall."

Instead, Pao An fell sick with dysentery when settling a clan dispute in the delta region of the Pearl River. So Viceroy Li sent him to Abundant Spring Mountain as his guest to rest, to heal—and to keep an eye on the river traffic on the Pearl.

"My worthless daughter-in-law runs the place," the Viceroy said. "I spend less and less time there. The house is like a prison, the memories too painful and deep. I sent my son and grandson away, before she turned them against me."

"It was a prison to me too," Pao An said.

"No box in the stable, this time, General, I promise," the viceroy said with a smile. "You can have the Upper House."

Pao An understood that despite the viceroy's overtures, he and Li could never be equals. What they shared were savage memories and the same crimes.

Abundant Spring Mountain, 1860-1863

At Abundant Spring Mountain, Pao An spent his days in the Upper House sleeping and watching for British ships on the river, and ate his meals with his guards. The Upper House had not been tended since the dead Tai Tai, Viceroy Li's mother, lived there. The old woman's bedding and clothes were still in piles on the floor of her sleeping chamber, waiting to be burned. He remembered the tunnel hidden in the walls, just in case.

He heard Mei Yuk on the terraces below, screaming at her maids or at her daughter. She often walked past his rooms and stopped with elaborate show to gaze into the spring outside his apartments. He saw that she had changed: the coquettish child bride had become a soft young upper-class matron. She changed clothes six times a day before she took the air on his terraces. He ignored her. In three weeks, when his exhaustion and dysentery lifted, she came to his room with fruits and hot wine.

"Forgive me, I've been a bad hostess. I shame my father-in-law. But now you are well, and I am so happy, General Chen. We will celebrate."

Pao An was sitting in a straight-backed chair of polished cane that Liang Mo had sent from the Fragrant Tree Islands. He had been looking out the moon window at the lily pond whose surface was dappled with afternoon light when Mei Yuk entered with three serving maids. He saw she was covering up the impropriety of her visit with a

storm of words, ordering her maids to set out plates of fruit, to open
the blinds here and close them there. He noted the blush that crawled
up her fine ivory throat to her cheeks. How different she was from
what he had first imagined.

She was as beautiful as the surface of a pool in the garden of a rich
man. She reflected the sky, the clouds, the stars. But none of those
things belonged to her. Rulan's beauty was entirely different, he thought
with pain. Like a tree or a mountain whose splendor one could not
fully appreciate at once, her beauty grew on recollection. If only he
could have rolled back the years and chosen now what he had rejected
then.

And still Mei Yuk prattled on, ignoring his displeasure at her presence, bringing him wine, and breathlessly praising his renewed vigor.

". . . and soon you will be the Tiger of Fukien again, for that is
what they call you. I am so pleased . . ."

"Aren't you ashamed to show your face to me?" he asked gruffly.

Everything seemed to stand still in the room. The maid pouring the
wine in two small cups spilled the tiniest drop. She put the pot down
and her hands began to shake as she wiped the spot with a small towel.
Mei Yuk's lips were unable to form another word.

"The last time I saw you, you denied me and called for your
husband," Pao An went on unrelentingly. "Where is your husband
now? Since he is not here, is it proper for a wife to expose herself to a
man outside the family? I think you had better go."

"Get out, all of you," Mei Yuk shouted at her maids. When she and
Pao An were alone, she spoke.

"Do I embarrass you?" she said, her old arrogance trickling back
into her voice. "I was not so proper when I came to you the first time,
but then your manners were not so refined. You were not a general
then. I abased myself, but you seemed to enjoy it. I am quite alone
here in this house, where everyone hates me. But no matter. I hate my
husband's family. Does that shock you?"

He did not answer.

"Do you think I have exposed myself unduly? . . . Well, then if you
will not speak to me, look at me!"

Recklessly, she began to pull at the fastenings of her coat, until it fell
from her shoulders with a sigh. She loosened the ties of her skirt, and it
slipped slowly over her thin hips. She pulled her tunic over her
shoulders, and stood naked in a pool of discarded silk.

Pao An saw with utter detachment that she was pale and flawless,
with limbs as lithe as bamboo and small breasts that motherhood had

enhanced. Her almost hairless sex swelled gracefully below her smooth belly.

Slowly, deliberately, he turned away from her to gaze again through the moon window.

A moment later, he heard her gather up her clothes with a sob and rush from the room.

He left for Canton the next day to see the viceroy, but because he was still weak, the viceroy sent him back to Abundant Spring Mountain. Mei Yuk was there with her daughter to bow his litter through the gate.

She sent fruit with her maids that day and the next. With her steward in tow, she brought quail eggs and cakes to his manservant, but did not ask to see him. The following day, she sent her small daughter to him. The girl gave him a healing amulet of peach jade and stared at him with huge, bewildered eyes.

On the evening of the fourth day, Mei Yuk came alone. Again he was at the window in her husband's cane chair.

"I know you do not love me. I don't care," she said. "I have no pride." She began to undress again.

This time, he loosened her garments himself and lifted her into his arms. Her bones were as delicate as a bird's, and the vein in her throat pulsed like a swallow's breast. He thought she had grown more fragile. But when he put her on the bed, she drew him down to her with arms as strong as iron.

"When you came here, I thought Father had sent you to tempt me or to kill me," she confessed after their first lovemaking. "I hated you for making me afraid."

"Why did you flap around me like a moth around a flame? Didn't you know I would remember how you ran away in your Grandfather's house screaming for my death?"

Her eyes widened. Nervously, she began to pluck at a tendril of hair that had fallen out of her matron's hair knot. "How else can a woman save herself except by flirting—or screaming? Men have always wanted to hurt me. My brothers, mean as red ants. My father, cold and unforgiving as a statue. My grandfather, who lay with me as a girl—"

Pao An sat up in the bed, horrified.

"Oh, did he not! Many times. Until I started a child, which died within me. Then he married me off to his greatest enemy, and I have been a prisoner in this house ever since."

Pao An tried to take the small, weeping woman in his arms, but she squirmed away and knelt at the foot of the bed behind the faded blue hangings until he summoned her. "Fox-spirit," he whispered.

And she came to him like a tigress. She made his rain fall many times before the sun rose.

"You do not know what it is like to be without a man for so long," she whispered against his chest.

"I know what it's like to be without a woman," he replied.

"It's not the same," she said. "I have not had a man since the viceroy sent Liang Mo to the Fragrant Tree Islands with my son five years ago." His hands moved carelessly across the smooth dome of her belly, and she held them still, protesting, "No, I don't mean that. It's just that I have been so afraid. I have never been so long without a man's protection."

He laughed at her fatuousness, until she silenced him with angry kisses.

From then on and at the viceroy's insistence, he came back to Abundant Spring Mountain twice a year to rest, to dream, to plan. And to bed Mei Yuk, whose husband was far away.

Why then, when he embraced Mei Yuk, did he remember Rulan? He was a man destined never to hold on to his dreams, he told himself. He did not know how to live in the present moment as his father had always advised. That was why happiness rushed through his fingers like a fast-moving stream. He had no real desire for women now that he had his fill of them. On campaign, there were always women. He didn't remember their names or faces. And when he returned to Kwangtung, he stayed in the rooms set aside for his use in the Upper House of Abundant Spring Mountain, and Mei Yuk came to him every night.

A Taiping curse clung to him. He remembered vows of fidelity and chastity; to erase the memory, he was all the more profligate. He used Mei Yuk badly. Sometimes he took her the way his soldiers took women after taking a town. But savagery only seemed to heighten her ardor. The fury of her lovemaking almost frightened him. She would faint after the clouds and rain. Then beg for more.

"I want to go on the swing in the willow garden."

"Go then," he growled, and turned his back on her in the Tai Tai's great bed.

"I won't go without you. I want to sit on your jade stalk and swing up to the moon."

"Little slut. You should have been a singsong girl."

"Do you want to hear me sing?" she whispered. She began to wail an unpleasant, off-key song about a girl who had become insatiable for her lover's organ.

Laughing, he covered her mouth. "Hush, do you want the maids to know you're here?"

"All the maids know. Maids always know."

It was true, of course. Why had he let himself think differently? He told himself that such folly could get a man killed—on the battlefield or in the bedroom. The more disturbing question, one that he refused to consider, was this: If the maids knew, why did the viceroy hold back his hand? Surely his usefulness in battle was not so great that it would rise above the viceroy's honor?

"Forget the maids. Remember that you are mine," Mei Yuk said. "When I see how the little dog-in-heat who cleans your room looks at you, I want to put out her eyes with my chopsticks."

"I hadn't noticed, but now I shall."

"If you touch her, I will betray you to the viceroy," Mei Yuk told him.

"And he will send you back to your family in pieces."

"What do I care? My Kung Kung's house does not even exist. You and the Hakka witch burned it long ago." She raked his back with her nails in such a way that she led him round again to making love, and then taunted him by crying out at the moment of release, "Liang Mo, Husband!"

"Your mouth will buy us both a death," he told her.

"I don't care. I hope your viceroy catches us together," she said, clinging to him. "Only let him strike me while your blade is jammed up to the palace of the child. At that moment I will welcome death. And take you with me." She bit the muscle of his shoulder until he cried out. But he too was seeking death, and there was more death in the granddaughter of Merchant Wang than at the front of battle.

"Do you remember the last time we were here?" the viceroy asked Pao An. They were sitting in a garden at Abundant Spring Mountain finishing a game of *wei chi*.

"Yes."

"How time changes men. I thought then that Magistrate Lam would be one of the great ones of the earth. Now he is melted away. And you, who lay at our feet covered in excrement, are the greatest general in the south of China. Believe me, it took every ounce of self-control not to vomit at the sight of you. My son, as I recall, did. Or was that another time? Liang Mo has no stomach for the world's excesses. That is why I sent him to the rim of the civilized world, this Fragrant Tree Island, where he will not get in my way."

"How could you send away a son of your heart?"

" 'Son of my heart.' Ah yes." The viceroy looked down at the small round playing stones on the game board. He did not like the question.

They continued to play in silence. Although the viceroy was by far the superior player, Pao An's skill had steadily increased over the years.

"There, I have you," declared Pao An.

"You would beat me in the field, too," the viceroy said with a sigh.

"I'm not so sure."

"No. Though I am by far the better tactician, Scholar Tseng and you have this essential: you command by admiration whereas I command by fear. When men follow you, it is like raising the black flag of your Taiping; they follow to the death. I may hold the high ground, I may outflank you, but even you cannot predict how you will respond or where you will take your men. They admire that streak of uncertainty. I fix and mold and shape my opponent. I learn his strengths and weaknesses in the same way that I might study every bump of dirt in the enemy's terrain, but I cannot trust that men will follow me to the end. In any given battle, I win. But in the ultimate battle, I would bet on you."

"Is that why you have fixed and molded and shaped me?"

"Of course," the viceroy said.

"You arrest my movement, cut me off on as many sides as possible?"

"See? You know all this."

"Tell me, how did you fix me?"

The viceroy beamed at Pao An as a tutor would at a bright student who has given a particularly good recitation. "Your hatred for Hung drives you forward. Your love for your father keeps you directed."

"And Mei Yuk?" Pao An ventured.

"Aaiiee," Li said softly, and reflected. "That is precisely my point, a direct frontal attack like that. A civilized man would never mention her name. You win the battle." He paused; Pao An waited. "The answer is that lust makes a man careless. You are dangerous to me. I must keep you off balance, and your guilt tips the scales in my favor."

"But your own son's wife, the mother of your grandson!"

"You don't know, do you?"

"Know what?"

"That I am at heart a sentimentalist." Li stopped to consider what he was about to say. "Her boy is yours. Surely you suspected." Pretending to study the game board, he watched Pao An's reflection in the bowl of tea. The big broad face changed, changed again, and then closed up. "But there, you have done it! Forced me out of hiding. I have fixed you, but you have forced me. I have revealed all, and you are free of guilt. I must watch you, General Chen, because now you are a dangerous man."

Moving his pieces as he talked, the viceroy surrounded Pao An's last pieces and took the game.

That year, the rains failed to come. A thousand years of fecundity seemed to have come to an end.

The servants said it was because of the whore and the turncoat general. There was no true Li living within the mansion's walls: two aliens were its masters. Whores and impostors were everywhere, they said, even in Peking. The Hsien Feng emperor had died two years ago blind and syphilitic, while his favorite, the former concubine Orchid, Dowager Empress and mother of the heir, plotted with the eunuchs to wrest the mandate from the hereditary princes. The Dowager Empress had already driven from court many of Viceroy Li's friends. Worse, she seemed to prefer Scholar Tseng to the viceroy. Surely the Li ancestors were showing their displeasure with all whores and impostors by drying up the life-giving water of the family spring.

When the summer monsoon failed to come, the fall was dry and brittle, the trees dusty and drooping, the heat unrelenting, the ponds thick with algae. Fruit trees planted centuries earlier withered and died. The horses in the stable were expiring from heat. Second Cook, who had served three generations and had no family to protect his rights, fell over dead in his kitchen; instead of being buried with honor, he had been thrown into the river at Mei Yuk's orders. She also turned out his legions of kitchen helpers and forced the oldest maids, who used to do no more than fetch tea and hot towels, to chop vegetables and stir pots. All the water had to be dragged uphill from the river, and because the river water was filthy, brackish, muddy, and smelled of sewage or dead things, it had to be boiled. Clouds of steam billowed from the water pots set on blazing fires in the courtyard. Night and day the fires raged. Dead oxen and pigs, bloated with water and the gases of corruption, clogged the river. Girl children, their hair drifting like seaweed, floated slowly by on the exhausted current. Then later in the summer, boy children. And still, no rain.

Pao An fed as many of the beggars at the door as he could over the protests of the steward and the hysterical tears of Mei Yuk.

"Why are you giving away our life? Can't you see this is going to be a long drought?" she pleaded.

"Yes, but if I feed a few, hope will keep the rest from burning down the house," he replied. They were sitting on the veranda of Meng's old quarters, which overlooked the river. On both sides of the river, the mulberry harvest barely filled a hundred small carts.

"Everything is old and broken in this ugly house. I wish I were with Liang Mo in the Fragrant Tree Islands. From his block of stores, Liang Mo makes enough money to equip a house of our own. He says the barbarians have more sense than we people of Han. If something breaks, why use it or fix it up? Throw it away and buy new! 'Mei Mei, you must come,' he begs. 'The mangoes fall off the trees into my hands. Everywhere I look, I see mountains and the sea. I wake up to the sound of rain.' Poor man, how he misses me."

"Go to him!" Pao An declared wearily. "I'll convince the viceroy to let you. The ban against women immigrating to the Fragrant Tree Islands doesn't apply to scholars' and merchants' wives."

"Cut your head and tongue! I won't go without you. I'd kill myself if I could not lie with you again."

They fought like man and wife now. Especially about the boy. He blamed her for not telling him that she had borne his son. He blamed her more for allowing the child to be taken away.

"Berate me. Accuse me. Beat me, if you like. My boy was snatched away from me, but you leave me of your own free will whenever you please."

"The viceroy needs me."

"Let the viceroy drown in vomit. He is a monster to his son and grandson, and to me. He is looking for an excuse to throw me out and biding his time until it can be done most cruelly. You go! Go fetch and carry and kill for that monster. Go open the guts of a few more mother's sons."

"I have my work. I do it."

"You mean that you are waiting to corner that pitiful, mad Hakka who thinks he is the son of the barbarian god. You are like a jackal sniffing at a rabbit in his hole."

Pao An half-rose from his bench.

"I know you want to leave me," she said frantically. "You are tired of me. I know I do not please you." Her long fingers were playing nervously with an empty teacup, tracing the thin cracks on its surface, scratching at the dark spots left by the deposits of past brews. "I'm getting old. I see you eyeing my maid like a dog smelling a bitch's bottom. So, leave me and die! I had a dream last night. I kept calling to you but your ghost vanished out of my hands. I woke up and you had left my bed. I was frightened. Why did you leave Mei Mei?"

"I couldn't sleep," Pao An confessed, made guilty by her need of him. "I went to look at the spring, and I found the source under a ledge of rock, a hole big enough to hold a man. It's covered over with a white crust that glows in moonlight, like the eye socket of a skull."

"Ugh. Don't talk like that," she scolded. "You make my flesh crawl."

"Everything was dry."

"Why do you care if it's not your house? My father-in-law doesn't worry. He lies with a new girl every night in Canton. I'm the mistress and I don't care. This house gives no protection to me. Aiya, let's get out of the heat." She came over to sit by him on the bench and put her small hand inside his shirt. "I'm going to have my maid wash me. You can watch, if you like, then we will play outside in my garden this evening when the heat breaks. The swing is tied up in the willow tree."

Wantonly she lifted her leg and put her small red shoe in his lap.

Liang Mo's next letter said that he would be coming home within the year to take his wife with him to the Fragrant Tree Islands.

Six months before Liang Mo was to arrive, the viceroy came to Abundant Spring Mountain with two of his officers to confer with Pao An on how best to build up his own provincial militia to rival Tseng's. But Li found his most able general sick of all talk of war. Pao An's wounds had not healed well. His stomach still hurt. Even Mei Yuk's tantrums seemed a relief from the endless round of killing. All he wanted to do was sit in the shade, watch the river, and forget. He complained to the viceroy of the pain in his gut and his old wounds.

■   ■   ■

The viceroy scolded, harangued, and threatened, but when he realized that Pao An remained unmoved, that he had indeed lost the heart for killing, Li sent the other officers away and spoke to his general alone.

"Have you forgotten that you swore an oath to fight my enemies?" asked the viceroy sternly.

Pao An stared forlornly at the ribbon of brown water below them. The river, with its swirling currents, seemed to beckon him. He imagined himself leaping into the bright, colorless space between the Upper House and the river. His head spun with heat and fatigue and the dizzying, tantalizing vision of bloodred cliffs hurtling past as he plunged into the cool bosom of the Pearl.

The viceroy's next words shattered Pao An's reverie. "The Taiping general called Iron Fist, the same one who slew Yang, your master, and the woman Rulan, has broken with Hung and come south into Fukien Province to gather cash and rebel conscripts."

The viceroy saw with satisfaction the incredible speed with which Pao An could assume the stance of war. Pao An's face suddenly became ugly, mottled with red. His nostrils flared, his hands tightened into fists. Viceroy Li remembered the box in the stable yard, and how this man had kept alive by controlling the *chi* pulsing through his body. A good tiger, thought the viceroy. Relentless, predictable, and as deadly as ever.

The viceroy drew out the tale of Iron Fist's entry into the south, focusing with relish on the atrocities that the rebel Iron Fist had inflicted on the people—the burning of monasteries, the slaying of nuns and monks, the forced conscriptions of boys.

Pao An rose to leave. "I will gather my men now."

"Not yet," ordered the viceroy. "Fukien is outside my jurisdiction. Scholar Tseng will doubtless demand that the Dowager Empress punish me for invading a neighboring province and will arrange it so that the governor of Fukien sends troops to attack you."

"Then I will fight in Fukien under my own banner," declared Pao An.

"Such talk is treasonous, of course," was the viceroy's unctuous reply. "You give me no choice but to disavow you."

"But not before supplying me with the necessary arms," added Pao An quickly.

Viceroy Li nodded, satisfied that once again Pao An was his instrument to direct. "And I will give you as many men as you need to conduct a long campaign."

"And after I destroy Iron Fist?" asked Pao An grimly.

"Turn on the Fukienese army when it comes after you. Slay the governor if you can."

"And when I do, your southern empire will be half-won," Pao An observed.

By way of answer, the viceroy chided, "You are putting me at risk. The Dowager has asked me to advise her about the rebellion. It seems that the imperial army is stuck outside Nanking, unable to dislodge the mad Taiping emperor from his citadel. The Taiping fight on and on, although the supply boats no longer come and the villagers no longer trade provisions for Taiping cloth. The Dowager grows impatient. So I will be in Peking to explain to the empress what the brilliant Tseng is doing wrong. Send the Dowager a letter demanding that she yield the entire south to you. She has a weakness for manly men and will leave you alone until the Taiping problem is solved, as long as you stay in the south and kill only southern Han, whom she deems expendable."

"I'll never understand you," Pao An confessed in a burst of candor. "Why do you place yourself in the trap so often?"

"But I am not ensnared—you are," Li pointed out with a smile.

"I go willingly," Pao An protested, "for revenge, for honor. But it's only a game to you!"

Pao An had touched a raw nerve. Against his better judgment, Viceroy Li snapped at him, "How do you know? How do you know?" Again he wished that Liang Mo, who had foolishly insisted on returning to Kwangtung to purchase laborers for his new sugar processing operation in the Fragrant Tree Islands, had half the ferocity of this general.

In three weeks, Pao An had the men and supplies he needed. The viceroy had departed for Peking amid the beating of gongs and clamor of official criers who ran before his palanquin shouting his rank and titles. Abundant Spring Mountain seemed as desolate and cold as a graveyard, and Pao An could barely conceal from Mei Yuk his eagerness to go. He told Mei Yuk that he was leaving the next afternoon and left her hysterically ordering her maids to prepare special foods for their last night together. At nightfall, he sent word secretly to his aide to have the horses waiting at the gates for a quick and unheralded departure for the border town where his militia was quartered. At the hour when Mei Yuk took her bath, he started down from the Upper Terrace dressed in battle gear. But as he passed the Second Terrace, he saw Mei Yuk's servants running with torches between the pavilions.

"What is the matter?" he called to a maid.

"The mistress! A devil has eaten her soul."

Pao An could hear the racket before he entered Mei Yuk's rooms. She was screaming at the servants, who were trying to calm her, and overturning the furniture. When he strode into her room, she was standing on the bed tearing down the draperies.

"Come see our bed now!" she challenged him. She spat on the covers. "Go to war. Leave me for her memory. See how warm the red grotto of a ghost is!"

"Leave us alone," he told the maids who cowered against a wall.

Mei Yuk's arms twisted around Pao An's neck like snakes. She would not let go and wept as though he had died. He finally broke her grasp and pushed her back on the bed, where she lay like a statue, legs straight out, tears spilling out of her wide, unblinking eyes.

"You think I don't know?" she hissed angrily. "I hear everything you whisper to your men." Her body began to shake with sobs. "Why do you love her instead of me? She is dead. A ghost. My arms are real. My body is flesh. Why do you reject me? You run off to avenge her memory and care nothing for me. What is left for poor Mei Mei?"

"Rest now," he told her wearily. "Liang Mo will take care of you when he comes back. You refuse to accept it, but he loves you."

"Who wants that eunuch's love? If you leave me," she whispered, "I will kill myself."

"You won't, I know you," he replied, anxious to be free of her.

"I will. I will. I will. I will. Do you think I am meaningless? Do you think I can do nothing? I will show you that I am as powerful as her ghost. I will—"

He slipped out of her arms and left her.

The soldiers cried out in alarm. Looking back from the ridge of hills beyond the mulberry groves on the other side of the Pearl River, Pao An saw that the Second Terrace was on fire. Flames raced along the rooftop of Mei Yuk's compound and touched the tops of the trees with crimson. A building collapsed and plunged headlong to the terrace below. The fire seeped down the dry slopes through the buildings and dead gardens. It coursed down the cliff like red water from the ancient spring. For an instant, the house of Li blazed into glorious life.

Pao An turned his back and spurred his horse toward Fukien.

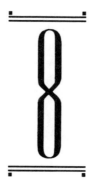

Fukien Province, Spring 1864

Pao An harassed Iron Fist's troops in several encounters, beating him each time, but Iron Fist always slipped away. He pursued him for all of 1863, and gradually reduced Iron Fist's army of thirteen thousand to a few hundred. Then his spies reported that Iron Fist was making a break for Anhwei Province. No peasants had rallied to his cause, and Iron Fist's dream of fomenting another Taiping rebellion in the south to challenge the one that was fast unraveling in Nanking had failed; now his troops were reduced to raiding the villages for money and supplies and terrorizing the same peasants they purported to free.

In the spring of 1864 in northern Fukien Province, Pao An met a column of ragged horsemen flying a yellow triangular standard with the insignia of two snakes intertwined—Iron Fist's symbol. The column, which numbered less than a hundred, retreated quickly before Pao An's more disciplined forces. Pao An left his main brigade and pursued the aimless rebels on horseback with a force of five hundred of his best men.

By nightfall, Pao An had tracked Iron Fist to a Taoist monastery on a rocky bluff. When Pao An saw the ancient fortress looming above him like a pale cenotaph against the dark sky, he had a moment of paralyzing doubt: something about the place recalled a deep, long-buried memory of the hillside graves of the Chen ancestors surrounding On Ting village. But then he spied Iron Fist's insignia flying from the gate, and he urged his men on.

Three times Pao An flung his troops against the walls of the monastery, and each time they were thrown back. Finally, when dark clouds rolled in to shroud the mountains, he took up a position on a knoll below the monastery and ordered his men to light fires, as if making camp. At midnight, he chose ten men and scaled the cliff on the western side of the fortress.

Once inside, Pao An's men ran through the grounds flinging torches into the storehouses and dormitories. In the confusion, none of the defenders saw Pao An race to the front of the temple to unlatch the gate. The rest of his men, who had left their fires to crawl up the mountain under cover of darkness, poured in, howling like curs and swinging swords and pikes.

As Pao An ran past the temple granary, a voice rang out. "Farmer Chen! You've poured pig shit on my plans again."

Iron Fist stepped out from the shadows surrounded by a dozen ragged men. Pao An was shocked at the man's transformation: the Taiping prince in gaudy finery now looked like a common beggar. His once brilliant Taiping uniform was tattered and filthy from the months of living on the road, and his long hair hung matted and unkempt.

"A bargain for an old ally," shouted Iron Fist. "You think you want me. But I have information that will make you run straightaway to Nanking to seize the real prize." The fighting in the courtyard had come to a halt as Iron Fist swaggered toward his adversary. "Come now, we talk alone."

"I know your tricks," Pao An retorted angrily. "A knife hidden in a sash, a Triad spell to make me fear the beating of my own heart. No, Nanking is only an illusion. My prize stands before me telling me lies."

"Aiya, eating from the same rice bowl as Viceroy Li has made you reason like an executioner," Iron Fist observed menacingly. "I swear on my oath as a Red Turban that the information I possess is valuable to you. You would be wise to listen."

Pao An shouted, "Why don't you swear on the bodies of the brothers and sisters you slew? I want nothing from you but your death. Why should I bargain with a dead man?" His men were closing in on Iron Fist, their swords pointed at his chest.

"A challenge, then," declared Iron Fist coolly. "A fight, just you and I. To the death. If you kill me, you have what you want. But if I kill you, your troops guarantee me and my men safe passage."

Pao An smiled and stepped forward without hesitation. "Agreed," he announced in a voice tight with hatred.

"Master," protested Pao An's aide-de-camp. "He's trying to trick you. Let me kill this turtle now."

"Of course it is a trick," declared Pao An grimly, as he stripped off his leggings and tunic for wrestling. "But I want the pleasure of killing him myself." The first icy breath of a thunderstorm swept the courtyard.

Iron Fist's control slipped. "Paddy boy. I should have choked you years ago."

"Have you turned squeamish so soon?" answered Pao An. Already he was arranging his soldiers to clear a ring for combat.

Iron Fist had not moved. "If I win, they'll kill me," he complained, pointing to the fast-growing crowd of angry, shouting men, all eager to witness his execution at the hands of their formidable general.

Pao An straightened up, his fist raised. "Hear me," he shouted. "If this man slays me, you allow him and all his men to go!"

"But General," interjected Pao An's aide, "you cannot let him go. His head is worth a treasure to us!"

"Swear!" Pao An ordered. Reluctantly, the aide raised his weapon, beckoning the others to follow. The men roared their agreement amid a sea of upraised swords and pikes.

"Come and be done with this," Pao An said impatiently to Iron Fist, while flexing his arms.

Iron Fist scowled. "You are younger and stronger. You have the obvious advantage if we wrestle."

"I can't give you youth," Pao An shot back in exasperation.

"A pike then," Iron Fist replied smoothly. "I will teach you as I taught Rulan, the Eastern King's daughter." He said the name with great deliberation.

Furious at the delay and unnerved at the mention of Rulan's name, Pao An seized a pike from his side. "Give him yours," he commanded a soldier, who immediately lofted a pike in Iron Fist's direction.

Iron Fist grabbed the pike while it was still in midair, whirled it above his head, and brandished it with a quick two-handed movement. His ragged band shouted insults at Pao An, already convinced that Iron Fist had helped them cheat death. "Paddy boy," taunted Iron Fist, crouching like a tiger. "Rulan. How well she moved. Remember?"

Anger nearly made Pao An strike blindly at his foe. He fought to keep from giving in to the violence of his emotions. "You should not speak her name." He circled to his left and saw Iron Fist smile.

"Ah, is she dead to you all these years? Have you suffered for her memory?" asked Iron Fist mockingly. He tossed his long hair out of his eyes. "I taught Rulan to wrestle, to ride, and to fight with sticks. She was a stalwart warrior, better than you. Still, I knew her weaknesses, just as I know yours by instinct. You are simple to read, pikeman."

With a cry, Pao An leapt forward, but Iron Fist skillfully parried the blow with a thrust that pinned Pao An's pike to the ground. Then Iron Fist moved his pike up viciously. The razor-sharp edge of the pike whistled past Pao An's ear.

They circled to the right. Iron Fist's ploy had worked. Pao An could not prevent the image of Rulan from dancing into his mind. Yet after his first, nearly fatal outburst of emotion, he realized that memory had not shattered his concentration, as Iron Fist intended, but had freed him from the dangerous grip of rage. He began to slow his breathing and felt his mind clear. He remembered Rulan's supple body dodging Mandley's blow as they boxed on the long march to Nanking. Had Rulan adopted her teacher's tricks? he asked himself. Could he trust the memory of her strength and skill? As Pao An thrust and parried, his mind rehearsed each move Rulan used to win against the barbarian. He found himself waiting for the high swing that was meant to make him pull backward in surprise.

The rebels were hurling curses at Pao An. He could hear his own aide screeching in gutter Cantonese. Iron Fist's stick crashed against his, and for a moment they strained together, face-to-face. Then Iron Fist punched him in the chest. The blow left Pao An breathless.

"All men must die, pikeman," Iron Fist panted. His eyes had vanished under the dark shelf of his brows. Pao An stumbled backward. A high passing slice smashed down at his head, but instead of jumping back from the rotating tip, Pao An ducked under it. When Iron Fist brought the stick low to catch his feet, Pao An was ready. He leapt over the stick and drove the sharp point of his pike deep into the rebel's belly.

His breath whistling in his throat, Pao An crawled off Iron Fist's twitching body and watched the dark blood streaming into the earth. He was about to turn away, when Iron Fist spoke. "Paddy boy, you still lose. When I took Rulan out of Yang's burning palace, I gave her to Hung. She is alive, but forever dead to you. She's in Hung's harem. The celestial bride is Hung's slave!"

Pinpoints of light exploded in Pao An's head. He wondered if he were going mad. He began to shake the dying man. "Don't mock me. I saw her—a body—a bloody dress on a bed in the Palace."

"Alive. And not alive," whispered Iron Fist.

"You are lying!" Pao An screamed and sought to squeeze the truth out of Iron Fist with his bare hands.

But although it took him a long time to die, Iron Fist said no more.

Pao An strode through the courtyard, his hair flying in the night wind, bellowing revenge on what remained of Iron Fist's men. The screams of the dying and the crackling of flames reminded him of the dreadful night that Rulan had perished in Nanking. Or had she? He told himself that it was only the cruel joke of a dying man and tried to harden himself to the dangerous wave of doubt that threatened to engulf him.

His victory over his old enemy was complete. Iron Fist's body crowned a mound of corpses in the courtyard. Why then did he feel empty, dissatisfied, wracked with indecision and despair? Suddenly, Pao An felt an overwhelming impulse to run away, to call an end to the horror, to fight no more. Did Rulan live? Do dying men lie? He believed in nothing and no one. Fate for him was a box with no hope of escape. All Pao An knew was that nothing had erased the loss of Rulan: not Mei Yuk, not the wealth and honor he had received at the viceroy's hands, and not this last bloody victory over Iron Fist, his greatest foe. With halting steps, he walked to the edge of the temple porch to survey the fiery scene: the burning halls where the monks slept and prayed were swept by a mighty wind that precedes a storm. The flames that were devouring the workhouses danced in the wind. Dead men lay everywhere. Had he ever lived a life that was not filled with the screams of the dying?

At that moment, the storm broke over him. Thunder pealed and lightning lit up the carnage. And in the silence between thunderclaps, the heavens opened and unleashed a torrent of rain. The flames in the temple roof hissed and crackled. He let the rain wash over his face. How he yearned to be clean!

Opening his eyes, he saw on the upper story of the burning temple two old monks who had climbed out on a balcony to escape the flames. They looked like figures in a comic opera, clinging together and crying out.

Without warning, an edge of the balcony collapsed, sending one of the monks backward with a pitiful wail into the burning rubble. The other stepped back with a feeble cry. The balcony shuddered, and the old man shifted his shoulders and tilted his head in a gesture of resignation that Pao An instantly recognized.

"Father!" he cried. The word was agony to him.

The old man gripped the broken railing of the balcony and with dim eyes searched the ground below. "Who's that? Pao An?"

Pao An dashed into the burning temple, but he was immediately felled by smoldering debris. "Father!" he shouted and, like a mad bull, hurled away the fallen timbers that had knocked him down and ran for the stairway. Burning cinders fell on him; hot air filled his lungs. He raced up the stairs while flames singed his thighs and crawled across the floor in a room thick with billowing black smoke. When he reached the balcony, he found that part of the floor had collapsed, separating him from his father who lay in the far corner, overcome by the heat.

Without hesitation, Pao An tensed his muscles, leaped over the gap, and pulled himself up on the shattered floorboards while fire licked at his feet. Then he crept through the dancing flames to where his father lay. Quickly, he swept the frail body over his shoulder and climbed over the railing. He landed off balance and fell to the porch below, wrenching his left leg.

Weeping, he turned the old man over. Li Yu's gaunt face was filthy and his robes were hissing from sparks that still sputtered in the tattered folds. Pao An pulled off the smoking cloth and wiped the dirt and soot from Li Yu's face. "Father," he called in a broken voice.

His aide came running to him. "Is it he? Is it really he?" asked the man, terrified by the fury of his master's despair.

Pao An sprang to his feet, screaming, "Ah, ah, ah, ah, ah—" His hands raked at his eyes, trying to tear away the sight of Li Yu's lifeless body. He clawed his chest, he covered his ears to stifle his own shrieks. But when he grabbed his knife and raised it above his chest, strong arms stopped his hand and wrestled the knife from his grasp.

"No more," said the aide with great gentleness.

"Let me die, let me die," Pao An wailed.

"Master," the aide said, shaking Pao An hard. "Your father is alive." When Pao An did not reply, he said again, "Master! Look, look."

Stunned, Pao An crawled to where Li Yu lay. Please, he begged whatever gods might listen, even the High God in whom he had never believed. The old man's face was cold under his lips. Please, Pao An pleaded, knowing that no god would heed him. Then, filled with wonder, he felt a faint puff of breath on his own wet cheeks.

Slowly, he took his father into his arms and stumbled toward the gate. The men had stopped their killing and looting to watch the odd sight of their general, whom they honored and feared, carrying an old man in his arms as tenderly as a father bears a beloved child.

"Master," called the aide. "What shall I order the men to do?"

"Tell them to burn the dead and gather up supplies and horses," Pao An replied quietly over his shoulder. "Our enemies here have fallen. We must prepare for the next battle."

This was fearful news to the aide. "Where are we going, Master?" he asked, dreading the reply. He had heard a rumor that General Chen intended to fight on in Fukien. The viceroy of Fukien was sending troops against them, claiming that Pao An's men were bandits fomenting rebellion. If General Chen ordered them to attack the Fukienese militia, surely the south would explode in a civil war. Then he and all the other Kwangtung men would never see their beloved farms and villages again.

Pao An's face was alight with an emotion that the aide had never seen in all the years he had served the dour general on campaign. If he didn't know better, the aide would have sworn that his general looked almost happy.

"Nanking," replied Pao An to his astonished aide.

Nanking, 1856-1864

The Grand Palace of Glory and Light had as many rooms as Hung had moods. Red rooms, black rooms filled with alabaster and teakwood, rooms hung with yellow silk for meeting barbarian emissaries, rooms for pleasure, rooms for pain. Rooms filled with women perfect as lilies who served his desire. The Golden Dragon Hall, built behind the former governor-general's yamen where the Heavenly Court now reigned, was marked by yellow colonnades entwined with circling dragons to set off the glory of the sovereign. There were pavilions for the taking of sugared fruit and tea, parks dotted with tiny lakes and bridges on which Hung could stroll with his favorites, small secret pavilions for dalliance, gardens in which to play chess, gardens for making poetry or making love, gardens for birdsong or for contemplation of the light.

All these rooms were the earthly dwelling place in which Hung would live with his celestial bride forever.

Yes, his sister Jiao had found her in Yang's burning palace and brought her to him. He gave her everything—his love, power over all the women in his palace—yet she reviled him and refused him the gift of eternal life.

Rulan perplexed him. She was his salvation, yet a reminder of his humiliation and his sins. To restore his purity, he had neither shaved nor cut his hair since Nanking was won, and his reddish-black beard now hung down his thickening body over necklaces of jade and gold. In Rulan he found immortality and yet beheld his earthly limitations— the examinations failed, the battles lost, and the crowds' adoration wrested away by a charcoal-carrier. She would not forgive him for imprisoning her and slaying her father, and stubbornly disclaimed all knowledge of the elixir of eternity! When rage overcame his remorse, he whipped her. He explained that the voice that spoke through Yang was the authentic Voice of the Father, but it had been corrupted by the body from which it issued. It was to preserve and protect the voice from the corruption of flesh that God had used the traitor Wei as His scourge. Yang was and was not God, just as Rulan was and was not the Key. She was only the Key when she acted in fulfillment of her sovereign husband's wishes. She was not when she persisted in her sin and stubborn pride.

"Give me your *chi*," he pleaded, although his eyes betrayed his fear of her.

Convinced that only Rulan's will stood between him and immortality, Hung had issued an edict: Rulan's feet must be bound with a chain of golden bells so that she could not come on him unawares. The chain was to hobble her, as one would a renegade horse, and to teach her to walk, eyes downcast, with humility and discretion. Two supervisors, armed with swords, stood watch over her to prevent her from suicide or escape. They taunted her, telling tales of how her father and Pao An had died. Once she had been the only woman with unbound feet in a great house; now she was the only woman with bound feet in an entire palace. And her soul was bound with many deaths.

How can anyone kill what one cannot touch? Rulan wondered.

To free herself from despair, she imagined herself in another place: in the foothills of Hunan with Cloud galloping beneath her and the vast army of brothers and sisters flowing out over the valley. In the small herb room at Abundant Spring Mountain, reading the dreams passing over Pao An's face. In her childhood bed next to Ailan, listening to her mother's tales of gods and goddesses and warrior women.

She had mourned the death of Pao An so deeply that all tears had been wrung out of her. Now her memories of him were a sanctuary in her mind to which she could escape her present horror.

And where were Wing and Mandley? Because there had been no word, no sign of them, Rulan half-hoped that they had been put to death and were therefore spared having to serve Hung, as she did. It was the only comfort she could salvage from the loneliness and degradation of harem life and the pain of her father's and Pao An's deaths.

▪ ▪ ▪

When Rulan examined her back in the gold-plated surface of her mirror, she saw fine white scars from waist to knees. The pattern was as delicate as lace, each fine strand a thread of purest pain. During her last beating, Hung had instructed Heavenly Glory to whip the part of Rulan's thighs that were not scarred. The reflection reminded her of the secret pattern on the old Tai Tai's Shouchou mirror. Like the entwined lovers, her back too was a record of desire, not that which arose out of submission but the desire that comes from the violent clash of opposing wills—an encounter far more erotic than sex behind the thick walls of Hung's harem.

"How beautifully you scar," he crooned, as if he were admiring the cracked glaze on an old vase. "I take recalcitrant stone and cut and polish. The living stone dies a little, but its shape assumes the creator's form. Even so, you are being shaped by discipline toward obedience. What art is higher than that?"

"Mercy, human kindness," she replied.

For speaking recklessly, Rulan was beaten again, while Hung watched.

A girl from Hang Chow was brought to sleep in Rulan's courts: Bright Orchid, daughter of a porcelain maker. She was fourteen, with a round face and dark eyes that twinkled mischievously when Heavenly Glory caught her gossiping with the girl who carried slop. At the meeting that night, Bright Orchid knelt next to Rulan as the supervisor harangued them by saying, "Harem talk and women's words must not go out. City talk must not be let in. Any moon who disobeys will be torn apart by horses."

"Aiya, I deserve to die!" Bright Orchid wailed in repentance for her crime. But when Heavenly Glory had forgiven her and gone away, Bright Orchid pinched Rulan's cheeks and winked.

The supervisors gave Bright Orchid, Rulan, and two others peacock-feather fans to cool Hung when he visited their court. He had sent the conveyer of heavenly decrees instructions for his reception:

> When the day is hot use your fan to chase
> flying insects.
> Then serve me hot tea and pure cold spring
> water, each thing in succession.
> Litter, torn paper offends my eyes.
> Shells and seeds should be hidden away,
> they offend my eyes.

■   ■   ■

During the summers, the heat clung about Hung's body like a blanket. The untended fields and barren canals around Nanking had long turned to rotten swamp, and wasps and flies swarmed up from the dank weeds and burial grounds and fell over the Grand Palace. They stuck fast to Hung's beard and hair. They left his skin red and feverish and peppered his belly and arms with itchy sores.

The four women in Rulan's court took shifts to fan him. And still, he screamed that they were deceiving heaven and ordered Heavenly Glory to stand over them with a willow switch to make them fan in orderly rhythm, each moon to a separate part of his body. His flesh was soft, fat, and oily, and insects were drawn to it like honey. He claimed Rulan's salves were to blame and made his women bathe him four times a day with scented water, which drew insects all the more. At night, he hid underneath gauze netting and silk coverlets, but he feared insects burrowing through the paper walls, chewing through the nets, hiding in the lining of his clothes. He threatened the four moons who wielded the feather fans that he would destroy them if they failed to drive the insects away. He accused Rulan of trying to kill him.

One winter day, when the rain fell through fog and the walls of the palace sweated like a dead body, Hung called for her.

Because she desired nothing and possessed nothing, she believed that there was nothing he could take away. Heavenly Glory came with six supervisors to escort her to the foot of his bed. He swung his feet off the bed and stood on a pure white rug.

"Do you like it?" he asked. "I had the tanners make it for me. I thought the color appropriate. White, the color of purity according to the new faith. White, the color of death in the old. Because I walk upon it, it signifies that I will overcome death, just as I overcame *Ku,* the demon of superstition. The hide comes from a white horse a woman used to ride; it was possessed by demons. It would not stand still for the reins that fastened to my cart. And so it graces my feet, a rug as white as a cloud. Someday, I will ascend to heaven on a cloud. Do you see, Rulan?"

When Rulan refused to answer, he had her beaten.

Bright Orchid lay naked on Hung's great bed while two women raised her small hips above a red silk bolster. Rulan was ordered to feed Hung a strengthening potion before he favored the girl with his fire.

The golden gong sounded. "Watch the heavens. Be upright, straight, and true," intoned a chancelloress.

Hung was fully dressed in formal gold headdress and gold robes and seated on a carved teak chair inlaid with mother-of-pearl. There were twenty moons in the room; all except the naked girl were dressed in identical diaphanous dresses. Their eyebrows and foreheads were unplucked, their long hair tightly knotted under a heavy veil so that no strands escaped, and their unbound feet moved silently across the polished floor in soft black slippers.

Again the golden gong sounded, and the chief concubines hastened to Hung and removed his lower garments. When he was naked from the waist down, they took clean towels and wiped his loins and legs.

Rulan held out to him the infusion of ginseng and powdered deer horn. Because he allowed no wine in Nanking, she had stirred the powder into hot water until it was as thick as soup. Hung drained the cup and a concubine quickly took it and wiped it clean. He beckoned, and two more knelt to caress him. The chancelloress repeated his edict.

> When the fire rises up, be diligent.
> Save the fire.
> Don't let it go out.

He stirred. Hung held out his arms, and two moons guided him to where Bright Orchid lay. Sighing loudly, he closed his eyes and put his hands on the girl. Rulan saw the girl's skin pucker in fear. The girl was trying to be brave, but she began to tremble.

Hung leaned back on the women while soft hands positioned him over the girl.

The chancelloress intoned

> Let yourself receive the sunshine!
> Make ready for the fire!

There was a snickering behind him.

"Eh? Who laughed?" he demanded.

He pushed the women aside, his eyes blazing.

"It was I," declared Rulan, still holding the empty bowl of ginseng. She watched as his ardor wilted. "You are ridiculous!"

For letting the fire go out, Rulan was beaten by the supervisors. They exhorted as they whipped her. "Repent your sin, and you will be forgiven." But because she refused to admit her guilt, Rulan was locked into a tiny chamber the size of a chicken coop. The only light came from a small grid in the door too high for her to see through. With the coming of night, the room was plunged into a darkness so deep that she could not see the back of her hand.

As a child, Rulan had hated the darkness because of the *kuei,* the demons, that filled it. But in the months she lived in her cell, she came to love the night for giving her back her freedom. In the dark, she was free of the disembodied eyes that peered at her through the door slit. She welcomed the night, for it brought her closer to the lost Pao An. She told herself that if he had survived four days in a box in which he could not rise, then surely she could spend months in a room as large as the span of her arms. She wondered how many men Pao An had slain before falling. What would Pao An do in my place? she asked herself. And she set herself a regimen of healing as he had done in the box at Abundant Spring Mountain. In the daytime, in full view of the guards peering through the window slit, she lay inert on the narrow plank bed. But all the while, she was flexing the muscles down the length of her body while breathing so deeply she could almost put herself into a trance. In the welcome darkness, she danced the sequences that the doctor in the women's commune had taught her. Hobbled by the shackles, she could barely manage to move, yet her mind made every gesture graceful, whole, complete. It seemed in these moments that Pao An, her ghostly lover, was at her side, moving in perfect harmony with her.

One night, she heard a scratching on the wall. She unwound herself from a difficult position and crept to the door. A small packet dropped down from the window-grid and landed with a thud on the dirt floor. A woman's handkerchief. Rulan untied it and found a handful of boiled peanuts and a tiny yellow orchid. She swallowed the peanuts, and hid the handkerchief in her shift. The next day, as she lay on her pallet, Rulan turned her face to the wall and pressed the flower Bright Orchid had given her against her cheek until it died from the heat of her hands.

That evening, before the night shadows bathed the room in darkness, she saw a small white object on the ceiling above her bed. She was sure that it was a silkworm that had spun itself into a cocoon. But how had that worm fed itself in the barren mulberry groves in Nanking? And how had it made its way into this tiny cell?

For weeks, Rulan lay on the plank bed gazing at the pale spot above. She stared so long and hard that her eyes seemed to pierce the small silken veil behind which the cocoon hid. She began to see visions on the iridescent threads: an island coiled like a green dragon in the middle of the sea. A mountaintop shaped like a sleeping woman, her belly swollen with child.

Rulan waited eagerly for the day when the glistening white egg would split, the thin veil burst apart, and the white moth escape the prison and wing its way to heaven.

Then one day, as she was studying the designs on the web, the door opened.

"Come out! The sovereign husband has forgiven you!"

She saw then that what she had gazed at for weeks was not a cocoon cradled in a silken nest but a dead spider's capsule thick with dust.

And yet the discovery brought her joy. She was sure that the vision had been granted her by Ailan, her watchful mother. Hung and the supervisors with whips seemed far less threatening, even as the ladies dragged her forth into the harsh, white light of early spring.

There was a springtime when the trees in the dank garden bloomed. The maids and chancelloresses walked arm in arm around the spot where the dragon boat was enshrined. The wives were carried in litters hung with yellow cloth. Rulan was made to pull Hung's cart.

Bright Orchid brought small gifts to Rulan. Because the girl loved *mui,* preserved fruits, and believed in their medicinal virtue, she tried to get Rulan to eat them. Rulan was as white as a salamander, she joked.

One day when Rulan was confined to her room, Bright Orchid was sitting on a stone bench near the old dragon boat with the newest wives. As she whispered to them, she made a small wet pile of fruit pits. The maids played games with their fans and sang songs. When Hung was carried through the garden, his eye fell on the pile of pits on the stone bench and on Bright Orchid, who was kowtowing to him.

Descending from the litter, screaming about flies, Hung began to hit the girl with a fan of ivory and gold. The blades cut her face, and although the girl wept and begged Hung for mercy, still he hit her again and again. She tried to protect herself, but he knocked her down. He stopped only when the fan was broken, and his hand was tired. By then Bright Orchid had fainted from pain.

When the women brought Bright Orchid to Rulan, she found the girl's face slashed to the bone. One eye was ruined. Rulan had the maids steal needle and thread, and she sewed up the flesh with silk.

"Now that I am ugly, maybe he will send me home," Bright Orchid told her through bruised and swollen lips. She cried happy tears that she would see her mother again.

The next day, Bright Orchid was gone. It was several days before Rulan learned that the girl was beheaded for breaking the Younger

Son's fan. Hunger began to age and sicken the women of Hung's household.

"What can we eat?" the famished women asked their sovereign husband.

"Why do you ask me these things?" Hung fumed. "My father in heaven will feed you even as he feeds the birds of the air. If you are hungry, eat the sweet dew of heaven that fed Moses and the Israelites in the desert."

Unable to find "sweet dew," the women gathered the grass growing between the stones of the courtyards and ate it.

Only Rulan seemed unaffected. She had taught herself to desire little and to eat almost nothing.

She took her place without protest at the head of Hung's carriage, but it was her spirit that screamed rebellion. Hers was the one eye that was raised too high. The foot that dragged too slowly. The ear that did not hear. The mouth that would not answer. The will that would not bend.

If one had *chi* like the Loi priestesses of old, one could send fire through the walls and across the distance, she thought. But she had no fire, and the guards that Hung had set around her were impossible to elude. How can I destroy him? she asked herself over and over.

The answer came to her like a wind from heaven. Think, Daughter, what drives this man from within? whispered Ailan out of the wind and fire. *Ku,* the lustful. *Ku,* the proud. *Ku,* the mad. Puff up his pride; feed the madness. Give him what he most desires. Then break the demon's back.

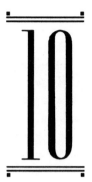

eavenly Glory was having trouble concentrating. She
stifled a yawn, then slid her eyes sideways to see if
Mandley had noticed. She was playing with a tendril of hair that had
come loose from her headdress and smoothing the wrinkles in her gold
gown. Jiao, Hung's sister, was listening raptly to the barbarian who
tutored the palace women.

Mandley went on reading from the Taiping testament, feeling his
own doubt and desperation grow with every new verse he intoned to
the two women.

When he had been kidnapped from the remnants of the northern army
that had straggled back to Nanking, Mandley was sickened by the
thoroughness of Hung's victory over the three kings, Yang, Wei, and
Shih Ta Kai. Hung had goaded the rivals into slaughtering each other.
Of the five original Hakka kings, their families and followers, only
Shih Ta Kai was alive now, a fugitive in the south with a ragged army
of conscripts. Mandley was sure Pao An had perished in the massacre,
although his body had never been found. Nanking's streets had run
with the blood of the slain brothers and sisters. Bodies were thrown in
heaps in the streets, and makeshift pyres smoldered in the squares. The
Porcelain Pagoda, which had graced Yang's section of the city, had

been blown up on Hung's orders, simply because Yang had loved it. To deride its dead owner, Hung placed an iron pot on the site of the ancient landmark.

Mandley had been given the title heavenly tutor and had been taken bodily into the hall next to the palace of "heavenly moons" to serve as tutor to Hung's women. While he was not exactly a prisoner, he found that he was followed everywhere and prevented from going beyond the walls of Nanking or into the inner depths of the palace.

Surrounded by the stolen treasures of captured cities, Mandley felt an utter poverty of spirit. After more than a decade in China, he accused himself, he was worse off than the sower who had cast his seed on stone, for his harvest was corpses, not souls. In bitter self-hatred, he accepted Nanking as his prison and Hung as his jailer. It took a year after Yang's death for him to rise above his terrible grief. He had heard—but not seen—that Rulan was alive, a prisoner like himself in an unnamed corner of the immense palace, and this news gave him renewed hope. Gradually, he fashioned the notion of transforming the Taiping nation from within. He focused his desperate purpose on the eighty-eight wives he was assigned to teach. Through them, Mandley told himself, there might yet be a chance to redeem the Taiping. Even if Hung had killed the grand theocracy that Yang had struggled for, winning the Taiping to the true faith was still possible. The women would be taught so that in the generation after Hung's death, Christianity might flower.

Yet here too, Mandley's lessons did not fall on fertile ground. The women were far too passive to consider any idea that challenged Taiping orthodoxy. Still, Mandley labored, hoping that Rulan struggled on, as he did, while keeping faith with Yang's dream of an enlightened nation. Occasionally, he found an ally from the old days who had escaped the carnage, and they would spend stolen moments together whispering sadly about the past. One of these was Wing, who was still in charge of the silk makers. She came to the palace with new garments for the women and Hung, but she too was prevented from seeing Rulan.

The palace guards soon grew accustomed to his comings and goings. On occasion, he was allowed to accompany the concubines into the gardens of the harem forbidden to men to call on Jiao, Hung's sister, who suffered from nerves and depression. It seemed that Jiao was frightened all the time. She feared revenge and assassins, and asked Mandley to pray for her. Heavenly Glory, who was always with Jiao, watched Mandley suspiciously.

.   .   .

Jiao coughed insistently, and Mandley looked up in surprise from his reading.

"I do not understand, Teacher," she said, "why the Great Book does not prophesy about the Younger Son, my brother."

Mandley noted with satisfaction that Jiao's face was knitted in thought. He had waited so long for her to wrestle with the glaring errors in Taiping dogma. Had it finally occurred to her that her brother's divinity was a massive deception? Mandley quickly turned the question back on her. "Why do you think that might be?"

Heavenly Glory interrupted boldly. "Because the Book is defective. The sovereign husband says that one cannot talk as the Triads do of restoring the Ming dynasty. What's gone is gone, and we are something entirely new. Clearly, we holy soldiers must persist even when the imps and demons devour us, for our example is necessary to guide the next generation in their struggle."

Mandley was shocked by the ease with which the Miao woman would jettison the guidance of the Scriptures. He turned to Jiao, whom he judged was more open to persuasion. "Do you ever feel the need to know Elder Brother Jesus?"

"I never think of him, Teacher," confessed Jiao with some trepidation. "I think I should be quite afraid of the Elder Brother, for the eldest always enforces the edicts of heaven on the younger members of the family."

"That is true in the Land of Flowers," Mandley admitted, "but in Elder Brother Jesus's teachings, the first must put himself last, so the last might be first in heaven."

Jiao looked frightened. "You're speaking in riddles like my brother. I don't understand and then I become quite afraid, especially when I think of Yang and the others who—"

"All demons!" Heavenly Glory declared vehemently.

Mandley quickly intervened. He was always ill at ease with the Miao girl, whose fanaticism frightened him. All he could think of to divert both women from an unpleasant quarrel was to recite the verse that had been ringing in his head. "As it is written in Isaiah, the book which the scribes have not translated, 'He was wounded for our transgressions; he was bruised for our iniquities. The chastisement of our peace was upon him, and with his stripes we are healed!' " He said it in English and then quickly translated it into Han for the curious women.

But as he repeated the familiar words, Mandley suddenly began to cry. The faces of those he loved passed before him: Yang, the carrier of charcoal. Rulan. Pao An. He heard her voice laboring to repeat the English and Hebrew words he had taught her on the long voyage down the Yangtze when the Kingdom of Great Peace was a glorious, still-untarnished dream. He struggled to control himself. "Do you know what that verse means?"

Jiao seemed perplexed by the barbarian's watery eyes. But Heavenly Glory regarded the tutor with open mistrust. It had never occurred to her that a barbarian might be subject to the same emotions as a Han.

"You mean that the Elder Brother would take a beating for someone else—willingly?" asked Jiao haltingly.

"Yes. Even die for another. And so every good ruler must first think of his people's sufferings before his own. He must be willing to give up clothes and money—and food, if need be—so that his people may live."

"Go without food?" scoffed the Miao girl. "Disrespectful! I would gladly starve so that the Younger Son might eat!"

Jiao, however, was silent. She was very much aware of how much her daily portions of rice were shrinking. If she was hungry, what was happening to the common citizens of the Holy City?

"I don't like that talk," Heavenly Glory continued. "It is not what the Younger Son preaches."

Mandley watched the fear and suspicion flood into the Miao girl's scarred face. Still, he was satisfied that Jiao, at least, had partially awakened to his message.

One day in the fifth year of his imprisonment, when he had been summoned to Jiao's rooms, Mandley got lost in the labyrinth of hidden gardens. He wandered aimlessly for a while until he heard the murmur of women's voices and the creaking of a cart. A sharp sound, like the popping of a toy gun, pricked his curiosity. He threaded his way through a maze of narrow corridors and leaned down to peek through a moon window. There he saw the warrior woman who had boxed with him on the plains beyond Nanking. She was pulling the slumbering Hung in a golden carriage in the garden of the dragon boat, as a lead ox pulls a plow. There were twelve women at the head of the carriage, six on a side, and both harnesses were tied around her waist. Rulan was bent over like an ox in harness. Her ankles were bound with a golden chain of bells, as were the traces, so that as the women hauled the carriage around and around the decorative rocks, the music made by their feet lulled the man in the cart to sleep.

The roar of blood in Mandley's ears was deafening. It took all his will-power not to burst through the window and break Rulan's chains. But he held himself back out of fear for her safety, because stationed around the garden were Hung's armed guard of women warriors. One of them was Heavenly Glory, who held a willow wand with which she lashed the backs of those who pulled too slowly or who let their fans droop.

Mandley wrapped his arms around his shuddering body until the thundering of his heart had eased. He leaned his feverish head against the cold stone. Rulan! he whispered to himself, savoring her name. He had lived so long without allowing himself to feel that any emotion now exhausted him.

When the procession passed out of view, Mandley began to run. On the other side of the wall, he paralleled Rulan's course, his feet automatically slowing to match the rhythm of the cart. He had no idea what to do, except to let Rulan know that he had seen her. He began to chant: "Bezer in the wilderness on the tableland for the Reubenites, Ramoth in Gilead for the Gadites, Golan in Bashan for the Manassites." He sang until the cart came round again.

Rulan's head shot up instantly at the old litany. He saw that her eyes were as brilliant and black as he remembered, and brimful of rebellious life.

There was a loud crack of a willow wand and a burst of angry shouting from the supervisors who shook their whips at him. The willow wand lashed at Rulan's back, and he saw pain explode in her eyes, but it was quickly replaced with a strange wild light that made him turn away in agony. She recognized his voice!

Again Mandley sang the names of the cities Moses had set apart in Transjordan as places of refuge for those devoid of hope or home. Long ago, they had recited these verses together, and she had been comforted.

"Bezer in the wilderness, Ramoth in Gilead, Golan in Bashan . . ."

Hung stirred from sleep, disoriented by the jostling of the cart and the angry shouts of the supervisors. But at the sound of Mandley's chanting, Hung smiled, sat up, and signed the women into silence. Listening intently to the litany, he began to sway rhythmically, and later he commended Mandley for his heavenly song.

Rulan decided that poison was the most likely way to kill him. Yet guards, her shackles, and Hung's suspicion prevented her from getting to him directly. She had to draw Hung to her. Heavenly Glory, she thought, might be the one to do so. Hung desired the secret of eternal life he believed Rulan possessed from her mother's Loi magic. Instead of the elixir of immortality, she would make poison for him. All she had to do was find a way to have the Miao woman deliver it.

• • •

"What is your secret?" Heavenly Glory asked Rulan. "Why are you the only one in the palace who does not mind hunger and want?" The skin on the back of her hands was so thin that the veins stood up like twisted blue worms.

"What makes you think I have a secret?" Rulan asked, pretending surprise at the long-awaited question. She knew how to survive on the grasses that grew between cracks in the flagstones, fungus that grew on a shady wall, even on the bits of bone that the starving threw away.

"Every woman in the palace ages, yet you are as young as ever," said Heavenly Glory. "You have been beaten and starved and bound in chains, but still you go on as before."

Rulan's smile was brilliant. "My mother was the same. She was thirty when she bore me, over forty when my brother was born, and she was as supple as a girl when she died." She prayed that Heavenly Glory would not see through the ruse.

The Miao girl frowned, her mind laboring over Rulan's words. "How is this so unless you have found the secret of immortality?"

Rulan managed a sigh. Even though she disliked Heavenly Glory, she hated using the girl this way.

"The elixir of gold! You knew it all the time!" exclaimed Heavenly Glory.

"Yes," Rulan acknowledged, pretending chagrin. "My mother taught me the recipe, and I believe it is the same as that dew that fell from heaven when Moses led his people through the desert."

Heavenly Glory grasped Rulan's hand so hard that Rulan winced. "You must make 'dew' for me," she demanded. "If I am young and whole again, then the Younger Son will turn the light of his favor upon me." Only she and Rulan, of all Hung's concubines and women guards, had never been brought to his bed—Heavenly Glory because she was ugly and Rulan because of Yang's curse at the betrothal.

Rulan felt a rush of guilt at the thought that she had been the cause of the girl's disfigurement in the attack on the powder train long ago. But she forced herself to set aside all sympathy for the girl, just as she tried to suppress memories of her life among the horsewomen, for they inevitably led to sorrow and tears. "Can you get the herbs I need?"

Heavenly Glory nodded, her happiness transforming her homely face. Rulan expected that as soon as Heavenly Glory left, she would run to Hung's bedchamber to tell him what she had discovered. After Heavenly Glory had told him the "secret," Hung would make sure that whatever herbs she needed would be found. "Then you must arrange it so that I am alone for an hour each morning. No one must see what I do when I prepare the elixir," Rulan said.

Only Hung, spying on her from a dozen secret places in the walls, would see.

Rulan searched her memory for the basic ingredients of the fabled elixir. When she was sure of the recipe, she gathered dew on the lotus blossoms floating in the fishpond outside her bedroom and collected it in a teacup drop by drop.

Hung, watching Rulan's every move, sent Heavenly Glory and a dozen others to gather dew from the lotus ponds in every garden of the palace.

Rulan ordered Heavenly Glory to find asparagus root, the longevity herb called *ho shou wu,* wild Manchurian ginseng, and several kinds of rare powders. She included one ingredient that was not in her mother's recipe: the herb henbane, which in small amounts quiets pain and in large quantities causes hallucinations, paralysis, and eventually death.

Hung sent men through enemy lines to procure the costly ingredients from medicine shops in Taiping-controlled cities, and made available a small quantity for Heavenly Glory to give to Rulan, while keeping the greater portion for himself.

From the powders that Heavenly Glory gave her, Rulan took cinnabar, red and yellow sulfur, and mother-of-pearl. She added peach-tree gum, mulberry ash, small pieces of asparagus root, ginseng, and *ho shou wu*—everything except the henbane, which she only pretended to use—and ground the minerals and herbs in a mortar. Then she heated the mixture with the dew and poured the infusion into a cup. Last, she took a gold coin from her necklace and dropped it in.

"A pity," she told Heavenly Glory, who watched Rulan's preparations with great interest, "that we are missing the vital element, the dragon's eye, the golden eye. But I will use the ancient lyrics my mother taught me, for these supply power—although not the kind the eye can summon."

Then Rulan intoned a childhood chant that she remembered from the Loi tongue, which Ailan used to sing when she gave Boy-Boy a bath: "fingers, toes, ears, nose." Rulan drank down the potion, plucked the coin from the bottom of the cup and pretended to swallow the shining disk, but slipped it instead into her cheek.

She had no remorse now about deceiving Heavenly Glory, for she was sure that the girl was not only betraying her secrets to Hung but was also looking for a way to destroy her as she had so many other young women in the harem on whom Hung's favor fell.

"If a person takes a hundred coins over the course of a year, immortality is assured," Rulan told Heavenly Glory. "But even a small amount enhances longevity. Here, I have a sprinkling of gold for you," and she pulled off two of the smallest links from her necklace, dropped them into the cup—which she filled again with the infusion— and poured it into a small gourd.

Heavenly Glory grabbed it greedily.

"If we had the eye," Rulan confided, "you might live like a goddess."

"Hung has such a stone," Heavenly Glory declared.

"Does he?" Rulan asked brightly. "Of course, he is already one of the immortals."

Hung was watching from a hole in the wall. Rulan felt the heat of his breath on her cheek. Or was it *Ku,* the demon, looking on with his red eye?

"You tricked me!" Heavenly Glory raged. She had dragged Rulan by her braid to Hung's room. Her scarred face was twisted with anguish for the man coiled in a fetal position on the bed.

Hung lay beneath a thin spread of gold silk. The women had just bathed him, and he smelled of scented water and sweet soap. Someone had combed his beard and tied the ends around his neck. His bloodshot eyes were turned to the right as if locked on an invisible terror, and his hands were clenched into claws.

You were too greedy, Rulan told him silently. A pinch of henbane might have eased the hunger pains in your stomach, yet you gorged on the poison, as you gorged on the wealth and titles of the brothers and sisters you slew.

Rulan set her wooden medicine box on a table cluttered with the elements for the elixir while Heavenly Glory screamed at her to undo the sickness that had felled Hung. There were round boxes of dried herbs, brown knobs of longevity root and wild ginseng, a stack of empty rice bowls, a mortar and pestle, a knife for cutting ginseng, a jar of honey, a teapot, and a bowl of dark liquid in which a large yellow orb was half-submerged. Rulan stirred the mixing bowl with a finger and recoiled at the cold, slippery feel of the jade egg in the viscous poison. It was a dragon's eye, the mate to the one that had shattered in the house of Wang. Hung had placed it in the elixir to make a more potent concoction, as she had suggested whimsically to Heavenly Glory.

Rulan peered into Hung's face, not daring to think what she might find. A demon? A snake-spirit? Although she had once believed with her mother that the world was filled with demons that fed on human souls, the years had taught Rulan that men themselves invent monsters out of their deepest fears. There was no demon, only a madman's emptiness in Hung's stare. Hung had fallen away from the High God into a realm of utter solitude and darkness.

"Witch! Infidel! Do not think yourself raised too high!" Heavenly Glory warned. "If the sovereign husband dies, you die too."

Over Heavenly Glory's curses, Jiao begged, "Use your power to heal him." There was no trace of her former arrogance; Jiao was once again a helpless woman afraid for her brother's life. "Come," she pleaded with Heavenly Glory. "We must set the women chanting."

The man who had whipped her, slain her loved ones, and battered her dreams lay helplessly before Rulan. She went to her medicine box and took out an envelope of henbane.

"You want the elixir?" she demanded, omitting all titles of respect. Hung's eyelids flickered. She filled a cup from the mixing bowl and poured the contents of the envelope into the cup. "The elixir I will mix for you will make you live ten thousand lifetimes of terror before you die. Plunged into chaos, locked in the dark box of your mind, haunted by the faces of those you killed." This was the moment for which her dying mother had prepared her. Now would Ailan's words be fulfilled. "I will give you what you most desire."

A small, strangled noise came from Hung's throat.

Trembling, Rulan set down the bowl of poison. "I understand so little," she told Hung earnestly. "I don't know what heavenly wind has blown us about like dry grass. Is the High God burning away the old and making us the altar of true sacrifice, as Man-da-li used to say?"

All she saw was her own face reflected in the pupils of his eyes.

Hot tears trickled down her cheeks as she took up the teapot and filled the bowl with the dark, tepid tea. The henbane spun round and round.

"You want life more than anyone I know. Why?" she asked brokenly.

Hung's face was contorted with unspoken rage. He moved his lips soundlessly, like a greedy child ravenous for a sweet, as she brought the poison to his lips.

And suddenly Rulan was ashamed. She pulled the cup away from his mouth and threw it against the wall, where it shattered in a hundred pieces. A stain as dark as blood ran down the tile. She went to her box and took out mung beans and mashed them in the mortar and fed him the antidote for the poison he had already drunk.

In minutes, Hung began to retch. Two hours later, Rulan gave him more antidote. There was movement in his hands now, although his body was still immobilized and he could not speak.

"You know that the imps are about to knock down the walls of the Holy City," Rulan told him. "Your Empire of Heaven on earth is finished. You could save millions of innocents if you repent and order the people to make peace. If you want to live, do as I say. I will write a document of recantation. You sign it and affix your seal. Do you understand?"

His eyelids flickered.

She wrote a short confession that declared that Hung was not the Younger Son of God but only a sinful man who had sinned grievously against heaven and the people, from whom he begged forgiveness. Rulan took the large oblong seal of office, pricked Hung's wrist with the small herb knife, and set his bloody seal on the paper. Then she guided his hand to write his name, Hung Hsiu Chuan, devoid of titles and rank. Finally, she gave him the last measure of the antidote and called Jiao and Heavenly Glory back into the room.

The women buried their faces in his bedclothes, touched his hands and his face with trembling fingers.

"Read this to them," Rulan ordered Hung.

Hung raised himself unsteadily on one elbow. Without warning, his hand flashed out, swept the document aside, and moved swiftly to rip the chain around Rulan's neck away. She fell backward with a cry of pain.

"You will not cheat me of all I deserve," he shouted hoarsely.

Hung lifted the string up to his mouth, and, like a thirsty man drinking from a jug, poured the coins down his throat. His mouth worked furiously, and his throat rose and fell as he swallowed the coins, every one, and washed them down with the bowl of henbane enriched by the dragon's eye of immortality.

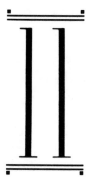

Temple Island, Summer 1864

Wing and Mandley waited for Pao An on an island off the west gate of Nanking. The ancient temples on the island had been turned into warehouses and mat-sheds when the silk guild's original quarters in the outskirts of the city grew too small. At the height of the Taiping silk trade, foreign ships sailed up the river to the island to exchange food and ammunition for Taiping silk. But after the imperial army and foreign mercenaries tightened their hold up and down the Yangtze, the silk trade ground to a halt and food shipments dwindled to an occasional mule train. The island was deserted now, and all the women had taken refuge inside the walls of the citadel as the enemy came nearer and nearer. The wide plain facing the river had been transformed by the besieging army into a huge barracks surrounded by deep trenches and a moat ten miles long that encircled the eastern and southern edges of Nanking.

Confusion inside the Taiping capital was so high and security so lax due to desertion, hunger, and loss of morale, that Wing and Mandley were now meeting openly outside Hung's palace. Their concern for Rulan had mounted when they heard rumors that Hung was engaged in a systematic slaughter of his wives. They had tried to smuggle in messages to Rulan but there was no way to reach her. Rulan was kept apart from the other women and guarded constantly by the sentinels appointed by Heavenly Glory who was now chief supervisor of the harem. Sick with apprehension, Wing and Mandley had watched Hung's palace change from a place of tribute to a cemetery, as more and more women died from starvation or beatings.

Mandley had hoped that Shih Ta Kai, Yang's old ally, would return with his army to lift the siege and wrest the kingdom away from Hung. But when months passed and Shih had made no move to save the starving city, Mandley admitted to Wing that there would be no salvation.

"Shih was always ambitious," he told Wing. "He'll carve out a kingdom of his own rather than seize one that is already dead."

Then they heard that Iron Fist had broken with Hung and taken his men south to raid in Fukien. The next rumor had Iron Fist warring with Shih. Finally, spies brought a report that filled them with terror, confusion, and joy: Iron Fist had been killed in Fukien by troops which were commanded by none other than Pao An, whom they had long believed dead and who fought as a general in Li's provincial army.

Wing thought the rumor preposterous. "What would make Pao An fight for Li, his bitterest enemy?"

"Desperation," replied Mandley. "Survival." He reminded her that Pao An was not the first Taiping soldier to change sides. Even before the siege, the Triads had been unable to stomach the religious ritual that Hung insisted on and had abandoned the Taiping cause. And when the tide of battle turned against the Taiping, hundreds of holy soldiers had deserted the Taiping camp for that of the imperial army, where looting brought more ample rewards. Mandley wondered if Pao An had become as depraved as these weak men.

Then came the astonishing news that a contingent of southern militia led by Pao An had unexpectedly joined the siege, much to the anger of Tseng, who had immediately sent a letter of protest to the empress that Viceroy Li was infringing on his field of operations.

Wing's hopes soared. It was her idea to send a message to Pao An. She argued that Pao An could get Rulan out of the harem and through enemy lines to safety. Mandley allowed himself to be persuaded that he and Wing too, with Pao An's help, might escape the attack that threatened to come any day. Wing chose a trusted woman in the silk guild and smuggled her out of the city in the last mule train carrying Taiping cloth to the outside world. If the woman reached Pao An, Wing was certain that he would follow her instructions: to come alone within twenty days to Temple Island to a spot marked by a red lantern.

Mandley, who had neither loved nor trusted Pao An in the old days, was not so sure.

This was the twentieth day, and Wing and Mandley waited in forlorn expectation.

Pao An came out of the river like a half-drowned rat a hundred paces downstream from the old Taoist temple. He came at the word of a water bearer who confirmed Iron Fist's last taunt: Rulan was alive but held prisoner by Hung. Ever since he had found his father, Pao An had been waiting for another miracle, a sign that would allow him to turn hope into action. He waited until Tseng's army was about to begin the final attack, and on a night when the camp was nearly empty, his men having been moved into position before the main gate, he slipped out and approached the island from the side opposite the point where he had seen the red lantern burn night after night.

There were no troops lying in ambush there, only a tall gaunt woman in a dark dress and a man in an embroidered headwrap and red vest. Pao An stepped out of the shadows and called softly, "Wing. Man-da-li, my brother."

Wing turned and came to him. "Every night we hung the lantern," she said weakly and touched him as if to test the reality of his flesh.

Trembling, Mandley stepped toward Pao An. His mouth moved, but no words came from the preacher who had turned a charcoal-carrier into a prophet. "I had given up hope—" he said finally. His voice was hoarse and strange to his own ears.

"How is she?" Pao An demanded.

Wing shook her head. "No one has seen her for two months. None of us have been allowed into the palace all that time." The bones of Wing's shoulders showed through the well-worn silk.

"What's the news in the city?" Pao An asked.

"Bad," Wing replied. "People falling dead in the streets. Kings fighting with one another over dogs and rats and a few radishes. Rumors everywhere. The brothers are planning a breakout. The sisters are planning mass suicide. Shih will not come. Tseng is struck by lightning. There is even a rumor that Hung is dead."

"Is that possible?" Pao An asked.

Mandley nodded. "I wouldn't have believed it a few weeks ago. But this rumor persists. It would explain why no one is allowed into the palace anymore. Why Hung's edicts have stopped. Why his brothers are fighting with the kings. Why the supervisors have locked the harem gates. No food goes in. They haven't even carried out night soil!"

"When will the final assault come?" Wing asked Pao An nervously.

"Tomorrow," replied Pao An grimly. "Tseng's brother has mined a tunnel under the main gate."

It was Wing who said what Mandley could not. "When the attack comes, if the walls are broken down, the kings have ordered the families to set fire to the city. The black flag is raised. The decree is death rather than surrender."

"Then there's no time to wait for the morning services to cloak our entrance," declared Pao An. "We'll have to go in now."

Wing nodded. "Before the night watch changes. The guard knows me. His men will be tired. You both will carry bolts of silk to hide your faces." A half-smile touched the corners of her lips. "And wearing women's robes over your swords."

Fog swelled up from the river while Pao An, Mandley, and Wing climbed into a launch with tall baskets piled with cloth. Two guildwomen, who brought along small baskets of small fish from the last of the guild's share, accompanied them. Pao An and Mandley wore the loose robes, embroidered hoods, and wooden name tags of guildwomen. As they poled the boat toward the western wall of the city under the shifting mantle of fog, each slap on the water sounded like muffled gunshots. The captain of the watch called down and Wing gave the password.

"Stay last in line," she warned Pao An and Mandley.

The captain came down to meet them in person. "You're late," he grumbled.

"We've been fishing," Wing replied archly. "I brought fish for you and your men."

"Fish! Praise the High God. She's got fish for us!" he yelled up to his men. The famished guards poured out through a small door in the gates. As they swarmed around the two women with the baskets of fish, Mandley, Wing, and Pao An hurried through the door.

By the first hour after midnight, all traces of fog had burned away. The full moon illuminated Nanking, a ghost city of ruined buildings and abandoned squares. Some streets were so torn by explosives that the broken stones formed secondary defense walls. Withered gardens grew in the exposed earth of the streets. Houses had been pulled down for fuel. Garbage was piled in courtyards.

Mandley guided them to a partially destroyed building whose weed-ridden courtyard abutted the rear wall of Hung's palace. "We'll wait until an hour before dawn," he said. "The palace guards are sleepy then." After a moment, he asked forlornly, hoping against hope, "Do you really think Tseng will break down the walls this time?"

Pao An replied with tight-lipped conviction. "Tseng has to succeed or he will be disgraced in Peking. This time the city will fall—if the charges are in place. If the powder isn't wet. If the sappers don't blow themselves up or suffocate in the tunnel before touching off the main explosives."

"So much death," Mandley said hollowly. "If I didn't believe—"

"I've never believed," blurted out Wing.

"Then why did you follow Hung?" an astonished Mandley demanded.

"Where else could I go after my sisters were slaughtered? Even trapped in an endless war, a woman like me was freer with the Taiping than bound to a mother-in-law."

"But were you never moved by the new faith?" Mandley asked, greatly disturbed by Wing's confession.

"Never," replied Wing curtly. "There are honorable principles in the faith you preach, Man-da-li, but we were asked to accept Hung, not those principles."

Mandley moaned. "I have failed utterly in bringing your people to God, failed all those souls I sought to save."

"Don't blame yourself," Pao An answered him. "You can save one person, and that is enough."

"There has to be the hand of providence in this," a tired, wan Mandley insisted. "I cannot believe that all the suffering has been in vain. Somehow, the people will be redeemed!" But even as he spoke, Mandley knew that his impassioned words were empty. It was fatal, he saw, to have begun with the wrong premise. The Taiping theology, which combined so much madness with the Gospel, had been an unnatural mutation that he could not reform; it had grown into a monster. Mandley had tried to teach the monster to act like a Christian gentleman, but it developed wings and fangs and claws and went ravening about. And he had been an accessory to the inevitable slaughter. "If only Yang had lived!" he cried out to Pao An. "If only there were a man like you, Pao An, to carry on the Eastern King's fight!"

"No, I am not the man you seek, my friend," said Pao An stiffly. "If I find Rulan alive, that is all I want. All else can burn." Suddenly, his face crumpled. "Is there anyone lower than I? Is there one person I have not betrayed? I can be manipulated like a child, traded like dirt. Truly, my poor father does not recognize the thing I have become."

"The blood of Christ will wash you clean," replied Mandley.

Pao An shook his head. "When?"

"I am like Pao An, a ruined city," Wing declared with sadness.

They slept in silence for a few hours. Then Wing clutched at her stomach in her sleep, moaning softly. Mandley stirred, but did not awaken.

Pao An watched the stars, faint pinpricks of light, as far away as the gods were from men. He decided he needed no gods, High God, or Jade Emperor. All he needed was his father—and Rulan.

When the hour came, Pao An alerted his companions. It was near the end of the night shift on the walls. The guards would be exhausted, most half-asleep. Inside the palace, there would be only women.

"It's time," Pao An announced as he flung off his long robe. "Get the hooks and rope."

Wing came out of sleep instantly and began rummaging through her basket.

Mandley rolled over and groaned. He sat up stiffly and rubbed his eyes.

"Are you sure you know the way, Man-da-li?" asked Pao An.

"I can find her," Mandley replied groggily.

The palace wall was twenty feet high, but there were no guard towers. Pao An swung his hook on the end of the rope in a widening arc and threw it high over the wall, where the top of a tree could be seen on the other side. The line caught in the limbs, slipped, caught again, and stuck fast. Wing, who weighed the least, went up first.

"There are pot shards on the top. Be careful," she whispered down to them. "I'll make sure the rope's secure."

Mandley went over next; then Pao An. They huddled under the scraggly branches of a dead willow, trying to see in the dim light. The garden they entered had dark mounds that rose to shoulder height. The place smelled of ashes, fertilizer, and decay. The trio moved slowly, hiding behind the mounds. A low moon came out from behind the clouds, and Wing leaned against a mound to escape the stream of pale white light.

"Aaiiee," she gasped, stifling her scream even as it began.

The mounds were stacks of unburied bodies. Scores of them. In the center of the garden was a huge circle of ashes where some of the bodies had been burned until death had outstripped the ability of the living to efface it.

"Lord God," Mandley exclaimed.

"It's true, it's true," Wing moaned, "he is eating them!"

"Don't be absurd," Mandley asserted, his mind grappling for order. "The bodies are whole."

Wing covered her eyes. Sniffling, she allowed Pao An to lead her away.

"Where are we, Man-da-li? Where do we go?" she asked.

Mandley tried to gauge their direction by the rooftops.

Just then, an explosion shook the earth and filled the sky with a ghoulish red light.

"They've blown the main gate!" Pao An said. "We must hurry."

They set off at a run. Guards were yelling outside the palace, but there was still no noise inside. Moments later, they heard the far-off roar of human voices and the popping of muskets. "They've broken through the wall," Pao An cried.

"This way," Mandley yelled, and pulled them around a corner. He stopped in confusion, scanning the rooftops. "There's the Gate of Golden Moons," he said finally, "the entrance to the pavilion of the wives. In there."

They ran under the open roof of a long veranda and dashed across the dusty floor of the Grand Palace of Glory and Light. Speed was their only hope now. Their footsteps clattered on the cobblestone walks.

The gates to Hung's private pavilions were closed and bereft of the usual team of women guards. They ran past the carved pillars. The first courtyard was empty. The second too. In the third, they saw a shadowy figure dragging a sack that bounced heavily on the ground. As the man rounded a corner, Pao An caught him fast around the neck before he could scream.

"Where is Hung? Where are the wives?"

"Dead, he's dead," the man wheezed. "The wives are praying over him. Everyone's run away."

"How did you enter where no man is allowed?"

"I figured to be the first looter. I won't be last when Tseng's men break in."

"Where are they praying?" Pao An released the man.

"In the small chapel. I heard the noise."

"Do you know the woman Yang Rulan, the celestial bride? Is she with them?"

He shrugged. "If she's alive. They blame her for his death."

"Oh Lord, no." Mandley shuddered.

By force of will, Pao An erased the gruesome images that sprang into his mind. He turned to the thief, but the man had already scuttled crablike into the shadows.

The next court was empty. And the next.

"I'm afraid, my friends," Mandley said. At that moment, they heard the singing.

As they raced toward the sound, the music swelled: women's voices praising the High God and His Younger Son, yet sung too high and off key.

They went softly now, Pao An and Wing with swords drawn. Mandley tried the small back door and found it ajar. One by one they crept in. The stench of incense and putrefaction was overwhelming. The main hall was ablaze with torches. Oil lamps burned in every corner and on every altar. Approximately fifty women in saffron robes, their hair and faces covered with dark veils, knelt around a yellow catafalque in the center of the hall. Lifted up on the dais, in a golden dragon gown and his crown of state, was the Younger Son of God. His face was blackened, and his body bloated with the gases of corruption. The hands that lay on his chest were cracked and running with fluids, as were his eyes.

"He is not dead," Heavenly Glory chanted.

"He is only waiting," Jiao replied over and over, as if to dislodge all doubts from her mind.

Wing whimpered and pointed. At the head of the bier was Rulan. Her hair hung down her back in a dark wave. Jiao and Heavenly Glory stood at her side, each holding up one of Rulan's arms in the dead man's direction. Rulan hung between them, sagging from exhaustion.

"They're trying to push the heat from her hands to raise him from the dead," Wing whispered, horrified. "They'll kill her!"

"Abomination," Mandley declared hoarsely.

The song rose again, unnaturally high.

"Do you know that hymn?" Pao An asked Mandley.

"Yes," he said.

"Then sing it. Make up words. Say the celestial bride must go out to meet her sovereign husband in the open air. I'll distract them somehow until you get her over the wall."

"Not you, Pao An," Wing hissed. "They remember who you are."

"I don't want to leave her," he insisted hotly.

"Wait for me by the courtyard," Wing ordered. She stuck her sword in her belt under her robe and walked boldly toward the bier, singing lustily.

Mandley began to sing too. The women, hypnotized by their grief, did not see them at first.

"We have come to bear the bride away," Wing told them.

"It is written," Mandley said, "that the City of God will come

down from Heaven to receive the Son. It is no earthly city." His mind
was a flurry of discordant words and images. The glassy stares of the
wives frightened him. Harpies, she-devils. Bacchae, he thought in
horror, remembering the savage priestesses of ancient Greece. They
might accept him, even adore him—or attack him with claws and
teeth.

The supervisors looked at Wing and Mandley with tear-swollen
eyes—was this part of the Younger Son's plan?

"The Younger Son charged me with the final things," Mandley
declared, his mind working feverishly. "He forewarned and he foretold. From among his wives, only one, his celestial bride, would meet
him at the dawning of the last day. That day has come. I must take
her to him."

Through a haze of incense, Rulan saw Wing coming toward her.
She recognized Mandley's voice. Surely this is the hour of my death,
she thought.

"But Teacher, the Younger Son is here," said Jiao, pointing to the
body.

"His earthly husk is here," Mandley insisted, trying not to look at
the thing rotting in its yellow robes. "He will awaken in the courtyard
where corpses are burned. Bear him out." None of what he babbled
made sense, but would it pass as sense to minds already crazed with
death and grief and hunger? "Lift him up!" Mandley ordered.

In a daze Heavenly Glory beckoned six of the supervisors to lift
Hung's bier.

"Only to the courtyard," Wing whispered to Mandley.

"You may follow as far as the courtyard, the anteroom of paradise,
and you may watch. But to paradise itself, you may not go," intoned
Mandley.

Wing and Mandley half-carried Rulan from the chapel. Holding
their torches aloft, the women followed behind Hung's bier, weeping
loudly and tearing their hair. The macabre processional wound through
the corridors and hidden gardens, while the clamor in the city swelled
louder. At the entrance to the courtyard, Mandley made the women
stop.

"We will bear the bride forward," he said. "You wait here."

Suspicion grew on Heavenly Glory's scarred, sullen face. She reached
out an emaciated hand to grasp Rulan's dress.

"He is waiting," Mandley said, gesturing impatiently to the mounds
of the dead. Jiao stepped forward eagerly.

"Surely the sister of the Younger Son is permitted." Wing's voice
was thin and shaky. "Surely the chief supervisor is permitted. Come,

Sister," Wing said. She held out her hand and Jiao took it eagerly. Heavenly Glory followed behind.

The five of them walked through the courtyard and behind the pyramids of death. The din outside the palace was deafening now. The noise seemed to bring Jiao and Heavenly Glory out of their stupor. They glanced nervously back at the wives, who were wailing at the entrance to the courtyard.

"Aaiiee!" screamed Heavenly Glory, brandishing her torch when she saw Pao An emerge from beneath the willow tree.

"No more sacrifices," Wing said. With one quick thrust of her arm, she pushed Heavenly Glory to the ground. "Quickly," she commanded Pao An.

Pao An gathered Rulan up in his arms. How amazingly light she was! The last time he had held her in their hiding place in the walls of the silk factory, she was almost as tall and strong as he. But this woman was as weightless as a shadow, a passing dream. He pressed his face to her neck and was surprised at the warmth of her flesh; the force of his emotions nearly brought him to his knees.

"Who?" she whispered, dazed and unbelieving, as if he were a phantom come back from the underworld. A slim hand reached up to touch his wet cheek. Amazed that her fingers touched real tears, she became afraid. "My love, you must not save me. I am beyond reaching. I will not endanger you—"

"Hush," he told her, as one tells a child. "You are safe. And you are mine. Nothing will harm you from now on."

Suddenly a cannonball exploded just beyond the wall. There was a shower of rubble, and all the wives came running.

Bacchae, thought Mandley again in terror as the clawing mass of women rushed toward him.

"Go up, Man-da-li!" Wing shouted.

He scurried up the trunk, his ears echoing with the savage cries.

"Take her!" Wing shouted to Pao An. She pulled out her sword and whirled to meet the frenzied women.

"You go first," ordered Pao An, trying to hand Rulan to Wing.

"Are you mad? I can't carry her," she cried. "Go, or they will get Rulan."

Heavenly Glory was pulling Pao An back, clawing at Rulan's hair and clothes. "Here, here!" she cried.

Pao An wrestled Rulan from the Miao girl's talons and clambered up the tree with Rulan slung over his shoulder. But as he was about to jump, Rulan's long hair snagged on the limbs of the dead willow. The women swarmed around Wing, who gave the horsewoman's battle cry and swung her sword viciously. They gave way at first but came back, like waves dashing against a stone. Two or three of the nimblest clambered up the tree behind Pao An. Hands tore at Pao An's legs and clawed at Rulan's sleeves.

"Hurry!" Mandley called beyond the wall.

Wing looked up and saw the dilemma. Wading through arms and legs and writhing bodies, she knocked the shrieking women aside. Heavenly Glory had flung her torch into the dessicated tree, which burst into flame. Now she was hanging on Wing's neck, her teeth bared. Wing shook herself loose and cut so cleanly with her sword that the blade went through silk and flesh like a scythe through dry rice stalks. Then she turned her back on the screeching, clawing mass of women and with a great arc of her blade cut Rulan's hair free.

With a savage cry, they were upon Wing, with flailing arms and nails and teeth.

Pao An climbed over the wall, his clothes afire, dropped Rulan into Mandley's arms, and jumped.

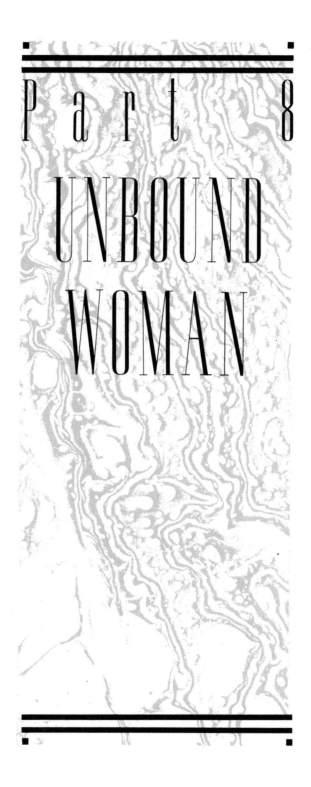

Part 8
UNBOUND
WOMAN

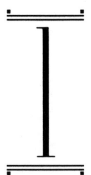

On the Road, 1864

"Such a formidable band of rebels has been rarely known since ancient times until the present," wrote Scholar Tseng to the child-emperor Tung Chih and his councillors after the fall of Nanking.

The Holy City of the Taiping was gutted, blasted, burned. Tseng reported that on the nineteenth and twentieth of July, a hundred thousand rebels drowned themselves in the dikes and ditches of the city. Thousands more set fire to themselves and their houses and jumped from the walls, "and so passed away without repentance" rather than surrender. The Grand Palace of Glory and Light was burned. No trace of Hung's body was ever found. The rumor in the city was that in his madness, Hung had poisoned himself by swallowing gold coins. The fires in the city raged for three weeks.

In that same letter to the emperor, Tseng claimed that the wealth of the Kingdom of Great Peace had been dispersed before the end. The heretics, having anticipated their doom, had smuggled their treasures south to the rebel Shih Ta Kai, whom Tseng proposed to pursue next. But the greatest treasures, Tseng alleged, had been stolen on the day the city fell by the turncoat general Chen Pao An.

Scholar Tseng blamed his rival, Viceroy Li, for plotting the theft with the traitor Chen, who had slipped inside the city on Li's orders before the invasion had begun. Tseng had given Li one last chance to atone for the crime: capture Chen Pao An and bring the treasure back.

Li would be looking for an illusion.

Rulan and Mandley lay Pao An in a small cart and took turns pulling. Pao An's face had been spared from the fire, although his back and legs were badly burned and he was racked with fever. Their destination was a small farmhouse a week's journey south of Nanking where Pao An had left Li Yu before joining the siege. Behind them, they heard, Viceroy Li was coming to exact retribution against his traitor general.

They were three among thousands fleeing the holocaust that erupted in the cities surrounding Nanking. Hollow eyed and big bellied from want and brandishing sharp sticks, the refugees were an army of the starving, one link in the endless chain of hunger marchers who traveled the roads in war.

Because the waterways and main roads were controlled by imperial soldiers, they marched through flooded paddies at night and hid in the copses outside the villages during the day. Once again, Rulan slept under the same blanket as Pao An, although this time he ate from her fingers.

"Where are we?" he asked her over and over, unable to focus his eyes.

"Together," was all Rulan could tell him.

Rulan was recovering physically, but she often dreamed of Wing's brave sacrifice at the flaming tree in the garden of the palace. Then Mandley would hold her trembling against his chest, and both would grieve for their lost warrior-sister as the mass of hunger marchers flowed like an endless river around them. Once napping in the heat of the afternoon, she awoke and called out in terror, "Man-da-li, where are you taking me?"

Mandley came quickly to her and stroked her forehead. "To the far horizon, dear girl," he answered. "To the gates of Paradise." When she asked him what he meant, he told her that they must flee overseas. There was no place in the Land of Flowers for them anymore. They were branded as much as Pao An, for a price was on the head of every holy soldier who had escaped Nanking.

After a few days, they left the horde of hunger marchers and journeyed alone to the farmhouse where Pao An had left Li Yu. They found Li Yu recovered from his ordeal, but Pao An was still desperately ill. Rulan managed to obtain medicinal herbs from the peasants who had cared for Li Yu, but her arts were not equal to the task of healing Pao An. Despite Rulan's anxious ministrations, he slipped in and out of consciousness; his strength ebbed, Rulan began to panic: after all they had been through together, how could he leave her now?

Still dreadfully weak, Li Yu insisted on helping Rulan nurse his son. Rulan marveled at the old man's ability to marshal his limited strength in smooth, small efforts. She concluded that Pao An's skill at *tai chi chuan* had been learned from Li Yu, who moved as if he were assisting an object to its intended place. With his huge eyes and half-smile, he seemed an ancient child still at some form of solemn play in the world.

He dipped a small bowl into a pot of hot water simmering on the makeshift brazier in the corner of the farmhouse and carried it between his hands across the room to where she sat. She saw how each foot was planted gently on the floor before another step was taken. He offered the cup to her with a gracious incline of his head.

"Thank you, Father," she said. She knew that Li Yu had been studying her for days and wondered what he had decided about her.

He sat on Pao An's cot, took a leaf from an aloe plant that Rulan had washed and peeled, and rubbed the cool sap on the burns that covered Pao An's broad shoulders. Pao An stirred, muttering, and turned onto the side that was badly burned. That was her main problem: how to keep him calm and quiet so the wounds could heal.

"Once when my son was four," Li Yu told her, "I took him along the riverbank. He led me to a banyan grove that was claimed by female-ghosts. All the children of the village were afraid of the place, but he pulled me into the center of it and we stood hand in hand in the shadows. 'Now,' he said, 'I will not be afraid anymore.' How I laughed at the little warrior. He was not afraid. In such ways did he show me that the son of my heart was not the son of my body, for all my life I have been afraid of the things that nature brings forth out of nothing to astonish us. Even in my youth, I was an old tortoise, while he from the first was a tiger." He turned his milky eyes to Rulan. "You, I perceive, are a true mate for him. Nothing frightens you. No ghost holds back your spirit. You are entirely whole."

"No, no, Father," she said, her eyes filling with tears. Why did he tell her such things when at this moment she was crippled by doubt? Surely he must sense her panic at not being able to find the right combination of herbs to break Pao An's fevered sleep, the right poultice to quiet his pain. Surely he must see that her greatest fear was the specter of death that hovered over the man she loved.

"When I left my son in On Ting, I knew that no cangue could hold him," Li Yu told her. "It does not surprise me that he rose to be a general in two armies. But it grieves me to think that he sacrificed himself for me. My time is almost over, but he has just come to the great turning of the river in his life." Li Yu lifted the swollen pad of his adopted son's hand to his dry, wrinkled cheek. "Before you came, I had a dream. Pao An was dressed like a barbarian with black boots and a wide hat. He came walking toward me with two babies held in the crook of his arms. When he reached the spot where I was standing, he went through me as if I were a mist or a memory. I turned to follow and saw him wade across a broad river like our Pearl with his babies on his shoulders to a wilderness without habitation. And when he reached the other side, he put down the children and with his hand built levees to hold the river back. From this I realized that he was meant to be the father of a great clan." Li Yu faltered. "Now I fear I have been the cause of his death and the truncation of his promise."

It was a long speech for the old man, and he sat back exhausted. Rulan honored him by not intruding into his reverie.

"How did he find me?" he asked Rulan after a while.

"By accident."

"There are no accidents. Only connections we do not understand. Consider this, Daughter. When I left On Ting I was determined to pay respect at the grave of my teacher in Fukien. Begging brought me to the monastery, and the monastery took me in. The monks thought to hide away from war. And yet the war blew into our very midst, bringing fire, death, and rebellion. And bringing me back my son."

Pao An groaned and opened his eyes. He looked like a shorn beast, for Rulan had cut away part of his hair to expose the burned scalp for medication. "Father," he whispered.

"Hush, my son. Rest."

"I found you. My life is whole again."

"Make mine whole, then. Eat. Rest."

Pao An fell silent and his eyes lost their light. Rulan tried pressing her nail hard on the pressure point on the groove of his upper lip to revive him, but the coma was too deep.

"He's slipping away," she cried. Frantically, without knowing what she did, she held out her hands to the now delirious Pao An and moved them back and forth, as if by will alone she could rouse him, but her hands were ice. She put them over her face and felt the cold pierce her.

"Has the fire gone out in you?" Li Yu asked quietly.

She nodded, not caring how he knew.

"Sometimes the tiniest spark can start a fire," Li Yu said.

He waited until she had cried herself to sleep, then crept to where she lay on a pallet next to Pao An. All night long, he moved his hands over her heart, willing his *chi* into her. His fingers did what his depleted body no longer could: they danced. And as they danced the patterned sequences, Li Yu sang the ancient songs he loved: he sang of a soul that had fled the body, a prince secluded too long in prayer on a mountaintop, a lover who had wandered far from his beloved. "Go back!" sang Li Yu, while striking the air with feeble fingers. It was his last, most painful, and most perfect dance—and no one saw.

Rulan dreamed of Ailan rising from the fire, young and beautiful as Kwan Yin. When her mother called out to her, Rulan awoke with a jolt, her hands and heart throbbing, her body on fire, and saw Li Yu's gnarled fingers and white face floating above her.

"Aaiiee! Father, what have you done?"

He dropped his hands and slumped against her, as weightless as a silken husk after the butterfly has flown. His words came in soft, nearly inaudible gasps. "I did not give him life. Now I can. I am only a tortoise as ancient as this kingdom, unable to swim in the waters of these times. Take my fire and heal my son. Go away from this place. Bear him sons and daughters. Learn the ways of the barbarians. Someday your children may come back to heal this dying land."

With her hands, Rulan poured strength into Pao An. The spark that Li Yu had bequeathed her seemed to make the *chi* flow with even more force than it had when she was young. Doubt and uncertainty melted away. She no longer wondered about the source of her power or whether she merited it; she simply accepted it, as she accepted the turning of the stars in the heavens, the dying and renewal of the land. And with that acceptance came a burst of skill. She discovered that she could make the heat flow with greater intensity and control than before. For the first time since the Tai Tai's death, she felt resolute, charged with promise. The warrior woman who had suffered and survived could do with her hands what the naive slave girl or the battered harem prisoner could not: the fire was an invisible cord pulling her man back from the pit of death, reeling him back to her.

But as Pao An gained strength, Li Yu seemed to lose it. The old man told Rulan that soon he would die. One morning, while the dew was on the grass, Pao An opened his eyes and recognized the grizzled head peering down at him. "Father," he whispered happily. He imagined himself in that other place in that other time. Pang and the others were waiting for him at the boys' house. A whole field needed to be flooded for planting rice that day. He must not be late for San Kwei's morning call. Pao An tried to rise; Li Yu needed a fire. But when he lifted his head, a wave of weakness—not only bodily inertia but an inexorable rush of memory—came thundering down on him. He fought against the awful weight and pushed himself up on his elbows.

Li Yu was laughing quietly. He touched Pao An's shoulder to restrain him. "How little you have changed, my son."

"I will take care of you," Pao An whispered.

Li Yu lifted an eyebrow, and Pao An was made painfully aware of his own debilitation. "Would you quarrel with your old father? No, no, you must go away from this barren place. This ground is mine for dying."

"Please, Father, not yet."

"Oh, a day or two. That does not matter. What matters is that at last I have made you the son of my spirit as well as my heart. My small flame rekindled your dying fire, my essence created you anew out of the abyss. Now you are wholly mine."

Rulan came running, running over the damp earth. Her tunic was undone, and her face was lit with such fierce, naked joy that Pao An had to turn his face away to keep from being unmanned.

"Come, dear child," Li Yu called out joyously. "Come and greet my son."

Three nights later Li Yu died on the pallet next to his son. Mandley dug a grave on the summit of the hill under a small pear tree.

Pao An, who was too weak to do more, swept the grave clean of debris, made a small, neat border of stones, and watered the pear tree with its graceful, bent branches so that Li Yu's ghost would have a place to rest when it returned to visit the world it left behind.

Mandley cut a cross into the bark of the tree.

Viceroy Li's troops swarmed into the area in search of his turncoat general to repay him for his deceit, but the hunt did not last long. In a farmhouse, Li discovered his former general, badly burned, a foreign devil in peasant dress, and the woman who was once his son's wife. It was obvious to the viceroy that they had no wagon full of riches, only the clothes they wore and their wounds.

"Who is the barbarian?" he asked Rulan.

"A holy man, an adviser to my father, the Eastern King of the Taiping," she replied without a trace of fear.

"Your candor condemns him to death. And Chen Pao An, my erstwhile general, sometime foe—why did he betray me and take his troops to Nanking?" The viceroy immediately regretted his words: the question made him sound like a discarded lover.

Rulan spoke as boldly as if her life and that of her companions did not hang on the subtlety of her words, and with no recognition of her lowly position and Li's lofty status. "Hung was holding me prisoner in his palace. Pao An came and brought me out."

Li tried not to show his displeasure. Why did the fact that they were lovers unsettle him? "He was always good at breaking out of boxes. In his present condition, I think a swift, clean cut rather than a slow death is preferred."

"He would appreciate that," Rulan replied.

"And you, Celestial Bride—isn't that your title among the Taiping?" Li said mockingly. "What would you appreciate?"

Rulan did not flinch. "To die with the same sword that sends him into the Void."

The viceroy was at a momentary loss for a response. Here was the woman who had invaded his dreams for years. He had cursed her and sought her and made her a symbol for the troubles that afflicted his house, his province, his empire. Perhaps Pao An had stolen a treasure out of Hung's palace after all. It was not one that the empress would want, but it was priceless, nonetheless.

Studying her, Li saw that Rulan was thinner than he remembered, but the gauntness made the bones of her face more striking. He noticed that she wore her hair short and unbound, as no decent women her age would do. What would it be like, he wondered, to grasp her hair in his hands, to bury his face in its thickness, to feel her long legs wrapped around his hips? He toyed lasciviously for a while with a demand that she would probably never grant of her own free will. "I'm not in the mood for dispensing favors," he ventured, raising an eyebrow eloquently. "Still, I might—"

"Liang Mo would be grateful for your kindness to me," Rulan said. She had lifted her head to stare defiantly into his face.

Li flushed. Had no one after all these years taught her womanly manners? he wondered.

That night, Li's senses were so aroused that he could not sleep. He rose from his pallet and wandered in his night robes outside the half-burned storehouse where the prisoners slept. He saw one small light burning in a back room and imagined Rulan stretched out on her cot, as wide awake as he. If she were any other woman, he would push her down and have done with it. Why did he hold himself back? Was it her valor? Yes, that was the word. Valor. Like the perfect warrior, she seemed pure and hard, ready at any moment to die. How marvelous a place, this Land of Flowers, he thought. It threw up blossoms of such exotic sort. Peasant-generals. Barbarians who aped civilized men. Warrior women. And when dynasties tottered and empires crumbled, there would always be some peasant such as Charcoal-carrier Yang to emerge from the slime to covet the throne.

Except for a few twists of fate, the viceroy acknowledged with satisfaction that he might have been entertaining kings instead of outcast rebels that night. And they might be having his head on the morrow instead of he theirs. All his life he had eluded one water pit after another. And finally, after all the risks and the losses, the victories and the vicious combats, he had jumped over yet another pit and would elude the judgment of his foes.

Why, then, did these thoughts bring regret instead of joy? Perhaps because he had enjoyed chasing the Rulan of the Age to the ends of the earth. The hunt had given flavor and purpose to a life that might well have been hopelessly narrow and frigid. Had the warrior woman really bewitched his mother, his wife, his son? Or was she merely the mirror in which their ambitions, desires, and passions had been magnified in all the gaudy colors of life?

The next morning Li rose with the sun and took his new bird to the summit of the hill to greet the day. How odd to think that this living treasure had come to him by chance in a ruined bazaar a hundred miles to the south. Li had purchased the bird from a man wearing a bedraggled scholar's hat with a gold button and robes so filthy and torn that they hung on his thin body in ragged strips. The man, an opium addict, was trying to find a buyer for his two small daughters and was devastated to learn that the viceroy did not desire the girls but the bird, a small creature with shiny red and gold feathers, which was borne in a small bamboo cage dangling from a stick. At first, the man refused to part with it, claiming that the creature was priceless, a firebird from the tropical forests of Nam Viet. But the beggar relented as soon as Li jangled his purse. It pleased Li to have spent almost nothing to obtain the very bird that he had scoured several provinces for—two strings of copper cash, enough to buy dirt for a week of dreams.

The bird was indeed extraordinary, unlike any species of red bird he had seen in the private aviaries of princes. Many wealthy men claimed to possess the firebird, but those were dim shadows next to this gorgeous creature. The bird was too rare to have been bred by men: obviously, it was a creature trapped in the wild. Li half-believed he had indeed stumbled on the mythical phoenix of the south, the "vermilion swallow" of the Tang poets, which embodied within its gleaming feathers the life-giving germ of the sun.

He observed that it was much more finicky than the average bird—a tightly feathered spark of intensity, hopping, turning, chirping, shrieking for food, beating its red-gold wings against the cage in the hope of escape.

"Peace, you obdurate creature," Li soothed his pet. "Take the morning light like the rest of your species with more song, more equanimity." But the bird only pranced along its wire to the very side of the cage where Li's face was and tried to peck him.

Li laughed. "Little warrior. Little fire of the south."

Li set the cage on a rock and gazed out across the valley. He saw familiar vistas like those of his southern homeland: a place half-land, half-water. He saw mist rising off the paddies, farmers and their wives trying to coax a few stalks of grain out of a sullen, waterlogged earth. The hard blue dome of the sky seemed to press down on him until he could not breathe.

"Were I in your cage and you out here with the key," he told the bird, "would you be as diffident as I? Would I be as proud as you?" He pushed his thumbnail through the slats of the cage, and the bird pecked it furiously.

The viceroy walked along the cliff until he came to a grove where a freshly dug grave under a pear tree was marked with a border of white stones. Here is a new bed, he thought. One we all must eventually lie in. Li picked up a handful of loose soil, tossed it gently on the grave, and went back to his bird. The grave, the solitude, and the bird had produced in him an unnatural keenness of vision that made him see his present predicament from a new angle. He had not leaped over the water pit this time. The trap was infinitely more intricate than he had at first perceived.

If there was treasure, Scholar Tseng had stolen it, he decided. What better way to deflect suspicion from himself than to blame the viceroy's general, Pao An, and hence the viceroy as well? That Pao An was a former Taiping, who had, moreover, been seen in the city before it fell, suited Tseng's plans perfectly. Whether Li brought back Pao An made no difference; only the treasure mattered to the empress. And Pao An had no treasure.

Li saw the folly of trying to fight his way out of the danger in which Tseng had placed him. Still, he refused to admit defeat. The trap was not yet sprung, he told himself; if one had no hope of untangling a net, one could buy time by avoiding it altogether. He would ignore the empress's summons and concoct a reason to go back to Canton, taking his chances that the fickle Dowager's ire would be directed elsewhere.

By the time the viceroy reached the yard outside the farmhouse where the prisoners awaited him, a frigid breeze was stirring the hairs on the back of his neck, and the bones of his back and shoulders were stiff and sore. Li mounted a horse that a servant held for him and gazed at the three white, strained faces staring up at him. Pao An limped forward slowly, sure of his sentence and prepared to plead for the lives of the others, the viceroy guessed.

Li waved him away with an arrogant flourish. "Go," he said sternly, as if he were disciplining one of the slop boys in his house. "Take them away from here. Your service has been unsatisfactory, and your presence is an encumbrance to me."

Rulan, he saw, was the first to recover from the shock. And the only one to demand an explanation.

"Why are you doing this?" she said boldly.

He had not expected their gratitude but felt a tinge of disappointment, nevertheless, that Rulan did not betray the weakness that any other woman in that position might.

"A whim that I'll probably regret before evening," the viceroy replied smoothly. He patted the birdcage that swung from his saddle. "But because it is a glorious morning and I have snared the vermilion sparrow, my hunger for wilder game is appeased."

Once he had lost sight of the farmhouse, the viceroy took a small key out of the purse he carried on his belt and opened the lock on the cage. The bird hesitated a moment, then hopped to the doorframe, spread its wings, and rose in a flurry of crimson feathers straight up into the sun.

"I so enjoyed the hunt," he told the swiftly disappearing spot of fire. "Let the chase go on."

When the viceroy's troops had disappeared, Rulan packed their meager belongings and they struggled south. Pao An was too weak to walk far. Each day's journey left him exhausted. Hong Kong was their destination, hundreds of miles away.

Peking, 1865

Yehonala, Dowager Empress of the Land of Flowers, posed barefoot in an artificial field of lotus blossoms in front of a painted backdrop of bamboo. Everything was perfectly arranged to please the hard, round eye of the barbarian picture-engine: her headdress of hanging pearls, the long white robes that brushed her slim ankles, the position of her small hands in graceful benediction. Her pose was an exact imitation of the statue of Kwan Yin rising from its stone pedestal out of the Kun Ning Lake in the old summer palace. The lake was artificial, as was the hill behind it, which thousands of coolies had dug up from the earth, although the vast stretches of water lilies and the thousands of goldfish sporting in the water were real enough. Nature and art were so cunningly mated that one could not mark where one ended and the other began. Remembering how the British had sacked and gutted that exquisite dwelling in 1860, Yehonala was suddenly sick with fury. Yet so perfect was her composure that not a trace of emotion marred the smoothly painted surface of her face. So much evil followed the year of the defiling of her pleasure palace by the barbarians: her husband's death, the breaking of the siege of Nanking by the long-haired rebels, who swept across both banks of the Yangtze closer and closer to Peking, as they had once before, burning government camps and calling on the people to switch to their side.

But the faithless Han had for once been true and turned against the rebels. The siege was renewed, and this time the rebels burned like paper soldiers in their citadel in Nanking, every one a martyr to their foolish dream of heaven on earth. She would insist that the people do the same to the arrogant British and their barbarian rivals who continued to seize territory and concessions for themselves, as if the Land of Flowers was a melon ripe for slicing. Yehonala was twenty-nine, ruler of two hundred million people. She had already accomplished a miracle: wrested her son, the nine-year-old emperor, from the hands of three powerful princes and stamped out a rebellion. And all because she had put her faith in the true source of power: the eunuchs, who had stolen the imperial seal as the Hsien Feng emperor lay dying and given it to her.

A small sigh came from the tall girl on her left with a mouth like a pouting angel.

Chief Eunuch An-te-hai, his gray hair hidden under a tall headdress of silver beads and mother-of-pearl, coughed eloquently.

Yehonala's dark eyes slid sideways. The girl burned crimson under her chalk-white makeup and dropped her peacock-feather fan. An-te-hai bent to retrieve the fan and handed it back to the girl with the merest hint of a smile.

Yehonala's small fingers dipped in a gesture of forgiveness. She spoke kindly to the girl, who shivered, despite her reprieve, at the sound of Yehonala's sultry voice, the "velvet voice" that An-te-hai claimed could command snakes out of trees. Such would Kwan Yin have done to a supplicant, even one who had broken court protocol and thus invited bad luck. It would never do to have the image of perfect mercy distorted by a low girl and then captured by the western engine of duplication for eternity.

Sweat was running down her neck under the heavy headdress and the veils that fell nearly to the floor. Yehonala's spine ached, and still the fool of a western portrait photographer fussed and dithered and mixed his evil-smelling powders. Finally, he stuck his huge hairy head and red face under his black veil and manipulated a machine as large and gross as a cannon. There was a loud explosion and the acrid smell of burned sulfur. The three girls flanking Yehonala screamed; even An-te-hai started and put a hand over his eyes. But Yehonala never moved. She had long forgotten who she was, so she knew no fear.

Had she ever been just Orchid, born in faraway An Hui to a minor provincial official inspector who was beheaded for some small neglect of duty? Had she ever been sixteen and the loveliest virgin of her clan, miserable at having to leave her dashing Tartar officer for the harem of the emperor? Well, she was never meant to pinch pennies and scold servants as mistress in a soldier's house in Tartar City. That was what Chief Eunuch An-te-hai had whispered as he carried her naked to the emperor's bed in the mantle of fur. "I will make you great," he promised, and he told her what games to play with the emperor, what instruments to use in lovemaking, and how the Hsien Feng emperor liked his opium mixed, for the emperor was easily bored and craved new sensations as a spoiled child craves his neighbor's toys.

By the time An-te-hai placed her at the foot of the emperor's bed, her tears were dry and her childish grief over her handsome soldier put away forever. Yehonala warmed at the memory of that first night. She found it easy to accomplish what An-te-hai advised. Soon it was, "Where is my Orchid? Where is my darling?" The emperor whined and pouted, complained that his first wife, Yehonala's cousin, was worse than a nun, and would have no other girl heat the opium for his pipe and rub his back but her. The nights stretched into years of opium-scented lasciviousness in which she ruled over the Ten Thousand Years.

Now the long wait was over. The Hsien Feng emperor was dead. Prince Su Shun, her greatest enemy, was dead, all his supporters stripped of titles and ranks and his immense wealth channeled into her coffers. She alone of all the palace women had borne the emperor a son. And how miraculous that the Dragon, half-paralyzed and riddled with pox, could sire such a great, fat boy—but that miracle too was wrought by An-te-hai, who had found a way for her to keep her handsome soldier after all. And now she and An-te-hai ruled not only in the harem but in all Peking. Princes who had once clamored for her head knelt for hours on the hard floor of the Audience Hall waiting for her to favor them with a whispered command as she sat behind the yellow curtain of state. Red-haired barbarians with guns and boats came with their impudent demands, thus proving that they were indeed apes, but intelligent apes, from which a civilized person could learn. And the sweetest victory—she, with An-te-hai's help, had vanquished the Taiping rebels. A woman and a half-man had triumphed where manly men had failed. The "Pure and Bright" Ching dynasty of her Manchu ancestors was safeguarded for another thousand years. So much for the old curse that a woman from her clan would bring the imperial house down!

No, thought the Dowager Empress as the barbarian babbled furiously. Kwan Yin—with the help of the eunuchs—would always look with favor on her faithful servant Yehonala. She moved her body into another semblance of the goddess. An-te-hai motioned the women to do the same.

To think that she had at first preferred the soldier Li over the scholar Tseng to lead the Han troops against the Taiping. The faithful An-te-hai had warned, "Never trust the men of the south outside their province. They hate us even more than do the Han of other provinces. Their blood is impure, for they are descended from barbarian snake eaters, yet they fashion themselves as the saviors of Han civilization against us Manchu."

Absurd, but true, Yehonala admitted, with their Triad and White Lotus and Golden Orchid and other secret societies of every sort that not even nature could have thought to spawn.

Viceroy Li had lied and lied again. He had sworn that there was no treasure taken from Nanking. Yet, as Tseng Kuo Fan pointed out, how could Li know there was no treasure if he had failed to capture the general who had stolen it? Either Li had abetted Chen Pao An's escape or had disposed of his turncoat general and taken the treasure for himself. Nor had Li returned to Peking to account for his error, as Yehonala had ordered: instead, he went straight to Canton, claiming that an uprising there required his immediate attention.

Always trouble with these men of the south, Yehonala thought. It was better to use them for a time and discard them before their conceit turned to rebellion.

"The silk cord," she said aloud. She must rid herself of this weakness for soldiers. Yehonala put down her hand abruptly and strode out of the elaborately decorated pavilion and down the open passageway to where her bearers awaited. Alarmed, her maids thrashed about in the field of artificial lilies in an attempt to follow her.

"Oh, oh, oh," squealed the photographer, who was dancing beside his three-legged portrait machine while white smoke spewed from his evil wand.

"Send the monkey away," she said to the clerk, who had stretched out in full kowtow as An-te-hai lifted the empress into the yellow chair of state. "Tell him to bring the picture tomorrow. If it is good enough, I will send it to the English queen. Poor thing, that little queen. Her life is not half so excellent as mine." She ignored the stream of gibberish pouring from the white devil's mouth as two clerks pulled him and the ungainly engine down the steps of the pavilion and out into the vast reaches of the Outer Palace. Eight eunuchs in bright green robes bore the barefoot empress quickly away on their shoulders.

In minutes, Yehonala was easing herself onto the yellow chair that served as an informal throne in the Audience Hall. As the women mopped the sweat from her smooth cheeks and strapped on her high Manchu boat shoes, she thought about how she might best deliver her happy decision to the faithful An-te-hai. The viceroy might have been an old ally, but eunuchs loved sending the silk cord more than friendship. Yehonala, who owed so much to the eunuchs, enjoyed feeding their appetites: she knew how much the castrati loved making nonmen. Death was their form of procreation.

She turned her head slightly and beckoned with one long jeweled nail. An-te-hai lowered his head so that the full lips, with their crimson center stain gleaming like a drop of blood, were at his ear.

"Old friend," she murmured. "Send a letter for me . . ."

That evening, after drawing up the edict, An-te-hai took it himself to the keeper of cords, who selected a cord of the proper color and length and placed it in a lacquered box with the edict tied and sealed on the top. This the chief eunuch gave to the captain of the morning guard, who dispatched it to an official courier.

The courier was carried to the Grand Canal in a litter hung with imperial yellow by four bearers, but because the Yellow River had mysteriously changed its course in 1855, wrecking the Grand Canal and flooding the countryside, the letter was diverted to a seagoing merchant ship. The merchant cried, begged, and finally bribed the courier not to waylay his shipment of silk. The result was that the courier won a bribe of a hundred silver taels and used his pass to board instead a government barge going south. The barge meandered past steep crags and burned-out monasteries and the midnight fires of hunger marchers streaming toward the cities, and the courier drank wine and ate the local specialties cooked for him by the captain while he joked with the salt agents. Occasionally, he went to the pleasure boats to try a girl or two, for the devastation of the rebellion had forced thousands of starving families to sell their daughters into "flower boats," the floating brothels at Hang Chow, Ning Po, and Shanghai. At Amoy in Fukien Province, he took a horse at the imperial way station and rode with a small but heavily armed retinue overland to Canton.

He did not go immediately to the viceroy's palace, but instead to a noodle shop across the river from the European factories and sent word to a member of the beggar's guild who had done him service from time to time. He dismissed his guards, took a room, and waited.

In such a decadent world, he reasoned, a prudent man needed money against the day that the Great One's favor dried up.

In two hours, the beggar showed up, his long filth-encrusted hair hiding a livid gash on his cheek, wearing a toothless grin from a fight not two days before. His gums were swollen and red.

"Ah, my Lord, I am glad to see you. You need a job done, *hai ma?*"

"You're so ugly, you might not do," the courier accused him.

"Aaiiee, you are unjust! I'll dress myself up. I'll chew tea leaves to sweeten my breath. What do you want done?"

"You said you knew someone in the viceroy's palace?"

"A worthless girl. Daughter of my wife's niece. Washes clothes for the wife of the personal secretary to the viceroy."

"I want you to give her a message."

In another hour, word got through to Viceroy Li that an important letter was going to be delivered to him from the Dowager Empress, and if he wanted to know the content of that message before he officially received it, he should send a trusted man with a certain amount of money to a certain place on the Canton waterfront.

It took another day and a half for bribes to be met and word delivered, but eventually the courier and everyone in between were adequately paid. The beggar got a set of wooden teeth, the little scrub girl bought her freedom, and the courier purchased a farm in the county of his birth for his widowed mother. And Viceroy Li was able to be absent from Canton when the lacquered box bearing the edict and the silken cord from Yehonala, the Dowager Empress, arrived.

Hong Kong, Spring 1865

Mandley and Pao An had been quarreling for weeks, ever since they, with Rulan, had gone across the bay to Hong Kong, where friends of Mandley lived. While Rulan visited the apothecary shops to sell the herbs she had gathered, Mandley sought out the Baptist missionaries in their schools and threadbare hospitals and houses, who might help them escape, and Pao An scoured the docks for rogue captains who would defy the emperor's edicts against emigration and spirit three fugitives out of the country.

Only Rulan met with any success. The coppers she earned fed them for two weeks with nothing left over for bribes or passage money. Word was being passed around the villages and the hillside caves where aboriginal peoples lived that Tseng Kuo Fan's troops were hunting three escaped rebels—the daughter of a Taiping king, a turncoat general, and a barbarian posing as a priest—who had escaped with the treasure from Nanking. As supplies diminished and the peril of their situation began to sink in, Mandley urged the others to try the missionaries one more time. The missionaries might be moved, he argued, if Pao An could beg to be taken on as a student for seminary and Rulan pretended to be his sister. Although his Baptist brethren had rejected them, missionaries of other denominations might yet be persuaded.

Perhaps Pao An's reluctance was all too evident, or the scars on his neck and hands too raw, for the ruse failed dismally. The head of the Basel Mission, an earnest Swiss who had seen many of his Hakka converts follow Hung into Nanking, took Mandley aside and explained that although he was not without sympathy for the Taiping, he could not help heretics because he was afraid for his family, for his career, for the entire cause of Christianity in China.

More determined than ever to wrest some concession from his race, Mandley went next to the Yankeee sea merchants, promising rich, though postponed, rewards in Hawaii if anyone would take himself and two Christian Chinese converts to Reverend Emmanuel Bosworth in the Sandwich Island Mission.

"What did you say to Man-da-li to make him so angry?" Rulan demanded of Pao An with a worried frown when Mandley had not returned after the second day. They were encamped on a deserted hillside in Kowloon.

Pao An stirred the fire with a stick. "Only that he refused to see that barbarians nowadays prefer to trade in coolie flesh, not souls."

"That was unkind," she chided him. "You know how he has suffered for us."

Pao An threw the stick into the fire, where it exploded in a shower of sparks. "So many years in Nanking made him forget that we are Han and he is—what he is," he grumbled. "He was actually serious about making me a priest—and you a white barbarian woman."

Rulan grinned and handed Pao An a cracked cup filled with aromatic broth. Despite their danger, she was happier than she had been in years. "At least my big feet would fit those enormous shoes! And you? I can picture you in a black suit like their holy men, all pious and sad. Perhaps you will grow fuzzy side whiskers like Man-da-li and recite poems to me from the Great Book every night." She laughed again and pulled his hair, which had grown long enough to hide the unsightly burns on the back of his head until she saw that he did not like her teasing. Suddenly uncomfortable, for she knew that Pao An was jealous of her affection for Mandley, she tugged her hair forward to hide her face.

Pao An was rehearsing to himself his terrifying plan. It was a last resort, when all hope had flown. He would not let it mar the beauty of this moment. Why was it, he marveled, that hardship only made Rulan more lovely? Their harsh regimen on the road had toughened her. The doomed, cadaverous look of the harem had been replaced by a serenity and self-assurance he had not remembered in the young concubine or warrior woman. It was as if Li Yu, in dying, had poured his strong and generous spirit into her along with his *chi*. By contrast, he himself bore the wounds and scars of war all over his body. His hair had grown back streaked with gray, while time had scarcely left a mark on Rulan. When she lifted her arm to shake out her hair, a great wave of sadness at what he might be forced to inflict on her rose in him. His hand shook and he dropped the cup, which splashed scalding soup over him.

"Are you hurt?" She grabbed up his hand to examine it.

He drew his hand back, but she took it again, held it to her cheek, and then kissed the scars on his fingers. "Once when I was a baby, full of mischief, I stuck my hand in the coals where my mother was cooking. It is my earliest memory. I remember her doing this." She kissed his fingers again. "So far I have been lucky," she added thoughtfully. "I have escaped the fire."

Both were intensely aware that they were alone for the first time since their secret meetings in the citadel before Yang's death. In the last few months of travel, they had lived as chastely as the Taiping brothers and sisters of old, with Mandley as a constant reminder of their old vows of chastity. Even when their bodies were whole enough to crave it, when had there been time to steal away for love? Slowly, deliberately, she closed her eyes and drew his hand under her blouse. Dizzy with longing, he cupped her warm breast and put his mouth to the tiny pulsing spot in the hollow of her throat. He bit the lobe of her ear gently. She turned up her face, allowing him to taste her lips and tongue, while unbuttoning her tunic for him.

When he put his mouth to her breast, she shivered from the intensity of her pleasure. She gripped his hair, panting, and pulled his head away. The sensation was overwhelming, even painful, after so many years of abstinence.

"Too much of Man-da-li has made you modest," he teased, his voice thick and his lids already heavy with desire.

"It has been a very long time," she admitted, no longer shy. "But I will show you how easily I remember!" Quickly, she stripped off her clothes and lay them neatly over the pile of leaves that served as her bed. Just as impatiently, he loosed the ties of his tunic and trousers, so that in minutes they stood face-to-face, naked, their bodies pale and glowing wherever the night shadows did not cling.

Her fingers crept up his scarred shoulders and touched his face in the darkness. Nimbly, she wrapped her legs around his waist, fastening her mouth on his with such hunger that he felt as if he was drowning. With a groan, he leaned her against the thick trunk of the banyan tree and quickly entered her.

They made love that way until his legs grew tired. And a dozen ways more until the fire had burned down into a pile of red embers.

Then as he lay back half-dreaming, she floated above him like an immortal rising into heaven and drew from him a shuddering exhalation.

When he awoke, she was kneeling naked to the waist before a fire which blazed up anew. And he saw that her body was no longer perfect: she was scarred by Hung's whip. Lines crisscrossed her back in an intricate design. Before his father's death, he might have cried out in rage and frustration at those who had marked her. Now he felt only sadness mixed with something he gradually recognized as ardor. He wanted to make love again.

Hearing him stir, she came to him quickly, with eyes downcast, holding a cup of broth balanced on her fingertips, like a well-bred lady offering tea to her lord. The heat of the fire had brought a faint half-flush to her skin. From the front, she was flawless: all ivory and gold tipped with rose.

He drank deeply, then gave the cup back into her hands and tapped his knuckles in the dirt in a small, grave gesture of thanks. When he spoke, his voice was hoarse, the words halting. "Sometimes when I think of all we have endured—" His voice caught in his throat. He stopped and began to stammer, "If we should ever be parted again, remember that, somehow, I will find you."

She cried out in alarm.

The wind blew up and rustled the leaves overhead. Low streams of clouds streaked the night sky.

"You're stronger than I," he murmured against her neck. His fingers caressed the thin scars on her back. Then impatiently, his hands were pulling away her thin trousers, making her ready for him again. "I am invisible, a no-name man. I leave no trace when I pass."

By way of answer, she kissed the burns on his neck and shoulder, kissed the old scar on his stomach where Wei's men had pierced him. Her fingers traveled down his hard belly and touched the wound where the Triad tattoo had been. She felt his silken softness harden to smooth polished marble.

They began to make love again, gently at first, Rulan straddling him, until their movements had reached a fierce and savage rhythm. Without warning, he lifted her up by the hips with his strong hands. She gasped in surprise.

He rolled her over quickly on the ground, holding himself away from her until she sought and found him and pulled him into her. Again and again and again, until she cried out like a phoenix surprised by the sharp, exquisite agony of the archer's arrow, "*Ah shi!* Oh yes!"

He pressed against her hips and pierced her hidden core. "Ahhhhhhh," she sighed, tears running from her eyes. And again. "*Ah shi!*"

"Why are you crying?" he asked when he could breathe again. His own eyes were wet.

She licked the salt from his lips. "From happiness, from fear. You have taken something from me. I no longer have resolve. I cannot bear to be alone."

While she slept, he watched the patterns made by the rain on the darkness outside their shelter. Her breathing was slow and regular, like a child's. He moved so that his lips curved around the soft tip of a breast. When his mouth was full of her sweetness, and the scent of the earth, the light warm rain and their lovemaking filled his head, he slept too.

Early the next morning, Mandley returned to their camp and found them sleeping under a thin blanket, which was tossed back on one side to reveal Rulan's naked thigh.

He sat down on a twisted root of the banyan tree and waited. She woke first and saw him, his back turned toward them.

"Please don't think ill of us," she said, dressing quickly.

"I'm a fool," he whispered.

"We are Han. The Taiping vows were too cruel. We—"

Pao An quieted her with a touch. "I'm sorry, my friend," he told Mandley.

"Forgive me," Mandley replied. "I've been sitting here for an hour thinking. I've known all along. For years, I've known, although I had hoped that Rulan and I—" He shook his head. "No matter. I've been thinking. Since you know each other and since in some way you have come to love the High God, please allow me one small place in your love."

He told them that he had found a couple from New England, a Congregational doctor and his wife, who would give them money for passage to Hawaii. Then he blessed them and pronounced them man and wife, according to his custom.

The next morning, Pao An and Mandley hastened to the harbor in Hong Kong. Pao An waited in a crowd of hollow-eyed women and children outside the missionary's dilapidated compound near the bay all day for Mandley. Mandley emerged from the gates hours later, unkempt and dejected. The missionaries were themselves penniless and had enough money for only one ticket to the Fragrant Tree Islands.

Grimly, Pao An left Mandley to set in motion the plan he had kept secret from his lover and his friend. He found a procurer for the immigrant agency Wohang and sold himself into the "pig trade" for a six-year term. The contract was for gang labor in the cane fields of the Fragrant Tree Islands at five dollars a month in addition to passage, food, clothing, and housing. He received ninety Mexican dollars, in advance, to be a crew leader. This he gave to Mandley.

"I will not have my wife go to a new nation as a slave. Take her there, not as your servant or your pupil but as a free woman. And tell her I will not say good-bye. She and I are not strangers to separation. I will meet her in the new land."

His ship left the following morning.

Barefoot, dressed in blue cotton peasant's pajamas with her hair tied up under a fringed bamboo hat, Rulan looked like one of a thousand Hakka vendors' wives on the wharves of Hong Kong. Crowds of half-naked coolies were being loaded like cattle aboard three ships, some with their hands tied behind them. The barbarian agent at the wharf was marking each coolie on the cheek with a writing brush. Those he marked with a *C* and a *P* were led away down the dock; those marked with an *S* were shuffling up the gangplank of a sailing ship named *Mei Foo* where they disappeared inside the hold.

"What do the marks mean?" she asked Mandley.

"The *C* is California to the railroads. The *P* is Peru to the guano fields. The *S* is Sandwich Islands, what you Han call the Fragrant Tree Islands—Hawaii to the natives."

"Then that ship where the men are being locked below is mine?"

He nodded.

"He went like that?" Her heart trembled with pain and hope. Pao An's ship had sailed five weeks before.

They studied each coolie clambering up the gangplank of the ship.

"Hawaii—California—Peru," Rulan repeated dully. The names all sounded the same to her. Empty. Ominous. Otherwordly.

Mandley fumbled in his pockets.

Rulan was staring past the junks and sampans that crowded the harbor to the small black dot of a ship disappearing below the horizon. He had tricked her into loving him, needing him, entwining his dreams around hers. Now she was alone with her whole life stretched before her, and she had no idea how to fill one hour of this day.

"He didn't want me to see him walking like a slave. Oh, Man-da-li, I can't bear to think of him locked in the belly of that ship! I was locked up once and it nearly killed my soul. I can't bear it if—"

"Don't weaken, Rulan. Not after what Pao An has sacrificed. It's all arranged. I have my fare. With the money he gave me by selling himself, you have yours. He says he'll find you in Hawaii. I told him where the Bosworths live in Honolulu, but I warned him not to try to escape. White people regard Chinamen as animals. They'll beat or shoot him for speaking his mind or disobeying an order."

Her eyes were bright with tears. "He won't stand for that, Man-da-li. He's too proud. He'll try to escape right away."

Mandley nodded sadly, acknowledging the truth of her words. "Of course he will. That's why I've decided to give you my passage money. Use it to buy his freedom if the chance arises. Or start a new life until he finds you. I can't go. I can't! I came to China to save souls and all I did was take lives. I owe your people one more effort—or one more death."

"No!"

"I've arranged everything. I sent a letter ahead to Bosworth yesterday. Bosworth's a Boston Congregationalist. His clan is old, but on the boat from San Francisco, he went out of his way to shake hands with me, a hill country Baptist. Said he was sick of sissies from Yale who thought anyone west of the Hudson River was a savage. We had big plans to join forces in China. We would have done it too, thumbed our nose at the old-timers in the missions, brought more Han to Christ—true believers, mind you, not rice Christians—except that Lucy lost her baby in Honolulu and couldn't go on. Emmanuel made the best of it. He signed on as assistant in the biggest Congregational parish in Honolulu, the one that serves the Hawaiians, kings and commoners alike. Now I hear he's dabbling in trade. He's got docking privileges in Honolulu, so the captain had better deliver you in good condition or he'll lose his commission."

Just then the captain came down the ramp, a red-haired man past middle age, with a large belly and self-satisfied air. Rulan had seen that look before, in Abundant Spring Mountain, in the Taiping army, in the harem.

As Mandley talked, the captain studied Rulan. She heard the word "missionary" and "convert." She took off her hat so he could see the lines around her eyes. She pursed her lips and squinted like a sour woman. When Mandley took the captain aside, she unleashed a torrent of Hakka invective at a passing coolie who dropped his carrying pole in surprise before creeping off in shame; she hoped she sounded like the "screaming women" in her village who had cowed men with their bad manners.

The captain's gaze passed over her. He seemed to decide that she was neither young nor beautiful nor tractable enough to suit his fancy. This would be a money deal, pure and simple.

Moments later Mandley returned. "Bosworth owns shares in this shipping line. The captain knows not to cross him or the Han girl Mrs. Bosworth has engaged as cook and maid. I paid him in Mexican gold for your passage and got three receipts. You keep this one with the letter of introduction to Bosworth that I gave you. This receipt goes to Bosworth in my next letter. The last I will hold."

Rulan was only half-listening. She was watching a man whose cheek was marked with an *S* climb up the plank to slavery and thinking of Pao An chained in a barracoon somewhere.

Mandley's voice was harsh. "What do you do if you are challenged by the officers at the harbor in Honolulu?"

"How long do they sell themselves for?"

"Rulan, we have only a little time!"

"How long?"

"Six years. Now what do you do if the harbor officials won't let you go ashore?"

She bit her lip and angrily clenched her fists. "What I ought to do is drown myself like the Wu Chang women so I won't be an affliction to those who love me." But for two weeks she had felt changes in her body, which her healer's eye could not ignore. She had missed her monthly bleeding, and not simply because of starvation or fatigue, because this time her breasts were sore and full, and the bloom in her cheeks was unmistakable.

"Rulan, please—"

"I won't, though I ought. So if the harbor officials challenge me, I will say that I am a Christian and show them the receipt to prove that my passage was paid and the letter to Reverend Bosworth, and demand to speak to him. I will fight to stay alive."

The bosun blew the whistle and the captain motioned Rulan aboard. Mandley pressed a small leather bag containing Mexican gold pieces into her hands.

"The gold I paid entitles you to a private cabin. You have the gun I gave you?"

She nodded.

"Use it if you have to. This captain is no better than the other scum that carry human beings as trade, but he understands money and about fulfilling a bargain. He wants to please Bosworth. And he wants to please me. He thinks I am a pipeline to more 'pigs.' He doesn't know that I will be helping our Taiping brothers to escape."

It was Rulan's turn to be frightened. She snatched his hand and held it to her cheek. "Man-da-li, you are in more danger than I. Come with me. There's enough money for us both. We will work, pool our money, and free Pao An."

Gently, he loosed his hand. "I would like that very much, but no, Rulan."

"When?"

He shook his head. "When I have finished here."

"Order your passenger aboard, Reverend!" the captain yelled.

"Don't leave me," she begged, realizing the awful finality of his words. "I'm frightened. Who will plan our return from exile, our march on the Forbidden City? Who will teach me barbarian ways?" She smiled wanly. "Who will ride with me to the far horizon, to the gates of Paradise?"

"Pao An," he replied. "Go in peace, dear girl. Live in peace. Don't plan revolutions that can't be won. Never come back. Seek the True God instead." He couldn't speak for a moment, but when he did, his voice was strong and deep, as in the harem when his song had kept her from despair. "You shall die in my country and I in yours."

She leaned close to memorize the angular contours of his face, the incredible color of his eyes, and wondered why she had ever thought him ugly. She smelled his cheeks, as she used to do Boy-Boy's. "Dear Brother," she said. "Remember me."

The captain took off his cap and greeted her with a low, mocking bow, before hurrying her rudely below out of Mandley's sight.

The trip, which was to have taken fifty-five days, took ninety-five. Of the two hundred coolies aboard, one hundred died of diarrhea, malnutrition, and suicide. These were acceptable losses in the pig trade, because the hundred who lived still turned a profit for the captain who ferried them across the ocean and the owner of the sugar plantation who worked them for six years. In the last month, although the captain allowed Rulan to keep her cabin, he fed her like the "pigs" below: one-half bowl of cold, maggot-ridden rice a day.

Hong Kong, Fall 1865

A charmed life, thought Merchant Li, as he watched his young wife make tea. The Hakka girl was clumsy, because her belly was full, and quite stupid, because her father was a porter and her mother a seller of ducks. She knew nothing of the art of making tea: how one must place the lid of the pot face upward as one tosses in the leaves, so the smell of food might not spoil the taste. How one must breathe in and out three times before pouring the brew into cups, pour it back into the pot to release the fragrance, and wait three more breaths before pouring it out finally to drink. How one must never replenish a pot more than once. The tea things she used were filthy, his cup was broken and brimful of the third bland infusion from the pot. In beauty and refinement, the Hakka girl could not compare to Meng and his ladies in Abundant Spring Mountain nor to the women who had warmed his bed in Canton in his days of power.

But the girl was tall, big footed, broad shouldered, and full of life. So strong and young and full.

She had gotten pregnant their first time together, and yet she wanted to make love every night. It pleased him to indulge her. It pleased him too to give in to pleasure, not to hold back seed to prolong both ardor and life. And perversely, the release of passion made him feel not undisciplined, but young.

Now he was viceroy of nothing and mandarin of nothing. The

Dowager Empress had sent him a golden cord to strangle himself. Instead Li had filled an oxcart with silver and had traveled south to Hong Kong. At last I am free, he told himself. Free of the cangue put around my neck by the first ancestor of the Lis. Free of the name that held me like bait at the end of an infinitely long string.

What tangled cords bind strangers, Li observed. On his last day of power, when he thought he had done with the Taiping rebels, the barbarian priest who had been with Rulan and Pao An outside Nanking had been caught with Taiping escapees in the city and brought by the bailiffs to the viceroy's palace.

"You will not find the others," the barbarian declared defiantly— and quite unnecessarily, since Li had no intention of conducting a search. "If you insist on punishing someone, there is only me."

The barbarian boasted that Rulan and Pao An had escaped across the sea, while he had returned to the streets of Canton to preach his message to the crowd, a message of insurrection.

When Li pointed out the folly of tempting fate and his own good humor too many times, the barbarian claimed that he was subject to no man but Jesus Christ. He waved a black book at Li, warning of its power. "I came to your house years ago to offer to teach you and was thrust out by an opium-besotted steward, so it was Yang instead who learned from me." The barbarian claimed that with the book to guide him, he had turned Yang into a prophet and a king.

Had the foreigner actually been to Abundant Spring Mountain? Was it his book that had overturned the empire? Li decided that the barbarian was too dangerous to let wander among the people. So Li confiscated the barbarian's book and had him beaten with a bamboo rod.

The madman ranted all the while that beating would not stop his mouth. He dared the viceroy to put him in a cangue or even in a hanging box in the public square, vowing that to the last he would preach his faith.

"You shall have your wish," Li said to the barbarian, who like a fool believed him and fell to his knees praising God. Li told his executioner not to put the man in the hanging box, but to take him to the stables and strangle him quickly. The body was thrown in the waste pit and covered over with lime, for it would not do to publicize such a death. The foreign devils used any excuse, particularly the untimely deaths of their priests, to steal another port city for their filthy opium trade. Therefore, eliminating the barbarian in this way attracted no notice whatsoever, and Li believed that he had snuffed out another rebellion at its source.

Disposing of the barbarian had given Li great satisfaction, for it seemed to mark the end of the Taiping disaster. Li would rein in his ambition and wait for his fortune at court to rise again. Li remembered going to his study and ordering tea to savor the moment. But then the scrub girl came to tell him that a messenger from the Dowager Empress was waiting. The cords of fate were never so neatly tied as one liked to believe, Merchant Li reflected.

And so the message had been given. Yet unlike the foolish white devil, Li decided not to welcome death but to refuse it. His life in the Land of Flowers was over. Abundant Spring Mountain was cinders and stone, returned to the earth dragon and rain dragon who had blessed and then cut his line. Had it been the work of Pao An, as his daughter-in-law claimed? Or the work of that madwoman herself? No matter. She was gone, as his ancestral dwelling was gone—out of his life forever.

And yet he had at the very last moment pulled his foot from the watery pit. Where a coward would have killed himself with the cord so conveniently supplied by his enemies, Li was determined to live.

His stalls, manned by a guild of fifty vendors in the marketplace in Hong Kong Harbor, were crammed with hairpins and combs, artificial flowers, rouge pots, music boxes, incense sticks, crude ceramic figurines of gods and goddesses, herbs and salves, cheap bolts of silk, and odds and ends that the maids in his household would have thrown away. From his stool looking out on the harbor, he saw a barbarian ship unfurl its huge white sails like a great bird about to take wing. His eye flicked without interest over the small, bent shapes of pigs, indigent youths and adventurers, who were climbing the gangplank into slavery in foreign ports, and paused to study the long low wooden buildings where the taipans and compradors stored their goods and met with barbarians. One-eyed junks and lorchas dodged barbarian sailing vessels and barges on the murky brown water. He turned his eyes to the peak of Victoria crowned with the magnificent granite residences where former opium runners lived. A forgotten island turned from a barren rock to a maritime empire in less than a generation by strange men who walked the streets like creatures fallen out of the sky.

Despite the ruin of his house, Merchant Li had kept many of his old friends, especially those in disfavor with the empress, and had built new alliances with his former enemies in the secret societies. Like him, they had lost their place in the order of things and were building new networks overseas. The Triads he had tried to root out of Kwangtung had established a base in Hong Kong. Now they came to his tiny stall to ask favors that he could still grant on the mainland. A bandit son sold into safety in the pig trade. Protection for grandmothers and wives left alone in the villages of women that were springing up in the Pearl River delta in the wake of the exodus of menfolk to barbarian lands. Someone had to help unschooled women translate letters, cash barbarian money sent from afar, arrange betrothals between a girl left in the village and a boy cutting sugarcane in Honolulu. Someone had to take charge of the opium and gambling concessions among the bachelors in the cane fields of Hawaii so that only Han profited from Han vices.

And so Li, with the help of the Triads, helped form "fraternal societies" for the protection of clan sons gone overseas. The very ones who despised him became his friends, and the ones who feared him sought his favors. Already Merchant Li had commandeered a gang of Triads to squeeze protection out of the Hong Kong merchants and had handpicked ten youths to sell themselves into the pig trade. They would work for six years cutting cane or hauling vats of hot molasses, and when their term of indenture was over, they would lose themselves in the alleys of Honolulu where rich and poor Han clustered together like pigs and chickens, ignoring the boundaries of clan or class or province or name. And thus the "fraternal society" would sprout another arm overseas under the very noses of the barbarian missionaries and native kings.

A new home, a new name, a new wife, and new sons. Already Liang Mo was making a profit from smuggled goods in the Fragrant Tree Islands. Merchant Li was founder of his own line across the sea, emperor of a new dynasty.

And as a simple merchant, he could admit what the general and the viceroy could not: he did not despise his son.

Merchant Li touched his Hakka wife as she bent over to fill his cracked cup. He slipped his hand inside her cotton shirt to squeeze the swollen breast.

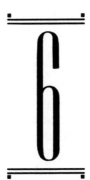

Honolulu, Fall 1865

Reverend Bosworth and his wife came with a horsecart to the harbor in the dusty town of Honolulu. Rulan saw that the man was a fatter, more prosperous version of Mandley, with the same strange mustache and the same ill-fitting black suit. Bosworth, like Mandley in the early days of the long march, wore the suit even in the sweltering tropical heat. Mrs. Bosworth was about thirty, with hair the color of dry straw, and wearing a gown that was pinched at the waist and cut low over a plump bosom.

Rulan understood some of their words. Mrs. Bosworth was horrified at Rulan's thin arms and legs and swollen belly and took her immediately to Dr. Houghtailing on Punahou Street, a broad lane lined with palm trees and two-story white houses. After poking and prodding her in a fashion that Physician Sung would have pronounced most indecent, he smiled broadly, told her to get dressed, and went out to the parlor to announce to the Bosworths, "You may have paid for one, but you're getting two. She's with child. That accounts in part for the swollen belly, though they starved her too. Can't tell what shape the child's in. Feed her. Try to get her to drink milk. These chinks don't go for it much."

Mrs. Bosworth, who was childless, took girlish delight in caring for her pregnant charge. She fixed over an old gown for Rulan and installed her in a small room off the porch of their white frame house in the hills of Nuuanu. Han women were scarce in the islands, and one like Rulan, who had little fear of westerners, knew a smattering of English, and had memorized long passages of the Bible, was a rarity indeed.

This is a new world, and I'm alone, Rulan told herself, so I'll practice their ways, dress as their women do, learn their medicine and language, and wait.

Rulan learned women's words and a myriad of indoor tasks. She went with Mrs. Bosworth to the leaders of the fraternal societies to undertake good works among the few women in the Han community. Together they nursed the ill and helped deliver babies, making sure that the daughters were saved. From Lucy Bosworth, Rulan learned the ways of the barbarians, as Li Yu had instructed her.

In Rulan's sixth month, as her belly grew, the child began to dance within the tight walls of the womb, pressing for freedom. Rulan was in the kitchen kneading dough for bread. She looked out of the kitchen window at the town of Honolulu sprawled below: clusters of low wood buildings with cheap tin roofs thrown on unnaturally red earth, surrounded by water the color of jade. She counted the new ships in the harbor. She sent inquiries into the work camps and the cane fields. No one had heard of him. She repeated his name constantly, as if repetition could make him return.

In her eighth month, the child began to kick and punch and turn somersaults in her belly. A boy, she decided. A strong boy like Pao An.

On the evening when the Bosworths were at the Bethel Street Mission teaching English to rice merchants and laborers from the cane fields, the child began to tumble in her womb like a badger in a box. The nausea was so great and her loneliness so overwhelming that Rulan decided to walk into town to buy cloth for an infant-size gown and cap. She put on the old gown Mrs. Bosworth had given her and tied up her hair under a faded bonnet with a low brim. The child kicked, kicked as she hobbled through the narrow dirt roads in the thick-heeled shoes that Lucy insisted Rulan wear to protect her bare feet. At last, Rulan said, laughing to herself, I can finally walk like a proper *mui tsai*. She went past the wharves to the narrow, muddy lanes of Chinatown to look for a silk shop.

The lights were just coming on in the small dirty hovels where Han merchants and their families slept. Only a handful of men had escaped the harsh, lonely life in the fields for an independent existence with wives and children. It took money for families to stay together: money for passage, money to pay off landlords and captains, and money to start small businesses in the city. Most of the stores were closed because the bachelors from the plantations were already in the noodle shops and gambling houses. Her nose drew her to a door between a fish store and a preserved seeds warehouse, which was marked with a narrow sign that said, in English and Chinese, Canton Trading. She smelled silk, spices, sandalwood, dried herbs—and the sickly sweet fumes of dirt. Rulan rang the rusty bell attached to the door. When no one came, she pushed the heavy door open and walked inside. Her shadow fell across the floor to the feet of a woman bent over a broom.

"Go 'way, lady. *Pau hana*, closee now," the woman scolded in the barbaric patois of the islands, without looking up. She was a small woman whose golden lilies were obviously giving her pain. Sighing loudly, she leaned against the counter with one hand while she swished her broom awkwardly around the dusty floor. Her high-collared Chinese dress of gaudy pink silk was filthy at the hem and her narrow face was pinched and tired. When Rulan made no move to leave, the woman cocked her head like a furious little bird and squinted at Rulan, whose face was hidden in shadow.

Rulan recognized her.

"Byemby you come back, alla same," the woman said, impatiently flicking her hand to shoo Rulan away. Under her breath she swore in good Punti dialect at the "great ugly white devil cow."

A plump man entered from a storeroom in the rear wearing western-style breeches held up by suspenders. A Chinese skull cap perched on the shaved dome of his head. He carried an abacus balanced on a grooved coin tray with one hand and was eating a roast-pork bun with the other. He gaped at the tall woman in the western gown silhouetted against the open door. Shyly, he put the half-eaten bun on the counter, wiped his hand on his trousers, and took off his cap to bow low. His queue fell over his bald pate.

"Missee so kin', catchum *hana-hana* tomollo. Missee, you wait pleasee tomollo. So kin'."

How different he looked, the viceroy's only son! She heard children squealing in the back room and slowly closed the door on Liang Mo and Mei Yuk.

Pao An, she cried silently. Don't leave me alone in a world of ghosts!

∎　　∎　　∎

The child was born in early winter while a gentle "plum rain" washed the peaks of Nuuanu clean. A girl, whom Rulan named Mulan. Bosworth baptized her in the tiny mission church in the valley with Rulan and Lucy looking on.

One morning when Mulan was seven, a tall stranger came up their lane. The child saw that he wore western trousers tucked into dusty black boots, a red bandanna around his neck, and a wide-brimmed hat like the men from California. Yet this one was not a *haole,* a white man, but Han, although he wore no queue. He limped up to their gate and stood with big, scarred hands tightly gripping the rough wood, studying her face without speaking. She tried to return his gaze directly, as her mother had taught her, but she was the first to look away. He frightened her with the intensity of his expression.

"Where is your mother, child?" he asked in Punti dialect. The words seemed to hurt him.

Then she knew that this was the man she had been taught to look for. Quickly, she unhooked the gate and pulled him in.

About the Author

LINDA CHING SLEDGE is a fourth-generation descendant of a foundling from On Ting village in Kwangtung, China, who came to Honolulu in the mid-1800s. A graduate of the University of California at Berkeley, she has a Ph.D. from the Graduate Center of the City University of New York, and lives in Westchester County, New York, where she has taught writing and literature for fifteen years. She and her husband Gary, an editor, have two sons, Timothy and Geoffrey.